QUEST for
HONOUR

Born and raised in New York, Sam Barone attended Manhattan College, graduating with a Bachelor of Science degree in 1965, with a major in Psychology. After a hitch in the Marine Corps, he became a software developer and manager. After spending nearly 30 years in the software development game, he retired in 1999 to start working on his second career: writing. Sam Barone is the author of *Dawn of Empire* and *Empire Rising*.

Please feel free to contact Sam at www.sambarone.com.

Book 1 – The Gathering

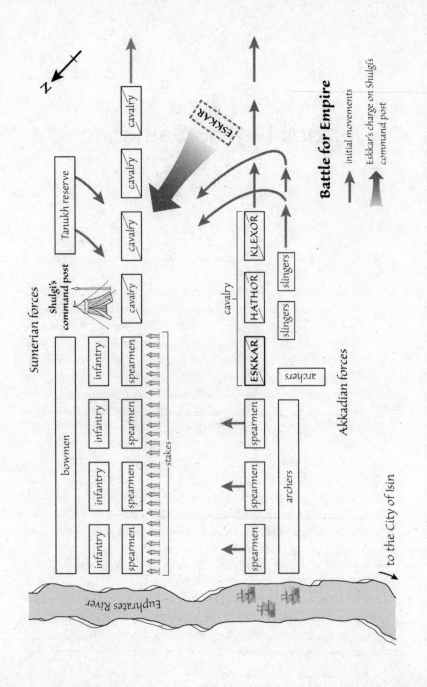

Battle for Empire

→ initial movements

⇒ Esskar's charge on Shulgi's command post

N

Sumerian forces

Shulgi's command post

Tanukh reserve

cavalry

bowmen

infantry

spearmen

stakes

Euphrates River

Akkadian forces

ESSKAR

HATHOR

KLEXOR

ESSKAR

slingers

cavalry

archers

spearmen

archers

to the City of Isin

SAM BARONE
QUEST *for* HONOUR

arrow books

Published in the United Kingdom by Arrow Books in 2010

1 3 5 7 9 10 8 6 4 2

First published in paperback in 2010 by Century

Arrow Books
The Random House Group Limited
20 Vauxhall Bridge Road, London, SW1V 2SA

Addresses for companies within The Random House Group Limited can be found at:
www.randomhouse.co.uk/offices.htm

The Random House Group Limited Reg. No. 954009

www.rbooks.co.uk

A CIP catalogue record for this book
is available from the British Library

ISBN 9780099536765

The Random House Group Limited supports The Forest Stewardship
Council (FSC), the leading international forest certification organisation. All our
titles that are printed on Greenpeace approved FSC certified paper carry the
FSC logo. Our paper procurement policy can be found at:
www.rbooks.co.uk/environment

Typeset by SX Composing DTP, Rayleigh, Essex
Printed and bound in Great Britain by
CPI Bookmarque Ltd, Croydon, CR0 4TD

To all those warriors throughout the ages who fought honorably
for their country. And to Bill O'Reilly, a different kind of
fighter, but a culture warrior nonetheless.

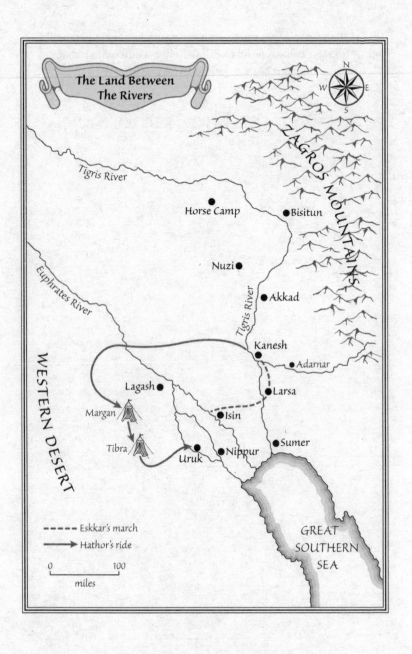

The Land Between
The Rivers

Tigris River

Euphrates River

ZAGROS MOUNTAINS

Horse Camp

Bisitun

Nuzi

Tigris River

Akkad

Kanesh

Adarnar

Larsa

Lagash

Margan

Isin

Tibra

Nippur

Sumer

Uruk

WESTERN DESERT

GREAT
SOUTHERN
SEA

- - - - Eskkar's march
⟶ Hathor's ride

0   100
   miles

1

3154 BCE – the city of Sumer on the great southern sea . . .

Yavtar guided the sturdy ship through the swirling water of the Tigris, toward the Sumerian dock, now less than two hundred paces away, that marked the end of the voyage. On shore a crowd of idlers followed his approach, ready to note the smallest mishap. A portly man attended by two guards pushed his way to the forefront. As Yavtar edged the *Southern Star* ever closer, he observed the yellow sash tied across the man's bulging stomach that marked him as one of the king's representatives, most likely the dockmaster. Arms folded, the man reached the head of the last empty dock and stood there, awaiting the ship's arrival.

For this important mission Yavtar had traveled day and night, racing downriver from Akkad to Sumer in less than four days. Now he almost regretted the haste, as he had to bring the *Star* ashore at midday, the peak of dockside activity. Since he hadn't made a single stop along the way, this would be his first landfall in almost four months. A sailing master who spent more time on land than water soon lost his skills, so Yavtar swallowed his pride and muttered a prayer to the river gods to help him achieve a safe landing.

The *Southern Star*'s extra length – she stretched almost twenty-five paces from stem to stern – made her unwieldy in cross-currents. If he misjudged the current when he turned the *Star* toward land, the swiftness of the water could drive him downstream, stern first, accompanied by laughter and catcalls from shore. Having to come about and pull upwards against the river's flow would be a humiliating and slow arrival.

Yavtar gauged the moment, then leaned hard on the steering oar, forcing it against the current and almost broadside to the flowing water.

"Drop the sail!" he barked.

A crewman stretched out his arm and jerked hard against the restraining rope. The square linen sail slid down with a thud.

"Pull, you dogs, pull!"

The four crewmen grunted against the sweeps, their bare feet straining for purchase. As the *Star* edged closer to the shore, the force of the river churned against the length of the hull. The vessel canted over as the pressure increased, and through his feet Yavtar felt the ship pitch up and down against the conflicting forces of water and oars. He caught a glimpse of his five passengers, huddled around the ship's single mast, and clutching at it for support, their eyes wide with excitement.

The *Southern Star* began to swing around, and now the bow was less than fifty paces from the dock. For a moment Yavtar thought he'd waited too long. His hand twitched with tension, gripping the steering oar with all his strength, as the Tigris's powerful current sought to roll the ship over and send the crew and their valuable cargo tumbling beneath the water. He forced himself to wait one more moment, then planted his feet firmly and pulled the steering oar in the opposite direction.

"In oars!"

Spray splashed over the *Star*'s bow, and Yavtar feared she might roll over. An instant later, the river relented. As smooth as a leaf floating on the current, the ship glided alongside the dock, and slid gently into its berth with the slightest bump against the rope-wrapped stanchions. Yavtar allowed himself a brief smile. Despite more than two months since his last voyage, his eye still hadn't lost the skill acquired in nearly thirty years on the river.

Two crewmen leapt onto the dock to secure the vessel fore and aft. The moment the *Star* stopped moving, the early summer heat struck down from the cloudless, blue sky like a hammer.

"Well done, shipmaster," Daro said, joining Yavtar at the stern. "I thought we were going for a swim. At least you didn't give those hooligans anything to hoot about."

Daro and his four soldiers were the passengers the *Star* carried, though that term didn't explain their presence. They were there to protect the ship's very secret and valuable cargo.

"Not bad for a farmer," Yavtar agreed with a laugh. Not that anyone thought of him as a farmer, especially now that he owned the largest number of ships in Akkad. His vessels carried cargoes on both the Tigris and Euphrates.

As Yavtar approached his fortieth season, he traveled less and less on the great Tigris, the river that, only a few years ago, had carried him into battle with Lord Eskkar and brought him so much wealth. Now he preferred to spend more of his days on the large farmstead south of Akkad, purchased with his victor's profits and surrounded by his two wives and a growing brood of energetic children.

Nevertheless, Yavtar still felt the urge to experience water flowing beneath his feet, so he often accompanied more valuable cargoes, if for no other reason than to keep a watchful eye on his hired shipmasters. This trip, despite the worth of its goods, had other, more urgent reasons for bringing Yavtar downriver.

"Is this vessel from Akkad?"

The dockmaster's abrupt words brought Yavtar back to the present, and he lifted his eyes to the wharf. The officious man with the yellow sash had advanced onto the dock, his bored guards still in attendance, and now stood frowning down into the boat. Looking up, Yavtar perceived the man's stomach in all its glory, bulging against his tunic from too much food and too little labor. "I'm Yavtar, owner of this boat and –"

"Do you come from Akkad?" The way the dockmaster uttered the name of the city turned a simple question into an insult.

"Yes, by the order of King Eskkar. We carry –"

"The only king I know is King Eridu of Sumeria," the man said, not bothering to hide the disrespect. "You will discharge your cargo as soon as possible. Only you and your sailing master will be permitted to leave the dock or enter the city. If any of your crew steps onto shore," he jerked his head toward the riverbank, "they'll end up as slaves."

The border disputes between Akkad and Sumer had intensified over the last few months, and now affected routine trade. Yavtar glanced toward the city walls and saw a handful of soldiers standing just outside the gate. He counted ten men and their commander.

"And before any cargo is landed, King Eridu has decreed a fee of three silver coins to be paid."

Yavtar frowned at the outrageous price. On his last trip to Sumer, little more than a year ago, the dockmaster had charged only a single silver, and that was more of a personal bribe than anything official. "And what do I receive in return for this large sum?"

"You are permitted to use the dock until dusk tomorrow. By then, you must be on your way, or you will be charged another three silvers," the man said, smiling broadly at Yavtar's discomfort. "If you can't afford to pay, take your ship and your goods back to your barbarian king."

Behind Yavtar, the crew and the Akkadian soldiers who guarded the cargo began to mutter at the slur. The last thing he wanted was trouble.

"Then it is my pleasure to make payment," Yavtar said. He climbed onto the wharf, reached into his pouch, and withdrew four silver coins. "And perhaps you could dispatch a messenger to fetch Merchant Gemama. Meanwhile, I would be most grateful if you could order your work crew to carry the cargo off the dock. I'm certain Merchant Gemama is waiting most anxiously for his goods." Yavtar dropped the silver coins in the dockmaster's open palm. The extra one would find its way into the man's private pouch. "And since I am my own sailing master, I will need one of my guards to accompany me in Sumer."

After a quick scrutiny to verify their quality, the coins disappeared. "Very well, one servant may accompany you into Sumer. I'll send a slave to Gemama." The dockmaster turned away and negotiated his way through the crowd until he reached the awning and chair that awaited him on the riverbank. As the man settled into his seat, he gave orders to the overseer of the work gang. At the slavemaster's command, they shuffled wearily toward the Akkadian craft.

Yavtar jumped back into the boat, where his four crewmen waited. "Hand up the cargo to the slaves, and make sure they don't spill anything. Don't let any of them into the boat, or the dockmaster will accuse us of trying to steal them." He stepped closer to his crew. "You heard what he said about staying on the dock. You might as well stay on board, unless you want to spend the rest of your lives in Sumer."

The transfer of goods began. The bulk of the cargo was specialty foods – peas, sesame seeds, exotic dates, spices, and sacks of the finest wheat for bread-making, all products in short supply in Sumer at this time of year. Once satisfied that his crew could manage the unloading, Yavtar turned to the leader of the soldiers. "My crewmen will keep the king's goods under their eyes until Gemama arrives with his gold. You make sure nothing happens to that pouch."

The vessel's real cargo, a double-bound leather pouch with a thick strap, now hung from Daro's shoulder. He nodded, and fingered the sword at his side. "We'll keep it safe, Yavtar."

"And tell your men not to stare at the guards on the shore. We're not here to pick a quarrel with the Sumerians."

The crew continued unloading, passing the bags, sacks, and bundles to the slaves on the dock. Yavtar watched the proceedings with care, counting each and every item from habit. The master crewman did the same. The work-gang slaves had to be watched carefully, of course. A dropped sack, a slit cut surreptitiously into the side of a sack, and goods would disappear in a blink. Besides, Merchant Gemama would recount and re-examine each item before he took possession, and the numbers would need to agree before payment would be arranged. The specialty goods would fetch a very good price, but then would come the real haggling over the ship's true cargo.

The leather pouch guarded by Daro and the Akkadian soldiers contained lapis lazuli, the finest to be found anywhere in the land. The precious stones had traveled a long and dangerous journey from the distant and almost unknown eastern lands to Akkad. The profit from that sack alone would more than triple the gains made by the rest of the cargo.

The bulk of the *Southern Star*'s cargo soon rested on the dock. Master Gemama arrived only moments later, attended by his own porters and three armed guards. His bald head shone in the sun, and he carried almost as much weight around his stomach as the dockmaster.

"Ah, Yavtar, good to see you, old friend," he shouted as he climbed down into the boat. "It's been a long time since you've landed here. A safe journey, I hope?"

"Smooth and fast, just the way I like it." Yavtar smiled at the Sumerian merchant, who also wore a yellow sash over his linen tunic, marking him as a king's man. They had known each other for more than twenty years, trading, arguing, and bargaining the whole time. Yavtar trusted the man, as much as anyone could ever trust a Sumerian.

The haggling over, the regular cargo went quickly, and Yavtar negotiated a bit more than he expected, no doubt Gemama's way of giving thanks for the speedy delivery.

After the gold exchanged hands, Gemama lowered his voice. "And you have something special for me?"

"Come and see." Yavtar gestured toward the Akkadian soldiers standing beside Daro.

"No, not here," Gemama said, glancing around. "We'll take it to my house. Afterwards, you'll join me for dinner."

Yavtar hesitated. The gems should be examined here, at the dock, and the price established and agreed to. Once on shore, anything could happen. Gemama could even change his mind.

The Sumerian saw the hesitation. "No, nothing like that." He lowered his voice. "I'll meet your outrageous price, whatever it is. But I'd rather not have everyone in Sumer know what's arrived."

Yavtar rubbed his black beard for a few moments. The rare gemstones, no matter what their worth, really mattered little. His true goal was to obtain information. "Very well." He moved closer to Gemama, lowered his voice, and named his price. "Half on account, and half in gold."

"Done," said Gemama, without a single protestation. "I'll return with the gold as soon as I get the regular shipment secured."

Before Yavtar could change his mind, Gemama dashed off, his guards and porters scurrying behind him, everyone keeping a watchful eye on the slaves shuffling under their burdens.

"Damn these devious Sumerians anyway," Yavtar muttered.

"Is anything wrong?" Daro asked, moving to stand beside the trader.

"No, nothing. You just guard that pouch and don't let anything distract you from it or the gold when it arrives. And you'll have to stay awake all night. Thieves sometimes slip on-board from the water, snatch what they can, then dash away in the current. And don't let anything that happens on shore distract you, either. That's another old trick in the game."

"The gold will be safe, noble Yavtar," Daro said.

Yavtar believed him. The Hawk Clan could always be relied upon, and Daro had proven his worth many times. Yavtar glanced at the shore. The officious dockmaster continued observing every detail, so Yavtar smiled at him, then sat down in the stern to wait. He used the time to study the busy dock with its throngs of hurrying people. Sumer appeared fully as bustling as Akkad, only under a hotter sun. A splash of water from over the side cooled his face, and he dangled his hand in the river, enjoying the push of the current.

Here, only a few miles from the Great Sea, the Tigris still had power, though much of its strength had diminished as the river divided again and again into ever-narrower channels. Those channels spread into dozens of streams that all emptied themselves into the vast body of water that marked the southern boundary of these lands. Sumer's inhabitants, in their pride, now called it the Sumerian Sea, as if they alone ruled its vast expanse.

The sun had time to move a hand's width across the sky before Gemama, breathing heavily and with his pate covered in sweat, returned, accompanied by his bodyguards. Ordering his men to wait on the dock, Gemama stepped cautiously down into the now much lighter boat, and walked unsteadily to the stern where Yavtar waited. Daro, the leather sack still slung over his shoulder, moved to join them.

Gemama reached inside his tunic and withdrew a fat linen sack that jingled as he handed it to Yavtar. "Fifty gold coins, most of them Akkadian, so don't blame me if they're short-weighted. The rest are from my own goldsmith, newly cast, so I can guarantee their purity. Another fifty coins are marked in my ledger, for whatever you wish to buy for your return voyage."

"Give Gemama the pouch," Yavtar said, accepting the coins. "And Daro, from now on, don't take your eyes off our gold." Yavtar handed Daro the Sumerian merchant's sack.

In return, Daro slid the leather pouch from his shoulder and offered it to the Sumerian.

"Good, then that's settled," Gemama said. Now we can return to my house." He slung the pouch over his neck, letting it hang down beneath his left armpit, and grasped the bottom with his hand. A thief would have to rip the pouch from Gemama's arm and neck before snatching it.

Gemama climbed cautiously off the boat, joined immediately by his guards. The largest led the way, shouldering the crowd aside with ease. Yavtar saw that dozens of eyes followed them as they left the dock, moved across the open space and entered the city of Sumer. Everyone, even the dockmaster, would be guessing about the contents of Gemama's leather pouch, wondering if it held gold, silver or precious gemstones.

Yavtar walked at Gemama's left, and the remaining two guards followed behind, everyone alert for any danger. The little party moved swiftly through the crowded lanes, dodging children, dogs, and the occasional cart. Yavtar heard Gemama's labored breathing as he kept up the rapid pace. The Sumerian, probably well over fifty, was getting on in years, and nowadays probably did nothing more strenuous than walking to and from the docks.

After two futile attempts at conversation, Yavtar gave up and concentrated on his surroundings. Gemama's house lay almost half a mile from the docks, and that through the oldest part of the city with its narrow and refuse-filled lanes that twisted and turned back on themselves. Inside Sumer's walls, the distasteful odor of too many people and animals living too close together blotted out even the scent of the sea that wafted up from the south. Yavtar noted the bustle of the crowds and the stalls of the merchants who seemed to occupy every available space, all of them calling out the worth of their wares to every passerby.

In the last few years, Sumer had grown almost as rapidly as Akkad, and now it matched the northern city in the numbers of its inhabitants. Untouched by the barbarian invasion in the north, thousands had migrated to Sumer and the other villages that nestled in the river's delta. Everywhere Yavtar gazed, new homes and shops were under construction, much of it paid for by Akkadian gold for overpriced goods needed during the barbarian invasion. Tallest of all, near the center of the city, stood the house of King Eridu, surrounded by walls more than seven or eight paces high.

Not really a house, but a large complex of buildings, barracks for the king's guards, storerooms and dwellings for the servants and slaves who attended their master. The walled compound provided security for the king and his followers. Yavtar saw soldiers pacing along the wall's parapets, and another half dozen hard-eyed men guarded the main entrance. The king apparently wanted to make sure he and his family had as little contact as possible with the rest of Sumer's inhabitants.

A bare pole rose up from the highest point of the walls. When in residence, a large yellow banner would hang limp in the moist air, announcing King Eridu's presence.

Lady Trella would call this place a palace, Yavtar decided, a compound built to showcase the glory and power of Sumer's ruler. The vast structure sent another, and not very subtle, message – that King Eridu didn't care about the rest of Sumer's people, as long as he and his possessions remained protected.

They reached Gemama's house and passed through the interior courtyard, where flowers bloomed at the base of the outer walls, and a good-sized tree shaded a long table pushed up against the side of the house. A fat lamb already turned on the fire pit beside the entrance. In Sumer, most of the cooking and food preparation took place outdoors, as the summer heat made any such work indoors too unpleasant. Gemama's wife and two daughters were presented to Yavtar, but he scarcely had time to mouth a few words of greeting before the Sumerian led the way upstairs and onto the roof. A small table, beautifully carved, sat under a wide white awning. A mix of red and yellow flowers floated in a bowl. With his guards watching the house and the grounds from below, the merchant and his visitor enjoyed their first private moment.

"Let me examine the stones first," Gemama said, settling in his chair with a deep breath of relief. He took his time unfastening the cord that bound the sack, then spread the opening wide. Carefully he removed its contents, each lapis stone wrapped in its own square of linen.

"There are twenty-eight stones," Yavtar offered. "Not all the same size, but some are truly magnificent."

Gemama unwrapped each stone, lining them up in three rows by approximate size. The intense blue color drew the eye, and the tiny gold flecks sprinkled within the stones glinted in the fading sun. "Incredible," he said. "I've never seen anything of such excellence before. These came from the Indus, you're certain?"

"Nothing of this quality is to be found in these lands," Yavtar said. "You know Nicar the merchant? His son, Lesu, traveled to the east and back. Took four months. Lesu started with forty porters and guards, but lost almost half his men to bandits and thieves. Only twenty-two returned. Even then, he might not have made it, but King Eskkar sent soldiers to the edge of the mountains to wait for his return, and escort him and his goods back to Akkad."

"How many stones did he bring back?"

Yavtar shrugged. "Nicar didn't say."

"Yes, I'm sure he didn't. Well, as long as the Akkadian doesn't flood the market with more gems, it doesn't really matter." Gemama returned his attention to the stones. He took his time, examining each, murmuring an occasional word of praise for every special attribute.

"These gemstones are worth the lives of fifty men," he said when he finished his inspection. "When polished and set into amulets and pendants, they will make any woman willing, every man a rod. Anyone who can afford the price will want one. Even the grindings will be collected and sold, used to heal wounds and keep the limbs healthy."

11

Yavtar knew the lore as well, though he had his doubts about the stones' effectiveness as an aphrodisiac. Still, what a man believed often became the truth.

Gemama set down the final lapis with a sigh. "When you quoted your price on the ship, I had my doubts. But after seeing these, one hundred gold coins seems very reasonable. I would have expected to pay more, much more. Even after gifting a few of the finest to King Eridu, I'll still earn a handsome profit."

"Well, I can certainly raise the price, if you're concerned."

Gemama ignored the jest and raised his eyes to meet Yavtar's, pulling his chair a bit closer to the table. "Perhaps there is something else you need. Something I can do in return for Akkad's and your ... generosity?"

Yavtar nodded. "Well, I would like to learn what I can about King Eridu and his plans for Sumer. If I had time to poke around the city myself, I would, but I see that Akkadians are no longer welcome here. Besides, I must leave Sumer by sunset tomorrow, so I have little time."

The Sumerian lowered his voice. "King Eridu's plans are secret. No one, not even the leading merchants, know all that he intends. And revealing what little I know could bring trouble down upon my house."

"I understand. But a little gossip between old friends ... and it might be possible to arrange another shipment of lapis lazuli in a few months. A more private shipment, one that perhaps will not pass through the eyes of the dockmaster."

Gemama took his time thinking over this subtle proposition. The dockmaster had certainly noted the well-guarded leather pouch, hence the need to gift a few of the lapis lazuli to King Eridu. A private delivery, perhaps concealed within a sack of grain or jar of oil, would be even more profitable. He weighed the risk against the chance of future profits. "I suppose old friends could gossip among themselves. As long as it remained among themselves."

"I will talk to Nicar about another shipment of lapis. It will be smaller, say a dozen stones, but I'm sure it can be arranged soon. And perhaps at a much lower price."

Gemama smacked his lips, then took a deep breath. "You are wise to learn what you can. How else can an honest trader prepare for the future? But what little I know will not help you or Akkad. You arrive too late, I fear."

"Too late? Too late for what?"

"By now everyone knows about the bandits raiding the borderland between Akkad and Sumeria. In the last few months, Eridu has assembled a strong force of well-armed horsemen. These are the 'bandits' pillaging the lands claimed by Akkad."

Yavtar couldn't keep the surprise from his face. As far as he knew, no word of this had reached Akkad. "Is King Eridu with them?"

"Who can say? Eridu dreams of conquest and loot these days. He might want to partake of the glory himself."

"Well, I expect that any fighting will be over soon," Yavtar said. "No doubt King Eridu knows by now that Lord Eskkar has marched south with a large force of archers and horsemen, to confront the bandits raiding across the Akkadian border."

"Ah, the border that is in dispute. Who is to say where the border starts or where it ends? And perhaps your King Eskkar may find getting rid of the 'bandits' not such an easy task. King Eridu left the city ten days ago with over a hundred soldiers, most armed with spears and shields. Twice as many more are promised to join him within a few days, all recruited and armed from the other cities. With these men, and his horsemen, Eridu intends to establish a new border, one that places all the fertile cropland to the north under Sumer's control."

Yavtar's eyes widened in surprise. A force of three hundred soldiers, supported by a large band of horsemen, would find Eskkar greatly outnumbered. If Eridu had departed ten days ago, the two forces might have already fought a battle. If not, the battle would be fought soon, long before Yavtar could return to Akkad and dispatch a warning.

He realized the silence had dragged on. "It was more than a year ago when Akkad established its southern boundary. No one in Sumeria disputed it then."

"At that time, King Eridu was busy consolidating his influence over Sumer and the other Sumerian cities," Gemama said. "Now that he has their allegiance, willing or not, the six cities of Sumeria now claim they need the rich northern farmlands to feed their growing numbers."

Six large villages made up the heart of Sumeria. Not really villages any more, Yavtar knew, but full sized cities, each with at least two or three thousand inhabitants. Sumer had grown into the largest of them all, but Larsa, Uruk, Isin, Nippur, and Lagash all contributed to the wealth of the region. He hadn't heard that the other cities had submitted to Eridu's authority. Joined together, they would form a powerful trading region, able to draw on trade from the Tigris and Euphrates, as well as the boats that crept along the coast of the Great Sea. If their fighting forces united ... if Eridu had accomplished such a feat, the southern cities would present a formidable threat to Akkad.

"Hmm, do all the other cities accept Eridu as their king?"

Gemama chuckled. "Well, it's only happened in the last few months, and it's not something anyone talks about. Nor does Eridu claim to be their king, not yet, but as he says, he is now the first among equals. In truth, I think he feels a bit jealous at Lord Eskkar's success. Too many people have been singing Akkad's praises for driving off the barbarians, and some in the countryside, thinking they will better themselves, have migrated north to place themselves under Akkad's protection. Eridu intends to put a stop to all that."

"So it will be war then." Yavtar shook his head in dismay. And this time the war would begin with Eskkar walking into a trap. "Trading will be the first casualty."

"Not our trade to the east and west. That will continue without interruption. It will likely even increase. And once King Eridu establishes his claims over the disputed lands, the regular trade with the north will quickly resume, I'm sure. The crops and herds from those lands will then move south, not north."

Rulers came and went, but the traders and merchants always found a way to exchange goods. Gemama spoke the truth. Trade would start up again sooner or later, no matter who won the battles.

"And the people of Sumer, are they as eager for war as their ruler?"

"The people do as they are ordered." Gemama lifted his shoulders and let them drop. "For the last year, Eridu's followers have blamed every shortage, every outbreak of disease, every problem on Akkad. The priests, seers, and even the merchants repeat the same message. By now, most of the city's inhabitants accept it as truth. Eridu has plenty of lackeys in his pay to spread the word and enforce his will, all of them eager to partake in any profits that will arise. He has already promised much of the northern land to his supporters. War, I fear, has already come. It may already be over by now, if your King Eskkar doesn't retreat to Akkad."

Yavtar had much the same thought. "And you, friend Gemama, what do you think of all this?"

"I think that all this fighting is foolish," the Sumerian said. "It would be easier and cheaper to trade for crops than wage war to seize the land

and then have to hold it. One lazy soldier costs more than ten farmers. But if King Eridu wins a quick victory over Lord Esskar's forces, then Eridu's reputation will be enhanced and profits will grow for everyone in Sumer."

"Quick victories are not easy to gain over Akkad," Yavtar said. "I've seen Lord Esskar's soldiers fight."

"Everyone knows of the skill of Akkad's archers. But with all the resources of the six cities and their thousands of men at his disposal, Eridu will soon rule most of the land between the rivers, perhaps even as far north as Akkad. In time, it may be that your city's new walls cannot withstand so many."

"King Eridu is not at Akkad's gates yet," Yavtar said. with more conviction than he felt. "Those who wage war against King Esskar may find themselves losing more than they could ever hope to gain."

"Win or lose, I must take care of my trading house and my family. Like everyone else in Sumer, I had no choice but to give my full support to King Eridu. For which privilege I am allowed to continue my trading ventures, and permitted to give one tenth of all my profits to him."

"A heavy price. What if the fighting continues and he demands more?"

"I pray to the gods for a quick end to the fighting. Though I warn you, old friend, that Eridu and his soldiers seem very confident of victory. His second in command, Razrek, knows how to fight. Apparently, they've been planning this for months, gathering men, weapons and horses, talking in secret with the leaders of the other cities. Even Eridu's son, Shulgi, plays a role in all this. In fact, many of the soldiers trust the son more than the father."

"Who is this Razrek?" The name meant nothing to Yavtar.

"A former bandit who grew powerful by killing all of Eridu's enemies on the trade routes over the last few years. I was fortunate not to compete with Eridu in those days." He sighed. "Hopefully the war will not last long."

He noticed Gemama didn't pray for any particular side to win. The merchant's words conveyed a grim optimism about the war. Gemama was no fool, and he knew the numbers of soldiers Sumer and the other cities could field. That knowledge must have convinced him that King Eridu would emerge victorious.

Yavtar kept the growing sense of uneasiness from his face. Lord Esskar had departed a few days before Yavtar sailed, expecting to confront bandits and marauders, not a well-trained enemy. By now defeat could have struck Akkad's forces, and the king himself might already be dead. "A war will provide profits for many."

"Yes, for some," Gemama agreed, "especially in the short term. But if the war drags on, Eridu will demand more gold from all of us, prices will rise, and the people will have less to buy goods."

"I'm sorry for all this, old friend," Yavtar said. "Should you need anything . . ."

"A few lapis lazuli will keep me in King Eridu's favor, for now at least. But in the future, who can tell? Perhaps one day I may wish to move to Akkad myself." He smiled at Yavtar across the table. "Well, there is nothing more I can tell you, but I think you've learned what you came for. At least our business is well concluded. Now it is time to feast. The lamb should be fully cooked by now, and there is some fine wine cooling in my cellar."

"My thanks to you, Gemama. You will always be welcome in Akkad. Though I think I will return there with a heavy heart."

"But with a full stomach." The Sumerian extended his arm across the table. "And a head swimming in wine."

Yavtar clasped Gemama's arm, the age-old gesture of friendship. "Then let two old friends celebrate a successful voyage."

"May it not be the last one, for either of us."

of horsemen who somehow managed to stay just out of reach. The chase had wearied everyone. The eight days of constant marching at such a fast pace had taken its toll even on their sturdy legs.

Esskar and Grond reached the base of the ridge and rode toward the Akkadian soldiers. Most lay sprawled about on the ground, winded from a long climb up yet another in the seemingly endless hills and grateful for every chance to rest. Only Hathor the Egyptian remained mounted, waiting for Esskar's approach. Hathor commanded the thirty horsemen that comprised Esskar's mounted force. They'd spent most of the day searching for the bandits, or riding patrols to prevent an ambush. The rest of the Akkadian force consisted of eighty-one archers.

"Are the scouts back yet?" Esskar hooked his leg over his horse and slid to the ground, handing the halter to one of the camp boys, who dashed up to take the king's mount. The boys, who had no status and received no pay, followed the soldiers and helped tend to the horses, all for the privilege of helping Akkad's fighters.

Hathor glanced toward the rear of the column, where the last two of his scouts had just crested a hilltop. "They're coming in now, Captain."

The soldiers who had fought beside Esskar the last three years called him Captain, from the days when he'd been Captain of the Guard. The city dwellers in Akkad called him Lord Esskar, while those in the surrounding villages called him king. Those who merely disliked his rule called him an uncouth barbarian. His enemies used worse language. Some claimed he was a demon summoned from the deepest subterranean fire pits by his witch-wife to carry out her sinister commands. Whatever men called him, all respected his ability to not only lead men, but to win battles.

All these names and titles held some truth to them. Born a barbarian, he'd fled his clan in his fourteenth season, when his family perished in a blood feud. He'd killed one of the executioners, stabbing the man in the back as he killed Esskar's younger brother. For more than fifteen years he wandered the lands of his hereditary enemies, the dirt eaters. He suffered abuse and contempt, each day expecting some ignoble death to strike him down but somehow managing to stay alive. As he survived each crisis, he grew stronger and more skillful, until the day came when he feared no one.

The chaos of a barbarian invasion had changed his fate. Esskar rose to Captain of the Guard, and with luck and advice from his new wife, united the people of Akkad and drove off their attackers. With the defeat of the invaders, the city's inhabitants pleaded with him to be their leader, ruler of the largest city in the land. Little more than two years had passed since that day, but new challenges arose to replace the ones vanquished, and each morning brought another struggle for survival.

By now Eskkar had ceased to fear the future or worry about the present. Each day was a gift from the gods, and a chance to defeat one more enemy. And a new adversary seemed to arise at every turn. Whenever men prospered, others appeared with a sword in hand, always ready to take what they had not earned themselves.

The two scouts reached the head of the column, dismounted, and joined Eskkar and the others.

"We saw more bandits coming up from the south-east, Captain." Alexar commanded the main force of archers. Now his face showed his concern.

"I saw another dozen following our line of march to the west," Eskkar said. "Probably more. They're following us on either flank, with more at our rear."

"With the forty or fifty we've seen, they already outnumber our horsemen," Hathor said. "Who knows how many more are waiting up ahead?"

"I don't like it, Captain," Alexar said. "They're leading us on, staying just out of our reach."

Eskkar, too, recognized the signs. All along the southern border, they found dead bodies, farm houses and crops burned to the ground, and the land ravaged beyond all reason. With each grim discovery, Eskkar's anger grew, along with the determination to make these raiders pay for their incursion.

Even barbarians didn't wreak such havoc. They might kill many men and take their women, but they left most of those they ravaged alive, so that they could be looted again on some future raid.

By now Eskkar and his commanders realized that the so-called bandits were anything but. Instead of scattering or fleeing at Eskkar's approach, they yielded ground slowly, staying well away from his force of archers, and confident in their superior number of horsemen. They retreated in only one direction, southward. With each passing day, the situation had worsened, as more and more of the enemy showed themselves.

"Commanders, follow me," Eskkar ordered. He strode a hundred paces away from the men and sank to the ground on a grassy swell. A lone tree provided some welcome shade from the late afternoon sun, and honey bees buzzed at the nearby flowers. One by one, his commanders – Grond, Alexar, Hathor, Mitrac, Klexor, and Drakis – joined him, sitting knee to knee as they completed the circle.

Looking at their faces, he saw the same anger and frustration that burned in his own belly. He had chosen his commanders well. All were Hawk Clan members and proven in battle.

The Hawk Clan formed the elite corps of Akkad's soldiers. After a near-fatal skirmish in the early days of the struggle against the barbarians, Eskkar and the few survivors of that first contact had sworn a solemn oath of brotherhood to each other, and to Eskkar, who had saved their lives and led them to victory.

In those days, most of his followers had been outcasts themselves, men without family, kin or clan. The creation of the Hawk Clan changed all that, providing each member with a new family, Eskkar's own. In Akkad, everyone recognized the bravest of the brave, for only through valor in battle and the acclaim of his fellow warriors could a man become a member of the Hawk Clan. To wear the Hawk emblem on his chest was the greatest ambition of each fighter that served in Akkad, the goal that each soldier sought above all else.

The binding promise each man swore united them as brothers and pledged their loyalty to Eskkar's leadership as head of the Hawk Clan. This new force of battle-tested warriors, now joined in bonds of brotherhood, turned out to be Eskkar's single most important contribution to defeating the barbarian horde. For what brave man could abandon his brother in time of need, or fail his family when danger threatened? The clan linked each man to every other, and promised a haven of safety when advancing age or wounds meant they could no longer fight against Eskkar's enemies.

As they fought together, the bond between the Hawk Clan grew deeper. Having gained their trust and respect, Eskkar repaid it by making sure his commanders and even his newest recruit knew not only what he intended, but what he was thinking. That knowledge made them confident of his leadership, and established that same trust in each other.

Eskkar's proven ability not only to fight but to lead men into battle enabled him to rely on simple instructions and to avoid complicated strategies, even in the chaos of battle. With his close commanders, he felt certain they had the ability to carry out his orders, act independently if necessary, and improvise where needed. That closeness made them a unique group of warriors, who not only thought as a band of brothers, but fought as one, too. Almost as important to Eskkar, none of them would hesitate to speak his mind.

"It's time to decide what we face and what we're going to do," Eskkar began. "We've been chasing these riders for three days, and still they elude us. Whatever city sent them – Larsa, Sumer, maybe even Isin – needs to be taught a lesson. In these lands, and with a force that large, I'll wager that these bandits are Sumerians, or at least in their pay."

The city of Larsa had the most to gain from the border lands, and their history of raiding Akkadian territory went back more than a generation. But Trella had a sufficient number of spies in that city, and Eskkar doubted their king, Naran, could organize such a raid without her agents noticing. Isin, farther to the south and west, had a king bold enough for such an affair, but King Naxos hadn't launched any raids on Akkad's lands since he came to power several years ago. That left the city of Sumer, ruled by King Eridu.

"Meanwhile we're moving further and further south," Alexar said, "and in another day's march, we'll reach the River Sippar. That will put us south of our own border, and into the lands of Sumeria. We don't have enough food or supplies to go that far south, and if we did, we would need to find some way to get across the river. If these bandits or Sumerians crossed over and took all the boats with them, we'd be trapped on the wrong side of the river, and helpless."

"No, we can't go further south," Eskkar agreed. "We need to finish these invaders off once and for all." He looked at Mitrac, who commanded twenty of the archers.

"Mitrac, what do you think?" Eskkar always started with the youngest of his commanders. His wife, Trella, had suggested that idea to her husband, so that the youngest would not feel the pressure of contradicting their elders.

"Our men can keep up the chase for another few days. If we can close within bowshot, I don't care how many men they have. So far, the scouts have seen no sign of longbows. We just need to get within reach, so our bowmen can kill them."

Klexor, who commanded half the horsemen under Hathor, spoke next. "We can't get close with their scouts watching our every move. The archers can't keep up with our horsemen if we try and chase the bandits. I think we need to learn more about them, how many mounted men they have. Maybe we should set a trap tonight for one or two of them. We'd have them by morning. We'd soon find out what they know."

"Even that might not tell us how many men we're facing, or what their leader's plans are," Drakis said. He commanded twenty archers. "There could be hundreds of soldiers just waiting for us to come within their reach. We move toward them, they fall back, and somehow increase their strength."

"I agree with Drakis. There must be a large force of archers or soldiers somewhere nearby." Alexar commanded all of Eskkar's archers. "Otherwise, the tactics of these men make no sense. Why else would they linger near our force, when they could just ride away?"

Eskkar turned to Grond, his bodyguard. "And what do you think?"

"I think they're luring us into a trap," Grond answered without hesitation. A large man, even broader than Eskkar, he'd been a slave in the western desert before reaching Akkad. "Somewhere up ahead, where the ground is favorable for them, they'll turn on us and attack. We've little more than a hundred men. If they strike hard enough and with enough men, we'll be overwhelmed. You need to find a way to get close to them, and soon."

All eyes went to Hathor, the last to speak. A few years older than Eskkar's thirty-two seasons, he was the oldest of Eskkar's leaders. While all the commanders recognized Hathor's ability, many of the men and inhabitants of Akkad remembered the past. The sole survivor of the band of despised Egyptians who had seized power in Akkad, Hathor had fought against Akkad's forces. He'd escaped death first by chance, and then by Lady Trella's intervention.

"Their horsemen," Hathor said, "outnumber ours at least two to one. They're well-armed and mounted on animals as good as our own. Not what you'd expect bandits or raiders to be riding. If we have to engage a force twice our size without support from the archers, it could get very bloody."

Eskkar started to speak, but Hathor wasn't finished.

"If we had enough men," he said, meeting Eskkar's gaze, "it wouldn't matter where we fought them. But our enemies have counted our soldiers, and still they remain close by, readying themselves for the battle. So they don't fear either our numbers or our weapons. If we're outnumbered, it would be foolish to fight them at a time and place of their choosing. That is the one advantage a smaller force cannot yield. Without a good plan of our own, I say we should retreat, march north toward Akkad for a few days, and send for more men and supplies."

All the other commanders dropped their eyes. No one wanted to propose an embarrassing retreat, and only someone with Hathor's experience and proven valor had the strength to make such a suggestion.

Eskkar grunted. "First, let's make it clear that these men are soldiers under good discipline. That means they're probably ready for whatever we do, and they won't be afraid to face us in battle. If we retreat, they won't just let us go. They'll nip at our heels all the way back to Akkad if we let them, attacking us at every opportunity. By the time we gather enough men to confront them, the countryside will be ravaged beyond repair, and a whole growing season lost. But Hathor is right. We must not fight on their terms. We must select the time and place of battle, and use it to crush them."

"And how will we accomplish that trick?" Grond asked.

"We must do what they don't expect," Eskkar said. "They've made their plans, and they're waiting for us to advance or retreat. Instead, we must devise something different. The first thing I want to do is stop moving south. Our men are tired from eight days of marching. They need a rest anyway, if they are to fight well. So we'll stay right where we are tonight and all day tomorrow. The next day, we'll begin marching back north, and at a good pace, as if we're afraid to remain this far south any longer."

He turned to Hathor. "If you were in their place, what would you do in response?"

"I'd send the horsemen to loop around us, get in front of us," Hathor said without hesitation. "They could delay our escape until their main force of fighters, if there is one, closed up behind us. With so many horsemen, they could easily slow us down."

"I agree," Eskkar said. He let his eyes reach each man, and saw that all of them, even the dour Egyptian, had smiles on their faces. They knew their commander well enough to know that he had something planned. The idea that Eskkar had mulled in the back of his head all morning had taken shape. The gamble would be great, and if his plan failed, his entire Akkadian force would be at risk. Nevertheless, he couldn't come up with anything better. He would put forth his plan. His commanders would add their suggestions and improvements, and when they were finished, their confidence would unite them once again into a deadly fighting force.

Eskkar returned their smiles. "Here's what we're going to do. The first step is to convince our enemy that their plan is working."

Every head leaned closer. Eskkar began scratching in the dirt with his knife. Soon stones and more knives marked the earth, each signifying places where forces could be arrayed. They talked and argued, offered suggestions and criticisms. Their voices rose and fell with the heat of their emotions. By the time the sun sank toward the western horizon, the plan had grown complete. As Eskkar expected, his experienced fighting men had expanded and improved his idea.

From a distance, the rest of Akkad's soldiers watched in silence. A few of the veterans had seen such a war council before, and knew that a difficult and dangerous plan would soon put them in harm's way. But those same veterans looked unworried. In battle after battle, Eskkar had always outwitted his enemies. At least, until now.

When the war council ended, the Akkadians camped for the night, grateful and all the more relaxed after they learned they would not be marching tomorrow. Eskkar and his commanders huddled about the campfire, reviewing and refining their plans. When yawning slowed the conversation, Eskkar told everyone to get some sleep. He took one last turn around the camp to make sure every man had prepared himself to fight in case of a surprise attack. Respectful of his adversaries, he'd readied his men for the possibility of a night or dawn raid. Finally satisfied, Eskkar rolled himself in his horse blanket and, for the first time in five days, slept as well as any of his men.

A strong guard kept watch over the camp and its horse herd. Whatever happened, the horses had to be protected. A night raid to stampede them would be ruinous.

In the morning, Eskkar's commanders woke everyone well before dawn. When the sun rose without any signs of enemies approaching, he let his men break their fast, though weapons remained close at hand.

Afterwards, Eskkar and Grond studied the land surrounding them.

"Those low hills over there," Grond said. "I think I saw movement along the crest."

Eskkar grunted. He'd studied those same hills, and hadn't seen anything. "I remember when I had eyes as keen as a hawk. Now I need others to search out any signs of life."

Grond had five less seasons than Eskkar, though most people thought they were of the same age. "Less than a mile away. Close enough to keep an eye on our camp and count our numbers."

"Swordplay will carry that far," Eskkar decided. "Maybe you can swing a blade with Klexor. He's big enough to make plenty of noise."

Grond laughed. "Who gets to win?"

Klexor's stocky body was the largest in Eskkar's mounted force. Hathor stood a bit taller, almost as tall as Eskkar, but lacked the bulk to his body.

"Decide for yourself. Then you won't complain afterwards. But let's start with the men. And send out scouts to the north and west first. That will give you and Klexor time to prepare for battle."

The hilltops that probably contained the closest enemy scouts lay to the south and east, and Eskkar didn't want to disturb their vigil by sending outriders in that direction.

Not long afterwards, a fight broke out in the Akkadian camp. A dozen men began pushing and shoving, fists swung, and men staggered to the ground, only to rise again and rejoin the fray. The commanders quickly broke up the quarrel, and the grinning men fell back on the ground, trying to look properly subdued.

Eskkar and Grond looked on with satisfaction at the performance.

"Now you can try your hand with a sword. I'm betting on Klexor."

"It would be close," Grond agreed. "But we'll put on a fight that should send the Sumerians a message."

"Let's hope it's the one we want them to hear."

3

On the day the Akkadians took their rest, Razrek, the leader of the Sumerian horse fighters, arrived at King Eridu's camp well after midday. Barrel-chested, with thick arms and muscled thighs, Razrek's very appearance struck fear into most men. His powerful jaw was half-concealed by a dark beard, and he wore his thick hair in a dozen bristling strands, each one tied with a bit of leather, that reached past his shoulders. For those who heard stories or rumors about his past, Razrek's deeds frightened them even more than his intimidating presence. He'd fought and killed his way across the length and breadth of Sumeria. Not a rogue in his murderous band dared challenge him to a fight.

Long before Eridu proclaimed himself king of Sumer, Razrek had murdered many of Eridu's enemies, and Razrek's killings, aided the ambitious trader in his rise to power. Two years ago, at the height of the battle against the barbarians in the north, Eridu provided Razrek with secret information about a valuable caravan returning from the Indus. Razrek and his band of marauders attacked and robbed the caravan, leaving no survivors. The loot from that one raid had doubled Eridu's wealth and soon enabled him to dominate every other powerful merchant in Sumer. Many suspected what had happened, though only a handful of men knew the true story, and none of them dared say anything.

Today Razrek rode into camp bringing with him a dozen veteran riders, all heavily armed and wearing leather helmets and vests. He guided his horse carefully toward King Eridu's tent, his eyes studying the large force of foot soldiers taking their ease. The king had made camp just north of the River Sippar, but well to the east of the usual crossings. Though early in the day, at least a dozen cooking fires sent smoke trails into the sky, and the smell of roasting meat permeated the air. That brought a grimace to Razrek's face. If they were his men, he'd have them working up a sweat training with their weapons, instead of worrying about their suppers.

Glancing around, Razrek saw more than three hundred men, most sitting or stretched out on the ground. As would be expected, those who could still afford to do so occupied themselves by gambling for whatever coins or belongings they possessed.

A strong force remained on guard, ready to repel any surprise attack from the Akkadians, and Razrek grunted in satisfaction at seeing that. He'd warned Eridu often enough to keep his men prepared and to continue at every moment with their training, but as the Sumerian king extended his sway over the land, he tended to bristle at his troop commander's suggestions.

Not that Razrek cared what Eridu thought of him or his ideas. Razrek cared only for the gold that Eridu paid him, with the promise of much more to come after the Akkadians were driven back north and the borderlands seized. For as much as Eridu was paying him, Razrek could ignore some of the man's pride and foolishness.

A large tent, the only one in the camp, sat near the edge of the encampment, close to a bubbling stream. Half a dozen soldiers guarded the tent's billowy walls and four horses picketed nearby. Razrek dismounted and tossed the halter to one of his men.

"I won't be long." He strode toward the tent flap, where two soldiers stood guard, one on each side. For a moment Razrek thought they might try to stop him, but one look at his brutal face and powerful frame convinced them otherwise. Razrek was, after all, the second in command. He shoved the tent flap aside.

Inside, King Eridu of Sumer rested on a cushion, two naked girls kneeling beside him offering him food and wine, among other things. A pleasant scent lingered in the air, some perfume that must have come from the distant eastern lands. Tall and thin, with a prominent nose, Eridu looked more like the merchant he once was rather than a warrior king. His reddish brown tunic, edged with an intricate design stitched on the collar, was bunched up around his waist. One of the girls held Eridu's rod in both hands, brushing her breasts against its tip. The second offered up a small platter containing dates and grapes for her master's consideration. Eridu spit out some grape seeds and glanced up in annoyance at Razrek's interruption.

"You should not enter my tent without permission."

"We're not in Sumer, my king. On the war trail such rules are best left behind."

"We will return to Sumer soon enough, Razrek."

The veiled threat was plain enough, but Razrek ignored it. "If I offend you, my king, I can take my leave. I'm sure my horsemen and I can find another leader to serve. Perhaps we could offer our services to King Eskkar. It's said that he, too, possesses much gold."

Eridu bit his lip. Razrek's horsemen were Eridu's most efficient force, not to mention the threat that had convinced the other cities to cooperate with the king of Sumer or have their lands ravaged. He took but a moment to swallow his pride.

"Leave us," Eridu commanded, shoving the girl away from his penis. She snatched up her clothing and ran from the tent, the other girl following. He pushed his tunic down over his still swollen member.

"What brings you here, Razrek? Aren't you supposed to be readying your attack on the Akkadians? Or have they turned back already?"

As soon as both girls were gone, Razrek sat down facing Eridu, hitching his sword across his lap as he settled himself.

"That's why I've come, to tell you what's happening, and to make sure you're ready to move against them."

Razrek had sent a rider to Eridu's camp this morning with word that Eskkar and his soldiers had ceased their march south. That inactivity continued to bother Razrek all morning, and he decided to report to Eridu himself, to make sure that the king of Sumer understood the import of Eskkar's action, or lack thereof.

"The Akkadians show no intention of breaking camp. They're resting their men, and the few scouts they sent out all rode to the north and west. That might mean they intend to move out to the north-west. This morning, a quarrel broke out among the soldiers. Not long after, another fight started, with two men hacking at each other with swords. The commanders had to break it up. My scouts could hear the shouting and clash of swords."

Eridu shrugged. "They could have been training. But all the better for us if they argue amongst themselves," he said with satisfaction. "That will make my victory even easier."

Razrek didn't bother to point out that it was his horsemen that kept Eskkar's forces from smashing Eridu's foot soldiers, more than half recruited or conscripted in the last few months. The Sumerian king still didn't fully understand the importance of trained and experienced fighting men in a battle. A merchant first and last, he believed that numbers were more important than skill and discipline, despite all of Razrek's efforts to convince him otherwise.

"Yes, my king," Razrek said, trying to be patient. "But this staying in one place is not what I expected from Eskkar. He's a barbarian who believes in closing with his enemy or giving way. That is the way the Steppes horsemen fight. They attack when they have the advantage in numbers, or retreat when the situation is unfavorable to them. When Eskkar does neither, then I worry."

Eridu selected a plump date from the platter beside him. He didn't bother to offer any to his visitor. "Eskkar's men are tired. Perhaps he is just resting them before he decides to retreat. We can wait one more day. Without food, he can't stay where he is, while we have plenty of supplies. And if he comes south, he falls into our trap. The chosen battleground is but a half day's march from here. By midday tomorrow, I'll be there waiting for him. Once he enters that valley, we will destroy him."

Razrek hesitated. Eridu's words made sense, but still Razrek felt uneasy. "It may be as you say. But I came to warn you to stay vigilant. Keep your men ready for anything. Eskkar is cunning, and by now he may even know about your presence. Still, if the Akkadian doesn't start moving tomorrow morning, I will try and engage his horsemen, to see if I can lure them away from the archers."

"My men are keeping a close watch to the north. I'll double the men on watch tonight. We won't be surprised, Razrek, you can be certain of that. And I've trained them hard enough these last few days."

While you took your ease with your women, Razrek thought. "Then my doubts are resolved, my king. I'll send word in the morning as soon as I see which way he's moving."

"Good. If Eskkar continues to come south, we'll meet him at the ambush site. If he decides to return to Akkad, you will have to slow Eskkar down until my soldiers can fall on him from behind. By then his men will be growing weak from hunger. The sooner we finish the barbarian off, the quicker I can claim these lands and get back to Sumer."

Razrek rose. "Of course, my king. I'll return to my men, and leave you to your pleasures."

He gave Eridu a brief bow and swept from the tent. Outside, Razrek found his second in command, Mattaki, frowning at Eridu's guards while he waited for his commander.

"Anything new?" Mattaki handed Razrek the halter.

"No, but at least I've warned him. He'll start moving north in the morning, which should be safe enough. He'll still be at least a good day's march from the Akkadians, maybe more, unless he learns how to drive his men faster. Eridu should have brought his son with him. The men would fight harder for the son than the father."

"Isn't Shulgi too young for this? That's what Eridu said."

"Shulgi has almost seventeen seasons," Razrek said. "He helped recruit and train most of these men. And he knows how to swing a sword, which is more than Eridu can say."

"So why didn't he bring him?"

"And risk sharing the glory? If Eridu beats Eskkar, he can claim to be a great warrior king. With Sumer and control of the river under Eridu's thumb, and the border area opened up, all the other cities will fall to their knees and accept his leadership. That's why Eridu wants this victory so bad he can taste it."

"While we do all the work and take all the risks," Mattaki said, spitting on the ground.

"That's what you're getting paid for. Besides, we outnumber Eskkar's forces almost four to one. Even if we lose half our force crushing him, we'll still come out with plenty of gold."

"And we can always recruit more men," Mattaki said. He received a share of the gold Eridu paid for each new farm boy eager to become a soldier.

In a moment both men were back on their horses, and Razrek led the way as they galloped through the camp, heedless of Eridu's soldiers, who were forced to leap out of their path.

Nevertheless, Razrek couldn't shake the feeling that something was wrong. He'd spoken to anyone and everyone who'd ever been to Akkad or knew anything about Eskkar. This inactivity didn't fit the barbarian's history. Attack or retreat. It was the only tactic the northern warriors knew, and the only ones Eskkar had ever used. If the barbarian didn't start moving tomorrow, Razrek would launch an attack on Eskkar's cavalry, force his hand somehow. Razrek knew how important it was to keep Eskkar off-guard and his men on edge, even if Eridu didn't.

The king had conveniently forgotten that it was Razrek who had planned this whole campaign months ago. And so far everything had gone as he envisioned. The border raids helped train Razrek's horsemen, even as they looted the countryside and Razrek grew rich in the process. Word of the attacks brought Eskkar rushing south, and the staged retreats drew him ever closer to the ambush site. Another day's march south, and the Akkadians would be destroyed. King Eridu would rule all of Sumeria and its surrounding lands, and Razrek would earn all the gold he'd been promised.

Nevertheless, Razrek fretted. With so much at stake, he didn't dare wait any longer. If the barbarian didn't start moving, Razrek would attack Eskkar's forces, and either drive him south for the quick finish, or follow his retreat north for the slow death. Either way, the Akkadian force would be destroyed, and with a little luck, their king would be among the first to die.

4

After taking a full day and night of rest, the Akkadians collected their horses and weapons, and prepared to move out. Scouts galloped off in all directions, but stayed close to the main force of archers. Eskkar didn't want to offer any tempting targets to the enemy horsemen. As long as the riders stayed within easy reach of the bowmen, they should be safe enough.

Before the Akkadians could begin the march, pushing and shoving broke out among the ranks. Instead of restoring order, Hathor and Alexar began arguing, their voices rising until they stood face to face, shouting at each other. Hathor struck Alexar in the chest with his fist, and the two men grappled. Soldiers shouted encouragement to their respective commanders, and a ring of cheering and shouting onlookers formed around them. Both commanders drew their swords. The clash of bronze against bronze once again echoed out over the grassland, as the two fighters weaved and shifted. Eskkar let the performance go on for a dozen strokes before he halted the brawl, stepping between the two and shoving them apart.

Raising his voice, he rained down abuse on both combatants, to the cheers and shouts of the men. The noise from the brief swordplay would have alerted any spies watching their camp, and Eskkar's bellows would have carried almost as far. The Sumerian scouts would report a second day of continued dissension in the Akkadian ranks. Satisfied, Eskkar ordered his commanders to break camp, and get the soldiers moving.

Hathor and Klexor split the thirty horsemen between them and moved out ahead, screening the archers. They headed north, back the way they came. Alexar and the bowmen followed, the leaders of ten moving up and down the column of soldiers as they marched, reminding them to look weary, as if they'd already been beaten in a fight. Esskar ordered a steady pace, but he rested the men much more often than he had in the last eight days. At mid-morning they turned off their own tracks, and headed westward, taking a different path than the one they'd followed when chasing after the bandits.

With Grond at his side, Esskar now led the way at the head of the archers. The countryside here wasn't entirely unfamiliar. His horsemen had scouted the countryside yesterday, and some of the archers and riders had lived in these lands before moving to Akkad. As the first of his scouts reported back, Esskar listened to each report, and he picked the next part of the march with care. The survival of his soldiers might depend on the path he chose through the hills and valleys that led to the west.

Not long after the Akkadians turned westward, enemy horsemen appeared brazenly on the hills behind them, as if tempting the retreating force to turn and give chase. Esskar ignored them, determined to avoid wasting his men's strength pursuing riders who simply rode away. His main worry this morning remained the possibility of an ambush. Sooner or later, the Sumerians would get in his path, and attempt to halt his force. Hopefully his change of direction westward would keep them off balance for the rest of today.

At midday, Esskar gave the order to halt beside a small stream, and the men sank to the ground while they ate stale bread. Some removed their sandals and soaked their feet in the water, while a few splashed their faces and hands. Esskar ordered that every water skin be filled. The countryside around them had been stripped bare of food and flocks by the enemy horsemen. Only a few loaves of stale bread remained to fill the Akkadian soldiers' stomachs. By tomorrow, even that would be gone and real hunger would set in. Nevertheless, Esskar no longer worried about food. That would soon be the least of his men's needs.

After a longer than usual break, the Akkadians abandoned the pleasant little stream and resumed their journey. The men trudged through the low hills and sparse grassland. The ground grew a little greener with each step nearer to the Tigris, still a few days' march away.

When dusk approached, Esskar gave the order to halt. The campsite didn't appear very favorable. No stream meandered nearby, just a half-mile-wide expanse of thick grass surrounded by low hills. Nevertheless, the seemingly haphazard choice had been selected with care. It had to serve Eskkar's purposes as well as his enemies'.

The men still had chores to do before they could rest. Eskkar made sure they collected plenty of wood and chips, and soon crackling fires sent smoke trails skyward, warming the men though they had little to put in their cooking pots. The scouts had seen no game during the day's march. Eskkar's marching orders kept the scouts close to the bowmen, and meant they had no opportunity to hunt.

As on the previous night, extra guards were posted, and a strong perimeter established. The last thing Eskkar wanted now was for his enemies to attack in force during the night. Grond brought over a small loaf of bread that he'd soaked in the last stream they crossed. Eskkar took half, and had to force the tasteless mush down.

For once, Eskkar didn't bother making the rounds of the camp. His commanders knew what needed to be done. Instead he gathered his blanket and tried to get some rest, stretching out on the ground and turning his back to the setting sun. Though he lay there unmoving, his mind raced with thoughts about the coming action. As dusk gathered, Eskkar managed to doze off, though he slept fitfully, as he always did the night before a fight. When Grond woke him, night had fallen, and the stars shone bright overhead. The fires already burned low, barely kept alive by soldiers tossing a few sticks on them now and again.

Eskkar took the hand Grond extended to him. "Is everything ready?"

"Yes, Captain. The men have already started slipping away. They're waiting for us."

Grond seldom wasted words, which might explain why the two had become good friends. As Eskkar slung his sword over his shoulder, Hathor slipped up beside him.

"My men are ready, Captain."

Eskkar looked around the campsite. Men still moved about, and blankets still circled the dying fires. Grond and Hathor had let him rest as long as possible. "You're sure you have everything you need?"

"Yes," Hathor said. "Good luck to you and your men."

"And good hunting to you."

With a final clasp of his hand on Hathor's shoulder, Eskkar disappeared into the darkness, following Grond. Hathor, Klexor, and all thirty horsemen would remain in the camp, tending the dying fires, acting as pickets, and trying to make themselves look as if they constituted all of the Akkadian forces. And praying to the gods that the Sumerians didn't decide to attack tonight.

A hundred paces from the nearest fire, Eskkar found the rest of his men waiting silently for his arrival. The seven horse boys were there as well, scattered throughout the archers to make sure they kept silent. He'd considered leaving them behind, but knew what their fate would be in the morning. Though sitting on the ground, the archers had formed a double column, each man a long stride apart from his nearest companion, and ready for the long night march. The chill in the air made more than a few shiver.

Every bowman carried two quivers full of arrows, thirty shafts in each. Every fifth man carried a water skin, but that burden would be shared as they marched. In a few hours most of it would be gone. Other than their swords and knives, the archers carried nothing else, no food, no cooking pots, nothing. They'd already eaten the last of the food. Morning might herald a long day of hunger and thirst, with the grim possibility of a fight to the death.

Eskkar moved to the head of the column. Lifting his eyes, he studied the sky and located the North Star. He would keep that at his back. Before long, the moon would rise, but by then Eskkar and his force of archers intended to be well away from their campsite, which would remain in place to reassure those watching the Akkadians' movements. With luck, he and his men would soon be far from the camp and any spying eyes.

It wouldn't be a full moon tonight, but should shed enough light to help mark the trail. At least, Eskkar hoped it would.

"Tell the men to move out, Grond. Pass the word to each man."

With that order, Eskkar had committed himself and his men to the risky plan. He waited until he felt certain the order had time to reach the rear of the column, and then started walking south, back along the trail they'd followed during the day.

Grond passed the order, then disappeared ahead into the darkness. He had the most dangerous assignment tonight. With two men, both experienced hunters, Grond would scout the way south and make sure Eskkar and the rest of the men didn't blunder into any enemy sentries.

Now Eskkar had plenty to occupy his thoughts. His men would worry about the spirits and demons that prowled the land, searching for living bodies to carry back to their caves beneath the earth. No one liked to travel at night.

Esskar, however, ignored any fears about the hunters of the underworld. Since childhood, he had heard many stories of people taken during the darkness, but he had never seen a demon himself. If they hadn't bothered any of his enterprises until now, he doubted the evil spirits would choose tonight to try and carry off a few of his men. Instead, Esskar worried more about someone tripping and breaking a leg, or stumbling over a bush and spraining an ankle. Any sound or movement could alert the enemy sentries, who might still be posted somewhere nearby, watching the Akkadian camp.

In the past Esskar would have led the men himself, but he knew his eyes had lost some of their keenness in the dark. Better to let another with sharper sight lead the way than for Esskar to stumble and fall, embarrassing himself in front of his men. Esskar didn't intend to allow his pride get in the way of his plan. Waradi, one of the youngest archers and raised in the hill country west of Akkad, had been assigned the lead.

Waradi moved out ahead, Esskar right behind. The soldiers gathered strength from his presence, and from the knowledge that he took the same or greater risks as any of them. Esskar ordered every warrior to follow three paces behind the man in front of him. That should be close enough to maintain contact with the man ahead, yet far enough apart so that if someone tripped, he wouldn't take the man ahead or behind down with him.

The first few hundred paces would be the most dangerous. If the enemy saw or heard them, and sounded the alarm, Esskar would have to call the whole plan off and return to Hathor and his horsemen. Then they would have no choice but to fight their way north. Alexar, Drakis, Grond, and the other commanders would have warned the men over and over about the need to keep silent, watch where they stepped, and keep the proper distance. Nevertheless, Esskar kept glancing behind him. Finally, he realized that the more he fretted about his men, the more he stumbled himself. Swearing under his breath, he concentrated on the ground before him.

That first part of the long night march moved with maddening slowness. Esskar worried that the enemy had detected them, might even now be gathering strength to attack. Still, as the Akkadians moved farther away from the camp, their chances of being seen lessened. All that mattered now was maintaining his place behind Waradi, and keeping silent. In that way, step by step, the column crept through the darkness and, despite the occasional stumbles, no alarm was given.

Waradi moved back beside Eskkar. "I think we're safe enough. We've traveled at least a mile from the camp."

"No sign of Grond?"

"No, not yet. He might be far ahead."

Eskkar, who tended to worry over every thing that might go wrong, had little concern for Grond's safety. The man was made of bronze, and it would take more than a few men to subdue him. If Grond encountered any of the enemy, the noise would carry over a great distance in the still night air.

"Speed up the pace, Waradi."

"Yes, Captain," Waradi said, risking the familiarity usually reserved for Eskkar's closest friends and commanders.

Eskkar grunted. He turned to the man behind him. "Pass the word, we're picking up the pace."

Each man whispered the order to the man behind him. Soon eighty-five men and the horse boys were stretching their legs at a fast walk, risking the occasional stumble over a rock or patch of high grass. A broken leg or even a sprained ankle would mean a man out of the fight, and Eskkar needed every archer he had. Thankfully the moon had risen, shedding a bit more light to mark both the hills around them as well as the ground beneath their feet.

They kept moving, covering the dark ground as fast as they could. Only when Eskkar's own legs protested did he halt for a brief rest. Every man sank to the ground, glad to be off his feet. Nevertheless, Eskkar paused only long enough to let the men catch their breath. The archers' legs would just have to suffer.

They resumed the grueling march. All too soon the moon rose to its highest point and began its descent. Eskkar estimated that they needed to cover at least fifteen or sixteen miles to reach the Sumerian camp. And, of course, that assumed that a Sumerian force existed, and that this unseen enemy had moved north to pursue the retreating Akkadians. If that held true, Eskkar was still gambling his enemy would camp at the most likely place, where the small stream would provide plenty of water. Still, for all Eskkar knew, they could have marched ten or twenty miles in the opposite direction, back toward Sumer.

Walking through the blackness, Eskkar wondered if his march was anything more than a fool's errand. The plan that had seemed so reasonable yesterday now seemed more like a dangerous gamble that would put the Akkadians in harm's way. If dawn arose without their encountering the enemy, he would have wasted more than just a long and dangerous night's march. Hathor and the horsemen would be miles away, possibly in as much danger as Eskkar's archers. And some of his men would gaze at him before looking away, wondering about their leader's ability. The thought of looking foolish in their eyes always bothered him.

"Look into the mind of your enemy," Trella had often advised him, "and try to think as he does." That single piece of advice from his beautiful wife had accounted for more of Eskkar's good fortune in battle than anything else. So he placed himself in the enemy's mind, and tried to think like the leader of the Sumerian force behind him. If the Sumerians wanted a fight, they would follow his trail, chasing after him as fast as they could, and counting on their large force of horse fighters to slow the Akkadians down until they could be caught from behind. Now the long string of assumptions seemed tenuous. Eskkar forced such thoughts out of his head. It was too late now to have qualms about appearing foolish.

More thoughts of Trella jumped into his mind. He always worried when he left her behind, though he knew she was safe enough. Akkad now had sufficient soldiers to man the extended walls, more than enough to repel any attacker and to defend Trella and their son, Sargon from any assault from within. With old Gatus guarding the city, and Bantor protecting Trella, Eskkar felt certain he had little to concern himself about in that regard. Those two were his most trusted and loyal followers, and both would defend Trella and her son while they had breath in their bodies.

He shook his head, angry at himself for letting his mind wander. Now was not the time to be wasting thoughts on Trella. Instead, Eskkar turned his mind toward the coming fight. He still didn't know for certain who or how many he would be facing.

Sumer, deep in the Sumerian south, had yielded little information to Trella's few informants in the last six months. They had gathered some rumors of war and of men training to fight. Loose talk provided only a rough count of their numbers, and Eskkar estimated that Eridu could have as many as two hundred men under his command. If supported by a strong force of horsemen, King Eridu might be tempted to attack the border.

Whatever enemy Eskkar faced in the morning, he guessed he would be outnumbered at least two or three to one, but that fact didn't trouble him. If he could achieve the surprise he intended, it wouldn't matter how many men his unknown opponent had.

But if Eskkar didn't come to grips with the enemy, if the campsite by the stream lay empty, Eskkar's split forces would be in deadly danger. Hathor would be lucky to rejoin the bowmen without a fight. Again and again Eskkar forced the ever-returning doubts from his mind. Dawn would answer all these questions.

As he strode along, he remembered another night march from almost ten years ago. That time Eskkar and a band of fighters led their horses, guiding the nervous animals through another long night of darkness. Luck had favored him then, and he closed with his enemy just in time for a daybreak raid through their camp. Now Eskkar had to hope tonight's march turned out as fruitful as the one long ago.

Waradi stopped short, raising his hand to halt the column. Behind Eskkar, the line of men stumbled and muttered at the sudden cessation of movement. To Eskkar's ears, the noise sounded loud enough to wake the demons below.

"Captain, it's Grond." Waradi's voice carried just enough to be heard a few dozen paces away.

Eskkar breathed a sigh of relief. "Pass the word for the men to halt."

Grond reached Eskkar's side, giving his captain a hug of delight. "We're making good time. Mitrac's hill is just ahead. My two scouts are on the far side, watching. But so far, we've seen nothing."

Eskkar digested the news. His archers had covered nearly two-thirds the distance to the stream. Best of all, they weren't lost, or marching in the wrong direction. "Good. Then we can increase our pace again." He moved back down the column, until he reached Mitrac and his group of hand-picked archers. "Mitrac. We're here. Gather your men."

The young archer had only nineteen seasons, but had more experience killing men than anyone in Akkad, including his captain. His bow had brought down countless numbers of barbarians, bandits and invaders, and even Eskkar stood in awe of Mitrac's skill with his chosen weapon.

Soon twelve of the archers stood behind Mitrac, all of them facing Eskkar.

"At least you don't have to walk any more," Eskkar said, in a feeble attempt at humor. Mitrac and his men would be left behind, to act as a rearguard and slow down any pursuit.

"Good luck to you, Captain," Mitrac answered.

"Is there anything else you need?" Eskkar wanted to say more, but there was nothing more to say. Everything had been discussed yesterday on the march up.

"No, Captain," Mitrac said. "You should keep moving. We'll catch up to you later in the day."

"Good hunting to you, then." He turned to Waradi. "Get the men moving. They've rested long enough."

With muted groans the column started off once again. Eskkar had time for a glance behind him at Mitrac and his men. The young archer had risked his life a dozen times, but always at Eskkar's side. Now Mitrac might have to face an unknown number of enemies, and Eskkar hoped he hadn't sacrificed one of his most loyal followers. Still, another dozen archers probably wouldn't make much difference in the morning, but here, if they could slow the enemy horsemen, they would strike a hard blow of their own.

The column of soldiers, now reduced to seventy-nine men and boys, pressed on. Once again Grond went on ahead to rejoin his two scouts. Their station would be at least a quarter mile in advance, alert for any signs of the enemy. Eskkar couldn't be sure, but estimated his men had no more than four or five miles to go to reach the camp site.

He glanced up at the heavens. The moon seemed to move faster now across the cloudless sky dotted with uncountable numbers of stars. The march continued, and the ground grew rougher, and more men stumbled or tripped as they tired. Eskkar's legs ached from the strain, and he heard the labored breathing of the soldiers behind him. They had covered several miles since their last stopping place. Better to halt now and let the men rest for a few moments.

"Waradi, we'll stop and rest. Pass the word to halt, then see if there's anything up ahead."

Alexar moved up from his post at the rear of the column. He joined his leader and sat down on the grass with a grunt of pleasure. Everyone was feeling the strain. "I left Drakis in charge of the rear, Captain." He glanced up at the sky. "Not much longer to sunrise," Alexar offered.

Eskkar's temper flared at the innocent words, but he caught himself. Alexar meant no criticism of his leader's plan. "Well, if we can't reach the camp by dawn, then all the men can enjoy a good rest."

"I meant . . ."

"I know what you meant, Alexar," Eskkar said, softening his tone. "We'll give it one more push. If we don't find anything, we'll build a camp of our own and wait for Hathor to join us."

That was the plan in the event of failure, or as much of it as they'd worked out. They would need food and water, and only the horsemen could bring that, and then only if they could avoid the enemy horsemen. In fact, Eskkar and his men would be trapped wherever they were, weary and helpless with scarcely any food.

"We've still got time," Alexar said. "Though I thought we'd have reached the stream by now."

Eskkar glanced up at the moon. It was fading, about to dip below the horizon. Not long after that, dawn would come. "We've rested long enough. Let's get the men moving." With a long sigh of soft murmurs, the column climbed back on its feet and started moving. By now Eskkar had no idea of how far they'd come, or how much farther they had to go.

"Captain! Captain!" Waradi rushed back to the head of the column. "One of the scouts, Myandro, he came back. He says he thinks they saw a glow in the night up ahead."

That might mean a single campfire, but Eskkar doubted any scouting party would burn a fire all night long. Only a large camp full of men would do that, to keep some fire available during the night should an emergency arise.

"Lead the way, Waradi," Eskkar said. "Alexar, get back to the rear and keep the men moving. Tell every one of them not to make a sound or I'll cut their tongues out myself."

In moments, and despite his orders, whispers of the sighting swept down the length of the column. Waradi and Eskkar pushed the pace even harder. The race against dawn continued, but now at least the Akkadians had some hope. It would be crushing to reach the enemy camp and find them awake and preparing for battle.

The archers moved quicker now, covering the next half mile almost at a trot. Then Waradi halted the column. Myandro, one of Grond's advance scouts, loomed up out of the shadows.

"Captain, there are campfires up ahead, at least three of them," Myandro said. "Less than a mile from here. As soon as we saw that, Grond sent me to find you. He and Ishme are waiting there, watching the camp."

A fire's light could be seen for miles at night. "You saw none of their sentries?" Eskkar bit his lip as soon as the words were uttered. Myandro, a

41

Hawk Clan warrior, had proven himself as one of the finest night hunters in Akkad. If the scout had seen anything of importance he would have spoken.

"No, nothing. If they have sentries posted, they're staying close to the camp."

"Let's keep moving, men," Eskkar said, speaking just loud enough to reach the archers now clustering around him. "Their camp is just ahead." Without waiting for a reply, Eskkar started jogging south. Myandro flashed by and raced ahead into the darkness with scarcely a sound coming from the thick grass beneath his sandals, while Waradi retook the lead position, stretching his own legs to keep pace with Eskkar's longer limbs.

Eskkar didn't stop jogging until he saw the glow of the fires up ahead. Then he slowed to a fast walk, breathing hard. A horseman born and bred, he hated walking, let alone running. Even after all those years living as an outcast among villagers and farmers, Eskkar still believed the farthest a warrior should walk was the distance from his tent to his horse. Villagers, who possessed few horses, had grown accustomed to walking great distances. Nor did they need many horses, living as they did jammed together in villages, with every man and animal within touching distance.

He glanced up at the sky. The moon had faded to a mere speck. But there should be just enough time to reach the enemy's camp. Myandro's figure again appeared out of the darkness.

"We'll need to be silent, Captain," he warned. "Every sound carries farther at night. We're close enough now that they might hear us coming."

"Just get us into position before the sun comes up," Eskkar whispered.

The Akkadians resumed their march, moving slower now and exercising caution with every step. They all followed Myandro, who led the way toward the base of a low hill. When Eskkar and the men started to climb, Myandro gave the order to halt.

"Keep the men here, Captain," he said. "You come to the top of the hill."

Soon Eskkar, Waradi, Alexar, Drakis, and Myandro lay at the top of the hill, facing south. Grond and Ishme were already there waiting for them, but one look over the crest told Eskkar everything he needed to know.

The enemy camp lay less than a quarter mile away, outlined by the fading glow from three watch fires. Eskkar could even make out the dozen or so trees that lined the tiny stream.

At this late hour, the guards hadn't bothered to replenish the flames, with dawn so near, even assuming they had any firewood left. The size of the encampment surprised Eskkar. He could even make out the hulking shadow of a large tent on one side of the camp. After one quick look, Eskkar raised his estimate of the enemy facing him to at least three hundred. No wonder the enemy felt confident enough to challenge Akkad.

"We won't be able to get a good count until dawn," Alexar said, thinking along the same lines.

"It doesn't matter," Eskkar said. "A hundred or a thousand, we have to attack. If nothing else, we need the food and water."

"Do you think they have any guards this far from camp?" Alexar had lifted himself up on one elbow to better scan the landscape.

"I haven't seen any," Grond whispered. "I've been watching, but the only sentries I see are those pacing the camp's perimeter. But there's at least ten of them guarding this approach."

"Let's see how close we can get before they spot us," Eskkar said. "It's the end of a long nightwatch, and their sentries will be tired. Alexar, you and Grond go back and tell the men what is up ahead. I don't want any of them falling down the hill because they're gawking at the campfires."

"Come on, Grond," Alexar said, excitement in his voice. "We'll bring them up a dozen at a time."

Eskkar rose and crested the hill. The sentries would be unable to see this far into the blackness, and every glance toward the campfires would reduce their night vision. He moved across the grass, feeling his way, until he reached a point about two hundred paces from the camp, as close as he dared go without risking detection. He stopped and waited until Grond crept up with the first group of men.

"Spread out along this line," Eskkar ordered, extending his arms. He kept his voice low, so that he couldn't be heard a dozen paces away. "We'll wait here until dawn."

Time seemed to race by, and the eastern sky began to lighten. Little by little, the Akkadian line extended as each group of men joined them. When all of them were in place, his line of seventy bowmen stretched more than a hundred paces. Eskkar walked up and down the rank of men, whispering to each one, telling them one last time what they were to do and what to expect. No one showed the slightest fear at the prospect of attacking an unknown force more than three or four times their size. These archers knew their trade, and knew what devastation they could wreak on unprepared men.

With everything ready, Eskkar found he had time for one more set of orders. He gathered the seven horse boys around him.

"Boys, remember what I told you. Spread out and stay a dozen paces behind the archers. Your task is to kill any of the enemy wounded. Use your knives, until you can pick up a sword. Just stay behind the line, and keep silent. I don't want the archers to hear you shouting behind them. You might frighten them."

A few giggled softly at the thought. The boys, ranging in age from twelve to fifteen, were nearly wild with excitement and fear. "Yes, Lord," they whispered.

"And just as important, I want you to keep an eye on our rear. If anything comes up behind us, you must let me know at once. Can you do that?"

"Yes, Lord, we'll watch the rear."

"Good. Then good hunting to you. If you do well, you'll have a full share in any loot we capture."

"Captain." Grond approached. "It's almost light."

Eskkar strode back to the center of the line. "Drakis, take the right side, Alexar the left. Grond and I will take the center. Keep the men moving forward, and keep the line as even as you can." He drew his long sword from his sheath and raised it in the air. It wouldn't be needed for some time, but it would do to mark his place in the line, so that every man would know where their captain stood, and could look to his position for orders if need be.

The men had already strung their great war bows, each one almost as tall as the archer holding it. Arrows were loosened in the quivers, and swords made ready. For well-trained soldiers, these preparations took only moments, so often had they practiced them. Then the men had a chance for one final rest. Most sank to one knee, but a few squatted down while they waited for the order to advance.

The enemy camp was awakening now, the sleepy sounds of men knowing that dawn approached, the cooks already up, the leaders of ten and twenty starting to move about, yawning as they shook the sleep from their own eyes. The first rays of the sun crossed the hill behind Eskkar, illuminating the land before him with a soft glow. The sun wouldn't be directly behind his men, but at least his archers wouldn't be staring into a rising sun. The time had come.

"Start the men moving," Eskkar said, extending his blade straight toward the enemy camp. Up and down the line, seventy-two men stood, nocked an arrow to the string, and started walking forward, long strides that covered plenty of ground. The fatigue from the long night march had vanished. The prospect of closing with their enemy gave every man renewed strength.

From his position at the center, Eskkar glanced to either side. The line remained as even as could be expected, rippling in places for a few steps before the men regained their position. The archers paced forward in silence, still in the deep shadow cast by the hill behind them. Fifty paces, then one hundred. Someone in the camp gave a shout, but Eskkar knew it didn't matter now. Another thirty steps and he gave the order. "Halt! Shoot!"

Seventy-two arrows flew through the air. The sentries went down, some struck three or four times. Another volley was already on the way, as the archers loosed their shafts as fast as they could. At this range, less than seventy paces from the edge of the camp, it was almost impossible to miss. And even when they did fail to hit the intended target, the shafts were just as likely to strike some other Sumerian stumbling to his feet in the rear.

Confusion swept over the camp. Men still half-asleep stumbled to their feet to find arrows hissing through their ranks. Wounded men screamed in pain as the heavy shafts pierced arms and legs. Everyone seemed to be shouting orders, and Eskkar knew that would only add to his opponents' panic. Any enemy who picked up a bow was targeted at once, the distinctive silhouette easily noticeable even in the half-light of dawn. The twang of the bowstrings and the buzzing of the shafts tearing through the air could be heard even above the din coming from the camp.

Eskkar used Waradi's bow to keep the arrow count. As soon as the archer had launched his tenth shaft, Eskkar gave the order to advance, while he kept moving up and down the line, encouraging the men to take their time and aim their shafts.

The line surged forward another thirty paces, the archers shooting as they walked, before Eskkar halted them. He wanted the Sumerians to fall back, but he also wanted to keep them in a close killing range, just far enough away so that the Akkadians couldn't be rushed by a desperate counter-attack. Another dozen volleys swept into the milling crowd, all discipline gone with the arrival of the deadly arrows that struck a man down with savage force at such close range.

"Forward, another thirty paces," he shouted. "On the run!"

With a shout the men jogged forward, the line still fairly straight. They reached the dead sentries and crossed into the camp itself, the scent of blood and worse already thick in the air.

"Akkad! Akkad!" The archers shouted their battle cry as they drove the enemy back. By now most of the bowmen had emptied their first quiver and began drawing shafts from the second.

"Select your targets!" Esskar bellowed, his voice carrying up and down the line. "Don't waste arrows!" He didn't want the men to run out of shafts until the Sumerians broke completely. "Forward! Another thirty paces forward!"

The line surged again. This time his men had to watch their step, as the dead and wounded littered the blood-slicked ground. Behind him, Esskar heard the horse boys' high-pitched voices crying out with glee as they hacked away at any wounded enemy that still moved. Horses bolted from behind the tent, and Esskar saw four men riding away, clinging to their mounts. Damn, that would be the leader of the enemy escaping. Esskar cursed himself for not telling a few of the archers to target the tent's occupants or the tethered horses.

By now the Akkadians had swept through half the camp, and the Sumerians gave up any attempt at defending themselves. Screams of the wounded rose up, adding to the survivors' confusion. Their leaders had abandoned them, and now every man thought only about how to save himself. Everywhere Esskar looked, he saw men throwing weapons to the ground and bolting to the rear. He knew broken men when he saw them. They would run and run until they fell exhausted to the ground.

The archers reached the far edge of the camp, leaving only dead and wounded behind them. They continued shooting their arrows, angling the shafts higher into the air, until everyone had emptied his quivers. On the plain stretching to the south, Esskar watched the surviving Sumerians run for their lives, escape from the deadly Akkadian arrows their only thought.

"HALT!" There was nothing else he could do. His men were too tired to chase after the fleeing men.

Esskar turned to face the camp. The sun had just cleared the top of the low hills, and he realized the entire battle had taken only moments. Each of his archers had loosed close to sixty arrows, and it didn't take long for his Akkadian bowmen to launch that many shafts. Bodies littered the ground, most with arrows protruding from them. Wounded men shrieked out for mercy or water. The smell of blood now mixed with the more powerful odor of vomit and human waste. Stores of food and piles of water skins, weapons, blankets, cooking pots, clothing, helmets, sandals and tunics lay scattered about, kicked over and trampled in the confusion. Even if the enemy managed to regroup, the survivors would have nothing to fight with and no food to sustain them.

Drakis joined his captain and Grond. "Well done, Captain. We caught them completely by surprise."

"We were lucky," Eskkar said, sliding his sword into its scabbard. Another battle fought without his needing to use it. The few enemy who had offered any resistance had been cut down at once, and he doubted if he'd ever been in any danger.

"Well, I for one hope that your luck doesn't run out."

"I'm sure it will." Eskkar laughed and clapped Drakis on the shoulder. "But not today. At least you survived this fight without a wound."

In the last battle, Drakis had fought like a lion, taken half a dozen wounds, and nearly died. He spent months recovering, while healers hovered over him.

Alexar arrived at almost the same time, a big smile on his face. "Another great victory, Captain."

"We've only won half the battle," he reminded them. "Now let's get busy. There's plenty of work to be done. Have the men collect their arrows first. We don't want to be standing here with empty quivers if the Sumerian horsemen arrive."

"Yes, Captain."

"Myandro, put out pickets to guard the camp. Drakis, have some of the men collect the weapons, then count and drag off the dead. Gather the food and anything of value in one place. Grond, come with me."

Eskkar led the way toward the tent, picking his steps through the bodies and waving off the already gathering flies. He swept aside the opening flap. Grond ducked in first, and Eskkar followed.

Big enough to hold seven or eight people, and almost high enough for Eskkar to stand erect, the tent contained cushions, a small chest, two wineskins, and scattered clothing. A sword hung from the central post, still in its scabbard.

"Our enemy travels well," Grond said, kicking a cushion aside. "All the comforts of home."

"Must be some soft merchant who ..." Eskkar reached out his arm and pointed to the far corner of the tent. Something had moved under a pile of blankets.

Grond drew his sword, the blade rasping as it came out of the sheath. "Come out! Now! Or I'll gut you where you hide!"

Eskkar saw the top of a head, then another. He laughed again, and let himself relax.

Two women appeared, clinging to each other, eyes wide with fear. Young girls, with probably less than thirteen seasons. One covered her mouth with her hands, and both trembled as they stood. They looked like terrified children.

"Please don't hurt us, master," one said, dropping to her knees, while tears streamed down her face.

The other girl, her eyes wide with fright, couldn't mouth a word.

At least they could answer one question.

"Who is your master?"

One girl swallowed. "Our master is King Eridu of Sumer."

Eskkar had to lean forward to hear the words. He grunted in disgust at the name of the former trader turned king. No wonder it had been such an easy victory.

"Get them outside. You'd better assign someone to guard them." If they'd been a few seasons older, Eskkar would have turned them over to his archers as a reward. Now he'd have to waste time and men to keep two useless pleasure slaves from harm.

The thought surprised him. A few years ago, he would have taken both girls himself. Even now, if he'd done any fighting, the thought of burying himself in a woman's flesh would have tempted him. Now he regarded them as just another problem to be dealt with. Living with Trella more than satisfied his urges.

"Maybe they'll tell us something useful," Grond said, when he returned.

"Yes, I'm sure they'll know plenty about Eridu's rod and what wines he favors," Eskkar said. "I doubt if they have the wits to remember what he dined on last night." Remembering Trella's advice, he took a deep breath. Women, even ones as young as these, still heard everything their master said. "But you're right. They may be helpful. We'll get back to them later. Now there's work to do. I want to be ready if the Sumerian horsemen arrive."

5

In the morning, Razrek was up before the dawn, inspecting his men and making sure they were ready for battle. He, too, had doubled his guards for the night, spreading them out around his forces and making sure his horses were protected. The Akkadians knew he was close by, and Razrek didn't intend to be surprised by a night attack, especially after warning Eridu to beware the same possibility. The first rays of the sun had just lifted above the horizon when Mattaki galloped up, his horse snorting and throwing clods of dirt in the air as its rider pulled it to a halt.

"Razrek! They're gone, all of them! The Akkadians have broken camp!"

A feeling of dread washed over Razrek. The Akkadians might be flanking him. They could attack at any moment. "Which way did they go?"

"South, damn them," Mattaki said. "I said they're gone. I watched the last of them ride off at first light, traveling fast."

"And the archers?"

"Gone as well. I rode to the top of the hill, but saw no sign of them. They must have left well before dawn."

Razrek clenched the hilt of his sword until his hand began to hurt. "What were our sentries doing? Sleeping again. You were supposed to keep..."

"No, I checked the guards twice last night, and watched the Akkadians myself. They settled in for the night. Damn the gods, they were all sleeping when the camp fires burned out."

"Then they can't be far ahead." Razrek took a deep breath. No sense appearing worried in front of his men. He hadn't survived so many years by panicking at the unexpected, and his wits told him to think the situation through. Eskkar was a cunning bastard who always had a trick or two ready to spring on his opponents. Razrek realized it didn't make much sense for the foot soldiers to leave an hour or two earlier. The Akkadian cavalry would overtake them soon enough, so what was to be gained by such a maneuver? Unless . . . unless the archers had left long before the dawn. Could they have slipped away without his men seeing them go?

"Demons below," Razrek said. "They're going back to attack Eridu's men. He thinks he's pursuing the Akkadians. Instead he'll be walking into a trap."

"Impossible," Mattaki said. "The Sumerians are at least twenty, maybe twenty-five miles behind."

"Not any more. If Eridu marched north yesterday, even his ragged band of cut-throats would have covered at least ten miles. If Eskkar's men can cover twelve or fifteen miles during the night, they can meet Eridu at daybreak."

Mattaki looked dubious. "Could foot soldiers travel that far in the dark? There wasn't much of a moon last night."

Razrek wanted to believe they couldn't. He knew Eridu's men couldn't manage such a thing, but Eskkar's soldiers . . .

"Marduk's bones, these Akkadians might." Razrek spat on the ground in anger. "Eridu had better hope to the gods Eskkar's men can't reach his Sumerians before dawn. If he doesn't have a strong guard posted, the fool might wake up with an arrow in his belly."

"Eridu's men outnumber the Akkadians by at least three to one, more if their cavalry won't be there."

"Numbers won't matter to Eskkar. Even if he can't destroy Eridu's soldiers, he'll maul them so bad they'll be ready to run home." Razrek looked up at the sky. By now Eskkar's archers might be closing on Eridu's men. "Get the men mounted, all of them. Call in the scouts. We'll have to ride hard to save whatever's left of Eridu's soldiers. I just hope they can hold out until we arrive."

"Which route will we take, to the east or west?"

"The shortest, which means we'll have to follow the path the Akkadians took."

"We're going to chase them? Are you mad? They'll expect us to follow, they'll set up an ambush for sure. We should swing around them, take a different route."

"No time. We'll have to take the chance." Razrek shook his head in anger. "Besides, it's the Sumerians Eskkar wants to smash, not us. By now he's figured out who his real enemy is. If Eskkar leaves a strong enough force behind to ambush us, he won't have enough to break Eridu's forces. We only have to get to Eridu before he's overrun, and that means we'll need to take the shortest path."

"You're going to get us all killed."

"No, at the first sign of an ambush, we'll just pull back, swing around them. If their cavalry tries to follow, we'll finish them off. Now get moving."

Mattaki took only moments to get the men ready to ride. Razrek waited, frowning at every delay. He felt his own doubts rising. Suddenly, he was dependent on Eridu's men holding their ground, and he felt certain Eskkar wouldn't gamble his forces like this if he weren't confident of winning. Or would he? King Eskkar believed in luck, that much was certain. Still, even the Akkadian might not be able to cover all that distance during the night. He might be counting on engaging whatever force he encountered before Razrek could arrive.

"Damn all the demons to the fires." Razrek swung onto his horse. "Let's ride!"

Mitrac figured he had more than enough time to prepare his position. Even if the Sumerian horsemen began their pursuit at first light, the sun would be nearly halfway to its zenith before they reached this valley. In fact, they might not even come at all, if they took another route to reach the enemy's camp ground. That would be the best solution, Mitrac knew, because it would delay the horsemen even more, and he wouldn't have to risk his men. Nevertheless, he hoped the enemy would take the most direct route. If the Sumerian horsemen followed Hathor's trail, then they would have to ride past Mitrac and his archers.

Eskkar and Mitrac had marked this position yesterday, on the march north. They'd been searching for a place where a few archers might hold off Eridu's cavalry. This gentle valley seemed a perfect place for the archers. The dale's walls were not particularly high or steep, but the slope was long and would be tiring for any horse and rider. At the valley's center, the walls pinched in, and a small hill jutted up a few dozen paces from the floor, leaving only one narrow path that circled the base of the hill.

Mitrac knew his archers could sweep the approach, and then follow the horsemen as they rode past. The hilltop might not be that imposing, but it would slow down any horsemen foolish enough to try attacking uphill and overrunning the archers' position. Unless, Mitrac corrected himself, the enemy was willing to risk taking plenty of casualties. Best of all, if the horsemen decided to avoid the killing zone and bypass Mitrac's archers, the enemy would have to turn around and ride back more than a mile, then find another trail south. That would waste even more time.

His mission wasn't to defeat or even stop the Sumerian horsemen, only to slow them down and give Eskkar enough time to finish off the foot soldiers. If the enemy didn't take this route, then Mitrac would have to find a way to join up with Eskkar's archers. Mitrac and his band would be needed, too, especially if Eskkar arrived too late to take Eridu's men by surprise.

All that mattered little now, Mitrac decided. "Let's get to work." He posted two guards on the top of the hill, and the others descended to the base and started digging.

The Akkadians had brought one bronze-tipped shovel with them on the march south, and Mitrac had requested it. He wanted to dig as many small holes as possible, to help block the expanse between the foot of the hill and the other side of the valley wall. The holes didn't need to be deep or wide. Half a sword-length deep would be more than enough to break a horse's leg.

The men took turns with the shovel. Mitrac didn't want any of them getting their hands blistered and impairing their archery. After Eskkar and the commanders had worked out the plan, Mitrac had picked his own men. He'd selected those who could draw and loose a shaft as fast as humanly possible.

Soon they were all sweating with the effort of digging. At least they'd gotten some rest waiting for dawn to arrive. Mitrac took his turn, like any of the men. They passed the shovel from man to man, while others dug with sticks or anything else they could lay their hands on. Soon the ground beside the hill was pock-marked with dozens of irregular holes scattered about. His men had just a few more paces of open ground to dig when one of the guards gave a shout.

"Riders coming!"

Everyone scrambled back up the hill, gathered their bows, and strung them. The quivers had already been laid out, so that the shafts would draw easily. By now Mitrac could feel the earth shaking as the horsemen appeared at the far end of the valley. As soon as the riders saw the hill, they halted. A few moments later, one of them waved his arms.

"It's Hathor!" Mitrac shouted. He gestured them to ride in. "Guide them past."

Hathor's tall and lean figure was almost as recognizable at a distance as Eskkar's. The Egyptian and his men cantered toward Mitrac's position, stopping when they reached the base of the hill. Mitrac and his men formed a line that forced Hathor to funnel his men close to the valley wall, in order to avoid the holes.

Hathor waited until his men had passed through. "They won't be far behind me, Mitrac."

"We've just another dozen holes to dig, and we'll be ready."

"If we get a chance, I'll send men back to guide you in."

Not likely, Mitrac thought. He'd recognized the same look in Eskkar's eyes. Both men thought there was a good chance Mitrac and his men would all be dead by noon. "Good hunting, Hathor."

The Egyptian nodded respectfully, then kicked his horse and galloped off, riding hard to catch up with his men. Mitrac knew that the Akkadian horsemen had as dangerous an assignment as his own. They needed to ride south at top speed, to link up with Eskkar's archers at the Sumerian camp. Hathor's warriors would be the final blow on the Sumerians, the stroke that Eskkar hoped would finish them as a fighting force. With luck, they might even get ahead of the Sumerians. Otherwise, they would follow their trail and try to hunt them down. Hathor would be facing plenty of danger of his own today. If anything went wrong, they'd be caught on tired horses in open ground.

The archers completed digging the last of the holes. Then, on their hands and knees, they spread grass over and around them, trying to erase all signs of their work. When Mitrac felt satisfied that any oncoming riders wouldn't see the deadly holes until they were right on top of them, he gathered his men atop the hill. They formed a rough half-circle that encompassed the hilltop. Swords were withdrawn from their sheaths and stuck into the earth.

Mitrac gazed at each of his archers. They looked nervous, excited, a few of the untested even looked scared. But all them appeared ready to gamble their skill against those of the Sumerians. Thirteen men would try to stop between seventy or eighty horsemen. On open ground, Mitrac knew it couldn't be done, not against a determined enemy, and these Sumerian horse fighters clearly knew their trade.

But the little hilltop might provide the archers with enough of an edge, and all of his bowmen could loose four aimed shafts in the time it took a man to count to ten. When the horsemen arrived, they would have to decide their course of action. Either attack at once and in full force, or turn aside and take the longer route south.

The waiting began. Mitrac realized he should have kept the men busy, even if it meant digging more holes than needed. The longer they waited, the more time they had to worry, and the more tense they got. He tried to talk to them, but quickly realized he was only making them more nervous. With a shake of his head, Mitrac suddenly understood why Eskkar always remained so grim and silent right before a battle. Better to say nothing, he decided, and just try to look confident.

This time they all heard the horsemen coming, and the ground shook even harder than from Hathor's passage. Mitrac no longer cared, and without realizing it, he let out a sigh of relief. Two advance riders came into view. They halted at the same place where Hathor stopped as soon as they saw Mitrac's archers, getting to their feet and readying their weapons. In moments the main force joined the scouts, and the troop halted at the top of the valley, just out of range. A heated discussion soon began, as evidenced by the gestures of the riders.

Mitrac smiled at their hesitation. They didn't know how many men might be hiding just behind the hill. For all they could tell, all of Eskkar's archers could be here, just waiting for the chance to slaughter their enemies.

That risk was too great to take. The two scouts turned their horses and began climbing up the valley wall, scrambling their way to the valley rim. Halfway up, the horses stopped, refusing to go any further, and the men dismounted and made their way up the last hundred paces on foot. From there they trotted along the valley rim until they could see behind the hill.

"They're afraid of our bows," Mitrac said, as much to reassure his men as himself.

The two scouts continued along the crest, until they could see well up into the valley beyond. They were within range now, and Mitrac considered loosing a few arrows at them, but decided not to waste shafts at such a long distance.

The two men turned suddenly and retraced their steps at a run. Soon they were slipping and sliding down the slope to where their horses waited.

Mitrac possessed very good eyes, and he used them to watch the two men report. They spoke to a rider on a large brown horse with a splash of white across its chest, and another man riding a gray speckled mount. Those would be the leaders. Without thinking, Mitrac took a quick count of his enemy. At least seventy riders, more than enough to wreak havoc in Eskkar's rear.

"Men, when I give the word, target those two riders." He described both horses, though he felt certain all his men had identified them by now. "Two shafts from every man, that's all. But hold until I give the word."

Now there was nothing to do but wait. Mitrac felt the excitement rising in his chest. He told himself that it wasn't fear, but that wasn't entirely true. He and his men had nowhere to go. If they left their vantage point, they'd be run down. His archers now had no choice but to stand together and defend this position. The battle was set, and the next few moments might determine his fate, as well as the fate of all the Akkadians.

"You're sure there's no more behind them?"

"Yes, Razrek," the scout replied, breathing hard from his exertions. "We could see all the way up the valley. And we saw fresh tracks, so the Akkadian cavalry must have just passed through."

"We're going to lose a lot of men riding through that gap," Mattaki said. "Let's go back and ride around this valley. Eskkar weakened his forces to leave these behind. Even Eridu should be able to hold them off. Why should we lose any of our men trying to get past a handful of archers?"

"They picked their spot well," Razrek said, ignoring Mattaki's advice. He studied the ground, searching for any advantage. "By the time we ride around them, the battle will be over."

"There may not even be a battle," Mattaki argued. "If the Akkadians haven't reached Eridu's soldiers, then we'll have wasted men and horses for nothing."

"And if they have reached Eridu's camp, Eskkar's archers and his cavalry will smash those fools."

"Against those odds?" Mattaki shook his head. "And if they do, it's all the more reason to save our men and horses."

Razrek shook his head. "No, we can't take the chance. Even if Eskkar attacks and pushes Eridu's men back, our men can turn the tide of battle. We're going through."

"Damn you, Razrek! What about the archers? Do we ride them down?"

"No, half of us would never make it up the hill. A few dead horses and the approach would be blocked. They'd pick us off like flies. We'll take our chances and ride through. We might still be able to smash Eskkar's force."

Even if he lost a quarter of his men, Razrek decided, he would still have enough to turn the battle at the camp. Mattaki thought like a raider, out for easy kills and quick conquests. Razrek perceived the real danger in the situation. If Eskkar broke through, there was nothing to stop him from moving all the way south into Sumeria, to Sumer itself if he wanted. In that case, Razrek and his horsemen might need some luck to get back to Sumer.

Razrek struggled to control his horse. All the animals had picked up the scent of fear and danger from his men, and wanted to mill about. The sooner they got past this handful of bowmen, the better. "Get our bowmen ready!" Razrek shouted. His horsemen had about ten bows, the shorter ones that could be fired from horseback. "Try and take a few shots as we ride through." It took only a few moments to ready the men.

"We're going straight through!" he shouted. "Now ride, damn you, ride!"

"They're coming!"

Mitrac smiled at the needless warning, shouted by an excited young archer in his first battle.

"Ready your shafts, men!" Mitrac had to raise his voice to be heard over the hoof beats of the approaching horsemen, but he kept his voice calm. "Aim for the horses and remember to lead your targets!"

Almost the same words Eskkar had repeated again and again at the siege of Akkad. Bring the horse down, and the rider is helpless, either stunned or injured, and suddenly on foot and unsure of himself. An easy kill.

The swiftly moving horses moved into range.

"Loose!" Mitrac gave the command and let fly his own shaft, with just the slightest arch to reach the riders out in front. Thirteen arrows flew toward the onrushing horsemen, galloping as fast as they could, every rider hanging low over his horse's neck. Well before the first arrows struck, a second flight flew off the bowstrings.

"Target the leaders!" Mitrac shouted the words with all his strength, to be heard over the din of the horses. He launched shaft after shaft at the enemy commander, loosing as fast as he could fit an arrow to the string. Not all his bowmen remembered. A few continued to shoot at the mass of riders, but enough arrows flew toward the enemy commanders, both riding on the far side of the valley, and keeping the moving mass of horses and men between themselves and the hilltop.

Nevertheless, even with at least ten arrows launched at them in the first volley, the two leaders rode through the humming shafts unscathed. Then Mitrac glimpsed an arrow striking the brown and white horse in the flank. The animal reared up, its cry of pain unheard over the thundering hooves, but Mitrac lost sight of his prime targets, now concealed by a mass of horses and men. Instead, he shot his arrows as fast as he could, aiming at the easiest target.

The first horsemen burst past the base of the hill. Mitrac swung his bow around and let a shaft fly. He saw one, then another horse go down, caught by the holes. Even through the din of battle, he heard the bones snapping and the animals' cries of pain. Some of the following horses jumped the injured animals, others swerved past them, bumping and colliding in the narrow passage, neighing and snapping their teeth in their confusion.

Another horse went down, screaming in agony, its rider pitching forward to land directly in the path of the remaining riders, crushed to death in an instant. But most of the riders swept by, though his archers followed their movement and continued to shoot arrows as fast as they could.

In the excitement, Mitrac had almost forgotten about the enemy commanders. He didn't recall seeing either of the two horses he'd marked ride past. Turning his gaze back up the valley, he saw five horsemen still remaining, obviously unwilling to chance the ride without the safety of numbers. One pulled a dismounted rider up behind him, and Mitrac saw the brown and white horse sprawled nearby. Once they'd recovered their leader, they took one look at the dead bodies littering the base of the hill. They turned away and galloped back up the valley.

"Archers!" Mitrac pointed with his bow at the retreating horsemen. A few arrows were launched after them. Mitrac loosed four shafts himself, and someone's aim must have been good, for one of the riders took a shaft in the back and pitched off his mount before the rest moved out of range.

"Good shooting, men!" Mitrac shouted. He had separated at least one, possibly both of the enemy leaders from their men. That alone should slow them down, especially if they had to decide what to do next. Satisfied, Mitrac looked around. One of his men lay on his back, an arrow in his throat. Another cursed steadily, as two companions tried to remove a shaft that had penetrated his arm. Other than those two, the rest of his bowmen were unscathed.

The wounded horses still cried out in their fear and pain, a pitiful noise that concealed the cries of any wounded bandits. "Finish off the wounded. Then put those injured horses out of their misery!" he shouted. "And don't forget to gather up your arrows!"

He had no idea if the bandits would return, but his men should be able to recover at least half the arrows they'd shot. The archers descended the hill and started killing the enemy wounded. A sword thrust in the neck finished them off. The horses were harder to kill and took longer to die, screaming like women under the clumsy sword strokes of the archers. Mitrac hated killing horses, and their cries only made it worse.

"Mitrac, here's a horse for you." One of his men led a horse to the foot of the hill.

Mitrac mounted the animal, and began counting the enemy dead. Back and forth he rode, guiding the skittish horse through the bloody grass littered with bodies. The task took longer than he expected, but at last Mitrac returned to the base of the hill. By then his men had captured two more horses, and waited there for him.

"How many?"

"Eighteen dead men, and twenty-three dead or captured horses. Good shooting, men."

They cheered at the news, as well they should. Every archer had loosed at least ten arrows, some as many as fifteen, at the enemy cavalry. Mitrac did the calculation in his head. At least a hundred and twenty to a hundred and sixty arrows had been launched. With the loss of a single man, his archers had broken the strength of the enemy horsemen. Even if those who got through reached Eskkar's forces, the surviving Sumerian horsemen would not be sufficient to overwhelm the Akkadians. And if the unhorsed enemy leader remained to the north, he faced a long and hard ride to rejoin his men.

The plan had worked, and Mitrac felt proud that he had suggested it. He might be the youngest of Eskkar's commanders, but after this, no one would ever doubt either his courage or his tactics. And that alone made the night's walk and the morning's work worthwhile.

6

"What happened?" A stupid question, Razrek knew, as soon as the words left his lips, but his head felt as if a horse had stepped on it. For all he remembered, maybe one had. He found himself sitting on the ground, his back resting against a large rock. A rough edge pressed against his spine, and Razrek shifted to remove the source of the pain. The movement sent a throbbing through his head. He had trouble speaking, and knew his thoughts were sluggish.

"What happened! I'll tell you what happened." Mattaki mouthed an oath and spat on the ground. "They littered the ground with our dead and wounded. Your horse took a shaft and went wild. You lost control and he threw you. If we hadn't stopped to pick you up, you'd probably be dead by now."

Razrek digested his subcommander's harsh words. He remembered riding toward the hill, as arrows struck all about him. After that, everything was hazy. He must have fallen hard. His shoulder hurt, too, he realized.

"Well, then, I suppose I owe you my life," Razrek said. He looked around. "Where are the rest of the men?"

"On the other side of the valley, damn you!" Mattaki shouted, his face a hand's length from that of his commander. "By the time we stopped to pick you up, the men had ridden past. We had to turn around and come back. There was no chance of getting through. I lost my horse trying to save your neck."

For a moment Razrek stared at him, his face empty of emotion. Then he realized what his subcommander's words meant. "We're not with our men?"

"Yes . . . yes . . . yes," Mattaki answered, "with at least a dozen archers between us and them. We'll have to ride around now, which is what we should have done in the first place."

Razrek sagged back, his head spinning again. He lifted a hand and gingerly touched the side of his head. A massive bruise met his fingers, but he didn't feel any blood. No doubt he was lucky to be alive.

Without him leading them, his men would find some excuse not to attack Eskkar's force. They'd lost men and horses. Some would be wounded. They wanted to hear his orders. Those reasons would be enough to stop them from moving farther south. Even worse, Razrek, Mattaki, and the two men with them would have to swing round the valley, a time-wasting trip, and then have to hope they could catch up with their men.

"Is it finally sinking in?" Mattaki said with a sneer. "Or is your head still addled?"

"Damn you to the pits, watch your mouth!" Razrek held out his arm and Mattaki pulled him to his feet. For a moment, he thought he would fall down, but then the dizziness passed, and he felt the strength returning to his limbs. A sharp pain accompanied every movement of his head. "Let's get moving. The sooner we catch up with our men the better."

"If they haven't scattered to the four winds," Mattaki said.

His subcommander, too, knew what kind of men they commanded. They fought for gold and loot, and a chance to pillage. For weeks they enjoyed nothing but easy raids on helpless farmers. Now they felt the reach of Akkad's arrows. They'd look for any excuse to avoid a dangerous and unprofitable fight.

Razrek managed to pull himself onto the spare horse. Whatever happened to the south, he wouldn't be a part of it. Eridu would have to hold off Eskkar's forces on his own. Razrek just hoped the Sumerian was up to the task.

"Lead the way, Mattaki," was all he said. There wasn't really anything else to say, not until they linked up with what was left of their men, and found out what had befallen Eridu and his foot soldiers.

As soon as he left Mitrac's archers behind, Hathor drove his men hard. Fortunately, a day of rest and yesterday's easy march had refreshed the mounts, at least enough to get one more day's push out of them. He alternated the pace between a canter and a fast walk, the ground moving steadily beneath their hooves. Mile after mile passed as they followed the faint tracks of Eskkar's bowmen. Whenever he turned his head to the rear, Hathor saw no sign of Razrek's horsemen in pursuit.

Yesterday, when the commanders worked out the details of the plan, Hathor had argued strenuously over the role his horsemen were to play. Eskkar wanted to gamble everything on his archers reaching the enemy camp before dawn. He wanted Hathor's cavalry to swing wide of Eridu's campsite, slip behind the enemy, and approach them from the south. It would be a cunning move if everything went well, but Hathor convinced first the other commanders then Eskkar that it was better to just follow Eskkar's men.

If the dawn raid worked as planned, Hathor's cavalry should be able to quickly pick up the enemy's trail, and would save the extra miles of riding needed to get behind the Sumerians. The Akkadian horses should still be able to ride down most of the fleeing soldiers, but more important, in the event that Eskkar's plan went awry, Hathor's cavalry would be able to provide support.

Most of all, as Hathor explained with all the energy he could muster, he and Eskkar would have a chance to communicate with each other. The longer two separate forces stayed out of contact, the greater the danger to both. That thought finally swayed Eskkar, and he had grudgingly given in.

He had never fought a large-scale battle with Eskkar before, but Hathor felt reassured that his commander listened to his subordinates, and didn't recklessly decide every issue himself. Satisfied with the new orders, the Egyptian looked forward to proving his worth and the worth of his horsemen. Then Hathor remembered that he had fought with Eskkar once before, but not on the same side. After Eskkar spared Hathor's life, it had taken a year before most of the Akkadians accepted his presence, and most of another year before they accepted his command. Now he had, for the first time, a chance to show what he could accomplish for King Eskkar, and Hathor did not intend to fail.

The sun had climbed halfway to its zenith before his horsemen rounded another of the endless low hills and saw a lone sentry ahead. The man took one look at the horsemen and disappeared, no doubt running as fast as he could to spread the word.

Hathor recognized the ground. "The stream is just up ahead!"

Down one hill and up another, they saw the Sumerian camp a quarter mile ahead of them. A line of bowmen had formed up facing them, but even at a distance Hathor recognized the longer bows that only the Akkadians could use so efficiently. He slowed his men to a trot until he recognized Eskkar's looming figure standing at the center of the line.

"It's Eskkar. He's taken the camp!"

A cheer went up from his men, answered by one from the men in camp.

In a few moments, Eskkar was slapping Hathor on the back, practically pulling him down from the horse.

"You did it, I see, Captain." Hathor glanced around at the ruined campsite, debris still scattered everywhere. The bodies had been dragged away from the stream, and the archers had pillaged every item the Sumerians left behind, searching for anything of value and adding to the litter that now covered the ground.

"Yes, we arrived just in time. Another mile and we'd have been too late. As it was, we hit them at sunrise." He looked at Hathor's weary riders. "There's food for your men, and a stream to water your horses. And a dozen water sacks to carry with you, if you want to carry them."

"Yes, we'll take them. They won't slow us down much before they're gone."

Eskkar nodded. "The Sumerians have been running since dawn, with no food or water. Most abandoned their weapons. They can't have covered much ground on foot."

Hathor understood. Eskkar always did everything as fast as he could drive his men.

"And, Hathor, we were right. It is King Eridu of Sumer that we're fighting. Apparently, he raised up this army to capture the border. He got away before we could stop him . . . probably halfway to Sumer by now."

Hathor nodded. That was Eskkar's way of telling him to be careful. If the Sumerians linked up with their horsemen, they would still be a formidable force.

The riders stuffed stale Sumerian bread into their mouths as fast as they could swallow, while they watered their horses. As Hathor regrouped his troop, Alexar and two of his men came over. They carried ten of the short bows that could be used from horseback, and as many quivers.

"In case you need them, Hathor," he said. "The Sumerians left them behind."

The brief rest, coupled with food and water, helped the men more than the horses, but Hathor didn't worry about that. The fleeing enemy couldn't be far ahead, and the weary horses still had at least that much distance in them.

They rode out at a canter, following the broad track made by the fleeing Sumerian soldiers, the ground littered here and there with discarded weapons, water skins, food, sandals, and even clothing. The horsemen had gone less than a mile when they came upon three wounded men, too injured or exhausted to run any further. Hathor's new bowmen finished them off, scarcely slowing down in the process.

That happened again and again. Some of the wounded pretended to be dead, but every Sumerian received an arrow or two, just to make sure. The Akkadians would collect the shafts on the way back.

The sun climbed higher in the sky, and the temperature grew hotter as well. The numbers of wounded Sumerians grew fewer. Those strong enough to get this far would not have been injured. But the lack of water would be taking its toll, slowing them down and weakening their limbs. A glance up at the sun showed midday would soon be upon them.

Hathor crested a hill and saw a large group of Sumerians ahead. Hathor's men started to cheer.

"Silence! Halt! Not the slightest noise." Hathor scanned the low hills ahead of him. About eighty or ninety men were grouped together. Some were already running, but most stood their ground. Then he understood.

"Give me your bow," he ordered the nearest horsemen carrying one of the captured weapons. Snatching the short weapon from the man's hands, Hathor raised it up over his head and waved it back and forth. "The rest of you with bows, do the same."

After a few moments, one of the Sumerians returned the gesture. Hathor lowered the bow. "We'll walk the horses toward them. With luck, they'll think we're their own cavalry. Try to look as tired as they are, and keep your eyes on the ground. And bunch up. We don't want to look like an attack line."

They started down the hill, plodding along. It wasn't as foolish a trick as it appeared. His men dressed the same and rode the same kinds of horses as the Sumerian cavalry. Those who had attacked their camp had no mounts. More important, the Sumerians would be expecting their horsemen to rejoin them, and might assume that this was part of their own force. When the Sumerians realized their mistake, it wouldn't matter. Hathor would give the order to charge. He had no doubt that his thirty horsemen, fresh and well armed, could scatter these poorly armed, exhausted, and thirsty opponents.

Their slow approach lulled the Sumerians. Men sank back to the ground, apparently relieved that they would not have to fight or run again. Hathor's eye caught sight of four horses. If these men still had mounts, they must belong to the Sumerian commanders, else they would have vanished long ago.

"Bowmen," Hathor said, "I don't want those horses or their riders to get away. Make sure they don't."

Two men moved out in front of the Sumerians. One was tall and lean, and dressed in a blue tunic that even at a distance stood out from the rest. He stood with one hand on the hilt of his sword, while the other waved Hathor forward, impatience showing in his every movement.

Hathor and his men drew within a hundred and fifty paces before the man's eyes widened in surprise. Close enough, Hathor decided. He needed some space to get the horses up to speed.

"Attack!" Hathor kicked his horse into a run and tightened his legs around the animal's body. In moments, the powerful animal raced over the ground, hooves pounding, ears flat, as excited as its rider. Hathor's sword flashed from its sheath, and he raised it up over his head and swung it around. "Attack! Akkad! Attack!"

As they'd been trained, the Akkadians shouted their war cries at the top of their lungs as they urged their horses forward.

"Akkad! Eskkar!"

The words struck fear into the Sumerians. Those standing turned and ran, already two steps ahead of those who had to first scramble to their feet. Hathor directed his horse straight at the man in the blue tunic, who turned and fled toward the horses waiting nearby. In a few long strides, the shoulder of Hathor's horse crashed into the man's back, knocking him to the ground. Then the Akkadians, still screaming their war cries, charged into the fleeing men.

Swords rose and fell, blood spurted into the air. Men screamed in agony, struck by sharp blades, knocked aside by the horses, or just trampled underfoot. Again and again swords descended, each strike eliciting a cry of pain. A few Sumerians tried to fight, but a tired and thirsty man on foot had little chance against a sword swung down from a horse. Even those Sumerians untouched by any weapon were affected, the age-old fear of men on foot caught from behind by mounted warriors.

In moments the Akkadians had swept through the scattering enemy, leaving a trail of bloody bodies. Hathor yanked hard on the halter, turned his horse around, then kicked it into a run once again. He rode straight toward the enemy horses. Tied to a bush, they had panicked at all the noise and the scent of blood, struggling wildly against the ropes that held them. One broke free and bolted back toward the north. A Sumerian struggled to untie another animal when Hathor struck him down. An Akkadian arrow slew another who flung himself across a horse and tried to escape.

"You!" Hathor shouted at the man who'd fired the killing arrow. "Guard these horses! Let no one near them!"

The Egyptian scanned the battleground. Bodies littered the earth, many of them shrieking in pain from their wounds. His horsemen had dispersed all over the area, already reduced to chasing down individuals trying to flee. Hathor ignored all the killing. His men knew what to do. They would finish off every man they could, until their horses could go no further.

Dismounting, he tied his mount's halter to the same bush that had restrained the Sumerian horses. He had time to give the animal a friendly pat on its shoulder before he walked back to the edge of the camp, toward the man in the blue tunic. He lay facedown, right where he had fallen, and to Hathor's amazement, the man hadn't been trampled by any of the following horses. A blood-spattered rock remained beneath the man's head. Hathor knelt beside him, and rolled him over onto his back.

The man groaned at Hathor's less than gentle touch. "What happened ... who ...?"

Hathor still had his bloody sword in his hand. He put the tip of the blade against the man's throat and pushed a little, just enough to draw blood. "What's your name?"

Fear widened the man's eyes. He gasped in terror, and lifted his hands as if to move the sword aside.

Hathor pushed the sword a bit deeper. "I won't ask you again."

"Eridu! King Eridu of Sumer! Don't kill me!"

"Well, damn all the demons below!" Hathor said, so surprised that he withdrew the tip of the sword from Eridu's neck. "King Eskkar wished me good hunting, but I doubt he expected me to catch you in my net." He lowered his sword, then reached down and using his free hand dragged Eridu to his feet. "You might prove useful, if you do as you're told and don't force me to kill you."

Eridu might have been as tall as Hathor, but he lacked both the bulk and his captor's powerful muscles. The king's shoulders sagged in defeat.

Hathor shoved him along until they returned to where he left the horses. A handful of his men were busy looting the bodies. "Tie this one up, hands behind his back. Use his sandal straps and make sure they're tight. We don't want King Eridu to escape, do we?" Hathor shoved Eridu to the ground, where he lay gasping as the breath fled his body. "And his feet, too."

While the soldier trussed up the prisoner, Hathor took another glance around. His men were returning, most leading horses that no longer had the strength to carry their riders. A few even herded prisoners along. Hathor frowned at that. He preferred not to bother with captured soldiers, better to just kill them and get them out of the way, but he knew Eskkar would want to talk to them, to learn why they fought, and what they believed in.

Such ideas reminded him of Lady Trella's influence on her husband. Hathor had the greatest respect for Lady Trella. She was, after all, the one who convinced her husband to spare Hathor's life, putting her will against Eskkar's rage and desire for vengeance, not to mention the demands of every inhabitant of the city of Akkad.

Trella, transformed in a moment from slave to queen, offered her enemy his life, even a chance to return to Egypt if that's what he wanted. Instead, Hathor had sworn an oath on his honor as a warrior to follow Eskkar wherever he led, and Hathor had included Trella in that promise. In the days that followed, when he was greeted with scorn and contempt, if not outright hatred by everyone in the city, only Trella's influence and firm acceptance of the Egyptian gradually convinced the people of Akkad to separate Hathor from the atrocities of the Egyptian Korthac.

Since that time, Hathor had discovered a measure of happiness serving Akkad's leaders. Never before had such feelings filled his life, and he welcomed the opportunity to repay Eskkar and Trella for what they'd given him. Destroying their enemies would help pay back the debt that could never truly be redeemed.

And Hathor had proven himself a skilled leader of horsemen, second only to Eskkar himself. In the last year, he'd worked long and hard with the men he now commanded, turning farmers and villagers into a skilled force of cavalry, a name he recalled from his days in Egypt. The Akkadian cavalry numbered less than fifty men in all, and Eskkar had brought only thirty-two with him on this expedition to the southern border. The rest remained in the city, patrolling the nearby farms. Hathor's riders had demonstrated their worth today. They'd smashed the remains of the Sumerians and defeated them for the second time in one morning. And he'd captured King Eridu.

His grinning and cheering men returned, congratulating each other and their leader. Every warrior had a story to tell, either a brave act that showed his worth, or something foolish the fleeing Sumerians had done. Even the normally grave Hathor couldn't resist a smile at some of the stories he heard.

"Enough celebrating for now," he shouted, at last putting a stop to all the chattering. "Count the Sumerian dead, and finish searching the bodies. Kill any of the enemy wounded that can't walk. Then gather all the weapons and anything else of value. The prisoners can carry it all back to Eskkar's camp. There's no water here, so we need to keep moving."

The men cheered again, and Hathor shook his head.

"Get moving, you fools. We've still got a long ride ahead of us."

More like a long walk, since the horses were nearly exhausted. Hathor looked down and saw Eridu staring up at him, his eyes wide and mouth open in fear. "And I'm sure King Eskkar will be most glad to honor his neighbor from the south."

The sun had begun its descent toward the horizon when Eskkar finished his second inspection of the camp. His men had established a strong position, digging a ditch across the easiest points of access, and positioning a good-sized number of pickets on the two main approaches. No force of horsemen would be able to sweep in unchallenged, not that he expected any would dare make the attempt.

Mitrac and his men had arrived a little after midday, struggling under the burden of all the weapons they had captured. Fortunately, they had rounded up a few horses, and used them as pack animals to carry some of the load.

One of the sentries gave a shout. "They're coming in, Captain! Hathor's men!"

Esskar strode to the southern edge of the camp. A ragged group of horsemen appeared. Not really horsemen, he decided, but tired men leading their weary animals. Hathor had sent a rider back earlier with the news of the battle. As soon as Esskar learned of Hathor's victory and the safety of his men, he let himself relax for the first time in two days. In fact, he took the opportunity to swim in the stream and clean his filthy tunic. At least the garment wasn't bloodstained.

That would please Trella, who preferred that he leave any actual fighting to others. They'd had that discussion many times. She insisted that his life was too valuable to risk on an insignificant fight. Esskar countered by reminding her that a leader needed to fight to maintain not only his honor but his reputation. That argument between them, he knew, would continue, at least as long as he remained alive.

Now Esskar wanted to hear the details of Hathor's battle.

Hathor led the ragged procession toward them. A cheer erupted from Esskar's archers as Hathor's men reached the edge of the camp, and soon every soldier was shouting and congratulating each other on their victory. The ragged noise soon turned into a chant. "Esskar! Esskar! Esskar!"

He shook his head at the praise. Once again he had accomplished something out of the ordinary. His soldiers and cavalry had defeated an enemy force that outnumbered them greatly, and had done so with very little loss of Akkadian life. Even Esskar had worried that he might lose half his men before he achieved this victory.

"Welcome back, Hathor." Esskar gave the Egyptian a hug that would have crushed anyone smaller. "You and your men have done well." Esskar said the words in a loud voice, so that everyone in the camp could hear. "Did you lose many men?"

"No, Captain, just two men dead and four horses. But we killed forty-four Sumerians, and captured three horses and fifteen prisoners, not a bad exchange."

"Take care of your men, Hathor, then join me at the tent. You look like you could use a bath and some food."

"Yes, Captain. Would you take charge of this prisoner until then?"

Hathor moved aside. Behind him stood a single prisoner, held upright by a grinning guard. Esskar glanced at the foot-sore Sumerian for the first time. Not much of a warrior, the man looked exhausted. Fear showed not only on his face, but in his every movement."

"King Esskar, may I present you with King Eridu of Sumeria."

"No!" Esskar couldn't believe his ears.

A laugh went up from Hathor's men, who crowded around to see their commander's reaction.

"I asked the scout not to tell you," Hathor said. "I thought you might enjoy a surprise."

"Now I want to hear the whole story," Esskar said. "Every word. But first take care of yourself and your men." He reached out, clasped his hand on Eridu's shoulder hard enough to make the man gasp, and dragged him into the camp. Esskar guided the Sumerian along until they drew close to the tent. Esskar had planned to put the prisoner inside, but now he changed his mind. He shoved Eridu to the ground about thirty paces away. "Stay there."

"Water, King Esskar. Please. I need water."

Eridu's voice sounded hoarse and dry. He might not have had anything to drink since last night. Well and good, Esskar decided. It would put the Sumerian in a more cooperative mood. "Perhaps later, after you tell me what I want to know."

Esskar entered the tent. Eridu's two playthings clutched each other at the sudden appearance of their captor. Despite his reassurances, they still believed they would end up dead or worse. He had spoken to them before, and even remembered their names. Both were pleasure slaves, fresh from the slave market. Berlit was the taller one, with brown hair that tumbled around her face. Girsu, shorter and darker of hair and skin, possessed an impressive pair of breasts. He sat down on the thick blankets no doubt once reserved for Eridu.

"Sit before me," he ordered.

"Yes, master," they said in unison, as they knelt before him.

"I want you to tell me some things," he said, keeping his voice firm. "If you withhold anything, if you try to lie to me ... there are a hundred men outside the tent who would be eager to show you their prowess."

"Yes, master, anything you command," Berlit said. She clutched Girsu's hand, as much to reassure herself as her companion.

Berlit seemed the one with the quicker wits, so he started with her.

"Describe Eridu for me. I want to know what he looks like."

The slave girl described Eridu, and after a few sentences Eskkar held up his hand. "Enough." The prisoner outside the tent was indeed Eridu, not some impostor sacrificing himself for his king.

"Now I want you tell me what Eridu's plans were, why he sent men across the border, what he wanted to accomplish. I want to know everything you've seen and heard for the last few weeks. If you do, I'll take you back to Akkad with me. My wife will care for you, find something useful for you to do. Otherwise . . ." He lifted his hand and pointed to the tent flap.

They started talking, and soon the whole story came out. They had only been with Eridu for nine or ten days, a gift from one of the king's wealthy merchants. Eridu had taken possession of them just before he led his men out of Sumer, and decided they should accompany their new master on his campaign.

As Berlit spoke, her voice grew more confident, and the words that had first come haltingly now flowed like a steady stream. Even Girsu joined in the conversation, waving her hands around as she spoke, filling in details left out by her companion.

They were well into their story when Grond and Alexar entered the tent, followed a few moments later by Mitrac. Hathor arrived soon after that, his tunic still wet from its encounter with the stream. The commanders sat behind the girls, so as not to appear threatening, and after a few nervous glances over their shoulders, Berlit and Girsu soon forgot their presence.

Eridu's slaves talked and talked. Eskkar even interrupted them once to have water brought in for them. The girls had been present during almost all of Eridu's planning sessions. For the first time Eskkar heard the name of Razrek, the leader of the Sumerian horsemen, who had ravaged the borderlands, and somehow managed to escape Mitrac's arrows. Even to both wretched girls, this Razrek appeared to be the mastermind of Eridu's plan.

At last Berlit and Girsu ran out of things to say. "That's all we know, Lord Eskkar. We were just waking up when the soldiers raised the alarm. King Eridu snatched his tunic and ran outside. That's the last we saw of him, until you arrived."

"You've done well," Eskkar said. "You will return with us to Akkad. Something will be found for you there." Better that than turning them over to his men. Two women tossed among eighty men would start half a dozen fights before the girls died. He turned to Grond. "Send someone to untie Eridu. Make sure he gets plenty of water and something to eat."

He turned to the girls. "Stay in the tent. You know what will happen to you if you leave. Hathor, come with me. I want to show you something."

Eskkar slipped through the flap, and all the commanders followed. Outside, he stepped around to the rear of the tent. "We found these in the camp, more than a hundred of them." He picked up a long wicker shield and held it up. Each shield was covered with hide, and was pierced in the center to form a grip for the hand. When Eskkar raised it up, it covered his body from the chin nearly down to the knees.

"Mitrac's been shooting arrows at these all afternoon. Our bows will penetrate them, but only at close range." He tossed the shield aside and stooped to pick up a slim, bronze-tipped lance. "Eridu's men had about three hundred of these. I think that's why he didn't fear our archers. He intended to have the shield-bearers form the first wave, with the rest of their men behind them carrying one or two lances. A quick charge to get close enough to throw the lances, then overwhelm us with their swords."

Hathor inspected first the shield, then the lance, wrapped at the center to provide a good throwing grip, and nearly as tall as a man. "In Egypt, many of our soldiers carried shields like these, just thick enough to stop an arrow. And the lances, flung with all a running man's strength, would be deadly at close range. If they could have closed with our archers . . ."

"Our archers would still kill half of them before they got into throwing range," Mitrac said.

"Perhaps," Eskkar said, "but if enough did get close enough, we might have lost more than half of our fighters."

He picked up the lance, and thought about what it implied. A simple weapon compared to the bow, which took months to shape, and relied on bowstrings that snapped all too often, and arrows that had to be straight and true, nocked and feathered, and tipped with bronze. A thrown javelin such as this would pierce a man's body with ease, the bronze blade emerging from the body's back. If Eridu had a few more moments to prepare, if he only lost half his men to Akkadian arrows, the remaining Sumerians might have cut down Eskkar's archers. A grim thought indeed.

"It was bound to happen sooner or later," Alexar said, breaking the silence. "Everyone knows about the skill of our bowmen. Our enemies will try to find a way to counter Akkad's archers."

"In the great siege," Grond said, "our archers fought from behind a wall. In all our battles outside the city, we've had to find a way to protect our bowmen. Even in today's battle, we were fortunate to arrive at dawn, and with the sun behind us. If the Sumerians had time to gather their weapons and take up these shields, our losses might have been much greater."

Grond understood the implication as well as Eskkar.

"We'll speak more about this when we return to Akkad. Now, I think it's time to talk to Eridu." Eskkar led the way back toward the tent. The Sumerian sat on the ground near one of the campfires, guarded by two men. His hands had been untied. Eridu looked up as Eskkar and his commanders approached.

"King Eridu of Sumer," Eskkar said. "Have you eaten your fill?"

Eridu, his mouth hanging open, stared at Eskkar and the grim-faced men surrounding him. "What . . . what do you want?"

"I want to know why you attacked our lands." Eskkar didn't bother to keep his voice down. The more his men heard, the better.

"The borderlands belong to no one," Eridu said, trying to put some authority in his voice. "Sumer and the other cities has as much right to the crops here as Akkad."

"Still, for two years you recognized the Sippar river as our southern border. You did nothing to lay claim to these lands, said nothing to anyone in Akkad. Instead, you sent soldiers pretending to be bandits to kill our farmers and devastate our lands. You marched across the border with your soldiers, to kill those you knew would be sent against you, and to seize all these lands, and perhaps even more."

Eridu wet his lips. His eyes darted around, and saw that the Akkadians soldiers had moved closer, all of them eager to see and hear what would be done.

The only sound was the crackling of the nearby fire. "I will pay you a ransom for my safe return to Sumer," Eridu said.

Eskkar smiled. "You came north to wage war upon Akkad and its people. You wanted to lead your soldiers to a great victory, and have everyone in Sumeria proclaim you a great warrior. But a real warrior should be able to fight his own battles." He turned to Grond. "Give King Eridu a sword."

The words had scarcely left Eskkar's lips before Grond slipped his sword from its sheath and tossed it, hilt first, on the ground, where it landed close to Eridu's hand. The two soldiers guarding the Sumerian moved back, as did Eskkar's commanders, creating an open space for the two to fight.

"I won't challenge you," Eridu said. He moved his hand away from the sword's hilt. "Your men will . . ."

"My men will give you a horse and set you free if you win," Eskkar said. "Hathor, Alexar, you will see to that. Give your oath to let Eridu go free if he wins." Eskkar took a step back and drew his sword. "You can ride back to Sumer and tell everyone how you killed Eskkar of Akkad in a fight. That should be enough glory for you."

This time Eridu had to swallow before he could speak. "I won't fight you. You're a barbarian . . . you're a skilled swordsman. I'll meet whatever ransom you set, anything. I swear never again to send men across the border. Two hundred gold coins . . . three hundred. Petrah, my steward, will see to the payment. That should more than repay for the damage done to the crops and farmers."

Eridu looked around the ring of men staring down at him and saw nothing but stony faces. He pushed Grond's sword away with the back of his hand. "I won't fight you. I'll pay four hundred coins for my freedom."

A staggering sum, enough to pay for all the damages and the cost of sending the soldiers south. Akkad could use all that gold, Eskkar knew. If he'd met Eridu in battle, Eskkar would have killed him without question or hesitation. But no one would pay for a dead man. The silence dragged on while Eskkar made up his mind.

"Your ransom will be eight hundred gold coins. From that sum, every one of my soldiers will receive one coin."

An intake of breath passed through the soldiers at the sum, followed by murmurs of approval. That would be several months pay for most of them.

"But first there is another price to pay, Eridu," Eskkar said. "You stretched out your hand to take my lands and kill my people. Helpless farmers tortured and murdered, their women raped and killed, their livestock plundered, and the crops burned. For that, there is a separate price. Get him on his feet."

Grond stepped forward and jerked Eridu upright as if he were a child.

"Alexar, Grond, take hold of his hands. Spread him out."

The two men extended Eridu's arms out to either side. Alexar used both hands, clasping Eridu's left wrist. Grond also used both hands, but he grabbed the Sumerian's right hand, leaving his forearm bare. Eridu started to struggle, but his captors held him fast, his arms spread wide. Before Eridu could understand what was to happen, before he could prepare himself or plead for mercy, Eskkar's sword flashed in the firelight, and the sharp bronze blade, delivered with all of his force, sliced through Eridu's right wrist. Blood sprayed out everywhere.

With a scream, Eridu collapsed on the ground.

"Get him in the fire," Eskkar ordered.

Grond caught the now helpless Eridu around the waist with one arm, and clasped the handless arm with the other. In a moment, Grond dragged the king toward the campfire and shoved the blood-spurting stump into the flames.

This time the screams went on and on, echoing throughout the camp. Grond needed all his strength to hold the arm in the flames long enough to seal the wound. The smell of burning meat wafted on the air before he pulled Eridu away. With a sob, the Sumerian king fell on his face, his knees drawn up, weeping into the dirt. The pain racked his body again, and he slipped into unconsciousness.

"Get someone who knows how to bandage that up," Eskkar ordered. Several of the soldiers knew how to treat wounds. He wiped his blade on Eridu's tunic. "If he lives," Eskkar raised his voice so all could hear, "he'll walk back to Akkad, where he'll stay until his ransom is paid. Tomorrow we start for home!"

A roar went up from the men, and this time it went on and on. They had won a great victory, and their king had outwitted and defeated Akkad's enemy. Most of all, they would receive a share of the ransom, and that gold made all the hardship and danger of the last ten days slip from their minds. Meanwhile, the Sumerian king had paid a harsh price for his evil deeds, one that he would remember for as long as he lived. And best of all, they were returning home.

7

Trella pushed a glass goblet half full of wine across the large table. Yavtar held it up to the light for a moment to admire the thick glass. Such goblets remained rare in Akkad, and those wealthy enough to afford them swore that they sweetened the taste of wine. A few skilled craftsmen had mastered the art, and learned the secrets of carving each one, hollowing out the green glass with painstaking care. Yavtar took a sip, then murmured his appreciation. Setting the heavy glass down, he lifted a pitcher of water and filled the cup to the brim.

"Since I took up farming, Lady Trella, I find I can't drink as much strong wine." Yavtar took another taste of the watered mix, and nodded appreciatively. "I must be getting old. The weaker the wine, the more I seem to like it."

"Isn't that how it should be? The more delicate the flavor, the better everything tastes. Still, for such an elderly man, you made a fast return trip to Akkad," Trella said. While he might be six or seven years older than Eskkar, no one would call Yavtar old. He had arrived at dusk yesterday, offering to visit Trella as soon as he settled his accounts from the trip to Sumer with Nicar. Instead, Trella suggested they meet tomorrow at mid-morning. Others would also want to hear his words, and the small delay would give the trader some time to rest and attend to his family and farm.

Lady Trella wore a simple red dress, cut square across her breasts. A silver fillet kept her dark hair from her eyes, but she wore no other jewelry. Her thick tresses, carefully combed by a servant several times a day, remained her best feature. She had seventeen seasons, and her body had matured into that of a graceful young woman. Though she would never be called beautiful, her inner strength and keen mind made her the envy of all of Akkad's women. Every man that gazed into those dark eyes felt the urge to possess her. The strong feelings Trella aroused made many call her a witch. Whatever they called her, no one who knew her doubted her sharp wits or her ability to command respect from friend as well as enemy. She studied everyone she came in contact with, and her thoughtful eyes noticed every body movement, every hesitation, every gesture that revealed to her a person's true thoughts.

In the same way, her mind analyzed every word and inflection. As her reputation grew, more and more people found themselves nervous in her presence, which only made it easier for her to divine their thoughts and secrets. Trella understood not only the traits and habits of men, but the ways of power.

Now six people sat in what everyone called Eskkar's workroom. The house had a second story containing only two chambers. After climbing the stairs and passing through the thick door, visitors entered the large workroom, which offered two good-sized tables, a chest, and an assortment of chairs and benches. Another door, equally sturdy, provided access to the second and more private chamber, Eskkar and Trella's bedroom. With a Hawk Clan guard at the base of the stairs, those gathered around the table could speak freely, without worrying about whether anyone could overhear their words.

"Merchant Gemama was pleased with the lapis lazuli you brought him?"

"More than pleased, Lady Trella, especially with the price. He knew he was being bribed for information, but for stones like those, he was willing to take a chance. It probably helped that Eridu wasn't in the city, and that I was leaving the next day."

"Did you need to leave so soon?"

"It seemed wise. Right now, the city is unsafe for anyone from the north, especially from Akkad. Talk of war was in the air. Besides, I didn't trust those Sumerians on the dock." Yavtar took another sip of wine. "With all that gold on board, I didn't want to take any chances. We left Sumer early, and didn't even put ashore for the night. The Hawk Clan soldiers helped us row. I worked them and my crew like slaves. Fortunately, we didn't have much cargo for the return trip, just enough to act as ballast."

The riverboats, Trella knew, behaved better when they had a certain amount of weight on board. When they rode empty and high, they tended to tip over, often from nothing more than a stiff breeze or a sudden movement.

"I did give him a good price." Nicar sat next to Yavtar. Nicar had once been Akkad's leading merchant. Now his son Lesu had taken over that responsibility, while the father acted as Chief Judge of the laws of Akkad. "Those stones were my share of the goods from Lesu's trip to the Indus Valley. I hope the information you received was worth the lower price."

"I think Gemama would have paid more for your stones," Yavtar said. "And I'm sure you could have set a higher price if you'd sold them here."

Nicar smiled. "Actually, I didn't want to cut into my son's profits. If we had both sold our stones in Akkad, the price would have dropped. There are, after all, only so many who can afford to buy such things."

"Then I think we made a good exchange, Nicar. Gemama spoke bluntly, but I heard the truth in his words. King Eridu would have cut the tongue from Gemama's mouth for what he revealed."

"So you're certain it's war, then?" Gatus, the oldest of Akkad's soldiers and the captain of the city's guard, leaned across the table.

Two others sat on either side of Trella. Annok-sur, Trella's friend and confidante, who also directed the large number of spies in Akkad and throughout the land that gathered information for Trella and Eskkar. Bantor, Annok-sur's husband, had the seat at Trella's right. He commanded all the soldiers in and around Akkad during Eskkar's absence.

"It's war," Yavtar answered, "and it's going to be bad. King Eridu left Sumer a week before we arrived, heading a large force of at least three or four hundred soldiers. No one knows exactly how many. Apparently, Eridu felt confident of victory. The other cities have submitted to his rule, or allied themselves with him, willingly or not. For whatever reason, they all contributed soldiers to his venture. For the last two years, Eridu has blamed every ill, every grievance, every problem on Akkad. Our name is like a curse to them now. The whole of Sumeria believes demons rule here in Akkad, and that our only purpose is to create misery for Sumer's inhabitants."

Taking his time, Yavtar recounted almost every word of his conversation with Gemama. When he finished, silence hung in the air for a few moments.

"Eskkar must have encountered Eridu and his Sumerians by now,"

Bantor said. "He has only a hundred men with him. Enough for bandits, but not for that kind of fighting."

"I'm sure my husband will know what to do," Trella said. "He knows when to fight, and when to retreat."

She made sure her voice carried conviction, though a tiny doubt remained in her heart. If anything happened to Eskkar, the whole balance of power in Akkad would shift. No matter how much she accomplished, or how well she administered Akkad's affairs, everything depended on Eskkar's presence. His fair rule of Akkad's few laws had created a trust in his leadership, while his warrior skills made everyone feel safe from danger. No woman could equal those feelings in the populace.

Unfortunately, those same warrior skills often led him into personal danger, and he trusted in his luck to carry him through, heedless of the risks he ran, not only to himself but to Trella and their son. Sargon, their firstborn, was only two years old, and while many in Akkad would acknowledge him as the heir to the kingdom, others would step forward to challenge the ascension of one so young. The danger would remain until Sargon grew old enough to share in their leadership.

"He's the luckiest bastard I've ever known," Gatus said, uttering words no one else in Akkad would have dared to speak. "One of these days his luck is going to run out."

"But not anytime soon, I think," Yavtar said. "This Eridu is not a soldier, though he preens himself as one, and seeks the glory of a conquest. And no matter how many men he has, they will not be as well trained as our Akkadian soldiers."

"I'm sure we'll hear from Eskkar in the next few days," Trella said. In truth, she had already expected news from her husband to reach her. If word didn't come soon, she would have Bantor dispatch a messenger to seek him out and report back. "But Sumer, as they now call their city, is preparing for war?"

"Yes, Lady Trella. The city is as active as Akkad, and growing each day. Walls, homes, markets, are constructed everywhere. The population grows even faster, feeding gold into Eridu's hands. The people feel no love for him or his family, but he has them under control, with plenty of armed men to enforce his orders. If he can wrest control of Akkad's borderlands, he will guarantee his food supply, and even more gold will pass through his hands. He's already promised farms and land in the border to those who support him."

"He'll change his mind after he meets our archers," Bantor said.

"Even if Eskkar drives off Eridu's men this time, it may not matter in the long run." Nicar's words sounded grim. "If Eridu has Sumer under his thumb and has gained influence over the other five cities, he will have to contend with us sooner or later. With deserts to the east and west, and the great sea at their backs, they can only expand northward. Akkad blocks the road to their expansion."

"How many people live in those cities?" Trella asked, directing her question at Yavtar.

"Sumer itself has almost as many inhabitants as Akkad, say four or five thousand. The other villages are not as large, but taken together, include another sixteen, maybe seventeen thousand."

"And all of them add new people each day, I'll warrant," Nicar said. "So they will all grow as fast as Akkad. And with large numbers of young men working the surrounding farms, Eridu will have plenty of volunteers, all dreaming of gold or glory, to swell his army. Not to mention a surplus of craftsmen and toolmakers eager to sell weapons and tools to the king."

In any large group of people, Trella knew, an abundance of unmarried young men could be found. There were always more boys than needed to work a farm or labor in the villages. Older men, especially those with wealth, took or purchased extra wives and female slaves for their pleasure beds, creating a shortage of marriageable women for the young men, increasing the pressure on them to find their own fortunes. Soldiering provided a way to fulfill that need, while the danger involved merely added spice to youthful dreams. Even in Akkad, plenty of boys and young men volunteered to join Eskkar's warriors, all seeking to improve their lives. More arrived each day, searching for work, and as often as not, getting into trouble.

"You think this will be a long war, then?" Trella asked.

"I think the lands of Sumeria have many more people than they can sustain," Nicar said. "So yes, even if Eskkar drives off Eridu's soldiers, the Sumerians will return. If not this year, then the following year or the one after that."

"I agree, Lady Trella," Yavtar said. "Gemama implied as much."

"Let them come." Bantor rapped his fist on the table. "Each time they do, we'll drive them off."

"First we'd better see what news Eskkar brings us," Gatus said.

"I agree," Trella said. "We'll know more when Eskkar returns. Then we'll decide what to do about this new threat." She glanced around the table, but no one had anything more to add. Trella stood, signifying the end of the meeting. "Yavtar, all of us give thanks to you for bringing us this information."

One by one, the men left, until only Annok-sur and Trella remained in the workroom.

"You said nothing during the meeting," Trella said.

"What was there to say?" Annok-sur put her arm around Trella's shoulders for a moment. "After two years of peace, war is returning to Akkad. This time it will be a different kind of war, and I think a long one. I only hope that Eskkar returns safely, and that he knows what to do."

"As do I," Trella said. "He understands very well why and how men fight."

"Perhaps. But these are not barbarians or bandits. His experiences as a warrior may not help him as much in the coming battles."

"Perhaps," Trella said. "But meanwhile, there is much that you and I can do, and I think we should begin by making our own plans for the possibility of war. Whatever unseen path the future takes, we'll need to be ready. I think there is going to be much more to winning this kind of conflict than just victory in battle. Our husbands will think only of winning the next fight, and the next one after that. We need to find a way to win the war, so that Akkad can remain at peace for many more years."

"The first step should be to send more spies – as many as we can – to Sumeria, to learn what they can about our enemies. We've relied too much on traders and merchants bringing us word of what they've seen."

"Yes, we can start with that." Trella turned to her advisor. "But much more needs to be done, and we'll need to start as soon as Eskkar returns."

"Let's hope Eskkar's battle went well, both for our own sakes and for Akkad."

"Yes." Trella's thoughts went to her headstrong husband. Accomplished warrior he might be, but even now Eskkar could be dead, lying face-down on some unknown battlefield. She and her son might find themselves exposed to any number of threats, their future destroyed. The sooner he returned, the easier she would feel. And the next time Eskkar went into battle, Trella resolved to provide him with every advantage she could.

That night, well after dusk, Eskkar rode up to Akkad's main entrance.

"Open the gate!" he shouted, staring up at the men guarding the walls.

At sundown each day, the guards closed the city's gates. Those travelers who arrived afterwards usually had to camp outside for the night. Now the soldiers peered down into the gloom, and saw a band of heavily armed riders. But before they could even issue a challenge, the commander in charge of the gate arrived. A torch in hand, he leaned over the parapet. A single glance told him all he needed to know.

"Open the gate," he ordered. "It's the king."

It took time to open the heavy gate, but at last the final restraining beam creaked out of its supporting brace. Eskkar, Grond, and a dozen riders cantered through. Once inside, they slowed their horses to a walk, and two Hawk Clan warriors led the way through the narrow lanes. This early in the evening, the streets and lanes held plenty of people relaxing after their day's labor and enjoying the cool air. Everyone stopped to stare at the horsemen. Horses were rare enough in the lanes during the day, and seldom seen after dark.

"It's Lord Eskkar." One by one, people repeated the words. "The king has returned!"

A few cheers followed, but Eskkar ignored them, guiding his horse steadily through the press. One voice asked about the bandits.

"We won a great victory!" Grond called out, to a roar of approval from the crowd. "The bandits are destroyed!"

At last the party reached Eskkar's house, and he swung wearily down from the sweaty horse. Grond dismissed the men, who would return to their barracks after handing the horses off to the stable boys. As soon as the soldiers washed the dust from their bodies, they would search out their favorite taverns. Soon everyone would know about the battle against King Eridu.

Inside the courtyard, Eskkar walked straight through the open ground until he reached the rear of the house. A private well provided a steady supply of fresh water for the household. He pulled up the bucket and drank deeply, careless of the water that spilled across his chest. By then servants had arrived in a rush, and one began refilling the bucket, while Eskkar stripped off his clothes and dropped them on the ground.

He washed himself as best he could, trying to remove five days of sweat and dirt from his body, though he knew he wouldn't really feel clean until he'd had a long swim in the Tigris. That would have to wait until the morning. With help from one of the servants, Eskkar scrubbed most of the dirt off his body, then dried himself with a large square of linen handed to him.

When he finished, he turned away from the well, to find the servants gone and Trella standing there, a clean tunic in her hand.

"Welcome home, Eskkar," she said, handing him the fresh garment.

He pulled it on, unable to resist a sigh as the soft cloth settled around his shoulders. Without a word he took Trella in his arms and held her tight against him. Once again he breathed in the familiar scent of her hair and felt the ease that she always brought him. After holding her close for some time, he bent down and kissed her, letting himself enjoy the sweet taste of her lips. Her arms went around his neck, and she pressed herself against his chest, rising up on her toes to answer his kiss with one of her own. She held him tight until he relaxed against her.

"It's good to be home, Trella. Is everything all right here?"

"Yes, husband. The city was quiet while you were gone. And the bandits from Sumer? Did you meet them?"

"Not bandits, but soldiers," he growled, putting his arm around her shoulder and guiding her back toward the entrance of the house. "And King Eridu was there as well, with almost four hundred men, trying to ambush us. He nearly succeeded, too."

"We just learned from Yavtar that the Sumerians were responsible. I wish you had stayed in Akkad, at least until we knew more about what you might face."

They reached the open doorway to the house, but instead of entering, Eskkar took her by the hand and guided her across the courtyard. A second structure there held six good-sized rooms in a row, each with its own entrance. Four were occupied by sixteen Hawk Clan soldiers who guarded Eskkar's house day and night. The other two were for guests who needed a place to stay.

"I've something to show you."

As they approached, Grond appeared from the last doorway, ducking his head under the low opening. "Ah, Lady Trella, it's good to see you."

"My thanks to you once again," she said, "for bringing my husband home safe and sound."

"Bring out our guest," Eskkar said.

Grond ducked back into the house and returned in a moment, half-dragging a man behind him. A hard shove, and the prisoner fell to the ground at Trella's feet.

"And this is . . . ?"

"King Eridu of Sumer, as he now calls both himself and his city," Eskkar answered. "He planned to lure us into a trap and kill us all, but we managed to avoid his snare and set one of our own."

Eridu looked up at them. He appeared weak and dazed. His eyes gazed around the courtyard without comprehension.

Trella called out for someone to bring a light. Soon a servant arrived and held a crackling torch above Eridu's head. She stared at him for a long time, studying his face, then reached out and touched his cheek with the back of her hand.

"He's burning up with fever. And what happened to his hand?"

"I cut it off," Eskkar said, "as punishment for trying to steal our land. I offered him a chance to fight me, but he refused, so I thought this would be a fair payment for his greed. He's also promised to pay a ransom of eight hundred gold coins. If he doesn't, I'll cut off more than his hand next time."

Trella leaned forward and inspected the burned and blackened stump. "I'll send for the healer, to attend his wounds."

Eskkar shrugged. "I'd let him take his chances with the gods, but I suppose his kin won't pay for a dead man."

He clasped Trella around the waist and turned her back toward the house. "Enough time to talk to Eridu in the morning."

"I'll send the healer over." Grond lived only a few houses from Ventor, the only healer Eskkar trusted. "I'll return in the morning, Captain."

"I'm sure Tippu awaits your return," Trella said. Tippu and Grond had married two years ago, and she now carried his child.

Inside the house, Eskkar and Trella mounted the stairs and entered the workroom. At night, one corner was used as a nursery for Sargon. Trella always wanted her son close by, should he need anything. A servant girl sat beside the tiny bed and its sleeping occupant. She would remain awake all night, to make sure no harm came to the boy. Too many babies died in their sleep, and Trella had no intention of letting Sargon suffer that fate.

Despite his weariness, Eskkar paused a moment to look down at his sleeping son. "Sargon seems to have grown again," he whispered. He reached down his hand and gently touched a finger to the boy's soft cheek.

"I doubt he's grown much in the last fifteen days," Trella said, keeping her voice low. "Come, let him sleep. He'll be chasing you everywhere in the morning."

"In the morning I'll take him down to the river with me. He likes to splash in the water."

They went into the bedroom, and she closed and barred the door. When she turned around, he took her in his arms and held her tight, almost crushing her against him.

"You've grown, too, my wife," he said, running his hands up her arms. "You're even more beautiful than when I left you."

"We should talk, Eskkar. I want to know what happened. Eridu . . . how . . . ?"

"Later. And only if you please me greatly." His hand brushed against her breast, and he felt her nipple harden at his touch.

Her eyes closed for a moment. "Perhaps you should think about pleasing me," she said, her voice husky with emotion. "Once again, you left me alone while you went off to fight."

"Perhaps I will." He kissed her, gently at first, then harder as his passion grew. Soon he lifted her dress up over her head, then pulled his own tunic off. "Each time I see you, I want to feel myself inside you."

She swayed against him, and he heard her quick intake of breath. He clasped his hands around her waist, holding her tight. Eyes closed, Trella lifted her head, her lips parted. He kissed her again, this time a kiss full of passion and promise. Eskkar moved one hand to the small of her back, enjoying the curving flesh, while the other lifted to cup her breast, squeezing it gently until she gasped in pleasure.

"I missed you, Eskkar."

"I promise to make up for it," he said, his voice husky with lust, the tiredness of the long ride to Akkad forgotten.

Then he had no more words. He scooped her up as easily as she lifted Sargon, and deposited her on the bed. She arched her back under his touch, and slipped her arms around his neck.

"We can talk later," she breathed into his ear. "Try not to wake Sargon."

"You're more likely to wake him than I am."

She buried her face in his shoulder. "I'll try not to cry out."

"Don't try too hard," he warned her. "I've been gone a long time."

8

Two days later, just before the sun reached its height overhead, a small procession wended its way out of Akkad's river gate. The party walked along the path that followed the riverbank for half a mile, then traveled across the fields to the sprawling farmstead owned by Rebba, one of the nobles who helped rule Akkad. Though the nobles had lost some of their authority after Eskkar's rule commenced, they still retained much influence, and ruling the city without their support would have made that task even more difficult. With this new challenge to Akkad's future looming, both Eskkar and Trella knew that the nobles' advice and consent would be critical.

Noble Rebba and his family owned several large farms, which made him the wealthiest farmholder in the lands close to Akkad. His crops and herds contributed much to the city's prosperity, and its inhabitants respected both his wisdom and courage. In the fight against Korthac, Rebba had gambled his life and that of his family on Eskkar's behalf.

Rebba's farm lay less than two miles north of Akkad and along the Tigris. Eskkar and a small force of soldiers had landed their boats there two years ago. He'd raced down the river from the village of Bisitun to recapture Akkad from the Egyptians who had seized both the city and Trella.

Trella and Eskkar led the way toward Rebba's holdings, accompanied by Grond, Gatus, Bantor, Alexar, Hathor, Mitrac, Yavtar, and Klexor. Annok-sur walked behind Trella. Though Annok-sur had no official duties, everyone knew she controlled the large network of spies and informers that Trella had established throughout the city, the surrounding countryside, and even in distant villages. Many considered her the third most powerful personage in Akkad, after Eskkar and Trella. Six guards accompanied the group, one of them leading Eridu by a rope tied around his neck.

The distance made for a pleasant walk in the open air, surrounded by breezes from the river and the clean scent of crops growing in the fields. Rebba had constructed a half dozen small footbridges over the intervening canals, which carried vital water to his fields. Travelers to and from his farm and Akkad no longer needed to splash through the muddy canal waters to reach their destination.

A small pack of dogs began barking as the group approached the farmhouse, but a servant quickly chased them away, reassuring the animals that the new arrivals meant no harm either to them or their master. Nevertheless, the half-wild creatures kept a watchful eye on the visitors as they walked past, and Eskkar heard their low growls.

The little cavalcade reached the main house, which was not much larger than the other half dozen structures surrounding it. They didn't enter. Instead they moved around to the rear, where they found the rest of the gathering waiting for them in the shade of two willow trees. Branches formed a green canopy overhead that blocked most of the sun's rays. Whenever a breeze sprang up, the leaves rustled and sighed in a distinct voice, depending on the direction of the wind.

Rebba had gathered three tables and placed them end to end. Another table off to the side held wine, ale, bread, water, and fresh fruit, enough to satisfy any hunger until the main meal would be served just as the sun went down.

As the host, the Noble Rebba sat at the head of the table, his cousin Decca sitting beside him; Decca had sponsored many of the craftsmen and small shops which served Akkad's inhabitants. Nobles Nicar and Nestor, who helped rule the city before Eskkar and Trella took control, had also taken seats. Noble Corio, the newest member of the ruling group, was the artisan who constructed Akkad's walls; he sat beside Yavtar and faced Nestor and Nicar across the table.

When Eskkar and his party arrived, everyone took time to greet and welcome each other. All the leaders of Akkad, all the men of importance to Eskkar's rule were there, with the exception of Sisuthros who governed the large village of Bisitun to the north. There hadn't been enough time to summon him. Under Eskkar's authority, these men made all the decisions that governed the daily lives of the thousands of people in Akkad.

At last everyone settled in, leaving only the guards and Eridu standing a few steps away. Eskkar took his place at the opposite end of the table, facing Rebba. Trella sat at her husband's right hand, while Annok-sur occupied a stool just behind her. Gatus and the other commanders occupied benches on either side.

"Noble Rebba," Eskkar began, "I thank you for welcoming us to your house. In this heat, to gather so many inside Akkad's walls would have meant a long, hot day. And I want to thank you for offering to guard Eridu. Trella believes that his wound will heal faster here than in Akkad. He's promised to pay eight hundred gold coins for his ransom, so we need to keep him alive. A Sumerian river trader arrived in Akkad from the north yesterday, and we entrusted him with the task of delivering the message to Sumer and Eridu's family."

All eyes turned to the Sumerian. Eridu appeared pale and weak, his tunic dirty and his feet bare, nothing like the ruler of a mighty city. His fever had broken, but bandages covered his right forearm, a yellowish stain marking the end of his stump.

"So this is King Eridu," Corio said, "who wanted to bring war and destruction to Akkad."

Elevated to his position as a result of Eskkar's rise to power, Corio could seldom restrain his impatience with what he called the old ways. He'd built the wall that had saved Akkad from the barbarians two years ago, and now directed the massive effort to raise newer, stronger, and higher ramparts around the expanded city that continued to grow faster than anyone thought possible. He never hesitated to speak his mind. As Trella once remarked, you always knew what Corio was thinking.

Eridu lifted his head and let his eyes take in the leaders of Akkad, but he said nothing. After a moment, he returned his gaze to the ground.

"He doesn't have much to say, does he?" This time the comment came from Nestor. "I owned two of the farms your men ravaged. One of my cousins is missing, probably dead at your hands. What do you know about those raids?"

"Answer him," Eskkar ordered.

Eridu's lips trembled at Eskkar's words, and his eyes revealed a glimpse of the hatred the Sumerian possessed. But fear overcame his hatred, and he knew better than to disobey Akkad's ruler. "I know nothing of your cousin. Many bandits raid the land on both sides of the border. I accompanied my soldiers to drive them off."

"You marched three hundred men on foot, from Sumer to well north of the Sippar river, to chase after your own horsemen," Eskkar said. "Did you intend to follow them all the way to Akkad?"

"We were preparing to return when you attacked us."

"He thinks we're fools," Corio said. "Perhaps we'd be better off separating his head from his body."

"King Eskkar has promised to return me to Sumer when the ransom is delivered," Eridu said, a trace of defiance in his voice. "Eight hundred gold coins. A boat took the request south this morning."

"It's not too late to change our minds," Eskkar said. "So I'll give you a choice. Tell us the truth, or I'll cut off your other hand. Your kin can feed you and wipe your ass for the rest of your life. I'm sure it's a duty they will look forward to."

Eridu's eyes widened. A glance at those seated at the table convinced him. Stony eyes showed not a trace of mercy. Not one would utter the least word to stop Eskkar from carrying out his threat. Eridu swallowed nervously. "What do you want to know?"

The story came out with a little prodding, none of it new or surprising. Sumeria needed the land, the cities in the south had a rightful claim to it, Eridu was merely carrying out the will of the people. After a while, the questions died out. The king of Sumer had wanted fresh lands and the glory of a conquest. Nothing more really mattered.

Eskkar nodded to Eridu's guards. "Take him away. Rebba's servants will show you where to put him."

"I still think we should kill him," Nestor said, when Eridu was led around the side of the house. "When he gets back, he'll just start preparing for war all over again."

"I think it's best to let him go," Eskkar said. He and Trella had discussed Eridu only last night. "Better to have an incompetent fool ruling in Sumeria. If he ends up dead, we may find ourselves facing someone worse."

"And the gold will be useful to compensate those who lost their farms," Nicar said. "The question now is, what are we going to do? The lands of Sumeria, including the six cities, possess four or five times as many people as we do, maybe more, and their wealth, taken together, is far greater than Akkad's. If they stand united, and are determined to wage war against us, we could be facing a long and bitter struggle just to survive."

"Our southern border stretches from the Euphrates to the Tigris," Gatus said, "and then follows the Sippar river to the east. That's close to two hundred miles from one end to the other. It will be impossible to defend it all."

"You can't patrol a border area with archers," Alexar added. "We'll need horsemen, and plenty of them."

"There aren't enough horses in the land for that," Rebba added "And the expense of maintaining so many animals . . . Eridu's gold will be long gone before you have a tenth of what you need."

Raising and maintaining good horseflesh took gold, and plenty of it. Corrals had to be built, cleaned, and maintained. A horse went through large quantities of grain and grass each day, and needed to be exercised as well. Then each beast had to be trained to fight, to charge ahead when its instincts made it want to falter or turn aside. That required skilled riders who understood horseflesh, who could teach both men and animals how to form a battle line, charge the enemy, and run a man or a horse down. It all took time. Even in Akkad, only the wealthy could afford the luxury of owning a simple riding horse, let alone an animal trained for war.

"Eskkar, you say that Eridu was ready to do battle with your archers?"

"Yes, Nicar. His men had a large number of shields, and even more javelins. The shield-bearers expected to charge our archers, supported by the javelins, until they could close the distance."

"And do you think this tactic would have worked?"

The table went silent for the first time, and every eye lifted to Eskkar.

"Yes, I think it would have succeeded. As long as they could close with us quickly, it might have worked. We were greatly outnumbered. Even if we drove them off, our losses would have been heavy. Without shields of our own, the javelins would have been deadly to our men. A few breaks in the line, and the enemy could have poured through and overwhelmed us."

"So our archers will not be able to overcome superior numbers, is that what you're saying?"

Eskkar poured some water into his cup and took a sip, using the moment to gather his thoughts. "Not necessarily. Our archers are well trained. We pick only those men strong enough to bend a bow and empty three or four quivers without weakening. As Gatus can tell you, it takes many months, four to five at least, to harden their muscles. An archer must learn not only how to loose an arrow, but how to gauge the distance, hit a moving target, and stand beside his fellows."

"When an archer is fully trained, he is a deadly and efficient soldier. But for all that, the archer has his own weaknesses. Unless he's in a defensive position, he's vulnerable to surprise attack, night attack, or even attack within close quarters. Outside of a city and its walls, he needs horsemen to scout for him, so that he can prepare to come to grips with his enemy. Archers also need someone to guard their rear. In the fight against Eridu's men, I had to use our horse boys to watch our backs."

"So you're saying our archers are of little use outside the city?" Nicar's voice held a trace of worry.

"No. What I'm saying is that up to now the archers have been our strongest force. But that will have to change. We need to prepare for a different kind of war, a longer conflict, and we will need new kinds of soldiers."

No one seemed happy to hear Eskkar's words, least of all his own commanders. Most of them had trained and fought as archers. Using their bows, they'd won yet another victory over superior numbers, and now they heard their leader say that their efforts might not be enough. The nobles were equally unhappy. A long and drawn out war would be a drain on all of them. Trade would be the first casualty. Already the nobles contributed large amounts of gold to pay for the building of Akkad's walls, and the ongoing support of the city's fighting men. In return for that contribution, they expected peace and security for their farms and trading ventures. A protracted conflict with the Sumerian cities would drain much of their wealth, with little to show for it.

"Do you think we can win this new kind of war?" Corio, impatient as always, drummed his fingers on the table.

"Yes, we can win this war," Eskkar said. "As we've all seen, battles are not won just by having superior numbers of fighting men. We drove off the barbarians, and we outfought Korthac to reclaim our city. Both times our fighters were outnumbered. Until now, we've taken great care in selecting recruits. Now we need to use all the manpower we have available to us, even those we've passed over when we select our archers."

Eskkar glanced at Gatus, the captain of the guard, and the oldest of Eskkar's commanders. Everyone respected both his courage and his words. More than that, the nobles trusted him. Born and raised in Akkad, he always spoke his mind and never cared whom he offended. Approaching his sixtieth season, he'd trained most of Akkad's fighters, and helped Eskkar develop his battle plans and tactics.

"What do you think, Gatus?" Eskkar shifted to face the old soldier. "Can you answer Corio's question?"

"Eskkar and I, and all the commanders," Gatus began, gesturing with his hand to include the rest of the soldiers, "have talked about such things for years. Now it is time to do more than talk. We'll need soldiers who can fight on foot, who can attack an enemy with sword and spear. And we'll need horsemen, many of them, to act as our eyes and ears, and allow us to strike at our enemies far from Akkad."

The old soldier spoke with passion. Gatus had seen every kind of enemy, and knew what to expect. Whenever he spoke, men listened. But everyone at the table knew Akkad had nowhere near enough men, nor horses, nor gold to pay them.

"If we have to fight an extended war with Sumeria," Nestor said, "the expense may be more than we can support. Perhaps it would be better to negotiate with the Sumerians, to make peace with them. They may have learned their lesson. We could even offer them some of the borderland."

Trella reached out and picked up her water cup. The simple gesture turned every eye toward her, as she knew it would.

"Lady Trella, what do you think?" Once again it was Corio who spoke first.

"Nobles, this conflict between our city and the south will not happen overnight. Eskkar dealt Eridu's forces a heavy blow. How many men did he lose, husband?"

Of course, she already knew the answer. Trella seldom needed to hear anything more than once. With her flawless memory, she could recall details even many months after hearing them.

"We killed about twenty or twenty-five of their horsemen, and over a hundred and seventy soldiers. Twenty-eight prisoners were taken, and I spoke with each of them. Then I let them go, so they could return to Sumer and the other cities and tell the story of what happened. There were many wounded who we left where we found them, to live or die. We captured most of their weapons as well."

"That means there will be no more war for the rest of this season," Trella went on. "And probably not next year, either. Eridu will need time to recoup his losses, and rebuild his reputation. The lost weapons will be expensive to replace, and he will have to pay the ransom as well. His supply of ready gold will be severely depleted, if not exhausted."

She paused a moment, to let everyone at the table digest her words.

"And, as my husband has explained to me, the defeat of the soldiers will be a heavy blow to their morale. They know they were vanquished by a smaller number of fighters. Their king was taken prisoner. Eridu will not find it so easy to recruit replacements. It will take time before he can again raise a large force of men."

"So you think we have a few years before the Sumerians begin to trouble us again?"

"No, the plotting will begin as soon as Eridu returns home," Trella answered. "But the next year or two will give Akkad time to prepare. In that time, there is much we can do. And as Akkad's leading merchants, perhaps you can find new opportunities for your trading ventures."

Corio laughed, a long chuckle that turned every head. "Of course, Trella, you're right. My business will prosper because the increased need for protective walls, not only here in Akkad, but in some of the smaller villages on the border. Nicar's trading will increase, too, as he supplies us with the ores needed to forge weapons. The city will grow again, as we hire new soldiers, and what we pay them will flow back to us in taxes and increased business."

"Yes, Corio," Trella said, letting a smile cross her face for the first time. "If we know what the future will bring, and if we have time to prepare, there is no reason why everyone's wealth should not increase, even as our soldiers grow in numbers. With Sumer's defeat, more people will seek Akkad's protection, more farmers in the borderlands will cry out to join with us. Already the city and the countryside are full of young men who have left their farms to come here. It may be that, in the long run, all of you here today will see your trading ventures prosper."

Nestor nodded. "Yes, that may all be true. But what happens when the Sumerians march north with thousands of men? How can we defend the border against such a force?"

"We're not going to defend the border," Eskkar said. "We'll patrol it with horsemen that Hathor will train. If the Sumerians come north again, we'll gather our forces and march south. Akkad's walls will protect the city, while we invade Sumeria. We'll ravage their lands and crops. Our threat to carry the war to their cities will be what secures the border."

"And if it doesn't?" Rebba didn't wait for an answer. "It won't be easy to invade Sumeria. You'll need supplies and food, and you'll have to march your men a long distance. And when you do arrive at Larsa, you'll find yourself facing a walled city full of defenders."

Larsa, the northernmost of the six cities in the Sumerian alliance, had always been the most troublesome. It would be the first one to face any attack by Akkad.

"Yes, Rebba, that's exactly what I expect," Eskkar said. "So that is what we're going to prepare for. When we tear down Larsa's walls and put what's left standing to the torch, the other Sumerian cities will understand the price of crossing our border and attacking our people."

"And have you considered how you will destroy Larsa's walls and capture it?"

"Not yet," Eskkar said with a smile. "My commanders and I meet tomorrow to begin planning for such things. While we train archers, horsemen, and foot soldiers, Corio and his kin will be busy figuring out ways for us to storm a city's walls. By the time such an attack is needed, we should have both the manpower and the skills needed to capture a city the size of Larsa within a few days. If we can do that, we can end the war."

"And if the rest of Sumeria fights on," Nestor said. "Then what will you do?"

"We'll march to the next city and destroy that one, too. Crush every city that resists, and spare each one that abandons war. Put yourself in their place, Nestor. Would you rather fight or make peace?"

"You assume much, Eskkar," Nestor answered. "How can you be so certain?"

"It's not just me," Eskkar answered. "My commanders think as I do." He glanced around the table. The soldiers were nodding agreement. "Don't forget, nobles, many of our preparations will soon be known to the Sumerians. That may help them choose peace instead of war. If they know what we might do to them, they may just decide to leave us alone. But as long as we have something they want, as long as our fertile farmlands tempt them, or they desire to control our trade, they will search for every opportunity to take what they want. If that means destroying Akkad, those who seek power or wealth will demand it. We must be prepared for war, whether it comes as an invasion or more raids across our border."

No one spoke, and it seemed as if the sighing of the trees gave voice to everyone's thoughts.

"We fought to save our city from the barbarians," Nicar said, breaking the silence. "We fought to take back Akkad from Korthac. Would we now give it away to the Sumerians? How much would it take to satisfy their demands? Half our land? All of it?"

"So you think war is the answer," Rebba said. "Attacking other cities and destroying them?"

"Only if they bring war to us," Eskkar said. "We have to prepare Akkad to meet whatever threat may come, either next year, or the year after that, or the one after that."

"No one wants war," Trella said.

"Then you think we can avoid a conflict?" Rebba directed the question to Trella. He knew she decided Akkad's future as much – if not more so – as her husband. And that she wanted peace.

"No, I think it will come," Trella said, "but we may be able to delay it, and we can hope to make any conflict a short one. And it will be better for Akkad if the war is fought in Sumeria, and not in our lands. Then it will be their farms and villages that are ravaged."

"Whatever course of action we decide, we must speak as one voice," Eskkar said. "If the people think we are not united, then their resolve will weaken and Sumeria's desire for revenge will grow stronger. My commanders and I have seen the face of the enemy. We believe Akkad needs to prepare for war. But if the nobles and leading merchants show disagreement, it will give strength to our enemy even as it weakens ourselves."

"I agree," Corio said. "We must prepare for war."

"As do I," Nicar said. "But with one condition. We must make every effort to maintain peace with Sumeria. I do not want our words or preparations to force them into war."

"Nor do I," Eskkar said. "And remember, they have little that we would want. If Akkad is to grow, we will grow to the north and to the west. Sumeria has nothing to fear from us. In time, they should have the wits to understand that."

"Then prepare for war," Nicar said. "The sooner we can achieve a lasting peace, the better."

"Prepare for war," Rebba said.

Nestor and Decca looked at each other, resignation on their faces. "Prepare for war."

All eyes went to Yavtar. As one of the most prosperous traders in the city, his opinion carried weight. The half dozen boats he owned plied the river, carrying cargo north and south.

And he had risked his life in the battle to save Akkad from Korthac.

"I spoke with one of the leading merchants in Sumer. Like us, he understands that trade is cheaper than war. It is their leader, Eridu, seeking the glory of a conquest, who brought on this conflict. If we treat them fairly in matters of trade, we may avoid any future raids."

"To accomplish that," Trella added, "we want to set up a trading village just inside the border. That will make it simpler to trade with Sumeria, to exchange food for their goods. A convenient trading outpost will make it easier for them to choose peace rather than war."

"Then we're all agreed. Good." Eskkar let his body relax. "Perhaps we can start by trying to convince Eridu of our peaceful intentions."

"It might be better if I spoke with him," Nicar said. "He's not likely to want to hear anything from the man who cut off his hand."

"No doubt," Eskkar said. He wanted nothing further to do with Eridu anyway. "Just make sure he knows what he'll lose if he tries anything like that again."

9

The next day, with mid-morning approaching, two members of the city's guard finally found the man they sought. Orodes lay sleeping on his side, stretched out against the wall of a tavern, ignored by the people passing to and fro in the lane. Bodies in the lanes, drunk, sleeping, or dead, were not an uncommon sight. The guards, one a seasoned veteran named Wakannh, and the other much younger, almost walked past the inert body, before the senior man slowed his pace and stopped a few steps away.

"Wait. I think that's the one she wants, and about time, too." Wakannh crossed to the man and peered down. "I recognize him." He prodded the unresponsive body with his toe. "Drunk and passed out. Get him on his feet."

"I'm not carrying a drunk all the way to the compound by myself," the younger guard protested.

"Carry him, drag him by his balls, I don't give a shit what you do." As a leader of ten, the older guard didn't intend to waste any of his own muscles on a drunk. That's what recruits were for. "Just get him moving."

Muttering under his breath, the second guard rolled the still snoring Orodes onto his back. "Demons' piss, the pig threw up on himself. Are you sure this is the one?"

Wakannh leaned over to look closer at the man's dirt and vomit-crusted face. "Ugghh, he stinks. Someone's pissed on him, too. But that's Orodes." He grabbed Orodes's arm and together they yanked him to his feet, waking him up in the process. The groggy man tried to protest, but the two soldiers gripped Orodes by his arms and half-walking and half-dragging, led the helpless man away, to the amusement of those onlookers who stopped to watch.

Two lanes over, the leader of ten stopped beside one of the public wells. "Might as well clean him up here. No sense bringing anything that filthy into Lady Trella's courtyard."

The second man shoved Orodes head first into the trough that collected the water, and held him there until he coughed and choked, flailing his arms but unable to lift his head. When the guard jerked Orodes's head up by his hair, he just hung there, helpless, too weak even to raise his arms. "What about his tunic? Stinks of piss and vomit. Probably full of lice, too."

"Get rid of it," Wakannh agreed. "It's worse than nothing."

The guard grasped the tunic with both hands and ripped it apart. Then he jerked the torn remnants from Orodes's body and kicked them aside. "Wash yourself up, you pig."

A few bystanders collected and laughed at the naked man's plight.

"What are you . . . ?" Orodes squinted into the morning sun.

"Open your mouth again and I'll cut your balls off," Wakannh warned him. "Someone at the Compound wants you, so that's where you're going. They probably want to hang you by your puny prick for stinking up the city. Now clean yourself up or I'll throw you down the well."

The Compound, as anyone living in Akkad more than a day knew, referred to the residence of King Eskkar and Lady Trella.

The guards stood there, while Orodes splashed water over his face and chest again and again, until most of the dirt and stench had faded away. By the time he finished cleaning himself, Orodes appeared to have regained his senses.

"By Ishtar's tits, I hope they do hang him by his prick," the recruit said. "He still stinks."

Orodes had never visited Lord Eskkar's courtyard, but he had little time for more than a quick glance around. Wakannh had happily handed him over to the soldiers at the entrance, who enjoyed a good laugh at the naked man's expense. But they found a cast-off garment for him to wear, and let him drink from the private well at the rear of the house.

When he finished quenching his thirst, he washed his face and hands once again, this time more to help sober up than get clean. When he finished his ablutions, Orodes turned to find that the courtyard soldiers had departed and a woman taken their place. Even with his head feeling like it might split in two, he recognized Annok-sur's tall frame.

"Do you have your wits about you?"

Orodes nodded, then grimaced at the movement. "What do you want? Why am I here?"

Annok-sur took a step toward him, examining him with care. "You're here because Lady Trella wishes to speak with you. If you have some other important business to attend to, I'll tell her so, and you can return to the tavern where they found you."

Orodes ignored the jibe. Whatever the reason, few turned down an opportunity to speak with one of the rulers of Akkad. "I can talk."

Annok-sur nodded agreement. "Good. Come with me."

She led him into the house, pausing only to speak to one of the women servants, then led Orodes up the stairs and into the workroom.

"Sit down," she said, pointing to the table. "Lady Trella will be here shortly."

Orodes eased himself onto the bench, then looked up to see the servant approaching, carrying a tray in both her hands. It contained bread, a handful of dates, and a hunk of cheese only slightly past its best. Orodes realized he felt ravenous. He hadn't eaten anything yesterday morning, before drinking himself into a stupor at the tavern. Two copper coins, stolen from a drunken patron, provided him with more than enough ale to drink himself unconscious.

By the time Orodes finished swallowing the first mouthful of bread, the serving woman returned with two cups. "Weak ale, and water." She put them down and left the chamber.

He reached for the ale, then stopped. His hand shook, and for a moment he couldn't control his muscles. Orodes closed his eyes, took a deep breath, and shifted his hand to the other cup. A meeting with Lady Trella was not the time to be drinking anything stronger than water.

When he finished eating, only crumbs from the bread and pits from the dates remained on the platter. Orodes allowed himself to take a small sip from the ale cup. His head had almost ceased throbbing.

The door to the inner room opened, and Lady Trella and Annok-sur came out. A child started crying in the background, but Annok-sur shut the door, and the sound faded. Remembering his manners, Orodes pushed himself to his feet and bowed.

"We've met before, Orodes," Trella began. "Almost three years ago, when your father fashioned Eskkar's new sword. You helped Asmar with the casting, as I recall."

"I remember . . . Lady Trella. I'm surprised that you do." Just before the barbarian invasion, Trella had visited Asmar's shop. At first his father had tried to patronize the young slave girl dressed in a shabby garment. But by her third visit, Orodes realized that Trella not only knew exactly what she wanted, but how it should be made.

She sat across from him, and nodded for him to sit. "Since then, I've learned some things about you. Have you reconciled with your father?"

Master smith Asmar. Orodes clenched his teeth for a moment. So Lady Trella had spoken with his father. That meant she knew all about the family quarrel, and probably about the reasons for Orodes's recent return to Akkad. He'd spent the last year and a half working at a mine in the eastern hill country operated by his uncle. Asmar and his brother both suffered from the same lack of imagination. Both believed the old ways were the best ways, and that the young should do as they were told. Orodes clashed so often with his uncle that he was finally ordered to leave. Otherwise he would still be there, slaving away for little more than his keep. He pushed those thoughts out of his mind.

"No. My father has ordered me never to return to his house." If Lady Trella had summoned him to talk about his father, he would take his leave.

"Then I may have something that may interest you. As you may be aware, I know some of the mysteries of gold and the smelting of ores. I've learned of a place that may have a good quantity of gold. I need someone to examine the site, and report back to me. If there is sufficient ore of high quality, I may wish to establish a mine there, to extract the gold and anything else of value. Your father Asmar says you know much about such things."

Orodes found it hard to believe that his father had said anything good about his wayward son. "There are several areas where copper can be found in the eastern foothills, Lady Trella," Orodes said. "Even my father has laid claim to one such place with the Chief Judge."

Copper, of course, was the most important metal. With copper and tin, combined in the right proportion, you could make bronze, and from bronze came tools and weapons. Where you found copper ores, you usually also found traces of gold, silver, lead, tin, and arsenic, as well as other useful metals. Each site would have these metals in varying qualities and quantities. But all the mines were in the far north at the base of the steppes, or the distant east, in the foothills of the Zargos Mountains.

"I know. But the place I'm speaking of is much closer to Akkad, and it is to the north-west."

Orodes shook his head. "There is little enough copper near here. You might find a few pockets of gold along the Tigris, but most of those have already been harvested."

"Still, I would like someone to examine this place and determine its potential. If there is sufficient supply of the noble metals, I might need a skilled smith to establish the mining operation. I'm told that you have the necessary knowledge for such a task. Is this something you would consider?"

Orodes would indeed. His father had driven him from his house partly because Orodes, in his twenty-third season, had already mastered all the mysteries of gold, copper and bronze. He also wanted to change his father's procedures for smelting the ores and refining the metals. Orodes believed that with some experimentation he could improve those procedures, and produce higher-quality metals in greater quantities.

Asmar, a capable and skillful metal worker, saw no reason to change anything in his craft, or try anything new. Father and son had disagreed often, until Asmar in his anger sent the disobedient son east to his brother's mine, where Orodes was supposed to remain until he learned to be a dutiful son, obedient to his father and elder brothers. Or, as it happened, until the master smith at the mine grew so annoyed at Orodes's constant and vexatious suggestions that he threw him out.

Of course, Trella would know all these embarrassing facts. Her spies, as everyone agreed, knew everything about every household in the city. And, of course, she knew about copper and where it was likely to be found. Telling her she might be wrong probably wasn't a good idea. He focused his gaze on her eyes. She sat there patiently, letting him collect his thoughts, waiting for him to realize the full import of the conversation. He noticed that her eyes never left his face, always seeking to learn more about him. Those same eyes also hinted that she knew more than she said.

The silence lengthened, and he realized that he hadn't answered her question. "Yes, Lady Trella, I can examine a prospective mining site, and tell you what's worth digging for. With the proper resources, I can establish the smelters, kilns, crucibles and furnaces, and convert the ores into the required metals."

Trella nodded. "All the gold and silver from the mine would come to Akkad, but the master smith in charge of the site would be well paid. How well paid would depend on what is found, and how much can be taken from the earth. Are you interested in such a task?"

Orodes opened his mouth, then closed it again. Those who oversaw a mine usually owned at least a part of it. Trella was offering to pay him for his skills, like any common laborer. Still, it was not an unreasonable offer considering he had no status as a master craftsman, no patron to succor him. He decided to ask for more. "What share of the mine would be mine, Lady Trella?"

She smiled at the bold question. "None. Not at first. You would be paid fairly, but if you wish to earn a share you will have to produce a steady and significant supply of ores, delivered on time, and without any being lost to the workers. If you can accomplish that, I would consider an arrangement where you would own a share of the mine's output in the future. As I said, this mine belongs to the king, and whatever is extracted from the earth will be used for Akkad's needs. And in selecting you for this task, I am taking something of a risk."

He would be a paid laborer, nothing more. Nevertheless, anything was preferable to starving in the streets of Akkad. And it would gall his father to learn that his wayward son had taken an important assignment from Lady Trella, even if it turned out to be nothing. "I would accept such a task, Lady Trella."

She turned to Annok-sur, who sat quietly across the room, apparently uninterested in the conversation. "Can you bring in Tooraj?"

Without saying anything, Annok-sur rose and left the room.

"You realize, Orodes," Trella went on, "that there must be no drinking, no wandering off, and not a word must be said to anyone about the mine. The first time you are found drunk will be your last. Remember that."

Orodes understood. Only a fool would risk Trella's displeasure. Besides, he drank only because he had nothing else. With an opportunity such as she offered, he would have no need to drink himself into a stupor.

Annok-sur returned, a soldier with the Hawk Clan emblem stitched on his tunic following her. The man wore a patch over his left eye.

Trella rose. "Welcome Tooraj. It is good to see you again."

Orodes felt surprise. The queen of Akkad had risen to her feet to greet a common soldier. Or not so common, he realized. Members of the Hawk Clan were few in number.

The soldier bowed, much lower than Orodes's simple incline of the head. "My thanks to you and King Eskkar."

"This is the young man I spoke of. His name is Orodes, and I place him in your care."

That sounded reasonable enough, but the cold stare that Tooraj's one eye fixed on Orodes made him realize that the soldier not only knew of Orodes's past indiscretions, but didn't intend to tolerate any more of them.

She said to Orodes. "Tooraj will be in charge of the expedition to examine the mine. Please obey all his instructions." She turned to the soldier. "Are you ready to depart?"

"Yes, Lady Trella. My men and I are waiting."

"Good. Annok-sur will accompany you both to the docks. If there is anything you need to take with you, Orodes, let her know."

With a shock, Orodes realized that they meant leave now, this moment. Realizing he had been dismissed, Orodes pushed himself to his feet, to find Lady Trella again smiling at him.

"Good luck, Orodes. I hope we can talk again soon, when you're ready to tell me what you've found."

Her smile, as much as her hopeful words, caught him by surprise. In that moment, he realized how beautiful she was, and how much he wanted to please her. The strange sensation stayed with him all the way to the docks.

10

That evening, Eskkar's most senior commanders joined him for dinner at the Compound. The gathering included Gatus, Bantor, Hathor the Egyptian, and Yavtar. No other guests attended. During the meal, the soldiers took their lead from their host. No one spoke about the coming war. That topic remained far too important to discuss in front of the servants and guards.

The setting sun hadn't yet touched the horizon, but the heat of the day was fading when Eskkar and his guests left the supper table in the courtyard. Eskkar led the way to the tiny garden at the rear of the house, a private place usually reserved for his and Trella's use.

The five men settled comfortably on their seats, relaxing after a long day and still pleasantly full of food after the bountiful meal Lady Trella's cooks had served. A servant brought a pitcher of ale, in case anyone wanted something stronger than water, and set it on the table before leaving Akkad's leaders alone. A pitcher of fresh well water and cups rested in the center of the table.

The evening air would be pleasant and far more relaxing than Eskkar's workroom. The inner walls of the courtyard, whitewashed to a cool white, formed two sides of a square. The house itself, rising up to the second story, provided a third side. The fourth side opened up into the rearmost part of the main courtyard.

A well nearby provided fresh water for the Compound, and Eskkar had washed the dust from his body many times in the last two, no, now nearly three years that he lived there. Four wooden flower boxes extended along the base of the walls. The first of summer's tulips provided tiny cups of purple, red and yellow scattered among the white lilies and the flax plant's blue flowers. A bench stood against the side of the house, and two young trees gave just enough shade to cover the small table centered beneath them.

Eskkar enjoyed the semi-private enclosure. The servants respected their master's special place, and ventured into the rear of the house only for urgent matters. He and Trella had made love here more than once, and they both enjoyed the peaceful surroundings. The trees had grown higher since he first took possession of the house. The assassin who had tried to kill Trella had been tied between those two trees and tortured until he revealed the name of the young noble who hired him. The noble's head now lay buried deep in the earth between those same trees.

For this meeting, Trella had arranged for extra chairs to be carried in. Of course, Eskkar wanted Trella there. After nearly three years at his side helping to rule Akkad, everyone sought her advice and counsel. He'd once asked her if she wished to be a member of the Hawk Clan. She had, after all, struck a blow against Korthac.

"A woman in the Hawk Clan?" She laughed, a happy sound that turned her into a young girl once again. "I'm flattered at the thought, but I think you should keep the Hawk Clan reserved for men."

A few moments later, Trella and Annok-sur joined the gathering. Trella's friend and confidante also had an important role to play in any coming conflict. The fact that she was a woman and Bantor's wife made no difference. At this table, everyone would speak as equals.

Before she took her place, Annok-sur spoke to the guards and made sure the sentries remained far enough away so that they couldn't overhear what would be said. Trella and Annok-sur sat on either side of Eskkar, facing the four men across the table.

"Yesterday you men attended the meeting with the nobles," Eskkar began without any preamble. "You heard their decision. Now it is time for us to talk about how the coming war will be fought. We need to decide what tactics we will use, how we will carry the war south, and what defenses Akkad will need. In the next few months, we'll face many choices and make many decisions. The more we can plan for the future, the easier those decisions will be."

He looked at each of them in turn. Gatus, almost twice as old as the others, had fought Akkad's battles all his life, and he knew more about training men than anyone. Bantor had served in Akkad's guard most of his life, and he'd proven both his leadership and fighting skills in the battle with Korthac. Hathor, while new to Akkad, had fought for almost twenty years across the length and breadth of Egypt. Yavtar had traded and sailed the Tigris all his life, and joined the fight when the Akkadians overthrew Korthac and reclaimed their city.

They had shared common dangers and fought together, in some cases side by side. All were Hawk Clan members, and each had sworn the oath to stand by his brothers. They all knew not only how to fight, but how to lead men in battle. Just as important, Eskkar valued their ideas, and knew that none of these four would hesitate to offer his honest opinion.

"So tonight the seven of us," Eskkar went on, "are going to start assembling an army for Akkad. And this army that we're going to build will be like no other anyone has ever seen."

Yavtar's eyes widened in surprise. "Why am I here? I know little about such things."

"Because, Yavtar," Eskkar said, "this new army is going to need vast quantities of food and weapons. You know every bend on the Tigris and Euphrates for that matter, as well as every tributary and stream between them. And who better than a river trader to know how to supply fighting men? Just as important, you know how to build boats, and how to train men to sail them. And I'm going to want boats that can deliver men and supplies wherever there's enough water to float a hull. So, the more you learn about how our new army is built, the better you'll know how to supply it."

Yavtar furrowed his brow. "How many boats will you need? You'll need crews to sail them, soldiers to protect them and their cargoes. All that will take months, perhaps years..." Yavtar's voice trailed off as he saw the smile on Eskkar' face.

"Yes, and there's much more, Yavtar. I also want boats that can carry large numbers of fighting men over long distances and at great speed. And I want other boats filled with men who fight on their own, to capture or destroy our enemy's vessels. You'll need to find and train men who know or can learn to fight from such a boat."

"And where will I find these men?"

"I don't know." Eskkar couldn't help laughing at the look on Yavtar's face. "Remember when you and your boats carried forty of us from Bisitun to Akkad in little more than a day? We were in the city long before

Korthac expected, because we raced down the river. That's when I first realized that boats could be for more than just transporting a merchant's goods."

He turned to Hathor. "We're going to need cavalry, too, but I don't just want men who can ride. I want men trained to fight from horseback, ride long distances on little food and water, and still strike a heavy blow at the end of the day. We're going to need hundreds of horses, along with all the things a fighting mount needs to be effective. That means plenty of grain, sacks to carry it in, leather, ropes, cloth buckets, everything you can think of to support a horse and his rider on a long campaign. And weapons, of course. Small bows that can be shot from a galloping horse would be best, but also lances, long swords, as well as leather vests and helmets for protection."

The Egyptian's eyes widened at the scope of the request.

"Hathor, please speak your mind," Trella said, her voice soft and gentle as always. "You bring knowledge of warfare from Egypt, and no doubt there is much we can learn from you."

"You'll need a great many horsemen, Lady Trella, probably more than you can find." Hathor looked at the others, but no one challenged his assertion. "The southern border is long, and distances between Akkad and the Sippar are almost as far. To project force over such a distance requires large numbers of horsemen. In Egypt we had many such horse fighters, all armed with sword and lance. But Eskkar has described the steppe warriors to me, and how they fight with bow and sword. If we can train and supply such horsemen, we would have an effective cavalry. That's what the Egyptians called their horse soldiers."

"Then we will call them that as well," Trella said. "But horses strong enough to carry a man and his weapons are in short supply, and Akkad has few men who can ride, let alone fire an arrow from the back of a moving horse."

Trella had learned much about the ways of the steppe warriors from Eskkar, including what weapons they used and how they fought.

"I've been thinking about that," Eskkar said. "The Ur Nammu have those skills, and we might ask them to help train our men. Perhaps they can gather horses for us as well. The horses will need training as much as the men. But a well-trained mount is worth at least two or three men on foot in a battle."

The Ur Nammu were the steppes clan who fought with Eskkar

during the battle against the Alur Meriki, who had nearly wiped out the entire Ur Nammu clan. Eskkar had rescued the survivors, and they owed him a blood debt for that deed. Though few in number, they'd offered assistance to Akkad, mostly as a result of Trella's generosity toward them during that conflict. For almost three years, she'd directed the city's trade with them, and ensured that they received fair treatment in all dealings. Now that foresight might prove to be helpful in the coming days.

"Even with whatever help you get from the Ur Nammu," Gatus said, "you won't have enough horses or trained riders. Besides, there are many battlegrounds in the hills or over rocky ground where horses are useless. We'll still need plenty of men trained to fight on foot, probably armed with spears and swords. Only such forces can take a battle to the enemy, occupy his land, and hold it."

"Infantry," Hathor said, offering another word from his native land. "In Egypt there were two kinds, heavy and light. The heavy infantry wore leather armor, and carried wicker shields and spears. The light infantry carried smaller shields and used hook swords."

"One line of spearmen won't be enough," Gatus said. "We'll need ranks of such men, at least three or four deep. Enough to present a solid wall of spear points against an enemy."

"Even cavalry cannot attack ranks of spearmen head on," Hathor agreed. "Not unless they greatly outnumber them. When spearmen are formed up in a solid line, they are vulnerable only from the flanks or rear."

"And how will we protect our own ranks of spearmen?" Eskkar had never faced such a line, and his instinct told him to attack such a formation from the rear.

"Well, our bowmen could defend the flanks and rear." Gatus rubbed his beard, as he usually did whenever he worked things out.

"Bowmen are as difficult to recruit and train as horse fighters," Eskkar said. "Our heavy bows require a strong man with powerful arms and keen eyes. And he must be tall enough to handle the weapon."

"We'll have to recruit them based on their skills." Hathor leaned forward on his bench, eager to impart his knowledge. "The tall ones with quick wits and sharp eyes become archers. The stronger, less mobile men become spearmen."

"If we can find them," Gatus said. "It won't be easy."

"We'll find them," Eskkar said. "Men still arrive in the city each day, searching for a better life, even if it means fighting. We'll use every available man we can find in Akkad and the countryside. We'll break them into four groups. Those with the strength and skills will become archers. Those who can use a spear and sword will be trained to fight on foot. Those who can ride will fight on horseback. And all those too weak or too small for anything else will be used as auxiliaries."

"As what?"

"Those who help the soldiers fight," Eskkar explained. He rose and went to the bench against the wall. When he returned, he tossed something on the table.

"It's a sling," Yavtar said, lifting the small leather pouch with its two long leather strips. "A toy for children to hunt rabbits, or farmers too poor to afford a weapon."

"Years ago, a woman nearly killed me with one of these," Eskkar remarked. The others glanced at him in surprise. He rarely talked about his days before arriving in Akkad. "And she'd just finished killing one man and wounding another with the same weapon." He glanced around the table. "If a woman can do that much with such a toy, then think what a well-trained and proficient boy or young man could do."

"Don't bother arguing with him, Yavtar," Gatus said. "If he's convinced these things can be deadly, then I suppose we'll have to give it a try."

"It's a weapon that costs almost nothing to make," Eskkar went on. "You can pick up stones anywhere and use them as missiles. Every shepherd guarding a flock of sheep can hurl a stone a hundred paces. Slings can be used on hilly or uneven ground where the slinger can't be easily attacked. Remember, there are many places where a horse can't go, or where an archer can't easily plant his feet to work his bow."

Yavtar tossed the sling back on the table and waved his hand in a dismissive gesture. "Most of the land in Sumeria is flat and open. Your slingers will be run down and killed."

"Not if they're supported by archers, soldiers, and horsemen," Eskkar said. "That's why they're called auxiliaries. They'll be used only in certain situations and protected by our soldiers." He turned to Gatus. "There are hundreds of boys and young men in Akkad who could learn to use a sling. How many such recruits do you turn away each day?"

"I'm not sure. Maybe ten, twenty, sometimes more."

"In the past we've turned down hundreds of recruits," Eskkar said, "either for being too young or too small. Now we could have an important role for them to play."

"Slingers will cost almost nothing to train, feed, and house. That's something, I suppose." Gatus knew how much the skilled bowmen received each month.

"And for each one killed," Eskkar went on, "there will be another ten ready to take his place."

Hathor touched the sling still resting on the table. "You can't send slingers against cavalry, but they can help protect the rear ranks."

"I can't see a bunch of boys with slings stopping spearmen or cavalry," Gatus said.

"That depends. Korthac had a few such forces in Egypt," Hathor said. "They did more than just protect the rear. They could harry the enemy before the fight, attack them from heights, or even battle enemy horsemen. Stones raining down on you from above, thrown by an unseen enemy, will unnerve even the bravest infantryman."

"And they could serve as foot scouts," Eskkar said, "to protect the bowmen and spear-carriers while on the march. They could also guard the supply animals. And maybe archers and slingers can hold their own against cavalry."

"We can always give it a try, I suppose," Gatus said. "Slingers would be a small part of our forces anyway."

"Don't discount them yet." Eskkar shook his head. "Trella and Yavtar are telling us that soon Sumer will be able to field an army four or five times as large as what we can expect to put together. They can pick the time and place of battle by invading the borderlands whenever and wherever they choose. There's nothing to stop them from crossing the border and fortifying a village or two. That's why Yavtar and his boats and crews will be needed, and that's why slingers may be useful. These new tactics could turn a battle."

He glanced around the table. "Since we'll be outnumbered in any conflict, we'll need an army that doesn't grow weak when they see the superior numbers of the enemy. Gatus and I have been talking about these things, and it can be done. In fact, poor Gatus here has the hardest job of all."

"I see nothing is going to change," Gatus grumbled. "I'll still have to do most of the work."

Everyone laughed with the old soldier. They knew he wouldn't have it any other way.

"Gatus is going to build an army of soldiers who fight on foot," Eskkar said. "Not archers. Mitrac will take charge of all the archers, and keep training them as before. But in our new army, the archer's role will be limited. We're going to have a strong force of men armed with spears and carrying shields, who can take the attack to the enemy."

"If you start arming and training so many," Yavtar said, "Sumer will learn about it, and redouble their efforts to recruit more men. They'll be convinced you're preparing to invade them."

"And if we don't prepare for war, they'll use the time to build up their army anyway and invade us." Eskkar shook his head. "No matter what course we choose, it always leads to war. But you're right about the build-up. The longer we can keep our efforts concealed, the better."

"And how will you accomplish that?"

"By training our new soldiers in small groups, and scattering those groups over the countryside, but especially in the north. We'll still train here in Akkad, but we'll keep men moving in and out of the city, so that the overall number here remains the same. If we manage it properly, we should be able to confuse Sumer's spies as to exactly how many men we have under arms."

"Will that work?" Yavtar sounded dubious.

"It will, though I'm not sure for how long," Eskkar said. "We'll work out the details on all these things later. Today we need to think about what our army will be like. Each of our soldiers will have to master at least two weapons, as Gatus says. The infantry will learn the spear and sword, while the slingers will master slings and short javelins. The bowmen already know how to use a sword, so there's nothing new there. And the horsemen will learn to use the short bow or the longer javelins, as well as the horse sword."

He turned to Gatus. "We'll need more training camps."

"We'll start training the men here," Gatus said, "as we always have. As soon as we establish some new camps, we'll move the more experienced men out to the north, some even farther north than Bisitun. We'll need a camp for Hathor and his horsemen, another one for the soldiers who'll fight with sword and shield . . . and spears." He sighed. "I thought I was going to be relaxing in my old age." A grin spread across his weathered face.

"Archers have been our primary weapon," Bantor said, speaking for the first time. "Our bowmen consider themselves the main force defending Akkad. Now you want to replace them with spearmen?"

"Not replace them," Gatus said, "but support them. It's true our archers can wreak havoc on our enemies, but they can't carry the battle to them. Exposed archers, with no shields, run the risk of being run down. But supported and protected by spearmen, they will remain a deadly force against our enemy. Remember, nothing scares men more than seeing a wall of spears coming at them, especially with bowmen following behind."

"So we'll use a combined force," Eskkar said. "Heavily armed foot soldiers, lightly armed cavalry and bowmen, and a support force of slingers. With those four groups of fighters, we should be able to face whatever the enemy sends against us."

"The Sumerians will have as much trouble finding good horses as we will," Hathor said. "They'll arm most of their men with swords and shields, and send them into battle. From what everyone has told me about Sumeria, they'll use many such fighters, what we called light infantry."

"Where will the gold for all this come from?" Gatus rapped his water cup on the table. "Even Akkad's nobles and merchants won't stand for such an expense, and that's assuming there's enough gold in the city. Have you figured out how much this is going to cost?"

"Yes," Eskkar replied. "We'll begin with King Eridu's ransom. That should be more than enough to get us started."

"I think I may have the solution to that, Gatus." Every eye went to Trella, including Eskkar's.

"A few months ago, I learned of a place not far from here that might hold a rich deposit of gold and possibly silver. The time has come to examine the site, to see if it can yield sufficient ores to meet part of our needs. If it can, perhaps we can pay not only for the men, but also for the equipment they will need."

"And no one has found this place?" Eskkar turned to Trella in surprise. "Wouldn't news of such a discovery be spread far and wide in a matter of days? Why didn't you tell —?"

Trella touched her husband's arm to halt the questions. "I didn't want to tell you until I knew for sure. Annok-sur brought a woman to me about a month ago. Her name was Calla. Her family had discovered the site and were gathering up surface gold when they were attacked by bandits. Everyone else was killed. Her husband, his brothers, Calla's two children.

She was raped and left for dead. The bandits took all the gold Calla's family had found and rode off. She survived and managed to return to Akkad, and told her tale to Annok-sur. We've been taking care of her ever since. I gave her a small house, and now she works with Annok-sur. In return, Calla has revealed nothing about the find to anyone else. Now you all must continue to keep the secret, until we can first examine the site and, if it shows promise, claim it for Akkad."

"And what of the bandits?" Eskkar understood how bandits would react. "If they're cunning enough, they'll be returning to the place every few months to do their own digging. They may even have taken all the gold by now. If the gold is on the surface, like nuggets in the river or dust in pockets, the site would be easily depleted with a few days' work."

"It's possible," Trella agreed. "But Calla thinks the bandits just moved on, satisfied with what they had taken."

"How do you know so much about gold?" Gatus asked Eskkar. "Something else from your past?"

"Yes."

The single word told Gatus and Hathor that nothing else about Eskkar's previous experience with gold would be forthcoming.

Trella returned to her story. "Calla knew she could not claim such a site by herself. I promised her a reward and a secure place of her own if she would keep the secret. Still, we won't know for sure until we visit the place. If the bandits are there or have returned from time to time, we'll take it from them."

"With a gold mine of our own," Eskkar mused, "we should be able to pay for many new recruits . . . and their weapons."

"The mine would belong to the King," Trella said, "to be used to pay for soldiers to defend the city and its people. Even the nobles would not object to that, especially if it would lessen the burden on them. The people will know we are not claiming the gold for ourselves. And the gold will flow through Akkad, helping all of our merchants, craftsmen, and innkeepers."

"You are looking into this?" Eskkar took Trella by the hand.

"Oh, yes, husband. I've already started. In the last few days, I've considered each of the goldsmiths in Akkad, to see who would best suit our needs. I wanted someone with quick wits, a man flexible enough to adapt to new ways. I settled on a young goldsmith who can inspect the site, estimate its potential, and develop the mine, if there is one. This morning we dispatched him north to examine the place, accompanied by a few soldiers. But do not get your hopes raised up just yet. As you say, there may be little or no gold remaining there. Either way, we should know in ten days or so."

Eskkar knew that Annok-sur had dispatched a handful of soldiers on yet another mission, but he hadn't asked the reason. "Any quantity of gold we could get . . . it could make a difference."

"We must all keep this a secret for now," Trella said. "As soon as I learn anything about the find, we'll know what to do."

"Forgetting the gold for a moment," Bantor said, speaking for the first time, "what are you going to tell our men about all these preparations? They'll want to know why Akkad is building up its forces."

"I'm not sure yet," Eskkar said. "We'll need to find something to account for it. Maybe we can say that the barbarians are returning into the northern lands. That would explain what we're doing. And it would please the Sumerians, I'm sure, to know that we face an old enemy."

Eskkar looked at each of them. "What I'll need from all of you are ways to make this work. Figure out what you're going to need, and how much we can tell the rest of the men. For now, we must keep this to ourselves."

"You're not going to tell Klexor and the other subcommanders?" Hathor looked uncomfortable about that.

"No, not yet. Trella and Annok-sur think we should tell as few as possible for now. We can keep them busy enough with the training."

"How much time do we have?" Yavtar settled his elbows on the table. "I mean, if I have to build boats and find crews, it could take months, even years."

Eskkar smiled at Yavtar's gradual acceptance of the plan. "We'll have to assume that Sumer will be capable of attempting another push into the borderlands as early as next year, but more likely the following year. That's why we need to start preparing as soon as possible."

"You're keeping watch on King Eridu?" Bantor asked.

"A boat from Sumer arrived this afternoon with the ransom. The gold is already under guard only a few dozen paces away. Eridu departs at dawn."

"Then that is settled," Eskkar said. "Now we know what we need to begin."

"Maybe more," Gatus said, "if Eridu has learned his lesson."

"Or less." Trella's voice held a hint of resignation. "It seems wars come suddenly, always catching one side by surprise. Yet Annok-sur and I have already taken measures to get more information from Sumer and its leaders. But we can't count on that too much."

"Let's just hope whoever is advising Eridu isn't working on new ways to wage war as well," Yavtar said.

"Then we are agreed," Eskkar said, satisfaction in his voice. "But it will be up to you four to make this plan work. If you believe we can do this, then the men will believe and accept these new ideas soon enough."

The commanders glanced at each other, all of them joined together now to face the challenge. Eskkar knew they would already be thinking of how they could begin.

"We'll start making our plans tomorrow. But now Trella has some more news."

"I wanted to tell you what Annok-sur and I have been planning," Trella began. "First, and most important, we will need many spies in Sumer and the other southern cities. We must search for suitable men and women as quickly as possible, so that they can be settled into the Sumerian cities. Once war is imminent, any new arrivals will be viewed with suspicion, so the sooner we can get them in place, the more likely they'll be able to provide us with information."

"How will they get information back to Akkad?" Gatus asked. "It's nearly nine days on horseback to get from Sumer to here. If your spies disappear for days on end, won't that be noticed?"

"Yes, but Yavtar can help with that. Merchants will use the river as much as ever. Boats come and go, often without anyone noticing. If we place some of our most trusted men among Yavtar's crews, they can gather information as they travel up and down the two rivers."

"We've talked about using the river for such things before," Eskkar said.

"I can always use more good river men," Yavtar said. "Soldiers make good rowers, and I wouldn't have to pay them. Well, not much, anyway."

Everyone chuckled at the idea of soldiers laboring to increase Yavtar's profits.

"At least you won't be using any of my horsemen for rowers," Hathor said.

"Have you any advice for us, Hathor?" Trella smiled reassuringly at the Egyptian, knowing that any mention of his past would bring a pang of sorrow. "You've fought battles with large numbers of soldiers on each side, so you must know what will be needed."

"Well, you will need supplies for the men. The less time the soldiers spend searching for food, the more they can march."

"Not only food and water, but weapons as well." Bantor, Annok-sur's husband and the most loyal of Eskkar's leaders, seldom spoke, but when he did, everyone heeded his words. "There are never enough arrows on the battlefield. A good bowman can empty a full quiver of arrows in a few moments. Once they are gone, he's of little use in a fight, armed only with a short sword."

"That means we will have to make and store large numbers of arrows, bowstrings, and even bows," Trella said. "But if Yavtar can bring your men fresh supplies of these things, then our archers will have plenty of shafts to prolong their part in the battle."

"You're assuming that all the battles will be fought near a river," Gatus argued. "Soldiers need to find the right kind of battlefield, and it might be a day or two's march away from wherever Yavtar can bring his boats."

"Then I would suggest that all of you stay as close to the river as possible," Trella said. "The advantage of having two or three ships deliver thousands of arrows or fresh food may be as important or even more so than choosing the right place. If we plan our battles in advance, we can make sure of being close to water. And all the major cities of Sumeria are located near one or the other of the two rivers, and there are dozens of smaller streams."

"Besides arrows and food," Bantor continued, "an army needs grain for the horses, torches and oil to light the night, ropes for the corrals, shovels, sharpening stones for the swords, even cooking pots. The more that we can load onto a boat, the less the men will have to carry and the farther they'll be able to march."

"That's another problem," Hathor said. "Our soldiers will travel different distances each day, depending on the land, whether it's hilly or sandy or grassland. In Egypt we never knew for certain how many days it would take to march from one village to another."

"We need to train the soldiers to march at least a certain number of miles per day," Gatus said. "No matter what the land is like." The others looked doubtful at that idea.

"Would it be of value to know how far you are from your destinations?" Trella paused for a moment. "We could measure the distances between here and the southern cities. Then if we knew the soldiers could march so many miles in a day, we would know when they could arrive."

"How will you measure the distances?" Gatus sounded skeptical, and rightfully so. No one even knew exactly how far it was from Akkad to Larsa, which was the closest city.

"We could train walkers," Trella said. "Men who would pace off a certain distance with each step. Every hundred steps, he moves a pebble from one hand to the other. That way we could count the steps between Akkad and the southern cities and villages."

"It would also be good to know when we've reached certain places on the journey," Hathor said, leaning forward on the table. "We should learn the location of every landmark between here and Sumer."

"And make a few landmarks of our own where there are none," Eskkar said. "If our walkers marked trees and rocks as they went, or built up piles of stones, we would know how far we'd traveled."

"That would be useful on the river as well," Yavtar said. "In time of war, the river is safer at night. If the landmarks could be seen at night, that would be even better. But when there's no moon, there's little that can be seen."

"The best landmark at night is a fire," Trella said. "It doesn't have to be a real fire. A candle in an open box, facing the water, can be seen over great distances, I think."

"You would need help from villagers living in those places up and down the rivers," Gatus said. "Can that be done?"

"Perhaps. Let Annok-sur and me think about that one. What else will your marching armies need?"

"Maps." Eskkar remembered the maps they had used to fight the Alur Meriki. "If we had good maps, we could mark our progress against the landmarks, and know how far we've traveled, and how far we had to go."

"Isn't that a lot to ask?" Bantor said. "Can we show that much information on a piece of cloth?"

"No, not one piece," Trella said. "But a dozen or more would be enough to show everything. You will need to take a few clerks with you to war, Eskkar. They could keep track of the maps and landmarks, and mark off each day's progress."

Eskkar groaned and everyone laughed. Since he'd become Akkad's ruler, and even before, the clerks of the nobles and Trella's own people followed him everywhere, marking down every expense on a pottery shard, a permanent record of every activity. Already the shelves in the storage rooms creaked under the weight.

"Clerks going to war." Eskkar shook his head at the idea.

"All this is well and good," Gatus said, "but what happens when we reach Larsa? We'll have to besiege it, fight our way in. And from what Yavtar tells us, all of Sumeria is building walls around every dung heap, let alone Larsa and Isin and the other large cities."

"Yes, you're right, Gatus." Trella thought about that for a moment. "I think we need to send Corio's people to visit all the cities in Sumeria. They should examine the walls for weak points, and determine the best method and place to attack each city. That way, when the army arrives, it can get right to work without having to worry about what to do."

"You're fighting the war in advance, Lady Trella," Hathor said. "But all these ideas are good ones. The more prepared we are, the more the men will want to fight."

"Men always fight better when they think they have some advantage," Eskkar said.

"I've one more suggestion to make." Trella turned to Annok-sur. "Actually, Annok-sur suggested it. You need a special place to meet and talk about your plans, a private place. A place with only one purpose. We could build another room here on the second level, and dedicate the new chamber to planning the war. We would enter it only from the workroom, so only the most trusted servants will ever see the inside."

"And we can display the maps there as well," Bantor said, "perhaps even paint them on the walls."

"Remember the model of Akkad that Corio's apprentices built for the first wall?" Eskkar had looked at it in astonishment: a miniature city displayed in perfect detail on a long table. "If we had something like that, something that stretched from Akkad to Sumer, we could use it to plan the marches, and even mark possible battlefields."

"That will take a big room, indeed," Gatus said, drawing another laugh.

"I'll speak to Corio about it," Trella said. "He'll have to build the new room anyway, so he'll be spending plenty of time here."

"If we can do all or even most of the things you've said," Hathor leaned forward, unable to conceal his eagerness, "I think we'll be able to wage a new kind of war. Such advantages would be worth a great number of men."

"The more we know about our enemy," Eskkar said, "the easier this fight will be. If our spies can learn about our enemies, how many men they have, how well trained, what weapons they prefer, how they're fed and resupplied, we can use that knowledge to help plan for battle. That will make our soldiers fight even harder."

"And if we train them," Gatus said, "really train them well, they'll stand up to anything Sumeria can send against us."

"You'll take charge of that, Gatus," Eskkar said. "No one understands how to train men as well as you do."

Everyone nodded agreement. During the battle with the Alur Meriki, Gatus's training had transformed more than a few Akkadians into the equal of even the strongest barbarians.

"So, Gatus, you will need to outdo yourself this time," Eskkar said. "And all of you will have more ideas on how to make our forces stronger in the months to come. I'm sure we can think of even more ways to aid the soldiers."

They continued speaking long into the night. Hathor had more to impart about cities fighting against each other, and Eskkar knew something about that, too, from his days as a soldier for hire. Trella asked many more questions, committing to memory every word that was spoken, every useful fact that she could glean from the men's words. In the coming weeks and months, she would know, or soon learn, everything that would be needed to prepare for and support such a war.

At last Gatus yawned and declared he needed to get to sleep. A glance up at the moon showed that midnight had come and gone.

Trella had the last words. "Let us hope war never comes. But if we must fight again, then let us be well prepared. Remember, like the days when we faced the Alur Meriki, this is a war we dare not lose."

11

Before retiring to their bedroom, Trella checked on little Sargon. The boy slept well, secure in his bed and with his nurse watching over him. She blew out the candle and slipped beneath the blanket, where Eskkar held her close against the darkness.

"I'm sorry that war must come again to Akkad. Trouble seems to follow wherever I go."

"War would come here whoever ruled," she answered. "The southern lands are needed to provide food for our people, and allow us to expand to the north and west. Without those farms, Akkad will not be able to grow, and would slowly begin to starve. That must not happen, especially now that we have Sargon to worry about."

"Yes, he will rule over all these lands someday. If our luck holds true."

"It's more than luck that has brought us this far, Eskkar. Say what you will, but the gods favor you."

"Yes, they brought you to me. Or my luck did."

She knew he believed more in his luck than any of the fickle gods, who needed constant appeasement through prayers and offerings provided by the greedy priests. Or so they claimed to those who believed their every word. Nevertheless, she knew fate or some higher purpose of the gods had brought the two of them together.

Eskkar kissed the curve of her neck and she relaxed against him. Each day is a blessing, she remembered her father saying. Death may come through your door at any time, my little daughter, so live and enjoy your life as much as you can.

Death indeed had come for her father in the middle of the night, when he least expected it. She was glad that for many years he had enjoyed his life and his family so much, finding some joy in whatever each day brought.

Eskkar's hands touched her breasts, and she put thoughts of her father aside. Instead, she sighed and arched her body against her husband's. His strong hands always aroused the fire in her loins.

"Do you still enjoy my touch?"

"Yes, master," she whispered. "This slave enjoys your attentions. I will try to please you."

He laughed. "You already have, Trella."

She laughed, too, and returned his kiss with one of her own.

Afterward, Trella remained in the circle of Eskkar's arm. Somehow she always felt safer sleeping beside him. To know that someone would fight to protect you, would risk his own death if necessary, meant so much more to her now. Trella knew how easily a life could cease. In the space of one day, she'd seen her parents murdered, her brother carried off to the mines, and herself sold into slavery. Her comfortable life had ended in an orgy of blood and tears.

Just when she thought all that was behind her, Korthac had done it again. After a single night of fighting, he forced her to kneel at his feet and beg for the life of her coming child. That time, Eskkar had rescued her, and he'd fought a desperate fight to save her life and that of little Sargon right in this very room. Korthac would have tossed the baby into the fires before turning Trella over to his brutal soldiers for their amusement for a few days before he put her to death.

Now another threat had arisen, this one less immediate perhaps, but just as dangerous. The thought of the Sumerians being a danger seemed odd. She herself was from those lands, as much a Sumerian as anyone born in the city of Sumer. Nevertheless, no one in Akkad ever mentioned it, most probably didn't even realize it. Almost everyone within the city's walls had come from somewhere else. Those born in the old village of Orak and the nearby farms were few in number, compared to those who had sought Akkad's safety. No, she, Eskkar, and now little Sargon were the first true Akkadians. Most of the city's inhabitants felt the same way, Akkadians first. The old name of Orak had vanished within a few months.

Now another trouble had arisen, to provide a new challenge to her plans for the future. The cities of Sumeria had grown in size almost as fast as Akkad, but the southern lands held much less fertile soil to feed their increasing numbers. They could only expand to the north. Eridu had tried and failed. His attempt would not be the last.

Trella had spoken to the prisoner several times, questioning him about life in Sumer and his city's plans, but he said little, ignoring her as a mere woman who should stay out of the affairs of men. No, Eridu was a fool, and sooner or later someone would take his place, someone who might be vastly more cunning, someone who would be an even greater danger to Akkad.

For that reason, the Sumerians needed to be stopped now. Her husband would be happy winning another battle, driving his enemies before him in defeat. But Trella wanted more. She needed the southern cities to be defeated so decisively that it would take another generation before they dared to think once again about the lands to the north. That generation would give Akkad all the time it needed. By then all the northern villages would be brought under Akkad's rule, and the lands to the east and west settled and cultivated. With most of the fertile lands under Akkad's control, the Sumerians would have no choice but to accept Akkad's borders.

The danger lay in the next few years. If the Sumerians again went to war, they would not make the same mistakes a second time. In defeat, they had learned much. Sooner or later, they would have stronger leaders who thought much as she did. They would come in greater numbers and be prepared to win out over any defenses Akkad could raise.

Hathor had indeed spoken the truth when he said they didn't know where or when the battle would take place, or even what kind of battle might face them. If Akkad were indeed greatly outnumbered, then a single defeat could end her dreams for the city's future. No, she must plan for a brief campaign that completely mastered the Sumerians, one that defeated them so decisively that they would never again threaten Trella's city.

So the battle must be fought and won starting today, years before the actual fighting took place. Trella would have to make sure Eskkar and his commanders planned for this great battle, the single stroke that would crush their enemies. That meant that the soldiers needed to be properly supplied, possible battlegrounds mapped, distances measured, spies set in place, food and weapons stockpiled, and men recruited and trained. The people of Akkad must be prepared as well, but subtly, so that they did not realize before time what they were being asked to do, and how much their existence was at stake.

Last, Eskkar and his commanders needed to think of total victory. Korthac had thought that way. He'd planned the battle in advance, gathered his forces in secret, launched an attempt on Eskkar's life, and captured the city in a single night. Trella had been helpless, and only Eskkar's determination and courage had saved the day. And his luck. Even he had not believed he could win back the city from the Egyptians, but had only intended to save his wife and son.

Now she needed to guide Eskkar's mind, as well as his commanders, along those same channels. Akkad might have only one chance at survival. If it slipped away, Trella might yet end up as a slave once again.

Her final thoughts before she slipped into sleep were that Akkad would need all the gold it could raise. Without gold to pay the soldiers and provide for their needs, the city would fall. Much of her future, and that of their city, now depended on Orodes and whatever precious metals lay in the ground to the north.

12

For Orodes, the next few days passed quickly, and he scarcely remembered all the events that took place following his talk with Trella. Once they left the Compound, Tooraj clasped his hand on Orodes's shoulder and kept it there, as if to insure that Orodes didn't bolt and run. The soldier might be missing an eye, but his hand felt as if it could crush Orodes's shoulder to splinters without effort.

At the docks, he found five soldiers and a woman waiting for them. Every soldier carried a bow and a quiver of arrows, and wore a sword belted at the waist. Horses were available for everyone, and two others served as pack animals. So many horses meant a serious expedition, Orodes noted.

"My tools . . . I'll need my tools at the site."

"Already taken from your father's house and loaded," Tooraj said. "Can you ride?"

"Yes, of course. I've ridden –"

"Good. Get him moving."

Tooraj directed his last words to one of his soldiers, who handed Orodes a halter. Within moments, they moved onto the ferry. It took two trips to get all of them and their animals across the Tigris. As soon as the second vessel discharged its contents on the western bank, Tooraj told everyone to mount up, and the little caravan started moving north.

The one-eyed soldier apparently preferred not to waste time talking, and he said nothing else to Orodes for the rest of the day. Tooraj, a competent horsemen, rode at the head of the party, with the woman, Calla, at his side. Orodes decided that she was the one who knew where they were going. Either the rest of the party didn't know their destination, or more likely, didn't care. Except for their leader, all the soldiers appeared less at ease on horseback. Like Orodes, they probably rode infrequently, and needed to pay close attention to their mounts.

They made good progress. The horses, while no doubt not up to Tooraj's idea of good horseflesh, were sound enough, and they plodded along without much urging.

They camped as soon as it grew dark. Tooraj ordered Orodes to gather firewood along with the rest of the soldiers. Calla prepared the fire pit while the men foraged for wood, animal dung, or anything else that would burn. Fortunately, this close to the river, they didn't have to wander far from the campsite to find water.

They ate in silence. One of the soldiers produced a wine skin, which was passed around to everyone except Orodes. Even Calla took a long swig, before passing the skin across Orodes's body to one of the soldiers. Orodes looked at it longingly, but didn't bother asking for a portion. Tooraj obviously had his orders about giving wine to a man found drunk and passed out in Akkad's lanes.

Still, the smell of the raw date wine made the skin on Orodes's hands and arms crawl with longing.

"You're the guide?" Orodes decided he might as well talk to Calla, since it didn't seem likely he'd have much to say to the soldiers. Besides, any conversation would take his mind off the now empty wineskin. Her hair had a few streaks of gray in it, and he guessed her age at about thirty seasons, too old to consider as a bedmate, at least not this early in the journey.

"Yes. My husband and his kin found the place with the gold a few months ago."

She told him about the mine, her family, and what evil had overtaken them all. Orodes asked her about the gold, its quality, how they'd extract it, but Calla knew little about such things. Mostly she had cooked the food, and stitched the leather skins into sacks to hold the gold the men gathered.

Frustrated by her lack of useful knowledge, Orodes put his feet toward the fire and went to sleep, ignoring the still-talking soldiers and Tooraj.

In the morning, Orodes felt better. A long drink from the Tigris refreshed him, and he splashed water over his face and neck. He hadn't slept very well in Akkad since his return, and certainly not during the night before, when he lay down drunk in the lane. Orodes shook his head in embarrassment at the recollection.

Breakfast consisted of bread and dates, and everyone climbed back on the horses just as the sun cleared the horizon.

The rest of the day and night was uneventful. But by mid-morning of the third day, Calla began to point out landmarks. For someone who had known almost nothing about the gold, she certainly seemed to know her away around this part of the countryside. Orodes wondered if her family might have been bandits themselves.

For two days they'd kept the river in sight, but now Tooraj, following Calla's lead, turned the party westward, and they soon moved into the low hills that overlooked the river.

Orodes frowned as they rode west. His father and his father before him had explored this part of the country many times. None of these hills had ever produced any significant amounts of gold or anything else useful. By midday they'd left the Tigris several miles behind. Orodes decided Calla had led them on a fool's errand, when she gestured to a barely noticeable opening between two hills. They followed a twisting track of rock-hard ground that led deeper into the hills. Soon enough Orodes looked up to see a steep cliff blocking their way. A blind trail, as anyone could see.

Calla continued toward it, and as they rounded a large boulder, Orodes saw where the cliff face had collapsed, revealing a narrow defile that twisted its way through the heart of the cliffs, until, several hundred paces later, the pathway opened up and revealed a good-sized valley nestled between the hills.

Orodes, riding alone just behind Calla and Tooraj, felt his jaw drop at the sight that awaited them. A stream meandered its way through the center, appearing from one side of the valley and disappearing into the other. Orodes didn't see any other entrances or exits to this hidden canyon, one full of large boulders scattered about that towered over horse and rider.

He scarcely noticed the ground before him. Instead, he stared at the rocks and jagged cliffs surrounding him. The land had changed completely. The soft hills with their occasional boulders had vanished, replaced by more rugged limestone deposits.

"By the gods," he muttered, as he looked around. He could almost smell the copper and lead his instincts told him lay buried beneath the surface. Orodes had never seen such a place. Some cataclysm had ripped the earth apart, and thrust these hills upwards, carrying with them all the ores once hidden deep within their depths. It had to be an earthquake, he decided. Only a massive earthquake could shake these hills, and lift the earth in such a fashion. If he hadn't seen it for himself, he wouldn't have believed it existed, not in these lands.

The party reached the center of the valley, and Calla called out that this was where her family had camped. Orodes ignored her and the soldiers. He rode to the far end of the valley, near where the bubbling water issued from the ground. He slid from the horse and knelt beside the stream. He ran his fingers into the moving water, ignoring the chill. A glint of gold caught the sunlight. Reaching down, he picked up a nugget the size of his thumb, washed clean and pure by the running water.

He tossed it aside, and moved away from the stream. Orodes knelt again, and began digging into the earth, letting the dirt settle through his fingers. He could almost feel the ores, just out of reach. Gold and silver lay buried here, he felt certain, waiting to be taken. But there might be more, much more.

Rising, he slapped the dirt from his hands. Calla and Tooraj and the others stood about two hundred paces away, in the middle of the vale, unloading the horses. Orodes cupped his hands to his mouth. "Tooraj! Come here! Bring my tools!"

His horse had wandered off, not that Orodes cared. He moved toward the base of the hills, where the stream had broken through the rock walls and begun its journey through the little valley. A pool had formed at the water's entrance, and he splashed through it, ignoring the biting cold on his feet. The sharp chill told him the water came from deep within the earth, forced upwards when the underground river struck the once buried cliffs.

The stream had pierced the limestone wall long ago, breaking off chunks of stone and dumping them into the pool. The rocky fragments had all vanished by now, washed away by the flowing water, but he knew they'd left behind nuggets of lead, copper, iron, and gold, buried not far beneath the silt at the bottom of the pool.

Orodes didn't bother searching. He knew the ores were here, felt it in his bones. Instead, he concentrated on the rock wall. While working for his uncle, Orodes had often descended deep into the mountain mine, scrambling down the treacherous shafts, going down gallery by gallery, following the threads of ore. He'd stood deep underground while he examined the interior of the mine by the flickering torchlight, following the veins of ore created when the earth and rock were crushed together, often separated by thin, horizontal lines.

Now, studying the rock face before him, those usual horizontal layer lines were gone. Instead, he saw the threads pointed almost directly up to the sky. This once flat earth from deep underground had not only been shoved to the surface, but it had been turned on its side.

The ground beneath his feet might once have been hundreds of paces beneath the earth's surface, deeper than any miner had ever delved. Orodes realized he might be standing at the bottom of a mine, instead of the top. No miner had ever seen such a sight, at least none that he'd ever heard of.

"What do you want?" Tooraj rode up and dumped the large sack that contained Orodes's tools onto the ground. "I'm not some servant to come when you call."

Orodes ignored him. He untied the sack and removed a hammer and chisel. "Set up the camp here, but not too close to the pool."

"We're setting up camp in the middle of –"

"Shut up, and do what I say. I want the camp set up here. And tell your men to bring shovels and join me. There's work to be done now, before it gets too dark."

Without waiting for a reply, Orodes moved back to the limestone wall beside the stream and began attacking the rock. In moments, the sounds of his bronze hammer striking the bronze chisel began to echo through the valley.

Tooraj, stunned into silence, stared at Orodes. Then he shook his head and rode back to where Calla and the others waited.

Orodes worked without ceasing, his movements quick and sure with his implements. Rock chips flew from the wall, many striking his face and arms. Dust flew into his eyes, but he knew how to lessen that by keeping his eyes half-closed. He forgot about the other members of the party, ignored everything until someone called his name. He turned to find two of the soldiers standing before him.

"You wanted shovels?"

"Where are the rest of the soldiers? I want everyone in the party digging."

"On guard duty or setting up the camp. Tooraj says we're all you can have for now."

He would deal with Tooraj later. Orodes set the two men to work a dozen paces away, after giving them orders to dig down from the base of the wall, until they reached solid rock. Then he returned to his own chipping, digging his way into the face of the rock. He worked steadily, ignoring the weariness in his arms, pausing only to wipe the sweat and dust from his eyes, or to examine some interesting bit of rock. Some of these he tossed aside, but others he deposited on the ground behind him. As he worked, a small pile of gold nuggets and irregular pieces of ore began to accumulate.

"Orodes! It's getting dark."

Calla stood beside him. The two soldiers had disappeared, and he realized he hadn't noticed them leave.

"It's time to eat," Calla said. "You need to rest. And Tooraj wants to talk to you."

Breathing hard from his exertions, Orodes glanced up at the sky. The sun had dipped behind the hills, and already most of the light had gone. He'd worked without ceasing for almost the entire afternoon.

"I'll come." His voice sounded hoarse, and he paused to take a long drink from the stream, washing the dust from his throat and careless of the chilly water that streamed over his face and chest. After he'd gotten rid of most of the dirt, Orodes dumped the rest of his tools on the ground, and filled the sack with the nuggets and samples he'd marked for further study.

When he tried to lift it, he could barely swing the sack up over his shoulder. Hunched over, he followed Calla back to the campfire.

"I thought you were going to dig all through the night," Tooraj remarked as Orodes let the heavy sack fall to the ground near the fire.

The smell of meat cooking in a copper pot assailed Orodes. He hadn't eaten anything since they'd set out this morning. Calla filled a bowl with stew and handed it to him. He clasped his hands around it, letting the warmth flow through his fingers for a moment, then began eating.

"What orders did Lady Trella give you, Tooraj?" He got the words out between mouthfuls.

The soldier looked at him closely. This wasn't the drunken youth picked up from Akkad's lanes, or even the sullen and quiet young man who had ridden north the last two days. Blood spatter marked his upper arm and tunic, and one of his fingers had taken a nasty cut, but Orodes didn't seem to notice. He had changed the moment he'd arrived at this place. Something in Orodes's voice now commanded respect. The soldiers noticed it, too, and their conversation ceased as they watched to see how their leader reacted.

"I'm to stay with you a few days, until you've had a chance to examine the site and settle in. Then I'll ride back to Akkad and report to Lady Trella, collect anything else we may need, and return."

Orodes shook his head and gulped another mouthful from the nearly empty bowl. He'd forgotten the first rule of camping, the last one to take his supper received the smallest portion.

"There's no need to wait. I already have all I need." He poked at the sack with his foot. "You and I will return tomorrow, and I'll give my report to Trella."

Tooraj frowned at Orodes's failure to use Lady Trella's title, but the young man was too busy licking the remains of the bowl to notice.

"But we've only arrived. I thought it would take many days before you –"

"I thought so, too. But I was wrong. This place has already told me all I need to know. Now it's time to return to Akkad, so we can come back here as soon as possible and start mining. If we leave right after dawn, you and I can be in Akkad well before dark on the following day." He stood and dropped the empty bowl in front of Calla. "Wake me before dawn. I want to be on the move at first light."

Without another word or glance at anyone around the campfire, Orodes rolled over onto his side, cradled his head on his arms, and closed his eyes.

Tooraj appeared ready to vent his anger, but Calla shook her head.

"Best do as he asks. Lady Trella will know what's best."

If Orodes heard her speak, he gave no sign. In a few moments, he started breathing heavily.

Tooraj muttered an oath and stomped off into the darkness, to vent his anger alone.

13

"A map room . . . very interesting. Yes, that would require quite an expansion, if you wished to work with such a large model. With the single entry you want, and to carry the weight of men using it . . . I think it would need special supports, extra beams, a completely new design."

"Then I'm speaking to the right person, Noble Corio," Trella said. The two sat alone in the workroom. She had requested a private meeting with Akkad's master builder to discuss a new addition to the house. "Who else can we turn to when Akkad needs something new and difficult?"

Corio hunched his chair closer to the table, and picked up the slim stick of chalk bound with a rag. A square section of slate, framed with wood and a rope attached to the top, served as his drawing board. An apprentice usually carried the slate around his neck, always ready should his master need his services, but this morning the apprentice waited in the courtyard below, while Trella alone met Akkad's master builder.

"No need to flatter me, Trella. Let me sketch something while we speak."

Trella leaned forward, always interested in learning something new. Corio's nimble fingers belied the silver hair that covered his head. He applied chalk to the slate, and with deft strokes he soon had a rough outline to show.

"We'll need to build it as a separate structure, almost like a second story with nothing underneath," Corio said, talking as much to himself as to Trella. "The roof over the rest of the house won't hold the weight, and the walls weren't built for it either. So . . . if we sink five or six beams into the ground on either side, we can bridge the house with planks, and use those to support the floor. The walls and roof will need to be wood, no mud bricks, because of the weight. Mmmn. You're sure you want it up here, right off the workroom? Easier and cheaper to build an addition to the house on the ground."

"Yes."

Corio lifted his eyes at the response, the single word offered without any explanation. "It would be more secure up here," he said, after collecting his thoughts for a few moments. "What you ask can be done, though I don't think anyone has ever built such a structure before. You'll need a good supply of various types of lumber, most of which will have to come from the north."

The land around Akkad boasted plenty of trees, but not the dense and strong wood needed to bear large amounts of weight. All those had to be brought downriver from the forests at the base of the steppes.

"Please use whatever materials you think best, Corio."

"All those beams will make it expensive. Are you sure? . . . I mean, will you have —?"

"The Map Room will be a great help in preparing for the coming war. We'll use part of Eridu's ransom to pay for it. And I'm hopeful that soon a new source of gold will be found. So, spend whatever you need. But the work must begin immediately, and be completed as soon as possible."

"Mmmn." Corio continued his sketching in silence for a few moments. "One door, you say, and only a few small windows to provide fresh air. That should make construction a bit easier."

"No one must be able to hear what is said, or catch a glimpse of what lies inside, Corio. That is most important."

He pushed the slate across the table. "Support beams on both sides, sunk deep into the ground. I can brace them against the house and each other, for additional strength. When we're finished, we'll need to conceal everything with some false walls, to hide the supports. Otherwise your house will be the ugliest in Akkad, and I'm sure you don't want that. It might be interesting to slant the roof, to allow the rain to run off, and prevent anyone from hiding on top of the structure. That will require more wood, of course. Mmmn."

Corio understood the need for privacy, always one of the most valuable of commodities for anyone living within Akkad. With so many people and the occasional farm animal jammed together in small rooms only a few paces across, the luxury of speaking without worry of being overheard was both rare and expensive.

"Use whatever you need, Corio," Trella went on. "Already Eskkar and his commanders have begun the planning, and this work room is not big enough to hold all those who will be needed."

"I can order the lumber today," Corio said. "It will take a few weeks to get exactly what I require. Meanwhile, I can divert a few logs from the wall's construction, at least enough to get started."

Trella nodded. "That would be desirable, I think. But that is the next matter that I want to discuss. Work on Akkad's outer walls must be speeded up. And you must revisit the design. If Eskkar and his men are fighting in the south, your walls may be all that keeps Akkad's enemies out of the city."

Corio arched an eyebrow. "It's almost too late to do anything with the design of the walls. We've been working on them for nearly three years."

The new walls called for heights of almost twenty paces on either side of the main gate. Facing east, Akkad's primary entrance still remained the most likely approach for any enemy force. The wall there had already been completed, including towers every fifty paces that projected out, allowing archers to shoot down at enemies massing at the foot of the walls. On the remaining three sides, the height of the walls would reach fifteen paces. With a ten-foot ditch ringing the city, the high walls would be unassailable.

"Perhaps nothing significant can be done," Trella said, "but I want you to think about how we would defend these walls with fewer soldiers and archers. The ditch might be dug deeper. If an attack is imminent, we'll have hundreds more craftsmen and farmers crowding the city, and I think we'll need to make use of them to help defend the walls."

"We've changed the plans for these walls at least ten times before we began construction," Corio said, shaking his head in frustration. "Now you want to add further changes. It must end sometime, Trella."

"If it were easy, Corio . . ."

He laughed. "I know, then you wouldn't be asking me. Still, we always assumed we would have hundreds of fighting men to defend us."

"Two years ago, that was true. Now we worry not about barbarians, but about thousands of Sumerians massing outside the walls. Men with thick shields, with ladders by the hundreds and capable of building ramps as well. Men with skills almost as good as your own, all thinking about ways to force their way into Akkad."

"Back to the flattery." He sighed. "Oh, well, I'll see what I can come up with. Perhaps I'll have one or two of my sons try to devise ways to break in."

Trella had been about to suggest that same thought, but it was always better if Corio arrived at the right conclusions on his own. "An excellent idea, master builder. And I'm sure Bantor could provide one or two senior commanders to work with them. That way, you would have the benefit of their experience. You could even offer a gold coin or two for whoever comes up with the most dangerous idea."

"Just when I thought I would be able to enjoy some leisure," Corio said, "now you give me new challenges."

"Unless you wish me to seek the help of some of the new builders in Akkad," Trella said with a smile.

"From flattery to threats. Oh, well, I should stop complaining. Better to have too much work than too little."

"We're going to need your skills more than ever, Corio." Trella's voice turned serious. "And we'll need your ideas on how to best attack the southern cities. Which is one reason why we need the Map Room. Do you have someone who can construct the models?"

"As soon as you told me what you wanted, I thought of my second eldest daughter. She refuses to learn to cook and sew properly, and prefers to spend time with her brothers and the other apprentices in the wood room, building models and sketching designs. She has a fine hand for detail work. Besides annoying her brothers, she embarrasses them with her skills. And none of them will eat anything she cooks."

Trella's eyes showed her interest. She'd always found it easier and better to work with women than men. Girls could concentrate more on the task at hand, follow instructions, and remain calm under pressure. And they didn't have to be constantly competing with the other boys.

"You never told me your daughter had such an interest. What's her name?" Trella knew the girl's name, of course, but preferred Corio to offer it.

"Ismenne. I only wish she were a more dutiful child."

Dutiful children tended to be of little use to Trella.

"Ah, yes, I remember her now. How many seasons does she have?"

"Almost twelve. Soon she'll be married off and someone else's problem."

"If you think she can keep secret her work in the Map Room, perhaps I can make use of her. May I speak with her about this?" Trella saw that her offer had caught Corio by surprise. Like so many other men, he probably had underestimated his daughter's value. Until now.

He took only a moment to grasp the implication of her words. "Of course, Lady Trella. Perhaps I should have paid more attention to her myself." He sighed again. "Now she'll come under your spell, and I'll have lost her forever."

"I promise I'll return her an even more dutiful and loving daughter, who will give thanks to her father for permitting her this chance to help both her father and Akkad."

"Let me speak to her mother first," Corio said. "But I'm sure she'll agree. I'll bring Ismenne here tomorrow. I should have some sketches ready by then."

Trella knew the girl's mother would consent. With the queen of Akkad showing interest in her problem daughter, Ismenne, she would have much greater opportunities for finding a good husband. Everyone would benefit from such an arrangement.

"Then again we will all be in your debt, Corio. You and your daughter may do much to defend Akkad from its enemies."

14

I f Orodes's early return surprised Trella, nothing in her countenance showed it. She sat beside Eskkar in the workroom, facing Tooraj and Orodes across the table. Both men still carried the dust and grime of a long and hasty journey. They had come straight to the Compound, despite the fact that the supper hour would soon be upon the household. Already the sounds of a large gathering floated up from the floor below.

"Well, what did you find?" Eskkar's voice sounded hard. He had little patience for those who failed to obey orders. "Why did you return so soon, Tooraj?"

"He came because I ordered him, Lord Eskkar," Orodes answered, cutting in before the soldier could reply. "In half a day, I learned more than enough to return to Akkad. I've made a list of what I will require to begin mining, and I brought samples with me." He reached down and hefted a good-sized sack onto his lap. "You'll want to check these samples with my father, or perhaps another goldsmith you trust, but I'm sure of what they contain."

"And that is . . . ?" Lady Trella's voice sounded gentle compared to her husband's.

"Gold, of course. At first it will be mostly loose nuggets lying about, or just under the top layer of dirt. We'll also find more pockets in the stream and nearby. We'll need to pick the valley clean of the surface gold first, otherwise the workers will steal it all. Once we've emptied the stream and the stream's pockets, we can get started digging into the earth for the real ores."

"What else did you find, then?"

"Almost all of the noble metals are present. There's plenty of copper and tin, as well as quantities of lead, antimony, iron and arsenic. But I think we'll find the real strength of the mine is this."

Orodes removed a jagged nugget from the sack and placed it on the table between them.

Eskkar reached out his hand, picked it up, and held it to the light. "That's silver, isn't it?"

"Yes, Lord. The rocks and ground at this place are full of native silver."

"What kind of silver?"

The fact that the king of Akkad didn't know what that meant startled Orodes, but Trella caught his eye, and he knew that she understood. He softened his words so as not to offend.

"Native silver is a rare form of the metal, Lord. This nugget is almost . . . it's very pure silver, with only a few impurities, which could easily be removed. But any silversmith could work with this nugget as it is. Most silver, as I'm sure you know, is obtained from smelting lead and copper ores. Silver is one of the residues left behind from the smelting process. But the ores I found at the site are heavy with silver. More silver than gold."

Eskkar handed the nugget to Trella. "And you say there is a good quantity of silver at this place?"

Orodes glanced at Trella, who had spared only a brief look at the nugget. "My Lord, I believe that this site holds large quantities of copper, lead, tin, silver, and gold. And iron, of course, but that's of no value to us. Someday we may learn how to make use of it, since it's so common."

Eskkar's frown returned, and Orodes decided now wasn't the time to speak about iron.

"But silver seems to be the most plentiful. The gold nuggets resting on the stream bed are of high quality as well." Orodes reached into his pouch, extracted an irregular clump of gold, and set it on the table.

Eskkar examined the nugget. He'd learned much about gold in his wanderings, but it had taken the siege of Akkad and Trella's guidance to explain the mystery of gold to him. Many villagers believed the golden metal to be the most valuable of all possessions. Its rich and warm color satisfied some deep-seated longing in men. They worshipped it in secret, clutching it close to their bodies before burying it deep in the earth.

"Tell me more about the gold, Orodes." Eskkar handed the nugget to Trella.

"Yes, Lord. As you know, gold is the most valuable of all the metals taken from the earth. Unlike silver, bronze, copper, or any of the metals, only gold neither tarnishes nor rusts. It can be highly polished, and hammered into any shape, even beaten to the thinness of a leaf. Malleable. That's a word that we . . . the goldsmiths call it. And because gold is so malleable, it can be easily divided, and so accommodate exchanges of lesser value. Also, gold can be carefully measured and its quantity determined. Merchants and traders, for all these and other reasons, seek gold. They hammer out their own coins, and use them to adjust their trades, since much value is concentrated in such a small area."

"And in so doing, they have created a medium of exchange," Trella added. "It is easier to carry a sack of gold than a herd of cattle."

Eskkar nodded. Barter might still be the most common way to trade, but gold, silver, and even copper coins made life in the villages possible. "Tell us more about the mine, Orodes."

Orodes explained what he'd found, and told of his idea that the earth had shifted in the distant past and pushed part of its depths to the surface. He spoke at length, describing the site and estimating its potential, and no one interrupted him with questions until he finished.

"I think you've done well, Orodes. Now what do you suggest?"

Trella's face held the hint of a smile, and Orodes suddenly understood that she knew exactly what needed to be done.

"I believe that we should mine this site, and we should get started at once. I believe we will dig a vast amount of silver from the earth. To accomplish that, we'll need miners, slaves or free men. There will be no trouble paying them. We'll need carpenters to build the sluices, some laborers to build a dam across the stream. They can establish some farms in the nearby hills, away from the mine itself, so as to avoid illness. We can use the stream to flush the waste. Then there's the fire pits that have to be dug and lined, sacks and carts to carry the ores, men to sort and grade the rocks, others to crush them down to manageable sizes. We'll need plenty of wood for fires, but there's more than enough near the river. It will have to be brought in, along with food for the workers. A lot of work will be needed in the beginning, to get the mine up and running. You might want to consider widening the trail between the mine and river, and setting up some docks to load ships. It will be easier to transport the ores by boat, I think. After that, we can use fewer workers."

Orodes stopped, a little embarrassed at his long speech. But the rulers of Akkad still showed their interest.

"Many of those who work the fire pits and dig the ores will die," Eskkar said. "So you'll need a steady supply of slaves or prisoners for those jobs. As well as soldiers to guard them and the site, and herders to care for the horses and other animals. Then there will be carts to be built, to transport the ores to the river, where boats will bring it to Akkad. And after working all day, the men will want women and ale. You're talking about establishing a whole village at one time."

"Yes, Lord. I hadn't thought of it that way, but all those things will be needed, I'm sure."

"And what do you want for yourself, Orodes?" Trella asked.

"Lady Trella, I wish to be allowed to run the mine. I may be young, and you have little reason to trust me. But I know I can extract as much gold and silver as can be ripped from the ground. And I can do it faster and more efficiently than my father or the rest of my kin. If I am worthy, whatever you decide to pay me will be enough. No one in Akkad has ever doubted your fairness, Lord Eskkar . . . Lady Trella. But remember, this site is unique in all the land. After we harvest all the surface metals, we can dig down, go deeper into the earth, but the site is not limitless. The other surrounding hills, which I didn't examine, probably hold little of value. After a few years, there may be nothing left to extract. The site is rich in metals, but I don't know how much it will produce after four or five years."

"I can see that Annok-sur and I will be busy for the next few weeks. We've never built a village before, and now we have to create one in a matter of days." Trella turned to her husband. "But I think that if the mine can produce a steady stream of gold and silver for that many years, it will be long enough, Eskkar."

"Yes, that should be more than enough to pay for the war."

"War? What war?" Tooraj spoke for the first time, leaning forward.

Orodes, too, appeared surprised to hear the word.

"I think you had better tell them," Trella said, rising. "They've both earned our trust. Orodes, my thanks to you. You will take charge of the mine, and your loyalty and skills will be well rewarded. Now, I think I should go attend to our guests downstairs."

Both Tooraj and Orodes stood as she left the room.

Eskkar smiled at that. No one had ever ordered or even suggested that people rise when she entered or left their presence, but everyone did it. He'd done it himself.

"Tooraj, we believe that there will be another, even greater, war with the cities of Sumeria in the next few years. The gold and silver from Orodes's mine are desperately needed to pay for the men and arms we must have to defend Akkad. Without that gold, or silver, as it may be . . . our city may not survive."

Soldier and goldsmith stared, mouths open. Both thought the days of war had ended. Now they learned that the threat had returned.

"Tooraj, you will be in charge of all the soldiers and men at the site, and there will be clerks and others to assist you. But your main task will be to give Orodes whatever he needs to start the gold and silver flowing. He will be the master of the mine, and all those who work the ores."

Eskkar fixed his gaze on Orodes. "Trella has placed her trust in you. I hope you will prove worthy. The future of Akkad may depend on what you drag out of the ground at your mine, Orodes."

Later, after both Tooraj and Orodes left the chamber, sworn to secrecy, Eskkar remained seated, lost in thought, until Trella returned.

"What troubles you now, husband? Our guests are waiting below." Her hand rested on his shoulder.

"With this discovery, this gold, we are committing ourselves to prepare for war. And this new kind of war will bring death to hundreds, even thousands of men."

"There is no other way, Eskkar. Sumerian armies would march on Akkad in any case. Now at least we will have a chance to ready ourselves with both men and weapons. Without this new source of wealth, we would have no chance to survive. Akkad is fortunate to have you here, my husband. The gods sent you here to found this city. Now they've sent us a mine of gold and silver to pay for what we will need to preserve it."

"We'll need a name for this mine," he said. "How about Nuzi? It's the barbarian word for silver."

"A good name. And we'll need a good leader to establish the village. I was thinking that Lani and her husband would be perfect to place in charge of the . . . Nuzi."

Eskkar had brought Lani down from the north two years ago. For over a year, Lani had fulfilled the role of mistress, helping Trella in many ways besides that of keeping Eskkar occupied. But then her yearning to have a child of her own had changed her heart, and she asked to be released from her promise. Now pregnant and married to Grannar, one of Nestor's sons, she and her husband would be an ideal choice to administer a new village.

"I'm sure they would both be grateful to leave Akkad, at least for a while."

Grannar's first wife and three children had died two years ago from the pox that had swept over Nestor's farmlands south of Akkad. Thankfully, the scourge hadn't reached Akkad, and the danger had passed. Grannar had escaped unscathed, while his family died around him. Something about him had touched Lani's heart, and in time, the feeling had been returned.

"Then that is decided." Eskkar took a deep breath and let it out. "Since we overthrew Korthac, I have longed for peace, Trella — for you, for Sargon, for everyone in the city. But it seems that there must always be one more fight, one more battle, if we wish to survive."

She rose and moved to his side, putting her arm around his shoulder. "I see no other path before us. If you do . . ."

He pulled her down onto his lap and sighed. "No, there is no other way. Only a fool puts down his sword while his enemies gather against him. Some day there may be an end to fighting, but it is not this day. Starting today, we prepare for war."

That night, after Eskkar had gone to sleep, Trella and Annok-sur sat next to Sargon's little bed in the workroom. The child slept peacefully, a far cry from the first six months of his life, when he clung to his existence, sometimes fighting to breathe. Sargon had arrived early, weak and fitful, living his first few moments of life with a battle raging round him. Trella thought him as brave as his father.

The Egyptian Korthac had captured the city and turned Trella into a slave once again, and she'd delivered her child in the afternoon of the famous battle. In his first night of existence, Eskkar and Korthac had fought in the same room where Trella and her new son were held prisoner. Little Sargon had nearly been crushed by the violent struggle between the two desperate men fighting to rule Akkad.

Annok-sur reached out and touched the child's head. "He's growing so fast. Soon he'll be running everywhere."

"Already I wish he were older. The city needs an heir, someone the people know and trust, one of their own."

"You worry about Eskkar and the fighting?"

"Yes. I see it in his face. Despite what he said tonight, Eskkar has his doubts about facing so many of the enemy. So he will think he needs to lead his men. That means my husband is going to fight once again. He'll put himself in danger in the forefront of the fighting." She sighed. "Tomorrow it will all begin. He'll meet with Gatus and the others, to go over more ideas about waging war."

"It is what your husband does best, Trella. Even the Alur Meriki chieftain acknowledged his fighting skills."

"I know. Still, he worries me. Eskkar thinks he'll lose the respect of the commanders if he doesn't lead the men in battle."

"Not Bantor, I'm sure."

"Your husband will be at risk as well."

"Don't speak of such things, Trella. Eskkar would not be the same if he didn't command men in battle. Unlike your Eskkar, Bantor knows only fighting It's the trade he's followed since he left the farm, little older than a boy."

"Then we must do everything in our power to make sure our men succeed and survive. The first thing we'll need are spies in Sumer and the other cities."

"They can be found," Annok-sur said, "especially now that the Sumerians have ravaged the southern lands. Many from those lands burn with hatred for what the Sumerians did. But just as important, we'll need a way to collect and send the information back to Akkad. That will be more difficult."

"Yavtar will help with that."

"We should tell him to buy or build two or three fast boats to use only for carrying information."

"Yes, but I want to do something else," Trella said. "What we really need is to get spies close to the ruling houses, perhaps even inside them. If we could do that, we'll gather more facts and fewer rumors. If we're going to have people risk their lives getting us information, it should be as reliable as possible."

"That will be difficult. The wealthy merchants trust only their own servants and kin. We'll have to bribe our way into those places. That will put the spies in great danger. Gold always attracts too much attention."

"I might have a different way," Trella said. "And I think a spy should be able to do more than just collect information. He should be able to kill the decision makers and other key leaders, if the opportunity presents itself. No leader has enough competent men surrounding them. Look how often Eskkar talks with the men, watching them train, trying to find good men to be leaders of ten or twenty."

"An assassin would be useful," Annok-sur said. "Even one killing stroke at the right time could tip the scales of battle."

"Which means the Sumerians will think of the same thing. We will have to increase our own guard, to protect Eskkar. He's still the most vulnerable target."

"And you. Even this Eridu will have enough gold left to dispatch a murderer or two, to seek his revenge. Perhaps Eskkar shouldn't have cut off his hand after all."

"No, it was the right thing to do," Trella said. "Eskkar understands the use of force and terror. Eridu will carry that fear with him for the rest of his life. It will cloud his thoughts. Everyone he meets with will know that hatred colors Eridu's words. But we must double our efforts to protect Eskkar. I want more eyes following his movements. I want the women to report any stranger who shows the slightest interest in Eskkar or Sargon or myself. Or the city. Gather as many as you need to do this."

"And this other thing you spoke of, getting someone into the ruling houses?"

Trella smiled. "I think it's time for you to send for Tammuz and Enhedu. I think they will be the perfect choice to send to Sumeria, if they're willing. But first we'll need to train them in secret. And for that I think we'll need a farmhouse somewhere north of here, away from the city's eyes. I'm sure Rebba can provide one near the river."

"And what kind of training are you planning for them?"

Trella told her.

"I'll send for them in the morning," Annok-sur said with a smile. "And what about Orodes? Are you still certain he's the man you want?"

Trella sighed. "I hope so. He has the quickest wits of any metalworker in Akkad. Even his father had to admit that his son knew his craft. It's just unfortunate that Orodes was born the third son, instead of the first. But then we wouldn't be able to make use of him."

"And if he can't stay sober? Once a man falls into drink, he finds it hard to abstain."

"There won't be anything to drink where he's going. That will give him time to change his habits. But if he's not the right person, we'll have to find someone else to work the mine."

"I suppose living in the hill country will do Orodes good." Annok-sur laughed. "Tooraj will keep him sober."

"If Orodes can't stay away from the taverns, then he's of no use to us," Trella said. "In that case, tell Bantor to make sure Tooraj gets rid of him. We want to keep the mine secret for as long as we can, until it's well established and producing gold. And we don't want anyone with knowledge of the site and its contents to be able to sell what he knows."

"That we can always do, Lady Trella." Her husband would kill Orodes or anyone else for that matter, if the request came from Trella.

"Then we might as well go to bed. I think our husbands will be up early tomorrow, talking war."

"Let's hope that if war does come, it will be a short one."

"Annok-sur, I think that is the only kind of war Akkad can win. If the strife with Sumeria drags on for years and years, our city will die."

Book II – Preparation for War

15

The city of Sumer, two months later . . .

Tammuz and En-hedu reached the city of Sumer a little after midday. Each carried a large linen sack slung over his shoulder. As proper, En-hedu's burden exceeded her husband's both in size and weight. Dirt, dust and sand covered the couple's worn and patched clothing, as well as their hands and faces. When the strong west wind blew over Sumeria, it painted everything it touched in shades of gray. Several times in the last few days they had to stop and huddle close together, backs to the onrushing air, until the stinging sandstorms sighed into silence.

They had traveled south for four long days, walking from the tiny village of Mari all the way to Sumer. At last, footsore and weary, they had reached the end of their journey. Now they picked their way through the growing lines of chattering people entering or leaving the city.

Four soldiers guarded the gate, inspecting those trying to enter as well as those seeking to leave. One stepped in front of Tammuz, blocking his way.

"No beggars allowed in Sumer," he said, glancing at Tammuz's crooked left arm. A cripple could do no real work.

"We're not beggars," Tammuz said. "My wife and I are farmers from Ubaid."

The two of them had spent ten days living in the village of Ubaid, learning to speak like any of the Ubaid villagers, lest their speech give them away as coming from Akkad. When they departed, they knew everyone and everything about the Sumerian village, and could answer any question as if they had lived there all their lives.

The guard's voice implied that he had heard that claim before. "One copper coin each to enter the city, then."

"I see others entering without paying," Tammuz argued, pointing with his good arm at a few people walking by.

"They live here. They have a right to come and go."

"How do you know they live here?"

"Do you see them loaded down with all their possessions? Now get away from the gate."

"We plan to live here as well," Tammuz said.

"Not unless you pay," the guard insisted.

Another soldier sauntered over. "Any problem with these two?"

"They don't want to pay," the first guard said, "or they can't."

"Get rid of them."

"Wait, we can pay," Tammuz said. He turned to En-hedu. "Give them the coppers."

En-hedu deposited her sack on the ground between her feet, reached inside her dress, and withdrew a battered leather pouch that remained fastened by a thick loop around her neck. Taking her time, she undid the knot, reached in, and removed two coins that she passed to Tammuz, who handed them to the guard.

The second guard's eyes followed En-hedu's every move as she withdrew the coins from the pouch. If these fresh-off-the-farm country bumpkins possessed two coppers, why not three? "And one more for King Eridu's guards."

With the speed of a striking snake, En-hedu snatched the coins back from the first guard's still open palm. "No! My uncle warned us that you would demand more. If there was any trouble, he said we should ask to see your commander and give the payment to him."

The guard frowned. A small group had gathered to watch the newcomers pay their entry fee. Hearing the commotion, they edged closer, as eager to see either the guards humiliated or the newcomers driven away. He glanced around, his hand on the hilt of his sword. "All right, damn you both, two coins to enter. Either pay or get away from the gate."

"Two coppers. No more." En-hedu extended her hand, and once again the coins dropped into the first soldier's palm. A few of the gawkers laughed at the guards' discomfort.

Tammuz grabbed En-hedu, jerking her to his side. "Be silent, woman. Remember your place." He bowed to the guards. "I thank you for your help."

Slinging his sack over his shoulder, Tammuz pushed his way through the gate, En-hedu following a step behind.

"Give her a good beating tonight," a woman called out.

"If you're strong enough," another voice shouted. A laugh went up, and this time the guards joined in.

"He already did," the first guard added in a loud voice. "Look at her nose."

En-hedu's first master had broken her nose in a drunken rage, and it had never healed properly.

More laughter greeted the jest, but by that time, Tammuz and En-hedu had stepped through the gate. The guard's words meant nothing; they had heard it all before.

As soon as they were well inside the city, Tammuz grinned at her. "That went well. I was expecting them to ask us our business or look inside the sacks."

"All they care about is taking bribes from ignorant farmers." En-hedu turned her thoughts to the present. "Now we have to find a place to stay the night."

Walking through the crowded lanes, they attracted little attention, just two more wide-eyed farmers moving into the city and carrying their handful of possessions. It didn't take them long to reach the poorer section of Sumer. Yavtar had described the city in detail to both of them, and they not only knew where to go, but already had some idea of what they would find.

They stopped at one of the taverns which also functioned as an inn, a humble enough place suggested by Yavtar. An older woman with long gray hair straggling down her back blocked the doorway, her hands on her wide hips. She appraised them from head to toe and appeared to find little opportunity for profit.

"What do you want?"

"A safe place to stay for a few nights," En-hedu answered, "and perhaps some food."

"Only if you can pay. Too many people without any coins in Sumer these days."

"We can pay something," En-hedu said, "and we can work until we're settled."

"There's no work here, but one copper coin, and you can spend the night. In advance. Supper only, one cup of ale." The woman's firm voice showed there would be no haggling.

En-hedu glanced at Tammuz, who shrugged. One place was as good as another.

She paid the woman, who stepped aside and let them enter. This early in the day, the tavern stood empty, except for an old man leaning back against the wall, dozing with his mouth open. Only a few flies buzzed about. To En-hedu's surprise, the place appeared to have been swept clean. By tonight, she knew the usual debris from the customers would litter the dirt floor.

"Since you're here early, you can pick whatever place you like to sleep," the woman said. "My husband will return before sundown. No ale or wine before then. If you want water, there's a well down the lane."

"Thank you, mistress."

They had already stopped and drunk their fill. En-hedu picked her way to a spot on the opposite wall from where they entered. It was far enough away from the table where the owner would dispense the wine and ale, and almost as distant from the door to discourage any would-be robber. Thieves sometimes kicked open the door in the middle of the night, grabbed whatever they could, and fled before the sleeping customers knew they were being robbed. It had happened before, in Tammuz's own tavern in Akkad.

They sat down, backs against the wall, grateful to be off their feet. As always, En-hedu sat at Tammuz's left. His left arm, crooked and wasted, lacked any strength, and he could use it for small tasks only with some difficulty. His right hand and arm, however, rippled with thick muscle that bespoke long sessions each day to increase its strength. The sharp knife he wore on his belt was a gift from Lady Trella. While it appeared to be an old and well-worn weapon, it had been forged from the finest bronze by Akkad's master swordmaker, then deliberately aged and nicked. A thief might give it a glance, but none would consider it worth stealing.

En-hedu carried her own knife, smaller but just as sharp, inside her dress. The baggy garment concealed both the weapon and her well-endowed bosom. In spite of her sturdy frame, as tall as her husband, both she and Tammuz could move like cats, quick and light on their feet.

"Rest, husband. I'll keep watch." She touched his leg, a little gesture of affection.

He smiled at her, then slumped down a little more. She watched him drift off to sleep. They would have to take turns staying awake during the night, lest some thief try to rob them. That was a risk they couldn't take. The sacks they carried contained five gold coins, ten silver ones, and twenty coppers, all carrying marks from Sumer's merchants.

Those coins, however, would enable them to establish a tavern of their own, much like the ones they had owned first in Akkad and then in Bisitun. En-hedu remembered the days not long ago when she would have stood in the doorway, making sure customers could pay or trade before they entered.

King Eskkar and Lady Trella had asked Tammuz and En-hedu to become their spies in Sumer. The couple had played a similar role once before, in Akkad. Nearly three years ago, Trella had rescued En-hedu from her brutal husband, who had beaten her so often that she begged for death. His last pummeling had broken her nose. After a few months to recover her health and spirit, Trella gave En-hedu as a slave to Tammuz, to help him run his little tavern.

He had just entered his fifteenth season, about the same age as En-hedu. Tammuz had treated his new possession with gentleness, and when the last of En-hedu's emotional wounds finally healed, she found herself in love with her new master. His tender feeling for her gave En-hedu the first happiness she could remember.

Tammuz, already operating as a spy for Trella, kept watch on the worst of the beggars and thieves in Akkad, those desperate enough to kill anyone for a few coins. To fit in with his less reputable customers, Tammuz bought and sold stolen goods, and protected the petty criminals from the city's guard as best he could. As a result, he gained his patrons' trust, and he saw and heard much of what went on among Akkad's dregs.

Trella neither wanted to know nor cared about the petty thievery that happened every day in Akkad, and every other village for that matter. What she sought was knowledge about anything serious, any whisper or hint of a planned deed that might threaten her husband and his rule.

By then few knew or remembered that Tammuz had ridden as a horse boy with Eskkar on his first skirmish. Disobeying orders, Tammuz joined in the fighting and killed an Alur Meriki warrior with an arrow. Then a horse and rider knocked him aside, shattering his arm in several places. Injured on the war trail and forced to ride while the fever raged in his body, Tammuz nearly died. Most leaders would have abandoned the friendless boy, but Eskkar did his best to keep Tammuz alive. A few nights later, when Eskkar and the other handful of survivors established the Hawk Clan, Tammuz, still racked with fever, had managed to swear the same oath that bound all of the surviving fighters together. At least that's what the others told him, though Tammuz had little recollection of the ritual.

Because of his crippled arm, Tammuz could no longer fight, and most of the Hawk Clan members soon forgot about the crippled boy. But Trella, struggling to deal with the corrupt and devious nobles, had found a use for him, setting Tammuz up in the alehouse to keep an eye on those most willing to do violence.

When Korthac seized Akkad, Tammuz and En-hedu felt as helpless as anyone. But within a few days, Eskkar returned from the north and, in the middle of the night, broke into the city. Fighting had raged everywhere, and Tammuz had rushed to join in. By then he'd grown proficient with a knife, and several of Korthac's Egyptian fighters died under his blade during the battle. En-hedu had killed one man herself, to save her master's life.

Nevertheless, the fighting and its aftermath revealed Tammuz's role as one of Eskkar's loyal followers. They could no longer pretend to be dealers in stolen goods or even plain innkeepers. Twenty days after Korthac died under torture, Lady Trella sent Tammuz and En-hedu north for their own protection, to the village of Bisitun.

That had worked for a few months, but too many soldiers moving back and forth between Akkad and Bisitun knew of Tammuz's role, and soon word spread that he was one of Eskkar's followers. After that, they settled into a dreary existence as simple tavern owners, conspicuously avoided by any of the local thieves or anyone trying to escape official notice. Trella had advised them to be patient, that something important would be found for them.

Then one day Annok-sur had arrived, accompanied by Hathor, to meet them. Annok-sur offered Tammuz and En-hedu another, more dangerous chance to spy for Akkad. They would have to move to Sumer, become two of its inhabitants, and stay for at least two or three years. There would be great danger. If they were discovered, death by torture would be their fate. However, if they remained hidden and provided useful information, they could return to Akkad in due time and step out into the open as respected members of Eskkar's inner council.

One look at Tammuz's face and En-hedu knew he wanted to accept. Since his arm prevented him from joining Eskkar's soldiers, he would take on any role that Eskkar and Trella suggested that gave him a chance to fight. To Tammuz's credit, he had turned to En-hedu to see what she thought. Whatever reservations En-hedu had had vanished.

In truth, she was as wearied of their life in Bisitun as her husband. So they agreed to go to Sumer. But it turned out there was much more that Annok-sur wanted. She and Trella sought information from the leading citizens of Sumer, not just the poor and destitute. And Lady Trella had figured out a possible way for En-hedu to gain entry to the wealthier merchants and traders.

Nor was Tammuz ignored. Hathor explained what Eskkar wanted. More training would be required for the both of them, so that they could not only defend themselves, but eliminate potential threats to their mission. That training had lasted more than a month before Annok-sur and Hathor considered them as well prepared as possible.

Then they traveled south, until they reached the village of Ubaid, in Sumer's northern lands. One of Yavtar's boat captains had come from the obscure village, and he escorted Tammuz and En-hedu there.

All that preparation had ended at last. They journeyed south, passing through several small villages before reaching Sumer. Now that they had arrived, they could at last begin their mission.

En-hedu settled herself against the wall, though she never relaxed enough so that she couldn't get to her feet in a moment. As the sun began its descent, customers by ones and twos arrived. The poorest carried something to barter for ale – a chicken, a few eggs, fruit, bread, cheese, or even firewood. En-hedu watched one man exchange a knife for supper and the promise of plenty of ale. Since he carried another knife on his belt, he'd probably stolen the first one. She guessed he would drink his ale quickly and depart, just in case the real owner of the weapon arrived.

Loud voices, laughter, and the occasional oath soon filled the inn. The sounds were so familiar to Tammuz that he didn't even wake up until En-hedu nudged his arm.

"Time to eat," she said.

Tammuz remained at their space, while En-hedu fetched two greasy bowls only half full of stew, each with a hunk of bread protruding over the top. She made a second trip to bring the ale, watered down to be little stronger than what came out of the well down the lane. The food took the edge off their hunger, but did little else.

The rest of the night went as would be expected in such a place. Men came and went, women arrived to sell themselves, a few lucky men drank enough to get drunk. Two fights started. As the darkness deepened outside, the customers' voices rose, and soon everyone had to practically shout to be heard. Twice men approached En-hedu to see if she were available, but Tammuz put his hand on his knife, and the men shrugged and turned away.

As the evening grew later and later, the grinning patrons left as they arrived, by ones and twos, until finally the innkeeper secured the door and put out the fire. Snoring men who had had too much to drink soon created another type of din, but Tammuz and En-hedu were used to that, too.

In the morning, they gathered their sacks and went out into the lane. They bought fresh bread in the market, then began searching for a tavern to purchase. En-hedu expected this to be a simple enough process. Buying an inn shouldn't be any more complicated than buying a house, just a slightly larger one. Anyone could call a one-room hut a tavern, and more than a few proprietors did just that. Larger establishments, like the one they stayed at last night, would cost more coins to acquire, but En-hedu thought that they should be able to purchase a good-sized place for twenty silver coins or so. Nevertheless, Yavtar had warned them of the difficulties they might encounter.

Before the sun reached its peak in the sky, they found one not far from the docks that looked promising. After studying it, they approached the owner.

"Can't sell to you," the prospective seller said. "Wish I could, but only King Eridu's men can buy and sell a tavern in Sumer now. A new law, passed only a few months ago. Just another tax, really."

"Then how do we buy one?" Tammuz asked.

"Fresh from the farm, I see." The man laughed. "Well, first, you have to bribe a local merchant or trader to represent you. Then he and the seller set the price, which will be higher than you expect, so they can both make an extra profit off you. And in addition to the price, you'll pay another silver coin to King Eridu's men."

"What trader would you recommend?" En-hedu asked.

"One's as bad as the other. You'll probably have to wait all day or even longer just to see one." The innkeeper lowered his voice. "Then, a few days after the sale, you may find yourself turned out of your place by Eridu's cronies at the palace. They don't like people from the countryside buying establishments in Sumer. So once they've taken your coins, unless the king and his people approve of you, they just take your property and turn you out."

The proprietor shook his head at the injustice. "If you find someone to help you, come back. I'd love to take a profit and return to Nippur. I was born there, and now I have a farm and wife waiting there for me."

En-hedu and Tammuz thanked the helpful innkeeper and turned away. They found a shady spot against a wall where they could sit. The smell of urine wasn't too bad, and the people passing by ignored them, as they would any beggars.

"We can't take a chance on something like that happening," Tammuz said. "If we're turned out, we'll never be able to buy another one without arousing suspicion."

"That means we'll have to go to Merchant Gemama. If he arranges it, we'll be able to buy this place without dealing with King Eridu's men."

Yavtar had advised them to seek Gemama's assistance if they needed it, but warned them of the danger as well.

"As soon as we mention Yavtar's name, he'll know we're spies," Tammuz said.

"Perhaps not. And even if he does, if he denounces us, we can do the same to him," En-hedu said. "And what we've heard of King Eridu, even an accusation would be enough of an excuse to seize Gemama's property, or at the very least demand a large bribe from the merchant."

Since Eridu's return to Sumer, his rule of the city had turned into a nightmare for its inhabitants. King One-hand, as he was now called behind his back, had already killed more than a dozen people for the slightest of reasons. He'd raised taxes twice, desperate to recover the ransom he'd paid, not to mention the gold wasted on the lost campaign. Men, weapons, horses, food – Eridu had expended huge amounts of gold in the last year and now had nothing to show for it. The people's unhappiness showed in their sullen faces, especially the women. Many had lost a husband or son in the fighting.

"Then we might as well get it over with," Tammuz said.

They walked the dusty lanes until they found Gemama's house. The guard at the gate refused them entry, of course, until they produced a copper coin to show their good intentions. So early in the day, Gemama wasn't home, so they waited, along with four other prospective clients, for their chance to speak to the merchant.

"We might be here for the rest of the afternoon, and he still might not see us," Tammuz complained.

"Then we'll return in the morning, or try and see him at the docks."

The other petitioners ignored them, two country bumpkins who looked as poor as any grubbing farmer. Fortunately for Tammuz and En-hedu, Gemama must have had a good day's trading, for he returned to his house well before the sun began to set.

As he walked through the gate, he glanced over those waiting to see him. When he caught sight of Tammuz and En-hedu, his eyes widened with curiosity. No doubt he seldom dealt with anyone as poor as they appeared to be.

Everyone still had to wait. Gemama had his own needs to satisfy before he bothered with seeing anyone who might wish to do business with him. Naturally, Tammuz and En-hedu had to sit patiently until the others had been taken, one by one, to conduct their affairs with the merchant.

When Tammuz and En-hedu were led inside the garden, they found Gemama sitting at a wide table not far from the entrance to his house. The merchant yawned, clearly looking forward to his supper. Two nakhla trees – as the date palms were called in Sumeria – provided a canopy to block the sun from their owner. A frowning clerk sat at the far end of the table, wet clay and wooden chisel in hand, ready to record anything of interest. A small wooden box rested before him, no doubt filled with a handful of coins received or dispensed at the merchant's pleasure.

"What do you want?" Gemama began, not wishing to waste any time.

"Please, Noble," En-hedu began, bowing low before raising her eyes. "We wish to purchase a tavern in Sumer. My Uncle Yavtar said we should speak with you if we needed any assistance in buying an inn. We are willing to pay you a small fee each month, if you can help arrange the purchase. My uncle said he has traded with you before. We come from the village of Ubaid. He has a farm there."

En-hedu watched Gemama's eyes at the mention of Yavtar's name, but the merchant didn't react. No one became a master trader who let his thoughts cross his face. Besides, while Yavtar's name wasn't a common one, neither was it unique enough to stand out.

"I don't remember anyone from Ubaid," Gemama said. He lifted his ornately carved wine cup, inhaled the aroma for a long moment, then drained it. "Bring me another," he said to his clerk, pushing the cup toward him. He drummed his fingers on the table. "You wish to purchase a tavern, you say?"

"Yes, Noble. We've found one —"

By then the clerk was across the garden. "First refresh my memory of your Uncle Yavtar."

En-hedu, whose mind excelled at matching faces and names, gave a good description of the Akkadian trader.

Gemama nodded. "Yes, I remember your uncle."

"We have the silver to buy the tavern, and we can pay you something for your help, Noble," she added. "My uncle said to tell you he would again be in your debt."

The clerk returned, carefully carrying the wine cup in both hands, so as not to spill any. A clumsy servant who drank part of it himself, or claimed to have spilled it, would find the price of the drink taken from his meager earnings. A slave would simply be beaten. The clerk set it down on the table close to his master's hand.

"Well, if you can pay, then I suppose I must honor an old friendship," Gemama said, frowning in his reluctance. "You will pay me one silver coin now, in addition to what the seller asks for his tavern, and the fee that must be paid to King Eridu. Then you will pay me one silver coin each month for a year. You have enough for all that?"

"Yes, Noble," En-hedu said, forcing a smile despite the steep prices. "We have just enough, Noble." With the clerk there, it wouldn't do to admit to have more coins. He might have friends of his own who would be interested in relieving two strangers of their wealth.

Gemama rose. "Return here in the morning. Ask for Melchior," he nodded to his assistant. "My clerk will take care of everything."

With a wave of his hand, he dismissed them. En-hedu and Tammuz both bowed several times before walking quickly from the garden.

Once in the lane outside, Tammuz led the way. "He suspects us already."

"More than suspects. He knows," En-hedu agreed. "Yavtar said Gemama knew war was coming. But he's earned even more of Yavtar's favor for this, and at very little risk. If the war goes badly for Sumer, Yavtar will protect him. If Sumer wins, then we can be denounced or killed at any time."

Tammuz spat on the ground. "Sumer will never beat Akkad. Look at the people's faces. They've been defeated once. They've had a bellyful of fighting."

"For now," En-hedu said. "But in six months, even a year, things may change."

"Only the gods know for sure." Tammuz put his arm around En-hedu's waist and gave her a squeeze. "Only one more night at that wretched inn. With luck, tomorrow evening we'll sleep in a place of our own once again."

"Then tomorrow night, I promise to pleasure you with my new skills."

"Then whatever we pay for the tavern, it will be well worth the cost."

16

King Eridu pounded his fist on the table so hard the heavy wood shook under the impact. "What do you mean, they cannot come? How dare they refuse my summons!" A fleck of spittle driven by the force of his words hung unnoticed at the corner of his mouth.

Five men sat at Eridu's council table, and not one of them lifted his eyes to meet the enraged king of Sumer. Razrek, in charge of the king's soldiers, sat at Eridu's left. Shulgi, Eridu's son and second in command under Razrek, sat at his father's right. The three remaining men represented cities in Sumeria: Hammurat, from Larsa; Kuara from Isin; and Emenne, from Lagash. The representatives from Nippur and Uruk had failed to arrive. Each sent a messenger pleading urgent business that kept them at home.

The sound of birds chirping came from the garden below, their cheerful notes enhanced by the silence that followed King Eridu's rage. At last Kuara, chief advisor to Naxos, the king of Isin, lifted his eyes. "They did not come, King Eridu, because they will not support a second attack on Akkad's border. They know the time is not yet right to start another war. As does my own King Naxos of Isin. Everyone knows the barbarian Eskkar keeps his promises. One more raid on his lands, and the war will come south. It will be the cities and villages and farmlands of Sumeria that will face devastation and destruction."

"So Isin is afraid to fight," sneered Eridu.

Kuara reached out with his right hand to lift his wine cup. He took a small sip before setting it back on the table. He possessed only a thumb and forefinger on that hand. The subtle gesture sent a message to Eridu. Kuara had once fought as a soldier for King Naxos, until an enemy sword stroke cut off his fingers. As men told the story, Kuara still managed to kill his opponent, despite the severity of his wound.

"Isin will fight when the time is suitable, when what we expect to gain outweighs the risks."

Eridu snorted. "Now your warrior king is a merchant, weighing profit and loss?"

Kuara shook his head in resignation. "The land Akkad holds is needed by Isin even more than Sumer. We will fight to take that land, take what is ours. Many men in Isin are eager to wage war against Eskkar, and King Naxos will supply more than his share of fighting men when the time is right. But now is not that time."

"That is the same concern of King Naran, which he wished to convey to you." Hammurat of Larsa spoke with a hint of passion in his voice. Tall and spare, he had advised the king of Larsa for many years. "Larsa needs time to strengthen its walls and build up its defenses. If the barbarian comes south, Larsa will be the first to feel his fury."

"Your King Naran was eager enough to cross the Sippar and seize the farmlands," Eridu said. "And to take the largest share of what we captured. Now you want to hold back? While the Akkadians increase their strength?"

"Larsa took the larger share because we took the greatest risk, and many of our men died in the fighting." Hammurat shook his head. "We will send our soldiers across the border when a victory can be assured. Perhaps in a year or two –"

"King Naran and the others will send more men at once!" Eridu's hand shook with anger. "The sooner we attack, the faster Akkad will be destroyed!"

"Neither Larsa, nor Isin will send more soldiers at this time," Kuara said. "Nor will the other cities. This is the message King Naxos of Isin told me to bring to you. Eskkar's forces are too strong to challenge again."

Mentioning the name of Akkad's ruler brought even more fury to Eridu's already red face. Veins bulged on his forehead. "The other cities will obey me! They will provide me with men and gold, or I'll have Razrek level their cities to the ground!"

Kuara turned his gaze toward the leader of Eridu's soldiers. "What do you say, Razrek? Will you lead your men against our cities?"

"Razrek will do as I ask," Eridu said, his fist clenching once again.

"Is the man who led the attacks on the border not allowed to speak for himself?" Kuara's words remained soothing, intended to calm Eridu's anger. "Is this a council of equals, or are we just summoned here to hear King Eridu's pronouncements?"

Everyone's eyes went to Razrek, who shifted uneasily in his chair. "I think it would be unwise to bring force against our allies," Razrek said. "It's one thing to call for war against a common enemy. But many of my soldiers are from these cities. They would likely desert rather than fight their own kin. The Akkadians are hated by all, but Larsa, Isin . . . all the Sumerian cities . . . the men would wonder why we went to war against our allies."

The fingers on Eridu's remaining hand trembled. "You are saying you cannot lead your own men? They . . . you will refuse my orders?"

"No, my king. My men and I will fight at your command. But I still think now is not the right time to resume the war on Akkad. Or to start a new fight against the other cities of Sumeria."

"Nor do I," Kuara said. "You're consumed with rage and hatred for Eskkar. You want to attack him and punish him for what he did to you, and you want to do it now."

"He will suffer. I swear Eskkar's head will hang over Sumer's gate. As will yours, Kuara, and all of you, if you do not obey my orders."

Kuara leaned forward and rested his elbows on the table. "The people of Isin are not yet your slaves, King Eridu. And if any harm should come to me – to any of us – Sumer will find itself at war with the other cities. King Naxos knows the ways of war quite well." Kuara glanced at Hammurat and Emenne, who nodded agreement. Clearly, Kuara spoke for all of them.

"You have less than half the number of men you had when you crossed the border," Kuara went on, "and many of these are replacements, raw recruits fresh from the farm. Even worse, any mention of attacks against Lord Eskkar convinces more and more of your experienced men to desert. They believe he cannot be beaten in battle, and they do not want to face his Akkadian archers again."

"He can be beaten!" Eridu shouted, half-rising from his chair. "He's an ignorant barbarian and he will be killed, his army destroyed!"

"How?"

The single word hung in the air. Eridu's mouth opened, but nothing came out.

"I ask again." Kuara kept all emotion from his voice. "How will you defeat him? By marching north? By walking into Akkadian arrows again? By attacking the man who defeated the Alur Meriki in three battles, and who killed the Egyptian and all his men who tried to capture Akkad? By challenging the man who just destroyed half your army and cut off your hand?"

At the mention of his lost hand, Eridu's fury increased until the large vein on his forehead bulged and threatened to burst and cover the table in blood.

"We'll raise more men," Eridu said. "We can raise three, four times as many soldiers as Akkad."

Kuara shook his head. "Ask Razrek. Ask your son, Shulgi. Will numbers guarantee success against the barbarian? You yourself had him outnumbered by four to one, yet your men were defeated, and he scarcely lost a man. King Naxos and I spoke to some of the survivors. They saw how few casualties the Akkadians took. Eskkar could have killed his prisoners or kept them as slaves, but he was cunning enough to let the defeated soldiers live, let them go free so that they would tell everyone in Sumeria what they faced. Eskkar spoke with all of them, and warned them of their fate if he ever captured them again. He knows how to bend even his enemies to his will. Our soldiers said his men treated him almost like a god. They were in awe of him."

"We were caught by surprise." Eridu's voice sounded hoarse, and he could barely get the words out without choking. "We should have beaten them . . . a few more moments and Eskkar's men would have been destroyed."

"Perhaps it is as you say, King Eridu. Like you, I believe any man can be beaten. But what is done is done. Raising another army is not a plan that guarantees success, not against a trained and experienced warrior." He glanced at his companions again. "So tell us, King Eridu, how you will defeat him this time?"

"Razrek and I will come up with a new plan. We'll find a way to lure him south and crush him."

Kuara tactfully didn't bother to mention that that plan had already been tried and failed.

"Eridu, all of us wish to see Akkad's ruler killed and the city destroyed.

We all wish to take our share of the lands north of the border. But our men will not follow you down that path again. You've fought Eskkar. He offered you a sword to fight him, man to man, and when you refused, he cut off your hand. Even if the soldiers obey your orders, they will march into battle knowing that you dared not face him yourself, knowing that their cause is lost, that victory always sides with the barbarian. They will fight poorly, and run as soon as the first Akkadian arrow flies over their heads."

"Your insolence will be remembered," Eridu said. "You, all of you will —"

"My king," Razrek cut in, before Eridu did even worse damage to his cause. "We must be patient. We have suffered a serious defeat, and it takes time for soldiers to lick their wounds and forget their shame and embarrassment. Give me a few months, and they will burn with thoughts of revenge against Eskkar. They will remember how he attacked them by surprise. Meanwhile, we need time to raise and train many more soldiers. And Kuara speaks the truth. We need to find a new plan to destroy Akkad. When we have that, the men will take heart and fight with all their strength once again."

Eridu wasn't ready to give up yet. He turned to his son. "Shulgi, you can take command of Razrek's men. You can lead the men north."

"No, Father. Razrek is right," Shulgi said. The son possessed his father's height, but broad muscles covered his chest, and thick arms showed the effects of years of training. He had only eighteen seasons, but he spoke with the voice of one much older. "Our soldiers believe that Eskkar is either blessed by the gods or protected by demons. They believe . . . they know, he will win if it comes to a battle. We must remove such thoughts from their memories. We can prepare for a future battle, but it will be many months, perhaps years before we are ready to fight again."

"Listen to your son, to Shulgi," Kuara said, his voice now soft and persuasive. "He grows in wisdom with every passing day. When the time is ready, the cities of Sumeria will provide men to defeat Akkad. But we must not move too soon."

Eridu pushed himself to his feet, his hand flat on the table for support. "Get out! Get out, all of you! You're nothing but cowards! I'll lead the men myself. Then I'll settle with each of you."

Kuara shrugged in resignation. He rose, as did his companions. He bowed graciously to Eridu, but left the chamber without a word, the other two representatives trailing behind.

Razrek started to speak, but Eridu cut him off. "You get out, too. You and your cowards left me alone to face the Akkadians. With all your horsemen, you failed even to get a warning to us."

Razrek started to answer the charge, but he caught Shulgi's eye and saw the shake of his head. "Yes, my king." Razrek bowed and left the room.

Father and son watched the soldier depart. Shulgi waited until the door closed. "Should I leave, too, Father?"

Eridu reached across the table to drag the pitcher of wine toward him, and he poured himself a cup. His left hand still didn't equal the right, and wine spilled across the surface, angering him further.

"How dare you not support your own father? You should have challenged Razrek. You keep telling me you're ready to lead the soldiers, but you're as weak as the others. You fear even to avenge your father. Go. Go back to your men and pretend to be a soldier. And send my steward to me."

"Yes, Father." Shulgi rose and left the chamber, as silently as the others.

Outside the gloomy chamber, Shulgi found Petrah, his father's steward, waiting in the corridor in case he was needed. The old man had served Eridu faithfully for more than twenty years, and in that time Petrah had developed an uncanny sense of knowing when he would be wanted.

"He asked for you, Petrah. Be aware, he's in a foul mood."

"Thank you." Petrah never bothered to waste words. He brushed past Shulgi and closed the door behind him.

Shulgi stared at the closed door for a moment, his lips tight. He turned away, went down a flight of stairs, and stepped out into the sun-filled courtyard. He walked past the private well and continued until he reached the rear of Eridu's quarters. A small but separate dwelling stood against the wall, one that contained only three rooms, the province of his half-sister, Kushanna. Flowers and shrubs grew along the side of the house, softening for a few paces the hard lines of the Compound. The king cared little for anything green.

Kushanna waited for him just inside her doorway. Like Petrah, she also seemed to know when she would be needed.

"I saw the others leave," she said, stepping aside to let her brother enter. "They had smiles on their faces. Did it go as you expected?"

Shulgi could restrain himself no longer. "No, it went the way you said it would, damn you!"

"Come inside," Kushanna said, ignoring the harsh words. "Tell me all about it."

He followed her through the main chamber and into one of the inner rooms, not her bedchamber but a small windowless alcove where her companion slave slept at night. Shulgi had never been invited into Kushanna's bedroom. Even she wasn't that bold.

Kushanna sat on a small chest, while Shulgi sat on the edge of the slave's bed and stared at his sister. The entrance to her quarters could be seen from here, but no one could hear their words, as long as they kept their voices low. And no one could see inside the alcove without being seen.

Shulgi took a deep breath to calm himself. "I told him . . . we told him what needed to be done, that he had to be patient, that he had to stop wasting his gold on weapons and men who can't be trusted. Marduk take him! It's my gold he's spending, Shanna. My birthright. Even your dowry. Soon there will be nothing left for us, and Sumer will be weaker than before. Already the other cities no longer fear us."

Kushanna smiled at him. She did not permit many to call her by her childhood name.

Nearly as tall as her half-brother, she had two more seasons than his eighteen. Graceful and willowy, with light brown hair that reached nearly to her waist, she attracted every man's eyes. Her white gown of the softest linen clung to the full lines of her body. A gold ring adorned each of her forefingers, and a pendant of the finest lapis lazuli dangled between her breasts.

"So, what will you do now, my brother?"

"I'm surprised you're not reminding me about Father. You warned me he would not see reason."

"I could have been wrong," Kushanna said, picking at a thread on her dress. "He might have listened to your advice."

"He still thinks of me as a child," Shulgi said. "I get more respect from my men – even from Razrek – than our father the king."

"I know Razrek wanted you to accompany the soldiers when they went north. Perhaps if you had been there, our soldiers might not have been defeated."

"Father did not want to share his glory with me," Shulgi said, unable to conceal the bitterness he still felt. "That's why the fool ordered me to stay behind, supposedly to protect his city and his gold. Not that I had managed to do even that much. His loyal steward Petrah made all the decisions, in father's name, of course."

"He's been our father's trusted servant for many years," Kushanna said. "Such loyalty deserves to be rewarded."

"Yes, it does," Shulgi said, his voice hardening as he envisioned a suitable reward for his father's retainer. "Petrah will obey our father's every wish, even if it means destroying Sumer in the process."

"Petrah gathered the gold as soon as he received the message from Akkad. He paid the ransom in less than a day," Kushanna said. "He was very concerned for our father's welfare."

Her calm words fed the flames of Shulgi's rage, not that he cared any more. "Eight hundred coins, wasted, for nothing! Eskkar will use it to strengthen his army. And now father wants to spend what little gold remains on another foolish attack on Akkad. He will ruin Sumer to gain his revenge on Eskkar."

"One day, when you rule here in Sumer and over the other cities, things will be different."

He lifted his eyes and met her gaze. For once he paid no attention to the lush body sitting before him. "I think that day has come, Shanna. My father's mind is consumed with hatred. He will destroy all of us. What we talked about . . . it must be done. Will you stand beside me?"

Kushanna met his gaze for a long moment, studying his face, as if measuring the depth of his anger and resolve. Satisfied, she rose from the chair and sat next to him on the narrow bed.

Shulgi felt the heat from her thigh through the thin garment as it touched his own.

"You know I will, Shulgi. You are the only man I have ever loved." She took his hand in both of hers and pressed it to her bosom, letting him feel the softness.

A rush of desire swept over him. His eyes closed for a moment. When he opened them, her mouth was close to his own. Shulgi kissed the soft lips that reached up for him. They had kissed many times before, stolen moments when their father was absent or the servants occupied, and each time his passion for her grew stronger.

This time, however, Shulgi sensed something more than a casual dalliance. He let his hand slip from her grasp, and used his fingers to push the dress off her shoulder, until her right breast swelled from the garment's confines. For once she didn't push him away. Instead her eyes closed, and she took a deep breath, her nipple firm and hard. The warmth from her skin seemed to burn his hand as he brushed his fingers over her, and the scent of her body roused him even more than the sight of her naked breast, perfect in its beauty. He cupped the heavy globe of soft flesh, squeezing gently.

Shanna leaned against him, her body reacting to his touch. Then she opened her eyes and held his gaze while she nudged the dress down from her other shoulder, then let herself fall back on the bed. She reached up and traced her finger along his cheek, enjoying the look on his face as he drank in the sight of her bare breasts. Shanna had never let him go so far. Then she placed both her hands behind his neck and pulled him toward her.

Shulgi leaned over and kissed her breasts, first one, then the other. Shanna moaned softly at his caress, and arched her back against him, while her hand reached over to brush against the rock-hard manhood straining beneath his tunic.

"When will you make me yours, my beloved?" Her voice, husky now with passion, inflamed him even more, and the touch of her hand made his already fierce erection even harder.

He moved his mouth to her lips, and kissed them, gently at first, then with growing passion. "Tonight, my Shanna . . . tonight. Before our father decides to send me off on yet another wasted journey to recruit men." He ran his hand over her breast, teasing the nipple until it swelled and hardened. "Besides, I can't bear to wait another day for you."

"The time for waiting is past," Shanna agreed. "Tonight you will make me yours." She returned his kiss one more time, then slipped from his grasp and sat up, smiling at him as she rearranged her dress. "But first we must talk about what needs to be done. We must plan with care, so that nothing can go wrong. Only when we are ready can we act."

Shulgi forced the sight of her bare breasts from his thoughts. His erection still throbbed, but after all these years, he could wait one more day. "Then let us talk."

The rest of the day passed soon enough, as Kushanna and Shulgi made their preparations. He felt no surprise at learning that she had already considered every detail, every step. And only when she declared herself satisfied with his role did she agree. One last kiss, and he returned to the soldiers' camp just outside the city, where Razrek had settled his men and horses.

New recruits – those too stupid or too desperate to find another trade – milled about, waiting for the day to end. Kuara had spoken the truth in the council, Shulgi knew. These men would make poor fighters. It would take many months before even half of them reached the level of training achieved by the men Eridu had led north to their deaths.

Shulgi didn't care. His own detachment of men – its survivors numbering less than thirty since the battle with Eskkar's forces – were as good as any of Razrek's core group of veterans. More important, they were loyal to Shulgi, not Razrek, not even Eridu. They were commanded by Vanar, formerly one of two of Shulgi's leaders of twenty. The other had died by an Akkadian arrow, and Vanar had taken charge of those that remained.

Shulgi found Vanar stretched out on the grass beneath one of the few trees large enough to provide shade.

"Taking your ease, I see."

Vanar opened his eyes, but didn't bother to get up. "We've finished training for the day, commander. The men are washing down the horses in the river."

"Make sure they give themselves a good cleaning as well. My father has complained about the horse stink of the guards at the house. When you're satisfied with them, I want you and ten men at the house at sundown. Our men will take the evening shift at the Compound, from supper to midnight."

That news prompted Vanar to pull himself to his feet. "Tonight, commander? Can't we start tomorrow?"

"If you're not there before sundown, I'll be finding a new sub-commander. So unless you'd rather be taking orders than giving them . . ."

"Yes, commander. We'll be there. But why so many men?"

"My father grows even more nervous about assassins from Akkad. So just get the men there." Shulgi turned and made a circuit of the camp, making sure all was well. The sun had touched the western horizon before he walked back toward Sumer's gate, ignoring everyone he encountered, many of whom gazed curiously at him as he passed by, wrapped in his private thoughts.

Shulgi had set the first part of the plan in motion. With Vanar and his men to back him, there would be no problem with the household servants or guards.

Meanwhile, Shanna would see to everything else inside the household. As they went over what they needed to do, Shulgi realized she had prepared for this day months ago, waiting until he came to his senses and saw what needed to be done. Shanna understood what it would take to rule Sumer, to turn the city into the mightiest in the land. She wanted that power, the same way Shulgi did. Together they could achieve it. If he had listened to her when she first proposed taking action, Shulgi would have been the one leading the soldiers north into Akkad's territory. Unlike his father, Shulgi knew he would have returned with a victory. The men trusted him, believed in him. They would have fought bravely. Instead, they had run at the first sign of attack, as did Eridu.

Too late to worry about that now, Shulgi decided. In a way, this might even be a better time to act. Where once Shanna had tried to coerce her brother to act, now she merely had to encourage him. They both understood the grim future that awaited them if Eridu continued to rule. No, this was best. And even better, she would help Shulgi rule a new southern empire, even as she pleasured him in bed.

A sense of calm settled over him, and he wasted no more time worrying about what might happen tonight. Instead, he let his mind recall Shanna's body. He'd wanted Shanna for years, dreaming about her, lusting for her, and now the time had come.

Long after Shanna reached the age for childbearing, her father had kept her at his side, little more than an intimate servant. Then, less than two years ago, Eridu offered Kushanna for marriage to unite a trouble-some village with Sumer. Shulgi had sulked in silent fury for days afterwards. Less than a month later, he joined the fighters defending the western borders of Sumer. Even killing his first man in combat soon afterwards hadn't helped lessen the despair Shulgi felt at the thought of another man enjoying Shanna's body, ordering her about, commanding her to kneel before him, to please him with her mouth and hands. Those visions had tortured him for months, and hardened his heart against his father, who had sold his daughter to a common merchant for a mere fistful of gold.

The marriage indeed worked well enough. Her husband, no doubt with prompting from Kushanna, had joined with Sumer and supplied both men and gold for Eridu's growing military.

Thankfully, the gods had answered Shulgi's prayers, and her foolish husband – an old man scarcely able to walk without a cane – had died little more than a year after the marriage. Since Shanna had produced no child, her husband's family welcomed the opportunity to send back the unfruitful wife to her father's house, even if they had to return part of the dowry. Eridu had been pleased to take her back under his roof, especially since she brought a fair share of gold with her.

None of that mattered to Shulgi now. For years Shanna had teased him, aroused him with her touch and caresses. Shanna had done almost everything to him, spilled his seed with her hands, everything but let him take her. Tonight would see the end of that game. Tonight she would be his, in his bed, his property. After tonight, there would be no more games, only an empire to build.

A little before sunset, Kushanna sat beside her father, at his right side, during the evening meal. Like her half-brother, she felt no qualms or doubts. She'd prepared for this night for years. Unlike Shulgi, her wedding caused her no anguish. She much preferred an old man for a husband, one who could be easily manipulated. Plenty of wine and more lovemaking than he could handle soon produced the desired death. Her constant antagonizing of his existing wives and family ensured her speedy return to her father.

Now Eridu in his blind rage had fallen prey to another kind of manipulation, subtly encouraged by her solicitous advice and suggestions. Tonight King Eridu, still angry at the council's decision, had decided to dine alone. Only his steward, Petrah, joined father and daughter at the table, sitting opposite his master.

Shanna had worked with the cooks to make sure the evening meal was one of Eridu's favorites, a roast leg of lamb, covered with rosemary and seared to a golden brown, the meat tender and juicy within. Knowing of her father's foul mood, she had ordered the servants to serve the king's finest wine, and she mixed the wine and water for her father herself, adding a bit more of the strong wine than he normally preferred.

She also cut the lamb for him, taking care to slice the steaming meat to just the right size. Since his return from Akkad, Shanna had filled the role of diligent daughter, helping her father overcome the lack of his right hand. He scarcely noticed, and treated Shanna like a servant, complaining about the slightest oversight. No matter how unfair, she never protested.

Tonight Eridu's mood was as dark as the wine Shanna poured for him. Several times she tried to start a conversation, but the king had little interest in talking, and certainly not with Shanna.

"Where is Shulgi?" The meal was well under way before he uttered the first words spoken since they sat down.

"He said he would sup at the camp, with his men," Shanna said. "He will join us later."

"His men." Eridu snorted as he stuffed another piece of lamb into his mouth, chewing loudly. "Cowards, all of them. And Razrek is the worst of the lot."

"You're right about Razrek, Father," Shanna agreed. "You should get rid of him. Shulgi can lead the men as well as anyone."

"I should get rid of both of them. Find someone with the will to fight. What do you say, Petrah?"

"Razrek is experienced in warfare, my king, and he leads the men well enough. He may still be of some use to you."

"He'd fight just as hard for Akkad, if I didn't pay him so much gold. He's bleeding me dry."

"Soldiers are expensive to maintain," Petrah said, deftly avoiding Eridu's comment.

"Give Shulgi more authority over the men, Father," Shanna said. "At least you can be certain of his loyalty." She refilled her father's wine cup, adding only a splash of water.

"When he's older," grunted Eridu. "He's too young yet for such responsibility."

They ate the rest of the meal in silence. When Eridu put down his knife with a loud belch, Shanna rose.

"I'll fetch the sweet cakes, Father." She left the chamber, but returned within a few moments, carrying the cakes and dates herself, covered with a piece of linen to ward off the flies. Shanna settled the platter down on the table. Eridu's wine cup was empty, and she started to refill it.

"No more wine," he ordered. "Are the slaves ready to attend me?"

Shanna stopped pouring, but the cup was already half full, and Eridu reached for it. He'd chosen two women for his evening's pleasure, new slaves whose fear and trembling would act as an aphrodisiac to their jaded master. He liked them very young, and to take them two at a time. And if one failed to please him, a good beating would encourage the other to try harder.

"They're waiting downstairs, Father. I'll summon them when you're ready."

The door opened, and Shulgi entered, closing it behind him. He still

171

wore his leather vest and sword, as if he'd just come from the soldiers' camp, though in fact he'd waited in the courtyard for Shanna's signal, a wave from the upper window when she went to fetch the sweet cakes.

Shulgi moved to the foot of the table, to stand opposite his father, placing himself almost directly behind Petrah.

"Now what?" Eridu demanded, a hint of petulance in his hoarse voice. He rose, wiping his face on a cloth and tossing it down on the table. Petrah stood also, prepared to utter his thanks for his master's generosity and depart.

"It's the men, Father, they're demanding more gold again."

Shanna returned to her place beside her father, though she did not sit down. The knife she'd carved the lamb with rested on the table. With a smooth motion, she picked it up, grasping it firmly as Shulgi had instructed her, then Shanna turned and drove it into the right side of Eridu's chest, thrusting the blade upward so that it would penetrate the ribs, not glance off the bone.

She struck with such speed and smoothness that Eridu scarcely gasped, even as he looked down to see the knife protruding from his body.

The steward, slow to react and shocked by Shanna's attack, never had a chance. As Shanna delivered her thrust, Shulgi jerked out his sword, twisted the steward around, gripped him by the throat, and drove the blade into Petrah's chest, forcing him backwards onto the floor.

Eridu, his eyes wide with fear and astonishment, tried to call out. But Shanna clapped her hand on his mouth. With his only hand, he struggled to push her away, but by then Shulgi had reached his father's side.

He drew a knife from his belt and plunged it into Eridu's heart, driving the blade deep with a brutal thrust. "I've waited long enough for this, Father."

Eridu's eyes flickered from son to daughter one last time before his knees gave way. He was dead before he reached the floor.

"Quick! Move Petrah's body closer." Shanna kept her voice low. She knew Shulgi would have ordered the guard away, but anybody might be outside the chamber, and the door might open at any time.

Shulgi returned to the other side of the table, and dragged Petrah closer to Eridu's body. The knife Shulgi used for the fatal thrust belonged to Petrah, taken from his quarters only moments before. Using both hands, Shanna jerked the blade she'd used from the king's body, and thrust it deep into the remains of the lamb. Any trace of Eridu's blood vanished. She turned to Shulgi.

"Are you ready?"

Shulgi had withdrawn the knife from his father's body and placed it in Petrah's hand. "Yes, hurry."

Shanna touched his arm for the briefest moment, and took a deep breath. Then she screamed, a loud piercing sound that carried through the upper chambers and through the open window to the courtyard below.

At the same moment, Shulgi picked up the wine pitcher and hurled it to the floor, where it burst into a dozen pieces, the red wine mixing with the blood and staining the floor. Shanna, using all her strength, tipped the table up as high as she could, before letting it drop back to the floor with a loud thud. Food, cups, and the remains of the meal clattered to the floor.

Shanna screamed again, then ran for the door. "Help! Help! Petrah stabbed the king!"

Before she reached the door, servants flung it open and rushed into the room, followed a moment later by the stunned guard. His face turned white with fear when he saw the king's body, and blood spattered everywhere.

"Send for Razrek!" Shulgi ordered. "I want him at once. And send my guards to me."

"Is the king . . . is he dead?" The guard could scarcely get the words out.

"Yes, damn you!" Shulgi snapped. "Murdered by Petrah! Now get moving!"

The guard opened his mouth as if to speak, but then changed his mind and darted off, anxious to do Shulgi's bidding. His voice echoed down the corridor, shouting the news of Eridu's death.

The rest of the night was full of turmoil and confusion. Shanna pulled at her hair, hard enough to bring tears to her eyes, and left it in disarray over her face. She told the story again and again, in a halting voice that paused every few moments to sob. Her father and Petrah had quarreled over the cost of the soldiers. Eridu had slapped his steward, and Petrah had retaliated by stabbing his master with his knife. Shulgi had then killed Petrah.

Shanna kept crying, her body shaking with emotion as she shouted again and again for her beloved father. She repeated the story to every new arrival. Soon servants and soldiers filled the room, everyone jostling each other to catch a glimpse of the dead king, still lying where'd he fallen in the midst of the remains of the evening's meal. Razrek arrived in haste, pushing his way through the crowded chamber, his meal interrupted, his eyes going wide at what he saw.

As Shulgi repeated what had happened, Razrek's eyes narrowed. "Petrah?"

Razrek's face mirrored his confusion, and Shanna moved quickly to stifle any questions. Razrek was, after all, the only one strong enough to challenge their story.

"This is your fault," Shanna shouted, standing before Razrek, her face now contorted with rage. "It was your guard who failed to protect the king, your guard who let Petrah bring his knife into the room. He should be put to death at once. At once!" Her voice broke down, and she began to sob again, her whole body shaking from her sorrow.

Shulgi caught Razrek's arm and pulled him aside. "Best to do as she says. Otherwise, she'll start claiming you put Petrah up to this."

"Are you sure Petrah . . . ?" His voice trailed off. Something in Shulgi's eyes told him not to ask any questions.

"Do it now," Shulgi went on, his voice low. "With my father dead, I'll take charge of the city and the army. You'll be getting paid by me from now on. Is that clear enough?"

Razrek recovered his wits in a few heartbeats. Suddenly, he remembered that Shulgi's men stood in the corridor outside the chamber, and in the courtyard below. "Yes . . . my king. I'll take care of the guard, and send my men to guard the Compound."

"No need," Shulgi said. "I have some of my men here already. The rest will soon arrive. Now go get rid of the guard. We'll talk about this in the morning."

Shulgi turned to see Shanna seated in a chair, her face covered by her hands as she rocked back and forth. Servants attended her, holding her hands, offering water, wine and cloths to dry her tears. Every part of her body showed her grief, as dutiful as any daughter. Razrek shook his head and departed, glad to have had no part in the night's turmoil.

It took most of the evening before everyone calmed down, the bodies removed, and the room cleaned. In front of the household, Shulgi ordered Shanna to sleep in her father's bed tonight, for her safety. And to ensure that, Shulgi ordered his own bed brought into the dining chamber. Two of his men stood guard outside the chamber when he finally dropped the wooden bar across the doorway.

Crossing the room Shulgi entered what had been his father's bedroom, but was now his. A single candle still burned, and Shanna sat on the bed, combing her hair. She wore a clean garment. She'd ordered the other one, stained with her father's blood, to be burned. Shanna rose and walked toward him. Before he could reach out to touch her, she bowed low, as humble as any servant.

"My king, is there anything I may do for you tonight?"

"Oh, yes." He heard the hoarseness in his voice. But it didn't matter any more. With Shanna, there would be no need to pretend or hide his emotions. "You can take off that dress before I rip it off."

She straightened, and the smile was back on her face. "Yes, my king. We wouldn't want the servants to see a torn garment in the morning." Shanna pulled the dress over her head and stepped back.

His eyes drank in the sight of the lush body. A quick breath extinguished the candle before he picked her up and dropped her down on the bed, as excited as the day he had taken his first woman. His father was out of the way, Shanna lay naked in his bed, and Sumer belonged to him. Soon all of Sumeria, then Akkad and the northern cities would follow.

17

One month later . . .

Eskkar and Grond, accompanied by four Hawk Clan guards, entered the grounds of Akkad's main barracks. As the sounds of busy lanes faded somewhat, Eskkar took a moment to enjoy the soldiers' quarters, where much of his life had been shaped. During the days when he held the post of Captain of the Guard, the barracks housed all the soldiers as well as their weapons and horses. The once familiar stable smell had finally departed, along with the horses. A large corral across the river now held most of the soldiers' mounts, with the remainder stabled at a smaller holding area just south of the city. When the time came to tear down the malodorous horse pens, the soldiers completed the task in half a morning, glad to see the last of the odor-rich structures. A favorite punishment for petty infractions, many men had labored there over the years, cleaning out the muck in the hot summer sun.

New barracks soon sprang up to accommodate the growing numbers of men learning the art of war. These provided additional housing for the recruits as well as weapons' storage. The training ground, located at the back of the barracks, remained untouched, however.

As he strode across the grounds, Eskkar missed the horse smell. He and a few others who grew up in horse country claimed they could still catch the scent of the endless streams of horse piss that had soaked deep into the earth. While others complained about the foul odors, even the faint scent of horse sweat always reminded Eskkar of his youth and life with the clan.

"Have you heard anything about the training?" Eskkar's long legs covered a lot of ground, forcing Grond and the guards to hurry to keep up.

Gatus had started training a group of recruits as spearmen less than a month after the meeting at Rebba's farm.

"Nothing much." Grond kept his tone non-committal. "I know Gatus added new recruits now and then, and lost a few, too, but he hasn't told me anything. And none of his men will say a word."

Eskkar glanced at his friend and bodyguard. Only Gatus could convince Grond to keep a secret. "It's been almost three months since he started training them. He better have something to show for it. How hard can it be to teach a man to use a spear?"

Grond knew better than to answer that kind of question.

They turned the corner at the barracks, and Eskkar found Gatus waiting across the open space for them, sitting on his stool and holding a wood rod the thickness of his thumb in his hand. The Rod of Gatus, as long as his arm, had become part of the soldiers' tradition, and few recruits managed to escape its touch. A good whack on the arm or back, Gatus explained, helped each man concentrate on the orders of his superior, usually shouted in the recruit's face at the top of his lungs.

The instructors, too, used their rods almost as freely as Gatus, until even the slowest witted of the recruits learned instant obedience to their superiors' orders, no matter how seemingly senseless or humiliating. During the early months of training, while the men's bodies grew hardened by exercise and constant practice with their weapons, that lesson remained the most important. All orders must be obeyed at once, with no exceptions and no excuses. The reason was simple enough. In battle, the enemy cared nothing for how weary or ill or hung over a soldier was. The sooner every recruit learned that bitter lesson, the longer they would stay alive in combat.

Over time, as the men increased their skill level, the physical abuse tapered off, and the trainers' efforts shifted to more and longer periods spent practicing with bow, sword, and knife. Another skill every recruit had to master was wrestling. It not only strengthened the men's bodies, but also taught them how to fight unarmed. And as the long and arduous days of physical effort passed, the men grew more confident not only in themselves and their skills, but in those of their companions at arms, the men who trained at their side, and who would someday fight beside them.

Gatus had long ago mastered the art of turning farm boys into soldiers.

Eskkar had acknowledged that fact early on, and given Gatus responsibility for training Akkad's archers. Still, while many knew how to train fighting men, the old soldier had learned the best ways to turn individual fighters into a fighting unit. Under his hard tutelage, the men gradually formed a bond with each other. As Gatus had explained many times, first you beat the recruits down, showed them how weak and pitiful their strength and skills were compared to their trainers. That humiliating demonstration usually sufficed to drive the recruits to train harder and harder to master the skills demanded of them. By then, every recruit hated his trainers as much as any enemy they would face in battle.

When done properly, the grueling ordeal helped the men learn to work and fight together, each one determined to prove to their hard taskmasters that they could not only withstand the brutal discipline, but take strength from it. As that happened, each man's sense of pride increased. With each improvement in his fighting skills, that sense of worth grew stronger and stronger. Gradually a fighting unit took shape. What started out as a rag-tag group of individuals developed into a band of brothers that learned to take care of its own, the stronger helping the weaker, and the more skillful assisting those who needed extra work.

Months later, when the recruits had turned into true soldiers, they looked back in awe at what they had accomplished. By then many had changed beyond recognition, muscles bulging where none had existed before. Skills with their weapons progressed as well, from barely knowing which end of a sword to pick up, to supremely confident. Only then did the men grudgingly admit that perhaps their vigilant taskmasters had known all along what they were doing.

Now Gatus had turned his attention to this new force of spearmen, letting others train the archers and sword fighters. What would result from all this remained to be seen.

"Well, Gatus, your men look fit enough," Eskkar said as he approached, raising his voice so that everyone could hear. He got the words out before Gatus could complain about Eskkar's late arrival. "What are you going to show me?"

"My spearmen are ready to show you what they've learned." Gatus tapped his rod against his other hand. He, too, spoke loud enough to make sure everyone heard. "Why don't you and Grond stand over against the wall, where you'll be out of the way?"

Eskkar and Grond moved to the side of the barracks, the Hawk Clan guards trailing behind them. Gatus waited until Eskkar and his guards complied, then slid off his stool, tossed it aside, and turned to face his spearmen. Behind him, thirty men stood in two ranks, each of them carrying a shield and a spear, and with a short sword at his waist. Leather helmets made the men look both taller and fiercer. Every spear rested on its butt, the bronze tip pointing at the sky, as the men awaited their orders. Half the spears, Eskkar noticed, extended a forearm length longer than the others. He realized something else. These men had awaited his arrival for some time, standing patiently in the warm sunshine without shifting about or shuffling their feet. No men Gatus ever trained would be found sitting about in the shade when the king arrived. Each man looked confident, and the eyes that followed Eskkar's movements showed no hint of fear or awe.

Eskkar knew the importance of hard discipline in building morale. Unlike steppe warriors, whose honor guided their training from the youngest age, villagers first needed to be taught to obey before they learned how to fight. Warriors had learned these lessons as far back as anyone could recall. Eskkar accepted these ideas without question, since that was the way of the steppe warrior. The villagers, without any real clan or code of honor of their own, needed a teacher like Gatus and his methods as a way to gain respect. By the time the recruits took pride in themselves and their fighting skills, they had also learned the most important lesson of all, that of trusting and caring for the soldier who fought beside you. The months of shared suffering they'd endured bonded them to their fellow soldiers. They learned to trust not only their own skills, but those of the man next to them.

Because, as Eskkar well knew, that's what made a man fight, not some cause or even hope for a few pieces of gold or loot now and then. You fought because your sense of honor demanded it; you fought because your friend stood at your side and you could not think of letting him stand alone. And you fought on when all appeared lost, because your friends had died beside you, and how could you do anything less to honor their memory than give your utmost? Most of all, you fought because you had mastered the skills that would carry you to victory, and that belief in yourself and your weapons made each man determined to stand strong against his enemy.

Over the years, while Eskkar wandered the land, he came to understand better the code of the warrior, and the way it helped keep him alive. His father Hogarthak had taught his son well in that regard, so well that even as an outcast boy struggling against an unfamiliar and harsh world those lessons remained ingrained in Eskkar's mind. Still, he had never quite mastered the teaching of the same lessons to others. Eskkar could lead men in battle, could even train them well enough, but Gatus could turn raw recruits into a fighting unit better and faster than anyone Eskkar had ever seen.

With this group of spearmen, Gatus had worked hard with each leader of ten to make sure his subordinates knew just how far to go with the men. Recruits needed to be cured of their former habits, but not broken in spirit. When they finished their training, they would be accepted into Akkad's warrior ranks, and have the status that came with their oaths to defend their king, their city, and their fellow soldiers.

For many, it was the first time in their lives that they had ever accomplished something so difficult but so rewarding. Whether it was hitting a target at a hundred paces with a single swiftly launched shaft, or taking a man down with three powerful sword strokes, men soon learned more about themselves, about what they could do and accomplish, than any weapon they took to hand.

Now Eskkar glanced at a small assemblage on the training ground. For more than a month, he had chaffed at Gatus and his slow and patient methods. Every few days Eskkar had asked Gatus when the first group of spearmen would be ready.

"Soon."

The laconic reply grated on Eskkar's nerves. Nevertheless, he'd learned during the siege of Akkad to leave the training to Gatus. In those days, Eskkar had been stunned to hear that it would take many months to train a competent archer. He'd fumed at the delay, amazed that so simple a weapon required so much time for a novice to master. But Gatus had proved himself right. One of the reasons why Akkad's archers remained so formidable was their complete mastery of their weaponry.

But did teaching a man to use a spear take as much time as learning to use a bow and arrow? This time, he held his tongue, just in case Gatus once again proved himself right. And Eskkar had plenty to occupy his time. He'd spent many days in Nuzi helping establish the gold mine and clearing the nearby countryside of bandits. Visits to Bisitun and the other northern cities took Eskkar away from Akkad for long periods as well. And whenever he returned, there were always the nobles, merchants, traders and craftsmen to deal with, all claiming some urgent need that no one besides the king could resolve.

Yesterday, just before the sun had set, Eskkar had returned from the north once again. This time Gatus met him at the Compound. "My first group of spearmen is ready for you to see. Come to the barracks in the morning."

Gatus's demeanor provided no hint as to what would await Eskkar at the barracks.

"I'll be there." He resisted the temptation to ask what he would see, or to add that it had taken long enough to whip a few men into shape.

Once again Eskkar studied the men. They all looked confident, and he recognized the nervous movements that revealed the excitement that lay just below the surface. Gatus had worked with these men for months, testing, changing, and refining his ideas on how spearmen should train and fight. No longer a group of raw recruits, the men standing behind the old soldier had suffered months of hard discipline and physical labor. Now Gatus felt satisfied that they had mastered their craft, and that they stood ready to demonstrate their skills.

"All right, you men," Gatus called out. His booming voice echoed over the training ground. "Let's show our king what we can do." He gave a command, and the men turned to the right, transforming themselves instantly into a column of twos.

"Carry spears!"

The weapons bobbed upward for a moment, then came down, until each spear hung naturally at the end of each man's right arm, the point held slightly outward, so as not to jab the man in front.

"March!" The barked order started the soldiers moving forward.

Gatus paraded them back and forth in front of Eskkar. The men marched in a straight line and moved in unison. Three subcommanders stepped along at the men's side, noting how each movement was executed, and correcting and encouraging the men, though not loud enough so that the king's group could hear the words.

Eskkar noted that every man took his first step with his left foot, so that their arms and legs moved together. That would be important, because if the men got out of step, they would be more likely to trip and fall over each other. The long spears they carried would make that dangerous enough. It wouldn't take much to poke out someone's eye.

The line of spears moved together, each weapon remaining level with the earth as the men marched back and forth. The drill continued, the men marching this way and that, until Eskkar felt his attention wandering. He expected more than just watching men march back and forth. And with the spear held loosely at arm's length, the spearmen didn't look particularly dangerous.

At last, Gatus gave the order to halt and the column stopped directly in front of Eskkar, resuming their original formation of two ranks, but about seventy paces away from where he stood. Another command swung the line around.

"Attack positions!" Every spear was raised in a smooth motion, held just above shoulder height, each man gripping his weapon with the palm facing upwards. The rear rank took one step forward, so that they stood just behind the front rank. Shields were raised to eye level, covering almost all of the man's body.

For a moment, all Eskkar could see were the soldiers' eyes peering over the tops of the shields. They stood almost shoulder to shoulder, the tips of the weapons extending to the front.

"Advance!" Gatus's voice again rang out over the training ground.

The spearmen, in perfect step with each other, moved toward Eskkar, and he saw that all the men carrying the longer spears now formed the rear rank. Their spear points protruded almost as far forward as those of the men in front. A compact line like that would brush aside any line of swordsmen, who needed room to swing their weapons. And even if you could get close enough to take a swing, the spearman's shield would deflect the blow, and any swordsman would probably be gutted by at least two spears for his efforts.

Eskkar saw all this at a glance as the line approached, covering the distance with long strides and without hesitation. If they didn't stop, he and Grond would be pinned like rabbits to the barracks' wall. Grond saw the same impending danger. His sword rasped from its scabbard and he took a half-step in front of Eskkar, just as Gatus gave the command to halt. The spear points hung in mid-air, two paces from Eskkar's chest.

Taking his time, Gatus walked casually from behind his men to stand at Eskkar's side. "Well, next time you're late, I may forget to give the order to halt."

The men didn't laugh. Gatus's rod, which he still held in his hand, would have instilled silence into their ranks. Still, Eskkar saw plenty of grins covering their sweaty faces. At least he hadn't been frightened enough to draw his own sword.

"Impressive. I wouldn't want to be facing them on open ground."

"Spears up, at rest!" Gatus shouted, and the men raised their weapons to the vertical, then let the butts drop to the earth. Gatus moved closer, but he kept his voice loud, making certain that his men heard the words of praise. "This line of spearmen would tear through any enemy."

"They would at that," Eskkar agreed, impressed by their skills. "But against archers, how would they stand up?"

"The shield covers most of the body," Gatus explained. "In a real fight, they'd be wearing bronze helmets. You'd lose a few to arrows, but attacking at a run, most of the line would reach the enemy intact."

Or so it was hoped, but now wasn't the time to talk about doubts. Eskkar took a step forward, stopping in front of the nearest spearman. He reached out to take the spear, but the soldier refused to let it go. Eskkar tightened his grip and pulled harder, putting his own muscles into it. The soldier slid forward, feet struggling to hold his position, but didn't release his grip. The man's arm, Eskkar saw, was as thick as most men's legs.

"They've been taught never to let go of the spear," Gatus said, tapping the rod against his thigh. "Give the king your spear, Drannah."

No doubt Gatus knew the name of every man in the ranks. The soldier let go of the weapon. Eskkar hefted the spear, surprised at its weight. Far too heavy to throw more than a short distance, it was meant to thrust, to push through a thin shield or a man's body. The slim bronze tip, carefully fitted and bolted to the shaft, would enter smoothly, and be withdrawn just as easily, with little chance of snagging on clothing, flesh or shield.

"Each man has been trained to thrust with the spear, and to fight with his sword if the spear breaks or gets entangled with the enemy," Gatus explained. "The shield gives plenty of protection, and each man is responsible for guarding the man on his left as well as himself. And the shield can be used as a weapon itself."

"Show me how they fight with swords."

Gatus nodded, and his trainers took over. The men broke ranks, leaned their spears against the barrack wall, and reformed. Once again, the soldiers repeated their maneuvers, now carrying their short swords. They advanced, striking out with the weapon as they moved. The sword, Eskkar noted, was never swung, only thrust with short, stabbing motions, either straight ahead or upwards. Using the weapon that way meant thrusts to the belly, chest and throat. That went counter to Eskkar's instincts. The long sword he carried was meant to strike in an arc, hitting with the edge of the heavy blade and cutting through flesh and bone from the pure force of the swing. The usual intended target was your opponent's head or shoulders. The sharp point allowed a mounted rider to vary his attack, or stab downward, but that was seldom the first choice in a fight.

Nevertheless, Eskkar realized the benefits of thrusting with the point of these much shorter weapons. Less muscle was used, and the stroke could be launched faster. He guessed a competent soldier could get in two or three thrusts before a warrior could swing his blade a single time. Also, a man went down as fast or faster with a blade in his stomach or bowels. As long as these men had the shield to protect them, that way of using the sword would be deadly to anyone in their path.

The soldiers broke into groups of two, and each practiced against his companion, thrusting with both sword and shield. Eskkar saw that they used the shield as efficiently as the sword, shoving it forward, or thrusting with the edge. Used together, they made a deadly combination. He'd fought against men armed with shields and swords before, but the shield had served mostly for defense against an attacker's sword, not part of the killing process. Gatus had learned something new about the craft of killing, Eskkar decided. Once the tactic spread, there would be one more enemy maneuver to worry about.

When the exhibition ended, the men were tired, hot, and covered with sweat. But not one of them had shown any sign of weakness in the way they carried their shield, sword or spear. Precision had marked every one of their movements, all thirty of the men moving as one. Gatus had not only trained them well, Eskkar decided, but he'd hardened their bodies to match with their weapons. He'd taken untrained recruits, selected the strongest men he could find, and toughened them up. And just as important, he'd shown them how to fight like a unit.

Eskkar had learned many lessons during the siege of Akkad, but one lesson had stood out. To win a battle, it wasn't necessary to have the most men on the field of battle. Quality and training could make up for numbers. A small force could defeat a much larger one. He proved that with his handful of archers against the might and numbers of the Alur Meriki. Eskkar remembered how many months the bowmen trained, until they could stand exposed on the wall and launch arrow after arrow without flinching, powerful arms drawing each shaft to its full length before releasing. Now Eskkar would have to do it again, defeat a much larger force with a smaller, better-trained one. Except this time it would be spearmen such as these leading the way.

And they would have to lead, he decided. Gatus had the right answer. The new army of Akkad would be built around men like these. Archers and horse-mounted fighters would still be critical, but Esskar realized their main function would be to enable the spearmen to close with the enemy. To support that effort, bowmen and cavalry would need to learn new ways of fighting as well. That training for the horsemen had also begun, far to the north in another training camp near Bisitun, and now yet another tactic needed to be taught – how to attack or defend against enemy spearmen. One thing Esskar had no illusions about – whatever new trick or tactic Akkad developed, their enemies would learn about it soon enough, and add it to their own capabilities.

"Are you satisfied?" Gatus demanded, breaking into Esskar's thoughts. "With a few hundred men like these, I could cut my way through any army."

"No, I'm not satisfied," Esskar said, raising his own voice. He wanted to be sure the men heard his words. "Tomorrow I want you to start marching these soldiers as far as they can walk, march their legs off, until they can cover twenty miles a day. When they can march that distance, carrying all their weapons and a day's ration of food and water, and still be ready for a fight, then I'll be satisfied."

He heard the groans from a few of the men.

Frowning, Esskar pushed past Gatus and stepped to within three paces of the spearmen. "Listen to me, you men. In the battle with Sumer, my archers marched twelve or fourteen miles *at night*, carrying their swords and bows, and then fought a battle at dawn. If they can cover that much distance in the dark, you should be able to do twenty in daylight."

That stopped the spearmen's complaints. Esskar didn't mention that the men had traveled light, with no food and almost no water.

"Twenty miles is a long march," Gatus said, moving up and standing at Esskar's side. "A man would have to be tougher than bronze to make that distance."

"Then start with ten," Esskar said, "and keep them at it until they can do twenty. I will want to cover even more distance than that in time. And I want all my soldiers to move quickly, as fast as we can move. If we've learned one lesson, it's that the side that can react and move the fastest is going to have the advantage." He strode up and down the line of spearmen, studying their faces up close, looking each man in the eye.

"Unless you're not as tough as my archers," Esskar suggested. "Or if you prefer to have the enemy pick the time and place of battle."

"NO!"

He smiled at the unanimous response that echoed around the training ground.

"Then tomorrow we'll see what you can do," Eskkar said. "And I'll march with you, just to show you it can be done. Will you march with me?"

A cheer went up this time. The soldiers were as excited as he'd expected. A long day's march had just turned into a challenge. To march with the ruler of Akkad, to show him what they could accomplish, that would be something to boast about in the alehouse.

"Dismiss your men, Gatus. We'll leave at dawn tomorrow."

Gatus turned the men over to the leaders of ten, with orders to prepare for tomorrow's march. Then he joined Eskkar and Grond.

"Can they do twenty miles, Gatus?"

"They'll do whatever you can do, Captain. But I'm too old for that kind of walking. I'll be riding my horse, laughing at all of you stumbling along in the heat."

"Maybe I'll join you," Grond said.

Eskkar knew his bodyguard hated walking as much as he did. He also knew that Grond would not allow himself to ride while his commander walked.

"You've trained them well, Gatus," Eskkar said. "Now I want at least five hundred more of them to start, maybe more if we can find enough men, each as strong and well trained."

"Five hundred! I was expecting to train only another hundred or two."

"You've got one year, Gatus, that's all. When they've completed their training, you can pay them the same as the archers. You were right. These men are going to be the core of our strength. Keep training them until they can march and fight in their sleep."

Trella estimated it would take at least one year before a new threat from Sumeria materialized, more likely two. But Eskkar knew it was always better to prepare for the worst.

Gatus shook his head. "Spears, swords, shields, helmets, sandals, pay, not to mention food, ale, whatever, it's going to take a lot of gold to support so many men. Not to mention time and work to train them."

"You'll find a way, Gatus. And the gold will be coming soon from the mine at Nuzi. Ask Trella about the training and weapons, too. She's always full of ideas. Oh, I forgot to ask. Can these spearmen stop a charge of horsemen?"

For once, Gatus was at a loss. "I'm not sure about that. We've never tried anything against cavalry tactics."

"Well, you'd better figure out a way. Spearmen are no use to me if a few hundred mounted riders can brush them aside. Sumer will have plenty of horseflesh, and I'm certain we'll see all of it sooner or later."

Eskkar smiled at the frown on Gatus's face. Catching the old soldier off-guard didn't come easy. "Come, Grond. We need to get back to the house. Gatus has plenty to do to get ready for tomorrow's march."

With the Hawk Clan guards leading the way, Eskkar and Grond left the barracks. Gatus remained where they left him, deep in thought. Eskkar knew the old soldier wasn't wasting any time worrying about tomorrow's march. His subcommanders could handle those simple preparations. No, Gatus would be wondering how to stop a mounted charge. Still, if anyone could think of a way, Gatus would come up with something, though Eskkar was willing to gamble that Hathor would be involved in the solution.

The following night, Eskkar blew out one of the two candles illuminating the chamber and eased himself down onto the bed with a small grunt of relief. His back hurt, his feet were blistered, and his face still burned from the heat of the sun. The bed's softness cradled him and he let himself relax with a groan of relief.

"You shouldn't have marched with the men," Trella admonished. "Turn onto your stomach and I'll rub your back."

"In a moment. I'm too tired to move. But at least I led the men out this morning, and back this evening."

"I watched a few days ago as Gatus led them through their drills. They looked very efficient, very dangerous."

He hadn't known she had visited the barracks training ground. Leave it to Trella, to want to learn something new. Only a few dozen villagers were allowed in, mostly soldiers or the wives of the more senior men. Of course, she had blended in with the women, no doubt with Annok-sur at her side.

"Gatus had an easy day, since he rode out and back." Eskkar let out another groan of satisfaction, glad to be off his feet.

"As you should have done. The men wouldn't have thought any less of you for riding."

"I wasn't carrying a spear or a shield. And by walking with them, I got to know them. I spoke with every man on the march, and I'll remember at least a dozen names. It was a day well spent."

He reached up and touched her breast. Her nipple hardened and he smiled at the sight. He liked arousing her, joining with her passion.

"First, roll over," she said, ignoring his attention. "I want to practice my massage."

Esskar turned onto his stomach and cradled his head in his arms. Trella knelt with her knees on either side of him. Her hands pressed hard against his back as she leaned forward, fingers probing deep into the muscles.

"Ahhhhaa," he said, giving a gasp of pain mixed with pleasure. "Is this more of what Zenobia taught you?"

Zenobia was the woman who operated Akkad's most famous and luxurious pleasure house. Trella had befriended her when she arrived, alone and vulnerable. After the Alur Meriki were driven off, Trella gave Zenobia the gold needed to buy and operate the house. Now the finest pleasure girls served the choicest wines to Akkad's leading merchants. The strong drink loosened their tongues, and everything they said reached Annok-sur's ears. Only a few of Esskar's closest circle knew of the relationship.

"Oh, yes, we all practiced on each other, especially on Tammuz and En-hedu. I can still see the blush on his face." Trella's hands, which had started kneading her husband's lower back, moved up to his shoulders, each new movement eliciting a further moan of pleasure.

"Zenobia has a slave girl named Te-ara," Trella went on, "who is well-practiced in the art of massage. Zenobia brought Te-ara to Bisitun to teach En-hedu the secret art. I traveled with them, to watch the training and see what I could learn for myself."

Esskar knew that she had gone north to Bisitun for a few days, near the end of En-hedu's training.

"When I left, En-hedu had learned a dozen new ways to pleasure her husband, sometimes with Zenobia and Te-ara and me helping."

"I'd blush, too, if four naked women were fondling my manhood day after day."

Trella laughed. "We spilled his seed so many times, he begged for mercy. His eyes went wide with fear when we approached. Zenobia and Te-ara drained his poor member so often, he could scarcely walk afterwards."

"He probably enjoyed every moment. Does he still care as much for En-hedu? Or did Zenobia and Te-ara steal his love?"

She laughed again, and moved her hands to the muscles across the top of Esskar's shoulders. "He cares for En-hedu more than ever. I've seldom seen a man so smitten with his woman. He would die for her, and she for him."

"I wonder how they're doing in Sumer. Have you heard from them?"

"No, nothing, but it's too soon. They may not even have arrived there yet. Besides, it will take them many months to settle in and figure out what is happening."

"And if they're discovered?"

"Then that will tell us something as well. It will tell us that King Eridu is wiser than we think, that his men are quick to guard his secrets."

"Tammuz and En-hedu will die slow deaths." His voice drifted lower, as the effects of a long day and Trella's ministrations began to take effect.

"They know the risks, husband. They both want to fight for you and for Akkad, and this is the only way they can."

"And Yavtar vouches for this merchant . . ."

"Gemama. Yes, as best he can. When the war comes, even Gemama may be of use to us. I think you should turn over now, husband, before you fall asleep."

She moved off his back, and he wearily rolled over, another long sigh of relief escaping from his lips. Before he could protest, she cupped his manhood in both hands and began to massage it.

"I may be too tired for that," he said, letting his eyes close. But his hand reached out for her breast once again.

"That's what Tammuz kept saying. Let me show you what Zenobia taught us for such times."

In moments he was rock hard and gasping at her grip. Satisfied, she moved astride him with a sigh of pleasure. "See how easy it is to arouse a man."

Wide awake now, Esskar thrust himself upward, feeling the heat from her body. "You are still the most beautiful woman in Akkad." Then he could say nothing as she twisted her body, tightening her muscles and grinding herself against him on and on, until his heart pounded and his seed burst inside her.

Later, as they lay in each other's arms, he had just enough strength to whisper in her ear. "You are the only woman for me, Trella."

She understood how hard it was for him to say such words. "And you are the only man for me." She kissed his neck, pressed herself against his shoulder, and held him until he fell asleep.

18

Five days later . . .

In Sumer, in the days before King Eridu died, Tammuz and En-hedu found each sunrise bringing some new challenge. The city of Sumer no longer resembled the sleepy trading village that bordered on the Great Sea. In the last five years, the city had grown faster than any other village in Sumeria. People from all over the region migrated to Sumer in search of a better life.

The steady influx of people had greatly added to King Eridu's wealth. During his rule, he fed Sumer's inhabitants with dreams of conquest and easy wealth. Over and over, Eridu assured them that only the city of Akkad stood in the way of Sumer's greatness and prosperity. Once that barbarian-ruled city was swept aside, gold would flow to Sumer's inhabitants from all the cities and villages of the land between the rivers.

Even as an outsider, Tammuz saw how Eridu's stinging defeat had humiliated the people of Sumer. Dreams of conquest had vanished, replaced by a sense of gloom and worry about the future. Everyone now feared attacks from the north. Eskkar and his demon archers would invade and devastate Sumeria. Villages and crops would burn, farmers murdered in their sleep. The gods had turned their back on Sumer and its people. A feeling of dread replaced the giddy excitement of Sumer's soldiers and its people.

After King Eridu's ransom and return from Akkad, fresh rumors of a new war were on everyone's lips. He increased the already heavy burden of taxes. Eridu One-hand, as many called him, remained full of rage and hatred for all things Akkad.

He seldom left his private quarters, and those few whose business took them into his presence reported a man seething with hatred and bitterness. Word soon spread that he wanted to create another army and take his revenge against Eskkar and Akkad. Once again, Eridu's soldiers searched the lanes and alleys looking for any able-bodied men to conscript. More than once patrols stopped Tammuz on the street, until they saw his crooked arm.

Despite Eridu's yearning for another march north, the mood in the city remained sullen. In Sumer's defeat by Lord Eskkar, many men had died or been wounded. Neither the survivors nor the city's inhabitants had any stomach or desire for more battles, not against an enemy that had done little or nothing to arouse them. Eridu's claims to the contrary, most people cared little for the borderlands that until recently had been ignored and untouched by any of the southern cities. Faced with the prospect of another war, many men and older boys left the city. Those that remained did their best to avoid the lanes and marketplace, unwilling to be forced into the training camps by Eridu's roaming gangs.

All this fascinated Tammuz, but he and En-hedu had plenty to keep them busy. As soon as they purchased the inn, they moved in and almost immediately trouble started. The following day, some local thugs decided to take advantage of the new owners, young and fresh from the farm. Three men entered the little tavern in the late afternoon and demanded payment for protection, as they called it.

The inn was almost empty at that hour, and the few patrons present, recognizing the men as troublemakers and thieves, scurried out as fast as they could.

"You're new in Sumer, cripple," the leader rasped, a burly man who carried plenty of muscles on his arms and chest. "You'll need someone to make sure your inn is safe. We'll take care of that for you."

A scar marked his face, long black hair hung greasily around his face, and he was missing a tooth. The combination gave him a fierce expression that he used to intimidate those weaker than himself.

"But first we have to collect payment for your protection. One silver coin. Pay us now, or I'll break your good arm." He fingered the knife in his belt for emphasis, while his two companions smiled broadly at the new owner's apparent helplessness. "After that, you'll pay us the same every ten days, or you'll find someone has pulled the inn down on your heads."

From their private chamber, En-hedu took a step into the common room. The three men's heads turned to give her a brief glance, but she stood there speechless, her hands crossed above her breasts. The gesture allowed her right hand to slip inside her dress and reach the haft of her knife.

Tammuz had expected something like this, though not on their second day. He took two steps back and to the side, so that En-hedu would be almost behind the three men.

"Why should I pay you anything?"

The one with the knife stepped forward. "Because if you don't, you'll wish you were back on −"

But Tammuz used the backward steps only to draw the man forward. Now his foot lashed out with all his strength, striking right between the man's legs with a swiftness that caught all three by surprise.

With a howl of pain, the leader clutched his groin. By that time En-hedu had slipped up behind the two henchmen, snatching the knife from beneath her dress as she moved. With muscles as strong as any young man's, she struck downward with the weapon's hilt on the back of the nearest thug's head. He dropped like a sack of grain, caught unaware by the unexpected attack from behind.

The third man, still watching open-mouthed as his leader crumpled to the ground, reacted slowly. First he fumbled for his knife, then turned toward En-hedu as his companion collapsed on the floor, but by that time Tammuz, who had never stopped moving, closed the gap between them. Before the rogue could draw his weapon or even decide what to do, Tammuz had his own blade out, and he smashed the hilt into the man's face. The thug stumbled backward, tripped over a stool, and crashed into a table before sliding onto to the floor.

Meanwhile, En-hedu slipped behind the leader, hunched over in pain from Tammuz's kick, and struck again. This time the butt of her knife landed on the side of his head, and he lolled on the dirt floor of the tavern, too stunned even to groan in his pain.

The encounter had taken only moments, but Tammuz found himself breathing heavily from the brush with danger. "Better fetch the watch, before someone else sends for them," he said, a grim expression on his face. "I'll see what they're carrying."

"I hope none of them are dead." She reached out and touched Tammuz's arm for a moment, her eyes still wide with excitement. For the second time in their young lives, they had fought together.

"They're breathing," he said, glancing at the leader to make sure. His wife had struck with all her strength. The last thing Tammuz needed was a dead body on their hands. No matter what the reason or excuse, it would bring down too much trouble on their heads. Newcomers such as themselves couldn't risk offending anyone, not until they were well established and known. But a few bloody heads meant nothing, he hoped, at least not to Sumer's guards.

While En-hedu darted out to find the city's watch, Tammuz went through the men's things. Two of them had nothing of value, except for their knives. He tossed those into the darkest corner of the inn. He might be able to sell them for a few coins later. The leader's purse held nine copper coins, a respectable amount for even an honest man. Tammuz collected his knife, too, and pitched it after the others. By then the leader had begun to recover. He groaned, and attempted to sit up, but slumped back to the floor, too dazed to move or grasp what had happened.

Tammuz slid his knife back into its sheath. He grasped the man's right hand, placing his thumb on the back of the hand, and his fingers on the palm, just as Hathor had shown him. A quick twist, and the man's wrist snapped. That brought another gasp of pain, but by then Tammuz had his knee on the man's chest. He drew his knife again, and placed the point against the rogue's throat.

"Move and you die," Tammuz said. Not that he intended to kill the man, but the thief wouldn't know that. Tempting as it might be, cutting the man's throat would cause more problems than it cured, and might even generate ill will from the man's kin or friends.

He remained on the man's chest until En-hedu returned with two guards from the watch, both of them breathing hard. She must have made them run through the lanes.

"What's going on here?" demanded the older of the two. He had at least forty seasons, and wore a sash of red across his shoulder that proclaimed him a leader of ten.

"I told you! These men tried to rob us," En-hedu blurted out, her hands again clutching her bosom in her excitement. "They came in and demanded all our copper, or they would kill us."

Tammuz rose. The leader of the thieves, his eyes filled with pain, tried to speak. Tammuz glanced down and kicked him in the ribs.

"Maybe you attacked them?" The younger guard said, his eyes first taking in the men on the floor, then settling on Tammuz. "You're not from around here, are you?"

"Keep your mouth shut, fool," the leader of ten ordered. "Do you think a man and his wife are going to attack three men? Besides, I know these scum. Thieves, all of them."

"May I speak with you?" Tammuz said, bowing respectfully. He tilted his head toward the darkest corner of the inn and fingered the purse in his hand.

The older guard turned to his companion. "Watch them." He followed Tammuz across the room. "My name is Jarud. What do you want to talk about?"

"Honored guardsman." Tammuz used his humblest voice. "We have just purchased this inn with Merchant Gemama's assistance. We are his clients and under his protection. It may be that, until we're better known in the neighborhood, we might need extra protection from the city's guard. Perhaps you or your men could stop in from time to time, even enjoy a cup of ale with our thanks."

Tammuz held out his hand, with the purse taken from the thugs. "This would be for your trouble, Jarud. And each week, I might be able to give you another copper coin. And I should have some girls in a few days, to repay you for your help."

The guard took the little sack of leather and hefted it, trying to guess how much it contained while he considered the offer. "Mmmn . . . everyone knows Merchant Gemama. A good man, or at least as good as any grasping trader can be. If you are one of his clients . . ." He made up his mind, no doubt influenced as much by the weight of the purse in his hand as Tammuz's claim on Gemama's name. "I'm sure we can stop in now and again. And your name is . . . ?"

"Tammuz. And my wife is En-hedu. We are new to Sumer, and not yet used to the ways of the city."

Jarud glanced down at the knife on Tammuz's belt. "You did well enough against these three."

Tammuz moved closer and half-whispered the words. "My wife

194

struck two of them from behind." He lowered his head as if embarrassed that he had to rely on his wife for assistance.

"We'll take care of these thieves," Jarud said. "The work gangs can always use some new slaves. A few months hard labor will settle them down."

One of the first things Tammuz and En-hedu learned in Sumer was about the work gangs. Supposedly a punishment for petty crimes, few ever returned from their forced labor. With able-bodied slaves in great demand, only those whose friends could pay for their release were ever seen again.

The three men were dragged to their feet and shoved out the door, their former leader cursing as he clutched his broken wrist with his good hand. Tammuz went to the doorway. A small crowd had gathered, peering in at the little drama that had played out with a very different ending from what they had expected. Obviously, these new innkeepers, despite their youth, would have to be treated with respect.

"We're still open for business," Tammuz called out, flashing his white teeth in his best welcoming smile. "Come in and sample our finest ale."

Two laborers looked at each other, shrugged, and stepped inside. "Are you under the protection of the Guard?"

"Of course, as you can see," Tammuz said, clapping the man on the back. "Which means you may drink your fill here without worrying about thieves. And we serve the finest ales and a hearty wine as well. Come in, come in. Welcome to the Kestrel Inn."

En-hedu had decided the inn should have a new name, to distinguish it from its former owner. The Kestrel, a small falcon that hunted during the day, killed its prey with its beak instead of its talons. Common enough in Sumeria and the northern lands, no one would call one a hawk, but Tammuz knew a kestrel could hunt as well as any falcon, despite its diminutive size. In a way, that's how he thought of himself. A member of Akkad's Hawk Clan, but who showed himself as small and agile as a kestrel.

The newly-named Kestrel Inn soon settled down. People came in to gossip about what had just happened. En-hedu served ale until everyone had a cup.

Tammuz moved beside his wife, both of them behind the table that hosted the stock of ale. "In a few days, word will spread through the neighborhood."

She nodded. "We've passed the first test. But only the first. There will be many more in the coming months."

Even with a growing reputation as people to be left alone, Tammuz and En-hedu had plenty to do. Starting up an inn remained a difficult business. Customers of the previous owner drifted off to other haunts. The local wine seller tried to overcharge them, then attempted to pass off the dregs of his stock. En-hedu stood in the man's shop and screamed in his face until he reconsidered.

Then problems started with the delivery. The wine maker's slaves delivered two wine skins, one half empty, and claimed it must have been damaged when they picked it up. No matter that wine stained their chests and chins. En-hedu snatched up a cudgel and demanded they carry it back. She refused to pay for any of the delivery until it was replaced. The slaves no doubt received a good beating from the wine merchant, who found himself covering the cost of the missing goods.

Food, bread, ale, everything had to be haggled over and argued a dozen ways until the Kestrel's suppliers realized that its new owners were anything but young fools fresh from the farm. And once the word got around that Jarud, a leader of the guard, had taken an interest in the place, the attempts to cheat the Kestrel faded away.

Three days later, En-hedu walked the lanes until she reached the marketplace, studying the women who sold themselves. Fortunately, Sumer had a plentiful supply of prostitutes. The recent fighting with Akkad had probably increased the number of women forced to fend for themselves. And just as in Akkad, girls fled the farms of their fathers every day to come to the city, where even selling themselves to anyone who could pay provided a better life than the absolute slavery of husband and farm.

The previous owner of the inn employed three girls who attended his customers, but En-hedu hadn't wanted to keep any of them. They would be much too familiar with the customers, and as liable to cheat the new owners as any grasping merchant or conniving thief. As she strolled around the marketplace, En-hedu ignored most of the women offering themselves. Some were covered with as much dirt as the ground itself, others stank of cheap ale even this early in the day. Many appeared dull or unkempt or diseased, traits that often combined as the women grew older.

Life was especially hard for those with no man to protect and provide for them.

At last En-hedu found two women searching for customers on the edge of the marketplace. Both appeared reasonably clean and presentable, though they looked as if they hadn't eaten well for some time. En-hedu approached them. Since they were working the streets, they obviously didn't have a tavern or inn keeper to shelter and look after them. "Are you looking for work?"

One woman had a few strands of gray hair sprinkled in amongst her dark tresses. She forced a smile to her lips and took a deep breath, pushing her bosom forward and nearly out of her garment. "Yes, mistress. I enjoy comforting a woman. What would you like?"

"Nothing for myself. My name is En-hedu, and my husband and I have just opened a tavern. I'm searching for someone to help serve the ale and take care of the customers." No need to explain what taking care of the customers involved.

The woman bowed respectfully. Anyone who owned a business was entitled to a good deal of respect. "My name is Irkalla, and this is Anu, my daughter."

En-hedu guessed Anu had fourteen or fifteen seasons. She looked much like her mother, except Anu's eyes lacked the sharp wits that marked Irkalla's. The two women resembled sisters rather than mother and daughter, but that made no difference.

"The tavern is called the Kestrel, just off Dockside Lane, opposite the shop of Dragush the carpenter. If you perform your duties well, you'll have a place to sleep, and you can keep a third of what you make from the customers. All the copper will first be paid to me or my husband, of course."

If you let the girls collect the coins, they would try and cheat you, or disappear one night with some man, along with the evening's profits.

"A third is not much," Irkalla said. "Many taverns let the girls keep half their fees."

"If the girls are beautiful and very skilled." En-hedu lifted her hands and let them drop. "Have you worked in a tavern before?"

"I have . . . but not for many years," Irkalla answered, lowering her head.

En-hedu guessed Irkalla had thought about lying, but changed her mind. "Many taverns don't give their girls a place to sleep, or feed them twice a day. That is my offer. If you're not interested . . ."

"Forgive me, mistress," Irkalla said, using the usual sign of respect for any head of the household. "Yes, we are interested, as long as I can keep my daughter with me. She gets frightened easily. We would work very hard to please your customers. When can we start?"

"Today. Now. My husband will want to speak with you as well. He will explain exactly what will be expected from you both."

"Then we will follow you back to the . . . Kestrel, to meet your husband." Irkalla took Anu's hand, and smiled. "Give thanks to our new mistress."

"We thank you," Anu said, dutifully.

The poor girl didn't appear very happy, despite the prospect of having a roof over her head tonight. En-hedu led the way back to the Kestrel, the two women, still holding hands, following behind.

Day by day, the Kestrel took shape. An artisan sketched an outline of the bird on the wall next to the door, then finished by coloring it in shades of gray and rose, a splendid image of the small but cunning aerial hunter. Tammuz expressed his satisfaction by serving the artist a second cup of ale in addition to the supper promised for later that day.

A woman living down the lane agreed to bake bread for the tavern, and her two children fetched buckets of fresh water each morning. After a few days, the baker accepted an offer to come each day at sundown to cook the usual pot of stew, comprised of whatever En-hedu had bartered or purchased that day. With the wine and ale sellers finally delivering what they promised, the Kestrel once again began to attract a good number of customers. Two laborers arrived with a cart loaded with clean sand to fill and smooth over the floor of the inn, which had degenerated into a lopsided layer of dirt that had more rocks than soil.

The location, so close to the docks, naturally attracted plenty of river men, as well as those sailors who traveled along the coast of the great sea. The unruly crowd needed watching, of course, but Tammuz had searched the dockside and marketplace for days until he found a former soldier named Rimaud.

Big and strong, Rimaud had taken an arrow in his leg during a battle with the desert horsemen, and the wound had never fully healed. He walked with a heavy limp, and pain still crossed his face from time to time.

Since he could no longer work all day, or even move quickly, he'd suffered in finding work on the docks. But for Tammuz and the Kestrel, Rimaud would have no trouble keeping order within its confines.

With Jarud and one or two of his guardsmen stopping by almost every night, word soon spread that the honest innkeeper and his wife provided good ale and decent food, in a setting where you could eat and drink without worrying about getting your throat slit or your purse cut.

A few evenings later, just as En-hedu and Irkalla finished serving the day's stew, a man rushed into the Kestrel, and shouted that King Eridu had died, murdered by his steward. Over their ale cups, heads huddled close together. Many whispered words that expressed satisfaction about the death of Eridu One-hand. Not one spoke a word of mourning or respect for the dead man. "Maybe now we'll have peace," one man said, muttering into his ale cup.

No one from the city's watch came that evening, and most of the customers left early, unsure of what the future would bring.

The next morning, Tammuz and En-hedu learned that Eridu's son, Shulgi, had taken command of Sumer and its soldiers.

Soon messengers walked the city's lanes, spreading word that King Shulgi had summoned all the inhabitants of Sumer to the marketplace at noon. Leaving Rimaud to watch the inn, Tammuz and En-hedu followed the crowd, and managed to secure a place just within earshot of their new ruler.

"A handsome man," En-hedu remarked, as Shulgi stepped forward and began to speak.

"Not much older than we are," agreed Tammuz.

After explaining how his father was murdered by his steward, Shulgi proclaimed that he would continue Eridu's rule. Then he called for a time of peace and healing. There would be no further war preparations.

Everyone cheered, and words of praise and support for their new king echoed throughout the marketplace.

Shulgi explained that peace would allow Sumer's people to work and plan for the future. No action would be taken or permitted against Akkadians, and trade would resume with the northern cities at once. King Shulgi also announced that he would send a deputation to Akkad, to inform King Eskkar of his desire for an end to hostilities between the two cities.

By the time Shulgi finished speaking, the throng voiced their approval for their new ruler. The war with Akkad was over, and a great weight had been lifted from Sumer's inhabitants. Mothers would not have to dread their husbands and sons going off to war, and families could work their farms and shops without worrying about being conscripted. Again and again, the crowd declared their thanks for the new king and his policy.

To conclude his speech, Shulgi declared three days of mourning for his father. After which, he continued, there would be three days of feasting to celebrate the coming peace. Of course, the people ignored the first pronouncement and started celebrating. None concerned themselves about the demise of the unloved and aloof Eridu One-hand, who had brought them nothing but grief and disaster.

Tammuz and En-hedu joined in the cheering, waving their hands and shouting as loud as anyone. But that night, when the inn finally quieted down, they lay in their bed and whispered to each other.

"If there is to be peace," Tammuz said, "maybe there will be no need for us to remain in Sumer."

"Yes, if there is to be peace," En-hedu said. "But men may say one thing while they think another. What better way to deceive your own people than to tell them what they want to hear? The next few months will tell us who this Shulgi is, and what he really intends."

"Well, meanwhile we can enjoy ourselves while we wait," Tammuz said. He ran his hand down her shoulder and across her belly, enjoying the smooth flesh that never failed to arouse him. There was a time for war, and a time for pleasure, and he didn't intend to confuse one with the other.

19

Three days later . . .

King Shulgi strode into his house, climbed the stairs two at a time, and stepped into the council chamber where not long ago his father had met with the leaders of the other cities. The house, the Compound, the soldiers, the city, all that once belonged to his father now belonged to Shulgi. The guards who patrolled the Compound reported to him, not Razrek. King Shulgi ruled over every man and woman in Sumer.

That included Kushanna. Eridu had treated Shanna as just another possession, forced to attend to his every beck and call, as much Eridu's property as any servant or slave; in due time, he would have again married her off to another petty noble either for a goodly supply of gold or to further Eridu's needs. There might not be much gold left in Eridu's secret places, but Shulgi intended to make better use of what remained than his father had.

Kushanna entered the meeting chamber a few steps behind her half-brother, and a moment later, Razrek arrived. Two of Shulgi's men guarded the room's entrance, and none of Razrek's men had been permitted into the Compound.

Shulgi unbuckled his sword and dumped it on the table before he sat down. Kushanna sat as well, taking the seat on her brother's right.

"Sit down, Razrek," Shulgi said. "We've much to talk about."

The soldier glanced at Shanna, who favored him with one of her most pleasing smiles. Nevertheless, he sat down warily. "What shall we talk about?"

"The war, of course," Shulgi said. No doubt Razrek hadn't expected Shanna to remain.

"Yesterday you spoke of peace in the marketplace."

"And peace is what we'll have for quite some time. In fact, there will be peace until the day we're ready for war with Akkad. And this time we'll strike so hard a blow that Akkad's walls will fall as easily as their barbarian leader."

"Your father wanted to fight . . ."

"You will never mention my father's name again, Razrek. His plans, his thoughts, all mean nothing. He was a merchant who thought his gold made him a leader of soldiers. You took his gold and let him play out his dreams of glory to further your own ends. You are as much responsible for the debacle on the border as he was."

Razrek bristled at the slur. "I did my best to warn him. Believe me, nothing would give me greater pleasure than killing Eskkar and . . ."

"You will address me as 'king' or 'my lord.' Don't forget that again, not even in private."

The soldier glanced at Kushanna, but her eyes were lowered, her gaze apparently fixed on the table.

"King Shulgi." Razrek bowed his head. "What do you want of me and my men?"

"Your men are no longer yours to command," Kushanna said, her eyes now fixed on Razrek. "From now on, all of them will be under King Shulgi's authority."

Razrek's eyes widened in surprise. "And what will I be doing?"

"You will be raising fresh troops and training them," said Shulgi. "I need bowmen, spearmen, and more horsemen. Thousands of them. You will take what gold I can spare, build a camp on the edge of the western desert, and start recruiting."

"But that would take months, years . . . Lord Shulgi."

"Yes, I know. It may be as much as two years before we are ready. But I'm still young, and I can afford to be patient. Our plans will take time to bear fruit. But there is much to do in the coming days to prepare for our attack. This war will be won not just on some battlefield, but in every city on the Tigris. Our victory must destroy Akkad so completely that it can never rise again. The land between the rivers will be ruled from Sumer."

"What will the people say when they learn of your plans?"

"They will not learn of them until I am ready to tell them. By then they will be as eager to fight Akkad as any bride on her wedding night is eager to please her husband. Until that day, we will talk only of peace and trade." Shulgi leaned closer to Razrek and placed his hands on the sword resting on the table. "Until that day, only the three of us will know my plans. So if people begin to speak of war, I'll know who is responsible."

"Then you already have made plans?"

"Kushanna and I have spoken of many things." Shulgi didn't bother to elaborate. Instead, he lifted his hand from the sword and placed it on her arm. "Meanwhile, you will be well paid, and when we complete our conquest, you'll have more gold and slaves and power than you can imagine."

"I can imagine quite a lot . . . Lord Shulgi."

"I'm sure you can, Razrek. Just make sure you remember to keep silent. We will speak only of peace while we prepare for war."

"People will notice sooner or later, Lord."

Shulgi nodded. "Eventually. But when they do, we'll tell them we're arming against the western raiders, or the barbarians to the north-east. Which, as it happens, is going to be true."

"We're at peace with the desert tribes." Razrek's face betrayed his confusion.

The Tanukhs and Salibs were desert dwellers who lived on Sumeria's western border, along the edge of the desert. The two tribes had fought each other off and on for as long as anyone could remember, occasionally joining forces to attack the Sumerian cities. But that tactic had failed in the last ten years, as the cities increased their strength, pushing the tribes back to the edge of the desert and beyond. In time, the tribes decided it was simpler to accept Eridu's gold than try to wrest it from Sumer's grasp.

"Yes, my father bought that peace with plenty of his gold. But soon you are going to approach the Tanukhs, to offer an alliance. In return for supporting Sumer, we will help them destroy the Salibs."

"Why the Tanukhs? We've dealt more often with the Salib tribes in the past."

"Because the Tanukhs are more numerous, and because their lands are farther to the north. That will make it easier for them to raid Akkadian territory when the times comes. And by waging our battles in the southern desert, there is less likelihood of Akkad discovering what we're doing until it's too late."

"What if the Tanukhs don't want to fight the Salibs, then what?"

"That will be your first new task, Razrek," Shulgi said. "You'll have to convince them to side with us. Agree to fight at their side. Promise them anything they need in trade. Use gold, threats, whatever it takes."

"And what do we want from them?"

"Horses, of course, and men. The Tanukhs must agree to help us make war on Akkad when the time comes. In that way, we'll be able to field a large number of mounted fighters to carry the battle north."

Razrek's brow furrowed.

"You seem uneasy about this," Kushanna said. "The western desert is the perfect place to train our own fighters."

Razrek glanced from Kushanna to Shulgi, who seemed unconcerned about hearing a woman's advice. "You want us to fight alongside the Tanukhs?"

"Oh, yes, Razrek." Shulgi leaned back and took Kushanna's hand in his own. "We're all going to fight the Salibs, until they're destroyed or driven deep into the desert where they belong. This way our soldiers will learn to fight against a real enemy, not wooden posts in training camp."

"The next Sumerian army that marches north will know how to fight, and how to win," Kushanna added. "It may take a few years to prepare everything, but this time Lord Shulgi will have experienced fighters at his back to face Eskkar."

"And what else do you have planned . . . Lord Shulgi?"

"Oh, there is more, much more. You will learn everything in time, after you have proven your loyalty. I may even let you rule in my name in Akkad, after we conquer the city."

Razrek considered that interesting possibility. He eased back in his chair. "And when will all this begin?"

"Tomorrow. Return here at noon, and we will decide what you will need, gold, men, everything will be planned for." Shulgi took a breath and turned to Kushanna. "Is there anything else for Razrek?"

"No, my king, except to tell Razrek to make sure his men know who commands them from now on."

"Ah, yes. We wouldn't want you to forget that." He saw the look of dismay on Razrek's face. "Don't worry, you'll soon raise a new force of men, one much greater than the handful you have now. Meanwhile, our work starts tomorrow. So go back to the camp, and tell all your men that peace is at hand. You'll keep training them, of course, but the fact that

Sumer no longer has an enemy should turn that into a pleasant enough task. And now you may return to your men."

Razrek accepted the sudden dismissal smoothly enough. "Yes, my king." He stood, bowed, and left the chamber.

Shulgi waited until Razrek had gone, then rose and went to the guards stationed at the door. "Make sure no one disturbs my rest."

He closed the door, barred it, then leaned his back against it while he faced Kushanna.

She smiled, then lifted her arms over her head to stretch. "And now what do you desire, my king?"

Shulgi strode toward her. "Get up."

She rose and faced him, her breasts almost touching his chest. She ran her tongue over her lips.

"Take off your dress."

"Yes, my lord." Taking her time, she reached down and gathered the dress in her hands. Slowly she pulled it up, higher, until the light brown patch of hair beneath her belly lay open to his gaze. Shanna held the dress there for a moment, then lifted it higher, until her full breasts were revealed, their pink tips already hard with desire. Suddenly she jerked the dress up over her head and let it fall to the floor. She shook her hair to straighten it, the long brown tresses swirling over her shoulders. Her hands went to her hips. She spread her legs apart and moved closer until her body pressed against his.

"Is this what you want to see, my king? I hope my body pleases you." She ran her tongue over the base of his neck.

With an oath Shulgi swept his arms around her. "Your body would please the gods, Shanna, my queen, my love." He leaned down and kissed the warm lips that lifted to his. Shanna returned the kiss, then her tongue darted inside his mouth, and her leg lifted up and wrapped around his thigh.

"Perhaps you would find me more attractive in bed, my king. Your queen would like to please you in many ways."

His manhood had swelled into a solid rod against the touch of her leg. Shulgi picked her up, carried her into the bedroom, and tossed her onto the bed.

Shanna laughed as she bounced on the mattress, then held her head on one elbow as Shulgi pulled off his tunic. He moved onto the bed and knelt astride her, his staff brushing her lips. With a smooth motion, she lifted her head up and took him in her mouth, her hands reaching around to clutch him firmly.

"Ahhhha," he gasped, as a wave of pleasure passed through him. "For this . . . I would kill a dozen men."

She looked up at him. "You will kill many more than that for me, my king."

Half the afternoon had passed before Shulgi and Kushanna once again sat at the table. This time she sat across from him. "We need to talk, Shulgi. At least for awhile."

"Talk about what?" He still could see her naked in his bed, kneeling on her hands and knees as he entered her from behind, pounding against her soft flesh, while she moaned in delight.

"Talk about the destruction of Akkad."

That took his mind off her body. "What about Akkad?"

"It will not be easy to defeat this Eskkar and his bowmen. And the walls of Akkad are strong and high. We will need to set many things in motion to destroy him and his city."

"And what do you suggest? Already Razrek knows that we will need more men."

"There are many other tasks that we must begin. First, we will need more informers and spies in Sumer and the other cities. In Akkad, Trella has her agents everywhere, and we must do the same. Nothing must happen in any part of Sumeria that we do not know about. The other cities are almost as dangerous to us as Akkad. The more we know about what happens in Larsa and Isin and the others, the better. Then we must dispatch spies to Akkad as well, so that we may learn about Eskkar's plans and discover the size of his army. When he becomes aware of the threat to his lands, he may even try to strike you down here in Sumer, so we must protect you from that danger as well."

"All that will cost plenty of gold."

"Trella spends that gold in Akkad without hesitation, and with no complaints from her husband. Can you do any less? Would you risk your victory over a few gold coins spent to gather information?"

"No, I suppose not. What else must we do?"

"Trella will soon have her agents here in Sumer, if indeed she does not already. We must find them out, and get rid of as many as possible.

The longer we can keep our plans a secret, the stronger we will be."

The idea of Eskkar and Trella spying on him hadn't occurred to Shulgi, but he didn't want to admit that. Shanna certainly had her wits about her. "Spend whatever you need," he said. "Just remember I need all the gold I can get to buy men and weapons."

"A few more men or swords won't make that much difference," she said. "Not if you don't learn everything about your enemy."

He sighed. "I suppose you're right."

"Good. Then I will start in the morning. You will also need to stockpile weapons, thousands of them, and I think I know how that can be done without anyone noticing, and without spending too much gold."

"How will you accomplish that little trick?"

"We will buy the weapons from the land of the Indus. Our traders go there now and again. I'm sure those barbarians will be willing to sell us all the swords, knives and spears we want. We can have the traders deliver what we buy to any of the cities, or even the western lands where you'll be training the men. That way, it will not look as if our craftsmen are working night and day outfitting an army. And perhaps we can establish our own forges in those outlying areas, staffed by slaves, to make weapons for us. That will keep the greedy craftsmen from asking such high prices for their goods."

Casting bronze swords and other edged blades took both skill and time, as well as plenty of copper and tin. He realized that building an empire might require more than just raising an army. Shulgi poured himself a half cup of wine, then filled the rest with water. "That is a good idea."

"I have another. If we can manage it, that is. We should try and make contact with the Alur Meriki. Maybe when we're ready to go to war, we can encourage them to attack Akkad once again."

"How will that help us? The Alur Meriki are not as strong as they once were. Eskkar can sit behind his wall and slaughter them even easier than he did before."

"Eskkar will not be there," Shanna said. "When you destroy Eskkar and his army, you must do it in our lands, or along the border. He must be drawn south, and he must bring all his forces with him. If we can find a way to have the Alur Meriki strike at that time, the city may not have enough men to defend itself. Even if the barbarians fail to capture the city, they can devastate the countryside, burn the crops, even foul the wells. Eskkar's soldiers will lose heart, and many will want to return to Akkad rather than fight your men. All of this will make your own success when you attack the city easier."

"If we could get the Alur Meriki . . . they certainly would like a chance to pay Akkad back for their defeat. And it would cost us almost nothing to encourage them."

"Meanwhile, you will recruit and train an army of men, thousands of them, more than any man has ever assembled. When you meet Eskkar and his forces, you must not only defeat them, but you must crush them completely. There must be none to escape back to Akkad and defend its walls. You must have an army so vast that no matter what tricks and schemes Eskkar comes up with, you can still destroy him on the battlefield."

"And how many men will that be?"

"I think you will need twenty thousand soldiers, perhaps more, to defeat him."

"Twenty thousand! No man has ever raised and commanded such a force. It would take years . . ."

"No, it must be done in less than two years," Shanna said firmly. "If we stretch and squeeze every gold coin from every merchant and city in Sumeria, we will just have enough to last that long. If we do not capture Akkad to regain our wealth, we will be ruined, our people starving. And if that happens, the farmers and villagers will rise up against us."

"But so many men . . . Eskkar cannot raise a quarter of that number. There aren't that many men of fighting age in the north."

"Nevertheless, that's what you will need to defeat him. He is resourceful, and despite everything we do, Trella and he will soon learn that we are preparing for war. And his soldiers are battle hardened, as Razrek says. They have already fought many battles, which makes them more dangerous. Don't forget, Eskkar will make his own preparations to defeat us, even as you prepare your men. And that is why he must be drawn to Sumeria and overwhelmed by your soldiers."

"When will this great battle be fought, my bloodthirsty queen?"

She smiled at the compliment. "In twenty-two months. The crops will be in, the soldiers trained, the weapons delivered, and our people ready. And that will be the best time for the Alur Meriki to strike. If we wait longer than that, the Akkadians will have gathered enough men to march on Sumer."

"Is that enough time?" The breadth of her plan stunned him, but the thought of commanding twenty thousand men in a battle . . . he would be remembered for a thousand years. With that many men, he would rule all of Mesopotamia, and possibly even the lands beyond. It would truly be an empire worthy of Sumer, and of himself.

"It will have to be," Shanna said. "Meanwhile, you must do as Eskkar has done. Train with your soldiers, fight as many battles with the western raiders as you can, make your men have confidence in you and trust your judgment. If the soldiers in your army stand behind you, none of the other cities in Sumeria will dare to disobey your rule. And when the Akkadian soldiers learn of your skills, they will begin to doubt their own leader. They will remember that Eskkar is a barbarian, and that he grows old. When you meet him in battle, he will have at least thirty-five seasons, perhaps more. Too old to fight himself, too old to command his army."

War, as everyone knew, was best left to the very young. Razrek had over thirty seasons, and he had grown soft of late.

"Twenty thousand men," Shulgi mused. "With so many, I can rule the world."

"With so many, *we* can rule the world. The empire of Sumeria will rule the land in every direction."

"How long have you been planning all this?"

"Since our fool of a father decided he wanted to wage war against Akkad. I sat at his side at every meeting, every war council, every dinner with Razrek, while he planned his pathetic venture. I could have told him he would fail, but, of course, he would not have listened to me. So I used the time to make my own plans, to decide what you and I would do if Eridu were out of the way. I gave thanks to the gods when Eskkar defeated him. If Eridu had won . . . I still shudder at the thought."

"With so many soldiers, we will not fail."

"If you heed my words, my Lord Shulgi, we will not fail. Together we can build an empire, and I can help you rule it. In time, gold, slaves, the most beautiful women, everything in that empire will be yours."

"Including you, my dear sister."

"Including me, my dear brother." She took a deep breath and leaned provocatively toward him. "Am I not worthy to be your queen?"

"More than worthy. Tomorrow I will tell the people that you are to be my bride, their queen."

"Then, my lord and master, let me thank you again tonight for the honor you will bestow on me."

20

Ten days after Eskkar's march with the spearmen, he and Grond splashed their horses across the Tigris. Accompanied by Hathor and twenty horsemen, they departed the northern village of Bisitun and rode to the north-west. The trip had taken months to arrange. Sisuthros, who ruled Bisitun in Akkad's name, had sent word through his traders that Lord Eskkar wished to meet with the leader of the Ur Nammu. But the clan of steppe warriors had migrated to the west, and it took endless days of often aimless and always dangerous riding to make contact with them. At last a message arrived at Akkad that a time and place to meet had been arranged.

As soon as he received word, Eskkar had dispatched Hathor and a group of horsemen to Bisitun. Only after Hathor's horsemen had departed Akkad did they learn their true destination. Meanwhile, Eskkar and Grond took passage on one of Yavtar's ships, and reached Bisitun five days later, where they rejoined Hathor and his men.

After a single night in relative comfort in Bisitun, Eskkar resumed the journey to the north-west. All were mounted on good animals, and each day they covered plenty of ground. After three days of hard riding, they passed into the rugged and mostly empty land of rolling hills and rocky crags. Wild goats watched their progress from the heights, and hawks soared overhead, but they encountered few men. The dry soil made for poor farming, and the ever present danger from bandits or barbarians made the occasional inhabitants wary of strangers.

For Eskkar, the journey provided a chance to forget the troubles and problems of Akkad, and enjoy the pleasure of traveling long distances by horse once again. The clear air, now with a hint of coolness, cleansed the smells of the crowded city from his body. And the trip provided time for Eskkar to grow close to his men, something he did at every opportunity.

"The more men know you," Trella said to him many times, "the more loyal to your cause they will be." So he took advantage of these days of riding with the soldiers. They spoke about weapons, horses, women, all the things fighting men had discussed and argued about since the dawn of time.

They remained alert for danger at all times. The land they traversed belonged to no one, though the Ur Nammu rode through these places often. Akkad had established a truce of sorts with the Ur Nammu, and both sides had managed to avoid conflict for over two years. They had fought together twice against the Alur Meriki, and after the final victory, Eskkar had established a small trading settlement north of Bisitun, to facilitate trade with the Ur Nammu.

Twice each year, traders from Akkad and Bisitun met with bands of Ur Nammu. The warriors had plenty of gold, usually taken from the dead bodies of their enemies, for which they had little use, and they needed the tools and higher-quality bronze weapons that the villagers could produce more efficiently. The trade benefited both the horse clan and the Akkadians. But Eskkar knew how fragile such agreements could be. A slur on some warrior's honor, an insulting glance, a drunken brawl, any incident could trigger an outbreak of raiding and looting along Akkad's northern border. And right now Eskkar needed an ally, not another problem to distract him from the enemy in the south.

On the afternoon of the third day, the Akkadians saw three riders watching them from a distant hilltop. Eskkar gave the order to halt. The horses could use a brief rest, and the lack of movement, either to attack or flee, evidenced the newcomer's peaceful intentions.

"Is that them?" Hathor, like most of the horsemen riding with Eskkar, had never encountered any of the steppe warriors before.

"Could be," Eskkar said, "could be anyone." He turned to their guide, a leader of ten from Bisitun named Meskalum. "How close are we to the meeting ground?"

Meskalum moved his horse forward to join the leaders. "Not far now, captain. We should be there by sundown."

Eskkar made the calculation. About ten or twelve more miles, if the guide didn't miss a landmark and get lost. Even after all these years, he still disliked following someone else's lead. But he had no choice. No man could master every trail and landmark in such a vast land. "Then it's not likely there would be any other bands of warriors nearby. Break out the standard."

Grond pulled the yellow streamer, as long as a man was tall, from his sack. Meskalum fastened it to the tip of his bow. The wind lifted the cloth and sent it billowing.

"Everyone keep your eyes open," Eskkar said. "It's an old barbarian trick to keep your attention on one band while another slips up on you from behind. Meskalum, take the point."

With the guide out front, Eskkar set the pace at an easy canter. He didn't want to tire the horses, since one never knew if they would be needed to run or fight. And whether they reached the agreed upon place by sundown or not didn't matter. Meetings like this, arranged so long in advance and through so many intermediaries over great distances, could never be exact as to time. Five, even ten days early or late would be considered normal.

The riders continued the journey and, after a time, the horsemen on the hillside matched their pace and direction. As the sun descended, the two groups of riders began to converge.

"Looks like they know where we're headed," Grond observed. He'd fought against men such as these twice before, and had a healthy respect for their fighting skills.

"Let's hope they're not getting ready to ambush us," Hathor said. "All this empty land – no villages or farms – makes me nervous."

Everyone remained alert, and Eskkar stopped twice more, to study the land and the obvious ambush sites. A little before sundown they topped a hill and saw a meandering stream, bordered with willow trees. Beneath their shade, a thick belt of grass grew down to the water's edge. Two tents marked a campsite, and the blackened remains of a fire pit showed even from the top of the hill. A small herd of horses, penned in by a rope corral and guarded by a mounted rider, gave Eskkar a quick count of the warriors. He halted the troop once again while he examined the terrain ahead.

"Twenty, maybe," Grond said, coming to the same conclusion. "Maybe twenty-five, counting the three behind us."

By then the Akkadians had been spotted by the warriors in the camp.

Within moments, a yellow standard fastened to a lance waved at them.

Eskkar grunted in relief. "That's the Ur Nammu. My thanks to you, Meskalum." Whether the guide knew the land as well as he claimed, or had just gotten lucky, he deserved a word of praise in front of his companions.

They cantered down the hill. The three warriors behind them swung wide around the Akkadians, and raced recklessly toward the camp, their horses flinging clods of dirt high into the air, shouts floating across the land as they urged on their mounts.

Eskkar smiled at the display of horsemanship. In his youth he might have attempted such a ride, but no longer. A rider needed to be astride his mount ten hours a day for years to master that kind of riding. As the Akkadians drew near, a warrior separated from the group and walked toward them. When they approached within fifty paces, Eskkar swung down from his horse.

"Wait here a moment," he said, then moved toward the approaching warrior.

"Greetings, Subutai, chief of the Ur Nammu."

"Welcome to our camp, Eskkar of Akkad."

The two men clasped arms in the way of the warrior, then paced side by side back to the camp. Eskkar waved his men forward. Subutai had marked a place for them about two hundred paces from the tents. The Akkadians would have easy access to the river without getting too close to his own camp.

Eskkar and his men tended to their horses first, making sure the animals were watered in the stream, and the Akkadians used the one rope they had brought with them to make a rough corral of their own, winding the cord around two willow trees and a bush. Not much more was needed to keep the mounts penned in. With plenty of water and grass to eat, they weren't likely to stray.

With the horses taken care of, Eskkar washed his hands and face in the stream, another gesture of politeness. To meet with a clan chief was a serious matter, and it would not do to appear covered with sweat and dirt. Eskkar drank his fill from the stream, but shook his head at Hathor's offer of a drink from one of the two wineskins they'd brought with them.

"You'll come with me, Hathor. By custom, each clan leader brings one subcommander with him, so that there may be no misunderstanding or forgetting of what is said."

They strode across the grass to the Ur Nammu campsite, where Subutai and another warrior waited for them. Subutai led the way upstream to a small patch of grass a hundred paces from the river. The two leaders sat facing each other. Unlike villagers, who might talk half a day before getting down to business, barbarians preferred to take care of serious matters first.

Meanwhile, warriors from both sides watched the proceedings with interest. The two Ur Nammu warriors eyed Hathor with curiosity. Probably neither had ever seen someone from the land of Egypt.

Eskkar introduced the Egyptian as his subcommander, then faced Subutai's commander.

"It's good to see you again, Fashod," Eskkar said, nodding at Subutai's second in command. "Have your men been in camp here long?"

Fashod, caught by surprise, couldn't prevent a smile from crossing his face. "Only three days, Lord Eskkar. And I am honored that you remember me at all."

"I always try to remember brave men who have fought at my side," Eskkar said. In truth, he had to strain his wits to recall the man's name when he first saw him. Two years was a long time, despite Trella's constant admonition to try and memorize every man's face and name.

Eskkar explained that Hathor didn't speak the language of the steppes. That proved to be no problem, as Subutai and Fashod both spoke the language of the dirt-eaters well enough.

"Your wits remain quick, Eskkar," Subutai said, nodding in satisfaction. A compliment to one of his men reflected on him as well. "Your mighty city grows stronger each day, and even in the far north we hear of Akkad's power."

"You have grown in strength, Subutai." The last time Eskkar had seen the warrior he'd been thin and undernourished. Now firm muscle covered his frame, the result of long hours on the back of a horse and plenty of meat in his diet. "And I hear your people have increased as well."

"We are much stronger, Eskkar. Now there are almost two hundred warriors under my standard. In another ten years, we'll be almost as strong as we were in the past." He smiled at the prospect. "The Ur Nammu clan has grown as well. After the fighting ended, there were many women without husbands or fathers abandoned in these lands, and these have sought our protection. Now there are many children playing around the campfires."

"Then I am glad for my friend," Eskkar said. "Perhaps I can offer a way to help you increase your strength even faster."

"I wondered what brought you so far north, even before the next trade gathering."

That meeting would have meant waiting another three months – far too long in Eskkar's mind.

"A new enemy of Akkad has arisen in the land of Sumeria," Eskkar began. "I wanted to speak with you about them."

"The land by the great sea," Subutai said. "I saw it once, when I was but a young boy barely able to sit on a horse."

Eskkar explained the growing conflict between the two cities, and described the recent battle. Subutai listened impassively until Eskkar finished.

"So a new war is coming to Akkad," Eskkar said. "And this time we will be facing not only a new enemy, but a different kind of warfare. The next conflict will be fought over claims to land, not the grasslands your warriors need for their horses, but the land needed by our farmers and herdsmen. And when this war comes, it will require a new way of fighting. This time I may have to take the fight to my enemy. Our warriors will meet face to face, both on foot and on horseback. In that kind of fighting, numbers are important, and Sumer will have a great advantage in men. So I must find a way to offset the greater numbers of my enemy."

"And that brings you here, to the Ur Nammu?"

"Yes. I need horses, a great many horses. Good horses, and good breeding stock, too. In a few seasons, I want to have at least five hundred well-trained and mounted warriors to protect my foot soldiers."

"There are not that many horses in these lands," Subutai said, avoiding a direct response.

Good mounts were scarce. And even when they were plentiful, not all proved large and strong enough to carry a man and his weapons. To be considered as a war horse, the animal needed to be at least fourteen hands high. Every warrior – and even the villagers – tried to breed the animals so as to increase each offspring's size and strength. Still, some smaller animals made excellent mounts, while other, larger horses lacked the stamina and speed needed for a war horse. The breeder's skill, Eskkar knew, lay in quickly determining each horse's capabilities.

"Good horseflesh is scarce," Eskkar agreed. "I will gather horses from every direction. But here, in your lands, are bred the finest mounts. And you could breed more, if you had a reason to do so. Wherever and however you obtain them, I will trade tools, goods, whatever you need, with your people."

Subutai rocked back and forth for a moment, always taking his time before replying. "We have a few surplus horses, but numbers such as you need . . ."

"This war will take time, perhaps years before it begins. I know that no one has as many mounts as I will need, but I must start gathering them now, as I must begin training the men to care for them, and to learn to ride and fight."

Eskkar had his eyes on Subutai, but he caught a glimpse of Fashod, who let a flash of excitement cross his face.

"And if I can supply you with a good number of horses . . . you can provide tools, weapons, cooking pots, all the bronze we need?"

"Yes, as well as grain, cloth, food, wine, even cattle or sheep." Eskkar kept his features impassive, but he thought he read something in Subutai's body language. Trella had helped Eskkar understand the subtle signs given off by a man's face and body. He guessed the Ur Nammu leader had extra horses, or at least knew where he could get them.

"Then we may be able to help you, Eskkar. That is, if you can break wild stock."

Now it was Eskkar's turn to rock back and forth while he considered his answer. The Ur Nammu had found a wild horse herd somewhere. Such animals would be beyond the villagers' skill to train. Villagers could breed and raise horses, and teach them to accept a rider, but a wild animal, that was different. Only the most skilled riders could break a horse that had lived most of its life running free.

"I have only a few men who could handle such animals. Could you not break the new mounts, and exchange your trained horses with us?"

"Where are you intending to hold these horses? In Akkad?"

Subutai clearly wasn't willing to talk about any exchanges, at least not yet.

"No, I will establish camps north of Bisitun," said Eskkar, "most likely on the west bank of the river. Even a place such as this would be suitable. There are many small valleys in these lands with good grass where horses could be held. Perhaps your warriors could break the animals for us, until my men learn how to master the skill."

"Yes, that's what I was thinking," Subutai said. "I have warriors who could break horses for you. In fact, I have too many young warriors, all eager for battle. With the Alur Meriki far to the east, there are few opportunities for them to prove themselves. I'm sure ten or fifteen would be glad for the chance to demonstrate their horse skills."

"Then for that help, I would be grateful," Eskkar said. "How big a horse herd did you find?"

Subutai smiled. "I see I must learn not to betray my thoughts so easily. At least a hundred horses. It was far to the north, at the base of the mountains. We took a few last year, and drove the rest into the foothills, then blocked their way out. They should still be there, or most of them. There may even be more. The grass was good, with plenty of water. We saw some fine stallions."

If the Ur Nammu could deliver a few hundred horses and help break them, Eskkar could assemble a basic cavalry force in months, instead of years. With the additional animals he would obtain through trading, he might have more horses in the next six months than men to ride them.

"My men at Bisitun are almost ready to establish the first camp. As you bring in mounts, we will trade for them. If you agree."

Subutai turned toward Fashod, who nodded his agreement. They had worked with Eskkar before, and accepted him as an equal. Now he was glad he'd come himself. The Ur Nammu would not have dealt with anyone else from Akkad or any other place for that matter.

Eskkar leaned back. There was still much to talk about, of course, but the basic arrangement had been made. In true warrior fashion, the details would be decided between Hathor and Fashod. That way, if there were disagreements, the leaders could correct the problems without anyone losing honor.

"You have something else to say?"

The question caught Eskkar by surprise, unaware that his own thoughts could be read on his face. The idea of so many horses arriving so soon had not been part of his plan. But now that the possibility existed, he might be able to improve on his original idea.

"I was thinking about bows for the riders. Your people can make them as well as mine. They would be a powerful weapon for my men."

"You think you can train men to shoot arrows from the back of a horse?" Even Subutai couldn't keep the skepticism out of his voice.

Eskkar grinned. "Not at first. But perhaps a few of your young men, with someone like Fashod to control them, could help train my young men in the ways of fighting from horseback."

Subutai laughed, the sound carrying across the grassland. "Dirt-eaters fighting on horseback! Enough talk for today," he said, rising to his feet. He extended his hand and pulled Eskkar upright. "Tonight we will feast, then tomorrow we will talk again. I wish to hear all about your new enemy, these Sumerians."

Eskkar felt the strength in Subutai's grip. The warrior had indeed regained his full strength. "Then we'll feast," he said. "I brought two wineskins from Bisitun for you and your men. That should be enough to get most of them decently drunk."

Later that night, after the feasting and singing and drinking, Eskkar checked the guards and the horses before readying himself for sleep. His head hurt from the third cup of wine – more than he'd drunk in some time. A footfall crunched in the dirt, and he looked up to see Subutai walking toward him.

The Ur Nammu leader squatted down beside him. "Eskkar, I think I may be able to offer you more help, if you can find a way."

"I'll take any help I can." He wondered why Subutai was bringing this up now, and without Fashod or his men present.

"As I said, I have plenty of young warriors, and not enough fighting or riding to keep them occupied. With nothing to accomplish, they grow restive. They fight with each other, and make trouble over women and horses."

And question their leaders, Eskkar knew. That's why the warrior clans needed to keep their young men fighting. "Warriors need to ride," Eskkar agreed, still not sure where this talk was heading.

"If you were interested in taking some of them into your army for a time, they would make fine fighters for you. They could learn much about the ways of war, and practice their skills on your enemy."

A force of steppe warriors, even a small one, would be a blessing from the gods, Eskkar knew. They could act as scouts and messengers, and could harass the enemy as well. "If any of your warriors wished to join my men, they would be welcome."

"Just for a year or two," Subutai cautioned. "I don't want them deciding to stay with your army when they're needed here. But what they would learn would be very useful."

It certainly would, Esskar decided. They would learn more about Esskar's army and his forces, their strengths and weaknesses, than he would have cared to share with the Ur Nammu, but that couldn't be avoided. Like Subutai, Esskar understood that the day might come when they faced each other across a battlefield. But such a day would not come soon, he knew.

"I think we can make a fair arrangement, Subutai, that satisfies you and your needs."

"Good. We'll speak of this again in a few days. Better to let my men get used to the idea of delivering and breaking horses for you first."

When the leader of the Ur Nammu had gone, Esskar stretched out on his blanket. A force of warriors under his command. Something he'd dreamed about as a young boy. He found the idea strangely satisfying, and knew his father's spirit would approve of his son leading horsemen into battle. The Ur Nammu might not be the Alur Meriki, but they shared a common ancestry, both clans riding down from the distant northern steppes many generations ago.

With their skills, Subutai's warriors would make a powerful addition to his future army. There would be risks, of course, and plenty of problems, but he felt sure he could manage it, with a little luck. Hathor would help, and he would make a fine leader of Akkad's horse fighters.

Esskar wrapped his blanket around him and closed his eyes. Horses and fighting men from the Ur Nammu. Trella would be pleased.

21

L ittle more than a month after King Shulgi took control of Sumer, En-hedu stood with her hands on her hips, looking about the crowded tavern full of happy patrons. Since their arrival in Sumer, both she and Tammuz had worked hard, but at last the Kestrel Tavern had settled into a satisfying routine. Irkalla and Anu handed out the food and ale, and serviced the customers, those able and willing to pay for their special services. The cook, helped by En-hedu and the girls, made the evening stew, while Rimaud carried ale and anything else of bulk to the Kestrel by day, and kept the crowd under control at night.

With Tammuz's reputation in the neighborhood established by knocking the three thieves unconscious, and Rimaud's massive arms and shoulders, not to mention the short sword he wore day and night, only the very foolish or very drunk dared to make trouble. Guardsman Jarud stopped by almost every night, often with two or three of his men who either had done something well during the day, or possibly just avoided their leader's ire. He usually arrived well after sundown, to enjoy a late-night cup of ale. His presence helped convince the gangs who lurked in the marketplace and roamed the lanes at night that it made more sense to leave the Kestrel and its new owners alone, and concentrate on more vulnerable and less popular prey.

Serving decent food and strong ale, the Kestrel soon earned a good reputation, especially among those sailing or working on the riverboats and docks, located only a few hundred paces away. Patrons could drink themselves senseless, fall asleep on the floor, and still find their purses, not to mention their throats, intact in the morning. Rimaud even accompanied an occasional sailor back to his boat at closing time or got them to the docks just after dawn.

Tammuz and En-hedu still labored from dawn to dusk each day. Everything and everyone had to be under someone's watch, lest problems arose. Even good customers would cheerfully take advantage of any lapse of the owners' guard, either by stealing ale or pilfering from another customer who might have drunk too much.

Still, people came to the Kestrel to eat, drink, meet and talk with their friends, or just to find a safe place to sleep at night. That kept the little tavern open for business from dawn until well after dark. En-hedu and Tammuz made sure that one or both of them were present to keep an eye on things at all times, though they soon realized that Rimaud could be trusted as well. His gratitude for their concern showed on his broad face. He made sure that neither the customers nor the staff could take advantage of the Kestrel's owners.

Like any trade or craft, the owners also had to exercise constant care to maintain a profitable business. En-hedu kept track of all the expenses, and informed Tammuz that, in another month or two, the Kestrel would be turning a profit. That was important, not only because they had to earn their own bread, but because an unprofitable inn that remained in business would attract suspicion. And there were plenty of informers, who dropped in to hear the latest talk on the river, ready to take notice of anything out of the ordinary. En-hedu and her husband soon knew who they were. Their clumsy attempts to gather loose talk and draw information from the northern boatmen made many of the regular customers laugh.

En-hedu was working alone one afternoon when a man entered the Kestrel, his eyes squinting into the shadowy interior. Not much light entered from the door or the roof hole, and it was still too early in the day to start a fire. He glanced around, then went to a table and sat down. The tavern was almost empty, except for two drunks snoring their heads off in the corner. Tammuz and Rimaud were out buying ale, while the girls were trying to snatch some sleep in the tiny room that they shared with Rimaud and those clients who were willing to pay extra.

En-hedu reached the table, sizing up the potential customer. He looked like a man with a coin or two in his purse. "Welcome to the Kestrel. Ale costs one copper coin for two mugs, or one cup and a loaf of bread." It was always best to get the prices clear in the customer's mind right away.

Otherwise, they would claim they'd been distracted and hadn't realized what things cost. Or they claimed to have forgotten, which she could almost believe from some of the more ignorant farm workers, especially after they'd drunk a few cups of ale. By now En-hedu had heard every trick and sad story a customer could come up with.

The man smiled, reached into his tunic, and pulled out a leather pouch that remained looped around his neck. "And to stay the night, how much is that?"

A customer with ready coins always received a smile and a softer tone. "For two copper coins, you can have as much ale as you like, with stew for supper and a place to sleep tonight." That wasn't as generous as it sounded. Almost no one could drink more than three or four cups of the powerful brew. One customer had downed six cups before passing out and cracking his head on a table. He didn't wake up until nearly noon the next day.

A man with plenty of coin might also be interested in Irkalla or Anu, especially after a few cups of ale. En-hedu would point this one out to Irkalla. The woman knew how to take advantage of such situations, and sometimes ended up doing little more than bring the man into her chamber and put him to bed. In the morning she would tell the confused customer how strong and virile he was.

"Two copper coins, then," the man said. "My name is Malok. I just arrived today from Akkad."

En-hedu showed no sign of recognition at the man's name. Lady Trella had said they would be contacted by a man named Malok. The name was half the password.

"If I were you, I wouldn't be quick to tell people I'm from Akkad. Travelers from that evil city are still not very welcome in Sumer."

Despite Shulgi's announcement of peace with his northern neighbor, people's feelings took a long time to change. And offering that bit of advice meant nothing. Sumer's spies kept watch on the docks, and would take note of anyone from Akkad, even a lowly riverboat crewman.

"I grew up here in Sumeria," Malok said. "I only attend my master, who travels up and down the river, wherever the trading takes him."

"Well, I hope you'll return to the Kestrel many times," En-hedu said.

She scooped up the two coins and went to the ale table. Pouring a generous amount into the wooden cup, she carried it back to the table. "Supper won't be ready until just before dark. The cook hasn't even started."

"The ale will do until then." Malok took a mouthful of ale, and sighed with pleasure. "And you are ...?"

"My name is En-hedu. My husband Tammuz and I own this place."

"I knew an En-hedu in my village where I grew up. A place called Ubaid. You remind me of her."

En-hedu laughed. "I am her, Malok. I remember now. There was a boy named Malok, son of Grimald."

"No, Grimald was my uncle. Tibor was my father."

They laughed at the seemingly chance encounter. En-hedu felt satisfied. Their little string of falsehoods agreed. Malok was the first messenger from Annok-sur, the man who would deliver and carry messages back to Akkad.

Like any old friends reunited, they spoke of Ubaid, and En-hedu realized that Malok was indeed familiar with the village. He'd probably gone there just as she and Tammuz had done, spending just enough time to blend in. Malok had chosen a good time to visit the Kestrel. That timing might not be by chance, she decided. A quick glance toward the snoring drunks reassured her. They would sleep the remainder of the afternoon.

"So, what's happening now in Sumer? I hear you have a new king."

"Yes, King Shulgi, son of Eridu, now rules here. King Shulgi is young, but wise for his seasons. Unlike his father, our new king wants only peace. Some evil people think he murdered his father, that he wanted to seize control and to take his half-sister to his bed." She laughed as she delivered the local gossip. "People always have to have something wicked to talk about. But I heard him speak in the marketplace months ago when he took his father's place, and I say King Shulgi's wits are keen, as are those of his new wife, Kushanna."

As if they were merely having a casual conversation, En-hedu told Malok everything she and Tammuz had learned. By the time she stopped talking, the ale in Malok's cup was gone.

"Well, at least there will be peace between Sumer and Akkad now."

"Yes, there is much talk of peace." En-hedu put the slightest emphasis on the word *talk*. One of the sleeping drunks might be awake and listening. "But the recruiters are still talking to every farmboy and goatherd that enters the city, though most of the training camps around Sumer have emptied. One customer claimed they have been moved to the west, near the edge of the great desert."

"That seems strange," Malok said. "Why so far from Sumer?"

"The desert tribesmen are raiding the border again. Farms and small villages have been burned. Sumer has to protect its borders." En-hedu shrugged. "Whatever the reason, it's bad for business to have so many men so far away."

"As long as Sumer wants peace, who cares how many soldiers your king recruits, or where he sends them."

"Perhaps. Meanwhile King Shulgi is most active in consolidating his rule. The other cities have not yet agreed to accept his leadership. But I think they will in time. King Shulgi is governing wisely, though the taxes remain high, because the greedy barbarian king in Akkad demanded so much in ransom for Shulgi's father."

Malok took another sip of ale. "I know little of such things. When warriors struggle against each other, a poor boatman like myself must just grovel in the dirt on his stomach and hope neither side steps on him."

En-hedu laughed at that. "Well, despite all that Akkad can do to stop us, Sumer is too powerful and too strong to not take the lead of the southern cities. People who travel up and down the rivers say that Sumer is now the largest city in the world."

"That's what they say in Akkad, but with Akkad's name instead of Sumer's," Malok said with a smile. "Still, peace is good for trade, which means my master and his grasping boat captains will be pleased."

"And good for the Kestrel. If all the men are at war, then there is no one to drink and entertain my girls. And our patron, Merchant Gemama would still demand his profit every month, no matter how many customers we had."

She wanted Yavtar to know that Gemama had decided to help them.

"Then I'll have another cup of ale, to drink to peace between our cities."

En-hedu fetched it. As she set it down, she passed the final piece of information. "Our new queen, Kushanna, is very wise and very powerful. She attends all the councils, and the king seeks her advice on everything."

"I'll remember that, En-hedu of Ubaid. Is she as beautiful as they say?"

"Oh yes, and a few seasons older than her new husband." En-hedu described Kushanna in detail, knowing that Lady Trella would want to know such things.

Two men stepped into the room, and one shouted for ale.

"No need to shout," En-hedu said, raising her own voice as loud as the newcomers. "I can see and hear you well enough." She rose and smiled at Malok. "Enjoy your stay at the Kestrel."

En-hedu said nothing to Malok for the rest of the evening, and didn't even tell Tammuz until they were in bed and she could whisper the words into his ear. "Make sure you see him before he leaves in the morning, so you can recognize him next time."

"You think he'll be back? Maybe they'll send someone else."

"He's working on a riverboat. Now that trade has resumed, boats will be moving up and down the Tigris. He'll probably be here every fifteen or twenty days. No one will be suspicious of a sailor spending an evening or two in a tavern."

"I wish we could tell Trella ourselves."

"The messenger will be both loyal and discreet. She will have seen to that. Now go to sleep husband."

He held her tight for a moment, then let himself relax. Soon he fell asleep, and En-hedu could worry without disturbing him. Tammuz was right, the most dangerous part of this enterprise was delivering the reports to the messenger. If anyone suspected him or them, a long and painful session in Shulgi's torture room would drag the truth out of even the strongest man. Or woman. En-hedu wondered what she would do if the hot irons were pressed against the most tender parts of her body. She shivered. Best not to be taken alive, she knew.

En-hedu cleared her mind of problems. Instead, she let herself enjoy the warmth and touch of Tammuz's body against hers, so different from that of her previous master.

Her first owner had been brutal and cruel, turning her into a helpless animal pleading to avoid his fists. He had broken her nose at least once, and shared her with his friends or anyone willing to pay for more ale. En-hedu cried every night, and begged the gods for a quick death to release her. Word of her mistreatment had reached Lady Trella's ears, and she and her guards arrived at the tannery owned by En-hedu's master, to stop the beatings that had offended and embarrassed everyone living nearby.

With Lady Trella threatening to drive En-hedu's owner from the city, he grudgingly accepted a decent price for his slave. Lady Trella took the frightened and still crying girl by the hand, and led her to a new life.

It took weeks for the pain and bruises to fade, and for her wits to return. As she regained her health and strength, En-hedu impressed Lady Trella. In time, she gave En-hedu to Tammuz, as young and inexperienced as herself. Like two wounded chicks in a nest, they found strength and comfort in each other.

Together they blossomed into something stronger than either of them could have ever hoped for. The crippled boy and the plain and ungainly girl fell in love with each other, even as they spied for Lady Trella. And they also managed to strike a blow against the usurper Korthac, killing several of his soldiers during the fighting. With Tammuz's quick reactions, he had saved Gatus's life as well.

Now she and Tammuz were two of Trella's most important spies, working in the heart of Sumer. If they were successful, En-hedu and Tammuz would be greatly rewarded, and they could live a life of ease in Akkad. To achieve that goal, however, would involve much danger. Lady Trella had warned them of what would happen if they were discovered or betrayed. Death would be a mercy if they were unmasked.

That, En-hedu decided, was not going to happen. Not if she had anything to say about it. If not for herself, then at least nothing must happen to Tammuz.

22

Forty days later, Shulgi and two hundred horsemen arrived at Razrek's camp, located just before the river that marked the edge of the desert. Every man rode a sturdy horse, wore a leather helmet, and carried a good bronze sword. The men in the camp ceased their tasks and watched the king and his Sumerians' arrival, looking for lame or weary horses, tired riders or signs of poor horsemanship skills.

No hint of any such weakness could be seen. The competent riders sat comfortably on their horses, appearing relaxed after a five-day ride across Sumeria's southern lands under the fierce desert heat.

Shulgi, riding at the head of his cavalry, ignored everyone's gaze. Since taking over from Razrek, he'd put these men through vigorous training, working them and their horses from dawn to dusk. Shulgi started by placing Vanar in charge. Between the two of them, they soon identified the troublemakers and slackers. Two executions for disobedience, one for desertion, and the transfer of another ten or so men to Razrek's western desert force left Shulgi with a solid core of horse fighters. By that time, they were loyal only to the king of Sumer.

As it turned out, Shulgi didn't even have to increase their pay. Instead, he just made sure their promised wages actually reached them. As expected, Razrek had skimmed a portion each month. Since Shulgi had no urge to possess gold himself, he could give the men their due. To the horsemen, it made the long days easier to bear, and the extra coins in their purses increased their respect and loyalty for their new king and his commanders.

Since Razrek's departure, the defeated horse fighters now under

Vanar's command soon recovered the swagger lost in the battle with the Akkadians. Now, only a few months after Eridu's debacle, men came to Sumer each day, eager to join the horse fighters. Already Shulgi had another hundred or so men training outside the city's walls.

"Welcome, my king," Razrek called out as Shulgi halted his horse, a powerful stallion almost sixteen hands high, before Razrek's tent. "The men look fit."

"Yes, my men are well enough." Shulgi placed just the slightest emphasis on the mention of his men. "But they need a real enemy to fight."

"They'll find one here, and soon enough."

"Then you've done well also. Has the leader of the Tanukhs arrived?"

Shulgi handed off his horse and followed Razrek into the tent. No one stood out in the sun if it could be avoided.

"Kapturu rode in last night, with fifty riders." Razrek filled two water cups and handed one to Shulgi. "The rest of his men – he claims he has over three hundred more – are in a camp a few miles away. But I doubt he has much more than half that number. Several of the tribes have refused to join the fight. Still, with the men you brought today, we'll have more than enough. And once we loot a few villages, more will join us."

"Good. Kapturu has taken enough of our gold in the last few months. Now it's time both he and you earn some of it."

"Since I sent word to you in Sumer, I've added another fifty riders to the hundred I brought here, my king. The recruiting goes well, considering what we've got to work with. Not all are well trained, but they can ride, and that should be enough for now. If we only had more horses . . ."

"We'll get them from the Salibs." He counted the men available. With those under Razrek's orders, Shulgi commanded over four hundred riders. If this Tanukh Kapturu had half of what he claimed, they could number close to six hundred horsemen. More than enough to sweep through the desert villages. "When can we ride south?"

The nearest Salib encampment lay almost eighty miles south, a two-day ride through the heat. "If Kapturu agrees, we can depart tomorrow. My men are ready."

Shulgi had no doubt that they were. He had known Razrek for almost three years, and the man knew how to recruit men, and lead them in battle. Razrek's weaknesses were his lust for gold, and his preference for relaxing in Sumer's alehouses. As long as Shulgi could keep Razrek away from the city's temptations, the Sumerian would help build Shulgi's army.

A soldier entered the tent. "The leader of the Tanukhs is coming, commander."

"They must have seen you riding in," Razrek said.

Shulgi nodded to the guard. "Tell Vanar to join us, and to bring the gift."

A few moments later, they heard the sound of horses. Shulgi stepped outside the tent just as Kapturu halted his horse, a white stallion even bigger than Shulgi's. A touch on the heels and a flick of the halter against its neck, and the animal reared up, its hooves flashing in the air before they plunged back to the earth with a spray of sand.

Satisfied with his impressive entrance, Kapturu swung down from his mount with a swagger. The Tanukh leader, tall and with a thick black beard, patted his horse on the neck, then glanced around, his eyes resting on Shulgi only in passing.

"Where is . . . ah, Razrek. The greetings of the desert to you, my friend."

"Welcome, Chief Kapturu, mightiest leader of the brave Tanukh clans." Razrek favored Kapturu with a near-fawning bow before straightening up and smiling. "Enter our tent. We've wine and water inside."

Before Razrek could say anything more, Kapturu strode past Shulgi, almost brushing him aside, as the Tanukh entered the tent. Four of Kapturu's men, either bodyguards or advisors, Shulgi couldn't decide, followed their leader inside. They, too, ignored Shulgi, who was left standing alone outside the tent.

Vanar walked up, pushing his way through the Tanukh horsemen. "You sent for me, Lord Shulgi?" He carried the gift under his arm.

"Yes." Shulgi took the bundle from his second in command. "Order your men to approach as close to the tent as possible. If there's any trouble with these Tanukhs, I want you to be ready. Then join me inside as quickly as you can."

Without waiting for Vanar to reply, Shulgi ducked into the tent. The last of Kapturu's men had just taken a seat, closing the ring that contained Razrek and the Tanukh leader, seated face to face with a small open space between them.

"This is King Shulgi of Sumer," Razrek announced, already aware of the awkward situation that had developed.

Everyone turned toward Shulgi, who smiled and stepped into the circle. "One of your men will have to wait outside, Chief Kapturu." Shulgi gestured toward the man seated at Razrek's right. "I don't think there's room for all of us."

"This boy is your king?" Kapturu's voice boomed throughout the tent, and his words carried easily to those waiting beyond. "I thought he was one of your playthings."

All the Tanukhs laughed, including Kapturu. Razrek tightened his lips, concerned that things had gone badly and could go worse.

"I've a gift for you, Chief Kapturu." Shulgi's words slowly ended the laughter. He untied the cord fastening the bundle, unwrapped the cloth, and held up a gleaming bronze blade. Unlike the straight swords the Sumerians carried, this one had a curve that started a hand's length from the tip, where the blade widened as well. "Would you like to see how well it strikes? I can kill that one now, if he doesn't get up from my place."

The laughter and smiles vanished. Shulgi stood in the center of the tent, his head barely brushing the roof, with a sword in his hand. Everyone else was seated. Even if they reached for their swords, they would be at a disadvantage.

"You dare to insult my men?" Kapturu's voice hardened.

The tent flap jostled again, and Vanar ducked inside. He took one look at Shulgi standing there, sword in hand, and instinctively dropped his left hand to clasp his scabbard.

"Ah, Vanar, are your men outside? How many did you summon?"

"Yes, my king. Two sections . . . sixty men."

"Good." Shulgi turned to face Kapturu, sword now held high in both hands. "You might as well tell all your guards to leave." Shulgi decided that these Tanukhs were mere bodyguards, meant to impress the Sumerians. "They won't be needed while we speak."

"My men stay with me. And I don't take orders from a Sumerian boy who calls himself a king."

Shulgi shrugged in resignation. "Very well."

He whirled around, striking as fast as any desert snake, the blade swinging sideways, narrowly missing Razrek's head before slicing deep into the neck of the Tanukh seated beside him. The blow came so fast that no one had time to react. Blood splattered everywhere, the spray covering Razrek. Without stopping after the killing stroke, Shulgi spun the blade around, its bloody tip now a hand's length from Kapturu's throat.

"Would you like a further demonstration, Chief Kapturu?"

"Stop!" Kapturu directed the word, not at Shulgi, but to the rest of his men, who had started to draw their weapons. Seated on the ground, Kapturu knew he'd be dead before anyone could strike a blow in his defense.

Shulgi's eyes flickered to Vanar. His commander remained in the tent's opening, blocking the entrance, and no one outside could have seen what happened. "Perhaps we should begin our meeting." Shulgi took a half-step backwards, then thrust the bloody blade deep into the sand. "As you can see, this sword will take a man's head from his shoulders with ease."

The moment of truth had come. If Kapturu gave the order, a death fight could break out within the tent, to be matched by another outside. Shulgi dropped his left hand to his own scabbard, the gesture telling everyone in the tent that he was as willing to fight as to talk.

Kapturu's smile had vanished. Jaw clenched, he considered his options.

Shulgi kept talking, as much to relieve the tension as to give the Tanukh time to reach the right decision. "After your men remove the body, tell them to wait outside, Chief Kapturu. Our discussion should be more private, I think."

No one spoke. Either the tent would erupt in bloodshed, or the Tanukh leader would realize how vulnerable he was, with Vanar and his men outside, and this boy-king facing him.

The silence dragged out, the Tanukhs still not moving, while Kapturu worked out the implications. Suddenly, he leaned back and laughed, then clapped his hands on his knees.

"Yes, it looks like a good blade. Perhaps one day I can give you a gift of equal value." He turned to his men. "Remove the body, and wait outside." Kapturu smiled up at Shulgi. "Then we can begin our talk."

Shulgi moved to stand beside Razrek. He stood there while Kapturu's three men rose and dragged the corpse of their companion out of the tent. A babble of voices rose up outside, as the Tanukhs saw the body. Shulgi kept his face calm, but he knew a moment of legend had come. Soldiers would talk about this story around the campfires for months, even years. How their leader had killed a Tanukh who offended him, how King Shulgi defied the desert-dwellers to strike back.

Kushanna had known the importance of such moments. She had urged him to seek out danger, to prove to his men that he was worthy of their loyalty and respect, to add to his reputation, and downplay the fact of his youth. "Just don't get yourself killed, my husband," she whispered in his ear.

Killing his father had been one such moment, Shulgi knew, but that had to remain an unspoken secret, only hinted at by those who could guess the truth. Now this story would begin to expand his reputation, and men would think twice before they dared to laugh at him or his youth.

At last only Kapturu and Razrek remained with Shulgi in the now uncrowded tent. The sword still remained in the tent's center, bloody sand crusted around the blade where it emerged from the ground.

"Let's us begin." Shulgi settled himself on the ground, hitching his sword around until he found a comfortable position. "We have much to talk about, Chief Kapturu. Together, we can destroy our enemies, loot their villages, and take their women and horses." He hadn't ridden from Sumer to mince flattering words with any desert barbarian. "First we'll destroy the Salibs, and then we'll turn our attention to the north, where the real wealth of the land between the rivers lies. To make all that happen, we need only to work together. A few years, a few battles, and the desert and all it contains will be yours."

Kapturu leaned forward, no doubt already anticipating the wealth that would flow through his fingers. He, too, knew how to speak directly.

"Then let us talk about the destruction of the Salibs . . . King Shulgi."

In Sumer, Kushanna frowned at the man standing before her, shuffling his weight from foot to foot. "Gone? Just gone? Gone where?"

"Yes, my queen." Sohrab kept his eyes on the chamber's floor. "I waited seven days in Akkad, but they never arrived. They must have continued north, probably by boat. Horses are scarce in Akkad, and almost none can be purchased at any price."

Kushanna resisted the urge to have the man flogged. It was not the fool's fault for being the bringer of bad tidings. The two spies she'd dispatched to Akkad had taken her gold and disappeared. They might even have sold their story to Trella, earning a few more pieces of gold before running to the north. Trella would be laughing at the Sumerians – at Kushanna – if that were the case. The traitors would stop laughing soon enough if ever they returned within the grasp of Sumer's guard.

"And the other cities? Are our men in place there?"

Sohrab lifted his eyes, grateful for a chance to present good news. "Yes, Queen Kushanna. We have people in place in all the southern cities. They are still settling in, but already they've provided useful news."

The most useful news of all would be the names of those who spoke out against Sumer's growing influence. In the next few months, that would prove more valuable than any news of Akkad's activities.

"Good." Kushanna leaned back in her chair. Sohrab would continue to stand in her presence, at least until he learned to bring better news. "And what of Razrek? What have you learned about our brave horse commander?"

Sohrab met her eyes for the first time. "Razrek is not his true name. His birth name is Sondar. No one knows where he was born, but he lived many years in a small village in the north-eastern part of Sumeria, named Carnax. A prosperous but dreary place, from all accounts. Bandits destroyed the village, killing or enslaving its inhabitants. Only a few farmers live nearby now. The rest remains in ruins, and men say the land is accursed."

"But our brave commander survived somehow?"

"More than survived, my queen." He glanced around, as if concerned that someone might be listening. "One person claimed that Sondar himself was involved in the village's destruction, that he killed his master, the village elder. At any rate, Sondar survived, and with plenty of gold. He formed a band of horsemen, and began plundering the countryside. Eventually, your father, King Eridu, took notice and ... persuaded Sondar to change his ways and fight for Sumer."

Kushanna's irritation at the mention of her father's name almost made her miss something. The name of the village, Carnax ... she'd heard that name before. It took her a moment, but then she recalled the conversation. One of the spies reporting on Akkad had mentioned that Lady Trella, as she preferred to be called, rather than queen, had come from a Sumerian village named Carnax.

She leaned forward and stared straight into the man's eyes. "What else do you know of Razrek's past?"

Kushanna dragged every bit of information she could extract from Sohrab, but he had little more to add. At first she'd been merely curious. Now she sensed something more useful might be gleaned.

"I want you to discover everything you can about this village of Carnax. Visit it yourself, talk to those living nearby, find out exactly what happened to the survivors. If you can, bring one or two of them here, so I can question them myself."

Sohrab had proved useful in finding things out, but he lacked the skill to probe beneath the surface. Any information about Trella would be useful, if only to understand how she'd gained her power over the men of Akkad. Kushanna didn't believe in the priests or their gods and demons, but witches existed. Everyone knew that some women could bend men to their will, or call down spells to render them impotent. More than a few in Sumer had called her one, too.

"Yes, my queen. I'm sure I can find a few survivors from Carnax. It was only four or five years ago that it was destroyed, so many should know about it."

"Good. And this time bring me back something useful."

When she dismissed Sohrab, Kushanna moved from the table to the balcony. She liked to sit and gaze out over the city. Her city. Already everyone obeyed her slightest wish, and in the coming months and years, her power would only increase. Shulgi desired only conquests, and there would be years of fighting ahead of him, leaving her more than enough time to solidify her grip on Sumer. And fighting could prove deadly, even to Shulgi. After a few years, if he fell in battle, she could continue to rule in his name, at least until she could sit another, even more pliable, man on the throne.

That brought a smile to her face. She'd already caught one of Vanar's commanders staring at her every time she passed. Kushanna had given him the slightest smile, just enough to keep his interest. Like many others, he was smitten by her beauty. Such a soldier would do well enough, should she need another man at her side.

Nevertheless, she hoped Shulgi survived the battles in the desert, and the coming war with Akkad. At least, survived until victory was assured. Then, she knew, anything could happen. In her private chest, hidden in the false bottom, was a small box containing three different kinds of poisons. Any one of them, their taste masked by strong wine, would free her of her husband's company, should he need to be removed.

For now, Shulgi worshipped her body, and that gave her all the power she needed. Together they'd killed their foolish father and taken his city. Now the son and daughter would build Sumer into an empire worthy of them both. And she would be right at his side, to whisper in his ear at night. Yes, such thoughts brought a pleasant glow to her body. Shulgi rode her well, long into the night, leaving them both exhausted and satisfied. She'd allowed only a handful of men to enjoy her body, and he was by far the most energetic.

Kushanna looked forward to his return. Perhaps by then, she would have learned all there was to know about Lady Trella. Possibly even enough to have her killed. There was, after all, plenty of poison in the box.

23

Mid-morning had come and gone before Eskkar arrived at the barracks, his long strides forcing his guards to hurry to keep pace. He hated being late, especially over such a petty interruption as the one he had just left behind. A dispute between two traders had escalated into a pushing and shoving match, which brought them before Nicar, in his role as Chief Judge of Akkad. For once, even Nicar's conciliatory skills had not managed to resolve the issue, and both sides had demanded an appeal before the king.

After three years of settling many foolish disputes, Eskkar had learned to control his temper and keep his patience. Today's crisis, however, required him to keep from laughing. The two men involved, both prosperous merchants, had practically come to blows over a prospective virgin bride. The girl's father had somehow managed to offer his daughter in marriage to both belligerents. The man who first received the promise demanded the girl at the original and agreed upon price. The second potential husband had entered the fray soon after, offering more coins for the girl. Naturally, the father had changed his mind as to his choice of suitors.

The men involved caught up with Eskkar just as he departed the compound for the barracks, and insisted on their case being heard right there in the lane. While the two traders exchanged insults and threats, the father demanded his right to sell his daughter to whomever he pleased, and the girl alternated between sobbing at her embarrassment or shrieking at her father. It seemed she preferred the first suitor, but Eskkar couldn't be sure.

His first thought, which he decided to keep to himself, was that whoever won the girl would be overpaying and getting a poor bargain.

By then the crowd included the families of the two prospective husbands, the father of the girl involved, and a few dozen onlookers as excited as if they were watching a wrestling match. The onlookers voiced their own opinions, calling out one or the other's name, each faction trying to outshout the other. A few placed bets on the outcome. At last Eskkar made his ruling. The girl was to go to the first suitor, but the father was ordered to pay half the dowry to the second man, because he'd offered something for sale that he didn't have, a clear violation of the marketplace rules.

Howls arose over the harsh ruling, but Eskkar ignored that. The next time a foolish dispute cropped up, those seeking settlement might remember and accept the Chief Judge's decision.

By the time everything resolved itself and Eskkar could slip away, the sun had moved high in the sky, and no one appeared satisfied, except perhaps the red-faced virgin and most of the onlookers, who always enjoyed watching someone else's discomfort. Eskkar's good mood had vanished into a black cloud of anger that showed itself on his usually calm face.

With Grond at his side, Eskkar entered the training ground and strode to where Gatus sat on his tall stool, taking advantage of a sliver of shade cast by the barracks. On the wall just behind Gatus and his stool, a charcoal outline of a man had been scratched into the mud. A small table stood nearby. Two young men Eskkar didn't recognize sat in the dirt beside Gatus. A few dozen paces away, half a dozen skinny youths waited with barely suppressed excitement, staring open mouthed at the king of Akkad.

Eskkar caught the look on Gatus's face, and knew the old soldier was tempted to remark about the lateness of the hour. Gatus resisted the urge, probably only because there were so many young recruits around.

"We were delayed by the Chief Justice, Gatus," Grond called out as they approached, thereby avoiding Eskkar having to say something that might sound like an apology.

"No matter." Gatus slid off the stool, and paused a moment to adjust his tunic. "At my age, I need the rest anyway."

"What have you got for me?" Eskkar asked, aware that his voice sounded harsh. He took a deep breath. No sense taking things out on Gatus and these men, older boys, actually, and probably too young to know what they were getting into.

"I've found a few slingers for you." Gatus nodded his head toward the two young men beside him. They scrambled to their feet as soon as they saw Eskkar. "They're ready to give you a demonstration."

Eskkar appraised the two. Both wore ragged clothing, tunics either too small or too large, both patched and worn through in spots. Each had long and wiry arms. Neither man came up to Eskkar's shoulder in height, and he guessed their age as about fifteen or sixteen seasons, barely enough to be considered a man, even in Akkad.

Gatus stretched his arm and pointed to the closest one. "This is Nivar."

Nivar had long brown hair tied back with a bit of leather.

"Shappa has fifteen seasons," Gatus said, gesturing toward the other. "He's the older, so I've put him in charge of Nivar and the others for now. They're the first of your detachment of slingers, if ever there is such a thing. As for the rest of them," he jerked his head toward the others standing nearby, "we'll see."

Eskkar ignored Gatus's remark, in part because he knew the old soldier was as interested as Eskkar in learning if slingers could play a part in Akkad's growing army. Nevertheless, Eskkar had proposed this idea, and he didn't intend to change his mind now, no matter how foolish it might turn out to be. He studied the two slingers. For a moment, he was reminded of Tammuz, a skinny thief who had disobeyed orders, taken a bow, and killed an Alur Meriki warrior in the first battle to save the city.

Another of Trella's sayings came to mind. If a thing is worth doing, then do it as well as you can. It was her idea, after all, to make use of Tammuz, and that had worked out well, despite Eskkar's misgivings.

He walked over to the table and picked up one the slings. Eskkar hadn't touched one of these since his boyhood, when he'd used one to hunt rabbits and other small game for his mother's cooking pot. This sling was longer, with a shaped leather pouch at the end of two long strands of flaxen cords. The cords, he noticed, were made of thinner, plaited strands that felt supple to the touch. One end of the cord ended in a small loop, the other in a thick knot. The pouch differed as well. Square-shaped, but fastened at opposite corners, the remaining points faced up and down. It had a hole the thickness of his thumb in the center.

"Well, Nivar and Shappa, I'm glad Gatus found you. Perhaps we can convince old Gatus that slings can be as deadly as an arrow, and even more useful in other ways."

The boys bowed, and only Shappa managed to mumble a greeting. They were clearly in awe of Eskkar, who towered over them both. In fact, everyone appeared tense, not sure what would be asked of them. He decided to relieve the tension a bit.

"Did I ever tell you, Gatus, about the time I was nearly killed by a slinger?" Eskkar raised his voice so that everyone could hear. "The stone flew right past my ear and splintered against a cliff face." He didn't add that it was a woman who'd nearly split his head.

"It would take a dozen stones to dent your head, Eskkar," Gatus said.

Grond laughed, while the boys standing close enough to hear gaped in shock at the rude jest directed at their king.

"It's true." Eskkar ignored the remark. "Then another time, I was on horseback and a . . . man nearly unhorsed me with a sling." He'd almost said the word "shepherd", but decided that it didn't sound very impressive to admit he'd almost been killed fighting a sheep herder over a band of foul-smelling sheep.

"But you survived," Gatus said. "So the slinger's stones didn't bother you too much."

"No, but they made me change my tactics, and that's why I want to see what can be done with these men." He turned to Shappa. "Show me what you can do."

Shappa took the sling from Eskkar's hand, and selected three slightly oval stones about the size of a fat walnut from a pouch at his waist. The boy could scarcely control his excitement. He slipped the middle finger of his right hand into the loop and grasped the knot of the other stand between thumb and forefinger. He dropped a stone into the pouch, and started walking away from the wall.

Everyone moved with him, leaving the wall empty. Two of the boys carried the table well to the side, and Gatus picked up his stool and took it with him.

Shappa stopped about forty paces from the wall, and looked at Gatus.

"Go ahead." He settled himself on the stool once again.

The slinger turned slightly away from the target, with his left hand closest to the wall. The pouch hung straight down from his hand. With a snap of the wrist, Shappa spun the sling toward the ground, stepping forward and extending his right arm as he released the cord.

A shower of mud showed where the stone impacted, close to the center of the target's body. For the first time, Eskkar noticed the many pock marks in the wall. Gatus must have had the boys practicing for some time.

Eskkar frowned. He'd been unprepared for the swiftness of the throw, and had missed what Shappa had done. "Again," he ordered.

Shappa picked up another projectile, with all of Eskkar's attention focused this time. As the stone fell into the pouch, he understood the reason for the hole in the center – to give the pouch a better grip on the projectile, making it less likely to slip out during the rotation. Odd that he'd never thought of that as a child, nor had anyone else in the clan. This time the slinger whipped the sling around twice, releasing the stone before the second whirl had been completed, again stepping forward with an overhand throwing motion.

With another spray of mud fragments, the second stone landed just below the gouge the first had made. Two good casts, Eskkar decided, but nothing that he couldn't have duplicated with a bow. He pushed that thought from his mind. Comparing bowmen to slingers made no sense. He didn't intend to use slingers as bowmen. These boys weren't strong enough, and the bows and arrows his archers required took plenty of gold to construct and the men months to train.

No one said anything, but every eye was fixed on Eskkar. He looked at Gatus, but the man had occupied himself cleaning a fingernail. Eskkar turned back to Shappa. "How fast can you make a throw?"

Shappa moved toward Nivar, who had brought a handful of stones with him. The slinger selected three stones, and then stepped back to his original position. He dropped the first stone in the sling, and this time he turned to Eskkar.

"Begin." Again Eskkar focused his attention on the slinger.

The sling swung round, the stone released at the top of the swing. As the pouch descended, the release strap flying through the air, Shappa extended his left hand, a stone held in his fingers. The still-whirling pouch closed over the second stone, the trailing release strap swung back to the slinger's right hand. He caught the knot and applied another powerful spin to the sling. The second stone was launched toward the target, while Shappa's left hand extended once again into the pouch's path. The third stone soon flew on its way.

Eskkar realized his mouth was open, and closed it. He'd never seen anything like that before, still didn't believe what his eyes had just told him. In fact, if anyone boasted they could reload a pouch like that, he would have thought him a liar. Eskkar guessed that the three stones had been launched before a man could count to five. Even Mitrac and his arrows couldn't match that speed, but of course, the arrow's flight had much greater range. Or did it?

"How far can you cast such a stone?"

"With a good chance of a hit, King Eskkar, about seventy-five paces," Shappa answered, looking more confident now that he'd proved his skill. "But with smaller stones, I've hit targets at double that distance."

That matched the distances an Akkadian archer had to hit his targets – three out of four at seventy-five paces, and two out of five at one hundred and fifty. Mitrac and some of the other master bowmen could hit targets at over four hundred paces, something else Eskkar once wouldn't have believed if he hadn't seen it for himself.

"Can you do better? Can the range of throws be extended?"

"No, my lord, not easily. The stones vary in weight and shape too much to make a perfect cast each time."

"Do it again," Eskkar said. "And this time do it slower, and explain what you're doing at every step."

He made the boy do it twice more, until Eskkar felt certain he understood the process. Then he turned to Nivar. "Let me see what you can do."

"Underhand, Nivar," Gatus called out, still sitting on his stool.

Nivar stepped forward and took Shappa's place. Where the first slinger had shown a calm demeanor, Nivar could scarcely conceal his excitement. The stone slipped from his fingers when he tried to drop it into the pouch. To Eskkar's surprise, not one of the onlookers laughed. Everyone kept silent, except Gatus, who scratched his beard noisily.

Nivar faced the target, his body turned slightly to the side in the same position as Shappa. This time the sling swung the opposite way, but the projectile flung itself forward almost as quickly. When the stone struck the target, it was still traveling at an upwards angle. A good shot, and just as much mud had blasted off the wall.

"Again," Eskkar ordered, his eyes narrowed as they watched every movement, determined to miss nothing of the process.

Another throw, the underhand motion similar to the way Eskkar had skipped stones across a pond in his youth. This time the missile struck in the target's head. No doubt a few more paces back, and it would have missed the target.

"A good throw, Nivar." Eskkar wanted to encourage the boy. "How fast can you throw three stones?"

Nivar tried to duplicate Shappa quick reload, but the second stone missed the target, and the third failed to stay in the pouch.

"I'm sorry, Lord Eskkar," the embarrassment in Nivar's voice was plain to all. "I only learned Shappa's way of reloading a few days ago."

"Which method will cast the stone farther?" Eskkar asked. At the same time, he motioned to Shappa to give him the sling.

"There seems to be a difference of opinion about that," Gatus said. "A lot depends on the individual slinger, of course, but it seems to me that the underhand method will throw the stone farther, but perhaps not with the same force."

"Better a stone falls on the rear ranks than in the dirt," Eskkar remarked, modifying the archer's old adage. By now he'd fitted the sling to his finger, and dropped a stone in the pouch. He whirled the sling, turning it over again and again, until he thought he knew when to release it. Imitating the two slingers, he stepped forward as he let it fly. The stone sailed right over the barracks and landed somewhere out of sight.

But not out of hearing. A loud voice began cursing the fool who threw stones in the air.

Eskkar had to force himself not to smile. He didn't mind looking foolish, not as long as he could master the skill. Again and again he threw, five, ten, up to twenty stones. At first he took two revolutions for each throw, but soon learned to launch the projectile with a single spin. A second revolution added little to the force of the stone. Eskkar's results ranged all over the barracks wall, the dirt between, and the sky above. But by the twentieth stone, he'd slipped into what had to be the proper rhythm, stepping forward and throwing his arm directly at the target.

He grunted in satisfaction when he struck the target twice in succession. By then sweat covered his face and bare chest. The task seemed simple enough, but he realized you had to concentrate on what you were doing. No doubt, over time, the skill of each slinger and the individual steps would merge into a smooth motion that required little thought. Just like an archer. When you mastered your craft, you scarcely needed to aim the weapon.

But not on the first day, or the second. He looked around, and found Gatus had gone, leaving Eskkar and Grond alone with the recruits. Gatus might have rounded up the boys, but it was the king who conceived their use, and it should be the king to whom they gave their loyalty.

"All right, I want to see every man throw. Line them up, Shappa. Nivar, get some boys and collect the stones."

Grond helped out, making sure the now excited boys stayed at their place in the line. Eskkar told them to start with the more usual, overhand throw. There would be plenty of time for practicing with the underhand toss.

One by one, the boys demonstrated their skill. Soon stones were flying all over the barracks area, and Grond had to clear everyone out of possible danger. That included anyone to their rear, as some boys in their haste sent rocks whirling behind them, into the dirt at their feet, or straight up into the air, with everyone dodging the missile's return to earth.

Eskkar took several more turns with Shappa's sling, which he decided he preferred after trying a few of the others. Everyone wanted to demonstrate his skill, and as the boys grew accustomed to Eskkar's presence, their nerves steadied, their voices rose, and the ability to strike the target improved.

Not that he cared much about an individual's expertise. Eskkar wanted to see how effective a group of slingers could be. Working with five at a time, he had them rain stones on the abused barracks' wall, which soon looked like it was in danger of crumbling back to the mud. He still had trouble imagining the force with which the stones landed. Any enemy struck in the head would be going down, even if he happened to be wearing a helmet. Hits on arms and legs would be painful and slow a fighter down, probably taking him out of the battle.

The sun moved across the sky, but Eskkar never noticed. Midday came and went, and he kept the boys at it.

"Are you enjoying yourself, Eskkar?"

He turned to see Trella standing behind him, Annok-sur at her side. Trella must have been there for some time. Her usual four bodyguards accompanied her, all of them watching the performance. Trella held a basket in her arms. The smell of fresh bread made him realize how hungry he felt, and that he'd promised Trella he would return to the house at midday to join her. A glance at the sky told him that it was closer to mid-afternoon than noon.

"Trella, I'm sorry . . ."

She laughed and touched his arm. "I haven't seen you this excited in a long time. All of you, playing like children."

He wiped the sweat from his brow. "Did you see them make throws? Some are good. Others . . ." he took her arm and guided her more to the side where they might be safer from an errant throw.

"Since you missed your meal, I brought you and Grond some bread." She handed a loaf to each of them.

Eskkar tore a hunk of bread from the loaf and took a bite. "We forgot to eat. We're were having too much fun."

"That wall is going to collapse soon. The whole barracks may come down."

"These stones . . . when they land . . . they could smash a man's ribs, knock him off his feet. They're hot to the touch after they strike the wall. I wonder why?"

"I don't know, husband. Let me think about it. Does it matter?"

"No. What matters is that a good slinger can cast stones very quickly and with good distance and accuracy." He finished another mouth of bread. "These boys are too small and weak to make good swordsmen or archers or spearmen, but they can still kill, if they're used right."

He glanced around, feeling guilty for having the bread when the others had none. A few boys were still slinging stones at the wall, but most of the others sat on the ground, taking a rest, watching the king and queen.

"Enough slinging." Eskkar's voice caught everyone's attention. "Come here and sit down."

The boys moved closer to where Eskkar, Trella, and Grond stood. Most of them had never seen Lady Trella, since she seldom left the house and its grounds. Of course they all knew the stories told about her, and curiosity had them staring at her with their mouths open. Some forgot their manners and stared, in the way of young boys, at the nipples pushing up against her dress.

Eskkar bunched them closer so that he could see their faces. Each looked tired, covered with sweat, and full of excitement, some still talking about what they had done. The moment Eskkar started speaking, they quieted down.

"Each of you came here today because you wanted to fight Akkad's enemies." Eskkar let his eyes meet each and every face. "To be an archer or spearman or swordsman requires both great strength and size. All of you would be turned away if you tried to join those ranks. I wasn't sure that a sling could be effective in a real battle. But today you've proven to me that men of smaller stature can fight and kill as well as any bowman or spear-carrier. I've seen that, in your hands, slings can be a deadly weapon, and soon Akkad will need all the weapons and men it can find. Those of you who want to fight our enemies will be given the chance. If you do not want to fight, then you should leave now."

He waited a moment, giving them time to consider, but, of course, not a boy moved. All of them were caught up in the moment. Right now, they would do anything and everything he asked of them.

"If you stay, you'll have a safe place to sleep and enough food to eat." Both those were important. Half of them looked as if they hadn't eaten in days. "You'll even be paid, first as a recruit, then after you master your skills, as a soldier. In return, you'll work hard and train every day. In time, the best of you will train the others. For now, Shappa and Nivar will take charge of your training, for as long as they show themselves worthy."

Food, shelter, and an occasional copper coin would be more than most of them had ever had or expected. Every upturned face shone with happiness and pride.

"When the time comes to fight, you'll be assigned to where you'll do the most good. But I promise you that Akkad's bowmen and fighters will be at your side, to make sure you do not stand alone. Are you with me?"

They all shouted at once, speaking so quickly Eskkar couldn't be sure of what anyone said. It didn't matter. They would join, they would train, they would fight. Many of them, he knew, would die, but that didn't matter now, either. He turned to Trella.

She nodded, and he knew he'd done well, binding more recruits to his side.

"Shappa, take your men to Gatus. Tell him to find quarters for you, and that you'll start training in the morning." No doubt Gatus was expecting them. He would have understood the implications of the sling at once.

"Yes, Lord Eskkar."

"And the first thing you'll do is make some real targets and repair that wall, before it falls down."

That made them laugh. Eskkar grinned, too. He placed his arm around Trella's shoulders and led the way back to their house, their guards falling in behind and in front.

That night, a weary Eskkar lay back in bed, Trella curled up against his side. Their lovemaking relaxed him, almost as if he'd fought and conquered a real enemy today. "My arm is sore."

Trella started to shift her position, but he held her tight. "No, not that arm. My throwing arm. And my fingers are still swollen. I can't believe how difficult it was to sling those stones, how much force it took."

"Do you really think slingers can help the soldiers? They looked so small, so young."

"Oh, yes, I'll find good use for them. Everyone sees the sling and thinks of it as a child's weapon, or something for shepherds to frighten off wolves. But those stones can kill. Akkad is full of boys and young men, all eager to join Akkad's army and fight Akkad's enemies. They'll cost almost nothing to arm and supply, and they might prove very useful in certain kinds of fighting. Now all I have to do is make sure that when we face Akkad's enemies, the slingers have a role to play, and possibly even a chance to survive."

"You think most of them will be killed?"

"No, not most, but many. If they come against swordsmen or archers, they'll be cut to pieces. But they're young, small, and quick, and that can sometimes keep a man alive when brute strength isn't enough. It all depends on how we use them in battle."

"What kind of fighting?"

The question held more than idle curiosity. Everything interested Trella, and every time she bent her will to a task, she found a way to improve it.

"Well, first of all, I think they could be very useful in hilly country, places where a horse can't go, places where sword or spear-fighters have trouble traversing. Slingers could harry an enemy from above. They could also act as scouts, or rearguards, to keep enemy horsemen at bay."

"Wouldn't horsemen just ride them down?"

"Everyone thinks so, but I'm not so sure." He shifted in the bed to face her. "These boys are small and quick. I think they could get out of the way of a charging horse, dodge the rider's sword. If they carried knives, knives with very sharp blades, they could hamstring the horse as it went by. I've seen that done before."

"The knife would need to be longer than most. Wouldn't a curved blade be more effective for such a task?"

All knives and short swords were straight. Some long swords were cast with a slight curve to them, but Eskkar distrusted them. It made the blade heavier without increasing the length, and favored a slashing cut, rather than a thrust. Sometimes that would be more useful, especially on horseback, but he'd fought with a straight blade all his life and didn't intend to change now.

"For men on foot," he said, almost thinking out loud, "a curved blade would be better. It would cut deeper and across a greater length of flesh or muscle." He pictured the scene in his mind. "If we armed the slingers with curved blades, and taught them how to strike at the horse's rear legs, I'm sure they could bring horse and rider down."

"Since the weapon wouldn't be used as a sword," Trella said, "it need not be as heavy, just very sharp and strong enough to slice through flesh."

He hadn't thought of that. A sword needed to be thick enough to block or deflect an enemy's stroke. A man on foot scrambling around and dodging a horse's hooves didn't have that to worry about. No knife, no matter how thick, would stop or even deflect a sword swung with full force from a moving horse.

"That's true. We don't want to weigh the slinger down with anything heavy. He'll be carrying a load of stones with him as it is, so there's no need to give him something else heavy to lug around."

"They might have special tunics, ones with many strong pockets sewn into them. That would spread the weight over their bodies and make it easier to move about."

"A thick belt would be useful, too," he added. "They could fasten a pouch of stones to it, then cut it free if they needed to move quickly."

She laughed and kissed his neck, then arched her body and let her breast fall across his chest. "You've gotten yourself a new force of fighters. But now it's time to sleep. We'll talk more about this in the morning. And in the next few weeks, I'm sure we can find ways to improve their effectiveness. After all, you turned villagers into bowmen. Why not boys into slingers?"

He pulled her close. "Why not? I'm sure you'll think of something special for them."

Eskkar knew his wife too well to ask her what she might possibly do. If she put her mind to a task, then something was sure to happen. He kissed the top of her head. "Then they're in good hands, with you worrying about their lives."

They drifted off to sleep, secure in each other's arms, thoughts of war and battle set aside for the rest of the night.

24

Ten days after the messenger from Akkad departed, two men stopped before the entrance to the Kestrel. Late in the afternoon, Tammuz and En-hedu had just finished enjoying the shade outside the tavern's door. The Kestrel had been open for business for more than a month, and a steady routine had established itself. The mornings kept them busy, serving bread and ale to anyone who stopped by or who had slept over. That meant rising with the dawn, to keep an eye on the customers still sleeping on the floor, or those who might have availed themselves of Irkalla and Anu. The ale had to be watched, of course, at all times, and it wasn't unheard of for customers to rob those still sleeping, then depart.

When the last of the patrons left the inn, preparations began for another day's activity. The common room had to be cleaned each morning. A man who'd drunk too much ale seldom bothered to step out into the lane to relieve himself in the middle of the night, even assuming he could get Rimaud to open the door.

While the clean-up went on, ale and provisions needed to be purchased. But most of the day's preparation ended well before midday. At noon Tammuz and En-hedu often carried a bench outside the Kestrel. They took time to relax and watch the people passing by in the lane, while they shared a loaf of bread and a cup of weak ale. Afterwards, they would take turns getting some sleep.

Late in the afternoon found Tammuz seated on his stool behind the ale table. He took one look at the two men standing before the entrance and frowned. One was a bodyguard, complete with sword and a sack he carried over one shoulder. The other wore the sash that proclaimed him a member of King Shulgi's officials.

"This is the new tavern, the . . . Kestrel?"

A stupid question, since an image of the bird was directly behind Tammuz's head, not to mention the one outside, next to the door. He rose from the bench. "Yes, master. Do you need a place to stay?"

The man snorted in annoyance. "I wouldn't waste my time in a filthy place such as this. I am King Shulgi's collector of taxes. Fetch the owner."

That was unfair, Tammuz thought. They kept the Kestrel cleaner than most taverns in Sumer.

"I am the owner . . . my wife and I."

En-hedu stepped from their bedroom, but the tax man didn't bother to acknowledge her presence. "Your tax is due. Three silver coins. If you can't pay, your tavern will be closed and your goods confiscated."

"Merchant Gemama told us that the tax would be two silver coins," En-hedu said, moving beside her husband.

"The tax for a tavern used to be two silvers . . . now it's three."

"We'll pay two," Tammuz said. The tax collector could easily be trying to take advantage of them, collecting three coins and turning in only two. "That's what Merchant Gemama told us we had to pay."

The tax collector tightened his lips. "King Shulgi announced the new tax ten days ago, when he spoke in the marketplace."

A small crowd of the always curious had gathered just outside the door, to watch the little drama. One of the bystanders called out. "It's true! The tax was raised to three silvers."

Tammuz turned to En-hedu, dismay on his face. "That will take more than we've earned."

She shrugged. "What can we do? We'll have to pay it."

"The king doesn't care about your profits, innkeeper. Now pay up, or the tavern is closed."

"I'll fetch it." En-hedu went inside, and a few moments later, returned. The taxman held out his hand.

En-hedu held her fist to her chest. "I want a stone first, to show that we've paid."

A small clay shard, marked with the king's sign, a different one starting with each new moon, provided proof that the tax had been paid.

"Not very trusting, are you?" The man's sarcasm was wasted on her.

"All right." He dug into the bodyguard's pouch and handed over the red-baked clay marker. En-hedu examined it, then handed him the tax.

Without a word, the man turned and left the tavern. Tammuz and En-hedu followed him to the door, and watched him walk down the lane, heading to the next place of business. With nothing to see, the crowd dissolved, and Tammuz and En-hedu stepped back inside the Kestrel.

"Wait!"

Another man followed them in. Tammuz recognized Melchior, Gemama's clerk. He muttered another oath under his breath.

"Merchant Gemama's fee is due today. One silver coin. Do you have it?" Melchior's voice grated in Tammuz's ears. Gemama's clerk spoke as if he expected them to plead some excuse or ask for a delay.

"Yes, I have it." He nodded to En-hedu once again. She handed over the coin. "Make sure your master gets it," Tammuz warned. "We won't be paying twice."

After a quick inspection to make sure the coin was sound, Melchior placed the coin in his pouch and let it slip inside his tunic. He, too, left without another word.

"There go our profits for the month," En-hedu said. She lowered her voice. "If we had to earn that from the Kestrel, we'd starve."

"No, we'd dilute the wine and ale, serve bad food, and steal from our customers, like every other innkeeper in Sumer."

"Still, we're going to need more copper coming into the inn," she said. "Who knows, perhaps the tax will be raised again in a month or two. Maybe it is time to start using Zenobia's teachings."

The owner of Akkad's finest pleasure house had taught En-hedu the secret skill of massage, the hidden pressure points on a body that would respond favorably to a knowing touch. En-hedu had mastered the teaching, learning quickly, and with her strong hands and powerful arms, she could push and prod and knead as well as any man.

Tammuz didn't care for this part of the plan at all. He didn't like the idea of En-hedu touching other women, not to mention men. There would always be requests for more intimate services from both sexes.

She saw his frown. "Don't worry, husband. I'll take care, I promise."

He took a deep breath and put his arm around her. "I know. But I still . . ."

Another man entered the tavern. This one glanced around, and seemed happy to find the inn still empty.

"What do you want?" Bad tidings always arrived in threes. Tammuz knew the man was no customer. He looked too well fed, and the long knife in his belt didn't go well with the run-down clothing.

"I want to talk to the owner. Is that you ... Tammuz?"

"Yes, I'm Tammuz. And this is my wife, En-hedu. We own the Kestrel. Who are you?"

The man smiled, then sat at the nearest table, and motioned for them to join him.

Tammuz eased himself down onto the bench facing the man, while En-hedu stood just behind him.

"I spoke to guardsman Jarud. He says you can be trusted."

Tammuz said nothing, still waiting for the man to give his name.

He took the hint. "My name is Enar." He paused, as if he had just imparted a great secret. "Jarud says that many of your customers are river men, some of them from up north."

"The Kestrel is close to the docks," Tammuz said. "Who else but boatmen would come here?"

"Can your wife be trusted to keep her mouth shut?"

"My wife speaks only when she's told to," Tammuz said.

"Mmm, a good woman. Then she may be useful, too. An innkeeper and his wife hear many things from their customers, especially when the customers have drunk too much ale. When you hear such things that may be of interest, I would like to know them. You would, of course, be paid for what you tell me, provided it is useful."

"What kinds of things?"

"Oh, anything of importance. Things that might be of some use to Sumer's rulers. Any talk about unrest, people complaining about the king's rule, gossip about Akkad, even information about trade and cargoes, boats, caravans. Anything of interest."

Tammuz and En-hedu had heard rumors that the new queen, Kushanna, wanted as much information as possible about the six cities in Sumeria, as well as the far north. Enar would be one of her informers, seeking such information from any source he could find.

He glanced at his wife, who nodded. "How much would you pay?"

"At least a copper coin for anything of value. More, if it is especially useful. Much more if what you hear is of real importance, such as anyone plotting against the king."

"The Kestrel is a good tavern," Tammuz said, "but not good enough for most ship captains or boat masters. All that come here are the crewmen, the rowers, and some guards."

"I know who patronizes this place. I've been here before. You must not remember me."

Tammuz didn't, which annoyed him. He should be alert enough to recognize a Sumerian spy.

"How would I get such information to you?"

"I stay at the White Gull. If I'm not there, you can leave a message with the owner."

Tammuz nodded. "I'll keep my ears open. If I hear anything . . ."

"Another thing . . . you might want to encourage some of your more interesting customers to talk. Slip them a little extra ale, if need be. Your wife . . . your whores . . . the more you can get your patrons to talk about home – especially those from Akkad and upriver – the better."

"We can do that," En-hedu said, joining the conversation for the first time. "As long as you pay each time."

A brief frown crossed Enar's face at her impertinence. Women should speak only when spoken to. "I'll pay when you tell me something useful." He returned his eyes to Tammuz. "Best if you didn't say anything about this to anyone else. Nor to Jarud. Even those who live here in Sumer might need to be reported, should they say anything against King Shulgi's interest. That includes members of the city's guard."

"I understand."

"Well, then, I'll be on my way. Your first customers should be arriving soon." Enar stood, nodded approvingly, and left the tavern.

En-hedu sat down beside Tammuz. "At least he didn't demand a silver coin from us."

"Who knows, but we may be able to make a few extra coins this way."

"It does only seem fair, with what we're paying in taxes and fees, to get something back."

They laughed at the idea of spying for Sumer.

The next day, En-hedu gave massages to Irkalla and Anu. Both women worked hard, and En-hedu knew they would appreciate a little attention. Mother and daughter kept the kitchen, common room, and their own chamber clean. They started working early in the day before the first customer arrived, and then sometimes labored until Tammuz fastened the door, and even after. Some customers wanted servicing long into the night, and again in the morning. As the Kestrel grew more and more popular, the number of customers increased, and Irkalla and Anu rushed back and forth carrying food and ale, in addition to occasionally disappearing into their chamber with a patron for a time, usually as brief an interval as the girls could manage.

Giving the mother and daughter a massage helped En-hedu, who needed the practice. Aside from Tammuz, she hadn't given anyone a massage since they left Akkad. She started with Irkalla, who had never received a massage before. This early in the day, there were no customers in the Kestrel. Anu covered a table in the common room with a folded blanket, and En-hedu told Irkalla to remove her dress, and lie face down on the blanket. With Anu watching, En-hedu began working the woman's neck and shoulder muscles. A few drops of oil helped warm Irkalla's skin, and soon En-hedu moved down to the lower back. By then, Irkalla sighed with pleasure as the stiffness in her body faded, and the muscles stretched without straining.

By the time En-hedu had finished, Anu, showing more excitement on her face than En-hedu had ever seen, pleaded for a similar rubdown, hopping up and down in her eagerness.

"Please, mistress," Anu said. "My back has been hurting for days."

En-hedu smiled at the girl. "Give me a few moments to rest."

While Irkalla dressed, Anu removed her garment and moved up onto the table. As En-hedu began, she saw that the girl's back really did need work. The muscles in her right shoulder were knotted. Now that she noticed it, En-hedu realized why the girl sometimes had trouble standing up straight.

"You are very stiff, Anu. We shall have to do this every day for awhile, until your back is straight."

Shadows blocked the door, and En-hedu glanced up to see Tammuz and Rimaud returning. The guard carried a wineskin under each arm, and Tammuz had a third one slung over his shoulder. Tammuz's mouth opened in surprise at finding his wife working on a naked Anu, who moaned and sighed at each touch of En-hedu hands. She smiled at her husband, who stood there, fascinated. En-hedu saw his eyes fasten their gaze on Anu's body, and a moment later, she caught sight of his erection pushing up against his tunic.

"Almost finished," she said to Tammuz. "Then you can take Anu's place. It's time we took care of you."

Tammuz blushed, which made Irkalla laugh. En-hedu moved her hands lower down on Anu's back, and began squeezing the globes of her buttocks. En-hedu slipped her hand between the girl's legs, and found her secret place wet and aroused. Anu moaned again at the touch, and opened her legs wider in invitation.

"Enough for today," En-hedu said, giving the girl a friendly slap on the buttocks. "Now it's your turn, Tammuz. I think the three of us should be able to satisfy you."

Before her still-blushing husband could protest, she took his hand and guided him to the table. En-hedu helped him remove his tunic, and then she undid his undergarment, letting it drop to the floor. With Irkalla's assistance, she eased Tammuz onto the table, on his back.

His unfettered erection throbbed in the air.

"So big," Irkalla said, brushing the member with her fingers. "He must give you much pleasure."

"Oh, yes. It feels so good inside me."

"Shall I relieve him for you?" Irkalla asked. "Or Anu?"

"No, his rod is mine alone," En-hedu said. "But you can use your mouth to satisfy him, while Anu and I will keep his hands and lips busy.

She slid her tunic down off her shoulders, and moved up onto the table, letting her breast brush against Tammuz's mouth. In a moment, Anu moved to the other side and did the same. At the same time, Irkalla knelt on the blanket between his legs, and took his staff into her mouth.

Tammuz's hands went to the women's breasts, and he cupped and squeezed them even as Anu shifted her body so that her left breast brushed his face.

Except for the training with Te-ara before they left Akkad, Tammuz had never had such an experience. Soon he was groaning and writhing in pleasure, as Irkalla's skilled mouth, tongue, and hands brought him to a massive explosion of seed into her mouth. She gagged a little as he came, but she never stopped moving her head up and down, draining every drop from his rod, while he clutched at Anu's breasts in his passion.

En-hedu reached down and kissed him. "I hope you enjoyed yourself, husband. Next time, we'll spend more time pleasuring you."

Dazed, Tammuz struggled to sit up. All the women had smiles on their faces. His penis might have emptied itself, but it remained hard. En-hedu knew it wouldn't take much effort to arouse him again.

She realized that Rimaud had watched the whole thing. He still stood there, his mouth gaping open, as his eyes went from one to the other.

"I think you should put your dress back on, Anu," En-hedu said. "The customers will be arriving soon. We wouldn't want them to think they should get the same service, would we?"

The next morning, En-hedu gave Rimaud a long and vigorous massage that left the big man gasping for breath and scarcely able to stand. But the day after that, the pain in his leg lessened, and he pleaded with En-hedu for another, even offering to pay her. After speaking with Tammuz, she decided to give him one every other day, with no charge. That would help relieve his pain, and by not charging him for the service, it would make him even more loyal.

The cook became En-hedu's next patient. Like many other women who performed hard labor all day long, she had lived with back trouble for years, and the massages brought the first relief she had ever known. The woman's gratitude was even more embarrassing than Rimaud's. She soon spread the word throughout the neighborhood, telling everyone at the market and along the river, where the women went to wash their garments, of En-hedu's wonderful talent.

Word of En-hedu's skill with her hands soon spread. Except for the wealthy, nearly everyone worked long hours, and many earned their bread and a place to stay by carrying heavy loads on their backs. Women, who lifted more than their share of bales and bundles, soon began appearing at the Kestrel, seeking to speak with En-hedu, and asking, in halting words and nervous voices, if they could have a massage.

En-hedu charged each one a copper coin, but most women could not afford to pay for such a luxury. Instead, they bartered their services or other goods to pay for each massage. Soon En-hedu had chickens, rabbits, bread, fruit, cloth, garments, and dozens of other items being traded for her skill. En-hedu and Tammuz's sandals, worn down from the long walk from Ubaid, were repaired for free.

The local carpenter across from the Kestrel and the leather worker down the lane started spending time on En-hedu's table, and paying for the service by doing work around the inn. The carpenter made her a narrow table to facilitate the massage, as well as some new tables and benches for the inn, and the tanner provided straps to repair the sagging bed and replace the door hinges. Another customer provided cloth and rope to create some privacy for a corner of the common room, so that the women could remove their garments without worrying about the customers gawking. At first a few grinning patrons tried to peek behind the curtain nonetheless, but Rimaud took care of that problem by tossing them out into the lane.

All this work took time away from running the Kestrel, but thankfully a normal routine had settled in. En-hedu and Tammuz gave Irkalla more responsibility, and increased her wage to compensate. The inn now filled up almost every night, so they added another one of the cook's daughters to help prepare meals beside the basic stew. Almost every night meat was served, depending on what En-hedu's customers brought in barter that day.

Two months after En-hedu gave her first massage, she found herself working almost full time, doing five or six people a day. Some of the customers who stopped in after a hard day's labor decided they would rather have a massage than two cups of ale. More customers flocked to the Kestrel, to take advantage of her expertise. Many, of course, wanted extra servicing afterwards, but Irkalla and Anu took care of that part of the business. A few quick strokes from their strong hands soon satisfied the relaxed customer.

As word of her success spread through the city, some of the other taverns began offering the same service, but these were generally mere serving girls who specialized in a more personal massage. They lacked En-hedu's special skills, and those in pain or suffering stiffness continued to patronize the Kestrel.

En-hedu came to enjoy the work. With practice, her arms and hands had grown stronger, and she no longer exhausted herself by a long day's work. She'd also learned to examine each back, and vary her efforts. Those who really had knotted muscles received the full massage, but those who merely wanted to relax or loosen up their backs were easily satisfied with a different routine that required less effort.

Tammuz changed his mind about her work. He saw the gratitude in the eyes of those she helped. Besides, everyone praised his wife's skill, which helped improve his own standing in the neighborhood. Best of all, and despite all the extra customers, the Kestrel operated so smoothly that it required less work on their part. By now they often forgot the real purpose of their being there.

One day, just before mid-morning, two men entered the Kestrel. One was dressed in a clean garment, fine sandals, and wore an intricately stitched belt around his waist. The other had the size and weight of a bodyguard, and carried a sword hanging from his belt.

"Is this the Kestrel tavern? Is there a woman name En-hedu working here?"

Tammuz had grown so accustomed to the first question that he no longer bothered to point out the painted bird next to the inn's door, which in his trusting way, he'd thought even a fool of a city dweller should be able to recognize. "Yes, En-hedu is my wife."

"My mistress has need of her services."

"And you are . . . ?"

The man seemed insulted that Tammuz didn't recognize him. "I am Joratta, steward to the House of Puzur-Amurri. My mistress, Ninlil, is his second wife. She desires that the woman En-hedu attend to her right away."

Tammuz glanced at En-hedu, who entered the common room from their private quarters, wiping her hands on her dress. He'd heard of Puzur-Amurri, one of the richest traders in Sumer, rumored even more wealthy than Gemama, but had never seen him or any of his wives, and knew even less about them.

"My wife's services cost one copper coin."

"That is for my mistress Ninlil to decide, after the massage."

"Well, where is she?" Tammuz knew the answer to that question before he asked it. "Tell her to come in."

The servant looked shocked at the suggestion that his mistress would enter a common alehouse. "The servant En-hedu is to come to Puzur-Amurri's house, and right now."

"That's a long walk from here, all the way across Sumer. My wife has work enough to keep her busy right here. I'd have to charge you two coppers, and you would have to escort her back here."

That much was true enough. Though he trusted En-hedu's ability to take care of herself, he didn't want her walking around unescorted in a strange part of Sumer, where she might not be as well known. Lone women could be easily assaulted, or even taken away. It had happened before.

"My mistress will decide that," Joratta repeated.

"She can't go right now," Tammuz said. "There's work to be done here. Maybe later in the morning."

"My mistress is . . . needs her services at once. Right away." Joratta glanced at the bodyguard.

The man stepped forward, moving past Joratta until he was right in Tammuz's face. "She's to come with us now, cripple. Or do you want your good arm broken?" He leaned closer and reached out to poke Tammuz in the chest.

Tammuz caught the man's wrist in his right hand and jerked him forward. In the same motion, he shifted to the side and extended his leg. The bodyguard went crashing to the floor, and before he could react, Tammuz had his knee on his chest and his knife at his throat.

"Touch me again . . . call me a cripple again, and I'll kill you." He emphasized his meaning by jabbing the tip of the knife into the guard's neck. A trickle of blood appeared and the man's eyes widened in fear.

A sword rasped from a sheath, and Joratta, still in shock at the sudden movement, turned to see Rimaud limping toward him, the short blade carried menacingly in his hand.

"Wait! Stop!" Joratta raised his hands. He couldn't conceal the fear in his voice. "Don't do anything foolish. There's no need for violence."

Tammuz regained his feet in a smooth motion and slipped the knife back in his belt. "Next time keep your bodyguard out in the lane where he belongs."

Joratta pulled the shaken bodyguard to his feet, and pushed him out the door.

"Husband, I can go now with Joratta." En-hedu's voice was properly subservient, a dutiful wife trying to mollify a gruff husband. "My other client can wait until I return."

Tammuz frowned at her for a moment, as if making up his mind.

"Well, then go. Remember to come back with two copper coins."

"I'll get my oils," En-hedu said, bowing to Joratta.

Tammuz followed her back into their quarters, and gave her a quick hug. "Good luck to you, and take care around Joratta and the guard. They'll be angry enough."

"You did well, husband. I'll try and soothe Joratta's feelings on the way, and the guard's."

She left the chamber and the inn. Tammuz followed her to the doorway and watched the three of them disappear up the lane. This was what Lady Trella had hoped for, planned for – a chance to move into the inner circle of Sumer's elite. Now he just had to hope he hadn't played his role too strongly.

25

En-hedu did soothe Joratta's feelings on the walk back to his master's house, and even the bodyguard stopped glaring at her. Servants and slaves of powerful families often became as arrogant as their masters, and expected everyone to obey their slightest command. Nevertheless, En-hedu felt worried that perhaps Tammuz had angered the servant so much that he would convince his mistress never to summon her again.

The house of Puzur-Amurri was an imposing two-story residence in the most fashionable of Sumer's quarters, not far from King Shulgi's Compound. It lacked a walled courtyard to separate it from the lane, but competent workmen had plastered the front of the house and painted it a light blue. The doorway, taller than a man and wide enough to allow two men to walk in abreast, announced its owner's wealth and position. En-hedu saw that a servant stood watch outside the door, opening it for expected guests, and making sure no one in the lanes used the walls of the Puzur-Amurri home to relieve themselves.

Inside, En-hedu found herself in a large chamber that seemed to have no purpose. An opening that reached up through the second floor allowed light and fresh air to enter the room. Benches faced each other from the side walls, and two doorways led to the interior of the house. The chamber provided a place out of the heat for clients to wait until Master Puzur-Amurri deigned to meet them. A real extravagance, she decided. Those wishing to visit his wives would also remain here until summoned.

"Wait here," Joratta ordered.

He disappeared through the door on the right. En-hedu had expected to be brought to the wife, Ninlil, right away, but apparently whatever urgency dispatched the servant had vanished. After awhile, En-hedu set her basket of oils on the bench and sat beside it.

The odd-shaped shadow caused by the sun moved slowly across the floor. Once a man came out of the second door, but he didn't even bother to glance in her direction as he left the house.

At last Joratta returned. "Come with me. Be respectful to Mistress Ninlil, and do as she asks."

He led the way through the other door, down an impressively wide passageway until he reached another chamber. A carved door stood open, but Joratta knocked anyway.

A listless voice bade him enter.

"Mistress, the woman En-hedu is here."

En-hedu timidly followed him into the room. A bedroom larger than anything she had ever seen in Akkad – even in the house of Lady Trella – greeted her eyes. A narrow window looked out into a courtyard that faced the rear of the house. A table rested near the window, flanked by two carved chairs. Three chests lined the opposite · wall, and En-hedu wondered how anyone could have so many possessions as to need that many. The remainder of the room was taken up by the largest bed En-hedu had ever seen. The merchant Puzur-Amurri must have plenty of wealth to lavish so much of it on a mere second wife.

Ninlil reclined on the bed, her head propped up by two cushions. A loose garment dyed light brown covered her breasts, but her shoulders were bare. She spared En-hedu a quick glance and wrinkled her mouth in distaste.

"She's filthy. I won't have her dirty hands on me. Are you sure she's the one?"

"Yes, mistress. En-hedu of the Kestrel Inn."

"Can you give a good massage, woman?"

En-hedu bowed low. "Yes, mistress." She let a quaver slip into her voice. Ninlil expected to be feared and obeyed.

"Oomara says you helped her slave. She'd injured her back, and she claimed you cured it."

"I am not a healer, mistress, only a giver of massages. Many times it can help ease the pain in a person's back."

Ninlil pondered her choices for a moment. "Clean her up, Joratta.

Scrub the dirt off her if you have to." She closed her eyes and let her head fall back on the cushion.

Joratta took En-hedu's arm. "Come with me," he said, his voice almost a whisper, as if he did not want to wake his mistress. En-hedu followed him through the door and into the passage, turning this time in the opposite direction, until they reached the rear of the house. He guided her to the well, which provided fresh water for the household, and En-hedu drew up a bucket. She washed her hands and face, drying both on her dress, while Joratta leaned against the wall, impatience showing in his nervous movements.

"I'm ready, Joratta."

"You'd best do a good job, or she'll take it out on me."

"Yes, I understand."

Back in the bedroom, they found Ninlil sitting up in bed. She dismissed Joratta. "Let me see your hands," she commanded. "Clean enough, I suppose," she muttered. "But take off that dress. I don't want your filthy clothes touching any part of me or my bed."

En-hedu wasn't a slave to be commanded or paraded naked for her master's benefit, but Joratta had closed the door behind him, so the two women had the chamber to themselves. En-hedu set her basket down on the floor and pulled her dress up and over her head. She held the garment in her hand, then dropped it on the floor. No doubt Ninlil would have protested if En-hedu's dress had touched anything else in the room.

Ninlil removed her covering, and flopped back onto the bed on her stomach. The movement drew a gasp of pain from the woman as she tried to find a comfortable position. "Begin. Do something."

En-hedu heard the pain in her voice. She ran her fingers down the woman's back. The first thing she noticed was how soft Ninlil's skin felt to her touch. Too soft. En-hedu probed with her fingertips and felt little resistance. The beautiful body was weak, with no firm muscles resisting En-hedu's probing touch. Ninlil had probably never done any physical work in her life, likely never lifted anything heavier than a wine cup. Fawning servants no doubt provided everything at her command.

"Watch where you touch, woman. That hurts!"

It probably did, En-hedu saw. A lump under the skin showed where the girl's pitiful muscles had contracted in a knot. The spine appeared crooked as well. She opened her mouth to tell Ninlil what she found, then closed it. Better to say nothing about such things.

"I'm going to knead the muscles on your back, mistress. It may feel painful at first, but it should give you relief."

En-hedu poured a few drops of oil across the girl's shoulders, and started working the muscles from the neck down. The base of Ninlil's neck had another clump of strained muscles, and she massaged that slowly, taking her time and letting the heat from the oil and her hands warm the flesh. Gradually the knot loosened a bit, and En-hedu moved her hands lower.

Groans and grunts accompanied her every touch.

"How long has your back troubled you, mistress?" Talking might distract Ninlil from the pain.

"None of your . . . damn you, that hurts! Can't you be more gentle?"

"I'm sorry, mistress. But I must work your muscles if you are to feel better."

"I fell and hurt my back about two years ago. Since then, the pain has grown worse each day. Now when my husband visits my bed, he complains that I can't pleasure him properly."

"How often does he come to you?" En-hedu moved her hands lower.

"Every three days. He has two other wives. Neither is as beautiful as I am, but they have no pain to deal with. They can do things to him that I cannot."

"How sad." She added a few more drops of oil, and moved her hands lower. Now the really deep massage would begin, and En-hedu had no doubt that it was going to hurt.

"If I can't please him, he may send me back to my father's house, and demand the return of his dowry. The other wives would be glad to be rid of me."

The story came out as En-hedu's hands kept pushing and kneading the soft flesh. Puzur-Amurri, a vigorous and wealthy merchant nearing his fiftieth season, had been captivated by Ninlil's beauty, pursued her with passion, and paid plenty of gold to her father for her maidenhead. But now Puzzi, as she called him, had grown annoyed at her problem, especially when she had been unable to keep his shaft firm, a task that apparently required quite some effort.

As Ninlil related her tale of bedroom failures, En-hedu's fingers kept moving, working the flesh, probing the weak areas, moving all the way down to the lower back and the curve of her buttocks. As she worked, En-hedu tried to recall everything that Zenobia and Te-ara had taught her –

the muscles must be massaged firmly and with pressure, to send the warmth of the oil and En-hedu's hands deep into the body.

By now Ninlil had reached the peak of the massage. Her breath came heavily, and she moaned at every movement, followed by a sigh of pleasure when En-hedu's hands moved away from the weak points.

"I think, Mistress Ninlil, that is all I can do for you today." En-hedu stepped away from the bed. Leaning over like that tired her own back, and the muscles in her forearms ached from the strain. "Now you should rest." She gathered up her dress and slipped it over her head.

Ninlil pushed herself up to a sitting position, her head swaying at the movement. "I feel weak." She stretched out her arm for her garment. "Owww! It hurts! What have you done to me?"

"You must lay still for now. The pain will pass in a few moments."

"Damn you! You've ruined me. I'll have you whipped for this." With a gasp of pain, she tried to sit up, then collapsed back onto the bed. "Joratta! Help me!"

En-hedu never got another word in. Ninlil kept shrieking, and Joratta, who must have been waiting just outside the chamber, rushed in and attempted to calm her. Her cries grew louder and soon other servants rushed into the room, all anxious to soothe their mistress.

Joratta turned to En-hedu. He mouthed the word 'Go.'

En-hedu snatched up her basket and slipped out the door. She practically ran through the house and back into the street. As she turned off the lane, she glanced behind her, to make sure no one followed. It would be bad if they caught her and brought her back for a beating.

But no one showed any interest in her passage. Dejected, she set a quick pace and started the long walk back to the Kestrel.

En-hedu was still distraught when she related the story to Tammuz. He poured a cup of ale mixed with water, and she drank it gratefully.

"Well, you tried your best."

"She should not have moved. I told her to lay still."

"At least you got out of there before they realized you were gone."

"If she had been pleased, others of her class would have sought me out. Now there will be no one."

A servant skilled at massage, especially one dealing with the wives and concubines of the wealthy class, would have access to much information.

Men talked too freely in front of their women, or boasted of what they knew to impress them. Either way, as Trella and Annok-sur had discovered, women knew much more than their husbands and lovers ever dreamed.

"Stay close to the inn for a few days," Tammuz cautioned. "She may send Joratta to search you out and have you beaten."

"If she does, you mustn't do anything. A beating is nothing. I can endure far worse. But you might risk everything we have if you try to stop her."

"We'll see." He patted her shoulder. "We'll see."

The rest of the day brought no news of Joratta or Ninlil's other servants, no threats or complaints. En-hedu returned to her regular routine, and saw her usual clients. As a result of her skilled hands that day, the Kestrel made a profit of two copper coins, two chickens and a handcart load of clean white sand direct from the beach to spread across the floor.

The evening passed quietly as well, and Tammuz pushed Joratta and his whip to the back of his mind. Tammuz and En-hedu had a business to run, and its demands soon took their thoughts away from Ninlil. Another day and night went by without any sight of Joratta. But mid-morning of the next day brought Ninlil's servant and his bodyguard back to the Kestrel's door.

Tammuz glanced up when the entrance darkened. It took a moment to recognize Joratta, but as soon as Tammuz did, he summoned his own bodyguard. "Rimaud!"

The Kestrel's guard stepped into the common room, and limped slowly toward Tammuz's side, left hand on the scabbard of the short sword.

Joratta, eyes blinking in the semi-darkness, either didn't notice their alertness or didn't care. "Where is En-hedu? She must return to my mistress as soon as possible."

"So she can be whipped?" Tammuz moved to his feet and rested his hand on his knife.

"What?" A look of disbelief crossed Joratta's face. "No, of course not. My mistress wants to have another massage."

Tammuz looked toward Joratta's guard in the street. This was a different man, and he paced slowly back and forth outside the Kestrel, showing no interest in his master's business. Joratta obviously had no thoughts of a beating on his mind. If the woman wanted another massage . . .

"Go back to your mistress while you can still walk." Tammuz returned to his stool, but kept his feet on the ground. "And before I remember you owe me two coppers for my wife's labors."

"My mistress will pay her whatever she asks, but she must come now."

Tammuz laughed. "Your mistress has no credit here. She'll pay what she owes, and pay in advance if she ever wants to see my wife again. Tell her that."

"You don't understand. My mistress..." he moved closer and lowered his voice, "she pleasured her husband so well that he wishes her to come to his bed again tomorrow. So she must have another massage right away."

"I thought she was screaming in pain when she threatened En-hedu with a beating."

Joratta grimaced. "She was in pain ... for most of the night. But in the morning when she awoke, she felt much better, and by the evening when the master came to her chamber, the pain was almost gone."

Tammuz couldn't keep the smile off his face. "Maybe your master should come here to spend time with En-hedu himself. She could pleasure him without getting your mistress involved."

Rimaud snickered at the jest, and Joratta frowned again.

"You owe me two copper coins." Tammuz leaned forward and pointed his finger at Ninlil's servant. "Plus another one for threatening my wife and letting her walk back here without an escort. Then two more for if your mistress wants another session. That's five coins. Pay now, or get out."

"I can't pay that." Joratta looked uncomfortable. "What if my mistress refuses to pay so much? Or if there is more pain?"

"I don't care. Go back to your mistress. Tell her what she must pay. If she agrees, you can return here. En-hedu will be back by then, and if she's willing to give your mistress another massage, you can walk her there. And back. And by all the gods in Sumer, if she walks back alone this time, she'll never set foot in your mistress's house again."

Joratta decided Tammuz meant every word. "Just make sure she's here when I return." He turned and walked from the Kestrel, shouting at his guard as he emerged. Their voices quickly disappeared up the lane.

"Do you think she'll pay?"

Tammuz looked at Rimaud and laughed. "A second wife who can't pleasure her husband? She'll pay that and more."

They were both still laughing when En-hedu arrived.

26

Two months later ...

Shulgi picked his horse through the bodies of men, women and children until he reached what had been the center of the village. Not that much remained. His men had put the torch to all the tents and reed huts of the Salib encampment. They'd stripped the bodies and the dwellings of anything of value first, of course. Flies buzzed about his head, and he brushed them away. They had more than enough to feast on. More than a few carcasses of horses, cows, sheep, goats and other herd animals lay scattered about, mixed randomly with the bodies of their former owners. Even a few dogs, who could have escaped easily enough, had died defending the animals entrusted to their care. Others howled from the edges of the encampment, driven away by the sounds and smells of death.

The wail of the surviving women and children hung in the air as well. The cries of anguish and sorrow seemed almost powerful enough to return the dead to life. Men lined up to rape the women, pushing and shoving to keep their places. Not that Shulgi or his men cared in the slightest about their victims, alive or dead. The Salibs, even more than the Tanukhs, had raided Sumer's lands too often in the past. Everyone in Sumeria hated them, even more than they hated the Akkadians in the north. Shulgi felt satisfaction at the thought that he would be the one to pay back the Salibs for their constant raids.

For generations, the villages of Sumer had been too weak to strike back at their tormentors from the desert. Now, as the cities swelled in number, that had changed, and the power of the sword now rested in Sumeria. Rested in Shulgi's own hand, when all was said and done. He'd led his men in the attack, guiding them straight toward the largest concentration of Salibs. Two who opposed him had died, though one was an old man and not really worth counting. Most of the Salibs fled when they realized the numbers of their attackers. More important, his men knew he fought in the forefront, not from behind their ranks, as his father would have done. From this day on, Sumerians could speak about their warrior king without any doubts as to his courage or skill.

Shulgi let his eyes scan the battleground. A few of Razrek's men galloped in from the desert, after chasing down the last of the fleeing tribesmen. By the desert-dwellers' standards, this had been a rich village, where men measured wealth in the number and strength of their horses. Now most of those horses belonged to Sumer, and would be used to build the ever-growing force of cavalry Shulgi demanded. Every mount captured would be a weapon aimed straight at Akkad. The rest of the loot, whether livestock, gold, jewels or women, would be divided into three parts, with two parts going to his Tanukh allies.

Razrek and two of his men rode up, their horses picking the way through the rubble and dead bodies.

"Hail, King Shulgi. A mighty victory."

"Did you get all the horses?" Shulgi ignored the words of praise. Defeating this desert scum meant little. They remained only the first step on his long march to Akkad.

"Nearly all of them. More than we expected. Many broke loose, and it will take a few days to round them all up. We should add at least two or three hundred horses. And I don't think we'll have any trouble with our friends after this."

The success of this first joint raid with Kapturu's men should ease some of the tension between the two groups. The Tanukhs had earned their share of the gold and women they prized so much. That should keep them from bickering and arguing over every little detail with their Sumerian ally. The fact that Shulgi had ridden at the head of his men would also be noticed, along with the Salib blood still staining his sword. Chief Kapturu had remained safely out of harm's way throughout the fighting.

"I suppose we'll have to waste a few days celebrating." Shulgi shook his head in disgust.

"No way to avoid that," Razrek agreed. "When that's over with, Kapturu will send some of his men back to his village with the women and spoils."

Shulgi had lost a handful of Sumerians in the fighting, and now the Tanukh chief would further weaken their combined force just to safeguard his share of the loot. Meanwhile, the next village in their path would have plenty of warning, either to flee or fight. From this day onward, it would be war in the desert, and Shulgi would need every man.

"I managed to grab a couple of women from Kapturu's men, so we'll each have something to keep us occupied." Razrek offered that to try and cheer his commander.

Compared to Kushanna, these would be ugly enough. Still, any woman was better than none, and by now Razrek knew enough to make sure his king received the more promising of the two. "Make sure you clean them up first," Shulgi ordered.

Razrek smiled at such fastidiousness. "Don't worry, my king. They'll be grateful enough that we haven't handed them over to the Tanukhs."

Shulgi turned away. His men would be erecting a tent for him. He would bathe in the oasis that had supported this village, then he would amuse himself with the captive woman for the next few days, as a leader should. There was nothing else he could do. Shulgi knew he had to be patient. It would take many months, maybe even a year to subdue the Salibs. Only after that feat ended could he think about preparing the Tanukhs for war against Akkad.

Still, word of this victory would spread over the desert. Even as the Salibs banded together, so would more Tanukhs rush to join Kapturu's standard. And Shulgi's losses would be steadily replenished from the training camps in Sumer and the surrounding regions. Most important, his men gained fighting experience. All this should happen without alerting Akkad's spies to what he intended. After all, he could afford to wait a few years for his empire. He would then have a long life, with Kushanna as the first of many wives, to enjoy the world he had conquered.

Kushanna frowned at the man on his knees before her. Big, but soft, she decided. Recent tears had streaked his dirt covered face, bruises covered his face and arms, and his bound hands shook as he held them against his chest. His eyes held a hint of wildness, as if he were not quite right in the head.

Sohrab, accompanied by two guards, had escorted the prisoner into her presence. Sohrab had returned to Sumer with his captive last night, and requested a morning audience.

"Is this the man from Carnax?"

"Yes, my queen. He's the only survivor I could find. His name is Dilse. I searched all over, but –"

"You had to force him to come to Sumer?"

Not that she cared, but something seemed odd with the situation. Any plodding farmer should be eager for the chance to earn a few coins and visit Sumer.

Sohrab licked his lips. "He's not exactly one of Carnax's survivors." He saw the frown and hurried on. "It seems he was one of the bandits who sacked the village. I think he's afraid he'll be killed for what he did."

Interesting, and perhaps even better than some ignorant villager who probably knew little about the raid. "Lift up his head."

One of the guards grabbed the man by his hair and twisted it back until the man's mouth hung open, and his Adam's apple bulged toward her. His eyes lost the wild look, replaced with fear.

"Listen to me, Dilse. I care nothing about whatever you've done in the past. But I want to know everything about the raid on Carnax. If you tell me what I want to know, you'll be set free and even earn a few coppers." She waved her hand at the guard, and he released his hold on Dilse's hair. "Now speak."

"My queen," he gasped, "I know nothing about any raid. I'm just a caravan guard who became separated from my master. Please . . . I've done nothing."

A child could have recognized the lie. "You should not try to deceive me, Dilse. Perhaps some time with the torturers will help loosen your tongue." She turned to the guards. "Take him outside and cut off his fingers, one by one, until he's ready to speak."

For a moment, Kushanna enjoyed the look of horror on the man's face. Then she turned away.

"No . . . I'll tell you what I know! Please! Mercy!"

She ignored the cries for mercy. The guards knew what to do. They'd cut off one or two fingers before dragging the prisoner back, no matter what he promised. She walked across the room to the balcony. "Come with me, Sohrab."

"Yes, my queen.'"

"Tell me what you learned." She gazed down into the courtyard. The two guards soon appeared, jerking Dilse along between them. A small table set against the outer wall held several small knives and other implements.

"I spoke with several farmers who lived nearby. They knew little of what happened that day. It was almost four years ago. Those who lived too close to the village were all murdered. Apparently, there was a power struggle among Carnax's elders. A trader named Fradmon sought vengeance for the death of his son, executed for murder by the village elder. This Fradmon hired some bandits, and they attacked the village at night. The village elder, a man named Ranaddi, perished at Fradmon's hand. Ranaddi had a trusted advisor, and he had a grown son and a young daughter named Trella."

"It's not that uncommon a name."

"No, my queen. But this Trella was favored by Ranaddi, favored enough that she attended many of his meetings. She was said to be keen of wit."

Kushanna frowned. That sounded like the witch of Akkad. "How old was this child?"

"Not a child, my queen. She had already been given the rites of passage. Despite that, no man had claimed her for a husband."

A shriek erupted from the courtyard. Kushanna glanced down just as the guard tossed the first finger into the dirt.

"And what happened to this Trella?"

"It seems that Fradmon, who planned the attack, was killed by the leader of the bandits, who turned on his master and then took all the gold for himself and his men. Instead of killing everyone, the bandit spared the women and a few young men. He took them with him when he departed, probably to sell as slaves."

Another scream of pain echoed against the walls. This time the guard looked up at the balcony. Kushanna signaled the guard to cease.

"And Dilse was one of the bandits?"

"That's what the people living nearby believed. He returned to the area a few months later, still with plenty of coins in his purse. Apparently, he is not quite right in the head. A few times he got drunk, and boasted of the raid on Carnax."

Down below, the guards were binding up Dilse's hand. It took only moments before they disappeared from view.

Kushanna turned away from the balcony. "Well, we'll soon know." She led the way into the chamber. The guards returned, dragging the prisoner between them. They'd wrapped his right hand in a rag, to catch the bleeding. They knew she didn't like bloodstains on the floor.

"He's ready to talk, Queen Kushanna."

They usually were, after a losing a few fingers. "Give him some water," she ordered.

Dilse managed to choke down a mouthful, but more spilled on his chest and the floor. "Mercy . . . mercy." His voice trailed off into a whimper.

"Tell me of Carnax," she ordered. "Tell me everything you know of the raid, or you'll lose more than your fingers."

The story came out between sobs. Dilse had been a servant for the merchant Fradmon. He and his steward had returned and slaughtered almost the entire village. But then the steward, a man named Sondar, turned upon his master, killing him, and taking the few survivors as slaves. They marched the captives, mostly women and children, off to a slave trader waiting nearby. Dilse even remembered the name of the slaver – Drusas.

The name made Kushanna smile. An odious little man, he lived right here in Sumer, flaunting his wealth and still dealing in slaves. A stroke of luck that Dilse remembered the slaver's name, Kushanna decided. Drusas took delight in every one of his slaves. She felt certain he would remember what happened to Trella and her brother.

"And this Trella and her brother were sold to Drusas?"

"Yes, my queen." Dilse had to pause to choke back the sobs. "Sondar sold all the captives to Drusas. Once they were gone, all of us rode north, eager to get away from Carnax."

"No doubt." She turned her gaze toward Sohrab. "Did you speak to Drusas?"

"I tried to, my queen. I went to his house last night to ask if he remembered anything about Trella's brother, but Drusas had departed yesterday morning for the slaver's camp upriver. He won't be back for several days."

At least Sohrab understood the importance of the information.

She decided there was little more to glean from the wretch, kneeling at her feet. Then she had another thought. "This Sondar . . . can you describe him?"

A few moments later, Kushanna glanced at Sohrab. He nodded agreement.

"I think we have no further need for poor Dilse," Kushanna said. "Take care of him."

The guards smiled and dragged the prisoner away. They'd take him to the rear of the courtyard and drive a sword through his heart.

"You've done well, Sohrab. Keep all this to yourself. It may prove useful. Wait here for a moment."

"Of course, my queen." Sohrab bowed at the compliment.

Kushanna returned to the balcony. She wanted some time to think. Sondar had changed his name to Razrek, and within a few months had become King Eridu's most favored leader. Not that Razrek's murderous past made any difference. He could have burned a dozen villages for all she cared. But there might come a day when such knowledge might be useful.

Even more useful might be Trella's brother, if he were still alive and could be found. At the least she should be able to sell him to Akkad for a heavy price. Depending on Trella's feelings of affection, perhaps even further advantages could be obtained. But first the witch's brother must be found. She turned away from the courtyard and swept back into the room.

"I want Trella's brother brought to Sumer. Go after Drusas and find out what he knows. Make sure he tells you everything about the raid on Carnax, as well as what befell Trella and her brother. Tell him if I'm not satisfied with what he remembers, he may find more of his property in Sumer confiscated."

"Yes, my queen. And if I find that the brother is dead?"

"I'll reward you well if you bring him back. But even if he's dead, knowledge of his fate might be useful." Kushanna smiled. Yes, alive or dead, Trella's brother would help Sumer.

27

The morning after he returned to Akkad, Eskkar went down to the barracks to see Gatus. Last night, at the evening meal, the old soldier mentioned some new training routines that he wanted Eskkar to see. Eskkar promised he would stop by the barracks at mid-morning. Even with Gatus's warning, Eskkar slowed in surprise when he entered the training ground.

Months had passed since Gatus's last demonstration. Eskkar had seen the men training during that time, but between governing the city, working with the slingers, visiting Nuzi and the horse camps, not to mention his own training, he hadn't paid much attention to the men's training. He had more than enough to occupy his time.

Eskkar's eyes widened at the size of the group. Today one hundred spearmen stood there waiting for his arrival, all of them carrying shields, swords, and resting the butt end of their spears on the ground. Every man wore thick sandals and each had a bronze helmet, the latest idea Gatus and Trella had come up with. It made the soldiers appear both taller and fiercer. They looked ready to march into battle. Gatus sat on his stool facing them, waiting patiently.

The men had assembled in four ranks of twenty-five each. Two of the ranks faced the other two, about twenty paces apart.

Gatus picked up his stool and strode over to where Eskkar stood. "Good morning, Captain. I think you'll enjoy this."

"Were you waiting long for me?" Eskkar imagined the men standing in the hot sun all morning, waiting for his arrival.

"No, I told a runner to let me know when you left the Compound."

Eskkar remembered seeing a boy dash off down the lane. And, of course, Gatus was too good a commander to let men stand about in the hot sun doing nothing. At least, not without a good reason.

"What am I going to see?"

"I've been thinking about Sumer's army. We know they'll have men armed with swords and shields, and I think we should expect them to have plenty of spearmen as well. So I decided to figure out what our first encounter might look like. We've been practicing this for the last ten days. Now you can see what we've been doing."

Gatus walked back to the men, and moved into the center area between the facing ranks. "You men know the rules. Today you will be the Eagle army," he pointed to the men on his left, "against the Hawk army." With his rod, he gestured to the men on his right. "First side to push an opposing man across the rope is the victor. The losing side will buy ale for the winning side all night long."

A murmur went through the men as they readied themselves. Eskkar noticed two ropes stretched out and pegged down at either end, about ten paces behind each side.

"And this time," Gatus added, "I don't want to see anyone on the losing side trying to join the winners."

That brought forth a brief laugh up and down the lines.

Gathering his stool, Gatus moved out of the open area, but stayed just on the edge of the ranks. Two of his subcommanders took positions on one end of the spearmen, and two others shifted to the opposite end. Eskkar, as he moved to Gatus's side, realized the subcommanders would judge the men's performance.

"Spears ready!"

The men, all serious now, lifted the spears off the ground, keeping the bronze tip pointing upward.

"What side do you favor, Captain?"

Eskkar smiled as he studied the ranks. Both sides appeared similar in size and weight, so there was little to distinguish one group from the other. "I'll take the Hawks."

"Ha! The Hawks always lose to the Eagles," Gatus said. "You'll be buying my ale tonight." He faced the two ranks. "Shields up. Spears forward!"

The spears moved into a horizontal position, held shoulder high and palm up, and facing the opposing side. The men in the second rank of each group moved forward as well, each man letting his spear jut out between the shoulders of the two men in front of him, the longer spears of the second rank reaching out as far as the front rank.

Two spear walls now bristled threateningly at each other across the open space. Even from where Eskkar stood, the line of bronze-tipped weapons looked formidable. Every shield was held at eye level.

"Slow march forward ... march!" Gatus leaned toward Eskkar. "This is where it gets interesting. Hopefully, no one will get hurt this time."

The ranks began to walk toward each other. Eskkar watched, fascinated. The men were going to gut each other. But as the opposing spear tips crossed, he saw the men angling their weapons up so that they would pass between the heads of the men facing them.

As soon as the spears extended out past the line of men, the ranks surged forward, taking the last step with a rush that brought the two ranks into jarring contact. Shield crashed against shield, the sound echoing around the barracks, and accompanied by the grunts and shouts of the men.

In an instant the lines were struggling against each other. The men's feet kicked up dirt as they fought either to remain where they were or push forward. Eskkar saw a few men in the rear ranks slip to their knees, but they immediately regained their position. The men in the front rank couldn't fall down, since they were held upright by the opponent as well as the man behind. The air filled with curses or cries of triumph. Spears shifted and waved in all directions, and Eskkar saw men struck on the side of the head by the thick shafts, whether by accident or on purpose, he couldn't tell. For the first time, he noticed the many dents on the bronze helmets.

The lines wavered and buckled, as different parts of the ranks moved forward or back. The earth beneath their feet churned into a cloud of dust that hovered in the air. In moments, sweat covered every man's brow, and red faces showed the effort the men were expending. The rearmost rank pressed their shields into the backs of the innermost rank, and used that as leverage to shove the leading man forward, leg muscles straining. Every man tried to use his spear as well, to knock aside the opponent's shield or just to land a blow.

By now Eskkar could have extended his arms and enclosed all four ranks, so close together had they jammed themselves. The two leading ranks, shield pressed against shield, were crushed up against each other not only by their own force, but the pressure of the men behind them.

Slowly the Hawk line began to move backward. Men shouted to their companions to hold on, to not take that step backward. But some had no choice. The Hawk line still gripped their spears, using them to try and dislodge their opponent. Nevertheless, the Hawk line grew more jagged, as the Eagles pushed deeper and deeper into their ranks. By now every man gasped for breath.

A man went down near the center of the Hawk line, and that marked the beginning of the end. Sensing success, the Eagle army pushed harder and broke through the ranks, knocking opponents to the ground, and trampling on them. Spears entangled themselves, or were torn loose from their owner's grip. The Eagle team's shouts rose up as they rushed forward. The Hawk line collapsed, its men either driven back or knocked to the ground, trying to avoid being stepped on by the surging Eagles.

"HALT!" Gatus's voice carried over the spearmen, who crowded against each other gasping for breath. Some jumped up and down in victory, while the losers shook their heads in defeat.

"Reform ranks!"

Eskkar saw how well Gatus had trained them. Within moments, the men disentangled themselves, everyone helping the fallen regain their feet. They gathered up their spears and reformed the ranks, guided by additional orders from the subcommanders. A few of the men needed assistance to regain their positions, helped by those still strong enough to stand. Blood lay scattered across the once smooth ground between the two ranks. Eskkar guessed that a few spears in the belly would have drenched the earth with blood and entrails.

"Perhaps you should inspect the men, Captain . . . congratulate the winners."

Gatus led the way back into the open space between the ranks. The blood smell now floated in the air. Several men had deep scratches or cuts, others bled from their mouths or noses. Two or three men looked seriously hurt, dazed and barely held upright by their companions. "Stand easy, men."

Eskkar started with the Eagles, moving up and down the smiling line, talking to the men, congratulating them on their victory. He inspected the Hawk ranks next. Here he saw only a few smiles. More Hawks had been injured. Most of the faces were grim. They'd lost the struggle, suffered embarrassment in front of their king, and tonight would have to pay in the tavern for their defeat.

When he finished his inspection, Eskkar knew he would have to speak to them. This was one of those moments, as Trella explained to him, where he could bind men to his cause. He turned to Gatus. "May I command them?" The polite request was for the benefit of the men.

"Yes, Lord Eskkar," Gatus replied.

"All of you, close up and face me."

The odd command confused more than a few, but the sub-commanders stepped in. In moments, one hundred men were packed together facing him.

"How many of you have fought in battle?"

A few voices answered him, but not more than a handful.

"What you've just done will give you a good idea of what to expect on the battleground. The enemy will not yield easily. Your spears and swords will have to push him back, step by step, until his line breaks. You'll need to be tougher and stronger than your enemy, because they will probably have the advantage in numbers."

He let his eyes scan the men's faces. By now they caught their breath, and he held the attention of every one of them.

"I've waged many battles, most on horseback, or using sword against sword. What you have just done here is different, and I don't know how well I could have stood against you in battle. But I'm certain this is very much the way real fighting will be. You will be tired and hot. So will your enemy. You will probably be hungry and almost certainly thirsty. But so will your enemy. What will be different is that you will take the fight to them. They will see you ignoring your hunger and thirst, marching toward them, spears pointing at their faces, and they will be afraid. When you smash into their ranks, their fear will overwhelm them as you drive them into the ground. You will be covered in blood, but it will be their blood, not yours."

He paused and a ragged cheer erupted. Eskkar let them go on for a few moments, then held up his hand for silence.

"And remember this, if you remember nothing else. The side that breaks first will be slaughtered, its broken line easy kills for the advancing enemy. You saw what happened when the Hawk line started to slip. No man can fight well moving backwards. And if your enemy turns and runs, his death is certain."

Heads nodded in agreement, and he saw the gleam of self-confidence in their eyes.

"You men will be the pride of Akkad's fighters, its first army of spearmen. Never before has anyone trained so many to fight as one. If our enemy has greater numbers, it matters little. If you work and fight together, as Gatus and his commanders teach you, no foe will be able to withstand your charge. When the enemy sees you approaching, his knees will go weak with fear. When you smash into his shield wall, he will turn and flee. He will do this because he will know in his heart that you are stronger, tougher, and better trained than he is. He will not stand against you."

This time another cheer went up, louder than the first, and it went on and on, despite Eskkar's efforts to silence them.

"Now you must continue your training. But I will join you tonight, to buy ale for Gatus. I will sit with the Hawk army, and complain about our bad luck as much as any of you."

A laugh rippled through them.

"Gatus, take command of your men again."

He waited until Gatus had given the orders and turned the men over to the subcommanders. The two friends walked away from the training ground, found an empty spot in the shade of a barrack, and sat down on the ground, both of them leaning back against the wall and gazing out of the common area.

"Gatus, you've done well. These men look good."

Gatus shook his head. "I think they can be better. I want to train them harder. I want to increase the training, and try some new tactics as well."

Eskkar glanced at the veteran. Gatus had always been an excellent trainer, a good second in command, but seldom initiated anything new.

Gatus caught the glance. "Hear me out. First, I want to toughen them up even more. That means longer marches, more spear practice. I want them to handle their spears as well as you handle your sword. They'll need to learn how to fight with a sword as well, so we'll need more sword work. And I want to change the spears. I want thicker shafts. Too many splinter or break at the first hard contact, even on the training ground. In a battle, many would be lost after the first thrust. Then we'll have nothing but an army of swordsmen."

Eskkar had seen it himself. Even men in training could thrust hard enough to penetrate a Sumerian shield, and that effort sometimes snapped the shaft.

"A heavier and longer weapon will slow them down on the march."

Such weapons would cost more, too, but neither man worried about that. Trella had already collected a good supply of gold from Nuzi, and the first shipment of silver arrived only days ago.

"That's one reason why I want to toughen them up. You saw this group. Almost all of them are bigger and stronger than most of the men in Akkad. With the right training . . . I want to train all the spear-carriers every day, work them until they can't even stand. Remember what Mitrac's father did with the archers."

"Working the archers didn't involve them ending up bleeding and bruised. You won't be popular with these spearmen."

"I don't care, and neither do you, for all your fine speeches. I remember when you couldn't say three words without stumbling over the fourth."

Eskkar grunted. Somehow Gatus always managed to annoy him, remind him of the days when Eskkar seldom spoke more than a dozen words from dawn to dusk. Trella, of course, was responsible for his new-found eloquence. But the two remained friends, the way that two men who have fought side by side against overwhelming numbers always do, no matter what words pass between them.

"Do what you like with them, Gatus. I know you will anyway. Just make sure that when the time comes, they'll march and fight better than any force Sumer can put in front of them. Remember, they'll be facing two or three times as many enemies."

"That's why I want to train them harder. First, I'll show them how soft and clumsy they are, then rebuild them, toughen them up, until they're stronger than any fighting men in Akkad. When I'm finished training them, they'll be the finest fighting force in the land. Just make sure you don't waste their lives to protect your precious horse fighters."

"I know how to use my riders when the time comes, don't worry about that. What else do you have planned?"

"I want them to master every possible way to fight with a spear. I want to teach them how to brace a spear against the ground, to stop a charging enemy, even if he's on horseback. I want my men to learn to thrust with the spear just using their arms, until they can hit a man in the face or groin every time. Another technique I want them to master is to hold the spear tight against their bodies, and deliver the thrust by stepping forward. Or use a long thrust with one hand, or two hands stepping forward, with one or both feet. When they've mastered all those ways to kill a man, I'll teach them how to throw the spear on the run. I've practiced it myself, and found it's best to release the weapon when the opposite foot is forward."

Eskkar felt the surprise cover his face. "How long have you been thinking about all this?"

"Months. Almost from the beginning. But I had to know what they could do before I tried to teach them any of these new tricks. The last thing I want them to master is swinging the spear. If a man swings the spear from side to side, the tip of the blade will slice right through flesh and bone. If the spear is moving fast enough, even the shaft will cause injury. That trick will give a spearman a chance, if he's alone and in open ground against more than one opponent."

"How long is all this going to take?"

Gatus laughed. "If I told you, you wouldn't believe me. But the wait will be worth it, I promise. When I'm done, these men will wield a spear as easily as you whirl your sword around. And they'll fight through twice their number with ease."

"They may have to." Eskkar shook his head, this time in admiration at what Gatus had already accomplished. "You've done well, Gatus. I mean that. And now, I'll get back to my work, and let you continue with yours. Just keep moving the men up north."

Gatus kept the number of men he was training in Akkad's barracks at about one hundred, more or less. What most people didn't notice was that as the men grew more proficient, small groups were moved north, to be replaced by new recruits. Sumer's spies would count the number of men in training, but hopefully wouldn't notice the gradual movement north, or at least not be able to count the entire force.

"Will you join us at the tavern tonight?"

"Oh, yes. After what you've shown me, and told me, I think I'm going to need a large cup of strong ale. Just make sure you tell Trella about the new weapons you want. I'm sure they're going to cost more gold."

"Which will be nothing compared to what you're spending on horses."

Eskkar pushed himself to his feet. "Talking with you makes my head ache. If you don't mind, I think I'll ride to the north tomorrow. At least up there I won't have to argue with you all day."

28

The first portion of Eskkar's journey to the lands north of Bisitun was by riverboat. In the last few months, he received several reports regarding the training at the horse camp, and wanted to observe the men's progress himself. Each departure from Akkad now required careful preparations. As usual, Trella wanted as few people as possible to know when her husband had left the city. Whenever Eskkar departed, the Hawk Clan guards increased their security around Trella, and Gatus and Bantor kept the soldiers on heightened alert. There would be no repeat of someone trying to seize the city by force while Eskkar was gone.

Any who enquired about Eskkar's whereabouts would be told that he was occupied with important matters and remaining in the Compound. To help maintain secrecy on this trip, the first stage of the journey to Bisitun would be by boat. Eskkar riding out of Akkad on horseback, day or night, would certainly have attracted notice. But few paid much attention to what went on at the docks, especially in the early morning. Eskkar and his companions boarded their vessels before first light, and the two boats departed as soon as the sun cleared the horizon.

Yavtar commanded the boat that carried the king and seven of his guards. Another eight rode in the second vessel. For this visit, the men Eskkar took with him had all been carefully chosen by Hathor. All were archers, and more important, all knew how to ride. For that very reason, Grond remained in Akkad. The big man could ride, but was no horseman, and Eskkar wanted skilled horsemen only. Meanwhile, Grond's presence moving about the city would convince many that King Eskkar remained within the Compound.

The river journey to the north had another purpose. Yavtar's men had finished two new boats, and he wanted Eskkar to inspect them. The boat captain had taken over a farm about ten miles north of Bisitun, and installed everything needed to build and test the new boats that Eskkar and his commanders required.

Two days after departing Akkad, the ships rowed past Bisitun during the late afternoon, and reached the small jetty of Yavtar's farm just after dusk. Every member of the crew slumped against the oars, exhausted from driving the boats upriver. Eskkar had taken a hand with the oars, unwilling to sit idle while others worked. Besides, he wanted to get a feel for the boats that plied the river, and he enjoyed every chance to work his muscles. By now he'd overcome his initial worries about being on the water, and almost managed to enjoy the trip.

Once on shore, they ate a quick meal, then relaxed over a few cups of ale. The difficult journey upriver made sure every man slept well that night. In the morning, as soon as the sun had begun its journey across the heavens, Yavtar brought the three soldiers stationed at the dockyard and more than a dozen villagers to meet their king. Since this was Eskkar's first visit, he took the time to ask each one his name, and say something encouraging. They might be mere carpenters or laborers, but these were the men who would build the boats Akkad needed. Most just stood there, wide-eyed, and afraid to say anything to the man who ruled their world.

Yavtar's shipyard, as everyone called the place, didn't look like much. Three small houses, a few sheds, and a corral that held the dozen or so horses that would take Eskkar and his guards on the next part of their journey.

The most impressive part of the shipyard was the dock itself.

Built with sturdy wood from the northern lands, it had enough slips to hold seven vessels. Three of the slips were occupied – two with Yavtar's boats that had just carried them up the river, while the third slip held a craft that had arrived yesterday from the north carrying more lumber.

"This may not look like much now, Captain, but when we have forty or fifty men building ships, all those slips will be filled, I promise. Almost all the wood needed to construct our ships comes down the river. Just not enough big trees near Akkad."

Most of the trees in the land between the rivers were willows or date palms, and even Eskkar knew that their wood wasn't hard or dense enough for major projects. Good enough for cups, bowls, small tables and chairs, but not for much else. The gates that provided entry into Akkad had all been built from trees floated downriver from the northern forests.

"With the docks in place," Yavtar continued, "we can load and unload all we need, at the same time we can keep two or three of our new boats floating there while we work on them. But now let me show what I wanted you to see."

Not far from the docks Yavtar had established four construction cradles. Boats in various stages of assembly rested on each of them. He guided Eskkar to the first cradle, where a half-finished boat sat on its blocks.

"This is the third one we've started. The first two didn't meet your needs, so we tore them apart and started over. But this one will, I think. At least, it will last long enough for us to learn all we need."

"It doesn't look any bigger than what's plying the river now."

"It is at least five paces longer than my longest riverboat. But what's more important is that it's almost two paces wider, and with a steeper pitch to its sides. That means it will ride lower in the water."

"Why is that important?" Trella had finally overcome Eskkar's reluctance to admit that he didn't know everything, and he no longer hesitated to ask questions. Making assumptions, he'd learned, almost always led to mistakes.

"You wanted boats that could carry plenty of men, especially archers, as well as large cargoes to resupply your fighters. But if we've got a dozen archers shooting arrows at the shore or another ship, the boat will tip over at the slightest movement. So we need to have a way to keep it stable. Since we won't be carrying any fragile cargoes, like wine or pottery, we can take advantage of heavier ballast. My builders have worked on an idea that we'll need to test, but I think it will work."

Eskkar couldn't help laughing. "I've never seen you so excited. You seem to enjoy building ships."

"These are new kinds of ships, Captain, and that's something to get excited about," Yavtar said. "I've got women in Bisitun stitching linen bags with a drawstring top for us. We'll fill the bags with sand or dirt, and spread them flat on the bottom of the ship. The archers and crew can stand on them if they need to. When we're ready to go into action, the ships' crew will shift the cargo to one side or the other, to compensate for the archers' weight. And if we have to carry cargo, we just dump the sand, and stuff bread or whatever into the sack."

"Will that be enough to keep the ship from rolling over?" Eskkar could picture archers trying to work their bows while the ship bobbled and wavered beneath their feet."

"You should have been a ship builder, Captain. No, it probably won't be enough. But one of my men thought of this. What do you think?" Yavtar took a few steps and stopped before two wooden sawhorses. A thick log about three paces long rested there. It had two support members fastened to it at either end. The supports ended in a thick crosspiece.

"What is it?" Eskkar had never seen anything like it before.

"We've been calling it a brace, but that doesn't explain what it does. When we're ready to go into battle, these crosspieces will fit into notches cut in the sides of the ship. The log will ride in the water. If the boat starts to lean toward that side, the log will be forced deeper into the river, and it will resist the boat's tendency to roll."

Eskkar had noticed that the unfinished boat at the slip had notches cut into its sides. "How will that keep the boat from tipping?"

"Ever try to hold a log under water, Captain? The more you try to submerge it, the more it resists your efforts. And since it projects out two paces from the side of the ship, it will be almost impossible to roll the boat over. It should keep the ship stable enough for your archers to loose their shafts."

"If you say so." Eskkar still wasn't sure how it would work, but if Yavtar thought it would be useful, he would trust the old sailor.

"Next time you visit here, you'll get a real demonstration on the river. But I think we can build boats that can carry fighters and supplies at the same time. A craft like that would be able to defend itself from horsemen and archers on the shore, or another boat for that matter."

"I'll need the supplies, Yavtar. In our last fight in the south, we were out of food. Another day or two and the situation would have been bad. If we have ten times the number of men, we'll never be able to carry enough food for them, not to mention grain for the horses and extra weapons. Besides, carts and wagons need more horses or oxen to pull them, and will slow our pace."

"The good thing about Sumeria is that the land is full of rivers and streams, and you should be able to march near one. If you do, we'll be able to bring you supplies."

"Something else that would be useful . . . can you build a few boats built for speed and nothing else? We could use them for carrying messages back to Akkad."

"Hmmm, I suppose we could do something. No one's ever thought about a ship that didn't need to carry cargo. Let me think about it. Now it's time to have some bread and ale for breakfast."

The next morning, Eskkar and his ten guards crossed to the west bank of the Tigris and rode north, to meet the Ur Nammu and learn how many horses the steppe warriors had brought with them. This side of the river held few farmers, and the land remained mostly empty, though Trella had predicted that in a few years, all of this would be under cultivation or support flocks of sheep and herds of cattle, with all the land under Akkad's protection. By the third day, the land had turned hilly, and the number of valleys began to increase. None of them were large or had steep walls, but they sheltered good grassland that would be ideal for raising horses.

Mid-morning on the fourth day, Eskkar saw Ur Nammu riders standing on a crest line, outlined against the sky. He gathered his horsemen around him.

"I think we've reached the place," Eskkar said. "Now remember what I've told you. Make sure you give no offense, no matter what happens. And the first man who puts his hand on a sword will wish he'd never been born."

They rounded the base of the hill and trotted the last few hundred paces until they reached the entrance to the valley. He counted fifteen warriors waiting for them. Subutai wasn't among them, but Eskkar relaxed when he saw Fashod. Eskkar halted his men a few paces from the waiting horsemen.

"A good day to ride," Eskkar said, one of the traditional greetings used by the horse people.

"A good day to ride," Fashod replied. "Welcome to our camp."

Eskkar glanced around. He didn't see any ropes blocking the valley entrance, and wondered what kept the animals from bolting out.

"How long have you been waiting for us?"

"Only two days. It took longer to bring the animals here than I thought. A few ropes broke, and twice a pesky mare slipped her noose."

"How many horses did you bring?" Eskkar couldn't restrain his curiosity.

"Thirty. Are these the men who will need to be taught how to ride?"

"No. Those should arrive tomorrow. There will be twenty to teach, as well as men with tools to build corrals and whatever else is needed. They'll bring plenty of rope. These men," Eskkar waved his hand to include those who had ridden with him, "need only to be taught how to fight from horseback."

"Good. Then the rest of today we can hunt and talk, and begin work tomorrow. Would you like to see the horses?"

"Very much, Fashod." Eskkar turned to the leader of his guard. "You stay here, and remember what I've told you."

Fashod wheeled his horse around and started up the valley, and Eskkar galloped after him. The rest of the warriors followed, and Eskkar had the strange sensation of riding with a group of warriors, something he had not done since his boyhood days with the Alur Meriki.

The valley curved slightly, and as they rounded the bend he saw the horses, already in retreat away from the approaching men. Fashod slowed his pace as they neared the end of the valley. The nervous animals watched them approach, ears flicking back and forth, a stallion pawing the earth as it kept its gaze on them.

"Good horseflesh," Eskkar said, his eyes examining the animals. You couldn't be sure, of course, until you worked with them, but he didn't see any dull coats or listless movements. Every head stretched upwards, and the wild look in their eyes showed plenty of spirit.

"A few good ones," Fashod agreed. "Better than most horses that dirt-eaters ride."

The horses were growing more restive, unsure of these strange men and animals. They'd been driven a long way, but they were still wild, and it would take a lot of hard work before they would let a man approach them, let alone slip a halter over their heads.

The horsemen rode back to the mouth of the valley and dismounted. Eskkar asked Fashod if he could meet his men, and Fashod obliged. Many of the warriors were young. In the Alur Meriki clan of Eskkar's youth, they would still have been considered boys. But the Ur Nammu had been devastated by war and nearly exterminated, and now the clan needed its boys to turn into men as fast as possible.

The warriors were cool to Eskkar. They didn't know much about him.

285

To them, he was just another clan deserter or outcast, someone who had joined with the dirt-eaters. Even worse, some suspected he had come from the clan of their hated enemy, the Alur Meriki. Most of all, the Ur Nammu considered themselves superior to any villager or farmer, and their words were cautious or aloof.

One warrior – Eskkar guessed he had about twenty seasons – did more than repeat Eskkar's name in greeting. "My name is Chinua. I know you, Eskkar of Akkad. I fought with you and your men when the Alur Meriki nearly overwhelmed us in the canyon of death." He raised his voice so that all would hear. "All of you have heard many times the story of that fight. I was there, and I say that Eskkar of Akkad is a mighty warrior, who saved my life and the lives of many Ur Nammu that day. Despite his many wounds, he helped Subutai slay the leader of our enemy."

Chinua, which Eskkar knew meant "wolf", moved to face the rest of his men. "Some of you have loose tongues and foolish words. If any of you insult King Eskkar or his men, it will be as if you have challenged me. I will not forget the blood oath that binds all Ur Nammu warriors with Eskkar of Akkad."

The little speech, coming from one of the warriors and not Fashod, did more to impress the men than anything either commander could have said. Eskkar wondered if Fashod had suggested it.

"Your words are wise, Chinua." Eskkar moved his horse beside that of the warrior and extended his arm. "It is always good to greet an old comrade again."

Chinua clasped Eskkar's arm in friendship. "We will break many horses for you."

"And help me train my men to fight as warriors fight." Eskkar didn't like to give speeches, but he knew that, at times, words were more powerful than swords. "As the Ur Nammu have fought against the superior numbers of the Alur Meriki, so will my men have to fight against great odds. That is why we seek your help, as brother warriors, so that we can overcome our enemies."

That was important to remind them, that Subutai and Eskkar had sworn the blood oath of warriors. The enemy of my enemy is my friend.

"It is true," Fashod added. "I, too, have fought at Eskkar's side, not once but twice. Though because of him, I have a wife that I must beat regularly, taken in a raid against the main camp of the Alur Meriki."

The men laughed at the jest, but the words of Chinua and Fashod, and even Eskkar, made them aware of the special relationship that existed between them. Eskkar saw some of the hostility and distrust fade from their faces. A good start, but much more would be needed to bridge the gap between them. With luck, they would have plenty of time.

"Now it is time to feast." Fashod turned to Eskkar. "Is there any wine in those skins I saw your men carrying?"

"Only one skin," Eskkar said. "But I will have more brought out, if you and your men think you can drink with my men."

"A fair challenge." Fashod turned his horse back toward the camp. "First one back to the camp gets an extra cup of wine."

In an instant the riders whirled their horses around and burst into a gallop, leaving Eskkar still struggling to turn his mount around. By then the Ur Nammu were thirty paces ahead of him, and Eskkar realized that he would likely be the one without any wine tonight.

After the men finished their meal, Fashod came over to Eskkar's campfire. He sat down beside Eskkar, so that both of them faced the fire. "Tell me of your plans, Eskkar."

"First we must break the horses and train the men. I will send orders back to Bisitun, and soon more of my men will come. They'll bring ropes, poles, shovels, everything needed to hold the horses. Wine and food, too. If this place seems suitable, I'll send for masons to build a wall across the mouth of the valley, with a gate. That way we'll be sure the horses can't break out."

"All that will take time," Fashod mused.

"There is time, but I intend to waste none of it. As long as you keep bringing me horses, I will have more men coming to learn how to fight."

"Bows, arrows, lances, those will be needed as well."

Eskkar nodded. "All has been considered, including what you and your men will receive in return for your help. If anyone is unhappy with the exchange, come to me and we will work things out between us. I want no Ur Nammu warrior feeling slighted."

"Will your men obey our orders?"

"They will. If you set the example. Treat them fairly, but no better than you would treat any of your own. They have much to learn, and the sooner the better. As you train these, they will help train those that follow them."

"It will be as you say, Eskkar." He stared at the fire for a moment. "Do you think you will be able to defeat your enemy, when you come to face him?"

"The future is never certain, Fashod, but I've learned one thing in the last few seasons, if nothing else. Well-trained and well-armed fighters can defeat almost any number of the enemy."

"Then I promise you, Eskkar of Akkad, that when the time comes, your men will be ready."

They started the next morning. Fashod gave half the warriors to Chinua and told him to get started on the horses. Eskkar told his men to form a line with each rider ten paces apart, facing Fashod's remaining warriors, who formed a similar line two hundred paces away.

"When I give the order," Eskkar said. "We'll walk our horses toward Fashod's line. His men will move toward us at a walk. Each of you will guide your horse into the gap between two warriors. At all times, keep the line intact."

Blank looks and open mouths greeted these orders. "We need to train our horses to fight, and this is how we begin. The horses must get used to seeing other animals coming toward them. They must also think that there will always be a gap for them to pass through. Otherwise they will not charge in combat. Or if they do, they may pull up at the last moment, turn aside, or dig in their heels and toss their rider. Now we begin."

He moved to the end of the line. "WALK!" At the same time, he raised his sword in the air, held it for a moment, then lowered it. Fashod repeated the same signal, and his men advanced as well.

The ten men started moving. Immediately the line grew ragged. Some animals were impatient, others too slow. The riders all had different ideas about what a walk meant.

"Damn you, look at Fashod's line."

The men lifted their eyes to stare at the approaching line of warriors, all moving evenly across the grass toward them.

"Straighten out the line!" Eskkar knew the warriors would be grinning at the clumsy dirt-eaters.

By now the two lines were drawing close to each other, and the nervous horses added to the confusion. They passed between Fashod's men in twos and threes, a sorry example of horsemanship.

"Keep the line even!" Eskkar made them continue pacing forward until they reached Fashod's starting point. "Wheel left! Reform the line."

Two riders turned to the right, which brought guffaws or curses from the mount they bumped into. Eskkar swore again. The idea of right and left wasn't clear to some of them. That, too, would have to be explained.

Nevertheless, the line eventually reformed. Of course, Fashod's line had turned smoothly, without a lost step and they now waited patiently.

"Walk!" the ten horsemen plus Eskkar moved forward, the line ragged within a few steps. "Keep the line even, damn you!" His voice would be hoarse by the end of the day if he kept shouting at this rate.

They did a little better the second time. When they'd finished the tenth pass, the line remained nearly straight. Still, Eskkar wasn't sure if it wasn't the horses who grasped the concept quicker than their riders.

"Now we'll try the same movement at a trot."

One rider started forward.

"Damn you, wait for the command!" Eskkar bellowed. At this rate his voice wouldn't last the morning, let alone the day.

The sheepish rider had to ride around his grinning companions to regain his place.

"Trot!"

This went a little better. A lot of the work depended on the horse, but gradually each animal got used to keeping pace with the horse beside it. After ten times, Eskkar gave the order for a canter. Once again, the horse and rider had to learn what that command meant, what gait to set, the faster horses being held back, the slower ones urged to move a bit faster.

Again and again Eskkar shouted to keep the line even. As midmorning approached, both horse and rider were getting weary. The drill seemed senseless, and only the fact that the warriors executed each pass with precision proved that they, too, had practiced such things.

The men were getting tired, which was what Eskkar wanted. Weary horses and men would be less likely to do something foolish or injure themselves. "Now we try a gallop. The sooner you get it right, the quicker you can rest."

This time the line held together better than expected, either by luck or skill, and the two lines rushed toward each other. Eskkar repeated the drill three more times, then waved Fashod's men in.

"Enough for now. Take care of your horses, wash them down, and return here. Move!"

Fashod discharged his men as well, but he rode over to join Eskkar. Both men dismounted and sat down on the grass.

"Your men did better than I expected."

"These men are experienced fighters, good archers, and decent riders, but they've never learned how to use a horse in battle. The next group will be far worse."

Fashod grunted at hearing that.

In ones and twos, Eskkar's men returned. He waited until he had all ten sitting on the ground before him. "Any questions?"

The men glanced at each other, but one man finally spoke. "Why are we doing this? We'll never walk our horses toward the enemy."

Eskkar kept the frown from his face. Better to let the men ask questions, even stupid ones. If he started cursing at them, they'd never learn to speak out.

"Do you know why the steppe warriors are so ferocious?" No one answered. "It's because they're better horsemen. They've learned that a well-trained horse is worth two or three men in a battle. And this – what we've done this morning – is how they train their horses. Their animals will charge toward an approaching group of horses, because they know there will be a gap for them to pass through. And they trust their rider to find that gap. In battle, they strike together, crashing into their enemy. When villagers fight on horseback, they ride up to an enemy, stop the horse, and start hacking at each other with their swords. The warriors let the horse do the fighting. They never stop. They know a wound is just as good as a kill, so they strike at the horse, the rider, anywhere they can, and they keep moving forward. They push through their enemy until they break through to his rear. Then they wheel around and attack again. They never worry about their back, because they're always moving forward."

Eskkar glanced at Fashod. "Tell them."

"What Eskkar speaks is true. We train the horse to use its shoulder to crash into an opposing horse, to step on anything in its path, and to always continue forward. When we attack dirt . . . villagers, they break quickly, because they suddenly find warriors behind as well as in front. The moment a horse fighter starts worrying what is happening behind him, what danger may be approaching, he's easy to kill. Either that, or he turns and runs."

Horses have a natural tendency to jump over obstacles in their path. They had to be trained to step on anything on the ground, man or beast.

"A good horse takes months to train," Eskkar said. "A warrior guards a prime animal as much as his wife, maybe even more, because he knows a good horse can save his life in battle. It's not likely we can ever do as well as Fashod and his men, but the Sumerian horsemen are not warriors. Mitrac proved that a few months ago. With a handful of men, he struck a heavy blow. So Akkad's horsemen just need to be better trained and better mounted than our southern enemy. And that," he waved his hand toward the valley, "is why we're here."

He stood. "Enough talk for now. While the horses rest, we will practice our sword fighting."

They worked with their swords the rest of the morning and early afternoon. Then they gathered their horses and repeated the morning's drill, moving quicker this time through the walk, trot and canter, and into the gallop.

When they finished, Eskkar collected his weary men. "Tomorrow, we'll start again. This time we'll narrow the gap a little each time, until there is just enough room for horse and rider to pass through Fashod's line. And then we'll start all over again, yelling our war cry and waving our swords. The horses need to hear and see all that, as well. In ten days or so, we'll slaughter a cow and cover everyone with blood. Your horses will need to get used to that scent, too. Now get some sleep. You're going to need it."

By noon the next day, both the men and their mounts stood exhausted before Eskkar. He ordered them to take care of the horses first, then find something to eat and get some rest. As they moved to obey, a shout turned Eskkar's eyes back to the mouth of the valley.

A small caravan had arrived. Eskkar dismounted and led his horse toward the newcomers. As he approached them, he took a count. Thirty men on horseback, another twenty on foot, and three small carts laden with supplies. Klexor swung down from his horse as his captain arrived.

"By the gods, Captain, if you were any farther north, we'd never have found you!"

The two men hugged each other for a moment. "Two days ride from Bisitun, and you're complaining."

"If you had to listen for two days to those carts squealing with every turn of the wheel, you'd be glad to arrive anywhere. Even the demon pits below can't be that noisy."

"Have you brought everything?"

"Not everything had arrived in Bisitun," Klexor replied, "and I knew you wanted to start the men training as soon as possible. Another caravan should arrive tomorrow or the day after. After that, Sisuthros will have you on a regular schedule, with a caravan arriving every three days."

"What have you brought?"

"Twenty men who claim they can tell a horse from a donkey. Half of them are liars, I'm sure. Three of my best riders, to help with the training. Five men to escort the carts and drivers back to Bisitun. They can leave in the morning. Half a dozen laborers to build your walls, three rope makers, two weavers, two cooks, and five farmers. The carts are full of grain, food, wine and ropes, as well as tools and weapons for the Ur Nammu." He lowered his voice. "Any trouble with them?"

"No. Fashod and Chinua, one of his leaders of ten, have spoken to them about us, enough for them to give us a chance to prove ourselves. You just make sure of your men."

"I've done nothing but pound that fact into their thick skulls for the last two days. The first one that gets out of line will wish he'd died in his mother's womb."

Eskkar grunted in satisfaction. It wasn't everything he needed, but it would do for a start. "We need to get an enclosing wall built across the valley's mouth as soon as possible, but we can manage with ropes for now."

He didn't want anything fancy or solid, just something tall enough to make the bravest horse turn away. Wild horses tended to be powerful jumpers, and ropes alone might not stop them long.

"Well, you won't see any walls for a few weeks. They'll have to make the bricks and let them dry before they can use them."

Eskkar nodded. He knew all about the construction of bricks and walls. Trella and Corio had seen to that. Probably he would need more masons and laborers as well.

"This valley is the perfect place to train horses, Klexor. We can seal off some of the small openings, and use them to keep the half-trained beasts from the wild ones. And more horses will be arriving in a few days. The Ur Nammu warriors who helped drive this herd here have already left to capture more animals."

"By the time you're finished here, you'll have built another village."

"No doubt. As soon as the walls are up, we'll start building some huts for the men. Until then, everyone sleeps on the ground. Now come with me. You and Fashod need to meet and decide how you're going to train the men."

The three leaders spent the rest of the day and most of the evening talking. Only when Klexor understood every part of the process did Eskkar relax. The new camp would slowly take shape, but over the next few months everything needed to train both men and horses to ride and fight would be in place. Supplies and fresh men would arrive on a regular basis, and as the men became proficient in their horsemanship, they would help train the newcomers.

As far as Eskkar knew, no one had ever done anything like this before. Usually a village anchored a training camp, or a place to assemble and work the horses. This valley would be dedicated to nothing but horsemanship. Raw recruits would arrive, and when they left, Eskkar was determined they would be efficient horse fighters. The longer he could keep this place secret, the better for Akkad.

29

Trella stood in the entrance to the Map Room. It had taken more than four months to construct, and she had watched the builders create it, plank by plank, brace by brace. When they finished, the last crew of carpenters cut the door into Eskkar's workroom, connecting the two chambers for the first time. During construction, the laborers entered by ladders from the courtyard, so as not to disturb Eskkar and Trella's private quarters any more than necessary.

This morning the last of the tables, benches and other furnishings had arrived and settled into place. The gleaming white walls added to the sunlight slanting down through the slit windows spaced around three sides of the room. Fifteen paces long and twelve paces in width, the chamber would provide a secure place for the commanders to plan Akkad's defense. Now Trella had only to add the final touches that would turn it into something truly unique.

"Well, Ismenne, are you ready to begin?"

"Yes, Lady Trella."

Corio's daughter clutched a bulky sack in both hands. Trella had offered to help her with it, but Ismenne, shocked at the idea that Lady Trella should actually lift anything herself, insisted she could manage alone.

Trella moved inside, running her fingers down the long rectangular table that sat in the center of the room. Almost as long and half as wide as the Map Room, the table's plank surface and its ten stools dominated the chamber.

"This end will point to the north," Trella said. She helped Ismenne lift the sack onto the bare table. "From Bisitun to Sumer. Are you sure you have everything you need to get started?"

"Yes, Lady Trella. The rest is downstairs in my room."

Bantor and Annok-sur had once used that chamber as their home. But over a year ago Bantor had purchased a house for his wife and daughter down the lane. Still, Annok-sur used her former home often enough, especially when Eskkar traveled to the north, to stay close by Trella's side. The idea of having a room practically to herself had excited Ismenne as much as working with Trella.

"I'll have one of the servants carry your models and sketches up to the workroom," Trella said. "You can move them into here yourself."

Ismenne nodded and started pulling thin strips of wood from the sack and spreading them out on the surface. For the last three months, she had prepared drawings of the major cities and villages whose shapes would soon be sketched, painted or modeled onto the table. The girl had attended every meeting where Annok-sur's agents reported to Trella about the lands to the south. Ismenne also sat in on those meetings where soldiers, river men and travelers discussed distances and landmarks.

It had all started with Gatus. Trella had him march his fully armed and burdened men one hundred paces across the training ground several times, marking the area with pegs each time. When Trella decided she had the proper length, Gatus trimmed a long spear the exact length of five paces. When the measuring spear fitted within the hundred paces exactly twenty times, Trella had her basic unit of measurement. Another strip of wood one pace long was matched to the measuring spear.

Now that she had a standard length for a soldier's pace, Trella provided that distance to her walkers and dispatched them to their destinations. Bags of pebbles would be used to measure the distances. After a hundred paces, a pebble would be shifted from the full sack to the empty one, a process that would be repeated as long as necessary.

Already Trella had calculated the distance between Akkad and the nearest villages, and her walkers had gone as far north as Bisitun. As soon as she trusted their skill, Trella sent the first one south, to measure the distance to Larsa, the nearest of the Sumerian cities. In the next few months, every distance in Sumeria would be paced on at least two separate occasions and the tally recorded in the soft clay shards used to keep records. Eventually the information reached Trella and Ismenne, who would then sketch the distances directly onto the table.

Gatus had provided more information in the last few months. He would march his men hard for five days, carrying extra provisions, and record how far they traveled each day, the pace naturally speeding up as the weight of supplies decreased. Now Trella had a figure for the average distance an army of spearmen could travel in any given day. It wouldn't be perfect, of course. Differences in the landscape, whether hard earth, tall grass or soft sand would alter the calculation, as would the heat of the day, wind or rain, or even the scarcity of water. But at least they had a beginning, and soon Akkad's leaders not only became more aware of the land around them, but knew the marching distance from one place to another.

Trella hadn't stopped with Gatus. Hathor had put his horsemen through the same process. Now he knew how far his men could ride in a given day. Even Yavtar had contributed, matching the travel times for various ships and measuring the distance along the Tigris and the other main streams that flowed to the south on their way to the great sea.

All these numbers and measurements found their way into the Map Room, where Ismenne worked from dawn until dusk. She attended countless meetings with Trella's walkers, as well as the city's traders and merchants. To them, the girl seemed nothing more than a minor servant or a clerk, helping Trella record their information. But the girl listened to every report, every story about the landscape, the hills and valleys, what the walkers saw and felt, everything Trella could extract from their memories.

When they were gone, Ismenne would begin a new sketch, matching what she'd learned against her previous attempts. Slowly the long table underwent a change, turning into a map that illustrated every major feature of the countryside between Akkad and the cities of the south. Every bend in the river, every stream that fed into the Tigris, every hill and valley, took its place on the map. Eventually the table ceased to exist, giving birth to the map that would guide Eskkar and his senior men through the coming war.

By the end of the first year, the map stretched from Bisitun to the great sea beyond Sumer. But the work never ended. Trella continued to gather new information from her spies, and she relayed it to Ismenne. Traders, travelers, even explorers, Trella spoke with them all, gathering information as innocently as possible.

In that same year, Ismenne passed from child to woman, her body filling out. She stood a hand taller than Trella now, with hair as dark as her mistress. Strangers often assumed Ismenne to be Trella's younger sister.

Fortunately, for Trella at least, Ismenne's change into womanhood bonded her even closer to her queen. Ismenne felt no urge to marry, no awkward feelings toward the boys and young men around her, no rush to experience the pleasure of the gods. She understood the importance of her work, and was determined to see it to completion.

In their workroom, Trella faced Eskkar across the table. After being gone for almost forty days visiting the horse camps in the north, Eskkar had worked up quite an appetite, and he consumed almost all the sausage, cheese, and bread the servants carried up to their chamber. Trella ate her fill, too. Like most people in Akkad, she preferred to eat only twice each day, in the mid-morning and at the day's end. At last Eskkar pushed his plate away and leaned back in his chair with a smile of satisfaction on his face.

"Are you ready to meet with your men?"

He nodded. "Yes, now I can face a long day of talking. I'm not sure why, but the food here at the house always tastes better than anywhere else." He reached across the table and touched her hand. "Perhaps our lovemaking improves the flavor."

She clasped his hand. He had practically dragged her into bed as soon as he arrived, pausing only long enough to wash up at the well. Before their passion subsided, the evening supper had come and gone, and they had dined on cold chicken and bread before he fell asleep.

"Your commanders should be arriving now." She could already hear Gatus shouting about something or other in the courtyard below. He and the others had been summoned by Eskkar to discuss what progress they had made, and to hear about his inspection of the northern camps. "I have a surprise for all of you this morning. The Map Room is ready for use."

Eskkar lifted his eyes to the door. When he had left for the north, two planks nailed across the entrance sealed the room shut. Now all traces of the planks had vanished, and the door stood ajar. "Let me see." He started to rise.

"Let it be a surprise, Esskar. None of your men have visited it either, so you might as well see it all together."

Heavy steps sounded on the stairs. "Esskar! We're coming up!" Gatus had a powerful voice that penetrated throughout the house.

Trella stood by Esskar's side as Gatus pushed the door open and the commanders filed into the workroom. "Good morning," she said, nodding in turn to Bantor, Hathor, Alexar, Mitrac, Klexor, Drakis, and Yavtar, who, like Esskar, had returned yesterday from another voyage to the south. "Today you will have your first meeting in the Map Room. I think you will find it quite a surprise."

"The gods know you've been building it long enough," Gatus said, but he softened his voice as he always did when speaking to Trella. "I hope it's worth the wait."

"Follow me, then." She led the way, pushing the door open.

One by one, they stepped across the threshold, and every one sounded a gasp or uttered words of astonishment. Esskar, the last to enter, found his men gathering about a long table that stretched nearly the length of the room.

Trella had moved to the far end. Standing beside her was another woman. "This is Corio's daughter, Ismenne. She has done most of the work on the map, and is the best person to answer your questions."

Trella could have explained it just as well, but wanted the soldiers to know how she felt about Ismenne. Trella wanted Ismenne to have their trust, and that would be best accomplished by keeping her not only in the room, but privy to all the questions and information the commanders possessed.

"You've grown into a woman, Ismenne," Esskar said as he approached the head of the table. He, too, gazed down at the map in wonderment. "And this is all your work . . ."

"Yes, Lord Esskar."

Now every man in the room stared at the map. They could see the miniature city of Akkad marked out by the curve in the river. The village of Bisitun, the gold camp at Nuzi, the horse and training camps to the north. Esskar moved down the table, his fingers trailing along the edge of the table, following the river, until he stood beside the city of Larsa, the first of the Sumerian cities. The city's outline looked different from what he remembered from years ago. He extended his finger to touch the map, then hesitated, and glanced at Trella. Eskkar knew a map sketched on papyrus required a pointing stick, to avoid damaging the material or smudging the image.

Ismenne understood the unasked question. "You may touch the map, Lord Eskkar. These colors will not smear unless you rub them too hard, and any marks can be easily removed or repaired."

"She has painted and repainted every spot on the map dozens of times," Trella added.

"What are these lines?" Hathor had leaned over the table and pointed at the model of Akkad. A series of short strokes radiated out from the city in several directions.

"The black lines show how many days' march any place on the map is from Akkad. The red lines," Trella extended her slim arm and pointed to another group of lines, "indicate a day's ride for a company of horsemen. As you can see, there are five black lines leading from Akkad to Bisitun, but only three red lines. Now you can understand why I have had so many questions about men and horses for Gatus and Hathor. And Yavtar, too, for traveling times up and down the rivers. Those are the white lines marking the downstream water routes, and the blue lines upstream."

"So it's three days march to the gold mine at Nuzi," Eskkar said, letting his own fingers step over the lines as he counted.

"As Gatus explained to me," Trella said, "that assumes the men are carrying their shields, spears, swords, some food and their water skins. And assuming there is one pack horse for every forty men. If the soldiers have to carry more, then each day's journey will take longer."

The pack horse carried the men's cooking pots, a shovel, and other odds and ends needed by the men. Hathor and Eskkar had argued over the cavalry's number of pack animals, before finally settling on one pack animal for every thirty men. A large train of animals would slow a fast-moving force. Both men had agreed that the cavalry should move at least three times faster than a company of men on foot.

"So it is five days' march to Kanesh," Gatus said, his eyes blinking as he strained to see the markings. "And from there, another . . . four days' march to Larsa."

Gatus, Trella knew, could see things at a distance without difficulty, but lately had trouble seeing things close up. Another problem of those who lived to old age.

"Yes. Our walkers have estimated these distances, and made adjustments for the terrain. So if the land is hilly or ground soft, it will take longer to cover the same distance."

"I can see where we'll need Yavtar's boats to bring supplies," Eskkar said, his finger brushing several places on the map. "And other sites where we should store food and weapons. Supplies, too, should be prepared in advance, perhaps hidden, or buried in the earth. Your boats are going to make the difference in the coming war, Yavtar."

Trella nodded. Her husband never failed to impress her by his knowledge of such things. As Gatus had once told her, Eskkar could take in a battleground at a glance and come up with the best plan of action. He did it without thinking, the natural skill of a man who had fought many engagements.

"I'm building three kinds of boats, Lady Trella," Yavtar said, lifting his eyes from the map for the first time. "You might want to add more lines for the different types of vessels."

"Yes, that's a good idea." Trella turned to Ismenne. "We'll work with Yavtar tomorrow, to get estimates of his fighting ships as well as his messenger craft."

The war vessels that Yavtar had designed, with their larger crews, could move faster than a heavily laden boat carrying cargo. The smaller, speedier craft would be mainly used to carry news and reports. For these, a crew of eight to twelve rowers would speed the craft up or down the river.

Eskkar stepped down to the other end of the table, to where Trella stood, before the great sea. The model of the city of Sumer was as large as the one of Akkad. "And this is what the city looks like now?"

"As best we can know. One of Corio's sons visited the city a few months ago and memorized the layout. But there is much building of walls going on, and it may have already changed. As we get new reports, Ismenne will adjust the model."

Eskkar lifted his eyes to the girl. A great deal of responsibility rested on her shoulders. If her drawings were wrong, if the information she provided incorrect, the results could be serious, even deadly.

Trella saw the look and understood Eskkar's thoughts. "Now that you have all seen the map, you can understand how useful it may be. Ismenne and I will be examining and testing each line on the map. And all of you will help provide any new information or corrections that need to be made. If we keep the map current and accurate, it should help you plan the war."

"It will, indeed, Lady Trella. Even in the land of Egypt, where many models of cities were built, I've never seen such a thing."

"Then I think, Hathor, that you and everyone here will agree that this room and its contents must remain a secret. The fewer who know of its existence, the better. Ismenne and I would ask that you tell no one of this, not your wives or lovers or even your subcommanders. If Sumer learns of this, and build their own Map Room, much of our advantage will disappear. All our lives may depend on keeping this secret."

"Who else knows of this?"

Eskkar's voice held that grim tone that told Trella – told everyone in the chamber – that he had made up his mind.

"Corio and Ismenne, of course," Trella said, "as well as Annok-sur and Grond. Others may know that this room will be used for planning, but no one else has seen inside. Aside from you leaders, no one else knows how much effort and detail went into building this. Even the servants have been forbidden to enter, or even to discuss its existence."

Since the chamber could be entered only from Eskkar and Trella's private quarters, the Map Room door would be seen by very few, which should help hold its secrets.

"Then I suggest that we all heed Trella's words," Eskkar said, the hard edge still in his words. "This place should not be mentioned to anyone else."

Everyone nodded. They were all Hawk Clan. She knew they would heed his words.

"Then we can start our planning," she said. "Who wishes to begin?"

30

Three months later, Eskkar and Trella rode into the mining village of Nuzi just after midday. Trella had never visited the place before, but Eskkar had stopped by twice since the digging began, both times when he traveled north to visit the horse camps. His descriptions of those brief stopovers hadn't satisfied her curiosity, and while Orodes's reports of steady progress had proved satisfactory, Trella decided she wanted to see Nuzi for herself.

Orodes had started sending gold back to Trella almost from the start. Within ten days of his return to the mine, the first sacks of gold dust had reached Akkad. Nuggets, sifted out of the stream or dug from the hills and borders of the flowing water, soon followed. Since those first deliveries, a heavily guarded boat arrived every five days, bringing gold and silver to Trella's coffers.

To safeguard the precious metals, Trella ordered a small house with thick walls and a solid-beamed roof built within the Compound. The new chamber also provided a place for the two goldsmiths to work. Under close supervision, they hammered and worked the gold, silver and copper extracted from the mine into coins. At Orodes's recommendation, each coin was carefully trimmed and worked into a round shape that carried the mark of Akkad on one side, and the Hawk emblem on the other.

Almost as soon as the coins appeared in the marketplace, they set the standard for quality that other merchants and traders were forced to match. "Good as Eskkar's gold" became the new criterion for value throughout Akkad and the countryside.

Despite Trella's best efforts to keep Nuzi a secret, word of the king's gold mine quickly spread. Gold seemed to loosen the tongue of everyone who came into contact with it. Every laborer, soldier and miner working at the site whispered news of the gold and silver deposits. Within months the hills and valleys surrounding the village held dozens of groups of ore hunters, all searching for another cache of gold. But Orodes had spoken the truth about the find. Whatever precious metals existed nearby remained locked deep within the earth, inaccessible to even the most determined seeker.

Tooraj, with the help of a handful of Hawk Clan soldiers, established a tight ring of security around the mine and surrounding valley. Gangs of laborers dug away at the hills, shearing them into vertical cliffs that only a mountain goat could have scaled. Soldiers guarded the single entrance to Nuzi day and night, and every person leaving the site – man, woman, or child – was stripped naked and searched. Some desperate laborers swallowed nuggets to conceal them, but that trick carried its own risks. In the first month, two men died clutching their bellies within days of leaving Nuzi.

Orodes issued a decree that anyone caught attempting to smuggle any precious metal out of the site would labor alongside the slaves for six months. Since a good number of the slaves and thieves forced to work at the mine died within that length of time, not many were willing to risk their lives for the handful of gold they might purloin. Nevertheless, Trella felt certain that small quantities of gold and silver still found their way out of the valley. But as long as Orodes kept such pilfering small and inconsequential, Trella didn't concern herself about the loss.

As Eskkar's little caravan approached Nuzi, Trella saw the smoke from the smelting fires rising over the hills. Well before they reached the entrance, the acrid fumes from the open furnaces assailed her senses. The smell alone would have told anyone within a mile that gold, silver, and the other noble metals were being ripped from the earth and burned out of the rocks and minerals that held them.

"About time they saw us coming," Eskkar said. "The lazy fools wouldn't have had time to close the gate before we cut them down."

The group had drawn within a hundred paces of the stout gates fastened to tall beams buried into the hillside before any of the sentries noticed the fifteen heavily armed riders approaching.

"I think they're more concerned about anyone trying to ride out, not in, husband."

Trella's effort failed to soothe Eskkar's annoyance.

"Four men," he muttered. "At least one of them should have been keeping an eye on the trail."

The chagrined sentries scrambled about belatedly. The half-hearted challenge died as they recognized Akkad's king. Trella heard the muffled chuckles of the Hawk Clan guards riding behind them. Like most fighting men, they enjoyed the spectacle of some other soldier receiving a tongue-lashing for failing to do his duty. They knew the king would point out this dereliction to Tooraj, who in turn would no doubt make the guards' lives miserable for a few days.

Eskkar gave the merest nod to acknowledge the salutes as they paced the horses through the gate and into the valley. Once inside, Trella wrinkled her nose at the powerful odors of burning wood and molten metal.

Inside the valley, more than seventy people labored. A mix of men, women and children were occupied digging, carrying wood or tending the half-dozen smelting fires. Others worked building mud bricks, using the water from the stream and straw that had been carried in by mule. Carpenters hammered bronze nails into wood, raising structures that enabled the slaves to move the heavy sacks of ores. Work also progressed on new flues and sluices to separate the ores. Stacks of lumber, ordered in prodigious quantities by Orodes, were scattered about. A shaduf, worked by three sturdy women, handled the heaviest loads, its long arm lifting and moving the weight with relative ease.

All this activity fascinated Trella. She turned toward Eskkar, but saw his eyes taking in the guards riding patrol on the hilltops overlooking the valley. Those crests held three watch stations, small shaded towers where a guard could see down into the valley and also anyone trying to gain access to the site from the surrounding hillsides. With so much wealth being taken from the earth, every possible security measure needed to be taken to prevent thefts. The noble metals required too much sweat and labor to wring them from the earth, and were guarded accordingly.

Eskkar helped Trella down from her horse as Orodes approached, wiping his hands on a filthy apron that stretched below his knees. To Trella's eyes, the mine master seemed older, more mature, and filled with confidence. Orodes had responded well to the responsibility she'd given him. According to Tooraj, everyone respected his skills. Perhaps the time had come to find him a wife, to help him settle down and keep him from falling back into his bad habits.

"Lord Esskar . . . Lady Trella, welcome to Nuzi. I didn't know you were coming."

"We didn't want to upset your labors." Trella spoke quickly, to forestall any biting remark from her husband about a surprise inspection. "We're eager to see what you've accomplished."

"I'll spend some time with Tooraj," Esskar said, as the leader of Nuzi's soldiers walked toward them, moving as fast as he could without breaking into a run. "I've seen the mine before."

Her husband might be interested in all the gold and silver the mine could produce, but he cared little for how they were obtained. Trella suspected there might be another reason for his lack of interest. Esskar had told her much about his past, but some parts of his earlier life remained a mystery. He seemed to know more about mining than he cared to admit.

"Then Orodes can show me around the valley."

The smile Orodes gave her announced that he would like nothing better than to have her undivided attention.

"Let me show you where it all began, Lady Trella," he said.

Orodes led her to the far end of the valley, where the stream flowed from the cliff face. Stones set in hardened mud now arched the water that spilled into the pool, creating a small waterfall. "This is where I found the first nuggets. Now all our drinking water comes from this place." More stones set in the pool provided easy access to the falling water. "Once the water leaves this pool, it's directed into the various sluices to separate the ores. After that, it's unfit to drink. Even the animals need to be kept away."

Trella studied the water, watching how the original course of the stream had been divided and diverted into three separate sluices. Orodes certainly knew his craft, she decided. Those water channels maintained an even flow to each trough, and with scarcely any leakage. When she lifted her eyes, she found him staring intently at her.

She recognized the look. Another man smitten by her position. Yes, Trella decided, Orodes definitely needed a wife.

Orodes realized he was staring and dropped his eyes for a moment. "Are you ready for the next step in the process?"

"Yes. And I want you to explain everything to me. Everything."

They walked and spoke until darkness fell. Orodes explained how the raw ores were washed, inspected, and separated again and again, until each particular pile contained a high content of specific minerals. Then the materials were crushed into smaller chunks, sifted again in running water, then heated in a furnace, sometimes with charcoal or other materials, some of which were delivered daily to Nuzi. When various impurities were burned off, the resulting raw metals were examined again. Some samples were reheated and reprocessed, others bagged into sacks for storage or transport. She recognized the green of copper ore – malachite Orodes called it – and the reddish tint that signified lead.

"With most of the surface gold already gone," Orodes went on, "we'll have to extract it in smaller quantities from the other processes that yield copper, tin and iron. Once everything is ground down to a fine powder, we can wash it again to extract the gold dust, though, as I expected, silver will soon be Nuzi's most valuable product. Already I need more toolmakers to fashion hammers and other implements. We're breaking tools almost every day, chiseling our way into the rocks and floor of the valley."

Trella paused and watched laborers hammering a bronze chisel into the rock face until it cracked, then levering the small opening until the rocks broke away. Fire, too, could be used to heat the stones. When they grew hot, a bucket of water tossed against the heated surface would split even the hardest rock.

"How many men will you need to bring Nuzi to full production?"

"Not counting the farmers and soldiers, just those working in this valley, at least a hundred slaves and as many craftsmen. With that many laborers, and the new process I've established to sift and sieve the ores, I think we'll be able to extract as much of the noble metals as feasible. Of course, I'll need a steady supply of firewood. With that I can make my own charcoal."

She'd already considered that request. Soon as many boats as departed from Nuzi would be arriving laden down with all the dozens of specialized tools and goods that Orodes needed to operate the mine efficiently. Trella realized it would be up to her to establish and maintain such a flow of materials, some from as far away as the northern forests. And it would take a good portion of the wealth extracted just to keep the flow of the precious metal coming.

Again and again Trella asked Orodes to go into more detail. At last Trella felt she understood every facet of how the mine worked. If another goldsmith were needed, she would know how to question him.

"Orodes, you've done well," she said, after he had finished his tour of the site. "When you first started, you asked for a share of the mine's profits. After what I've seen today, I believe you've earned it. From now on, one part in fifty of every shipment will be yours."

"My thanks to you, Lady Trella, for having faith in me. It is more than sufficient."

By the time Nuzi ceased operating, Orodes would probably be the richest man in Akkad.

As the setting sun signaled the end of the day's labors, Eskkar arrived, walking with Tooraj. Her husband would have spent the afternoon discussing ways to stop thieves and raiders, ensure the soldiers stayed honest and alert, and keep the ever-growing number of slaves under control. Tooraj's labors would be almost as difficult as Orodes. Tooraj would also need to be properly paid. She would see to that as well. He, too, could probably use a wife.

"Have you finished your inspection, husband?"

Eskkar couldn't keep the smile off his face, as happy for the good news Tooraj had given him as for avoiding a long session with Orodes. What Trella found fascinating would have bored her husband to death. Besides, Eskkar knew he could trust her to keep Orodes in check.

"Yes. Tooraj has everything under control."

"As does Orodes. He has built a very productive site, as I'm sure Tooraj has already informed you. The silver from Nuzi will flow to Akkad, and it will be enough to meet our needs for some time." She placed her hand on Eskkar's arm. "Now I think it is time for supper."

The three men standing facing her all looked guilty. None of them had given a single thought to a proper evening meal. Oh, well, that would be one more task she would have to perform.

31

Queen Kushanna frowned at the man kneeling before her. The guards had made a half-hearted effort to clean him up at the well, probably by throwing a few buckets of water over him. They knew better than to bring someone filthy into her presence. Nevertheless, the wretch still showed the thick black bands of dirt under the chipped and cracked nails on his hands and feet, and no quick scrub with a rag could remove all the grime imbedded into his face. His thin arms and legs had almost no flesh on them, and the unruly shock of black hair already streaked with gray nearly concealed his face. Death from either hunger or exhaustion would have taken him soon, she realized.

"Are you sure this is the one, Sohrab? I'd hate to think you brought back the wrong man after all this time."

Sohrab had departed nearly a month ago, and had returned by boat at dusk yesterday.

"Yes, Queen Kushanna. It took some time to find him. The original buyer sold him to –"

She waved her hand to silence him. "Hand me the whip."

Her chief spy removed the leather lash from his wrist and offered it to Kushanna. She used the stiffened plaited leather grip to lift the man's head so that she could read his eyes. A man's eyes revealed so much about him, much more than a woman's. This one's gaze appeared dull and listless, the eyes of one grown accustomed to the brutality of others. The ability to think would have been beaten out of him long ago. Now only fear of the whip could motivate a slave this far gone.

"What's your name, slave?"

The man stared at the whip. No doubt Sohrab had used it often enough on the slave's back.

"Almaric, mistress."

The voice was properly humble, the brown eyes downcast. He'd been a slave for more than three years, and the gods must have blessed him to keep alive so long at the mine.

"Look at me when you speak," she commanded. "Where are you from? Who was your father?"

The eyes blinked, as the man struggled to remember. His mouth opened, but no words came. Kushanna struck him across the face with the whip, not hard enough to break the skin but sharp enough to raise a welt. Almaric flinched at the pain, but knew better than to raise his hands or protest.

"Carnax, mistress. I'm from Carnax." He glanced about, but saw no mercy from Sohrab or the two guards.

"And your father?"

"Ahhhaaa ... my father was ..." His brow furrowed, as he struggled to recall the past.

Kushanna raised the whip again, but before she could strike, Almaric found the words.

"Sargat, mistress ... my father was Sargat of Carnax, advisor to the Village Elder."

Any imposter or properly coached slave might know those facts. Kushanna, however, had spoken at length to Drusas the slaver. Even facing the usual threats, he'd recalled little about Almaric, not even the boy's name. But Drusas remembered a wealth of detail about a young girl named Trella, how she was offered for sale as a virgin who could count and read the symbols, even that she possessed the healing knowledge. He'd sold her to a trader named Nicar on his way home to Akkad, now Eskkar's Chief Justice.

More important, Drusas recalled having Trella kneel naked before him, while she read the symbols and counted her numbers. "Tell me about your sister. What's her name?"

The question startled Almaric, but Kushanna lifted the whip again.

"Trella, mistress. My sister's name is Trella."

"Good. Very good, Almaric. Perhaps you would like some water." She gestured to the guard, who filled a cup from a pitcher and handed it the prisoner.

Almaric gulped the contents down in a few swallows, spilling a good portion on his chest and the floor between his knees.

Kushanna forced a smile to her face. If a servant had spilled that much water, she would have had the unlucky offender whipped. "Now describe your sister to me, slave. All you know of her."

The story required many promptings, but Kushanna only used the whip once more. Eventually, the detail Kushanna sought emerged, as the brother recalled a small brown mole beneath the sister's left breast. Drusas had remembered the same mark on the slave girl he sold to Nicar. No one else would know that fact, not even Sohrab.

Satisfied at last, Kushanna handed the whip back to Sohrab, then turned to the guard. "Take him down to the slave's quarters for now. Feed him well, and give him some ale. Tell my master steward Almaric is not to be whipped except by my order."

She waited until the guard removed the slave, then turned to Sohrab. "You've done well. That is indeed Trella's brother. We were doubly fortunate to find him still alive. In his condition, I'm surprised the mine's owner didn't have him killed."

"Yes, Queen Kushanna. He knew the symbols, so at the first dig, he was put to work helping count the sacks of ore. That kept him out of the pits. After two years, he was sold to a second mine. They had no need of a slave who could count or read the symbols, so he went down into the mine. He would have been dead in a few more months. They sold him for a single silver coin, and were glad to take advantage of me."

"You could have taken him for nothing," Kushanna said. "They would have given him up fast enough at my order."

"I thought it best not to use your name, my queen. This way, no one knows of your interest in such a laborer."

She smiled at Sohrab's ingenuity. He was learning to anticipate her commands. "I see I chose wisely when I sent you to find Trella's brother. Now we have to make use of him. His wits are addled, but perhaps with rest and good food and plenty of time, he may recover. The healthier Almaric is, the more value he will have. For now, take him to my farm south of Sumer. See to it that he is given only simple tasks and treated well. And watch over his progress. If he remembers how to think, we will send for him again."

"Yes, my queen. And you think he will be useful in the coming war?"

"Perhaps. He is the only one of Trella's kin that remains alive. Who knows, she may care more for him than her husband. At the least she'll pay well to have him returned to her."

"Shall I send such a message to Trella of Akkad?"

"Not yet, Sohrab, not yet. In due time you can deliver the message yourself."

32

Eskkar frowned at the well-worn tracks that led to the valley north of Bisitun. Three months ago, when he and Hathor first visited the place with a dozen Ur Nammu warriors, the ground showed no sign of anyone's passage through the land. Now the pristine emptiness of the hill country had changed. From the depth of the tracks, he knew horses, oxen, wagons, cattle, sheep, men, women and even children in increasing numbers had followed the same trail over the last three months, no doubt all of them bearing burdens of one kind or another. Probably not a day went by without another group of men or wagonload of supplies arriving. Still, when Eskkar crested the last hill, a little before sunset, and saw the valley below, he halted his horse in surprise.

"A walled village!"

Grond halted his horse beside that of his captain. "Well, I suppose it is. Not much of a wall, though. Or a village, either."

Eskkar let his eyes take in the site below. A mud-brick wall, just tall enough to keep a horse from jumping over it, ambled its way across the entrance to the valley. He guessed it to be at least two hundred paces from end to end, maybe even more. A wide gate near the center provided access. Beside the gate, a lone lookout tower twice the height of the gate rose up, its skeletal logs providing little more than a platform where a man or two could stand. Farther behind the wall, huts and tents extended a good distance into the valley, and Eskkar could see three separate horse pens, one of them empty. Smoke rose from several cooking fires, the gray streams curling lazily into the blue sky before following the wind to the east. The ringing sound of a bronze hammer pounding on a shaping stone echoed off the valley's walls.

As he watched, an empty wagon pulled by two oxen emerged from the gate, no doubt headed back to Bisitun to pick up another load of whatever goods Hathor and his commanders needed. The men conveying cargoes between Bisitun and here would be earning plenty of coins for their hard labor.

"All this, in only three months." While Eskkar had seen how well villagers could dig and build during the siege, this matched anything he'd seen at Akkad.

"Hathor knows his business," Grond said. "You picked the right man to build your cavalry."

They rode down the hill, followed by the ten Hawk Clan guards who had accompanied Eskkar all the way from Akkad. The lookout guard saw their approach, and raised a shout that must have carried halfway up the valley. In moments, six bowmen appeared from behind the wall, readying their weapons efficiently and taking their stations without anyone shouting orders at them.

Eskkar grunted in approval. The camp's discipline appeared sound. By the time he and Grond reached the gate, the guards had already unstrung their bows and waved them in greeting. Hathor arrived to join those standing by the gate, hands on his hips, waiting for them.

"Welcome to Horse Valley, Lord Eskkar." Hathor had a grin on his face. "And good to see you again, Grond."

Eskkar swung down from the horse, and the two men clasped each other's arms. "I'm glad I decided to come. It looks like you've built a village here since the last time I was here."

Hathor glanced around and shrugged. "This is nothing. Wait until you see the training ground. Come, I've much to tell you." He called for his horse, and a soldier brought out a fine brown stallion. "Follow me." He put his heels to the horse and cantered up into the valley.

Eskkar mounted and rode beside him. Beyond the horse pens the valley curved, and he saw another, much smaller wall blocking a cleft into the valley's walls.

"That's where the Ur Nammu keep their animals." Hathor gestured with his hand. "They camp there at night. The masons built it for them in three days."

Halfway up the valley, Hathor halted. A long house had been built here, along with another corral filled with ten or more horses. "This is where my commanders and trainers sleep. We'll stay here tonight. That will give me time to order up a feast in your honor, and prepare the men for tomorrow. Too late in the day to start a goat roasting, but we have some chickens, enough to make a good stew. We'll save the goat to celebrate another day."

Eskkar glanced up the valley. In the distance, he saw a small herd of horses roaming free. "A feast? Trella told me you were starving up here."

"Well, we were for the first month. Now we've plenty of food, and ale, too, for that matter. Grain, chickens, vegetables, everything we need comes from Bisitun. As the women arrived, they started building ovens, and now they bake bread, dozens of loaves each day. More than enough for everyone. We started giving some to the Ur Nammu, and they started bringing game into camp at day's end. So everyone is eating well."

"How many men do you have up here?"

Hathor had to stop and think. "About two hundred men, and another hundred women and children. You'll see most of them here tonight. When we heard you were arriving in a few days, the first two companies of cavalry had just finished the first part of their training. So I promised everyone a feast in your honor. They'll all want to see and hear their king."

That meant another speech. Still, Hathor and the others had made remarkable progress establishing the training camp. Eskkar hadn't expected any of the soldiers to have completed their training this soon, so they deserved at least a few words of praise. Unlike the steppe warriors who started riding as small children held in their fathers' arms, many villagers knew little about horses. For them, learning to ride and fight from the back of a racing animal meant overcoming their fears, real enough considering the size and speed of a horse.

By the time Eskkar, Grond and his guards took care of their horses and washed off the dust of their journey in the stream, the preparations for the feast were well under way. Soldiers carried armfuls of wood and started new campfires. Women and children crowded about, as curious to see the man who ruled their lands as to do the cooking. Two grinning soldiers dispensed and guarded the ale supply, but provided each man and woman with at least a cup of ale. Eskkar guessed that a few soldiers would be drunk before dark.

Everyone wanted to talk to the king. Every soldier, every recruit, found some excuse to visit Hathor's little camp. Even the laborers and craftsmen soon heard about Eskkar's presence and joined the crowd. Children, some barely able to walk, wandered over to stare in open-mouthed silence at the dark-haired man, though most soon decided that the tall and somber figure looked no different from any other man, and they wandered off to play their games.

Many people brought their own food with them, content to sit on the grass as close to Eskkar and his companions as they could get. He wanted to talk to Hathor, to learn what progress had been made, but it proved impossible. When Fashod, Chinua and four other smiling Ur Nammu warriors joined them, a shout of welcome rose up. Eskkar had never seen or heard anything like that before, villagers cheering barbarians. He still felt it odd that excited people often shouted out his own name.

With a smile, Eskkar forced himself to relax. The feast would have to come first, and from the looks of the ale being poured, it would go on for some time.

In the morning, Eskkar's head throbbed with pain. He'd eaten too much food, drunk too much ale, and in general behaved more like a half-drunken warrior than a king. Now he stood outside, pissing on the rocks that lay scattered behind the house and sighing in relief. The ground in front of the house had been trampled flat, but at least none of Hathor's men lay there in a stupor. The Egyptian had seen to that, making sure everyone got a few cups of ale but no more. By now every man, aching head or not, had returned to his station.

When Eskkar walked back into the house, he found Grond waiting, holding a cup of water that contained only a splash of ale.

Eskkar drank it down without pausing. It helped, but it took a second cup to quench his thirst and ease the pounding in his head.

"Grab some bread, Captain," Grond suggested. "Hathor's waiting with his commanders."

Eskkar clenched his jaw. More embarrassment. They had let him sleep while others had gotten up at dawn and gone about their business. Yesterday's ride to the valley had been long and tiring, but probably no worse than the day's training many of the men had undergone. No doubt everyone believed he was getting old and needed his rest.

The gloomy thought darkened his brow, and he followed Grond out to the side of the house, where Hathor had set up his command post.

The Egyptian greeted them. His face had resumed its somber look. Now that Eskkar thought about it, last night was the first time he'd ever seen Hathor laughing or even smiling so much.

He motioned for Eskkar to sit on the ground beside him, and Grond took his station just slightly behind his king. Instead of the usual circle, seven subcommanders faced their leaders, and one look at the ground explained that arrangement. A rough model of the valley had been dug into dirt, showing the long valley, the horse pens, and the training grounds.

"We'll start here, Lord Eskkar," Hathor began. "After we explain what we've done, we'll inspect the training grounds, and my commanders will give you a demonstration of their men's horsemanship."

"Good." Eskkar tried not to sound impatient, though he wanted to see the recruits in action, not stare at the dirt. Still, one had to begin somewhere.

"I'll start with the horses," Hathor began. "The Ur Nammu still break most of them, but a few of my best riders have started helping them with that. It's a difficult task. The men get thrown, stepped on, and one particularly clumsy fool managed to break his arm."

Eskkar realized that one of the men facing him had his left arm in a sling. A few of Hathor's commanders chuckled at the remark, and Eskkar saw the sheepish look of the man with the injured arm. Eskkar nodded in sympathy. Such accidents happened to everyone sooner or later. Men were thrown or fell from the horse, stepped on, scraped against trees and shrubs, and even bitten. Horses that would charge full speed into a battle might take fright at a blowing bush and either bolt or start bucking. Any such sudden motion could launch their unsuspecting rider through the air. And, of course, these things usually happened just when you thought you had the animal under your control.

"Once the animal can be ridden," Hathor continued, "we spend most of the morning riding them around the valley and the nearby hills, getting horse and rider used to each other. The Ur Nammu showed us their way of caring for their mounts, so now each rider cleans, grooms and feeds his own horse. We even have a few extra mounts for the trainers. We rest the animals during midday, to save them from the heat, while the men train with swords, knives, lances and bows. We don't have enough bows to go around, but the bowyers in Bisitun are working as fast as they can, and the Ur Nammu have contributed a few more every time they return from their main camp. We've a good supply of lances already."

315

"Can our men handle the bow while they ride?" Eskkar had worried about this since he first envisioned using cavalry much the same way as the barbarians did – to charge their enemy, loosing shafts as they rode, before wheeling off and forming up for another attack. If fifty men launched five or six arrows during each charge, that meant close to three hundred arrows raining down on the enemy force, with very little opportunity for them to shoot back. Barbarians considered this their most important tactic, especially when used against dirt-eaters or, in the case of Sumeria, massed infantry.

"We've less than twenty men learning to use that weapon, and their progress is slow," Hathor admitted. "But they're improving, and I think it can be done, at least for some of the younger and better riders. We'll have to see, but their Ur Nammu teachers expressed satisfaction with their progress. Those who can't are taught how to throw a lance. That's difficult enough to do from horseback, but some of our men are getting good at it."

Barbarians such as the Ur Nammu learned to ride and shoot from a horse's back almost from birth. Eskkar understood that villagers would never achieve a steppe warrior's level of skill in a few months, if ever. He knew he could not do it himself. His training with the clan had been interrupted before he had a chance to master the bow from the back of a horse. Not that he would ever have been very proficient. Eskkar was too tall to be a good archer from horseback, and his large hands lacked the dexterity needed to draw and nock an arrow while riding at a dead run.

"If using a bow can't be done, Hathor, don't waste the men's time. I'd rather have a good rider flinging a lance and swinging a sword than a poor archer fumbling with a bow."

A lance – usually not any taller than a man – made for a deadly weapon when thrown from the back of a charging horse. With the speed of the animal to add strength to the rider's arm, a flung lance could pass right through a man's body or impale a horse. In the last few months, Eskkar had spent quite a bit of time practicing with that weapon. Since he knew he could never shoot a bow on the run, the lance gave him the best weapon to strike an enemy at a distance.

"We have many months before we have to make that decision," Hathor replied. "And you're right, not many will be able to master that kind of archery. Right now the main thing is to teach the men how to ride and fight from horseback. Learning to ride well is a difficult and painful task that takes months to master. We've had two men killed so far, and lost a few horses to broken legs. Both men had their necks broken after being thrown. Now as soon as we think a man won't make a good rider, we stop his training. No need to waste men or horses. And I've had to send back a few men, those who couldn't control themselves or the horse while swinging a sword.

More than a few. Eskkar had heard the reports of those who couldn't master the needed skills. Still, the numbers were fewer than he'd expected. Not everyone had the strength in their legs and back that enabled them to keep their seat while guiding a galloping horse across rough ground with one hand, and swinging a sword with the other.

Just as important was each rider's sense of balance. A man needed to know how and when to lean forward or to the side, how to move with the animal. Striking with a sword required plenty of balancing ability. Otherwise the rider would crash to the earth with the first blow. To use a bow from a fast-moving horse required even more balance, since you needed two hands to use the bow. And you still had to guide the horse with your legs, voice, and the halter, while snatching another arrow from the quiver and fitting it to the bowstring, another task that took plenty of practice. Hand and leg movements had to guide the horse with precision, while the rider kept his balance with the animal racing beneath him.

Hathor waited a moment, then continued. "To train so many horses at the same time requires plenty of work. Like their riders, some horses, even after they're broken, aren't meant for warfare. Almost all of the horses we select are about thirteen to fourteen hands high, which gives them the size and bulk needed to carry a man and his weapons. Still, some taller animals don't have the endurance, and a few smaller ones do as well as their taller brethren, though we make sure those mounts are matched with a small rider."

Every barbarian, including Eskkar, preferred to ride his largest and strongest horse into battle. "And the Ur Nammu have found enough horses of that size to bring to us?"

"Yes. Subutai has his men out riding all the way to the steppes, to gather more wild stock.

"At least those animals will know how to fight. Unlike the tame horses raised in the villagers' corrals."

A horse raised in the wild could be a fearful fighter. Life in the herd involved biting, kicking and banging into other horses. Stallions fought and often killed to protect their mares, and the mares fought to protect their colts. Those same instincts made for a good warhorse.

As the sun rose higher in the morning sky, Hathor explained the rest of his training procedures, stopping often to answer Eskkar's questions. Twice, Hathor turned to one or another of his commanders for a more precise answer. By then Eskkar knew all their names and responsibilities.

"Now I think it's time to inspect the horses, Captain. And while we're doing that, my men will prepare for the demonstration. We're going to have two forces charge each other, so you can see how they ride and how they fight."

Eskkar climbed to his feet. His head had cleared, and he felt rested and refreshed. It would be good to feel a horse between his knees again. "Come on, Grond. Let's see what these men can do."

"They can ride, Captain," Hathor assured him. "And I think they'll fight well when the time comes."

"Then my trip was well worth the effort. After your commanders have finished, I'd like to ride with your men and take some practice with a lance. I don't always get enough time in Akkad."

Hathor nodded. "Then I'll join you, if I may. We can hurl a few dozen lances and see how many targets we can hit. And since I saw you practicing your swordsmanship with a lance in your left hand, I've been doing it myself."

"I learned that from Gatus. He has his infantry using their spears in all manner of ways. You never know when it might come in handy to have a second weapon."

"Let's hope we never need it in a battle," Hathor said. "But always better to prepare for trouble than be caught by surprise."

33

Shulgi lay back in the comfortable bed, enjoying the feel of the soft cloth against his naked body. The chatter of birds floated through the window, as well as the fainter sounds of Sumer's inhabitants bustling about their morning business. Dawn had risen some time ago, but no one would disturb the warrior king of Sumer in his bedchamber. All the city's inhabitants envied their king his good fortune to have the voluptuous Queen Kushanna in his bed, no matter what they might think about her strict rule over their lives. Brother and sister had brought peace and a measure of prosperity to the city, and few even remembered their father, dead now for over a year. The rumors that Eridu had died at his son's hand had faded from memory.

Three months had passed since Shulgi's last return to Sumer. In all that time he'd seldom slept on anything softer than a blanket stretched over hard ground. In truth, he hadn't spent more than a few months in the city since taking power. Instead, he'd ridden up and down the length of the desert, chasing the last of the Salibs, even those who fled deep into the west to escape. Their destruction had taken longer than he'd expected, but he felt more than satisfied with the result – an army of horsemen at his command. Before Shulgi reluctantly turned his horse's head back toward Sumer, he'd conquered another six desert clans and covered more than half the distance to the fabled land of Egypt. With the elimination of the last of the Salibs, the mocking title of Boy King vanished as well.

Egypt would be his next conquest, after he'd crushed Akkad and forced its people into his new Sumerian Empire. Once he had the additional manpower from Akkad and the northern lands, he would have an army large enough to invade Egypt. But that effort would have to wait a few more years. When he finished conquering Akkad, Shulgi knew he would need at least another year or two to solidify his rule over the remnants of the Akkadian lands, as well as the other cities of Sumeria. After Shulgi eliminated their petty rulers and installed men loyal only to himself, he would reign supreme, the only king in the vast land between the rivers. First Akkad, then Egypt, then only the gods knew how far Shulgi could stretch his reach.

"What are your thoughts, my brother?" Shanna ran her fingertips down his arm and onto his stomach.

Shulgi's thoughts of empire vanished at her touch, and his manhood stirred even before her hand closed around it. He'd taken her twice last night as soon as he returned to Sumer, and once again this morning. No matter how often he possessed her, it needed only a word, a look, the feel of her breast, to make him hunger for her body again. Shulgi wondered how she'd learned to arouse such passion in a man. Perhaps Kushanna, too, was a witch, like the queen of Akkad. He wondered if Eskkar felt the same lust for his wife. Not likely, he decided. Those who had seen both women voiced only disdain for Trella's plain looks and simple attire.

"I was thinking how soft your lips are when they touch my body, Shanna."

"Mmm, yes, such a beautiful body. So strong, and so fierce a rod. Since you've ridden to war, you've grown even more handsome. A true king." She tightened her grip, and his erection sprang up, throbbing. Taking her time, she moved down the bed, settled herself comfortably, and let her breasts dangle against his thigh. She brushed her lips lightly against his staff, teasing him until he squirmed under her touch, the urge to penetrate her body growing ever more demanding.

"Take me in your mouth," he commanded, unable to restrain himself. He used the same voice he would give orders to any soldier.

"Oh, yes, my lord. Whatever you command." Still taking her time, she closed her mouth over the tip of his member, and used her tongue to force a moan of pleasure from his lips. Slowly she took the full length of his manhood into her mouth, her hair now scattered across his loins, until her lips touched his hard stomach.

"You are a witch." No other woman had ever managed to take the full length of his aroused staff into her mouth.

She lifted her head and took a breath. "If I'm a witch, why do I do your bidding?" Before he could reply, she began stroking his staff, this time using her cheek against the tip.

Waves of pleasure rushed through him. He'd taken plenty of women while away from Sumer, but none of them compared to her. Unable to restrain himself any longer, Shulgi reached down and pulled her toward him.

With an easy movement, she knelt over him and guided his staff inside her body. Kushanna sighed in pleasure as she sank down on him. She clasped her hands behind her neck and leaned back. Without moving her hips, she used the powerful muscles deep inside her womb to squeeze his rod.

"Do you like that, my brother?"

"Oh, yes, Shanna," he panted. "There is no one like you."

"Then let me take you to the pleasure of the gods." She began to move up and down, grinding her hips, thrusting herself harder and harder against him, keeping him deep inside her.

He felt the warmth of her body as he gazed upon her breasts, swaying above him. Faster and faster she rode his manhood, twisting and pushing against him, until with a cry he burst inside her. Even that did not satisfy her. She kept moving, squeezing him, until he protested and pushed her aside.

"Enough. Any more and I won't be able to ride for days."

She brushed the tangle of hair from her face and stretched out beside him, cradling his head against her breasts. "Tonight you will be strong again for me, I promise you."

His arms encircled her as he lay there, scarcely able to move. Shulgi breathed in the warm musk of her body. His eyes closed, and he let himself relax. Within moments, the feel of her face against his shoulder lulled him back to sleep.

When he woke he found Shanna dressed and standing beside the bed. She wore a soft gown of pure white, and her slaves had combed her hair artfully to frame her features. A tray of fruit, bread, and ale rested on the table. She leaned over and kissed the sleep from his face.

"It's time you woke up, my brother. Sumer's noble merchants and traders will assemble here at midday, to hear of your latest conquests. And you don't want your body to grow weak from too much time in bed."

Shulgi smiled at that. The long days spent on the back of a horse had tightened every muscle, including, it seemed, his manhood. He'd never spent his seed so often, and with so much force before. For a moment Shulgi considered telling her to remove her dress. He shook the temptation from his mind and pushed himself into a sitting position.

She handed him the ale cup, and he drained its contents. Some day, he knew, Shanna might hand him a cup of poison with as much grace and concern. But not today. And not while there remained so many lands to conquer.

"Tell me of the desert."

Her voice had lost its pleasure-slave tone. The cunning queen of his empire had returned. He tore a hunk of bread from the loaf. The sour-sweet taste seemed like nectar after the foul-smelling desert fare.

"The last of the Salibs are destroyed. Except for the lands Chief Kapturu claims, the desert is ours."

"Then there will be no more slaves arriving in Sumer?"

For the last year, captive Salibs, mostly women and children had paraded through Sumer's lanes, to be sold as slaves throughout Sumeria and even as far north as Akkad. Shulgi's profits from those sales had nearly equaled the gold and gems taken from the desert-dwellers.

"Kapturu's horsemen still range the desert fringes, and will continue to supply slaves, though the number will be fewer and the cost higher."

"We need all the gold we can raise, Shulgi."

He nodded. "I've brought another thousand gold pieces with me, plus three sacks of gemstones. Perhaps that will satisfy you for a time."

She shook her head. "Another month, perhaps two. But more gold will be needed in the coming year. Unlike Trella in Akkad, we lack a steady supply of silver."

The mine at Nuzi had flooded the northern lands with the precious metal. Silver coins with the mark of Akkad paid the wages of Eskkar's soldiers.

"Have you exhausted all the gold from Sumeria's mines? It seems you spend my spoils of war as fast as I win them."

Kushanna saw the look of frustration on his face. All the established mines within Sumer's reach had been confiscated months ago, and their ores used to pay his own soldiers. But the output had always been small, and Kushanna's demands had exhausted most of them. Hundreds of slaves had died extracting what little remained. Nuzi was a recent find, and could be expected to produce large quantities of gold and silver for some time.

"Don't chide me with such a frown, brother. My agents have been busy on your behalf. Your captured treasures have bought you support in every Sumerian city. Hundreds of voices throughout the land now clamor for war against Akkad. Your victories in the desert, along with the gold we've spread around, have won support for your cause. Larsa, Uruk, Isin, all the cities are raising troops of their own, eager to share in the spoils of Akkad conquest."

"Just so they're ready to follow my standard into battle."

"That campaign, too, is already under way. With the Tanukhs under your command, Sumer will field the largest part of any combined army. Because of that, the rest of the cities already accept your leadership, willingly or not. They understand it's best to direct their wrath against Akkad than each other. The heavy bribes we've paid to their merchants and traders help see to that."

"Especially now that they know what happened to the Salibs."

"It's more than that, Shulgi. Sumer continues to grow. We're now twice as large as Nippur, and the other cities are even smaller. Their rulers know they will fall under your sway sooner or later. The wise among them will seek to gain as much influence from you as possible. And as much gold and power as they can wrest from Akkad's defeat."

Kushanna had indeed done well. Shulgi had thought it might take another year or two before all of Sumeria acknowledged his leadership. Instead in less than a single year he had already accomplished far more than his father ever dreamed.

"Then it's time to issue a call for more of their soldiers to join me in the desert. The sooner they learn how to fight under my command, the better."

Hundreds from the other cities had already flocked to his standard, desperate men searching for loot, young men seeking glory, petty thieves and outcasts seeking escape from their crimes. Razrek had accepted them all, feeding them into his training camps. Already many had turned into competent fighters and even subcommanders.

"Yes, my brother, that can be done. I'll dispatch messengers tomorrow."

"Any news from Akkad?"

"Of course. I have a dozen agents living there, and reports come from every trader who visits. Esskar continues to recruit men and train them in the north. He shuffles them around from training camp to training camp, trying to keep their numbers secret. But more than a few have deserted, thanks to your gold. We know all about his spearmen and cavalry. But no matter how hard the barbarian tries, he won't be able to raise more than three or four thousand fighters, perhaps a little more."

Shulgi already had more than that number in his own camps at the edge of the desert. With the hordes of Tanukh horse fighters, Eskkar of Akkad was greatly outnumbered.

Kushanna saw the look. "Don't count your victory yet, brother. Eskkar is trying to make up for his smaller force with greater training. His force of infantry spearmen is reputed to be fierce, and his horsemen grow more proficient every day, thanks to those accursed steppe barbarians in the north."

Shulgi knew the remnants of the Ur Nammu had been assisting the Akkadians. Kushanna had tried to reach out to them, offered them gold and trading opportunities, but the clan had rebuffed her overtures. The Ur Nammu would deal only with Akkad, despite her bribes and offers of friendship.

"My men are training each day as well, and we've fought a dozen battles with the Salibs."

"All to the good, Shulgi. But don't grow overconfident. You will need every man from every city in Sumeria. Crush the Akkadians with numbers. Eskkar and his men will not go down easily."

"Agreed. But with an army that small, Eskkar knows he can only fight a defensive war. He expects us to invade his land and besiege his city. He hopes to wear us down until we abandon our attacks. I'll do that if I have to, but I prefer to force him out from behind his walls. Make him fight on my terms."

"You've a plan for that?"

"Yes, I've been working on it for months, with Razrek and Vanar and the others. We'll bring Eskkar out of Akkad, then destroy him."

Kushanna didn't answer. Instead she picked up a date and split the skin, removing the pit. "Our father tried that."

Shulgi took another mouthful of bread before answering. "Our father was a fool. He wanted to defeat Eskkar himself. The man means nothing to me. It's his city I want. If Eskkar wants to keep it . . . well, then he'll come to me, fight me on my terms."

She waited a moment, until she realized he didn't intend to offer any more information.

"Be aware that Trella continues to raise Akkad's walls higher and higher."

"She can raise them as high as the mountains for all I care." He smiled at her and patted her hand. "And her spies? Have you found them all?"

"Most of them. And I've put many others to the torture." A smile crossed her face at the memory. "Some have confessed spying for Trella. But I'm sure there are still a few within the city."

Shulgi knew that Kushanna, even as a young girl, enjoyed watching men tortured. It was one of the few things that excited her.

"How do you know when they're telling the truth?"

"It's simple. If they use Trella's name, I know they're lying, saying anything to stop the pain. When I hear Annok-sur's name on their lips, then I know we captured a spy."

"Clever, my sister. I see I'm in good hands with you guarding my city."

"There will always be more spies."

"I know. Don't worry about such things for now. Did you learn anything more about her brother?"

Kushanna accepted the change of subject. "Oh, yes, we found him working in the copper mine less than fifty miles from here. His name is Almaric, and he is Trella's older brother. His wits were almost gone when Sohrab brought him here. But he's recovering, and he may be of some use to us. At the very least we can exchange him for some gold. Or use him to distract Trella right before we strike. Much will depend on how much he recovers."

"You're sure you have the right slave?"

"Drusas remembers Trella, all right, and how he sold her to Nicar of Akkad. Apparently, Drusas felt himself bested in the exchange. She was still a virgin when Nicar took possession. Trella's brother was sold to the Minga clan, who operated a silver mine about three days' journey from Sumer. After a few years, he was sold again to a copper mine."

Shulgi shrugged. "Let's hope we can make use of him."

"He will serve some purpose, of that I'm sure. Trella knows nothing of her brother's fate. It might distract her at the right time."

Shulgi considered that for a moment, then dismissed it from his thoughts. "And what of the Alur Meriki? Did you ever reach them?"

"Yes, it was difficult, but a meeting place was arranged. Who can we send to meet with them? It's far too dangerous for you to go."

"Well, Razrek claims he has dealt with them before. I'm sure he's ready to visit the barbarians again." He smiled. "By now he's had enough of the desert. And what better way to prove your courage than to put your head in the lion's mouth?"

"Then all that remains is to be patient, Shulgi. Assemble your forces, and train your men. When the time comes to strike, I'll have all the supplies and food that will be needed."

"I'm ready now, my sister. We could defeat Akkad today."

"One more year. By then your army will have grown even stronger. At the end of next summer, as soon as our crops are in, you can strike."

The harvest in Sumeria – if the gods acted as they normally did – would take place ten or twenty days before Akkad began to take its crops from the field. Sumeria's warmer climate meant that her farmers would reap their harvest before the Akkadians. That would leave Esskar's men short of food at the start of the campaign. Still, a year seemed such a long time.

She guessed his thoughts. "It will come sooner than you think, my brother."

"And what will my beautiful queen be doing in the coming year?"

"Helping you raise your mighty army. The other cities must prepare as well. They will each need to raise and arm thousands of men, and they will need to be trained as well. Our gold has already bought the support of their kings and ruling nobles. When you are ready, fighting men will march forth from Larsa and every other city, to follow your banner."

"I will need to visit each of those cities, then, see to their training, meet with their rulers . . ."

"More than once, I'm sure, my brother. But when you ride into their strongholds at the head of your cavalry, strong and confident, all will accept your leadership."

He nodded. Kushanna spoke the truth. Best to wait until victory was certain. "Then I will wait one more year. But starting tomorrow, we begin. I want every city in Sumeria to begin recruiting and training more men."

"They will, my king. They will."

326

34

Three months later...

Razrek licked the blood from the corner of his mouth, and tried to ignore the pain. One of his teeth felt loose. He probed it with his tongue and grimaced. His hands, bound tight behind his back, hurt even more than his swollen face. All this meant nothing compared to what was likely to come next. He lifted his eyes toward the tent where the leaders of the Alur Meriki had gone to talk, very likely deciding his fate.

At least Razrek hadn't given in to his fear, not yet. He glanced at his two companions, brave enough men and willing to accompany him in a meeting with the barbarians. Both had already given themselves up for dead. They shook with fear as they knelt on either side of him, tied up as tightly as he was.

The carefully arranged meeting between Sumer and the Alur Meriki had gone horribly wrong from the beginning. Razrek had reached the agreed place early enough. After two days of waiting, a band of twenty warriors had galloped into his campsite just after sunrise. Razrek held up his empty hands and called out the name he'd been given – Urgo of the Alur Meriki.

Razrek might just have well shouted out his own name. The warriors burst upon the three of them. They were knocked to the ground and their weapons taken from them. Neither Razrek's protests or curses made any difference. A vicious-looking warrior with a thick scar across his face led the group. The barbarians called him Rethnar. A clan leader, Razrek decided, identified by the small copper medallion hanging from his neck.

After a quick look, Rethnar shouted a few orders, and Razrek and his companions were lifted onto their horses and led off.

A long ride followed that lasted most of the day. Mid-afternoon had arrived when they crested a hill and Razrek saw the main camp of the Alur Meriki below him. Even Razrek's eyes opened wide in wonder at the vast traveling village. He'd seen the camps of the Tanukhs and Salibs, but those desert tribesmen didn't compare to the barbarians. At least a thousand horses, hundreds of wagons and tents, small herds of sheep, cattle and goats filled a small valley.

His captors had led their prisoners through the camp, until they reached their destination, a large tent set somewhat apart from the others. Razrek caught the word "*sarum*", which he knew meant king or leader, before the warriors bound his hands and pushed him to his knees, along with his men. When Razrek protested, a fist had hammered into his face, knocking him to ground.

"Keep silent, dog," the warrior said, "or I'll cut out your tongue."

Razrek had no doubt that the man meant what he said. Razrek clamped his lips shut. He should never have let Shulgi talk him into this meeting.

Voices that rose and fell came from the big tent. Several warriors were having a heated discussion within, and Razrek felt certain it concerned him. The arguing went on and on, and the pain from Razrek's knees began to hurt worse than his hands.

At long last the tent flap jerked aside, and four clan chiefs, including Rethnar, came out. The three warriors guarding the tent followed behind. Not that they were needed, Razrek decided. The clan leaders appeared as hard and powerful as any of the warriors they commanded.

One warrior wore a copper pendant, much larger than those of his companions, on his chest. That would be the emblem of the Alur Meriki, the sacred medallion that identified their leader, Thutmose-sin. The leader of the clans stopped two paces away and stared down for a long moment at his prisoners. About forty years old, he stood taller than any of his commanders, and every muscle on his body might have been chiseled from stone. An odd, circular scar marked his forehead, just above his right eye. The rest of his face was untouched, though there were scars enough on his arms and chest to attest to his fighting strength.

The other three men ranged themselves alongside their leader, who folded his arms across his chest. Thutmose-sin gave Razrek's men little more than a dismissive glance, but took his time studying the Sumerian leader.

"You are the one called Razrek."

A statement, not a question. Razrek found his mouth dry, and had to swallow before he could answer. "Yes, Sarum. My name is Razrek, and I've been –"

"You've been sent by the leader of the village called Sumer. You wish to wage war against the village of Orak, now called Akkad, and you want us to join you in your fight. Why? Are you not strong enough to fight your own battles?"

Razrek knew better than to answer that question either yes or no. "My Lord . . . Sarum . . . the people of Sumeria are determined to fight Esskar of Akkad, who is your own sworn enemy. My king wishes to offer the mighty Alur Meriki a chance to join in the spoils of battle. Akkad is a rich land with much gold and silver, large herds, and thousands of possible slaves. Is not the enemy of my enemy my friend?"

The saying meant the same to the barbarians as to the tribes of the desert.

"The Alur Meriki will fight their enemies at a time of our own choosing," Thutmose-sin said. "For dirt-eaters to suggest that we fight alongside them is an insult to our honor."

"Sarum, I mean no such thing. I spoke as one warrior to another . . ."

Rethnar took a step forward and kicked Razrek in the chest. The savage blow knocked the breath from his body, and he toppled over.

"Do not dare to compare yourself to true warriors," Rethnar shouted, his face red with anger.

Razrek twisted his body upright, and managed to get back on his knees, gulping air into his lungs. If he were going to die, he didn't intend to grovel before these barbarians. "Untie my hands and give me a sword," he said, "and we'll see who is a warrior and who is a coward!"

Rethnar reached for his sword.

"Hold your anger, Rethnar," Thutmose-sin commanded, his hand staying his companion. "He is only a dirt-eater seeking a quick death. Do not give him what he wants."

"We did agree to meet with these Sumerians," another man said. He was the oldest of the four clan leaders, probably approaching his fiftieth year. "We should hear his words. We can always kill him later."

"As always, Urgo, you give good counsel," Thutmose-sin agreed. "Bring this one into my tent. We will hear what he has to say. Give him some water. It seems his mouth is dry."

The guards untied his hands and handed him a water skin. They kept him on his knees while he drank, but that was expected. No warrior, let alone their Sarum, could admit treating a dirt-eater as an equal.

Inside the tent, the guard pushed Razrek back on his knees before leaving. The Sumerian found himself facing the four clan leaders. He explained his purpose for visiting. A war was coming, a mighty conflict with many thousands of men on each side. The purpose of this war was to crush Akkad into the dust, to leave no stone of the accursed city standing atop another. The forces of Akkad, led by Eskkar, would find themselves arrayed against the might of all the cities of Sumeria. The Akkadians would be forced to leave their walled city and march south, to face the army of Sumer. That would leave the city almost undefended, its walls guarded by old men, women and children. The time would be ripe to pluck the city.

Razrek spoke until his voice gave out. They gave him more water, and he went on. Razrek told them he would have brave men inside the enemy's city, men who would lower ropes for the Alur Meriki to scale the walls. Once inside, the city's inhabitants would be no match for the fury of the mighty Alur Meriki warriors. Finally, Razrek had nothing more to say. The faces of his captors revealed nothing about what they felt.

"Take him outside," Thutmose-sin ordered.

Razrek bowed. In his chest, he felt relief. At least the Sarum hadn't ordered him to be tortured. Not yet.

Thutmose-sin waited until the guards dragged Razrek out. The four commanders of the Alur Meriki shifted to face each other, sitting cross-legged on the thick blanket with only a small space separating them. Thutmose-sin looked at each man in turn. "Tell us what you think, Urgo."

The oldest clan leader shook his head. "We should not get involved in the affairs of dirt-eaters. Akkad is too strong for us to challenge for now. In another five or seven years when we have recovered our strength, then it will be different."

"This is our best chance to attack Akkad," Rethnar said, his voice harsh in the tent's confines. "We need to take our revenge now, before the accursed dirt-eaters grow even more numerous. Our blood stains the ground around their filthy walls and cries out for vengeance." He fingered the scar on his cheek. An Akkadian arrow had torn his mouth and cheek open during the final battle. "If fighting on the side of these Sumerians gets us over the walls, so much the better."

"We can afford to wait," Urgo replied. "Each year more of our young men become warriors. If we strike now, if we rely on these Sumerians, we may risk more than we can gain."

"If you're afraid . . ."

Thutmose-sin held up his hand to stop Rethnar's hot words. "No one here is afraid. But we must do what is best for our clan." He turned to the other commander, by far the youngest of the group. "What course would you choose, Bar'rack?"

"My blood cries out for vengeance against Eskkar and his dirt-eaters. My brother lies dead and unburied in some nameless ground, ambushed by the renegade Eskkar and the cowardly Ur Nammu. Since that day, I've sworn to take Eskkar's head from his shoulders. But, like Urgo, I do not think we should let ourselves be used by these Sumerians."

Rethnar swore under his breath. "Our warriors cry out for revenge, and none of you want to fight. The young men think their leaders are weak, unwilling to fight. When they learn that we have let slip an opportunity to strike Akkad, they will burn with fury." He set his gaze on Thutmose-sin. "What do you say, *sarum*?"

Thutmose-sin ignored the hint of insult in the use of his title. There was already too much bad blood between Rethnar and himself, fanned to a red-hot heat since the defeat at Akkad's walls. Rethnar was right about one thing. Word of this offer of alliance would get out. Rethnar would be the first to tell every member of his clan.

"I, too, want to see the renegade Eskkar killed." Thutmose-sin touched the scar on his forehead. "I fought him the night he burned the wagons, and would have killed him if my sword had not shattered. One more stroke." He shook his head at the grim memory.

"In the years since that battle, we have added hundreds of warriors. But Akkad has grown by thousands, and we know they have learned from Eskkar the way of a warrior. They are no longer simple villagers who can be swept aside. They've trained themselves to fight with bow and sword and lance. Even if we get into the city, the fighting will be fierce. If we attempt this, we would need to send every warrior we have into the battle.

Anything less will fail. Even if we win, our losses will be heavy, and might well doom the Alur Meriki."

"That is wise," Urgo said, speaking quickly before Rethnar said anything to make things worse. "If we lose too many warriors, we may never recover. Already we face a growing number of enemies."

"But if these Sumerians can get us over the wall," Rethnar said, "I don't care how many men they have inside the city. If the dirt-eaters are at war, we can take advantage of those staying behind. Once inside, we can slaughter thousands, burn the city from within. If the traitor Eskkar is not there to lead them, they will be no match for my fighters." He glanced at the other commanders. "I will lead the raid with all the men in my clan, if no one else has the courage to fight. I will take the help of the Sumerians. We can deal with them later."

"Your three hundred warriors will not be enough," Urgo said. "Better to not attempt any raid unless you have enough men to be certain of success."

The Alur Meriki now counted almost a thousand warriors fit to ride and fight. But most were young and inexperienced. Thutmose-sin had more than four hundred under his standard. Two other clan chiefs, both absent on raids, controlled another two hundred. But all four clan leaders present knew these other leaders wanted no part of a return to Akkad's walls. Whatever decision would be made, would be made by those present.

Both Urgo and Rethnar turned toward Bar'rack. His clan was the newest of the Alur Meriki, made up of survivors of three other clans that had taken heavy losses in the fight against Akkad. More than a hundred and fifty warriors rode under Bar'rack's banner.

Bar'rack glanced at Thutmose-sin, and caught the slightest inclination of his head. Rethnar, caught up in his rage, didn't notice. Bar'rack took but a moment to comprehend what Thutmose-sin wanted. "If the *sarum* approves, I will ride with Rethnar," Bar'rack said. "Between our clans, we have enough warriors to punish Akkad. But if we cannot get over the walls by stealth, then I will not waste my warriors' lives attacking the city."

"I accept Bar'rack's warriors." Rethnar couldn't hold in the smile of satisfaction. "We will destroy Akkad."

"If we cannot get in," Bar'rack repeated, "then we will raid the countryside and devastate the lands of Akkad. That will be more than enough to repay us for the risk, at least for now."

Thutmose-sin looked at Urgo.

"It is almost enough," Urgo said. He, too, had caught the Sarum's signal. "I will contribute fifty warriors to fight under Bar'rack's orders. That will give Rethnar at least five hundred men. He speaks the truth when he says our warriors need to fight. A raid such as this will give them a chance to avenge their honor."

That many men would constitute a major raid, more than enough to destroy the crops and herds of the Akkadians. No matter what happened at the walls, the devastation to the countryside would be crippling to the city.

Thutmose-sin nodded in acceptance. "Then the Alur Meriki will raid the lands of Akkad next summer. But both of you will safeguard your warriors. I do not want lives thrown away."

Rethnar climbed to his feet. If he heard the Sarum's words, he didn't bother to agree with them. "Then I will go and speak with this Razrek. There is much that needs to be discussed, but we have nearly a whole season to prepare."

Later that evening, as most of the vast camp prepared for sleep, Thutmose-sin and Bar'rack walked to the edge of the narrow stream. They reached a small boulder and sat down, facing each other. No others were within a hundred paces.

"You are satisfied with the Sumerian?"

Rethnar and Bar'rack had spent most of the night working out the details with Razrek.

"Yes. He's brave enough for a dirt-eater, and he has planned out every step that will be needed. There will be more meetings in the coming months, but if things happen as the Sumerian believes, we should be able to get into Akkad."

"And if not, then I will count on you to save as many warriors as you can. Do not let Rethnar throw away the lives of his men or yours. Remain calm in the heat of battle, and think not of the glory of fighting, but of winning."

"You do not think this plan will succeed?"

Thutmose-sin took a deep breath. "I don't know. If it were so certain, the Sumerians might try it themselves. I do know that Eskkar is no fool. The night my father put his family to death, Eskkar managed to escape the warriors, even though he was but a boy. He even killed a man before he fled. Then, instead of dying in the lands of the dirt-eaters, he survived and grew strong. Now he rules one of their largest cities. He will not be defeated easily, either by these Sumerians or by Rethnar."

"Still, we may win a great victory."

"Rethnar is right about one thing. Our young men grow restless. They need a challenge like this if they are to grow strong. We lost much honor when we were defeated outside of Akkad's walls. This would regain much of that."

"Then I will do my utmost to make sure Rethnar succeeds."

"In that case, every member of the clan will praise your name, Bar'rack." He paused for a moment, then shrugged. "I should give you my thanks now. Because if Rethnar destroys Akkad, then when he returns with his victory he will be Clan Leader of the Alur Meriki. And I will be dead."

35

With each passing month, Tammuz and En-hedu watched in satisfaction as business at the Kestrel improved. As trade among the Sumerian cities picked up, traffic on the river had grown. Boats arrived almost each day from the north, venturing down the Euphrates and Tigris rivers, as well as the numerous streams that flowed between them, to deliver cargoes to anxious buyers waiting on Sumer's docks. After the boats unloaded, their crews sought refreshment from the many inns or simple taverns that sold ale or wine.

The Kestrel, now open for business almost a year and a half, attracted many of these crewmen, most eager to part with a portion of their pay for a chance to drink with their friends and new acquaintances, eat a good meal, and in many cases obtain relief from their more basic urges. Tammuz told En-hedu that they would soon need another girl to help Irkalla and Anu.

En-hedu's massage business had grown even faster than the Kestrel. With Ninlil paying for a massage every other day, more women from the better classes soon enquired after En-hedu's skills. Since the wealthy in Sumer now included many wives of the senior soldiers, women of all classes and ages sought En-hedu's soothing hands. Within a few months, she earned as much from her massages as Tammuz did from the Kestrel.

Despite her success, En-hedu enjoyed her evenings helping Tammuz in the alehouse. The need to provide massages at night had vanished, and except on rare occasions, the last massage ended at sundown.

Tonight, customers filled every available table and bench in the inn.

A trading boat from Akkad had made port today, as well as two from Larsa and another from Nippur. With such a large crowd, Tammuz and En-hedu kept a close watch on the ale, while Rimaud kept the more boisterous patrons under constant observation, alert for any signs of trouble. Despite their vigilance, an occasional fight still broke out, but Rimaud's reputation for flinging any offenders out into the lane lessened the number of such conflicts. Why fight, when there was good ale to be drunk in the company of pleasant companions? Those with more serious issues resolved them outside in the lane.

After sundown, the cook and her staff departed, their work for the day finished. Anyone still hungry at this hour would have to make do with bread from the basket hanging on the wall behind the ale table.

When Jarud stepped through the open door, Tammuz waved a greeting and started filling a pitcher. Most of the ale he purchased each day at the market was of only fair taste. But now he could afford to include a few jars of better quality brew that he reserved for his best customers.

The recently promoted leader of twenty for Sumer's watch settled into his bench just as Tammuz arrived with the ale and a reasonably clean cup. Four other members of the night watch were already crowded around the table, but they made room for their leader.

"Hello, innkeeper." Jarud scooped up the fresh cup the moment Tammuz placed it on the table. "I've worked up a thirst tonight. Two fights already broken up, and a thief caught in the act and sent to the work gangs. And it's still early in the evening."

"Greetings, Jarud. Are you through for the night?"

"No, I just stopped in for a cup of ale and to get a bit of rest. One of my men is guarding two boatmen from Nippur outside. If their captains don't want to pay for them in the morning, they'll do twenty days' labor in the work gang."

Tammuz smiled. "They always pay, don't they? Not many captains want to pull an oar themselves, especially upriver."

Everyone laughed at that. Only in dire circumstances was a boat captain likely to pick up an oar. Some boatmen claimed they'd never seen one do any real work. That fact helped Sumer's guards make themselves a few extra coins when desperate ship owners, no doubt with a schedule to keep, had to purchase their sailors' freedom.

"A full house tonight." Jarud glanced around the inn. "Anyone causing problems here?"

"Not a one. Your men have been helping keep the place quiet most of the night."

"Well, then at least they're doing something to earn their pay, besides sitting on their lazy asses. What they should be doing is walking the lanes, looking for troublemakers. But I'll have to take them with me when I leave."

"Not all of them." Tammuz let the dismay sound in his voice. Except when he was short-handed, Jarud could usually be counted on to leave at least one of his men at the Kestrel.

Jarud shook his head. "New commander in charge tonight, so we can't afford to look like we're loafing on the watch. He'll be here a few months, until he gets a command of his own."

"I thought you just got a new commander."

"That was thirty, forty days ago." Jarud laughed and took another mouthful of ale. "You need to get out of your tavern more often. Still, Kourosh won't be here long. He's too good to be wasted guarding Sumer's fat merchants and lazy shopkeepers. He brought a few of his men with him from the desert, and they worship him like a god. King Shulgi is already preparing a command for him."

Sumer's king had returned from the desert months ago, and immediately started recruiting and training an army, supposedly to wage further war against the desert tribes, though only a fool believed that. Desert fighting belonged to those on horseback, and King Shulgi already had a vast contingent of cavalry. Now he spent his time visiting the other Sumerian cities, helping them raise their own forces, supposedly for protection against future desert raids.

Tammuz showed no particular interest in Jarud's new commander. Instead, Tammuz held out his hand. "One copper for the pitcher. I still have to make my living."

Jarud pointed at one of his men. "Pay the innkeeper."

A worn copper coin appeared, and was grudgingly handed over, despite the fact that the pitcher had been a large one and contained the best ale in the house, in honor of Jarud's appearance.

"Good luck with your new commander," Tammuz said, after giving the coin a brief inspection. Sumer's night watch came into contact with plenty of fake coins, and had little compunction about trying to pass them off. "Come back when your watch is ended. I'll save some good ale for you."

"You always say that," Jarud countered, "and it's always the same piss."

"I collect it just for you from the piss pot outside. At least it's always fresh."

Everyone laughed, and Tammuz went back to the table where En-hedu was busy helping Irkalla. He stood beside his wife, until Irkalla left the table to deliver another cup of ale. "I just heard Sumer's going to have a new captain of the guard, a man named Kourosh."

En-hedu nodded. "Those three in the corner table look like trouble."

"I'll keep an eye on them." He knew that En-hedu would remember Kourosh's name. Between the two of them, they often picked up bits of information. They already knew the names of most of Shulgi's commanders and their assignments. But Jarud's few words about the new man's skill were much more interesting. A popular leader, especially one who knew his trade, would rise quickly in Sumer's military hierarchy. Men who could lead were always in short supply, whether in Akkad or Sumer.

Such a man would be worth watching, and his name would be reported to Akkad by the next messenger. By then Tammuz would know quite a bit more about the man, his origins, his skills, and his strengths and weaknesses. En-hedu had already collected a wealth of information from the commanders wives, most of them eager to talk about what their husband or lover was doing.

During the first few months, Tammuz had wondered about the usefulness of what he and En-hedu were learning. Now he saw the value in the reports that went to Akkad every month or so. In the last year, Sumer's soldiers had regained both their pride and their confidence. Once again they swaggered through the lanes, benefiting from the stern training instituted by King Shulgi and Vanar, his infantry commander. Border patrols to the east, and the desert fighting to the west, had toughened them up. To Tammuz and En-hedu, the sheer size of the forces being recruited could have only one ultimate objective – the city of Akkad.

Still, life in Sumer had grown quite pleasant for them. One year and half of another had passed since their arrival. The city's population had increased greatly in that time, and by now the Kestrel and its owners were accepted as if they had lived there all their lives. Tammuz and En-hedu had gathered and dispatched many reports to Akkad during that time. Perhaps, Tammuz decided, it was time to start doing more than just gathering information.

More than thirty days later, Tammuz glided through Sumer's darkened lanes, as silent as a shadow and attracting as much attention. Most of the city's inhabitants had secured their doors and settled in for a good night's sleep. Only those few returning from the ale houses remained up and about. And Sumer's night watch, of course, prowling about and keeping an eye on things.

The new moon shed almost no light, but Tammuz knew the way through all of the city by now. Since he first heard Kourosh's name mentioned as the latest leader of the night watch, Tammuz had learned much about the increasingly popular commander. Bits of conversation heard in the Kestrel had helped, as members of Sumer's guard offered plenty of praise for their new leader. A stern but fair taskmaster, Kourosh forced recruits and veterans alike to train each day with sword and spear, often from dawn to dusk. Despite the petty grumblings, Tammuz noticed a hint of pride in these men. Kourosh knew his trade and, more important, he knew how to train his men and earn their respect.

Twice in the last ten days Tammuz had slipped out of the Kestrel late at night and walked the lanes. As tonight's work ended, he had watched Kourosh drink with some of his senior men at a tavern he favored, one closer to the barracks. The new commander of the guard had never visited the Kestrel, but over the last month Tammuz had seen Kourosh several times, training his men and escorting them to and from the docks, a route that often took him past the Kestrel.

Now Tammuz stood in the shadows at the end of another long day and half of the night. No more ale would be sold until the morning, and those who had no place to go would sleep in the tavern or find an empty spot in the lane. The taverns had already disgorged the last of their customers and started fastening their doors. The evening's drinking had ended, and both innkeepers and their patrons needed to sleep, if they were to work hard the next day.

Kourosh and five soldiers came out of the tavern fifty paces away, talking loudly, one of the usual effects from too much ale. Two men departed down the lane, but Kourosh – recognizable by his stocky build – and the other two began walking toward Tammuz.

Staying in the shadows, Tammuz slipped away and moved ahead of the three, hurrying toward the king's Compound, where Kourosh had his comfortable quarters. If the two soldiers accompanying their commander returned to the Compound with their leader, then Tammuz would have wasted another night. But if they turned toward the barracks, then Kourosh would complete the last few hundred steps of his journey alone.

At this time of night, the broad lane leading to the compound should be free of soldiers and passersby. Tammuz felt his heart racing, and tried to restrain his nervousness while he anxiously peered down the lane. Kourosh should have been only a hundred paces behind, but perhaps he had lingered to talk to his men. Either that or he had decided to sleep in the barracks tonight . . .

A single shadow loomed up out of the darkness. Tammuz gave one last glance to the lane behind him, saw that it was empty. Taking a deep breath, he shuffled forward, taking short steps and limping a little. Kourosh's long strides closed the gap between them in moments, and the soldier walked straight down the center of the lane.

Tammuz, still hobbling along, moved to his left, as if to yield the center to the approaching soldier. At the same time, he slipped the knife from its sheath and pressed its length down the back of his leg.

"Get out of the way, old man," Kourosh said, his tone pleasant enough despite his words.

"Yes, master." Tammuz shuffled more to his left, then sprang to his right, crashing into the soldier. Before Kourosh could react, the knife had buried itself in his chest, just under the breastbone, Tammuz driving the blade upwards with all his strength into the heart, just as he'd been trained.

Kourosh gasped, more in surprise than pain. His hands seized Tammuz's shoulders, and he tried to push his attacker aside, but by then the knife's blade had already sucked the strength from his arms. In a moment Tammuz tore free of Kourosh's grasp, jerked the knife from his body. Ignoring the spurt of blood that spattered over his arm, Tammuz struck again, this time through the ribs and into the lungs. The second blow wrenched a gasp of pain from Kourosh and sent him sprawling on his back to the ground.

Tammuz glanced up and down the lane, ready to flee if anyone had noticed. But he saw no one. Satisfied, he reached down. His hands shook, and it took three tries before he could cut the soldier's purse free from his belt. Kourosh wore a short sword, and it would be one of quality, so Tammuz slid that from its sheath, shoved it under his left armpit, and began trotting down the lane, back the way the soldier had come.

At the first joining of two lanes, Tammuz turned to his left. A hundred paces further was one of the city's wells. As he drew near, Tammuz emptied the contents of the dead man's purse into his hand, then dumped the coins into his tunic. He scooped some dirt from the lane into the purse and tossed it into the well. With luck, it would sink to the bottom and never be seen again.

By now Tammuz had reached the poorer quarters, and he saw the homeless or drunks sleeping in the lanes. He set the sword down near two unconscious forms who reeked of ale. With luck, they'd awake in the morning, find the sword, and try to sell it in the market.

Moving with caution, Tammuz retraced his steps toward the Kestrel. He stopped twice, to make sure that no one was following him, and doubled back once just to be certain. Then he crossed one more lane and in another few hundred paces reached the inn.

The inn's front door would be closed, but he turned down the side lane until he reached the narrow door that led into their private chamber. The door that was always barred opened silently as Tammuz approached, and he knew En-hedu had watched for him and seen him coming down the lane.

Tammuz slipped inside without making a sound. He moved to the edge of their bed and slumped down, exhausted more from the tension than from the physical activity. He felt himself shivering, and couldn't seem to catch his breath. He'd never killed someone like that, in cold blood.

En-hedu took her time securing the door's many bolts and braces, working silently so as not to awaken any customers. She finished up by moving a sack filled with dirt against the bottom of the entrance. With luck, that portal wouldn't open again for months.

Then she stood before him. "Take off your tunic," she whispered.

He rose and unbuckled his belt. The coins taken from Kourosh's purse spilled onto the sandy floor with scarcely a clink of metal on metal. En-hedu helped pull the tunic over his head. She tossed it aside, stepped away, and returned with a pitcher of water and a piece of cloth. Taking her time, she scrubbed his face, neck, arms and legs, anywhere blood might have spattered.

"It went well, husband?" No need to ask what had happened. His shaking hands told the story plain enough. Nevertheless, her voice couldn't conceal how worried she'd been.

"Yes. He never even cried out."

She continued with her ministrations. In the morning she would bathe him again, to make sure no bloodstains appeared on him. His tunic would be wrapped inside one of her dresses and taken to the river at first light, to be scrubbed clean against the rocks. Any stains that remained would be taken for wine spills, an occupational hazard for any innkeeper.

"Lie down," she whispered, as she guided him down onto the bed.

He started to tell her what happened, but she silenced him with her fingers on his lips. "In the morning, Tammuz. Now it is time for you to rest."

She knelt on the floor beside the bed and began kissing his body. For a moment he tried to protest, then to his surprise his penis stiffened into rigidity, and he felt her long hair brush his stomach as she took him into her mouth. His passion raged, either from her deft touch or the murder of Kourosh, he couldn't tell.

En-hedu kept stimulating him, driving his lust higher and higher, until she felt him throb with desire. She moved on top of him. He couldn't hold back a gasp of pleasure as he entered her softness, but if any of the inn's occupants heard that kind of noise, they would just roll over and return to their sleep.

She moved her body against him, and within moments his seed burst inside her with a force he found difficult to believe. Then he slumped back exhausted. En-hedu took him into her arms and held him tenderly until he fell into a deep and untroubled sleep.

36

Four months later...

The priests of Marduk, after many long nights consultation with the stars, finally declared the end of summer. Most of Sumeria's farmers had finished their harvests, and now offered thanks to the gods. As En-hedu knew, that meant spilling a drop or two of ale on the Kestrel's floor, then gulping down the rest of the cup as fast as possible. Tonight the tavern would be packed with as many grateful farmers as river men.

King Shulgi had ordered the usual three days of feasting, which ended yesterday. Nevertheless, Sumer's inhabitants continued to relax and enjoy another benefit from the gods – the blazing heat of the season had broken as well, and balmy days and cooler nights would soon be in store.

For En-hedu the time of feasting brought plenty of customers, as the wealthy wives indulged themselves. One of the richest women in Sumer now sighed contentedly under En-hedu's ministrations.

"Ahhh, that feels so good."

"Yes, Mistress Bikku." En-hedu leaned forward, her body's weight helping move the muscles in the woman's naked back. A pleasant enough body, En-hedu mused, in better shape than many of her customers. Wives and mistresses of the wealthy tended to possess soft bodies, unused to any physical work. Probably the hardest labor they performed consisted of vigorously satisfying their husbands' needs in the bedchamber. Unlike Tammuz, whose rod tended to stiffen at En-hedu's lightest touch, Sumer's merchants, even some of the younger ones, apparently required long and strenuous efforts to bring them to arousal, especially after a long night of feasting and drinking.

Mistress Bikku had first summoned En-hedu several months ago, after hearing many and glowing recommendations from Ninlil, wife of Puzur-Amurri, En-hedu's first client from Sumer's upper class. Since that first precarious start with Ninlil, En-hedu's list of wealthy clients had grown to over a dozen.

The pampered wives, both old and young, relied more and more on her massage skills to relax and to prepare for their husbands' nightly visits. Her customers paid her as many coins in a few days as the Kestrel earned in seven or eight.

To please her new employers, En-hedu had purchased two new dresses that showed her rising status. No woman of wealth wanted to be visited by someone from the poorer classes, no matter what skills she possessed. So En-hedu dressed like the wife of a prosperous merchant or respected craftsman. A porter carried fresh water to the Kestrel each morning, so that En-hedu could wash her body before donning her finery. She scented the water with crushed flower petals, to create a pleasant scent that lingered in her hair.

To her surprise, Tammuz found both the fine clothes and sweet-smelling water exciting, and often when she returned from working on one of her customers, they would retire to their private chamber to relax and make love.

All of the well-off women En-hedu massaged liked to talk, especially to someone of no consequence. The fact that her ministrations were probably more enjoyable than what many received from their husbands also helped loosen the women's tongues. Most of the wealthy merchants and traders cared more about their own pleasures. They had little time or interest in satisfying their women, who were often relegated to the role of pleasure slave or a symbol of the man's status within the city.

Aside from the usual gossip such women indulged in, sooner or later the conversation turned to the talk of the coming war. En-hedu had picked up many odd facts, one here, one there, that occasionally added up to a significant bit of information, which soon found its way to the Kestrel and from there to the boats going upriver to Akkad and Lady Trella.

Between the loud banter from the soldiers and other patrons of the Kestrel, and the giggling gossip of En-hedu's clients, she knew more about the coming war than most of King Shulgi's soldiers. The most important facts, however, still eluded her – when and how the war would begin. Rumors had predicted the start of the war several times, and all had turned out to be false.

On the bed, Bikku groaned in pleasure once again. "Your touch is making my loins grow moist, En-hedu."

"You flatter me, mistress." En-hedu received many such invitations, but always managed to deflect them. Most of them. At least that's what she told Tammuz when he asked her about such invitations as they whispered at night in their bed. "I'm sure I'm too clumsy for such things."

A chattering of women's voices rose up outside Bikku's very sumptuous bedroom, saving En-hedu from making further excuses.

"Bikku, are you not finished yet?" Ninlil, her face flushed with excitement, entered the room and rushed to the head of the bed. "Your servant says that En-hedu has been here for some time." She managed to spare En-hedu a quick glance.

"Don't shout so." Nevertheless, Bikku turned her head on the pillow to face her visitor. "En-hedu's hands feel so good I never want it to end."

"Who else are you inviting for supper tonight?" Ninlil ignored the last comment. "Everyone wants to come and enjoy your table."

"Ahhh . . . oh, yes, En-hedu, right there." Bikku had no need to answer Ninlil's question. "That's where it feels so tight."

"Yes, mistress. I can see your muscles stretching beneath your beautiful skin. This will help you please your husband tonight."

Bikku was seven or eight seasons older than Ninlil, and first wife to Jamshid, perhaps Sumer's most prosperous merchant, reputed even wealthier than Gemama. Accompanying her husband, Bikku had dined at King Shulgi's table seven or eight times in the last six months. Queen Kushanna favored her company, or so Bikku related to any and everyone. The queen of Sumer's presence and beauty overawed every other woman in the city, and every wife hungered for the chance to dine at Shulgi's large and impressive residence. Such invitations now marked those in favor with the king, or those who needed to offer more gifts and gold as a sign of loyalty.

"Not tonight," Bikku said in response to Ninlil's question. "At least, not until much later in the evening. Only the men are meeting at King Shulgi's palace, no doubt to drink too much wine and talk business long into the night. We wives will be dining alone tonight. A simple meal, but my cook promises no one will go home hungry."

Ninlil laughed, and En-hedu joined in to the extent of a brief smile. She continued her work, kneading the woman's lower back, occasionally adding a drop or two of warm oil. By now, En-hedu could ask the servants to heat the oil before her arrival, so that it would help soothe the delicate skin of their mistress.

Tonight Bikku's table would be covered from end to end with delicious food of all kinds, but the women would only nibble at the cook's grandest efforts. None of these women dared allow themselves to grow fat. They all needed to please their husbands and lovers, at least until they'd delivered a healthy son, preferably two. Which meant, as En-hedu knew from experience, that tonight the household slaves and servants would dine well, albeit on cold food and leftovers, after the guests departed and Bikku finally retired to her bedchamber.

"Are they going to talk about the war? I am so tired of hearing my Puzzi talk about all the gold he's getting for the supplies he delivers."

"Of course they're going to talk about the war, you silly girl. Why else would Queen Kushanna invite them? Do you think she cares to hear their tiresome stories of trading and bartering? My husband says that tonight they go to learn what new demands King Shulgi has in store for them."

"I wish we could be there," Ninlil said wistfully. "Imagine, Kushanna will be –"

"Queen Kushanna," Bikku corrected her younger companion. She reserved to herself the right to call Kushanna by her name. "She rules when King Shulgi is at war or visiting the camps. He returned late last night, and soldiers came and went through the lanes until nearly dawn. We could hear their loud talk from our window."

"Will there really be another war? Puzzi says it may not be good for his trading business."

Puzzi's trade ventures mainly went north on the Tigris. War with Akkad would shut him down, at least temporarily.

"Yes, it will be war. It's about time those barbarians in Akkad learned their place. It's because of their threats that Jamshid is forced to pay so much gold. King Shulgi intends to wipe them from the earth, to avenge the insult to his father."

En-hedu never stopped working, but she kept her ears open. Of course, everyone in Sumer talked about the coming war, but no one knew

346

anything for certain. The soldiers in and around Sumer had not received the call to arms. Training continued, and recruiters still scoured the countryside, but none of the early signs of war she and Tammuz watched for each day had occurred. No demands for extra cattle to be herded north, no movement of grain from the city's well-stocked storage places, no large movement of troops out of the camps. Without these and other preparations, war remained only a threat, not something real.

Yesterday, the messenger from Akkad had departed Sumer with little more information than what he'd carried the month before. Still, in the next day or two, En-hedu knew she would learn all about King Shulgi's dinner. Whatever Shulgi and his half-sister said or did was soon whispered throughout the city.

The conversation between Ninlil and Bikku turned to a new delivery of fine cloth from the east. Nothing more was said about the war, and soon En-hedu finished her massage, thanked Bikku profusely for the privilege of serving her, gathered up her things, and departed, stopping only to collect her fee of two copper coins from the household steward. At least En-hedu had finished the morning massage early enough so that she could look forward to breaking the midday fast with Tammuz. She strolled contentedly through Sumer's crowded lanes, glancing at all the goods displayed in the stalls and on the tables, and enjoying the warmth of the sun.

At the Kestrel, she found Tammuz standing in the doorway, watching the lane. Though he leaned against the door casually enough, she quickened her pace. He seldom waited for her return. Something was wrong. When her husband saw her coming, he disappeared into the inn.

When she stepped inside, her eyes blinking in the dim light, she saw only two skins of ale or wine on the counter. There should have been eight or nine. En-hedu greeted Rimaud, but went directly to their private quarters.

"What's happened?"

"The docks have been closed since mid-morning," Tammuz said. He didn't bother to lower his voice. "Soldiers dragged all the boats onto the shore and posted a guard over everything. No boats of any kind are allowed on the river. Nothing has come down the Tigris since yesterday. I asked the sellers in the marketplace about our goods, but they said all ale and wine, all food, in fact, is being taken to the king's warehouses. All the women were ordered to bake extra bread. Almost everything coming into the city now must go straight to the soldiers. Rimaud and I protested to the guards. They knew who we were, and slipped each one of us a skin, just to keep us quiet. But they warned us, there won't be any more for some time."

"How long will this go on?" En-hedu was beginning to worry. "They can't keep the docks closed forever."

"I asked the guards, but they really didn't know. They thought only a few days, but they know less than we do."

"Tonight there is a meeting at King Shulgi's house. All the leading merchants and traders are required to attend, and without their wives. I thought . . ."

En-hedu realized tonight's meeting would not be to discuss the coming conflict. It would announce to the city's leaders that the war had already started. No doubt King Shulgi would be telling them more about their future contributions to that effort.

"Then it's war, for certain," Tammuz said, completing her unspoken words. "We have to get word to Akkad somehow. There must be some caravans going north."

An innocuous message delivered to an elderly widow in Akkad would warn Lady Trella that war was imminent. If the message ever arrived. En-hedu knew it would be risky and unreliable to give such a message to a stranger, but until the regular messenger from Akkad arrived in the next few days, they had no other way to get news to Lady Trella. And that assumed his boat actually reached Sumer.

"I'll visit the caravan camp outside the city," En-hedu said. "Perhaps we'll find one leaving soon."

But she returned by late in the afternoon with only more evil tidings.

"The city is sealed. No one can leave, not even the local farmers who spent the night. All the caravans are guarded. Soldiers are riding and patrolling every road and trail, stopping anyone who tries to leave. They say it's to protect them from raids by the Tanukhs and Salibs. They say a large force of barbarian horsemen is on the loose, raiding north of Sumer."

Tammuz shook his head. "Most of the Salibs are dead or driven into the desert. The Tanukhs have been quiet for years, especially since King Shulgi broke the last resistance of the Salibs. Why would the Tanukhs raid here, close to Shulgi's army. Why would . . . ?"

His voice trailed off, and En-hedu knew his thoughts. If it were the Tanukhs, then Sumer's cavalry would be mustering to chase them down, not sit idly by in their camps outside the city, or patrolling the roads.

"The war has begun," she said. "Whatever is going on between Sumer and Akkad is already happening."

"But what can it be? Most of the army is here in Sumer, or camped nearby. Even Razrek's cavalry."

"Maybe the first attack on Akkad will come from Larsa, or one of the other cities."

Not that En-hedu believed it. The other cities were reluctant allies, and not likely to be willing to strike the first blow against Akkad. They would join the fighting, but only after Sumer initiated it, and when victory seemed likely.

"It's a good thing the messenger got out yesterday," Tammuz said. "Otherwise he'd be trapped here like the rest of us."

This time En-hedu shook her head. "No, husband. It's bad that by chance he avoided the patrols. He will carry the news that open war has still not come to Sumer. At least if he were trapped here, those in Akkad might wonder why he didn't return. I wish we had more ways of getting a message north."

Tammuz and En-hedu knew they had become Akkad's most important spies in Sumer, so important that only a few in either city knew of their presence.

"There must be some way to get word out," Tammuz said. "There has to be something we can do. I can't believe we failed to –"

"By the time we get word to Akkad, they will know the worst. The war will already be on them. Now we can only hope that Shulgi's first blow isn't fatal."

He clasped her hand and held it tight. "Don't worry. Akkad is strong."

"Yes, I know."

But in her heart, En-hedu worried. After more than two years of living in Sumer, she realized just how vast an army the city could raise. And an army that size might not be denied.

From his balcony, Shulgi gazed out over the Compound. Beneath him, his commanders moved about, coming and going, or gathering in small groups. The orders to start the war had already been issued. Now the men, animals and supplies needed to conquer Akkad would be brought together, to begin the long journey north.

Even from the balcony, Shulgi couldn't see much of Sumer, but the hum of excitement from its inhabitants carried over the walls. By now even the dullest would have figured out that Sumer was going to war. The long awaited day had finally arrived, and Shulgi would depart the city at dawn to join his army, already on the move north.

"Any last thoughts, my brother?"

Kushanna moved to his side, her bare feet soundless on the wood floor. He put his arm around her shoulders.

"No, everything is well begun. The messengers departed two days ago to the other cities, ordering their armies to join me at Kanesh. By tomorrow, that outpost will have fallen. After that, the border lands will be swept clean and the crops destroyed. Then we'll begin moving north."

Shulgi intended not just to invade the Akkadian lands, but to build and fortify a half dozen posts along the way, occupying the countryside in stages. Eskkar would have to come out and fight and, when he did, he'd be attacking the entire Sumerian army, over twenty thousand strong.

"You will take care of yourself, my brother. Trella may send her assassins against you."

"I'll take precautions. But surrounded by my army, I'll be safe from the witch queen." He kissed the top of her head. "You just make sure the supplies flow steadily north. It will be thirty or forty days before we stand outside Akkad's walls. And then who knows how long it will take to starve them into submission."

"Eskkar will challenge you before you reach Akkad's walls."

"Then the north will be conquered even sooner. If he fights, he loses. If he remains behind his walls, then he starves."

"Be wary of his tricks."

"In the last two years, Razrek and I have thought of everything Eskkar can do. We'll be ready."

"Then I'll await your return, my brother. Your victorious return."

"Just keep my city under control, my sister. And keep the supplies flowing. Everything depends on that now."

Book III - Battle for Empire

37

Daro sat cross-legged near the bow of the boat, watching the land flow by. As he gazed at the green ribbon of trees and bushes lining the banks of the Tigris, a flock of small birds burst into flight, startled by an approaching hawk that wheeled back up into the sky once its prey took flight, too wise to chase after them. The birds darted across the water, to resume their hunt for food on the opposite shore, their latest brush with danger already forgotten. The river's flowing water soothed every spirit, man or beast.

The sun descended closer to the horizon, and before long darkness would spread across the river. By then the vessel would be tied up alongside the jetty at Kanesh, and the grinning crew would be well into their first cups of ale inside the walled village. Once again Daro swore at the bad luck that had kept him riding ships up and down the rivers for the last two years.

It had all started even earlier than that, when Yavtar sailed to Sumer and needed an armed guard to protect both himself and his precious cargo of lapis lazuli. A few days earlier, Daro had made the mistake of telling his commander that he knew something about boats. As a boy, he'd worked a few seasons helping his father row up and down the Tigris. When Yavtar requested an escort who knew something about the river, Daro happened to be in Akkad, and found himself volunteered for the duty.

That trip had gone well, and Daro thought that would be the last time he sailed up and down the great river. Instead, once safe and secure back in Akkad, Yavtar had requested Daro be put in charge of another cargo.

After a few more such voyages, Daro grew bored with the task. Riding the water gave him little time to practice his archery, so he asked for a return to duty with his fellow bowmen.

The next day Alexar, recently promoted to commander of Akkad's archers, summoned Daro to his quarters. When he arrived, to his surprise Daro found Yavtar there as well. Daro knew the boatmaster and Alexar remained good friends. Both had fought together against Korthac's forces.

"Yavtar heard you want to leave the river," Alexar began. "He wants you to stay."

Before Daro could protest, Alexar held up his hand. "It's already been decided. Much as I could use your help, Yavtar needs to build a force of archers to defend the trading ships and their cargoes. He also has some wild idea about building fighting ships – ships that can carry archers and provide a platform for them to fight from. In a few years, there may be a hundred bowmen guarding and fighting from Yavtar's new fleet of boats. You've more river experience than any of my archers. And if you do well, you might end up commanding all these men. You could soon find yourself a leader of one hundred."

Fighting boats? River archers? Before Daro had time to ask a question or utter a protest, Yavtar spoke. "Well then, that's settled." The river-master placed his arm around Daro's shoulder. "Come with me, lad. I've got a lot to tell you."

Later Daro learned that Yavtar had asked Eskkar for Daro's services. After Eskkar's approval, no further discussion seemed necessary, at least to Yavtar. The shipmaster obviously had no qualms about using his position in Eskkar's inner circle of advisors to obtain what he wanted.

Even then, Akkad's boatmaster didn't tell Daro everything, but Yavtar revealed enough to make Daro's eyes widen at the prospect of war with Sumeria.

Two years had passed since then, the war approached, and by now Daro had made countless trips up and down the rivers. Months ago he'd earned the title of commander of one hundred, and his force of river archers continued to grow. With the threat of war looming ever closer, Daro decided to make every third trip down to Kanesh, to inspect those of his men stationed there.

The trading outpost would be the first target for Sumer's army, and Eskkar had stationed a strong garrison there. As the tension between Akkad and Sumer increased, Daro wanted to ensure that his archers had prepared themselves and their boats. That inspection would take most of tomorrow, but tonight he would sip some ale with his men, relax in their company, and try not to think about what the future might bring.

Once again he let his gaze sweep over the riverbank and the farmland stretching beyond. Despite the peaceful setting, something felt out of place. Still, Daro saw nothing unusual.

"A fine evening, commander."

Daro turned to see Scria, the ship's master, standing beside him. Scria's face reminded Daro of a rat, thin and pointed, with yellow teeth that protruded from his lips. The lank, greasy hair added to the resemblance. But despite his appearance, the man knew the river and could sail his boat well enough. Yavtar apparently thought as much.

"Yes. I'll be glad when we dock."

"An empty river makes for a fast voyage," Scria said, looking out over the prow and scratching his chest.

When Daro didn't reply, Scria turned away and began weaving his way back to the stern.

"Wait! Come back!"

Now Scria's rat face held a frown. He didn't like to be ordered about by some soldier, even a commander.

"You said the river was empty." Daro rose to his feet, bracing himself against the boat's motion and stretching upwards to see downriver. "How long has it been . . . we haven't passed a boat coming upstream."

Since they started out early this morning, they'd waved greetings to at least a dozen ships headed north. But as the morning turned into afternoon, the sightings of ships bound for Akkad and other cities upriver had ceased.

"Mmm . . . has been a long time. This late in the day, we should have seen a few, unless they decided to stop in Kanesh." Scria scratched his chest again, this time in a different place. "Maybe they pulled ashore to rest."

A stupid answer, Daro knew. No boat captain worth his salt would sit idly on the riverbank while the sun remained in the sky. Especially with a way station not that far upstream. There should be boats. Something was wrong. He glanced at the river, then up into the sky. He saw no birds, heard no sounds other than their own soft passage through the water.

"You men! On your feet. String your bows."

Daro had brought only two archers with him, more than enough to drive off any casual bandits or pirates. Suddenly, he wished he'd brought a dozen, though that many would have overloaded Scria's boat. As his men scrambled to their feet, Daro turned to the boat captain.

"Get the boat in the middle of the river, away from the bank."

The man at the steering oar followed the current, and at this point in the river, that brought them closer to the left bank, scarcely fifty paces away. "Why . . . what's the problem?"

Daro gripped Scria's shoulder and squeezed. "Just do it. Now!" He pushed the man away and reached down to grasp his own bow. With the ease of years of practice, he strung the weapon, then slung the quiver over his shoulder, letting it hang down to his waist on his left side.

The boat had already turned into a curve of the river. Scria's shouts to his steersman brought the bow around, and the vessel moved sluggishly toward midstream, struggling against the current. Daro rested his foot on the prow, to get a better look.

A flight of arrows burst from the brush along the river's left bank. They hummed through the air, striking the boat, the crew, and the water on either side. One shaft grazed Daro's arm, and two struck the boat on the left side.

"Get down!" Daro shouted the order, but those who survived the first flight were already ducking as low as possible. An archer lay sprawled beside the mast, and one of Scria's three crewmen had taken two shafts and fallen overboard.

The boatmaster – his voice rising to a hysterical shout – had an arrow protruding from his arm, as he crawled along the bottom of the vessel. Daro loosed a shaft at the shore, now filled with men emerging from the bushes and splashing into the shallow water, some still launching shafts. Fortunately, the crewman steering the boat had survived, and he kept the vessel moving toward the center of the river.

A quick glance at their numbers told Daro all he needed to know. At least twenty archers had attacked them, maybe more. He dropped his bow and picked up an oar. "Everyone row!" A few arrows launched toward the riverbank weren't going to accomplish anything.

Moving to the right side of the vessel, he took shelter behind some sacks of grain and began pulling as hard as he could, thrusting the paddle deep into the river and dragging it through the water. His surviving bowman, Iseo, did the same, crouching down as low as he could and working the dead crewman's oar. The boat moved farther from the left bank, slowly passed through the center of the river, and glided closer to the opposite shore. Arrows continued to fall on the ship and splash into the water, but by now Scria's boat had moved well past the point of the attack.

"We should get to the opposite shore!" Scria's right hand clutched his bloody left arm. His voice had lost none of its panic.

Daro lifted his head and let his eyes scan the right bank. He saw a party of horsemen – at least twenty – following the course of the river and matching the pace of the boat. Many of them had bows in their hands. They rode easily, as if they didn't care if the boat slipped away from them. A third party of perhaps a dozen riders trotted into view on the left bank, going down river as well. The boat was trapped between the two forces.

"Turn the boat around," Daro shouted. He pointed to the horsemen on the right bank. "We have to go back up river."

Scria's eyes widened. "We can't go back!" he screamed. "We're too heavy to pull upstream!"

The boat captain had started with three crewmen. One had died, another lay on his back, an arrow in his shoulder. Only luck had saved the most important crewman, the one steering the boat. If he'd taken an arrow, the ship might have swung broadside and swamped. But Daro knew they couldn't continue south, and both sides of the river appeared to be crawling with who knew how many mounted men.

"Keep the boat in the center of the river! Scria, start dumping the cargo. Iseo, help him. Get the body over the side, too. Hurry!"

Scria, crouched on his knees, remained motionless. "We can't dump the cargo. It's worth at least thirty –"

"It's worth nothing to you if you're dead! Iseo! If he doesn't start helping, throw him overboard."

Daro reached down and lifted the first sack, lifted it onto the gunwale, then pushed it over the side. Soon the boat was rocking back and forth, threatening to capsize at any moment, as the three of them tossed sacks, bales, and clay pitchers overboard.

He paused to look at the shore. The horsemen still kept pace with the boat's progress. The enemy didn't bother wasting arrows. They seemed satisfied as long as the boat went south. That meant more enemy would be waiting ahead, and likely with some way to force the boat to shore, perhaps a vessel of their own filled with armed men.

Daro scrambled back to the rear of the boat. The steersman, his face white with fear, clenched the steering oar with a grip that made the bones in his hand stand out.

"I'll take the oar!" Daro snapped. "You help Scria dump the cargo. Make sure we don't dump what we need for ballast." An empty boat would capsize at the least movement.

In a few more moments, the craft rode higher in the water, with almost all of the cargo over the side.

"Iseo, we're turning upstream. Start rowing, all of you. Steersman, as soon as we come about, get that sail up. Then stay low, and row for all you're worth."

He pushed hard on the steering oar, turning the boat first toward the right bank, then swinging it back across the center of the river and turning it upstream. As soon as he got the boat headed north, the men on shore took notice. Once again arrows flew through the air, splashing into the water, thudding into the sides of the boat, and a few striking inside the vessel.

The frightened steersman raised the sail faster than he'd ever done in his life. The soft breeze didn't help much, but it enabled the boat to keep headway against the river's current. As soon as Daro had the boat centered in the river and moving north, he ordered Scria to take the steering oar. With his wounded arm, the boatmaster would be of more use guiding his boat than trying to row.

Daro scooped up Scria's oar and began stroking. His powerful arms, strengthened from years of archery, helped push the boat up the river. Soon they retraced their way and reached the point of the first attack. As he watched, a dozen horsemen moved into sight, and guided their horses down the slope toward the river's edge. All of them carried bows.

Daro swore, dropped his oar and collected his bow. The enemy would ride into the stream as far as they could, which would bring them into killing range. They'd rake the little boat, and riddle everyone with arrows. "Iseo! Keep rowing!"

But the horsemen weren't close enough for that yet. Daro stood, aimed, and launched his first arrow. He'd aimed for the nearest rider, but the shaft struck the lead horse in the shoulder. The animal went mad with pain, rearing up and twisting its head to tear at the arrow with its teeth. The rider slipped from the animal's back and went into the water with a mighty splash. The wounded animal kicked out with its hind legs, and the next horse panicked as well.

Aim for the horses, you fool. Remember Eskkar's advice. Daro shot arrow after arrow, as fast as he could nock them to the string. The slippery slope leading to the water didn't provide the riders much room, forcing the horsemen to bunch together. With the animals all taking fright, either from their own wounds or hearing the cries of the other horses, they dug in their hooves and refused to enter the water.

A few of the enemy gave up the effort and dismounted, trying to find their footing in the slippery mud and continue shooting arrows at the boat, but by then the craft had swung by the curve and moved out toward the deeper center channel. The moment the curve blocked the enemy from sight, Daro dropped the bow and picked up his oar. "Stay in the center! And row, damn you, row!"

He kept Iseo and the steersman rowing until well after dark, matching them stroke for stroke, an agonizing effort that sapped every bit of strength he possessed. By then everyone was exhausted, but the evening breeze had strengthened, and allowed the craft to keep moving slowly upstream, despite the tiring rowers. Daro let each man take a turn resting, always keeping two men pulling the oars. At least they could quench their thirst easily enough, scooping water from the river with their burning hands to refresh themselves.

The moon sent a pale glimmer of light down the water, providing just enough light for the steersman to keep the boat in the center of the river. They dragged the oars through the water in silence, everyone struggling against the pain, until even Daro thought his heart might burst. As midnight approached, the boat slid around yet another curve in the river.

"Daro! The way station's up ahead!" Scria's shout echoed his relief.

"Keep your voice down, you fool."

Daro lifted his eyes and saw the single rickety jetty protruding from the east bank. It looked peaceful enough, with one boat tied up at the little dock and another drawn up on the shore. No fires burned, but any crews pausing here on their way south would be asleep by now. He made up his mind. Daro knew he'd never get to Akkad with just the men onboard the boat. If the breeze died, which likely would happen at any moment, certainly well before dawn, they didn't have the strength to keep the craft moving northward.

He looked down and saw the gleam of his sword at his feet, then took a deep breath. "Akkad! Akkad!"

The shout floated out over the water and brought a challenge from the soldier on night watch, a shadowy figure who sprang to his feet, surprised to hear a boat approaching at this time of night.

"There's a boat on the river! Everyone get up! Get up!" At the sentry's loud command, other shapes appeared. Men sat up, fumbling for their weapons and trying to shake the sleep from their eyes. Another voice called out. "Who's there?"

"Daro, leader of one hundred from Akkad." He let himself relax. The guard's voice held the accent of someone who'd lived in Akkad all his life. "Bring us in to shore, Scria."

When the boat ground against the sandy bank, Daro had to concentrate to keep his footing. He felt lightheaded and weak as a newborn lamb. Hands reached out from the darkness and dragged the boat up the sandy bank and out of the river's grasp.

"Commander, what are you doing going upriver at night?"

"Enemy horsemen between here and Kanesh. The outpost may have been taken." By the time Daro finished explaining, everyone was on their feet, the soldiers belting weapons around their waists and the rivermen getting their belongings back into their boats.

"I'll take all the soldiers with me in Scria's boat. Six men on each side, we should be able to make good time going upriver."

"There won't be anyone to guard the ships," a boatmaster Daro didn't recognize protested from the darkness.

"Doesn't matter. The enemy will be here by morning, maybe sooner. Sink one of the ships, dump the cargo of the other, and double up your crews. Take the one ship and row for all your worth back to Akkad."

Daro climbed back into the boat, shouting his words over his shoulder. He settled in at the steersman's station. With twelve men pulling oars, he'd be back in Akkad by noon, if the wind stayed favorable. He didn't care what happened to the traders. As soon as the last of his men settled in, Daro gave the order. "Push off and start pulling on those oars. I want to be halfway to Akkad by dawn."

38

Adarnar outpost on the Sippar river, at sunset . . .

Enkidu made his rounds of the outpost three times each day – just after dawn, at midday, and when the sun touched the western horizon. He took his time, talking to the guards, making sure none had gotten drunk, forgot their weapons or failed to take their posts. After four months under his command, such occurrences seldom happened. The nearly thirty soldiers and equal number of craftsmen and their families knew Enkidu and his ways by now.

Like every fort on the edge of Akkad's lands, the group of soldiers assigned to the Adarnar outpost contained the usual number of fools and dullards, slackers and the sharp witted. These provided a daily trial to the more professional soldiers. Enkidu had worked hard training all of them with equal parts firm discipline and helpful encouragement, and while some of his men might not be good enough to strut up and down on top of Akkad's walls, they had all become proficient enough for patrolling the border. They now took as much pride in their duties as their commander, and he in turn felt satisfied with every man under his authority.

As always, pride in their skills proved helpful, as Adarnar possessed few amenities either for its men or its horses. Compared to Kanesh, which lay a good two days' march to the west, Adarnar was scarcely large enough to hold the barracks and corrals for the twenty-two horses. The small fortified settlement sat on the northern edge of the Sippar river, its single dock running along the water's edge just wide enough to berth three ships.

The boats that sailed along the Sippar, as well as the occasional caravan following its banks, were Adarnar's main reason for existence. All trade and commerce throughout the land had to be protected from bandits, if Akkad were to continue to grow stronger. Since taking command of the post, Enkidu had not lost a single sack of trade goods, which was more than most of the other outposts could say.

The wealthy merchants in Akkad often acted as though only the trade on the Tigris and Euphrates mattered, but plenty of goods flowed along the Sippar and the other streams that branched off or merged into the two giant rivers. With the threat of war making everyone uneasy, most boats carried their cargoes only as far as the market at Kanesh, but that settlement enabled the local farmers and herders to obtain all the goods anyone could buy in Akkad or Sumer for that matter, and usually at cheaper cost. For humble farmers struggling to survive, places like Kanesh and even Adarnar provided both security and a convenient place to exchange goods. As soon as King Eskkar established the protective string of forts along the Sippar, the adjacent land with its bountiful farms had flourished.

Not that Enkidu cared about trade. Four years ago he'd fought at Drakis's side in the desperate battle against Korthac. Both of them had nearly died that night. In fact, most of the men they led in the bloody fight for the city's gates had succumbed to death or taken serious wounds. Enkidu not only survived, but earned his entry into the Hawk Clan. He soon progressed to a leader of twenty, then fifty, and four months ago Alexar and Drakis had given Enkidu command of the post at Adarnar.

Already into his twenty-sixth season, Enkidu knew he would command even more soldiers in the coming war. In two more months he'd return to Akkad with half of his best-trained men, leaving behind a well-run garrison for the next commander and the latest batch of raw recruits, who would start the process all over again.

Enkidu inspected the last guard on the northern wall, found nothing to require his attention, and headed back toward his quarters. He enjoyed the private room that – as commander of the post – he shared only with one local farmer's daughter, who was quite pleased to have caught his eye and grateful for the chance to escape life on the farm. Enkidu's wife and two sons remained in Akkad with her family, waiting for his return. He still hadn't decided if he would bring his concubine with him when he returned to the city. The girl pleasured him well each evening, but

Enkidu's wife had a sharp temper, and he didn't know how she would react to a second wife. He shook such thoughts from his mind and thought instead about the evening's pleasure.

"Commander! South Post! Hurry!"

The voice held urgency mixed with fear, and Enkidu's pleasant thoughts of the future vanished. He burst into a run across the outpost, reached the wobbly wooden steps, and climbed them two at a time.

The guard had his hand extended toward the river, and one glance told Enkidu all he needed to know. "Get everyone in the fort. Close the gates!" He bellowed the last words, but already the other guards were raising their own alarms. "Everyone to their posts! Prepare for an attack."

He'd given that order many times before, but only to train his men, never in a real attack. Enkidu turned back to stare across the river. One hundred, two hundred, perhaps more riders had emerged from the low hills and scattered trees that hugged the far side of the river. The lead elements already splashed their way into the Sippar, churning the calm waters to froth beneath their hooves. The river here was wide but shallow, and they'd be across in moments. With a chill, he realized he could do nothing to stop them.

"Get men on horseback. Ride for Akkad. Tell them . . . we're under attack!"

He'd almost said what he already knew, that they were all already dead. The marauders, now that he could see them better, looked like Tanukhs, but those desert-dwellers hadn't raided this far east in many years, not since Eskkar took command at Akkad. Enkidu's second in command, a veteran named Sargat, arrived, took one look across the river, and swore.

"We'll never be able to hold them off. Ready the horses," Enkidu said. "I'll try to slow them down. We'll have to break out of here."

That meant abandoning the villagers living in the fort, but he couldn't help that. Enkidu shouted another order, and the handful of men on the palisade began shooting arrows at the advancing horde, in a futile effort to slow them down.

Enkidu dashed down the steps toward the rear of the fort. "Get everyone into the boats. Pull for Kanesh." That place might have already fallen, but this could be an isolated raid, and if the boats escaped, they might find safety at the larger fort or ashore somewhere in between. At the corral he saw men moving about, throwing halters on the skittish animals.

They'd reacted to the unfamiliar scent of fear in the men handling them. A leader of ten reached the corral at the same moment. Enkidu grabbed him by the shoulder and shouted in his ear.

"Take five men and try to get through before they encircle us. Fight your way past them if you can and warn Akkad."

The man nodded, and began shouting his own orders. Frightened villagers pushed past him and through the open rear gate, heading for the jetty. The two boats rocked wildly as panicky men, women and children tried to pile into them. One ship pushed off, already heavily loaded. A few villagers jumped into the river, to try to swim to safety downstream. They knew that drowning would be a better fate than to be taken by the Tanukhs. Anyone captured on shore would die within moments, if a worse fate didn't befall them.

Five horses burst out of the gate, heading north. For a brief moment, Enkidu felt tempted to take a horse and go after them. But he couldn't leave his men. With an oath, he turned his back on the coral and snatched a bow that one of the departing riders had abandoned.

"Fall in with me! Form a line! We've got to hold them off for a few moments!"

Enkidu bellowed the words to make himself heard. The undulating Tanukh war cries floated over the confusion in the fort. Then the drumming of hooves on hard ground told him the enemy was only moments away.

Six men moved to his side, bows in hand. Another handful of soldiers struggled to catch their horses. "Go! Ride for Akkad!"

They burst out through the gate, kicking their horses to a gallop. Enkidu saw the fear mixed with relief on their faces. Then the din of screaming Tanukhs drowned out everything. The enemy horsemen had reached the main gate. The first one swung over the top of the now undefended palisade. Enkidu put an arrow right through his chest. But a dozen more pulled themselves up and over. The archers beside him loosed their shafts, but it only slowed the wave of attackers for a moment.

"Get to the horses! Ride for Akkad!"

The rest of his men dropped their bows and dashed for the remaining horses. Enkidu followed them, moving backward, and still shooting arrows as fast as he could. A handful of the attackers flung open the main gate, while dozens more continued to scale the fence and drop from the parapets into the fort, screaming their war cries and waving swords.

Another group of soldiers galloped out, but the din of exultant war cries and approaching hooves told Enkidu that the Tanukhs had already reached the rear of the fort. Women screamed in fear, pushing their way toward the water. Enkidu reached the rear gate, still shooting shafts as fast as he could nock them to the bowstring. Already he'd emptied one quiver. He snatched up another from the ground.

The Tanukhs, shouting in triumph, rushed toward him. "Mount up!" Enkidu shouted. He continued launching arrows, dropping a man with every shot, the powerful long bow of Akkad deadly at such close range. Bodies, arrows protruding, lay scattered over the inside of the fort, mixing in death with those villagers too slow to get to the boats.

Enkidu glanced over his shoulder. Sargat swung up onto his horse, and held the halter of the last horse for Enkidu. An arrow already nocked on his string, Enkidu drew back his arm, loosed the shaft, and turned to run. Instead a burning pain shot through his chest, and he saw the point of an arrow protruding from his side. He took two steps, stumbled and fell to the ground. Each breath felt like fire, too hot to take into his body, and the strength drained from his legs. He lifted his eyes. He knew he wouldn't be able to mount a horse. He met Sargat's eyes.

"Go! Get to Akkad." He managed to get the words out.

Sargat shook his head in frustration, dropped the halter, and put his heels to his horse, drawing his sword as he galloped out of the fort. Enkidu heard the clash of bronze as Sargat and the last of the Akkadians charged into the Tanukhs attempting to force their way toward the rear gate. Enkidu tried to get to his feet, his hand fumbling for his sword. Something knocked him over, and he fell against the side of the gate. Somehow he managed to drag the suddenly heavy sword from its scabbard.

A Tanukh, his teeth bared, appeared before him. The man raised his sword with a grin and swung down. Enkidu saw the blow descending and managed to raise his weapon. But the Tanukh's powerful stroke brushed aside his feeble resistance, and he felt the blade bite deep into his neck. A rush of pain exploded through his body, blinding him for a moment before the blackness fell over him. The pain vanished, and he had time for only one thought before death took him. At least he'd died a warrior's death, with a weapon in his hand and facing his enemies. There would be no evil voices calling him a coward to haunt his way through the underworld.

39

Esskkar stood at the entrance to the Map Room, watching Trella and Ismenne make yet more of the never-ending adjustments to the pictorial that depicted all the major landmarks and marking stones between Akkad and Sumer. In the two years since Trella had unveiled it, the map had changed again and again, rebuilt and redrawn countless times to include ever more detail, and to take into consideration the steady stream of new information that, month by month, flowed to the map maker's hand.

Trella's walkers had paced off the distances between nearly every village and city from north of Bisitun to as far south as Sumer. Discreet landmarks, recognizable only to those who knew what to look for, marked the most direct paths a man might travel. Marking stones indicated the length of the journey between various points. Both horsemen and walkers had trod many of the same routes, recorded their travels, and confirmed their findings. Piece by piece, Ismenne's deft fingers added each new bit of information to the map.

After so many years of effort, the layout held a prodigious quantity of information. Since neither Esskkar nor his commanders knew for certain what might end up being useful, they tended to add everything they could. Esskkar's doubts about the Map Room's benefits had vanished long ago. It had already demonstrated its worth, and as long as it remained a secret known only to a few, it would prove even more useful in the coming war.

With so many details to represent, Trella and Ismenne had created new symbols to explain the map. Esskkar and his commanders had memorized these new symbols out of necessity, but Ismenne still received an occasional question over how to comprehend some of the less familiar markings.

Today Ismenne took the lead in the latest adjustments, and Trella, standing at her side, deferred to her decisions. While his wife could complete almost any task she undertook, Eskkar knew Ismenne understood the map better than anyone in Akkad, and could interpret its patterns of lines and images without effort. When one of the commanders had a question, Ismenne could convert the scale on the map at a glance, and she seldom made even minor mistakes.

Eskkar remembered that, not many years ago, he had needed Trella to explain to him the meaning of the word *scale*. Now he could grasp the distances, landmarks, rivers, and paths with ease. It helped that he had ridden to and from many of these places on his training visits, and had verified much of the information with his own eyes. With his experience and that of his commanders, routes could be planned, difficulties accounted for, and the necessary supplies and equipment calculated. No one man – no leader of any group of fighting men – could keep so much information in his head. The map, however, held it all.

The map maker, as everyone called Ismenne, worked as hard as any soldier sweating in the training camps. Not that many in the city knew either of her existence or her skills. The Map Room's master craftswoman seldom left the Compound. When she did, Hawk Clan soldiers provided an unobtrusive protective guard. Not only did Ismenne know more about the Map Room than anyone, but she had heard every plan, every strategy, every resource that would be used in the eventual conflict with Sumer.

Every fifth day, Eskkar and any of his commanders whose duties kept them in Akkad met in the Map Room to review the latest information from Trella and Annok-sur's agents in the south, and to work on the various plans they would set into motion when the war began. This morning's meeting had included some new information from the city of Isin. King Naxos of Isin had strengthened his walls yet again, and increased the number of men under arms in the nearby camp. This report required a slight reworking of the map at Isin. Eskkar and the commanders had discussed the new possibilities until midday, when his leaders took a break from the morning's work to return to their homes for the midday meal.

Eskkar had stayed behind, waiting for Trella to finish her discussion with Ismenne. He and Trella would dine together in the workroom. The midday meal often provided the day's only opportunity for them to relax in each other's company. He could have taken his place at the table and started without her, but it pleased him to watch his wife work.

She had come to him as a slave more than four years ago. From that humble beginning, Trella had worked day and night, often at his side, until the city's inhabitants had raised their voices and demanded that Eskkar take power in Akkad. Now Trella helped rule the city which she helped create. Thanks to her guidance, the people prospered. No one starved to death, while others had too much food on their tables. The King's Judge made sure that the laws of Akkad applied to all, rich and poor.

Eskkar and his wife set the example for the more wealthy of the city dwellers. No one wanted to flaunt their riches while the king lived in more humble surroundings, with no public display of his power. As a result, the prosperous merchants and craftsmen held the respect of those beneath them. Everyone knew the king and queen of Akkad ruled for *all* their subjects, not just those who possessed wealth.

Since the barbarian invasion, Eskkar and his soldiers had worked hard to keep at bay all of Akkad's enemies. Nevertheless, many gave as much credit to Trella's plans and guidance. Between husband and wife, Akkad's inhabitants slept peacefully at night. The approaching war would change all that. From all the stories and tales trickling into Akkad, Eskkar expected the outbreak of hostilities soon. The coming conflict made these peaceful moments even more precious.

At last Trella straightened up, and Eskkar knew that the latest difficulty had been resolved. She looked at him, surprised to find him standing in the doorway. Trella was, he decided, even more beautiful than that night when he saw her for the first time. Then she'd been a young girl, but one already past the usual age for marriage. Now she was a woman grown.

Eskkar had taken her to his bed that night, and even that first time he knew she possessed something special, that she was unlike any woman he had ever known. For her part, Trella had worked her magic on him. Facing threats from within and without, they learned to help each other. Soon their lives were bound together, first as master and slave, then as partners working to save the city, next as husband and wife, and finally king and queen of Akkad. They had saved each other's lives, they had fought together, and now they ruled together. Trella was, as the barbarians said, a gifted woman.

Eskkar knew that some men grew tired of their women, or needed second and third wives. While he had taken other women from time to time, he remained under Trella's spell, if that were what it was, as much today as when they'd first joined.

Even now, he felt the stirrings of desire pass through him, as he watched the firm muscles move beneath her simple dress. Shaking himself from his thoughts, Eskkar entered the Map Room, strode down the length of the table, and placed his arm around Trella's shoulder. "I think it's time for you and Ismenne to take some food and rest." He leaned down and kissed the top of Trella's head.

"Yes, Lord Eskkar," Ismenne said. "As soon as I finish making these changes."

"Eat first." He couldn't help smiling at the girl. "Or you'll be too tired to get through the day."

Not that he believed it, of course. The young girl had plenty of energy and strength. Still, some fresh air and a bite to eat wouldn't hurt. Perhaps some day Trella would bear him a daughter who might grow up as beautiful and wise as Ismenne. Despite her youth, Corio's daughter and her efforts might yet help win the war with Sumer.

They left the Map Room. Ismenne closed the door behind them, then disappeared down the stairs to tell the servants to bring food to Eskkar and Trella. Before they could sit down, shouting erupted from the courtyard below. Hoof beats drummed on the earth, a horse neighed, and Eskkar's own mount, always close at hand, answered it. A guard called out the challenge.

"Another problem," Eskkar muttered, "and always as we sit down to eat."

Eskkar moved to the stairs and started to descend. But before he descended halfway to the common room, two men burst through the main entrance and headed for the stairs. The first man looked up and saw the king standing there. Eskkar recognized the leader of twenty who guarded Akkad's main gate.

"Lord Eskkar! The outpost at Adarnar has been attacked!"

Guards, servants, even some tradesmen, followed the others into the room. Bantor and Grond, who'd been taking their meal outside, pushed the onlookers aside and followed the messengers, their eyes as wide with excitement as the youngest recruit.

Eskkar turned his attention to the second man, an older soldier swaying on his feet, a bloodstained bandage on his left arm, and a large bruise on his cheek. Flecks of dried blood still stained his neck and tunic.

"Come upstairs," Eskkar ordered. "Everyone else wait outside in the courtyard." He found Trella standing behind him. Her expression told him she understood. The long dreaded war with Sumer might have begun.

Grond had to help the wounded man up the steps. Eskkar dragged over a stool and the soldier slipped onto it with a long gasp of relief. Trella handed him a cup of wine, then had to help hold it while he sipped. Despite her efforts, his trembling hand spilled half the liquid onto his chest, staining the ragged garment as red as the blots of color on the dirty bandage.

"Send for a healer," Trella ordered. "This bandage needs to be changed." Her fingertips traced the nearly black bruise on his face. "His cheekbone may be broken as well."

"What's your name?" Eskkar snapped the words out. The man appeared ready to slip into shock, and needed the sharp words to keep his focus.

"Sargat, my lord." He coughed, then again lifted the cup to his lips. "Second in command to Enkidu at Adarnar."

"What happened?"

Alexar and Gatus, both breathing hard, joined them in the workroom. Drakis entered a moment later and completed the senior commanders in Akkad.

Sargat kept his eyes on the king. "Yesterday . . . no, three days ago, a little before sunset, a band of Tanukhs rode across the Sippar and attacked the outpost. Adarnar was overrun in moments. We tried . . . there were too many of them, hundreds and hundreds. We couldn't stop them."

A barbarian raid, Eskkar decided, but perhaps only an isolated attack.

"How many were there? How long did Adarnar hold out? How did you get away?"

Everyone had a question. At this rate, the man's story would take the rest of the day.

"Let Sargat tell us what happened," Eskkar cut in before anyone else could speak. "Take your time. Start at the beginning, and tell us everything that you remember."

The events at Adarnar came out in halting words. Trella refilled the wine cup, this time mixing the strong wine with plenty of water. No one said a word while Sargat spoke, every man in the room knew how the Tanukhs fought, all of them could visualize exactly what had taken place at the fort. The soldiers would have fought to the death, rather than let themselves be captured and tortured. Then would come the villagers' turn, tortured and killed for their captors' amusement, the women raped before being murdered, after watching their children butchered before their eyes. When only the dead remained, the Tanukhs would have burned the fort to the ground.

While Sargat spoke, the healer entered the room, put down his heavy box of implements, and without a word began attending to the wound. The soldier scarcely noticed when the healer used his obsidian knife to cut open the wrapping, cleaned the deep cut, and applied a fresh bandage around the man's arm. At last Sargat ended his tale and slumped back in the chair, his eyes closed.

"Did anyone else get away?" The soldier needed rest, needed more attentions from the healer, but Eskkar had only two more questions.

The eyes opened. "Yes, lord, one other. I was the last one out the gate. I caught up with the last handful of men to ride out. We had to fight our way through the Tanukhs. Only myself and one other soldier managed to get though all the confusion . . . there were so many of them, and all trying to get into the fort. He was wounded as well, and I left him behind at the first place of safety. I took his horse and rode for Akkad, as Enkidu wanted."

"How sure are you that these raiders were Tanukhs?"

"They were Tanukhs. I saw them and heard them speak. Enkidu recognized them as well."

Not Sumerians pretending to be tribesmen then.

"My thanks to you, Sargat." Eskkar reached out and touched the man's shoulder. "You've done well. Now get some rest." He nodded to the healer. "Take him downstairs and do whatever else you can for him. Tell the servants to put him in the guest chamber."

Eskkar strode across the room and into the Map Room. Bantor, Grond, Alexar and Gatus tramped after him, the floor flexing from their weight. Trella, Ismenne and Annok-sur came in together, and closed the door.

Standing over the map, Eskkar studied the land around the symbol that represented Adarnar. "Two or three hundred Tanukhs . . . that's a lot of men to slip across the border and travel so far east without being noticed, all to attack an insignificant outpost. They could have found plenty of farms to raid closer to home, on both sides of the Sippar."

"They could be halfway to Akkad by now," Gatus mused. "Or they could be on their way back to the desert."

"This doesn't make sense," Bantor said. "They would have had to cross over Larsa's territory. They must have been seen. We should have gotten word of their passage."

Esskar turned to Trella and Annok-sur.

"Nothing, my lord." Annok-sur's voice showed her concern. It was her task to gather information, in order to prevent such a thing. "I spoke with a trader yesterday who came from Larsa. He heard nothing out of the ordinary, only the steady preparations for war. Even to the people of Larsa, a band of Tanukhs would be noticed and talked about."

"Unless they crossed over further south." Esskar traced the Sippar river with his finger. "It's longer, but Sumer could also have given them passage through part of their lands. The Tanukhs could then ride north and strike anywhere they wanted."

More muffled shouting came from the common room below, until one voice rose up over everything else.

"Lord Esskar! I must speak with Lord Esskar at once!"

They heard the heavy tread of footsteps on the stairs. Esskar had just opened the Map Room door when a soldier pushed his way into the workroom. Esskar recognized Daro, one of Yavtar's commanders.

"Daro? What's wrong?" The man looked almost as weary as Sargat. Bloody bandages covered both his hands. "What happened to your hands?"

Daro lifted his hands as if seeing them for the first time. "From working the oar. We've been rowing upriver for almost two days." He shook his head. "The enemy has taken Kanesh. They've stopped all the traffic on the river. No boats are coming north."

Esskar glanced at Gatus, then nodded to Trella. One attack might be just a raid, but two – that meant hostilities had broken out. The same force that attacked Adarnar couldn't have reached Kanesh so quickly. Nor would Kanesh have fallen so easily, with its force of more than ninety defenders. Esskar guided Daro back to the workroom table and gestured him to the same stool just vacated by Sargat.

"Sit down and tell me what happened. Take your time, and don't leave anything out."

When Daro finished his tale, Eskkar ordered him to see the healer and remain in the Compound. Now only the commanders remained, sitting around the table in the workroom.

"How can this have happened?" Gatus asked the question none of the others wanted to voice. "We expected to have days of warning, plenty of time to reinforce Kanesh."

They had argued over sending more soldiers to Kanesh, but in the end they decided it might provoke the conflict.

"I'm sorry, Gatus." Trella's voice showed her concern. "Our last reports – one arrived only yesterday – showed nothing unusual in Sumer or Larsa. The Sumerians showed no signs of moving to the attack, no increase in the number of men, no large-scale movement of supplies."

"And yet they took us by surprise, captured Adarnar, Kanesh, and who knows how many other outposts." Gatus clenched his fist and rapped it on the table. "All by using the Tanukhs against us. Now the way is clear for them to ravage all the countryside south and east of Akkad."

"How they did it doesn't matter now," Eskkar said. He felt the same anger as Gatus, but Trella had provided them with good and timely information for almost four years. "Somehow the Boy King of Sumer has struck the first blow. By now his infantry forces are on the move, marching at top speed toward Kanesh. They'll be there long before we can muster enough force to recapture the outpost."

"Once they've strengthened Kanesh," Bantor said, "they'll move north. They could be at Akkad in five or ten days. But they'll never be able to take the city."

"They'll come in force, and prepared for a long siege." Gatus shook his head in frustration. "We'll be trapped inside Akkad. With so many men, they could just starve us out, while they harvest our crops and herds in the countryside."

"We need more reports on what their strength is." Eskkar kept his voice calm. Even with his closest commanders, he didn't intend to show any fear or doubt. "We'll need strong troops of cavalry to range the countryside, learn how many men we face. Once Hathor arrives with all the horsemen and we can dispatch them on patrols, we'll know better what to do."

"We may learn more from our spies in the next few days." Annok-sur waited until all the bad news had sunk in. "And those fleeing the Tanukhs may be able to tell us more."

"Meanwhile, we should not let the city see how grave this situation is," Trella said. "If they see us looking worried . . ."

The commanders understood that problem. If the people living in and around Akkad saw doubts and fears on their leaders' faces, they'd flee the city, and the defenders would have even fewer resources to withstand Sumer's armies.

"We need to do more than that." Eskkar looked for a moment at each of his commanders. "We need to tell . . . no, show the people that we will not only strike back, but that we will defeat Sumer. We need to remind everyone in Akkad that the one who strikes the first blow may not be the one who strikes the last. In battle, anything can happen. Our first defense has been broken, but we've many more weapons we can bring to bear. The people need to know that we will not only avenge the loss of Kanesh, but punish Sumer and the other cities until they beg for peace. We need to show more than strength. We need our people to understand that we are determined to avenge our losses, and that we will win."

"The people already believe it," Trella said. "You saved Akkad once from certain destruction. If we show strength, then they will remember that above all else. You will protect Akkad."

"When I march our spearmen through the city's lanes," Gatus said, "the people will believe in our victory."

"And as Annok-sur says," Eskkar reminded them, "we'll know more in a few days. There is no real danger to Akkad yet, and we've enough time to prepare."

"Still, we're going to need a new plan," Gatus said.

Almost all of their tactics had relied on Kanesh withstanding any attacks, at least for a few days, until help could arrive or an orderly retreat set in motion. Now ninety good fighting men were dead or captured in Kanesh, and another thirty in Adarnar. Other outposts along the river had probably met the same fate. Akkad would be cut off from all information about the borderlands.

"Oh, yes," Eskkar answered, wondering if his face revealed his own doubts. "We will most certainly need a new plan."

At sunset, Eskkar and Trella dined alone in the workroom. Neither had much to say. She had set aside their usual evening meal, eaten outside in the courtyard and always with the company of one or two of Eskkar's commanders and their wives, or a few important tradesmen. Tonight they needed to be alone with their thoughts.

Eskkar had given all the necessary orders, and his commanders had taken over. Within the city three hundred archers readied themselves for a possible attack. Messengers galloped off to the north, announcing the arrival of war and summoning all the soldiers from the training camps.

Over the last few months, in preparation for the call to arms, Akkad's horsemen and spearmen had moved closer to the city, shifting in small groups from the northernmost camps to newer ones closer to Akkad. Only a few miles away, just across the Tigris, close to three hundred of Hathor's best-trained cavalry stood ready to ride at a moment's notice. And on the east bank of the river, less than three miles away, five hundred tough spearmen waited for Gatus's orders. The complete force of Akkad's army needed only a few more days to reach the city.

Other riders had ridden to the outlying farms and villages, warning them to seek protection within Akkad's high walls. In the next few days, grain, herd animals and other supplies would flood into the city, in preparation for a siege of long duration. Storage rooms would be filled to capacity with everything needed to withstand a siege. Akkad's leaders had prepared as best they could for exactly this event. In the coming days, weeks or months those preparations would be tested against swords and spears.

Eskkar ate without tasting, pushing the warm chicken into his mouth, washing it down with well-watered ale. He left untouched the plate of still warm vegetables that he usually enjoyed, especially when dipped in oil.

At last Eskkar pushed his plate away and lifted his eyes to find Trella's gaze on him.

"The barbarians are coming once again," Trella said. "It's almost as it was the night before the Alur Meriki attacked. We've done all we can to prepare. Now we have to fight to learn our fate."

"The Sumerians aren't barbarians."

"Yes, they are, husband. Of a different sort, but just as eager to destroy what we've built. It seems as if mankind is divided into two kinds of people: barbarians who want to take from others, and those of us who want to make something better for ourselves, our friends and our children. All the progress we've made in the last few years, it's all the work of a few good men working together. In a way, the Sumerians are even worse barbarians than the Alur Meriki. At least the steppe people know no other way. But Sumeria's rulers should know better. They should work for their own people. Instead they crave triumphs over their own kind and others. They create disaster everywhere. They must be stopped."

Eskkar accepted the gentle rebuke. Trella understood his concerns, his worries, his fear of failure. But she also wanted him to stand strong, and do what had to be done.

"Not stopped, Trella. They must be crushed, beaten down so hard that they never attempt this kind of war again. To give passage to the Tanukhs, the enemy of their own kind ... everyman's enemy, so that they can pillage our lands ... you're right, they're worse than the Alur Meriki ever could be."

"You are the man to do it, Eskkar. There is no other in Akkad who can do what needs to be done."

"It will be a hard fight," he reminded her, though she as well as anyone understood the ways of war. "Many will die."

"If you do not win, everyone in Akkad may die. Remember that, Eskkar. Do what you must to make sure this doesn't happen again. Sargon and I will await your return."

Without realizing it, Trella had uttered much the same words that every mother in the Alur Meriki and other barbarian clans spoke when they bid their husbands and sons a final message before departing for war – return victorious over your enemies, or die bravely. Only by victory could the women and children left behind be truly safe.

Eskkar reached out and touched her hand. "Then I'll return with a victory, wife."

40

Five days later the Tanukhs continued raiding the southern countryside, but they had not moved as far north as Eskkar expected. Instead they remained close to Kanesh and the Sippar. Hundreds of farmers and villagers had fled the desert horsemen's advance, running in fear to Akkad, some continuing on to even more distant villages. Most of the land between the city and Kanesh lay empty. There would be no harvest this season, and crops not burned by Tanukhs would wither in the fields. Only mounted scouts from both sides now ranged the empty land, each probing the other's strength and gathering what information they could.

As Eskkar predicted, the same day the Tanukhs attacked Kanesh, the Sumerians summoned their men, gathered their forces, and moved northward. Shulgi's vast army of soldiers traveled slowly, carrying a mountain of food with them, and making sure their supply lines remained intact. To everyone's surprise, they halted when they reached Kanesh, and soon word reached the Akkadians that Shulgi had begun strengthening the village's defenses.

With the war now openly proclaimed, Trella's spies and informers had gleaned the basic thrust of Shulgi's plan. He intended to march to Akkad north along the Tigris, but he also planned to establish half a dozen fortified outposts along the way. If that required twenty or thirty days, or even longer, it didn't matter. Shulgi intended to ensure that supplies from the south could continue to reach his massive force. If attacked by Akkad's army, the Sumerians could simply fall back to the nearest outpost and regroup before resuming their northward trek.

Trella had even learned the planned location of the last outpost, a mere four miles from Akkad. From there, Shulgi's men would encircle the city. Crowded with people, the city would have to surrender in a few months when the food ran out.

Eskkar spent half the morning with his commanders discussing the latest reports, though they added little to what he already knew. When he had heard all the evil tidings he could stomach, he dismissed his men. Now only he and Trella remained in the Map Room, except for Ismenne. Eskkar wanted her there, in case anything in the map's terrain affected his plan.

He closed the door. "I've decided on a way to defeat Shulgi's forces. Before I tell Gatus and the others, I wanted to share it with you both. I need to know if it can work."

Ismenne's eyes darted back and forth, but Trella merely looked curious. She knew Eskkar had spent most of the night alone in the Map Room. "Whatever way we can help, husband."

He put his hand on the map beside the city of Akkad. Step by step, he went through what he wanted to do, what he would need at each step of the way, and how he expected the Sumerians to react. When Eskkar finished, he stood at the foot of the table and his hand rested on the city of Sumer.

Ismenne's eyes were wide with astonishment. Trella merely nodded. "A dangerous plan, Eskkar, but what else would I expect from you? Come, Ismenne, let us see what we can do to help Eskkar. We must think of everything that may go wrong as well, and at every stage."

They returned to the head of the table, and started there. One by one Eskkar worked through Trella's suggestions and objections until they again reached the end of the table. At last Eskkar felt satisfied with what he would propose to his commanders.

"It's the only way to win," he said.

"Better to risk much to win everything," Trella said. "The danger is great, but no worse than staying here. It's the only way to end this war."

"And the map," he added. "The plan could not be done without it."

"Speed will be your only ally."

"Then it's time to tell Gatus and the others. My thanks to you, Ismenne."

With the decision came a certain peace of mind. The last few days had taxed even his strength. Tonight, Eskkar knew he would sleep well for the first time since word of the fall of Kanesh reached Akkad.

He left the Map Room and descended to the courtyard. The sun had passed mid-afternoon. Eskkar hadn't realized how much time he'd spent talking to Trella. He found Grond waiting for him, feet up on the table, dozing in the shade of the house. His bodyguard had learned to sleep when and where he could.

"Wake up, Grond. Dispatch runners to the commanders. Tell them I want them all here tonight for a meeting in the Map Room. Then get your sword. I need to feel the weight of a blade in my hand."

"Yes, Captain." Grond's feet hit the ground, and a broad smile covered his face. "It's about time we got down to business."

Eskkar spent the remainder of the afternoon practicing his swordplay against Grond, first with wooden swords, then beating two training poles into splinters with his bronze blade. When they had finished, Eskkar felt satisfied and glad to have accomplished something, if only a good sword-practice session. He washed up at the well and returned to the workroom, just as the commanders began to arrive.

All of the senior men were there: Gatus, Yavtar, Bantor, Hathor, Mitrac, Klexor, Drakis, Alexar and even Shappa, the commander of the slingers. Hathor had arrived two days ago, with the last of the cavalry. The remaining spearmen and archers had reached Akkad only that morning. Yavtar's boats and fighting crews waited at Rebba's farm, trying to stay out of sight of Shulgi's spies.

Trella, Annok-sur and Ismenne completed the group. Ismenne closed the door when the last man filed through. They took their positions behind the map. They knew what faced them. The decisions they would make this day would seal the fate of Akkad, for good or evil.

"They're digging in at Kanesh." Gatus started the session, rapping one of the wooden pointer's on the table for emphasis. "The last of Shulgi's infantry arrived, along with a huge supply caravan. A few more days' work fortifying Kanesh, and we'll never retake it. It will be a secure base for all of Shulgi's forces."

"The Sumerians still have to come to Akkad," Alexar said. "We'll meet them halfway and attack. We know the ground, and can pick a favorable site for our spearmen."

"If we're defeated, we'll have no other course of action but to hold out in Akkad," Bantor argued. "We might as well just wait for them here. We're still getting all the supplies we need from the north."

"Enough." The single word brought everyone's attention to Eskkar. "We have been over all this before. No need to repeat it again." He stationed himself midway down the table, with Larsa within easy reach.

"Our situation is grave," Eskkar began without preamble. "Shulgi has moved with caution, and has left us with few options. We can either stay within the walls, or march down to Kanesh and fight. If we fight him there, we'll be outnumbered four or five to one. With the outpost under his control, he can take a defensive position and wait for us to attack. By the time we get to Kanesh, Shulgi will have fortified it against any assault, even assuming we can cut through his army to reach it."

Eskkar took a sip from his water cup, and let his eyes touch each of his commanders. He could see it on their faces. No matter how willing to fight, their grim demeanors already hinted at eventual defeat.

He went on, softening his voice as if speaking about the weather. "If we stay here, in the next few days – ten or fifteen at most – Shulgi will begin moving north, taking his time and protecting his rear. In a month or so he'll trap us inside Akkad, cut the river supply lines, strengthen his position surrounding us, and starve us into submission. Two or three months after that, our food will run out, while he'll feed his men with Akkad's grain, taken from our croplands."

No one said anything. As Eskkar said, they had been over this before.

"So I propose to carry the fight to him. Tomorrow we'll begin the march south. We'll leave behind just enough force for Bantor to hold the city."

"That's what Shulgi expects us to do," Gatus countered. "He'll be waiting . . ."

"I'm going with you," Bantor said. "I'm not staying behind."

"You have to stay." Eskkar made his words final. "You've been preparing the city's defenses for two years. You know better than anyone how to hold this place. Every man within Akkad knows and trusts you. It's likely that you'll end up facing the full force of Sumer's attack. No one in this room can defend the city better."

"After you've been defeated at Kanesh!" Bantor couldn't conceal his anger.

"I don't intend to be defeated at Kanesh," Eskkar said. "In fact, I don't intend to fight at all, at least not yet, and certainly not at Kanesh."

They stared at him, some smiling for the first time, others surprised at the hint of a new strategy.

Gatus laughed, his coarse guffaw breaking the tension. "So you've come up with some new hare-brained idea to get us all killed. I've been expecting some strange barbarian tactic to pop out of your mouth."

"It's dangerous enough, Gatus," Eskkar said, "but you're the one who made it possible. So if anything goes wrong, it will be as much your fault as mine. Now, do you want to complain or would you rather hear what I've got to say?"

He went through the plan for the second time that day, explaining every task he expected to complete, and the role each of them would play. Eskkar plotted each day's position on the map, laid out his forces and their objectives. He spoke slowly, covering every essential point. Men, horses, boats, supplies, weapons, Eskkar explained how he intended to use each of them. Slowly, his commanders began to nod their heads in agreement.

Nevertheless, every one of them had a half dozen objections and as many suggestions. Eskkar answered them all, one by one, and in as much detail as he could. Then Gatus started answering the questions, followed by Hathor. By then, Eskkar could lean against the Map Room wall and watch. He turned to Trella and saw the slight movement of her eyes that meant approval. Eskkar's commanders had accepted his plan, and soon they would make it their own.

Gatus had the last question, and he directed it not at Eskkar, but Trella. "And you think this can work? Ismenne agrees with this? Annok-sur?"

"We see no other way to win, Gatus," Trella answered. "Every other course of action merely delays our defeat. Eskkar's plan is not something Shulgi will expect. It is dangerous, to be sure, but no more dangerous than remaining inside Akkad and waiting for the end. And we'll be on the offensive."

Gatus snorted. "Offensive, is that what you're calling it? Well, I always said your husband would get us all killed one of these days. I just never expected anything like this. Still, I do like it better than hiding behind Akkad's walls and waiting. Doing that once was enough." He glanced around the table. "When do we march?"

"Tomorrow." Eskkar glanced up at the narrow windows, and saw only grayness. Dusk had fallen. "You've got the rest of the night to prepare your men, all of you."

The next morning, just before dawn, Esskar rode out of the Compound, Grond at his side. Twenty picked warriors from the Hawk Clan waited in the lane outside, his personal guard. Ten rode in advance, and ten followed close behind Esskar's horse. The horsemen kept their eyes moving and their hands on their swords. War had come to Akkad, and treachery could strike at any moment and from any direction. The city always held a good number of strangers, and even Annok-sur's army of women couldn't watch all of them all the time. A single arrow shot from a rooftop could bring down even Esskar.

But the lanes of Akkad remained almost empty of life, and the few sleepy tradesmen who happened to be up and about shrank in fear against the nearest wall or ducked back into the first doorway they could reach as the grim riders trotted by. Esskar's guards never slowed, and they soon reached the city's main gate, which creaked open just in time to let the king and his guards ride through without breaking the pace.

They followed the well-packed dirt of the road until it forked, then took the southern route toward the first assembly point, about six miles away. In the last few days, Esskar's commanders had assembled the army in four such camps, each a few miles apart. With such a large number of soldiers under arms, Esskar didn't want the men wandering loose in Akkad, with its numerous temptations for women, wine and gambling. Not to mention any possible spies from Sumer, or even traders who might talk too much about what they'd seen or heard. And so the men had said their farewells days ago, and now waited for the order to march.

Esskar had said his goodbye to Trella last night, when they held each other tight. They had never endured a parting such as this. Often enough, Esskar had ridden off to do battle, but this time he went to wage war on the land of Sumeria, and for this conflict there would be many battles to be fought. Both of them knew that this might be the last time they could cling to each other. Even Esskar's final words had acknowledged the risk. "Watch over Sargon, our son. Train him well."

A poor choice of words, Esskar decided in the light of dawn, almost as if he expected to fall in battle. He felt no such premonitions, no hint from the gods that this time his luck might desert him, but only a fool tempted fate with such words. The one sensation he experienced was relief. More than two years of preparation had created a well-trained and superbly equipped army. Now would come the true test of all that time and training. The sooner he closed with Shulgi's invaders, the quicker the war would end.

At the first camp Hathor waited with three hundred horsemen mounted and ready to ride. In addition to their weapons, each man carried a water skin and a sack bulging with food. Twenty pack animals brought up the rear, each burdened with a cooking pot and as much bread and grain as it could carry. No fires burned, and only a few women and boys stood watching in silence, many with tears streaming down their faces, as their menfolk rode off to war. Eskkar and his guards fell in beside the Egyptian, who gave the command that started the entire force moving in a double column.

"Any problems?" The two leaders rode close together, feet almost touching as they cantered along at an easy pace.

"None, Captain. Not even a horse going lame. The men are eager to ride."

"Let's hope they feel that when they see Razrek's cavalry."

Hathor laughed. "One battle at a time, isn't that what you keep saying?"

This time it was Eskkar who laughed. "My father used to say, don't count the number of your enemies, just kill the man in front of you."

"Your father must have been a great and wise warrior."

"He was."

Something in Eskkar's words told Hathor not to pursue the subject. Not many knew about Eskkar's early years and his wanderings before coming to Akkad. He preferred to keep that part of his life a well-guarded secret.

They reached the second camp without speaking further. Klexor pulled himself onto his horse as they approached, and swung in beside Eskkar and Hathor, who slowed their pace but didn't halt the men. "Good morning, Captain. My men are ready to ride."

"Well done, Klexor." Eskkar reached out and placed his hand on the man's shoulder.

As the original column rode past, Klexor's five hundred and thirty riders fell into place behind them. By the time they gathered in the scouts on patrol and the Ur Nammu riders, there would be close to eight hundred and fifty horsemen.

The third camp stood ready when they arrived. Gatus, wearing a wide-brimmed reed hat to shade his bald head from the sun, sat astride a gentle mare. At least for this campaign the old soldier had decided to admit his age. Gatus had promised his men that he would march and fight on foot beside them, but they had protested until he agreed to use the mare to keep pace with his men. Now he waited at the head of twenty-eight hundred spearmen.

Eskkar halted the horsemen, and waved toward Gatus, who ordered his men to move out, marching them four abreast and taking the lead. Except for those riding patrols around the main force, the horsemen would follow in their path, leaving the way free of horse droppings for the foot soldiers.

The bowmen, slingers, and the remaining men waited at the fourth camp. Eskkar could see a few of them still taking target practice as his men approached. When they saw Eskkar approaching at the head of the army, Alexar and Mitrac summoned their men back into ranks, and they fell in behind Gatus and his spearmen.

The city of Akkad was going to war, with a mighty army larger than anything Eskkar had ever imagined. Counting everyone, the army numbered just over five thousand, an incredible number of fighting men. He knew they were good men. Many had trained for this day for over two years, and even the least experienced man among them had at least six months to learn his trade. Those with less experience remained in Akkad, to continue their training and defend the city's walls under Bantor's command.

Eskkar's most loyal commander, Bantor had protested his assignment most of the night. Finally Gatus ended the argument. "We're leaving our women and children in your care, because you're the best man to protect them. So follow your orders and stop complaining just because you can't go off and get killed with the rest of us."

Eskkar had smiled at that. In reality, he had wanted to leave Gatus behind as well, but he knew all the spearmen would fight better under Gatus's eye. Besides, he would never have obeyed such an order.

As they marched south, Eskkar studied the men. The soldiers' training had been arduous, even brutal at times, but as Eskkar and every barbarian knew from childhood, you trained long and hard so that the actual fighting would be easy. Not easy, but at least something familiar to each man. He had to remind himself that more than half of these men had never raised a weapon in anger. For many of them, real battle would be something new and frightening, something beyond anything they'd ever dreamed of.

Fortunately, the Sumerian soldiers were much the same, at least as far as battle experience. But what the Sumerians lacked in experience, they made up in numbers. Trella's spies had come up with all kinds of numbers, but they all agreed on one thing – at least fifteen thousand men were under arms, controlled by King Shulgi. Other estimates had placed the number of Akkadian enemies at as much as twenty-five thousand, a number so vast that Eskkar had trouble grasping it.

Six cities, plus the half-barbarian scum that lived and raided along the western desert now served under Shulgi's banner. The Sumerian king might be little more than a boy, but somehow in two short years he had assembled and trained the largest army the world had ever seen, and now he intended to use it against Akkad.

Eskkar understood what risks lay ahead of him. If he faced Shulgi in battle and were defeated, it might mean the end of Akkad. Even if Eskkar and part of his army survived and managed to retreat behind Akkad's walls, such a huge enemy force could take its time and starve the city until it surrendered. And these new besiegers would not repeat the mistakes of the Alur Meriki. The Sumerians would establish their resupply lines and take their time, until the city was ripe for the taking. Eskkar frowned at the thought. The idea of someone other than himself and Trella ruling Akkad's people and lands was unbearable.

"Worried about something, Captain?"

Hathor's words brought Eskkar back to the present. He straightened up, and pushed the dark thoughts from his mind. "Just thinking about what's ahead of us."

"Shulgi has raised a powerful force, but our men are better trained. And he's young, and lacks experience. As long as –"

"As long as we don't fight him on his terms." Eskkar laughed. "Well, let's hope our plan for that works."

"It will, Captain. It will."

41

The army of Akkad marched south at an easy pace. They stayed close to the Tigris, both for access to fresh water, and to be resupplied by Yavtar's boats. For the last two years, while Eskkar worked and trained with his commanders, Yavtar and Trella had planned ways to supply the army. In preparation, they established eight temporary docks and way stations between Akkad and the border outpost of Kanesh. As soon as the army commenced moving south a steady stream of boats loaded up their cargo and pushed away from Akkad's jetties. Trella's supply clerks, many of them women, had planned each march of the campaign and knew what particular supplies would be needed at every step.

Those cargoes would make sure Eskkar's forces traveled light and fast. The army would stop briefly at each way station on their journey south, and Yavtar's fleet of boats would bring grain for the horses and fresh bread for the soldiers. Eskkar knew that Trella would keep the cooking ovens in Akkad burning from dawn until well into the night, and that supplies and even a few extra men would be ready for him at every stage of his march.

Shulgi's army also relied on the river for food and supplies, but if Trella's spies knew their business, the Sumerians had less than fifty boats working the river. Yavtar, meanwhile, commanded over sixty supply vessels, plus ten ships fitted specifically for battle. Each warship carried at least sixteen to twenty archers in addition to the regular crew of sailors and rowers. These ships would provide protection for the supply ships.

The Sumerians had captured the trading post at Kanesh, established two years ago to facilitate trade between Akkad and the Sumerian cities. Located at the juncture of the Tigris and the Sippar, the post had little value, except as a place to store goods being shipped north or south, and to provide travelers and traders a safe place to meet and haggle over prices. Nevertheless, almost a hundred archers and swordsmen had been stationed there, and the villagers dwelling within had increased that number to well over three hundred.

Eskkar had hoped, when the inevitable war broke out, to either reinforce the outpost or get the soldiers guarding it out in time, but Kanesh had fallen in a single morning, cut off and taken by a heavy force of Tanukh horsemen before the first rumor of war arrived from the south. All the supplies awaiting shipment in Kanesh had been taken intact. The defenders, now all dead or enslaved, probably had no time even to destroy the goods.

Now all of Shulgi's army had camped there, digging in and waiting for Eskkar to march south and meet them in battle. The idea of Sumerians enjoying Akkad's supplies while they waited to crush his army rankled Eskkar more than he showed.

As the men marched, Eskkar rode up and down alongside the men, observing their faces, looking for signs of fear or doubt. After the first of these inspections, the soldiers stopped being nervous about his passage. They smiled or waved, showing no more concern for their fate than if they were on yet one more of Gatus's strenuous training marches. Eskkar's careful scrutiny of his men impressed all the leaders of ten, twenty, fifty and one hundred. The idea that the king of Akkad might find fault with some equipment, or even the careless handling of their weapons, made every man in the army conscious of their duty.

He did the same reviews – at least three or four per day – on the cavalry, archers, and especially the slingers. Their relative youthfulness made it hard for them to restrain their excitement. From their looks and gestures, they might have been rushing back to Akkad to fill the local taverns for a night of feasting.

Five days after departing Akkad, at mid-morning, Eskkar saw three riders returning at a gallop. The leader of the scouts raced down the column of soldiers until he reached Gatus and Eskkar, who recognized the man, Tarok, another veteran who had fought in the battle to recapture Akkad from the Egyptian Korthac. Tarok pulled up and guided his horse alongside the Akkadian leaders.

"We saw the Sumerians." Tarok couldn't keep the excitement from his voice. "It's a great force, spread out on the plain just north of Kanesh. Their cavalry drove us off."

"How many?" Eskkar, surrounded by his commanders, waited to hear Tarok's estimate.

"We saw at least two or three thousand horses," Tarok said, his eyes wide with wonder at the number. "We didn't have time to take a better count."

Eskkar heard the murmur spread up and down the column at the news. "Well, then I'm glad you got away. No sense in fighting such a large force with just the three of you."

Everyone laughed, and the tension was broken. "You've done well. Report to Hathor. Meanwhile, we'll keep moving according to our plan." Eskkar and his commanders had known of the size of the enemy's cavalry. Tarok's sighting merely confirmed it. "In a few hours we'll reach the Tigris and obtain supplies from Yavtar's boats."

"They'll be expecting us to do battle in the morning," Gatus said. "They know we can't just march down here and then turn back without a fight. Even more likely, the Sumerians will expect us to launch a surprise attack tonight."

The easiest way for a smaller force to defeat a larger one was to attack at night, catching the enemy asleep and unprepared.

"We'll give them a surprise all right," Eskkar said, "but not the one they're expecting. Push on to the river."

The army continued its movement, turning slightly westward, to reach the Tigris before nightfall. About two miles north of Kanesh, they made camp along the river, and Gatus made certain that a strong force of pickets and skirmishers patrolled the land. By then Razrek's scouts had drawn ever closer, ranging up and down the column, galloping every which way, and trying to entice their enemy into giving chase. The Akkadians kept a wary eye on their enemy, but otherwise ignored them. The soldiers might have grown nervous at the sight of the Sumerians, but they saw their commanders' unconcern, and drew strength from that.

Before dusk fell, eight boats carrying supplies from Akkad slid ashore. Draelin, another of Yavtar's leaders, splashed ashore even before the first boat ground its bottom against the riverbank. "Take me to Lord Eskkar," he commanded.

Moments later, Draelin stood before Eskkar, Grond, Gatus, Hathor and the other commanders, all of them crowding around the messenger. "Lord, I bring word from Bantor. A large force of barbarians has been sighted to the east, riding hard. Bantor thinks they may not be Tanukhs, but Alur Meriki. They might be coming to strike at Akkad."

Eskkar swore at the news, a grimace on his face. "How soon before they reach the city?"

"Another three or four days," Draelin answered. "No more than that."

"Any word on how many?"

Draelin shook his head. "Hundreds ... a thousand ... no one knows."

"Well, if it's Alur Meriki, they don't have a thousand warriors," Gatus said. "If they mustered every fighter that can sit on a horse, they might have half that number."

Eskkar nodded. For almost five years he'd waited, knowing that some day, when the Alur Meriki had recovered their strength, they would return to Akkad to settle their blood debt. But Trella's spies had not neglected the eastern lands where the Alur Meriki had gone, and he had a rough idea of the forces they could muster. "If they send a raiding party, even a large one, it won't be more than two or three hundred men."

"That's not enough to take Akkad," Gatus said. "Why would they risk provoking us, making us come after them, unless ..."

"Unless they knew all our fighters had gone south to fight Sumeria." Eskkar shook his head. "This is another of Shulgi's plots. Demons take the boy king! He must have allied himself with the Alur Meriki, or at least warned them of his plans. So they decided this is the time to strike, to take their revenge."

"Three or four hundred barbarians on horses aren't going to scale Akkad's new walls," Gatus said. "Our men there can hold them off."

Eskkar had left four hundred and fifty fighters in Akkad to defend the city, barely enough to guard the walls properly. Many of those left behind were considered to be too old or too young for a vigorous campaign in the south. The city's inhabitants would have to join in the defense as well, and Bantor's men had been training them too. Many had taken part in the defense of the city during the Alur Meriki siege, and would supplement the soldiers. And with so many people crowding into the city seeking safety, there should be more than enough to withstand any attacks, at least for the next few weeks.

The Alur Meriki raiders would terrorize the countryside, but they couldn't do any real damage to Akkad itself. Gone were the days when its inhabitants trembled at the name of the dreaded barbarian horsemen.

"Unless they're betrayed from within." Esskar turned to Draelin. "You're going back on the river at once. Double up the crew and get back there as fast as you can. Tell Bantor to be wary of treachery, some plot to open the gates or scale the wall somehow."

"I was hoping to stay with you, Lord Esskar, and join the fight here."

"I think you'll find all the fighting you want back in Akkad. Take my message to Bantor and Trella. Go now."

"Yes, Lord." Draelin turned and ran off, back toward the river.

"Damn the Alur Meriki!" Esskar said. "I'd hoped we were done with them for a few more years."

"May they all rot in the demon's pits," Gatus said, not caring that Esskar had once belonged to that clan. "You think Shulgi has men inside Akkad?"

"We have men inside their cities." Some of Trella's deep-laid plans over the last two years were still to be put to the test, but Shulgi and Kushanna were just as crafty. "If the Sumerians have been talking to the Alur Meriki, they must have talked about some way to get inside."

"We can send some men back to the city," Hathor said. "A few hundred horsemen ought to be enough to drive them off."

"No, that's what Shulgi wants, for us to try and defend the city. If we send men back, we won't have enough to fight the Sumerians. We need every man we have." Esskar took a deep breath. "Akkad will have to hold out by itself."

"Draelin should be back before the Alur Meriki arrive," Gatus said. "It's only going to take him a day or so to get upriver."

"Trella will be watching for any treachery. As soon as she heard of the Alur Meriki's approach, she'll know what to do."

"I could send some horsemen, in case Draelin doesn't get through," Hathor suggested.

"No, we're already surrounded by Razrek's fighters. You'd never get a man through on horseback. Only the river is safe now."

"Then we continue on?"

"We continue. Make sure the men get as much rest and sleep as possible. I want us to be well on our way before daybreak. This may be their last good night's sleep for quite a while. You know what to do. Make sure everything is ready."

Esskar strode away, to try and get some sleep if he could. He had forced himself to sound confident before his men, but worries about Trella and little Sargon's safety would be with him for the next few days. No one wanted to return to Akkad more than he did, but he had to trust in Trella and her instincts. She would know what to do, and Bantor would heed her advice. Between the two of them, Akkad would be well defended. When Esskar did finally fall asleep, he dreamt of the days when he stood on Orak's walls, defending the village from the ravaging Alur Meriki.

The rest of the Akkadians settled in for the night. Nearly a quarter of the men remained awake and alert, and even those who slept kept their weapons at hand. Torches burned all night, lit by oil delivered as part of the boats' cargo just for that purpose.

He slept uneasily, waking often. Once Esskar roused himself enough to speak to some of the guards, all of whom urged him to return to sleep. When Grond finally woke him, Esskar glanced up at the sky. The waning moon indicated dawn was still far off, but that made no difference. In moments he was wide awake, slinging his sword over his shoulder.

"Is everything ready?" Esskar knew that Grond would have awakened even earlier, and would have checked on Gatus and Hathor's preparations.

"Yes, Captain. Gatus will be ready to move out in a few moments."

Esskar strode among his men, stepping in and out of the light cast by the flickering torches. Faces turned toward his, and for the first time he saw a hint of fear and nervousness on their faces. The night held its own terrors, and made even brave men afraid.

He found Hathor, Klexor and Fashod together, making their final preparations. At the last moment, Fashod of the Ur Nammu had decided to join the expedition and take command of the forty warriors who had volunteered to fight Akkad's enemies. Most of them were young and looking forward to their first battle. All three men faced him as he approached, and in the flickering torchlight he saw no signs of doubt or concern on anyone's face.

"We're ready to begin, Captain."

"Your men are going to be surprised."

"That they will," Klexor said. "Half of them will piss themselves with fright when they finally learn of the plan."

"And the other half will be too scared to piss," Esskar answered, the old adage never more true than now. "Good hunting to you all. I'll see you on the twelfth day."

"On the twelfth day. We'll be there, Captain."

For a moment Eskkar felt tempted to go over the plan once again, but he caught himself in time. Both Hathor and Klexor knew what to do. Their subcommanders would learn the news once the sun had risen and the horsemen were safely out on their way."

"Then get your men moving. Make sure my way is clear until dawn."

At the next campfire, he found Gatus and Alexar waiting for him to arrive, both of them ready to move out. "It's time to go, Eskkar."

"Well, then, Gatus, lead them out." Eskkar glanced behind him, and saw the first column of Hathor's riders on the move.

Everything had been discussed and planned and readied for this moment. Once the horsemen moved out, Eskkar, his commanders, everyone would be committed. If he had misjudged their enemy, or something unforeseen cropped up, they might all be dead by midday.

Grond approached, leading two horses, and Eskkar took Boy's halter. He'd named his favorite warhorse after the fine stallion he'd ridden many years ago. Boy stood even taller than his namesake, and Eskkar had worked with him until the two of them merged into a single fighter.

"Well, Boy, today's the day you earn all that grain you've been eating all these years."

He swung up onto Boy's back. The stallion bucked once, just to show his spirit, and then settled in.

The sun edged over the horizon, casting a rosy glow into the sky. The soldiers shoved the torches into the earth and gathered up their weapons. Gatus started the spearmen moving south. Screened by horsemen on either side, the men walked in a column four abreast, every man grunting under the heavy load of food and bulging water skins they carried, along with their weapons.

Shouts echoed from the darkness all around them. The Sumerian sentries heard the activity, had probably crept up close enough to see what was going on. That didn't matter, as long as they didn't try to contest the passage, which wasn't likely. Shulgi and Razrek had probably expected a night attack. When that had failed to materialize, the Sumerians would assume an attack at dawn. They would expect the Akkadians to move toward them, would be waiting for them when dawn broke. Indeed, Eskkar felt certain King Shulgi and his Sumerian allies had prepared well for any assault on his position.

They were going to be surprised indeed when the sun rose.

42

By mid-morning a crowd of soldiers milled about near King Shulgi's command post, blocking the path cleared and marked so that scouts and other messengers could bring messages to their leader. Swearing at the stupidity of villagers turned soldiers who couldn't seem to remember the simplest of orders, Razrek rode his gray stallion to within fifty paces of his destination before he swung down from his horse.

He pushed his way through a group of laughing soldiers, knocking one man aside and sending another stumbling to the ground. The offended soldier rose with a curse that died on his lips when he saw Razrek's scowling face, even before the man recognized the Sumerian army's second in command. King Shulgi, seated on a stool before a narrow table scarcely larger than the map that covered its surface, glanced up at Razrek's approach.

Shulgi's handsome face looked grim, either from lack of sleep or the failure of Eskkar to attack. "Where is the barbarian?"

Thousands of lips had mouthed the same question since well before the dawn. The Sumerians had remained awake all night, catching what rest they could while they stood at their posts, expecting an attack from the Akkadians. Before sunrise, word spread that Eskkar's forces were on the move, and every Sumerian forgot their weariness, snatched up their weapons, and again prepared to meet his attack.

But the dawn revealed nothing but an empty plain facing the alert and ready Sumerian force. The soldiers had breathed a sigh of relief when they realized that there might be no battle today, and fallen back into their careless habits.

"He's not coming, Shulgi." Razrek's voice sounded as harsh as the expression on his face. "Eskkar's moving to the south with his infantry."

"And the cavalry?"

"They've ridden off in another direction. As soon as it was light, the Akkadian cavalry galloped upstream about ten miles, then crossed over the Tigris before my men could catch them. I sent a thousand horsemen after them as soon I learned they were riding out. Our men stopped when they reached the river, and sent word back."

Shulgi's fist slammed onto the table. "Your riders should have followed them, crossed the river after them, attacked them! Instead, you let them get away without even a skirmish."

"Perhaps. But why waste the men? The scouts say Eskkar is with his spearmen. If he's fool enough to send his horse fighters back to Akkad to defend the city, or off on some raid, so much the better for us."

"If they were going back to Akkad, why cross the river?"

Razrek shrugged. "Maybe they wanted to slow down our pursuit. Or they didn't want to take a chance encountering the Alur Meriki. The Akkadians must have gotten word about them by now. Forget his cavalry. We should go after Eskkar. If he's stupid enough to go south, we can catch up with him, block his path, and crush him. He's only got a few dozen horsemen with him."

"I'm not moving my men until I know where Eskkar is. If we break camp and take up the pursuit, he could double back and attack us while we're spread out, maybe destroy the vanguard. It took a whole day to get the men prepared to face him here. And all our supplies are here." Shulgi unclenched the fist that rested on the map. "Where will he go? And why south? And why divide his men? He's already outnumbered almost five to one."

Shulgi had over twenty-one thousand men with him, with more trickling in each day. His spies told him the Akkadians could scarcely muster five thousand.

"What does it matter?" The thought of looting an entire city – especially one as rich as Akkad – brought a grin to Razrek's face. "Now we can march on Akkad, capture his city while he's away, and end the war with a single stroke."

"And what will Eskkar be doing all that time? It will take us at least a week to march to Akkad, and who knows how long to fight our way inside. Akkad's walls are thick and high. The Akkadians have had plenty of time to prepare for our attack. It might take months to capture the city, and even longer to starve them out. In that much time, the barbarian would ravage all of Sumeria. He could force the other cities to submit, or even change sides. He might end up camped in front of Sumer."

Akkad's new walls and mighty gates were the envy of every other city in the land. With a new and even deeper ditch carved beneath them it would take plenty of resources and preparation to surmount them. More important, it would take time, days, months, no one knew for certain.

"The city may have already fallen to the Alur Meriki." Razrek hadn't lost his desire to go north. "If not, our men are still inside. They might still open the gates for us."

"If that's true, then the city will wait," Shulgi said. "We need to destroy Eskkar and his infantry, before he destroys us. I think he's going to Larsa. He's going to try and take the city and cut off our supplies."

Nearly every wagonload of food and grain needed by Shulgi's army passed through Larsa. Boats and pack trains stretched all the way back to Sumer and the other cities, all with Larsa as their first destination. Ships and their cargoes stopped there, too. Shulgi's men consumed enormous quantities of food, far more than could easily be obtained from the countryside, and the horses needed grain. It would take eight or ten days to send word south and direct the supply caravans to a new destination. With so many mouths to feed, food for the men was already in short supply. The nearby farms had been stripped clean days ago.

"All the more reason to march on Akkad. There's plenty of food up north."

"If Larsa falls, Isin and Uruk might be tempted to ally themselves with Eskkar and his men. Even worse, they could demand the return of their forces, weakening us when we need them most."

Razrek rested his hand on the table and leaned over. "Larsa's walls are strong. They can hold out for weeks, maybe longer. It will take Eskkar five or six days to march his foot soldiers there. I can have five hundred horsemen there in three days. With that many extra men to strengthen the defenses, Larsa can laugh at Eskkar's puny force."

"Send eight hundred," Shulgi ordered. "And I want them moving today. I don't care if they don't eat or drink until they reach Larsa, or their horses drop dead from exhaustion after they arrive. And use the rest of your men to slow Esskar down. Engage him in battle, harry his flanks, attack his rear, anything you can think of."

"And what will you be doing, my king, while I'm sacrificing my men by attacking Akkadian bowmen and infantry?"

"By dawn tomorrow, as soon as we're certain he isn't doubling back, I'm coming after him. You just have to buy me time to catch up with him. Slow him down, while we give Larsa time to prepare. Hopefully, we'll finish him off outside the gates of Larsa, catch him between our forces and the city's walls."

"All right. I'll send Mattaki and —"

"No. You go yourself. Take the eight hundred. I want you inside Larsa if Esskar ever reaches there. He's liable to get there faster than you think. Leave Mattaki in charge of the remaining horsemen. Let him nip at Esskar's heels. And once you're inside the gates, make sure the city's elders don't decide to change sides, or fail to mount a real defense. Cut off a few heads if you have to, but make sure you can hold out until I arrive."

Razrek considered his orders. At least he could take his ease in the city while waiting for Shulgi. And Larsa's merchants were rumored to have plenty of gold.

"As you command, Lord Shulgi. I'll be on my way by midday. Even if Esskar reaches the city, he'll not get in."

Shulgi's eyes returned to the map. "Make sure that he doesn't."

Kushanna flung the cup clattering across the room, the water it contained splashing over the polished wood floor. Rage suffused her face, her lips narrowing in anger at Sohrab's words.

"Are you sure you conveyed my message exactly as I gave it to you? You left nothing out, added nothing?"

Sohrab quailed before her wrath. "I delivered your words with care, my queen. I added nothing, I swear it." He'd expected her to be angry, but not like this. Someone would pay for this tonight. Sohrab just hoped it wouldn't be him.

"Tell me again what she said. Every word, every gesture."

Sohrab took a moment to compose himself. A messenger who couldn't deliver a precise message soon found himself out of work. Trained almost from birth, he could memorize and recount even a long conversation between several participants.

"Lady Trella told me to give you this reply. She made me repeat it twice, to make sure I wouldn't forget." He closed his eyes for a moment, to return his thoughts to the meeting with Lady Trella. Sohrab would echo every intonation of Trella's words.

"She said . . . 'Queen Kushanna of Sumer, I thank you for discovering my brother Almaric and removing him from the mines. That mercy will be returned to you. Please tell Almaric of my love, and that I expect to see him soon. But the ransom you request of eight hundred pieces of silver for his delivery to Akkad is not possible in this time of war between our cities. I will, however, pay twenty silver coins for his quick and safe return. That is more than twice the price for a young and healthy male slave in Akkad's market. If that price is not acceptable to you, please hold my brother safe until my husband Eskkar reaches Sumer. At that time, you can make whatever arrangements you can with him.'"

"She dares to threaten me? When her husband reaches Sumer? I should have cut off the slave's ears and had you take them with you."

Sohrab winced at the thought. Handing over Almaric's ears to the queen of Akkad would likely have been fatal. Sohrab lowered his eyes and kept silent. Anything he said would only enrage Kushanna further.

Kushanna wasn't finished. "'That mercy will be returned to you . . . when Eskkar reaches Sumer!' The little slave bitch is trying to frighten me with her barbarian husband. I'll have her brother's eyes cut out and sent to her in a box!"

Kushanna stepped across the room to the table and snatched up another cup. This one she filled with wine. "And what of the king's army? Has he encountered the Akkadians yet?"

Anything to change the subject, Sohrab decided. "Not yet, my queen. Eskkar and his army had marched out of Akkad three days before I met with Trella. By now King Shulgi may have already met and defeated the barbarian's forces."

Queen Kushanna shook her head. "I've received no reports of a battle yet. In another day or two we'll know." She lifted the cup and drank. The strong wine helped her regain her composure.

"Shall I go and remove the slave's eyes?"

"No. Not yet. When Trella is captured and kneeling at my feet, I'll do more than pull out his eyes. I'll cut her brother's balls off and make her eat them. That will repay her for the insult."

Kushanna smiled, as if imagining the sight. "Go to the farm. Have the slave beaten. I want him whipped so hard that he can't stand."

"Yes, my queen." Anything for an excuse to get out of the room. "Would you like me to bring him here in the morning and have him whipped in your courtyard?"

She considered that for a moment. "No. That can wait. Go."

With a deep bow, Sohrab scurried from the chamber. Kushanna grimaced and stepped onto the balcony. An Akkadian trader hung by his hands from the punishment post. She stared at him while she thought. Trella seemed confident enough of victory, to send such an insulting message. Of course, that was to be expected until Shulgi destroyed Eskkar's army. Then Trella would send a different message – a message begging for her own life.

Killing the brother now wouldn't help, Kushanna decided. Alive, he might still be useful. Not that she expected Eskkar would ever show up at Sumer's gates, but in war, as everyone said, anything could happen. No, she would wait to avenge the insult. That would make it even more pleasurable.

But for now . . . she called out to one of the soldiers standing guard below. "Guard. Guard! Have the prisoner whipped until he's dead."

"Yes, Queen Kushanna." He trotted off to do her bidding.

Soon the sounds of the man's agony would fill the courtyard. That would be some small satisfaction, at least until she had Trella in her power.

43

Day 1

Even as Razrek delivered his report to King Shulgi, Eskkar and his infantry splashed their way across the Sippar river. The invasion of Sumeria had begun. The Akkadians had marched south at a rapid pace, swinging wide of the post at Kanesh to avoid confrontation with the enemy. Eskkar's men, despite struggling under the extra food and water they carried, had still managed to flank the Sumerian infantry with ease. A few hundred Sumerian horsemen had shadowed Eskkar's forces, but they hadn't come close, no doubt respecting the accuracy of the Akkadian bowmen, who now ringed the spearmen. If Shulgi had managed to get a few thousand of his men in position to block the Akkadian crossing, Eskkar would have had to fight his way through. Fortunately, that hadn't happened.

The Akkadian force had halted as soon as they crossed the stream. Eskkar gathered his commanders – Gatus, Alexar, Mitrac, Drakis, Shappa, Grond and Chinua – around him. Chinua of the Ur Nammu commanded the fifteen Ur Nammu warriors, the youngest and wildest of the barbarians who had decided to ride and fight with Eskkar's army. Fashod had taken the rest of the Ur Nammu with Hathor.

"As soon as the men have eaten and drunk their fill, call them to assembly. I want to talk to them. All of them. It's time they knew what they faced."

"Might as well. It's too late for any of them to run back to Akkad," Gatus said, a grin on his face.

As word spread that Eskkar wished to speak to them, the bowmen, spearmen, slingers, even the supply men and Ur Nammu warriors, crowded around their leader. Eskkar climbed to the top of a man-sized boulder, and waited until the soldiers had gathered around him, jammed together shoulder to shoulder and filling every space. At last they quieted down. More than four thousand men surrounded him, most of them still pushing and shoving, so they could get a step closer to better hear his words.

For once Eskkar had no qualms about talking. These were soldiers after all, not traders or merchants who might hide their smiles at his way of speaking or his still-strong accent. He knew many of these soldiers, and all of them knew and trusted him.

"Soldiers of Akkad, you've trained and marched for this day. Some of you have been cursing Gatus and myself for more than two years."

Eskkar waited until the ripple of laughter rose and fell. "Now all that hard work will be put to the test. Our enemy outnumbers us, but they can't fight as well as you, and I know they can't march as fast as you can. The Sumerians have drawn men from all the cities of the south, and even the outcast clans of the western desert. They have no love for each other, and no common cause to fight for. They fight only because King Shulgi commands them."

Such words came easily to him now. He knew what he wanted to say, and understood what they needed to hear.

"We fight because we are all brothers, all Akkadians. Like myself, most of you were not born in Akkad, but by taking up our cause, we have all become Akkadians. We fight for our families, our homes, our future. Now we will march to Larsa, the first of the six cities of Sumer. We will take Larsa, and punish its leaders for raiding our lands. And its spoils will be ours."

A ragged cheer arose at the mention of spoils. Most of the soldiers owned little more than the clothes on their backs. They'd come to Akkad to better themselves, to leave the hardships of the farm and countryside behind, and most had joined the army to fill their bellies and earn a few copper coins each month. Few of them understood the life-or-death situation that Akkad and its leaders faced. A chance for the spoils of battle meant more to some of these soldiers than any cause. And if they had to kill a few Sumerians to get at them, then they would fight all the harder.

Esskar waited until the cheering had faded away. "The Sumerian infantry will try to follow us, but they'll be too slow to keep pace. Their cavalry will try to hold us back, but our bowmen will keep them at bay. All you have to do now is march, march and march again, until your legs are too weary to keep you standing, until you're cursing Gatus and me as you've never done before. Until we reach Larsa, we cannot – will not – waste a moment. Meanwhile, obey your commanders, stay together, and we will defeat the Sumerians."

Another cheer went up. In a single swift motion, Esskar drew his sword and raised it over his head. A roar from over four thousand throats rose up at the gesture. He kept the blade pointed to the sky and filled his lungs with air. "March for Akkad! March for revenge! March for gold! Are you with me, Akkadians?"

An even louder clamor echoed out over the river, startling birds and even the Sumerian horsemen observing them from across the stream. The pandemonium went on and on, as every man raised his sword, spear, bow or fist in the air. "Akkad! Akkad! Akkad!"

The outcry continued, until the men's voices grew hoarse.

Esskar lowered his sword, then pointed it toward the south-west, the direction that would lead them to Larsa. "Then march! Show these Sumerian scum that you're not a bunch of old women. Commanders, get this pitiful excuse for an army moving!"

More laughter swept through the men. They surged away from Esskar, returning to their places, gathering up their supplies and weapons, jostling their way back into formation. Even before everyone was ready, Gatus gave the command to move out, and the invasion of Sumeria began in earnest.

Gatus organized the column into three groups. The spearmen formed the core of the marching formation, with the supply men, builders, even Esskar's two clerks, directly behind them. Bowmen and slingers surrounded them on all sides. The archers would keep any enemy horsemen at a distance. Esskar had only twenty horsemen with him, in addition to the dozen or so Ur Nammu warriors. These, supported by groups of slingers who acted as skirmishers, would scout the land and act as messengers if needed.

The Sumerian cavalry – from what Eskkar had seen of them – didn't possess many bows, and those who did carried the smaller kind meant for use on horseback. The Akkadian longbows had almost twice the reach. If the Sumerians charged his archers and tried to overrun them, the spearmen and slingers would be ready and waiting to deal with them. Those who survived the hail of arrows would find themselves impaled on a wall of spears.

Gatus led the formation, riding his mare and wearing his battered reed hat. Grond and the other commanders had insisted Eskkar march with the spearmen, out of range of any arrow launched high into the air. He didn't mind. It gave him a chance to talk to the men, and he moved up and down the ranks they traveled speaking to many, answering questions, or even listening to stories the soldiers told about other battles.

They kept a fast pace, but the Akkadians halted often, taking short breaks that never seemed to last long enough to rest. The sacks each man carried gradually grew lighter, as the bread, cheese, and dates were consumed. Better to carry the food in your belly than on your shoulder.

By mid-afternoon, the scouts galloped back to report. A large force of cavalry was coming up behind them, driving hard.

"How many?"

"Seven hundred, eight hundred, perhaps a thousand," the scout replied, his eyes still wide with excitement.

"Not enough to attack us," Gatus said. He had one leg swung over the mare's neck. "Probably reinforcements for Larsa."

Eskkar knew how hard it was to count moving horsemen, but the number seemed about right. "The rest will be at our heels soon enough. They'll try to slow us down."

"We'll see about that," Alexar said. "Our bowmen have been waiting for a chance to test their weapons."

"Keep the men ready for anything, an attack, an ambush, anything."

Eskkar didn't fear the horsemen. No horse that ever lived would charge a bristling line of spears, no matter how hard its rider urged it forward. Archers could be ridden down, if the enemy were willing to take the losses, but men armed with shields and spears were a different matter. If the Sumerian horse attacked the archers, they'd find themselves crushed by the spearmen. And even the Sumerians didn't have enough cavalry to dare a true frontal attack. As long as Eskkar stayed away from Shulgi's infantry, his force of Akkadians would be safe. At least, that was what he told himself several times each day.

The Akkadian army kept moving. The tactics and marching orders used in months and years of training now proved their worth. The odd commands and alignments, which once had made the men shake their heads at their leaders' apparent stupidity, now provided a safe zone for all his men. Almost none of the soldiers were aware that today's formation had been planned months and years ago. Only Eskkar's most trusted commanders knew the whole story.

Darkness had fallen before Gatus gave the order to halt near a small stream that provided fresh water. Weary men dropped their sacks and shields, but there was no time yet for rest. The commanders marked out a square camp, with the slingers, archers, horses and supplies in the center, the spearmen surrounding them.

After objections from Eskkar, Gatus had come up with the idea of the night camp. "The men need a place to sleep while on the march," he declared. "If we provide a secure place each night, they'll sleep better and march farther the next day. Or would you rather be attacked while you sleep and wake up with your throat slit?"

Eskkar had thrown up his hands and given in. The idea of spearmen infantry belonged to Gatus. If having the men fortify a camp each night appeased the old soldier, Eskkar would go along. That night, Gatus and Eskkar walked the camp, inspecting the preparations. Only when Gatus declared himself satisfied with their preparations to repel any attack during the night did the men receive the command to rest.

Fires were soon burning, but most of the soldiers ate a simple dry meal of bread and dates and whatever else they had to hand. Within moments, those not on guard duty were snoring away, loud enough to be heard back in Akkad. At least it seemed that way to Eskkar.

He and his commanders sat huddled in the center of the camp, hunched over a cloth map spread out in the dirt. Trella's agents had started mapping this entire area years ago. Now Eskkar could see the location of every stream, well and landmark between Kanesh and Larsa, with the route they were to take stitched out in red threads.

"It took longer than we expected to reach this place, and we had no opposition. Tomorrow's march will be even longer, and if Razrek's horsemen attack . . ."

"The men will be carrying less weight tomorrow," Gatus said. "And we'll start moving at first light. We'll make up the time."

Eskkar decided there was no sense in arguing about it. Tomorrow's march would tell the tale.

Gatus leaned over and studied the map. "How far did we come today?"

"About twenty-two miles," Eskkar said, checking the map, though by now he had little need of it. He'd memorized it months ago. "Tomorrow we need to do twenty-four, almost twenty-five miles if we want to reach fresh water."

Even as Trella's spies had mapped the land, they had also measured the distances. For two years a dozen men had mapped and paced off much of the land of Sumeria. Hopefully, no one in the southern lands had noticed any of this activity.

Eskkar thought it quite remarkable to know in advance the exact distance one had to walk or ride to reach a destination, and even more remarkable to know approximately how long such a journey would take.

"These spearmen are tough," Gatus said. "They'll make the march. They've done it often enough in training."

Once again, Eskkar kept silent. The men were carrying more weight now than they usually did in training. No one else answered Gatus's comment, but every commander knew that training had ended, and that this was real war. And the spearmen had the most equipment to carry. An archer could travel fairly well carrying a bow, two quivers full of arrows, and a short sword. The slingers carried even less. But a spear and shield were both heavy and cumbersome to carry, and spearmen wore helmets of bronze as well, which were usually tied to a man's waist as they walked. With all those items of warfare attached to his body, a spearman needed to press hard to keep up with the archers.

"I'm going to get some sleep." Gatus stood and stretched, ignoring the silence regarding tomorrow's march. "I suggest you do the same." He strode off to throw his body down on the ground beside his sub-commanders.

"Well, we'll know where we are tomorrow night," Eskkar said. "Let's hope Gatus is right. Meanwhile, make sure everyone gets some rest. We're going to need all the sleep we can get."

44

Uvela sat cross-legged on the ground, with only a thin blanket to soften the hard earth beneath her. To make herself more comfortable and catch a bit of shade from the midday sun, she leaned back against Akkad's outer river wall. Before her lay a sun-bleached linen cloth, upon which rested an assortment of leather straps, necklaces, carved figures of Ishtar, as well as the other various spirits that brought luck or long life or fertility or strength to a man's rod. Every so often an idle laborer or visitor from the surrounding farms would wander by, let his eyes glance over her wares, and move on.

Few of Uvela's wares would attract a second look. By custom, such a prime location close to the docks and the river gate should have been occupied by a reputable seller of more valuable goods. But though she managed to sell one or two items every few days, no one asked Uvela to give up her station. Not even the more aggressive merchants, eager for additional selling space bothered to complain about her presence.

Uvela's station included the younger woman who sat beside her, tending the small cooking fire burning in a thick clay pot. A battered bronze kettle full of stew hung suspended over the low flames. Occasionally, a boatman or even one of Akkad's dockside guards would offer a copper coin for the kettle's contents, a more than fair price for such basic fare. Both mother and daughter were known to the city's guards, who made sure that no ignorant farmer or foolish vendor disturbed their places, trinkets or even themselves.

From where Uvela sat she could see everyone entering Akkad

through the river gate. For more than two years she'd watched an assortment of people step on or off the docks, coming and going, and by now she could read their faces almost as well as Lady Trella.

Most strangers entering the city for the first time looked about them in awe, impressed by the high walls, surprised by the size of the docks, overwhelmed by the dozens of craftsmen selling everything conceivable. Gangs of laborers from the market loaded or unloaded the steady stream of boats, adding to the confusion. Gawking newcomers – their mouths open and clutching most of their few worldly goods – would walk slowly into the city, jostled about by those whose regular business brought them in and out of the gate, usually at a hurried pace.

Some people, their eyes downcast, arrived wearied or troubled by some anguish or misfortune that brought them to Akkad. These usually wore ragged clothes and carried all their possessions in a simple sack slung around their necks. Uvela could guess their stories, how bandits or Sumerians had ventured across the border to harass and plunder those weaker than themselves. With their homes destroyed and their crops burned, these desperate folk hungered for a new life in Akkad. Since the outbreak of war with Sumer, their numbers had swelled, as everyone sought the safety of the city's high walls.

After years of such observation, Uvela knew families could usually be ignored, as could the very young and very old. That left only a few who caught her eye, but when someone did, she stared at them carefully. None of them ever noticed her gaze. With her lank gray hair practically covering her face, her eyes could scarcely be seen. If they did happen to gaze at her, they saw only an insignificant old woman, whose patched and faded shift hung loosely over her thin shoulders, and marked her status as one of those who often needed to beg for food to supplement their meager earnings.

Now two men walking off the docks and toward the gate attracted Uvela's attention. Their poor clothing couldn't conceal the strong muscles that lay beneath the worn garments. They strode up the slight incline with ease, despite each carrying a heavy sack almost as large as the ones used by a merchant's porters as they transported goods from city to city.

The new arrivals gave the city's walls the briefest of glances, then moved forward, letting the crowd carry them through the wide open double gate only a few paces away from where Uvela sat.

"Have you see those two before?" Uvela rose to her feet as she spoke, determined to have a second look.

Her daughter, sitting beside her, didn't raise her head or her voice. She, too, knew how to use her eyes. "Never."

"I'll follow them." Uvela pulled a scarf from a pocket in her dress, and swept it over her head and across her neck. The gray hair vanished in an instant. Meanwhile, her daughter removed her own hat, a large reed affair that would cover both head and scarf if need be, and handed it to her mother.

Uvela moved quickly through the gate. The guard there gave her a glance, but said nothing. No one questioned or even spoke to one of Annok-sur or Lady Trella's women when they went about their business. In fact, the guards made sure that no one else disturbed them, either by accident or on purpose.

In moments, Uvela caught sight of the two men moving deeper into the city. She slowed her step, staying about twenty paces behind them, the usual crowd of men and women filling the lane between them. The men glanced around from time to time, but a ragged older woman blended into the throng, almost unseen and beneath notice in any event. Nevertheless, Uvela kept well behind the two as they moved closer to the center of the city. They stopped only once, to ask directions from a vendor, before they continued on until they reached the Spotted Owl, a tavern often used by travelers.

This time both men glanced around before they entered the dwelling, but if they saw a woman wearing a large reed hat, they never noticed.

Uvela found a place to stand and waited. The Spotted Owl, while not one of Akkad's finest, provided good food and decent ale at reasonable prices. After a river journey it was only natural for travelers who could afford the price to want to partake of some ale and food. She settled in, the scarf and hat held out of sight behind her back, expecting to wait some time while the two men quenched their thirst. But before long, one of the men came out and turned up the lane, away from where Uvela sat. She moved to her feet, prepared to follow the stranger, but before she'd taken more than a few steps, he ducked under a low doorway and disappeared into one of the endless huts whose uneven walls formed the lane.

Retracing her steps, Uvela returned to her vantage point. With a little stretching she could see both tavern and hut from where she stood, and her slight stature made her almost invisible as she leaned against the wall.

Before long, the second man stepped out of the tavern, glanced up and down the lane, and followed his companion's steps to the same house.

By now her interest was more than idle curiosity. Even before the outbreak of hostilities with Sumer, Annok-sur's network of spies and informers had kept their eyes open for any suspicious strangers. With the armies of Akkad and Sumer marching toward each other, Uvela and others like herself had heightened their activities. Any stranger, boatman, merchant or uncouth farmer could be a spy for Sumer, even a possible assassin. Before Lady Trella became queen of Akkad, or even Eskkar's wife, she had nearly succumbed to an assassin's knife.

Now Trella rarely left the Compound, and when she did venture forth, a compliment of Hawk Clan soldiers guarded her person as zealously as they protected the king's. And although Eskkar had marched south with Gatus and the army, there were still other possible targets for hired killers within Akkad.

An attractive young girl, her hips moving suggestively, strolled down the lane, smiling at potential customers and trying to talk to the any of the passersby who showed the slightest interest. Her shift, cut low, revealed much of her breasts. As she drew close to the spot where Uvela waited, she gestured casually, and the girl approached.

"Good day, Uvela."

"And good day to you, Martana. Are you busy right now?"

"No, only one customer so far today, and that took but a few moments." She laughed at the memory. "He had to rush back to his wife and four children."

Uvela smiled at the story. "Then perhaps you can do some work for me." She told Martana about the two men, and described them in detail, including where they seemed to be staying.

"See what you can find out about them from the people in the tavern." She reached inside her dress and handed the girl a copper coin. "You'll earn a silver coin if you discover anything useful. But be careful. Don't arouse any suspicions. They could be dangerous."

Martana tossed her head. "Everyone knows I'm curious about men. Will you be here long?"

"No, I'll be up the lane, where I can watch the house better." And where she could send a message to Annok-sur to ask for help, but there was no need to tell Martana that.

Uvela waited until the girl disappeared inside the tavern, then moved up the lane, just another old woman beneath the notice of most men in the city.

A street vendor Uvela knew was happy to dispatch one of her daughters to carry word to Annok-sur, and just as eager to provide a doorway from which Uvela could keep a close eye on the stranger's hut. She settled in for a long wait, but at least she knew she would soon have plenty of help.

The next day, just after dusk, Trella, Annok-sur and Uvela sat at the table in the workroom, their heads almost touching. Though the room provided plenty of privacy, Bantor and a few of his commanders lingered in the Map Room, so the three women kept their voices low, out of habit as much as for any other reason. Successful women learned almost from childhood to keep their thoughts and conversations to themselves, lest what they think or say upset or anger the men in their lives.

"They've settled in for the night," Uvela said. She had just arrived from her post in the lane, where three other women now kept watch on the strange men staying at the Spotted Owl. "It seems they've joined up with seven or eight others who've been hanging around the inn. Some are staying at a house just up the lane. This morning the two newcomers split up, and spent most of the day wandering around the city, each accompanied by one of those who'd been living here. None of them appeared interested in seeking work, or buying anything but food and ale. They don't look or act like laborers. They might be just thieves."

"Or assassins," Annok-sur said. "Bantor, or even Trella could be their target."

Trella frowned. "And you think one of those who arrived yesterday is the leader?"

"Yes, the others seem to defer to him. Jovarik is his name, and he's also a little older. No one knows if this is his first visit to Akkad. We followed him around today. He walked all over the city, and spent some time near each of the gates."

"If the others, who have been here longer," Trella said, "have also learned what they want about the gates and its guards, Jovarik may not need to see much more."

"We could bring in the innkeeper," Annok-sur said. "He might be able to tell us more about them."

"No, if he's in league with them, they would be warned. And we've nothing from Martana or the other prostitutes?"

"No, nothing," Uvela said. "Martana serviced two of them this afternoon, but always with one or two of the others watching. They said nothing, except that they're in Akkad seeking work. Last night four of them took another girl back to the house, but even after pleasuring all of them, she heard nothing suspicious. They say little when anyone is nearby, it seems."

"We need to overhear their conversations," Annok-sur suggested. "Perhaps one of your girls can get close enough without being seen."

"No, I don't think so," Uvela said, after pausing a few moments to consider the possibility. "Those staying at the Spotted Owl say little, and the ones living in the house would be suspicious if they thought someone was trying to spy on them. They always keep someone at the door and they even watch the smoke hole every so often."

"Perhaps we should just have Bantor's men take them into custody," Annok-sur said. "Some time with the torturers would tell us what we want to know."

"Eskkar and the soldiers have been gone for five days," Trella said. "And we know that enemy horsemen are approaching the city from the east. Those marauders must have some plan in mind, some way they think they can get into the city."

"Unless they just want to raid the countryside." Uvela hitched her stool a bit closer. "That's happened many times in the past."

"No, I don't think so," Trella said. "The war with Sumeria started suddenly. We had no hint of the threat. How is it then that the barbarians arrive on our doorstep at the same time? That seems too much of a coincidence."

"Then we should have these strangers arrested, brought before Bantor's questioners. That's what Eskkar would do."

"Yes, that would be his first reaction," Trella agreed. "But that wouldn't stop the horsemen from raiding our lands, and they might devastate the countryside, destroy all our crops. If Eskkar remains in the south more than a few weeks, there might be nothing left when he returns."

Neither Annok-sur nor Uvela said anything. Eskkar and the army might never return, or if they did, they might arrive on the run, a broken force, with the Sumerian hounds right behind them.

Trella read their silence. Such thoughts, while never voiced, were no doubt often on the minds of those who knew the true situation. "I want to know what these men are planning. We need to get someone close to them, someone who can hear their words."

"Any women in the inn would attract attention," Uvela said. "Others like Martana would likely learn nothing."

"I agree," Trella said. "I think there may be another way. Send for Wakannh. He's good at finding people."

From the shadows Wakannh studied the small tavern up the lane. Not really much of a tavern, more like a hovel whose owner sold some overpriced and watered-down ale in the evenings to half a dozen drunks and thieves. Not that there was much to see, just a dim outline of a low doorway.

"Is that the place? What would someone at the Compound want with any of that rabble?"

"Shut your face," Wakannh said. As a leader of ten in Akkad's guard, he commanded this little group of four men tonight. Annok-sur had given him the information that the thief Sargat might be found within the tavern, but Wakannh didn't intend to share Annok-sur's name with any of his men, let alone a recruit of less than a hundred days.

"Sargat is one of the quickest thieves in Akkad," Wakannh said. "So here's what we'll do. I'll go in the front. You two go around to the next lane. There's probably a secret way out to the back. And you ..." he grabbed the talkative recruit by the shoulder, "look agile enough. You get up on the roof. If Sargat tries to get away, make sure you stop him. And so help me, if you make a sound up there and give us away, you'll be digging latrines for the rest of your miserable life."

"Yes, commander," the recruit said, fingering his sword in the darkness. "I'll be quiet."

"Better give me your sword," Wakannh said. "It will only get in your way on the roof. And I want Sargat alive, remember that, all of you. The folks in the Compound can't talk to a dead man. Now get going, all of you."

Regretfully, the recruit handed over his sword. His leader of ten always seemed to take particular satisfaction in picking on him.

Wakannh waited while his men moved into position. He couldn't see them in the next lane, but they were veterans who would do what they were ordered, without asking stupid questions or trying to do any thinking on their own. When he saw a darker shadow appear and disappear on the rooftop, Wakannh started down the lane.

At the entrance, the smell of fresh urine greeted his nose, even stronger than the usual night odors to be expected. A greasy blanket hanging at an angle half-covered the doorway. A fire burned inside, its light leaking out from around the edge of the door covering.

He pushed it aside, ducked under the door stile, and took a quick glance around the room. A single candle burned, adding its flickering light to that of the fire. A quick count showed eight men within, all of whom looked up as he entered. The sight of one of Akkad's guards stopped all conversations. Annok-sur had described Sargat, so Wakannh's eyes searched the little gathering, soon eliminating all but two of the group.

"I want to talk to Sargat. Which one –?"

The figure farthest away from the doorway burst into motion. Before Wakannh could react, Sargat had sprung to his feet. Two quick steps and he launched himself at the ladder that led to the roof, his foot landing unerringly on the third tread before the slow-reacting Wakannh started moving. Sargat's legs had almost disappeared up the ladder before the ceiling shook and rattled. The thief's body came tumbling down, to crash onto the earthen floor with a thud.

To Wakannh's astonishment, the fall hardly slowed the man down. Sargat twisted to one side and leapt to his feet, but by then Wakannh had barreled his way through the patrons, knocking two men aside. He shot out his hand, caught Sargat by the hair, and jerked him back with all the strength of his bowman's arm.

This time the thief landed flat on his back, and Wakannh planted a knee on Sargat's chest and the tip of his sword on his neck. "Going somewhere?" With a quick flip of his wrist, the sword's pommel struck down on Sargat's forehead, stunning the man. "I don't think so, scum."

"I got him good, didn't I, commander?" The recruit had swung down from the roof and now stood beside his commander.

Wakannh opened his mouth to bark at the recruit, but changed his mind instead. If Sargat could move that fast, he might have slipped past a less alert guard, even one waiting on the roof. "Yes, you did, for once. Good job. Now go get the others."

Within moments, the four guardsmen had Sargat's hands bound behind his back, and his legs hobbled together, so that he wouldn't try running away. Wakannh didn't intend to take any chances with someone who moved that fast.

"Where are you taking me?" Sargat had regained his wits quick enough.

"To the Compound. And if you open your mouth again, I'll deliver you with your balls cut off and shoved down your throat." He turned to the still smiling recruit, busy massaging his right fist. "Put a sack over his head. The less he sees and hears, the better."

45

===

argat's fingers dug into the wall, and he swung himself onto the
ledge, taking care to keep his silhouette as inconspicuous as
possible. Once on the inner side of the ledge, he settled in and
remained motionless. Over the years, he'd learned many things about
climbing about on other people's rooftops, but the most important lesson
was to fade into the shadows and avoid the slightest movement. Many
times the creaking of a ceiling beam or rustling of cut branches had caused
a head to pop up from the smoke hole and look around. Thick shadows,
dark clothing, and the absence of the slightest motion tended to render
him unseen.

Another lesson well learned was patience. He'd reached the roof
adjoining the hut that held Jovarik and his companions. Now he needed to
assure himself that anyone below who might have heard something
became reassured, until whatever sound from the sagging roof faded from
memory.

While Sargat waited, he thought about what had happened earlier.
The guards had caught him easily enough. Sargat hadn't thought anyone
even knew he'd returned to Akkad. He'd only slipped into the city twenty
days ago. In that time, he'd robbed only three houses, descending through
the smoke holes, taking what he could, and disappearing into the night as
silently as he'd come. He would have sworn that no one had seen him.
Despite all his care, the guards had come straight to the tavern. Someone
had planned his capture with care, to ensure that he didn't escape and
vanish once again into Akkad's criminal underworld.

He soon learned who that was. When his captors removed the sack covering his head, he found himself sitting across the table from Annok-sur. Lady Trella sat just outside of the candlelight, a half-step behind the older woman. When he glanced around, Sargat realized he was in the king's Compound, the so-called workroom where Lady Trella dispatched her agents to spy on Akkad's troublemakers. Which included him, Sargat decided. As his eyes grew accustomed to the light from the single candle, he realized that no guards or servants stood nearby. They would be within call, of course. Still, their absence meant that something private needed to be discussed.

Annok-sur's hands remained below the table, and he guessed a weapon would be in her hand, ready should he make any sudden movement toward either of them. His own hands remained bound, but the rope looped about his ankles had been removed before they had escorted him up the stairs, and not replaced.

"Welcome to the Lady Trella's house," Annok-sur said. "Do you know who I am?"

"Yes." Still trying to collect his wits, he didn't trust himself to say more. The less he spoke, the harder it would be for the witch-queen of Akkad to read his thoughts. Or so he hoped.

"Good. We only learned of your return to the city a few days ago. You should know that guards are waiting in the courtyard to bring you before the King's Justice. I expect that you'll be found guilty of enough crimes to warrant you being sentenced to the slave gang for the rest of your life."

Sargat heard the threat, but they hadn't brought him here in the night to remind him of his fate. Sentenced to the labor gang meant that they would break his legs first, so that he couldn't run, then, when he had recovered, he'd work for the rest of his life. He put that thought out of his mind. They wanted something from him, but what?

"Of course, you may be able to avoid the work gang, and earn a few silver coins in the bargain. If you're interested, that is."

His eyes flickered to Lady Trella, but the shadows hid her eyes, and he couldn't read anything from her expression. Whatever she wanted, and it must be something important to warrant her presence, he'd find out soon enough.

"What can I do for you, and . . . Lady Trella?"

"There are some men in Akkad who may be plotting with our enemies," Annok-sur continued. "We want you to discover what it is that they plan. You would need to get close enough to hear what they're saying."

"And if I do that . . . ?"

"If you learn what they're plotting, you can go free. And you'll have ten silver coins as a reward."

Another glance toward the still silent Lady Trella. Obviously, they wanted to use his skills as a thief to gather the information they wanted. Sargat knew how to play that game. He'd dealt with men who'd hired his services for such tasks before. But never a woman, let alone the one in charge of the city's spies and informers. "And if I can't learn anything?"

"Then I fear you will have to face the King's Justice. Of course, if the men discover you, you'll probably be killed outright."

Death, or mutilation and slavery for the rest of his life. "For ten silver coins, I would be happy to help you." Promise them anything, he decided. The minute he was on his own, Sargat would be over the roofs and gone. They wouldn't catch him again, and he knew of several ways to slip out of the city undetected. "What do you want me to do?"

Annok-sur told him about Jovarik and his companions, and the place where they were staying. He knew the lane, but didn't remember that particular rat-hole. Still, it was familiar enough ground for him.

"And you need this information . . ."

"Tonight, if possible. They are still eating their supper and sipping ale, and there is plenty of night remaining before they sleep. If you don't succeed tonight, you may not have the chance to try again."

The haggling began. He asked for more coins, more assurances of protection, more promises of safe passage while in Akkad. Annok-sur had agreed to them all. Sargat let himself relax the tiniest bit. All those tales he had heard of Annok-sur and her power now sounded foolish. She was just another woman, one willing to believe whatever she was told.

"Then I should go and see what I can learn."

Annok-sur smiled, but turned to Lady Trella. By now he had nearly forgotten her presence.

"How many seasons do you have, Sargat?"

Lady Trella's odd question surprised him, and despite the soft tone of her voice he felt a hint of his prior nervousness return.

"I have eighteen seasons, Lady Trella."

"You shouldn't lie to us, Sargat. You have only sixteen seasons."

He started to protest, but she held up a slim hand.

"That doesn't matter, of course. But lying about helping us, when instead you plan to just disappear again, that is something we cannot tolerate. You may be a very agile thief, but your eyes, your face, all show your lies."

"Lady Trella, I ..."

"Be silent!" She raised her voice. "Wakannh!"

The door opened at once, and Wakannh stepped inside the room. In one hand he carried a large block of wood. In the other, a small bronze axe. The block, Sargat noticed, appeared stained a darker color.

"The penalty for lying to us is to have your tongue removed." Trella leaned closer for a moment, and Sargat caught a glimpse of her brown eyes fixed on his own, as if staring into his heart. "The penalty for being a thief is to have your right hand cut off. Which of these would you prefer to have done to you first?"

She uttered the words in the same soft voice a woman would use with her lover, but Sargat felt a chill pass through him.

He glanced back at Wakannh, standing there, patiently waiting for the order to begin. Suddenly he realized that she would as easily give that order as not. "I ... Lady Trella ..."

"You had a friend named Tammuz once. Do you remember him? He befriended you many times, even saved your life once by hiding you from the guard. You undertook a similar mission for him once, just before Korthac seized control of the city."

Sargat felt his heart racing. How did she know about these things, events that happened years ago? He'd told no one, and only Tammuz knew. "Yes, I remember him, Lady Trella. But Tammuz left the city years ago."

"And I know where he went. Before he left, Tammuz told me you could be trusted. Was he wrong? Or would you let Akkad's enemies capture the city and put everyone to the sword, yourself included?"

Sargat remembered that Tammuz had fought against Korthac when the king recaptured the city. Sargat had thought that a foolish risk at the time, but now he realized that even then Tammuz must have been working for Lady Trella. That meant ... what did any of this mean?

"I ... I will do as you ask, Lady Trella. I swear it on Marduk's –"

"No need for that, Sargat. Just your word as a thief. And you will be rewarded, and I will be able to tell Tammuz how well you served both him and his city. If you try to escape, you will find no one will help you, no hiding hole so deep that I cannot find you. And if you give away your presence to our enemies, then you will spend many days with the pain-givers before you repay your crimes. So think carefully before you speak again. Will you learn what these strangers want in Akkad, and will you bring that information back to me – if for no other reason than it would give honor to your friendship with Tammuz?"

Sargat found his throat dry, and had to swallow before he could answer. "I will not fail you, Lady Trella. If you speak for Tammuz, then I will do what you ask."

She kept her gaze on him for a moment, as if searching for the truth in his words. "Wakannh, take Sargat to where the strangers are staying. Give him whatever help he needs, and when he is finished, bring him back to me."

"Yes, Lady Trella."

Sargat saw the guard bow, but caught a glimpse of disappointment on his face. No doubt the man would have preferred to use his axe.

All that had transpired not long ago. Now Sargat lay stretched along the roof of the adjoining hut, his weight spread out over as many roof poles as possible. The poles had creaked a little when he settled in. Unless one kept to the edges of the mud-brick walls, a little noise was unavoidable. Sargat had squirmed and wriggled his way over the tops of people's heads for more than ten of his sixteen years. Victims, he'd learned, might wake at any little sound, but if they then heard nothing, they were likely to fall back asleep, or attribute what they'd heard to some bird, cat or rodent moving about.

This roof was scarcely two body lengths from end to end. He picked his way across, taking his time and always letting part of his weight settle before he moved the rest. When he reached the small ledge that separated the two huts, he heard movement on the other side. Either someone was sleeping on the roof, or a guard was keeping station.

Gradually he lifted his head, moving so slowly that, even if the guard happened to be looking in that direction, he might not notice the tiny change in the ledge's silhouette. When Sargat's right eye cleared the top, he saw a man laying on his back, staring upwards, his hands behind his head. The relaxed position told Sargat that the sentry didn't expect anyone to disturb his rest.

Sargat settled back down and considered his choices. Despite all of Annok-sur and Wakannh's warnings, Sargat hadn't expected to find anyone up on the roof. At worst he'd expected the thieves or whatever they were to stick their heads up occasionally through the smoke hole and look around. That was usually enough to ensure privacy for those below. But the guard's presence ended most of Sargat's easy plans. It also confirmed that these strangers were up to no good, and were probably dangerous.

He took another glance over the wall, studying the prone form of the man less than four good paces away. Before Sargat ascended to the nearby roof, Wakannh had sketched the layout of the two chambers that formed the structure below. Twice as long as wide, the men were likely gathered near the back end of the house. That meant that Sargat could hear whatever conversations were being held below without coming too close to the smoke hole. If he could get across the ledge, and take up a position directly behind the guard, he might lie there unnoticed, even if the sentry should glance around. With nothing breaking the line of the roof, Sargat knew the guard's eye would skip over the darkness, and search only for the contrast lines where dark and light met.

Ordinarily, this would be foolhardy, and Sargat had never been a fool. But the chance for plenty of silver – not to mention placing Lady Trella in his debt – made the risk worthwhile. Besides, if the guard did notice Sargat's presence, he would be up and running over the rooftops to where Wakannh and his men waited. Despite what Lady Trella had said, he didn't think they'd kill him if the strangers detected his presence.

The decision made, Sargat rose up and began climbing over the dividing ledge. Moving each of his limbs one at a time, he resembled a spider more than a man. The sentry never moved. The man remained relaxed and at rest, lost in his thoughts. The idea that someone might try to creep up beside him on the roof never entered his head.

Sargat kept his eyes focused on the guard. The slight creaks that his slow movements created were not what was important. Those down below would attribute any noises to the guard shifting about. As long as the sentry didn't decide to turn his head and study carefully the rooftop behind him, Sargat kept moving forward.

At last he reached his position, about an arm's length from the back of the guard's head. Turning his eyes downward, he eased his face against the roof poles, his weight spread out over as wide an area as possible. He didn't worry about the poles giving way under his slight weight, since those who dwelt inside would be used to sleeping on the roof during the hot weather, and most families added more trimmed branches than they really needed.

Beneath him, he could see almost nothing. Vague shadows outlined heads, and he guessed about five or six men were in the main chamber. Wakannh had made the same estimate, so at least none of the strangers had slipped away. No candles burned, and only a little moonlight filtered down through the smoke hole.

At least now he could hear them talking, actually make out what they were saying. But the men spoke about women, ale, even the warm weather. One complained that he preferred the ocean breezes of Sumeria. The desultory conversation went on and on, without Sargat hearing anything of use to anyone. It looked as if he would have to remain where he was until they decided to fall asleep. Even Sargat started relaxing, despite the presence of the guard less than an arm's length away.

Then another voice broke into the conversation, one that Sargat hadn't heard before. He realized that another man had entered the hut and joined the group. All the idle talk ceased, and the men shifted about, as if preparing themselves.

"Rattaki! You awake up there?"

The newcomer's low voice sounded harsh, the voice of someone used to giving orders.

The sentry jumped at the words, and shifted his body to lean over the smoke hole. "Yes, I'm awake. Think I can sleep up here without a blanket?"

"Stay alert, then. You can listen from up there."

The sentry shifted his position, twisting his body and swiveling his head, and Sargat knew the man's gaze had swept over Sargat's prone figure. But the man saw what he expected to see, which was nothing. Sargat lowered his gaze, so that the whites of his eyes didn't show.

"The rest of you, pay attention. I've gotten word back from the horsemen. They'll rush the wall tomorrow night when the moon reaches its highest point. It should give us enough light, and most of the guards will be half asleep by then. All we have to do is kill a few sentries, and get the ropes over the wall. Then the eight of us will hold the Akkadians off until the barbarians mount the wall. Each of us will wear a strip of cloth tied around the right elbow. Otherwise these bastards are as likely to kill us as anyone else inside the city."

Tomorrow night! If barbarians captured the city, Sargat's own plans would be disrupted. The barbarian horsemen would put everyone to the sword, men and women, honest men and thieves alike. And they'd be trapping everyone inside the city, to make sure no one escaped with anything of value.

"How many will be coming, Luroc?"

A new name, one that Annok-sur and her agents hadn't learned. Sargat decided that this Luroc was staying somewhere else, away from his men. He peered down through the branches. He couldn't see much of Luroc's features, but the man possessed a barrel-like body and a thick beard that concealed much of his face.

"How should I know? Five hundred, a thousand. They've got a dozen ladders prepared, and they'll head for the gate as soon as enough of them are over the wall. More than enough to brush aside these old men and new recruits."

Sargat concentrated on Luroc's voice. He possessed a strong accent, marking him as a man from the southern-most lands of Sumeria.

"You're sure they know where to attack? Can they find –"

"They've already marked the Tanner's Lane," Luroc said. "They'll be able to find it even if clouds hide the moon."

"And our gold? When do we get paid?"

"As soon as we get back to Sumer. A boat will be waiting to take us south and we'll be there in four or five days. Queen Kushanna will be eager to hear of our victory. And you'll take onboard whatever loot we can pick up when the barbarians overrun the city. So just keep your mouths shut for another day. That means no drinking, no women, and no talking. Stay in the house as much as possible. And no one goes anywhere alone. I'll cut the heart out of anyone who even thinks about doing or saying anything stupid."

Luroc answered a few more questions, until he grew annoyed with the process. Sargat decided that all these things had been discussed before, probably more than once. Luroc had come only to inform his men about the date and time of the attack, and go over the plan one final time. He would slip back into whatever hideout he had prepared for himself, one where his name would not be Luroc.

At last the men grew silent. "Enough then. I'll meet you at the wall just before the moon reaches its peak." With one last word of warning to keep quiet and out of trouble, Luroc left the room. The sentry on the roof swung his legs over the smoke hole and skimmed down the ladder, his eyes focused only on his descent.

Sargat waited until the first snore wafted up through the hole. Then one by one he stretched his muscles for the first time, making sure he could move without any problem. Taking his time, he retraced his movements back to the ledge. This time he used the ledge to travel across the back of the huts, until he reached a place where he could drop lightly down to the ground. A dozen paces away, Wakannh and one of his men waited, but neither of them heard or saw Sargat's approach until he stepped out of the shadows.

"Demons below!" Wakannh swore. "Where did you come from?"

"Did you see someone enter and leave?" Sargat couldn't keep the excitement from his voice.

"We saw a man enter, but didn't see anyone come out. Thought it was just one of the men returning from taking a piss. Why?"

"Never mind. Take me back to the Compound. I need to talk to Annok-sur and Lady Trella."

"It's the middle of the night. Are you sure . . . ?"

"I'm sure. Now let's get moving, before any more time slips by!"

Lady Trella sat across the table from Bantor, his face framed by the two thick candles burning at either side, despite the lateness of the night. He'd just arrived from the barracks, at Trella's summons. Annok-sur sat next to Trella, as she usually did. An excited Sargat, accompanied by Wakannh, had just completed the second recitation of what he'd heard for Bantor's benefit, before leaving Akkad's leaders alone.

"And Sargat is convinced the attack will come tomorrow?" Bantor's face showed his concern. "There's been no word of any horsemen loose in the countryside, at least not anywhere near here. Our scouts have reported nothing so close. According to them, the barbarians are still many miles away."

"That's what he heard them say," Lady Trella said, "and I believe him. If we had any word of barbarians drawing near, you would have doubled the sentries on our gates and walls. Shulgi must have prepared this attack the same way he plotted the assault on Kanesh, a sudden strike by horsemen without any hint of their movements. Food for the riders and grain for the horses could have been hidden along their way, awaiting their arrival."

"It is possible, isn't it?" Annok-sur leaned forward. "If they wanted only to attack Akkad, and not raid the countryside, could they reach here without any word?"

Trella saw Bantor clench his fist on the table. He'd brought the news of the Alur Meriki raiding to the east and coming this way, and he didn't like the idea that his outriders might have failed to detect their close approach. But despite what he lacked in imagination, he was no fool when the possibility of danger to Akkad arose. He knew the Alur Meriki could travel vast distances when necessary.

"If they swung to the north-east, then rode straight in. They'd have to cover a lot of ground at night, at least fifty miles from daybreak to midnight. That's a lot of riding in the dark."

"Skilled riders, with extra horses, carrying torches, and a well-marked trail prepared in advance." Trella kept her voice persuasive. Bad enough Bantor had to deal with his wife's authority from time to time. "We've done such things ourselves. We've no reason to believe Alur Meriki can't do such things even more efficiently."

He gave in to their pressure. "I guess they could manage it. But there's only one direction they could take to make this work. I can have riders out in the morning. As soon as we see them coming, we'll have plenty of time to prepare." He glanced up at the window, to gauge the progress of the moon. "Plenty of time left tonight to round up the Sumerians. It won't take much to make them tell us who their leader is and where he's hiding."

Trella took her time replying. In the interval since Sargat had completed his story, and Bantor's arrival, she'd thought long and hard about the choices facing her. The easiest and safest solution was to do as Bantor said. Capture the Sumerians, put them to the torture. Even if they didn't know where their leader was, they knew enough of the plan to confirm Sargat's story. And once confirmed, the city could prepare itself. No force of horsemen, no matter how fierce or numerous, could scale Akkad's high walls once they were properly defended.

Nevertheless, that solution left her unsatisfied. Like everyone else, she wondered what Eskkar would do faced with the same facts. Unlike Bantor and the other commanders, Eskkar would seek to gain some opportunity from this information, to turn the enemy attack into a defeat. She knew he would not enjoy sitting idly behind Akkad's walls while raiders – foiled in their attempt to slip into the city – terrorized the countryside.

"Is there something else you would consider, Trella?" Annok-sur realized the time for a quick reply had long passed.

"I don't want these horsemen destroying the farms and crops," Trella began, still working out the idea in her head. Eskkar always had his battle experience to guide him, but she had lived and fought beside him for over four years, and in that time, she'd insisted he relate every tale, every adventure, every fight that he'd even been in. And not just once, but time and again, asking him to explain each choice and the reasons behind it, and the likely consequences.

"We're another thirty or so horsemen coming down from Bisitun," Bantor said. "They can patrol the countryside around the city."

She made up her mind. "No. I don't want these men driven away. I want these barbarians destroyed, or at least defeated. Otherwise they'll do as much damage to the crops as Shulgi and his whole army. Between them they'll destroy almost every farm supplying Akkad."

Bantor shook his head. "They won't attack in force once they see we're ready for them."

"I know." Trella let the smallest hint of authority strengthen her words. "So perhaps we should let them into the city."

Even Annok-sur looked askance. "What are you saying? Let them in?"

"Remember during the Alur Meriki siege, when Eskkar proposed the same thing? He had a plan to let them over the walls, then attack them."

Bantor snorted. "I remember that . . . idea. Gatus and the rest of us didn't care for it then. Eskkar likes to gamble, but we all thought the plan too risky. And we had a larger force of bowmen at our command than we do now."

"Ah, but then we didn't have the leader of the Sumerians to help us invite them in." As she spoke, Trella felt her own conviction increasing. Not only was this the right choice, it was what Eskkar would do if he were here. And the risk to Akkad could be managed. "With Luroc helping us, I think we can make it work."

She went over the ideas sketched out in her mind during the night. Annok-sur sought to find weakness in the plan, improving on some of Trella's suggestions. By then Bantor, either half convinced or unwilling to argue with both his wife and Trella, decided that it might, just might, be done without too much risk .

"Good." Trella stood and placed her hand on Annok-sur's shoulder. "Now all you have to do is find where this Luroc is hiding and bring him here. Bantor, you'll have to prepare what we need, and all without telling anyone except your most trusted subcommanders what we're planning."

Bantor got no sleep for the rest of the night, nor did his wife. While Bantor summoned those men he felt certain he could trust for the coming day's work, Annok-sur started the search for Luroc. By dawn, more than twenty women walked Akkad's lanes, whispering Luroc's vague description to dozens of other women, who in their turn spoke to others. In this way, every hut, tavern, shop and residence in the city came under their scrutiny, but without arousing suspicion.

Nevertheless, midday came and went without any sign of the elusive Sumerian. For a man who'd been in Akkad for several days, he'd managed to stay out of sight. As the day grew short and they ran out of places to search, Trella suggested another possibility, namely that Luroc might be staying at the home of some Akkadian merchant.

With that in mind, Annok-sur turned her attention to the upper-class traders and merchants. She soon discovered that only one merchant, Ramal-sul, had departed the city that morning by boat, heading north to Bisitun. And he had taken his family with him, leaving his servants in charge of the household.

With that fact, Bantor gathered some men. Then he went to Ramal-sul's house and knocked on the door. When the servant opened it, Bantor asked to speak with the master's guest, and the servant had duly let Bantor into the inner courtyard.

Luroc, sitting comfortably on a shady bench, took one look at Akkad's Captain of the Guard, and reached for his sword.

"Don't do anything foolish, Luroc," Bantor said, holding up his hands. "The house is surrounded, and there are men on the rooftops. We know all about your plan for tonight, so it's not like you have to betray any secrets."

Bantor spoke quickly. He wanted Luroc to know the situation before he attempted anything foolish.

"My men could have taken you prisoner any time in the last few days, even last night after you gave your men their final instructions and left their hideout. Or I could have entered the house with a dozen men and rushed you before you knew we were there. Instead, I've come to offer you an arrangement. Lady Trella wishes to speak with you. I'm to bring you to her."

"Who betrayed me?" The gruff voice held more disgust than anger.

Bantor leaned carefully against the courtyard's entrance. He didn't intend to get any closer to a desperate man with a sword in his hand. "I really don't know. Does it matter?"

Luroc, the sword in his hand, shook his head.

Bantor saw the man preparing himself for a death fight. "If you want to live, I suggest you come quietly and listen to what Lady Trella has to say. You'll find she can be quite generous. Otherwise . . . best fall on your own sword."

Before Luroc could decide what to do, the Captain of the Guard turned and left the room, leaving Luroc standing there still holding his naked blade.

Luroc took only moments to make up his mind, perhaps assisted by the sight of two armed men who appeared on the roof of the house, peering down into the inner courtyard. One man carried a bow with a shaft already nocked to the string.

Stepping out of Ramal-sul's front doorway a few moments later, Luroc found Bantor and two guards waiting there. The Sumerian's sword rested in its scabbard. The soldiers looked competent, and Bantor was known to be a powerful fighter.

"No need to worry, Luroc," Bantor said. "Walk beside me, as two old friends would do."

Together they walked the lanes of Akkad, crossing half the city before they reached Eskkar's house. At Bantor's approach, the guards opened the gate and the little group passed inside.

Annok-sur waited just outside the entrance to the house. "Please give Bantor your sword, Luroc. Only the Hawk Clan is permitted to carry weapons in Lady Trella's presence.

For a moment, Bantor thought the man would try something stupid. But Luroc kept control of his emotions. He reached for his blade, and Bantor's two men moved in closer, just in case Luroc decide to start hacking at everyone. Using his fingers, he drew the sword from its scabbard and handed it to Bantor.

Annok-sur led Luroc into the house and up the stairs, to where Trella waited for them at the big table in the workroom. Another guard stood beside her, in case the Sumerian decided to leap across the table. Bantor remained just behind their guest.

"Please sit down, Luroc," Lady Trella began. "I imagine you could use some wine. Or ale if you prefer."

Annok-sur moved around the table to stand beside Trella. Annok-sur reached down and filled a cup with watered wine, which she handed to Luroc.

The man took it with both hands, as he slid into the seat across the wide table. By now the shock of his capture had started to sink in, and he looked like a man who knew he would soon be dead.

"As Bantor may have told you," Trella said, "we know of your plot to help the barbarians slip into the city. Since that will not succeed, you may want to consider another option. How much gold did King Shulgi promise you?"

Lady Trella's pleasant voice contrasted sharply with the harder tones of Queen Kushanna. Nevertheless, both women expected to be obeyed when they spoke.

"Twenty gold coins to prepare the men." He took another gulp from the wine cup. "Fifty more if the attack succeeded."

"The king of Sumeria is generous, but I am willing to exceed that price. I will give you safe passage to one of the northern cities and seventy-five Akkadian gold coins if you are willing to help us. With that much gold, you should be able to find a place of safety far from this war."

Luroc's eyes widened at the sum, and he decided the wild stories of Akkad's gold mine at Nuzi were true. With that much gold, he would never need to work again. "How can I help you?"

"By making sure the barbarians enter the city, of course. The city's guard is even now collecting your men. They'll be sentenced to the labor gangs for the rest of their lives. Bantor's men will replace them and you will be on the wall at Tanner's Lane tonight to bring the barbarians into the city."

"You want the barbarians to cross over your walls?"

"Yes. Our men will be waiting for them, of course."

"They'll capture your city. Even if they don't, they'll kill so many of your soldiers you won't be able to resist Shulgi's army when it gets here."

"Perhaps. But that will not concern you. You will have your gold and be on a boat going north. Unless you prefer the alternative."

Luroc glanced behind him. Bantor still stood there, but now his right hand rested on the hilt of his sword. The guard standing just beside Lady Trella had not taken his eyes off Luroc for a moment.

Luroc wet his lips, then realized he still held the wine cup. Another mouthful seemed to ease his choice.

"How do I know you will keep your part of the bargain?"

"The word of Lady Trella has never been broken," Annok-sur said. "If you do as we ask, you will not be harmed. You and the gold will be free to leave at sunup. Several boats will be departing to the north. Or you can even return to Sumeria, if you wish."

Returning to Queen Kushanna's presence without the destruction of Akkad to report didn't appeal to Luroc.

Trella gave him a moment to work things through. Then she nodded. "I give you my word you will not be harmed."

Luroc drained the wine cup, and pushed it toward the center of the table. Like any good gambler, he knew when he was beaten. "I don't think I'll be going back to Sumer. What do you want me to do?"

The long day had finally given way to dusk, then darkness. Since Luroc decided to change his allegiance, if indeed the mercenary ever had any, Trella had remained with Bantor most of the day. She and Annok-sur questioned the spy at length, obtaining the names of all his men, and ascertaining that no other Sumerian agents remained in Akkad. Bantor had dispatched Wakannh, who had been present at last night's meeting, to gather up all eight Sumerians, and they now languished in a single room at the barracks, guarded by a dozen men.

Trella insisted that Bantor go over every part of the plan. She knew the way her husband's mind worked, and she'd watched him in enough planning sessions over the last five years to know how he would proceed. Every step, every part, had to be discussed, responsibility assigned, every commander and his second in command had to fully grasp and understand the role he would play.

The carpenters had to be summoned and given their instructions. The rest of the city had to remain guarded as well throughout the night, as the barbarians might have more than one plot. No soldiers would be sleeping tonight. Those not involved at Tanner's Lane would be manning Akkad's walls, alert for any attack.

At the barracks, behind its closed gates, the soldiers prepared torches and poles, readied shields and spears, while archers tested their bows and changed to new bowstrings. The handful of spearmen remaining in the city prepared themselves for this new way of fighting. Even food and water had to be readied, to make sure that no one lacked for anything.

All this needed to be accomplished before sundown. Tonight, Trella wanted everything in Akkad to appear as normal as the night before. Only when the city lay cloaked in darkness were the men and equipment quietly assembled, brought together in small groups, and taken to their stations.

The waiting began. Trella leaned against a wall a hundred paces from Tanner's Lane. Annok-sur had wanted her to remain in the Compound, but Trella insisted on being there. Bantor protested as well, but gave way when he saw her determination.

"I must be there," she said. "I know how Eskkar would think and act. Tonight you will think of me as you would of him."

"But if it fails, you may be in danger."

"If I am sending men to fight and die, then they need to see me there, standing beside them. Would Eskkar do any less?"

No amount of words changed her mind. Before midnight, she arrived at Tanner's Lane, accompanied by her four Hawk Clan guards. She wore the short sword Eskkar had given her belted around her waist. He had taught her how to use it after Korthac's defeat.

Near one of the watch fires, Bantor and Luroc waited together for her arrival. Even in the flickering light, she saw the worry on Bantor's face.

"The men are ready, Lady Trella." At least Bantor knew better than to argue with her in front of the Sumerian.

"Nothing was said about me being tied to a rope." Luroc's words, though spoken just above a whisper, sounded bitter.

Luroc had been forced to remove his tunic, and a slim but stout rope was fastened around his waist, then fed out through a hole cut in the back of the garment. Wakannh had the other end of the rope fastened around his body.

"That's just in case you decide to slip over the wall and rejoin your companions," Trella said. "Though they'd probably kill you anyway at the first alarm." She had been the one who suggested the rope to Bantor. "Wakannh will stand next to you at all times, as if one of your trusted men. If you try to escape, or give us away, you'll find yourself hanging over the fire pit in the morning."

"I'll keep my end of the bargain."

"Then all will be well for both of us," she answered.

The waiting began. The moon still climbed upward in the heavens, slower than it usually did, it seemed to those watching. But at last the moon reached its zenith.

"Clear the wall," Bantor ordered in a low voice. One by one, the sentries on the wall ducked below the wall, then dropped to the ground below or moved rapidly but silently down the parapet's steps. The barbarians, if indeed they were out there, would have been waiting for the guards to be taken out.

Luroc, with Wakannh at his side, moved to the top of the wall, now empty of sentries. Luroc leaned over and waved a bit of white cloth.

Neither man could see much, but then Luroc stiffened. Wakannh saw them, too, and his hand tightened on the rope.

The ground beyond the ditch seemed to be alive, like a field covered with locusts, as crouched men moved quickly and silently over the empty ground. In moments, a wave of men dropped down into the ditch. Bent low, they raced to the base of the wall. It took only moments to locate the two ropes Bantor's men had thrown over the edge.

The ropes tightened as men started the climb. Ladders bumped softly against the wall as well. Then a figure swung up over the top, glanced around, and saw the two men standing there. The whites of the barbarian's eyes shone in the moonlight. He swung over the wall, his hand on his sword.

"Wait!" Luroc whispered just loud enough to be heard. "I'm Luroc. The way is clear."

Without waiting for a reply, Luroc turned away, and he and Wakannh moved to the steps and raced down the steps. They disappeared into the shadows at the entrance to the lane.

Bantor waited for them there. He could hear the small sounds of bodies scraping and slipping over the wall. Soon he saw the barbarians, their number swelling, readying weapons.

From the shadows a few steps away, Trella watched the parapet fill with the enemy. More and more kept coming, helped up and over by their companions. She heard the faint rasp of swords being drawn from scabbards, and noted the silhouette of one or two bows.

Behind her the soldiers shifted, their breathing coming faster as they tensed up for the coming struggle. But their small sounds were masked by those on the wall. In the faint moonlight, Trella saw that everyone had moved to their assigned places. At last she heard the sound of wood scraping against wood as the barricades moved into position, blocking off the parapet. If the barbarians detected them, they made no outcry.

"It's time." Bantor's whisper sounded harsh.

Trella moved silently across the open space at the end of the lane. Behind her the soldiers formed up in silence. Looking up, she saw the wall now swarmed with men. Some began to drop down off the parapet, others found the steps and ran down, and still more heads and shoulders crawled over the wall into the city.

Wakannh's voice boomed out over the lane. "Hoist the torches!"

The Alur Meriki froze in place as the first torch flared into being and was pushed out over the lane from the rooftop. Every eye watched as the long pole extended its flaming contents over the intruders, joined quickly by another and another, until five torches sputtered and blazed on each side of the open space and the barbarians could see the line of bowmen facing them, with another line of spearmen kneeling just in front of them, lances extended upwards. The Alur Meriki had time for that one glance.

"Loose!" Bantor's voiced echoed off the walls. For a brief moment the barbarians didn't move, not until the first wave of forty arrows crashed into their midst.

Warriors dropped like stones, screaming in pain as the arrows struck them. But the arrow storm unleashed the fury of men who suddenly realized they'd been lured into a trap. In the torchlight they could clearly see that every house and stall in the lane was boarded up, giving them no place to go but into the arrows ahead of them.

Bantor drew his sword. The leader of the bowmen continued to call the cadence and another flight of arrows, aimed low, struck at the invaders. Those barbarians still standing rushed forward, screaming their war cries as they charged at the forty men in front of them. Other Alur Meriki reinforcements continued to climb over the wall, eager to join the fighting and as yet unaware of what was happening.

Bantor's third wave of shafts included shafts from other archers on the rooftops, as bowmen climbed into position and added their own arrows to the carnage below them. The barbarians had only to cover about thirty paces to come to grips with their opponents, but the shafts flew again, and this time the charge broke.

The warriors had brought few bows of their own, certain that swords would be the most useful weapon once inside the walls. Instead they found themselves attacked by bowmen under the blaze of torches that lit the scene all too clearly.

Some tried to tear down the boards that blocked entry to the houses but the archers on the opposite roof turned their arrows on them. Others tried to move along the parapet, but the heavy wooden barricades, positioned to extend out over the parapet's edge, blocked that path, too. Behind those barricades stood villagers and soldiers with spears, who thrust at every head or hand that tried to climb over or swing around them. A few Alur Meriki managed to leap up and grasp two of the torches and dash them out, but it made no difference. Even two or three torches would have provided enough light for the archers.

Suddenly, the Alur Meriki began moving back, jamming the steps or pulling themselves up to the parapet, with no other thought in their minds but to get back over the wall. The archers' shafts continued to find them. Bantor shouted another order and the bowmen moved slowly forward, shooting together under command, shooting again and again until they reached the base of the parapet. By then nothing moved, not even the wounded at their feet, who died from a quick spear thrust. Shouting continued from the walls, as archers kept shooting at the surviving barbarians as they fled back across the ditch.

Bantor bellowed out a command to secure the wall, and soldiers began clearing the dead off the steps and parapet. Trella knew the fight here had finished. She turned to find Annok-sur at her side, a short sword gleaming in the torchlight.

A cheer went up from the men, the volume increasing until everyone had joined in, shouts of victory mixed with laughter at the barbarians, who had carefully planned their assault yet still stumbled into a deadly trap. Trella found herself surrounded by gleeful soldiers and villagers, as she turned away from the carnage and headed back to the Compound.

"That should send them running back to their clan," Annok-sur said. "It looks like we've killed more than half of them, I'm sure."

"The cavalry from Bisitun will hunt down any stragglers in the morning," Trella agreed. "I think those who escape will have little inclination to raid our lands."

"You planned this as well as Eskkar."

"Let's hope he has as much good fortune in the south. Send word in the morning. It will be one less worry for Eskkar."

"And what should I do with Luroc?"

"Pay him and let him go," Trella said. "He's not likely to trouble us again. Besides, once word of this gets out, the Sumerians will think he betrayed them."

Annok-sur put her arm around Trella's shoulders. "Let's hope the Sumerians fare as badly against your husband as these barbarians."

Trella's satisfaction at the victory lessened at the thought of her husband's danger. "Tell Yavtar's men to get word to Eskkar as soon as possible. The last thing he needs is to be worrying about Akkad."

46

Day 2

The soldiers plodded through the heat. Every strap rubbed the skin raw, and many men had taken off their sandals, to insure that they didn't wear out and to save them for combat. The sun grew hotter as they moved south, especially to men unaccustomed to it. The Sumerians had that advantage. Most of them were born and raised in the dry lands, and could withstand the sun and wind better than the men from the north. The soldiers wiped the sweat from their eyes and kept walking, though at every stop to rest men drank as much water as they could hold. Fortunately they splashed across several of the numerous streams that eventually found their way into the great sea.

The Sumerians kept horsemen at their rear and flanks, but only small bands, to keep track of where the Akkadians marched. So far, the enemy hadn't tried to launch any attacks. Just before midday, while the men were resting, one of the guards called out.

"Riders to the rear!"

Eskkar swung up on his mount to get a better look. In moments, the land behind him began to fill with horses. The large band of Sumerian cavalry that had followed them yesterday was coming closer, but not, as Eskkar realized, coming straight at them. They would pass the Akkadians on their left. These men were not Tanukhs, but they rode easy in their mounts, and Eskkar had to admire their training. These horsemen might be the pick of Sumeria's horse fighters.

"They're passing us." Grond shaded his eyes with his hand. "Probably headed to Larsa."

As the enemy came abreast of the Akkadians, Gatus gave the order that got the men back on their feet and into marching position. "Stop gawking at that scum! You'd think you never saw a horse before!"

Enemy horsemen or not, Gatus got the men moving. He wanted to make camp tonight where they planned, and he was determined that his spearmen would lead the way, even if they collapsed when they reached the destination.

"They're going to Larsa, all right," Eskkar said. "They'll be waiting for us when we get there."

Gatus came over to join them. "Think they'll try anything?"

"Not this bunch," Eskkar said. "I'll bet that Razrek is leading them. He'll be glad to take some comfort in Larsa for a few days."

"Then the people of Larsa may be happy to see us when we arrive," Gatus said, not entirely in jest. "Razrek with that many men accompanying him will be a demanding guest."

Eskkar grunted in agreement. A large force of men and horses might not be too welcome in Larsa. They would eat and drink and chase the city's women, and if all the tales told about Razrek were true, his men would pay not a copper coin to the city's inhabitants.

Before long, the riders disappeared in the distance. "Well, tomorrow we'll see the rest of the cavalry," Eskkar said. "We'll have some fighting before tomorrow's march ends."

"Good." Gatus didn't sound concerned. "The men need to be blooded anyway, so the sooner the better. The more fighting they do, the better they'll get at it." He pulled himself up onto the mare and cantered to the front of the column, where he shouted orders for the men to pick up the pace.

"Bloodthirsty old bastard," Grond commented.

"That he is," Eskkar said, laughing. "But more than that, he wants to see his training in action. For that, he's willing to ride an old mare, wear a foolish hat, and sleep on the ground. And that's why he refused to stay in Akkad, where he belongs."

"Well, let's hope that it isn't us who get bloodied." As Grond made the wish, he spat on the ground for good luck.

The forced march continued, with the men stretching their legs in earnest. They had a long way to go, but Gatus and his men didn't disappoint during the long day. They made their distance, reaching the tiny stream just a little before sunset. That gave the men time to gather some firewood, and start a few fires burning. The more ambitious men had collected some sheep and cattle during the day's march, and soon the smell of burning flesh floated in the air.

The Akkadians had taken everything useful from the few farms they passed, stripping the land of anything edible. If they could have ranged out, they could have taken more, but the enemy horsemen shadowing their march were waiting for just that occurrence. Eskkar knew he had to keep his force close together. If they spread out, the Sumerian cavalry would cut them to shreds.

No doubt Razrek's horsemen were doing an even more efficient looting of the countryside. They'd grown so used to terrorizing those living within Akkad's borders that they had no qualms about looting Sumeria's own people.

Most of the farmers in their path had fled at word of the Akkadians' approach, but a few animals were still to be found, and they provided a bit of fresh food to stretch the now stale bread that filled a man's stomach but didn't satisfy hunger. A handful of red-faced men had discovered a skin of wine hidden somewhere along the march and drained its contents in moments, before the rest of their companions even knew what they'd found.

The food sacks contained less weight by now, and would be even lighter after the men washed down their evening bread with water. Most would rip the loaf in half and soak the stale bread in the stream to make it easier to chew.

Everyone settled in for the night, groaning in relief at the opportunity to stretch out and give their tired legs a rest. Behind them, the Sumerian cavalry's camp fires glowed in the distance, and Eskkar saw that the number of horsemen pursuing them had increased. Trella's estimates of Sumer's horse fighters had ranged between thirty-five hundred and four thousand, and except for those who had ridden on to Larsa, Eskkar guessed that the remainder were camping little more than a mile from his own campsite.

Gatus posted even more guards tonight than yesterday. Eskkar and the rest of the commanders were waiting for him when he returned.

"The sentries are out and alert," Gatus said as he squatted down beside the fire, stretching his back with a sigh of satisfaction. "I warned them to be especially alert for any Sumerians sneaking up on them in the night, either to slit their throats or launch a few arrows at us from the darkness."

"Two can play at that game," Eskkar said. "I've asked Chinua and Shappa to join the commanders from now on. We're going to need their skills for the next few days."

Shappa, still short of his sixteenth birthday, seemed in awe of the men gathered around Eskkar. The slingers Shappa had helped train were attached in groups to sections of the archers and spearmen, so until now no single leader to speak for all of them had been needed.

Eskkar, however, had wanted some men to act as pickets and skirmishers, men or boys short in stature and quick on their feet. Shappa had picked out twenty such men during the long months of training, and he kept command of that group. They had trained to creep out into the darkness, gathering knowledge of the enemy's position, killing any enemy sentries they could, and protecting the Akkadian camp.

During the training, many of the older soldiers had laughed at the need for such men, but Eskkar ignored them. He'd slipped up on enough sleeping enemy encampments to know what could happen, and he didn't intend to take such a risk with his own camp.

"Shappa, I want your slingers out there beyond the sentries. It's likely the enemy will be sending bowmen against us during the night, trying to pick off our guards or just trying to shoot a few arrows into the camp. We need to kill or drive them off. Otherwise, we'll be dodging arrows all night while the men are trying to sleep."

"Yes, Lord Eskkar." Shappa's voice cracked at the words, and the rest of the group smiled.

Most of Shappa's slingers were short and slim, and their weapon made almost no noise when it launched a stone. A bow's sharp outline could often be seen against the night sky, and its twang heard. For this sort of action, the skirmishers had practiced using another way to cast a stone, whirling the missile around their heads. It wasn't as accurate a way to launch a missile, but it could be done while hugging the ground, and at close range was almost as effective.

"Collect your men," Eskkar went on, "and get them ready. I want them out in the darkness tonight." He turned to Chinua. "I know the Ur Nammu can move silently in the darkness. Do you think a few of your men could reach the enemy camp?"

Mindful of the warriors' pride, Eskkar had taken pains not to give them a direct order. Better to tell them what was needed, and let them offer to help.

Chinua had said little to anyone during the last few days, and the rest of the Akkadians had left him and his warriors alone.

"I can take three or four men out into the night," he said, speaking slowly, to make sure everyone understood him. "We can hunt those the enemy will send against you."

"That would be good. Perhaps you and your men might even get close enough to loose a few shafts at their herds. A stampede would slow them down."

The warrior took his time before answering, and Eskkar had almost decided to drop the matter when Chinua spoke.

"I will speak to my warriors. After we have killed anyone approaching us, the way should be clear to reach their camp."

Eskkar drew his knife and scratched out an outline of the camp in the dirt. "Shappa, you will take your men out here and here. This path," he indicated a line that led directly toward the nearest Sumerians, "will be for the Ur Nammu. The rest of your warriors, Chinua, should guard that path, so that your men are not attacked when they depart and return."

Shappa darted off to find his slingers, while Eskkar and the commanders made sure everyone knew what was happening. He didn't want fifty archers launching arrows into the darkness while some of his men were out there.

The Akkadians were settling down for the night. Snoring loud enough to wake the spirits soon drowned out all other sounds. Meanwhile, Chinua and five men slipped away in the darkness, and soon afterward, Shappa took two groups of five into the night.

"You think the Sumerians will come?" Grond sat at Eskkar's side, alert as always for any danger to his commander and friend.

"They have to do something," Eskkar said. "Otherwise Shulgi is wasting his time having them follow us when he knows where we're going."

"They may wait until we reach Larsa. Then they can attack us from behind."

"Perhaps. Still, I think they'll try and worry us tonight. They'll do something more direct tomorrow," Eskkar said. "Remember, they're just trying to slow us down so that Shulgi can get to us."

Gatus laughed. "If that boy can march his army fifty miles in two days, I'll give him my hat when I see him. By the time we reach Larsa, he'll be at least three or four days behind us."

If there were no delays in the march, and if the men could keep up the pace in spite of any Sumerian attacks, Eskkar expected to reach Larsa in less than two more days. But something always went wrong, he reminded himself. Battles were often little more than a collection of mistakes, with victory going to the side that made the least. Which was why he and Trella had worked so long preparing the men and equipment needed to fight this war.

"Let's hope we can take the city before Shulgi arrives," Eskkar said. "And that will depend on Trella's people."

"She knows what's needed. As long as your luck holds out, barbarian, we'll take the city."

Eskkar grunted. The gods who controlled men's fates could change a man's fortune in a heartbeat. "Then you'd better offer some extra prayers, Gatus. I think we're going to need more than luck for the next few days."

47

Day 3

In the pre-dawn darkness, Eskkar rubbed the sleep out of his eyes. Not that he'd gotten much rest during the night. He woke at every odd noise, and walked the camp, talking to the sentries and worrying about the skirmishers and Ur Nammu. If the slingers were killed or captured, it would be a small loss. Nothing they knew could change the battle plan. But if too many of the Ur Nammu were lost, then the rest of Chinua's fighters might just decide they'd had enough of Eskkar's war, pull out, and head back home.

None of the men he'd sent out last night had returned yet, but he really wasn't expecting them before dawn. The sentries Gatus posted had kept a sharp lookout for anyone trying to creep up to the Akkadians. During the night, odd noises out in the land between the rival camps kept every sentry on edge. Just before midnight, a few arrows had come flying into the camp, and one sleeping soldier in the middle of the camp had taken an arrow in the leg. But the arrows stopped almost as soon as they had started, and never restarted.

Nevertheless, Eskkar greeted the dawn at the camp perimeter, watching anxiously for his men. As the sun rose he saw them, crouched over and moving quickly toward the camp. As they drew closer, the returning skirmishers broke into a run, waving their hands and they raced back as swift as a young horse to the camp's safety. Eskkar saw that two of them had blood on their tunics.

Shappa, out of breath but grinning like he'd just taken his first woman, jogged over to where Eskkar stood.

"Captain, we killed three of them, and drove the rest off. Did any get through?"

Eskkar had taken a quick count and saw that all of Shappa's men had returned. "No, only a few arrows launched from a distance. One man was wounded."

The slinger glanced around. "And the warriors? Did they make it back? We glimpsed them moving toward the enemy camp."

One of the sentries gave a shout, and Eskkar looked out to see a small herd of horses galloping toward the camp, urged on by the war cries of the Ur Nammu warriors.

"I'll be damned," Gatus said, yawning as he walked over to join them. "I thought you told them to stampede the horses, not steal them."

Eskkar shook his head. "You can't send warriors near horses. It's a sign of weakness not to try and steal a few. I should have known they would try something like this."

"Well, no thanks to you, but now we've got another ten spare horses to use as pack animals. I can put the wounded man on one. Another fool sprained his ankle, so he can ride, too, instead of tiring out his friends."

Eskkar had seen the man during the march, fighting the pain and supported on either side by his comrades, while others struggled under the extra weight of the man's gear.

Chinua rode up, his body drawn up to its full height, head held high and proud of his men's accomplishments. "Hail, Lord Eskkar. We killed six men, and captured ten horses."

Eskkar bowed in recognition of the Ur Nammu's success. He saw that one of the returning warriors had a bloody arm. "The horses are yours, of course, Chinua, but if my men may have the use of them . . . we will be in your debt for the animals."

Chinua turned to his men, speaking rapidly in their own tongue, explaining the arrangement.

"Get the men moving, Gatus." Eskkar raised his voice. "At least we've taught the Sumerians not to try and sneak up on us during the night. Now it's time to march."

They broke camp quickly. The men were used to eating as they walked, and it took little time to gather weapons and begin moving.

"Your skirmishers did well," Gatus said, when Eskkar guided his horse alongside the old soldier.

"And not a man lost," Eskkar agreed. "Now we'll see what they can do at Larsa."

Gatus drove the men hard the rest of the morning. They complained and groaned at the pace, but their legs kept moving, drawing closer to Larsa with each step, and no one dropped out. The archers, slingers and the rest of the company dared not complain, since they all carried less weight than Gatus's men. Instead they matched the spearmen's pace, and covered the ground with long strides that ate up the miles.

The Akkadians soon had their usual escort of enemy horsemen at their flanks and rear. By now, seeing so many of the enemy close no longer worried the infantry. It didn't matter how many Sumerian horsemen surrounded them, as long as the archers protected the spearmen, both were safe from Razrek's cavalry.

The enemy hadn't tried to stop them yet, but Eskkar expected that to happen soon enough. Once the Sumerian horsemen on Eskkar's left drew a little too close. Eskkar called out to Mitrac, who noticed the same encroachment and with a few swift orders, prepared his men.

When the enemy drifted a little closer, Mitrac barked out an order. One hundred archers stopped, strung their bows, and launched five arrows each. Many of the shafts fell short, and the riders turned and ran as soon as they saw the first flight of arrows, but at least half a dozen horses and men went down, caught by surprise by the rain of arrows. It wasn't much of an exchange for the five hundred arrows launched, but it would teach the Sumerians not to come too close.

In moments the archers jogged back to their place in their ranks, and the moving column hadn't even slowed its pace.

But just before noon, the scouts riding a few hundred paces in advance halted as they crested a low hill. Eskkar put his heels to his horse and rode out to join them.

Hundreds of Sumerians waited about eight hundred paces ahead. They'd built up a low breastwork of dirt and a few trees, and now stood behind the makeshift barrier. All the ones in the front had bows, and more men, some on foot, others on horseback, took position behind them. Eskkar glanced at the Sumerian horsemen who'd been shadowing them, and saw they had formed lines and moved in closer. They would attack if the Akkadians ranks stretched too thin. And if he decided to avoid this encounter, his men would waste valuable time.

It didn't matter. Before Eskkar had finished studying the enemy formation, Gatus took charge.

"Spearmen!" Gatus's voice rose up over the excited soldiers. "Take battle positions." His subcommanders shifted the men quickly from the column into a wider front, the spearmen three deep. They shrugged off their sacks, pulled bronze helmets onto their heads, and readied their shields and spears.

"Slingers!" Gatus's bellow could be heard by every Akkadian. "Form up behind the spearmen!"

The slingers, even more excited than the spearmen, took their position. This was their first test. They would have to provide support for the spearmen when they charged.

"Alexar, position the archers at the rear and flanks. Keep the horsemen at bay." Eskkar gave the command but Alexar knew what had to be done and had already dispatched his subcommanders. Every bow was strung, and arrows nocked to the string.

Gatus wheeled his horse from in front of the spearmen. "Prepare to advance at a walk!" He waited while the command was echoed down the line by the subcommanders. "Advance!"

Every left foot took the first step, and the line of spearmen strode confidently toward the Sumerians. They carried their heavy wooden spears low in the right hand, to conserve strength, while holding their shields high to protect the face and upper body. The second, third and fourth ranks, when they were in range of the enemy arrows, would raise their shields up to cover their heads.

The whole shift from a marching column to battle formation took only moments, and to the Sumerians it must have looked as if the Akkadians had hardly slowed their march.

Eskkar took position with his horsemen, pacing along behind the slingers. When the Sumerians broke, his small group of Akkadian and Ur Nammu riders would charge into the enemy rear.

Gatus had dismounted and handed his mare over to one of the camp boys. He walked just ahead of the slingers, guarded by two spearmen on either side.

Mitrac, bow in hand, led the archers only a few paces behind the slingers. A few more steps, and the enemy position was within their range.

"Archers! Prepare to shoot!" He, too, waited a moment for the command to travel up and down the line. "Shoot! Keep shooting!"

Seven hundred archers stretched in a line three deep behind him. Without breaking stride, they raised their bows and launched the first volley at the entrenched Sumerians. Another was on its way before the first landed, and a third a moment later.

Almost two thousand arrows struck the Sumerians with devastating effect, and before their own bows could even reach the approaching spearmen. But the enemy's first flight of arrows flew toward the advancing line. Most fell short, but a few struck the shields. One man went down, an arrow in his leg. More enemy arrows flew toward steadily advancing infantry, who now presented a shield wall to the front and overhead. The Sumerians could manage only a jagged volley that showed the nervousness of their archers, daunted by the sheer volume of shafts raining down on them. Eskkar saw their faces turning to the left and right, looking for the first man to turn and run, all of them hesitant now to stand in place against their Akkadian counterparts while the frightening line of spears moved steadily toward them.

By now the spearmen had covered half the distance. "Ready weapons!" Gatus had to bellow the command this time, as the noise and din of a battlefield began to grow.

As if it were a single movement, the spears were raised and held above the right shoulder. The second and third ranks moved even closer to the front, the raised shields now covering almost every part of the ranks.

"Charge!"

The spearmen broke into a run, but kept the line even and their shields held out before them. For the first time they voiced their war cries as they charged toward the enemy. "Akkad!" burst from twenty-eight hundred lungs as they charged.

Eskkar saw the first of the Sumerians turn and run. Fear spread quickly and more men abandoned their position. The Akkadians closed the gap in moments. Arrows continued to rain down on the fleeing Sumerians, and now stones from the slingers whizzed through the air, striking with a loud thud when they struck a shield, or with the softer sound of crushing flesh.

Almost none of the enemy stood their ground, and the few that did accomplished nothing by their bravery but their deaths. With shouts of "Akkad!" still ringing out over the ground, the spearmen smashed into the now abandoned barrier, scrambled over it and kept going at a run.

The Sumerians – caught by surprise at the rapid and deadly advance – turned to escape. But due to the speed of the attack, confusion reigned, as Sumerians bumped into each other as they tried to reach their horses. Stones from the slingers arched up into the sky before raining down on the confused mass, sending horses bucking and tossing riders from their backs. The archers followed, but they held their arrows until they climbed atop of what was left of the breastwork. That gave them a slight height advantage, and they stopped and began shooting.

The spearmen closed with those Sumerians still surging backwards. Most had thrown down their bows and now struggled to catch and mount their horses, escape their only thought. Eskkar never heard who gave the order, but the first rank of spearmen had reached within forty paces. They cast their long spears, drew their swords, and closed with the enemy.

The Ur Nammu – without waiting for the order – charged, sweeping around to the right, where a narrow piece of empty ground let them bypass the exultant spearmen. The rest of the Akkadian horses followed.

As Eskkar reached the crest, he pulled up and turned to see the rear. The Sumerians at their rear and flanks had hardly tried to approach. The remaining archers, staying close behind the charging ranks, had kept them at bay.

By the time he returned his gaze to what remained of the Sumerian position, the carnage had ended. Bodies littered the ground, horses and men, victims of arrows, stones, spears, swords. The Sumerians were still fleeing as fast as their horses could gallop, and more than a few were on foot and running for their lives, trying to reach the safety of their still-mounted brethren before the shouting Ur Nammu, shooting arrows as they rode, ran them down.

Gatus finally halted the advance. He gave the men a few moments rest, which they used to loot the dead of anything valuable. The Ur Nammu, too, broke off the pursuit, and devoted their time to collecting another two dozen horses.

Drakis strode up to Eskkar. "Gatus took the count, Captain. Forty-six enemy dead, probably as many again wounded. One of our men was killed, struck in the eye by an arrow. Five more wounded."

Eskkar grunted in satisfaction, the results more favorable than he had expected. Not many enemy dead, but only because the Sumerians had fled before the spearmen reached them. A good exchange. "Get the wounded on horses, and tell Gatus to get the men moving again." He glanced up at the sun. "We've wasted enough time here." Before Eskkar's order could reach him, Gatus and his commanders started regrouping the men, getting them into formation, and resuming the march.

That evening, after the men had eaten, Eskkar gathered his commanders around him.

"Today the men proved themselves, as did their commanders. You all fought bravely. There was no confusion, no doubt, no fear. The men followed Gatus's orders, and went forward without hesitation. Watching the Sumerians run like rabbits will give our men confidence. Meanwhile, the Sumerian cavalry will spread the word of their defeat. I doubt they'll be willing to face us again."

The smiles on their faces showed they agreed with his words.

"Now we'll face the next test. Tomorrow we'll reach Larsa. The Sumerians will be in the city and the cavalry will still be nipping at our flanks at every opportunity. We're probably three or four days ahead of Shulgi's army, but we won't have any time to waste. We need to take Larsa quickly. If we let Shulgi get too close, he might decided to sacrifice his horsemen just to slow us down."

"Razrek won't go along with that," Gatus said, "not from what we've heard."

"Razrek will do whatever he's told," Eskkar said, "provided there's enough gold in it for him. I don't want to take the chance. Remember, Shulgi will do what he thinks is needed to win. For him, victory makes up for any losses, no matter how steep. If he doesn't win, and soon, his soldiers may begin to wonder about their leader's plan."

"Then we'll make sure they all have plenty to worry about."

"That we will, Gatus. Now let's get the men to stop boasting about what they did today and have them get some sleep. Tomorrow is going to be another long day, with maybe a hard fight facing them. They may not have a chance to get much sleep again."

48

Just after mid-afternoon the Akkadian army rounded a bend in the Tigris and saw the city of Larsa, about two miles ahead. A ragged cheer arose at the sight, and Eskkar didn't know if his men were just glad to stop marching or if they looked forward to coming to grips with their enemy.

Without any distractions from the Sumerians, either last night or today, Eskkar and his soldiers made good time and reached the outskirts of the city with plenty of daylight left. Gatus had pushed the men so hard that even the strongest complained. By now the army had been marching at top speed every day for nine days, and some of the men who'd traveled down from the north even longer. Their legs might be tired, but muscles rippled on every limb. Yet all the mutterings ceased as soon as the men caught a glimpse of their destination.

In four days the Akkadians – unprotected by cavalry – had marched almost one hundred miles, a distance that Eskkar would not have believed possible two years ago. His men had accomplished something never before done, and he felt proud of them.

"Is that the farm?" Gatus had ridden up to join Eskkar and Grond atop a little hillock that gave them a better view of the city's outskirts.

"Yes, the one with three willow trees." Eskkar had just identified it from Trella's description. He'd visited Larsa twice before in his wanderings, but never paid any attention to the countless farms scattered over the landscape. This particular farm was about a mile from the city, and had the slight distinction of possessing two rickety jetties extending a few paces from the riverbank into the Tigris.

"Let's hope that Yavtar can find the place," Gatus said.

"He will." Eskkar had complete confidence in the master sailor, who long ago had memorized every turn and twist in the mighty river. "Now let's get there and make camp so the men can get some rest."

Gatus shouted to his commanders, and pointed the way forward. The Akkadians soon covered the last mile of their journey. Eskkar and Grond swung down from their horses in front of the humble house. The farm's owners had abandoned it as soon as they caught sight of the approaching soldiers, and Eskkar could still see the family running toward the city, carrying a few possessions and driving three cows before them as they fled. A good sign, he decided. That meant that word of their arrival hadn't yet reached every part of the countryside, or that his Akkadians had moved faster than anyone expected.

The soldiers settled in around the farm and started building their night camp. As soon as that task got under way, Gatus released the men in shifts, so that they could splash and bathe in the river, soak their feet, and clean themselves and their clothes for the first time in days.

Eskkar decided not to waste any daylight. "Bring the prisoners."

The Akkadian horsemen had rounded up fourteen men and women during the last half of the morning's march, all farmers except for one trader and his three porters, caught before they could scurry their way into Larsa. Every one of them looked terrified, not knowing what fate awaited them. Escorted into Eskkar's presence, he saw the trembling in their limbs and fear on their faces, no matter how well they tried to mask it. One or two seemed hardly able to stand, so great was their fright.

Instead of death or torture, Eskkar greeted them with a smile. "I am Eskkar, King of Akkad. I want you to forget what tales you've been told about me and my men. You are all free to go to Larsa. But I want you to carry a message for me to King Naran. You are to tell him to surrender his city to me by sundown. Tell him I offer the people of Larsa this one chance to save their homes and their lives. If King Naran does not surrender, I will destroy it and all those who resist."

Silence greeted his words at first, then quick smiles as they realized they might not be killed or enslaved. Eskkar made them repeat the message twice, to make sure they wouldn't forget it, and sent them on their way. They kept glancing behind them as they stumbled out of the camp, as if still expecting to be slaughtered.

"I never understood why men like that fear death so much," Grond said. "We all die sooner or later. Any chance of Larsa surrendering?"

Eskkar shook his head. "No, not with Razrek and his men inside the walls. He knows he only has to hold out for a few days, until Shulgi catches up with us. Even if King Naran were willing to take a chance on our mercy, Razrek is the real power in Larsa by now. But I had to give them the chance. It's something they and others will remember later."

"Good. I'd rather see this place torn down anyway. It's been a thorn in our side for years. When do we attack?"

"If Yavtar arrives by sundown, we attack tonight. If he doesn't come, we'll go tomorrow, with or without him."

"Do you want me to send some scouts up the river?"

"No, we don't want to call any attention to it yet. The Sumerians might try to intercept the ships, and we need those cargoes."

Eskkar stepped into the farmhold's main house, then climbed up the rickety ladder to the roof. It gave him a good view of the camp, bustling with activity, and he could even see upriver a little way. When Eskkar turned his gaze to the south, he enjoyed a good view of Larsa's walls rising up over the swells of land. He'd kept his worries to himself, at least as best he could, but the moment of truth had nearly arrived.

If they couldn't captured Larsa, which meant take it before Shulgi's vast army arrived, the Akkadians would be trapped between the two forces. In that case, Eskkar and his men would have to ford the Tigris and try to battle their way north, back to Akkad, his entire battle plan in ruins. If he failed here, his commanders, every man in the army would know the truth, and he would see it in their eyes.

He shook his head, and forced the gloomy thought from his mind. Eskkar had a powerful army at his disposal, and the enemy behind Larsa's gates would be fearing disaster. The city's inhabitants had been told that all the battles would take place in the north, that no Akkadians would ever step foot on Larsa's countryside. Now they knew that Shulgi had failed to deliver on his promised protection. Few would be resting comfortably in Larsa tonight, despite Razrek's reinforcements.

Below the farmhouse, Eskkar saw the orderly preparations of his men. They were ready for the coming battle, and as yet they had no doubts of success. Most of the soldiers believed in Eskkar's good fortune, his ability to snatch victory from any desperate encounter no matter what the odds. That belief had served him well, but it needed only one setback to shatter the aura of invincibility and luck they all believed in.

No sense worrying about defeat now, Eskkar resolved. He considered descending the roof and helping organize the men, but decided not to. Gatus and the others knew what needed to be done. Instead, Eskkar stretched out, flung his arm over his face, and closed his eyes. He wasn't as tired as most of his men, and the sun still shone brightly down on the land. Still he knew he needed to get as much rest as he could, because there would be no sleep for him tonight. Despite the noise and bustle surrounding the farmhouse, he fell asleep, hoping his luck would hold for one more day.

Inside the city of Larsa, late afternoon

A spy should not be such a pathetic creature. At least that's what Dragan told himself often enough. Still, being a cripple made him beneath notice, almost invisible, and today of all days he needed that. Dragan eased his way through the crowded lanes, trying to keep his balance, until he reached a nook where two huts joined and he could watch Larsa's main gate without getting trampled on. Nearly every step he took brought a burning pain that traveled the length of his right leg and up his back. The faster Dragan tried to move, the worse the spasm, almost as bad as those times when he stumbled and fell, or someone bumped into him and upset his balance.

Most days he managed to control the affliction, but today's hurried movements made his leg hurt even more than usual, and he forced himself to ignore the searing agony. Instead, he studied the crowd of people congregating near the gate. In the last two days, farmers and herders filled the city, bringing their families and even their animals. They had all abandoned their homes and sought refuge within Larsa's walls, desperate to avoid the dreaded Akkadians rumored to be coming toward them.

Larsa had never held so many people before. Two days ago Razrek and his eight hundred haughty horse fighters had arrived, bringing word of King Eskkar's rapid approach. The Sumerian cavalry filled the city, most of them drunk within moments of stabling their horses, often within the homes of the inhabitants, who protested futilely to King Naran. The city's guards, outnumbered by Razrek's men, could do nothing to stop the drunkenness, fighting and the assaults on Larsa's women, which often took place in the lanes while the crowd watched.

The Sumerian horsemen turned into gangs of heavily armed men who roamed the city and knocked down anyone who tried to stand in their way. At least a dozen men had died, killed for one reason or another by the Sumerians, and their murderers remained unavenged.

With the addition of those fleeing the countryside, the city's normal routine had collapsed, unable to sustain such numbers. Boisterous soldiers filled the shops and common areas, while their horses, causing almost as much trouble as their riders, were stabled in the marketplace and every open area. No one tried, or could, restrain Razrek's Sumerians. Larsa's regular guards refused to leave their barracks, and not even King Naran in his fine house could keep Razrek's men in check, even assuming he had the slightest interest in doing so.

Dragan cared nothing about Larsa's discomforts. He leaned against the house wall and took the weight off his leg, easing the pain somewhat. A hundred paces away, the big gates that sealed Larsa's main entrance began to close, a dozen men straining to push the thick beams into position. One last handful of people, screaming in fright at the thought of finding themselves locked out and left to the mercy of the Akkadians, squirmed through the narrowing opening, to fall to the ground exhausted.

But the two parts of the gate joined at last, and the gatekeepers grunted under the effort to bar the entry. Two good-sized logs rose into the air, hefted upward by more than a dozen arms, and were dropped into place, the men breathing heavily from the effort. The head gatekeeper then hammered the four wooden blocks into place, jamming the restraining beams to prevent them from moving. Shut fast, Larsa awaited the coming attack of the Akkadians. They'd been promised that the relief forces of King Shulgi would soon arrive to destroy the invaders. But the king of the Sumerians had also promised that their city would never face the wrath of the Akkadians, led by the barbarian demon Eskkar. With the enemy without, and Razrek's men within, no one in Larsa felt safe.

Satisfied with the security of the gates, its keepers returned to their posts within the watchtowers that rose up on either side of the entrance. Dragan waited until he was sure that nothing further would be done to seal the gate, then he straightened up, and limped painfully back to his home.

Between the press of the crowd and his leg, dusk had settled in by the time he reached the single-room dwelling that sheltered him and his brother, Ibi-sin.

"They closed the gate early. I could hear a few wretched people left outside, pleading to be let in." Dragan sighed in relief as he let himself slip to the ground, extending his twisted right leg. Laying flat on the dirt floor gave him the most comfort. The tiny room held only a stool for furniture and a carrying box that contained their tools. A pile of moldy leather skins rested in a corner and, spread out on piece of hide, were the leather goods Dragan and Ibi-sin made and sold to stay alive – wrist straps, arm protectors for the archers, rings, laces, and plaited leather bands to hold back a man or woman's hair, and a few other trinkets.

"Nothing more, just closed it?" Ibi-sin sank onto the stool. A leather patch covered his left eye. Almost three years ago, a horse fighter from Larsa had smashed the eye into jelly with the hilt of his sword, and Ibi-sin kept it covered to keep out the dust. A fleck of dirt lodged in the eye caused great irritation, and required immediate washing to hold down the pain.

"Just closed it, thank the gods. At least they didn't nail it shut. Now we just have to wait until the Akkadians come."

"Either tonight or tomorrow. They won't dare to wait any longer." Ibi-sin lowered his voice even more. "Then we'll have our revenge."

"Perhaps. If the gods approve." Dragan glanced at the open door to the house, covered only by a ragged blanket. "You'll have to go out and listen for the signal."

"I'll go now. It feels good to be doing something at last, after so long."

"Be careful, little brother," Dragan said.

He watched his brother leave, the blanket swaying from his passage. One of them always remained in the room, to guard against thieves who might slip in and steal anything they could get their hands on. In this poorer section of Larsa, none of the dwellings boasted a door, and each owner or tenant made sure a wife or child stood guard over their property every day.

Fortunately, their poverty and wretched existence provided a measure of protection from the Sumerian horsemen, who would otherwise have pushed their way in and taken whatever they wished. Razrek's men wanted women, ale or gold, not humbly made leather trinkets.

Just as the raiders had done to his family's farm, Dragan remembered.

Almost four years ago, soldiers from Larsa had ridden across the Sippar and pushed north, looting farms and murdering their inhabitants. The evil raids had continued until King Eskkar drove them back across the river.

But by then, Dragan's mother and father were dead, his two sisters raped and carried off to some unknown fate. Ibi-sin had been knocked unconscious, which had saved his life even though it cost him an eye. Dragan had tried to run, but one of Larsa's archers put a shaft into his leg. Dragan managed to crawl into the wheat field and hide in the tall stalks, and fortunately the archer had no interest in following after his wounded victim, not when women and loot waited for the taking. Dragan had passed out from loss of blood, and Ibi-sin, holding a bloody rag over his face, had finally found him half a day after the raiders had departed.

Both brothers had nearly died, but next day, after the raiders had gone, their uncle, who had a nearby farm, arrived and managed to nurse them back to health. But with so many mouths to feed, the injured brothers could only impose on their kinsmen for so long. Their uncle, with his crops and house destroyed, decided to move north, to a farm given him by the Akkadians. At any rate, he had little extra food to share with two cripples. As soon as the brothers could walk, like many others whose families had been murdered or driven off, they plodded north to Akkad. It took them almost a month to make the painful journey.

Dragan and Ibi-sin found Akkad crowded with other refugees from the south, as well as those seeking something beyond long hours laboring on their families' farm. Since the brothers' wounds prevented them from doing manual labor, they became beggars in the lane, pleading with passersby for food.

Then one day a woman had stopped before their begging bowl, looking them over before she dropped a copper coin into the bowl.

"May the gods send you blessings, honored mother," Dragan said gratefully. A copper coin meant a good meal for them both tonight.

"My name is Uvela," the woman said. "You are from the borderlands?"

"Yes, Mistress Uvela. My brother Ibi-sin and I were farmers there, until the raiders from Larsa came and killed our family."

To Dragan's surprise, Uvela squatted beside them. "Tell me what happened."

No one had ever asked for their story before. They told Uvela what evil fate had fallen on their family, answering every question about the hated raiders from Larsa. By then Dragan guessed that Uvela was one of those women who worked for Lady Trella, wife of King Eskkar. When he finished the last of their sad tale, Uvela offered her sympathy and left.

After that, she would stop by once or twice a week, giving them a copper coin each time, but never staying to talk. The days passed slowly, and Dragan and his brother grew weaker. Food might be plentiful in Akkad, but if one wanted to eat well, one had to work to earn it. Almost two months slipped by, and Dragan knew he and his brother were going to starve to death.

Then Uvela returned, but this time she dropped no coin in their bowl. "Would you like to earn some copper?"

"Of course, mistress," Dragan answered. "Anything we can do, anything . . ."

"Then follow me," she said, "but not too closely. It's best that no one knows our business."

With the two brothers trailing a dozen paces behind, she led the way to a small house near the river gate. Another woman was there, and food was spread out on a blanket. Dragan and Ibi-sin dropped to their knees and devoured bread, cheese, dates and the first ale they'd had in many days.

When they finally finished eating, the other woman spoke to them.

"My name is Annok-sur. Would you like a chance to strike back at Larsa for killing your family?"

Three months later, Dragan and Ibi-sin had regained much of their health and strength. During that time, a tanner had come by each evening to teach them how to work with leather. Tools, the most valuable things the brothers had ever owned, and for which an apprentice might work two years to obtain, were provided as well.

Annok-sur told them what they needed to do, how they needed to act, what tale they would tell while living in Larsa. When their training and instruction ended, a boat had taken them downriver, dropping them off at night a mile from Larsa's gate. Annok-sur's coins enabled them to enter the city and rent the hovel there that they now called home.

For almost two years, they lived in Larsa. Every month or so a man stopped by to give them a few more copper coins. The man, who never gave his name, listened to what they'd learned, and told them what they needed to do. He even gave them weapons, two long copper knives like those Dragan had seen for sale in Larsa's market.

Those weapons, wrapped in a sack and buried beneath the floor of the hut, had waited for over a year until the day when they would be used.

Annok-sur's caution and their long preparation had succeeded. Since the war had broken out, King Naran's men had scoured the city, searching for any strangers or spies who might be in the pay of Akkad. Naran's agents collected every able-bodied newcomer to Larsa and set them to work in the slave gangs, to make sure no one tried to betray the city from within. But Dragan and his brother had lived for so long in the city that they were beneath notice, not that any soldier would pay the slightest attention to two cripples.

As soon as Dragan learned of King Eskkar's army camped on the plain outside of Larsa, he knew that today or tomorrow would be that day – the day when he and his brother would take their revenge against King Naran and his murderers.

"Wake up, Captain." Grond's head poked up through the hole in the roof. When the sleeping man didn't move, Grond reached over and shook Eskkar's leg.

Eskkar lifted his head, his hand already on his knife. "What is it?" His voice sounded heavy with sleep, and he knew he'd slept well, though not long enough.

"Boats are coming down the river. I think it's Yavtar."

By the time Eskkar reached the riverbank, a whole fleet of approaching riverboats were strung out like jewels on a necklace. He counted twelve boats, more than he had expected. The first craft angled its way toward the shore, swung smartly against the current, and slid alongside the jetty. In a moment, Yavtar jumped onto the little dock as, one by one, the other vessels birthed themselves on the riverbank, where eager hands pulled them up onto the shore.

"Good to see you again, Captain." Yavtar clasped his arms around Eskkar's shoulders.

"You brought more ships than we expected."

"Bisitun sent two more ships, and the builders just finished two more. I had to scrape Akkad's docks to find crews, but we're here now with everything you need, including a dozen ladders."

"Food and the fire-arrows?"

"Yes, along with twenty-five jars of oil. And plenty of bread and meat. At least you won't be fighting on an empty belly."

Gatus and Alexar strode up to the tiny jetty, and exchanged greetings with the boatmaster.

"He's brought the fire-arrows," Eskkar said. "Let's get them off the boats first. If we can, we'll attack tonight."

He turned back to Yavtar. "Did you see any sign of Shulgi on the way down?"

"Yes, and he saw us, too. We tried to slip by at night, but some sentry taking a piss spotted us and gave the alarm. There was nothing they could do except shoot a few arrows at us, but we were well away from shore and the light was poor. His horsemen caught up with us the next day and followed us along the river. We shot a few arrows at them, just to give the archers some target practice."

This far south, the Tigris flowed wide and deep. Without boats of their own, the Sumerians had no way to intercept the vessels. And two of Yavtar's boats were fighting ships. They carried little cargo, but plenty of archers.

"How far back is their main force?"

"At least two days," Yavtar said, "maybe three. If he gets here any sooner, his men will be too tired to walk, let alone fight."

"I don't intend to give him the chance," Eskkar said. "Make sure everything gets unloaded. It will be dark soon enough. And I've a few wounded men you can take back, plus some loot the men have picked up."

Alexar shouted some orders, and the dock burst into activity. It didn't take long for two hundred men to empty the twelve boats, distributing the food and weapons. Other soldiers filled sacks with sand and dirt, to ballast the boats for their return voyage upriver. In what seemed like no time at all, Yavtar and his boats were being pushed back into the water, their crews cursing at the clumsy soldiers whose excess zeal threatened to swamp the boats. Then oars bit into the river and they headed upriver, not to Akkad, but a resupply point halfway between the city and Kanesh. Only one boat remained – a small but fast craft – to carry word upriver of the army's success or failure at Larsa.

As soon as the last boat departed, Eskkar, Grond, Gatus, Alexar and the other commanders sat around a campfire, wolfing down bread only a few days old and sharing a small cask of ale, the first since they'd left Akkad. Eskkar paused between mouthfuls.

"Get everyone into position. We'll have to bring the archers and spearmen close to the wall, in case the horsemen try to attack our rear. Mitrac, you know where to direct the arrows. Gatus and his spearmen will protect your rear and flanks, along with Alexar and the rest of the archers. If nothing works, Drakis and his men will attempt to scale the wall. Grond and I will hold three hundred spearmen and a hundred archers in readiness, in case the gate opens."

"You should let someone else lead the way, Eskkar," Gatus said.

His men had argued about that before, but Eskkar refused to stand around and do nothing.

"No, that's been decided." He finished his bread and stood. "Grond, send the signal."

"If the gate doesn't open, we'll use the ladders." Alexar sounded confident. His men had practiced scaling walls in the dark and under the covering arrows of the archers.

Grond walked off into the darkness. Before long, a drum began to sound. Five slow beats, struck with full strength on the widest drum the Akkadians carried, then a long pause before the drummer repeated the same five beats. Each stroke on the drum brought forth a powerful boom that echoed through the twilight, loud enough to carry all the way to the city's walls. That sound would be heard through Larsa, and men there would ponder its meaning. Eskkar intended to keep the drum going until the assault began.

Meanwhile, the commanders positioned the troops, checking their equipment to make sure no man forgot his sword or second quiver of arrows, which had already happened enough times when the men got excited. Once in training a spearman had forgotten his tunic, and Gatus insisted he stay naked all day.

At last Eskkar moved to where his force of men were assembled, and nodded in satisfaction. The battle for Larsa had begun.

Ibi-sin returned to the hut. His brother sat at the back of the chamber, waiting. "They gave the signal."

Dragan nodded, the movement unseen in the dark. "I heard it even here. Watch the door while I dig."

He took his time, making as little noise as possible. Now would not be the time to alert any neighbors or soldiers passing by. It was slow work, as the three sacks were buried deep and the weight of their bodies had packed down the earth firmly over the months, but eventually Dragan pried loose the first sack from the earth and handed it to Ibi-sin.

The next two took longer, as they were much bulkier and heavy. But at last all three had been removed from where they'd been buried for so long The knives were removed from one sack and unwrapped from their covering cloths. Ibi-sin loosened the simple fastening on the other two, but didn't open them. Each contained a thick rope, knotted at every arm length, and long enough to stretch twenty paces. The section of the wall they had chosen wasn't that high, but the rope needed to be fastened securely across the parapet.

Dragan put his arm on his brother's shoulder. "My heart is racing, Ibi-sin."

"I know. Mine too. I'm afraid. Not of dying, but of failing."

"We won't fail, brother."

"Now we just have to wait."

"It won't be long. King Eskkar moves quickly against his enemies."

The brothers sat in the darkness of their hut, waiting. Outside the city's walls, the Akkadian army was on the march toward Larsa, its dark mass illuminated only by the moon and a few torches that bobbed about in the slight breeze. The entire force – or so it appeared to the nervous sentries on the walls – moved across the main entrance to Larsa and marched toward the south side of the city's wall.

Larsa's defenders moved with them, shifting most of their men to the southern wall, to prepare for the Akkadian assault. Weapons were readied, torches lit along the wall, as men pushed and shoved their way into position driven by their cursing commanders. Beneath the parapets, the city's inhabitants shouted or wailed, everyone in dread of the coming attack.

Outside the city, Gatus directed the men toward the southern gate, one of the three entrances into Larsa. A hundred soldiers carried the same number of torches, delivered by Yavtar's boats. One by one, each torch was lighted, until they all burned in the night, illuminating the Akkadian army as it moved into its attack position. The Akkadian archers halted first, stopping just out of effective range of the archers on the city's walls.

Mitrac lined up two hundred of his archers. Behind them, more bowmen waited their turn, and behind them, pots of the oil that burns were opened and made ready for use. The torches were driven into the ground, one between every pair of archers. The fire-arrows were laid out in easy access.

Each fire-arrow had been carefully crafted in Akkad. A bit longer than the usual shafts, the extra distance between the point and the bow was wrapped tightly with thin cloth wound over and over, and then fastened tightly with threads. The many layers of cloth would absorb the oil, sustaining the flame until it reached its target.

Alexar ranged his men to protect Mitrac's bowmen, guarding their rear and flanks, and held other archers ready to replace any man killed or wounded by shafts from the wall. Mitrac strode up and down the line, directing the men where to aim. He had studied the maps Trella had created in Akkad, and knew the general layout of Larsa. More important, he knew the most likely locations where Razrek would be stabling his horses. Those places were to receive the bulk of the arrow storm.

"Ready the line." He gave the command to start the battle. Men dipped the shafts in the oil and waited a few moments to let the thick liquid soak into the cotton, then stepped forward to where the torches waited. "Light your shafts! Shoot!"

Two hundred shafts flew up into the night, fleeting flecks of flame marking their flight. Almost every shaft carried over the walls, to land where the gods directed. Larsa's wall stood crowded with men, its archers firing back at the Akkadians. But the range was great, and for this work Mitrac had selected his strongest bowmen using the most powerful bows.

A second volley flew up into the night, then a third. Mitrac didn't try to keep the volley shooting. Better to let the men take plenty of care with the oil and fire, and shoot whenever they were ready. Mitrac had eight thousand arrows ready, but he didn't plan on using them all. Thirty arrows per man – or six thousand flaming arrows – should be enough to put Larsa to the torch.

From the wall, Razrek watched the arrows arching over his head. While in flight, they showed only the slightest trace of light, but when they struck something, they turned into a finger of flame that licked at anything within reach. Many burned out uselessly, striking mud walls or the dirt of the lanes. Others were snatched up and smothered by those standing nearby. Still, plenty burned long enough to set something alight.

Damn these Akkadians and their barbarian king! Razrek hadn't expected fire-arrows, and no one had expected a night attack, especially tonight. Esskar's men should be exhausted by the long march, besides being short on food and sleep. They were supposed to attack tomorrow, at dawn or during the day. Not tonight, tomorrow. Half of Razrek's men had to be rounded up from the ale houses and brothels.

Mattaki stood beside his commander, shifting from one foot to the other in his excitement. Once Mattaki realized his cavalry wasn't going to slow down the Akkadians, he had ridden on ahead, to warn Razrek. "They're shooting hundreds of arrows at us! Where did they get so many?"

"Thousands, not hundreds," Razrek corrected. "All brought downriver by those miserable boats, Marduk curse them all! Why didn't Shulgi stop them?"

Those ships made the attack possible, Sondar realized. They must have carried the fire-arrows, the oil, even the ladders he could see out there, as well as the food that gave the Akkadians strength for tonight's attack.

"The city is going to burn," Mattaki said. "Those arrows will set enough fires . . ."

"Let the city burn. The walls will remain upright."

Another of Razrek's men dashed up the steps to the parapet. "Razrek, the Akkadians are targeting the marketplace, the stables, everyplace we've put the horses! They've killed dozens already, and the rest are panicking, out of control! The fires are driving them wild with fear!"

With a start, Razrek realized the implications. A good horse was more valuable than any fighter. Without the horses, there would be no escape from those cursed Akkadians if they ever got over the walls.

"Get the horses inside the huts. Make sure they've got something over their heads to protect them. Throw people out of their houses if you have to!"

Even as Razrek gave the order, he knew it wouldn't work. Dragging a skittish horse into a hut through a low doorway wasn't an easy task. The houses were burning, too. While most of the city was made from mud bricks, all the roofs and awnings were wood, usually bundles of sticks, or wrapped cloth stretched over the open roofs. All dried to the bone by a long summer of blazing sun. King Naran had done nothing to prepare for a fire attack. No water jars stood ready to put out fires, no piles of dirt to smother flames, no lines of women and children helping to fight the blaze. Larsa was going to burn, all right.

King Naran rushed up the steps, a sword at his hip and a gleaming bronze helmet on his head. "Razrek! Do something! Have your men put out the fires before the city burns to the ground."

"No. We've got to keep the men on the walls. The Akkadians are waiting for us to weaken our strength. Then they'll rush the walls."

"But we'll have nothing left, nothing."

Razrek grabbed the King and pushed him to the wall. "Look out there, you fool! See those spearmen with ladders. They'll be coming soon enough. If you want to fight the fires, use your own men. Smother all the fires! Get your women and children to work carrying water!"

He glanced back at the Akkadians, moving and shifting behind the lines of archers. From what he could see, the entire force was mustered before the south wall. They would be coming soon enough.

"What about all your men behind the Akkadians?" King Naran gestured out into the darkness, where he knew the rest of the Sumerian horsemen were watching the assault. "Why aren't they attacking? Are they cowards?"

Razrek ignored the king's words. "Mattaki, get every man who can fight on the wall. Forget the fires."

King Naran shook himself free of Razrek's grip. "Damn you, Razrek! You said you came to protect Larsa." His voice rose shrilly over the parapet. "You and your filthy horsemen have brought this down on our heads!"

Razrek jerked his knife from his belt, and shoved the point against Naran's throat. "Talk to me like that again and I'll kill you. Now get off the wall!" He shoved the king away.

Naran stumbled backwards and fell, almost toppling off the parapet. He scrambled to his feet, his hand clutching his throat. He looked aghast as blood seeped through his fingers from where Razrek's knife had nicked him, and fled, calling out for his guards to protect him.

"Do you think our men will attack their rear?" Mattaki kept his voice low, so that the other men crowded on the wall couldn't hear.

Razrek stared at the Akkadians. "No, they're not coming. This caught them by surprise, and they'll use that as an excuse not to attack. They won't want to risk the horses in the darkness, and they're not going to face the spearmen on foot. We're on our own."

461

"May the gods help us!"

"Forget the gods," Razrek ordered. "Just keep the men on the walls."

Larsa's north side had no gate. The main entrance was on the east. The other two gates faced the south and the river to the west.

From the doorway of an abandoned hut a hundred and fifty paces away from the city, Drakis lay on his belly and watched the north wall. He had no trouble making out the sentries on guard. The fires burning in the city behind them provided enough light to outline the dark forms moving about. At present, the sentries didn't concern him. Drakis had his gaze fixed on a point midway between the wall and the ruined huts that King Naran had carelessly allowed to intrude so close to Larsa's walls.

One of Drakis's men had crawled to that halfway point, to get close enough to the wall to discern the signal, should it come. The man would relay the signal to Drakis and his forty men, now bunched up behind him, all keeping low and hopefully out of sight from the guards pacing the wall.

The men waiting patiently behind him were a mixed lot, slingers, archers, swordsmen and even two men who carried no weapon except for a large hammer apiece. Drakis had trained them for this operation months ago, up in Bisitun. Now Lady Trella and King Eskkar's foresight would be put to the test. And Eskkar's luck, of course. That would be needed, too.

"See anything?" His friend and subcommander, Tarok, sat with his back to the crumbling wall.

"Nothing yet."

"How long do we wait?"

"Until we see . . . wait!" Something was moving out there. The shadow midway between Drakis and the wall had lifted its arm and waved.

"That's the signal. Send out the slingers."

Tarok pulled himself to his feet and whispered the necessary orders.

Drakis kept his eyes on the wall. Plenty could still go wrong, but the next few moments might give him and his men the chance to be the first Akkadians to enter Larsa.

Dragan and Ibi-sin walked toward the north wall. Each carried a heavy sack over their left shoulder. Both were too tense to say anything, that curious mixture of fear and excitement that often accompanies men when they go into battle, magnified as always by those with no real experience in fighting. Dragan understood that a trained soldier might face an enemy, but he and his brother were farmers, and with little knowledge or skill in fighting and killing

With his injured leg, Dragan couldn't walk too fast, especially when carrying the heavy rope. But they finally reached their destination. Guards lined the wall every twenty paces, but the open space beneath the parapet was empty of life. Every man that could be spared had been summoned to defend the south wall, where the Akkadians were massing, or to put out fires.

The brothers reached the foot of the steps, but before they could start the climb, a sharp voice halted them.

"What are you doing here?"

Dragan took his foot off the first step and faced one of the guards striding toward them. "We were told to bring bread to the sentries on the walls." Each sack did contain a single loaf of bread, in case anyone wanted to glance inside. Dragan kept his voice low and properly subservient. The men who made up Larsa's soldiers were known for their brutality even toward their own inhabitants. "We can leave it here, and you can take it up if –"

"Let me see what you've got in there."

The guard stepped closer, and Dragan struck, bringing his hand up from alongside his leg and plunging the knife in the man's stomach. A moment later, Ibi-sin's knife flashed into the man's neck. The guard fell to the ground, legs thrashing, a low gurgling the only sound he could make, a noise that went unheard against the shouts of those fighting the flames burning throughout the city.

They wiped their hands and blades on the dying man's tunic as they'd been taught, gathered the sacks, and made their way up the parapet. Once on top, they took only a few paces before another guard moved away from the wall to see what they wanted.

"Bread, master," Dragan said. "Your commander said to give each man a loaf."

The sentry scarcely gave them a glance. "About time. Half the men have deserted their posts. I've been up here for half the night with nothing to –"

The man died before he could finish his words, struck down by Dragan's fierce thrust. One of Akkad's soldiers had taught him how to make that move, driving the blade quickly up into the man's ribs with all his strength. It was, Dragan realized, easier the second time.

The unexpected attack made even less noise, and that, too, was easily drowned out by the tumult coming from the south. Ibi-sin shoved the second guard's body close to the wall, where it might escape notice.

They moved down the wall to the next sentry. He died as quietly as the others. That gave them over forty paces of wall to themselves. Ibi-sin pulled open the sacks and dumped the heavy rope. A support beam projected out over the ground beneath the parapet, and he looped one end of the rope around the beam and fastened the knot, just as he'd been trained on Akkad's own walls.

Ten paces away, Dragan did the same. Before he had finished, Ibi-sin leaned over the wall, clutching a long strip of white cloth and waving his arms. Neither brother could see anything in the darkness, but he hoped Akkadians were out there and watching.

"What do we do now?" Ibi-sin's whisper sounded excited.

"We wait until . . . there! Someone's coming."

A crouching shape rose up out of the earth like a spirit and flitted toward the wall. Suddenly, the rope went taut and, in moments, faster than Dragan thought anyone could climb up the wall, a boy slid over the top. At least, he looked like a boy to Dragan. He carried no weapons, just another rope slung around his neck.

He ducked his head and shrugged the rope off his shoulder. "Take this." He handed the third rope to Ibi-sin, and pulled something from his tunic. "Help them up."

Both ropes went taut again, and two more men pulled themselves up and over the wall.

Shappa, the first Akkadian to breach Larsa's walls, ignored them. He dropped a stone in his sling and waited. The guards were visible enough, but most of them were facing inwards, watching the city burn. Smoke hung in the air, stinging the eyes, rasping the throat, and already carrying the stench of burning flesh throughout the city. Fire-arrows continued to rise and fall through the sky, but fewer now that most of the fires had taken root.

The first six men up the ropes were slingers, and they knelt against the wall, staying in the shadows. Shappa walked along the parapet, forcing himself to move slowly and purposefully, as if he belonged. He carried the sling in his left hand. His left hand was as his right, and he could use his sling almost as well with either hand. His right hand held a long copper knife concealed behind his leg.

The next sentry never saw the knife that flashed into his stomach. Shappa pressed his sling against the man's mouth to muffle any cries, but the man went down without a sound. Within a few heartbeats, the rest of the slingers followed. Soon two more ropes were being fastened to the parapet supports.

Shappa returned to find Dragan and Ibi-sin still helping men up and over the wall. Archers, their bows strung and looped over their shoulders, were pulling themselves into the city. The bowmen fanned out along the wall, and Tarok led them toward the ramparts steps.

"Guards! Guards! Akkadians on the walls! They're inside the city!"

Someone had noticed the mass of men slithering over the wall and sounded the alarm.

Drakis, almost the last man to scale the wall, pulled himself up over the edge, his white teeth showing either a grin or a grimace as the enemy sentries sounded the alarm along the north wall. "Too late now, fools!"

The noise echoed down into the city, but it didn't matter. With four ropes providing access, the last of Drakis's men pulled themselves up and over.

"Let's go!" Drakis commanded.

Forty men raced down the steps and into Larsa, pounding through the lanes, heading for the main gate.

Dragan and Ibi-sin watched them rush off, hard men intent on a single purpose. In a moment, they had the parapet to themselves.

"What shall we do now?"

"I don't know, Ibi-sin. But we'd better get off this wall before someone notices us."

Drakis had taken a good look toward the main gate before he descended the steps. He knew the way from studying Ismenne's map, but in the darkness, nothing looked familiar. The lanes twisted and turned, even more confusing than those in the older parts of Akkad. Some of the houses were burning, and his men pushed and shoved through crowds of people frantically trying to put out fires, save their possessions, or escape the flames. No one seemed to recognize them as Akkadians, or if they did, had any inclination to try and stop them.

Just as he thought he'd taken a wrong turn, the lane turned into a wider passage, and Drakis knew the gate lay just ahead.

"This way! Archers, take to the roofs."

He led the men in a wild charge straight at the gate. Two houses burned along one side, and a watchfire burned along the top of the wall. Sentries continued to sound the alarm, and now Drakis heard the panic in their voices. An arrow struck the ground beside him and skittered off into the darkness. The sentries on the wall had finally grasped the situation.

But Drakis and his men were moving too quickly to stop and too fast to hit. They made it to the foot of the gate before they encountered any opposition. Two guards died trying to stop them, and the others backed into the towers that led upwards.

Drakis didn't care about them. "Get that gate open!"

The two men with the hammers went to work. As soon as the first stroke pounded on the brace, the gate shook, and everyone knew what was happening. The city's guards started shooting arrows at anything that moved, including the city's inhabitants, and a group of soldiers who had collected themselves to ready a counter-attack. But by then the twenty Akkadian archers had reached the roofs. Now Akkadian arrows, as well as stones from the slingers, began to fly from the darkness, first striking down anyone who seemed in command, then searching out anyone with a bow. That stopped the counter-attack against Drakis and his twenty swordsmen.

The first wedge broke free, then the second a moment later. "Get the beam out!" Drakis's voice cut through the chaos.

Some of his men dropped their swords and moved to the gate. Four men lifted the top beam, grunting as they shoved it up over their heads. Then they had to move it aside. One man went down with an arrow in his chest, and the log sagged dangerously before the remaining trio could hurl it aside, letting it roll off into the darkness. They had to get it far enough away from the gate so as to not hinder it swinging open. The hammers kept pounding behind them, and Drakis glanced back to see the last wedge splinter into fragments.

He slid his sword into the scabbard and helped his men shoulder the second, and lower, beam. They had to stoop down to grasp it. An arrow slammed into the gate a hand's width from Drakis's head, but it didn't matter now. With a grunt the beam rose up, scraping along the wood, and Drakis moved away from the gate, his feet stumbling in the dirt, trying to maintain his footing. The soldier with the hammer began pounding on the gate with all his might, the signal to those waiting outside.

"Throw it!" Drakis gave the command and the men heaved the beam to the side. Behind them, the gate burst open, and the first man through was Eskkar, at the head of a wave of two hundred and fifty spearmen, and fifty archers. He recognized Drakis.

"Drakis! Stay here. Make sure the gate stays open until the rest of the men arrive."

That didn't take long. Soon the entire force of spearmen jogged through the gate, breathing hard. The first part of Eskkar's army was pouring into Larsa, and nothing could stop it now.

Eskkar, carrying a shield like any of his infantry, led the initial force straight down the widest lane. He remembered to count his strides, and when he reached eighty a lane appeared on his left and he led the men that way. Fires burned everywhere, and the people shrank out of their way, frightened by the river of fierce men all wearing bronze helmets that glowed blood-red in the flickering light, and carrying shields and long spears whose tips glinted as they reflected the flames.

Another two hundred paces and the house of King Naran appeared, an imposing structure surrounded by a wall taller than the height of a man. Four soldiers, swords in hand, guarded the gate, but they took one glance at the charging Akkadians and fled. Two ran up the lane, and the other two ducked inside the gate.

"Open that gate!"

Eskkar dashed up the lane, his personal guards and the spearmen trying to catch up with their leader. He heard a bar snap into place as he reached the entrance, but no gate this small would stop him now. He raised his shield and flung his weight against the gate. A moment later, four more bodies hit it, and more hands reached out to push against it.

Something snapped, and the gate burst open. Eskkar stumbled through the opening, falling to his knees from the press of men behind him. Grond caught him by the arm and jerked him upright. Akkadian soldiers shouting war cries rushed into the grounds, brandishing spears or swords. Any who resisted were slain. Those who tried to flee were caught and slammed to the ground. The spearmen fanned out, filling the spacious grounds and moving to the rear of the courtyard.

In moments the king's house was taken. Eskkar strode through the open door, stepping over a body. Two torches burned in the long common room, but it was devoid of life. A broad flight of steps led upstairs, marked by a bloody trail. Eskkar pointed with his sword and his men rushed up the steps. Another barred door held the soldiers up for a few moments, before they ripped it from its hinges, and poured into the upper chamber.

Eskkar mounted the steps and entered the room. Two thick candles mounted on the walls illuminated the first of the three rooms he knew to comprise the house's second story. Women were dragged from the other rooms, and soon a dozen stood crammed together in the corner. Eskkar looked at the terrified women shaking in their fear, clutching each other in their panic. One, older than the others, wore a rich gown. A pearl necklace hung from her neck. Two younger women, likely her daughters, clung to her arms, as Eskkar moved to face her. She tried to shrink back, but there was no place to go.

Eskkar studied her for a moment. King Naran had several wives, but his first wife had given him two daughters. "You are Naran's wife?"

"No!" The woman lifted her chin and held her daughters tight against her body.

"Then you're of no use to me." He turned to Grond. "Kill her, and the two with her."

Grond, his powerful frame as frightening as any man alive, drew his sword from its scabbard and stepped forward, raising the blade over his head.

"Wait! Stop!" The older of the two girls holding their mother upright shouted the words. "My mother is first wife to my father, King Naran."

"Where is he?" Eskkar's voice rasped into the older woman's face.

She hesitated. "I don't know." Her voice quivered as she spoke.

Naran's wife had courage, but the daughter would tell him what he wanted. Eskkar reached out, caught the mother's hair, and twisted it back, making her gasp with pain. "That's twice you've lied to me, woman. Next time I'll cut out your tongue. Where is he?"

Grond grabbed her by the face, pushing his thick fingers into the sides of her jaw, forcing it open. He shoved the sharp blade into her mouth, and a trickle of blood formed in the corner.

"Inside! Inside the bed chamber!" The same girl, sobbing now, pointed to the way.

Eskkar released his hold on Naran's wife. "Bring them." He entered the second chamber, a comfortable room where Naran no doubt took his pleasure. A large chest rested against the wall, the only concealment possible.

Grond went to it, placed his foot against one side, and shoved. The chest slid aside, revealing an opening cut into the wall.

"Get him out."

Grond would have to bend over double to squeeze inside the dark hiding hole, and he knew better than to do that. Instead he took a spear from one of the grinning soldiers, and thrust it into the darkness.

"Stop! I'm coming out."

On his hands and knees, King Naran emerged from the hidden chamber, his bronze helmet still on his head. If he had a sword, he'd left it behind.

A soldier arrived with a torch, shoved it inside, and inspected the hiding hole. "It's empty, Lord Eskkar."

"Don't take any chances. Tear the wall down. There might be another hole concealed within this one. Check all the rooms, break open every wall. There will be more hiding places for his gold."

Grond jerked the helmet from Naran's head, turned him around, and began tying his hands behind his back.

"Guard him and his women well, Grond. I'll be back for them later."

The moment Razrek heard the alarm about Akkadians entering the city, he knew it was time to go. Already the mass of soldiers outside the city had begun abandoning their position and started jogging toward the main gate. The threat against the south wall had been a ruse.

"Damn that demon Eskkar!" Razrek shook his head in frustration. "Summon our men to the river gate, and get them mounted. We've only moments before these bastards seal us in."

He raced down the steps and ran as fast as he could toward Larsa's river gate. Fires burned everywhere, and the heat from the flames would have given him pause at any other time. With swords in their hands, Razrek, Mattaki and his men rushed down the lane, forcing their way through the terrified mob of people pushing and shoving in every direction.

"Use your swords on the rabble," Razrek shouted. "Clear the way to the corrals!"

Mattaki shouted orders to every horseman they passed, and soon hundreds of men milled about in the stable area. Razrek reached the house where he'd stabled his horse, and those of his commanders. Some were already there, others arriving breathless, pausing only long enough to fit a halter over their horse's head.

Frantic soldiers tore loose the gate's fastenings and flung it open. Men kicked their horses hard and burst through the opening, riding south along the river toward safety. Razrek saw a few arrows reach out from the darkness and strike down several of his men. The shafts didn't descend in force, but he knew that would soon change as more archers reached the rear of the city.

Razrek finally fitted the halter to his nervous mount's tossing head. He swung onto his stallion and hunched over his horse's shoulder as he urged the big animal forward. With a thunder of hooves, Razrek and the rest of his men fled into the darkness, away from the walls and burning debris. Behind him came hundreds of the city's inhabitants, desperate to escape before the Akkadians sealed them in. Shouting and pushing, they forced their way through the gate, running for their lives.

The Akkadian bowmen, slowed down by the tangle of broken huts that littered the ground, finally pushed their way toward the river gate, trying to seal off the most likely escape route. But only a few arrived before Razrek and hundreds of his men galloped out. Arrows flew at them, but the leader of the first group of breathless archers didn't have enough men to contest their escape. He shot arrows at anything that moved, and emptied his quiver with the last shaft launched into the darkness.

More archers kept arriving, and now Razrek's stragglers were cut down, arrows killing horses and riders, driving them back into the city. When men and horses littered the space just outside the gate, the exodus stopped. A few defenders tried to close the portal, but Eskkar's spearmen arrived and took control. The last escape route out of Larsa had been closed.

A mile downriver Razrek halted in an open field. He and Mattaki bellowed commands, stopping the panicky gallop. Men and horses were breathing hard from the desperate dash through the night, and it took a long time under the moon's feeble light before Razrek finally collected all his men and took a count.

"Damn those Akkadians!" he shouted at Mattaki's white face. Only two out of every three of Razrek's horsemen got away before the Akkadians sealed the city. He'd lost valuable horses, men and weapons, not to mention the city of Larsa. Shulgi would not be pleased.

49

Day 5

Eskkar woke to find the morning sun in his eyes. Something felt odd, until he realized he hadn't slept on hard ground for the first time in almost ten days. He remembered dragging the remains of Naran's bed close to the window, so that dawn's first light would wake him. By then Eskkar felt as tired as if he'd fought a dozen fights.

Midnight had come and gone before he managed to snatch some sleep, throwing himself down on the king's fancy blankets, exhausted by the long day's march and the night attack on Larsa. Now the sun shone brightly, well above the horizon, and Eskkar realized he'd slept right through sunrise. Throughout the city, his men were up and about, while he slept in comfort on a thick spread of rich cloth that until last night had no doubt pampered the soft flesh of King Naran, his wives and concubines.

For a moment, Eskkar lay there thinking about last night's events, ignoring the sounds of activity in the courtyard below. His mouth felt dry, and his head ached as if he'd been drinking all night, instead of capturing his first city. He was, he decided, getting too old for this kind of warfare.

Grond entered the room, carrying an ornate carved tray in both hands. "Everything's under control, Captain."

Leave it to Grond to make sure his commander knew the situation first.

"There's fresh water, bread, hot chicken, and some dates. And a cup of Naran's finest ale." Grond set the tray down on a low table beside the bed.

"We;d better drink as much of that as we can. Probably won't see anything as good as this again."

Eskkar pushed himself up. The smell of smoke still lingered in the air, and every breeze brought more of the acrid smell inside. Most of the fires from the attack would have burned themselves out by now, but the charred embers would linger for some time.

Despite the small amount of sleep, he felt rested. He grasped the cup of ale, drank half of it, then filled it again with water. This time he emptied the cup. "Demons, that's good ale. You're sure everything's under control?"

"Oh, yes. The city's still burning here and there, but our men and supplies are all inside the walls. The Sumerian horsemen have moved in closer, to watch us, but they're not going to attack a walled city."

"Useless fools. Shulgi should have known better."

"I'm sure he knows by now." Grond sat down on the bed, which sagged under their combined weight. "No sign of Razrek. That wolf must have gotten away before they closed the river gate."

"How many men did we lose?"

"The commanders are still counting, but not many. Less than fifty, I'd guess. Another forty or fifty wounded. Half the men are still busy chasing women or looting."

"The wounded will thank the gods for Yavtar and his boats."

"A quick river trip back to Akkad, if they can get through. By the time they recover, the war will be over."

"Or we'll all be dead." Nevertheless, Eskkar had a smile on his face. "And Naran's gold?"

"Piled up in the next room, under guard. We found the third hiding place after you went to bed. Very small, but stuffed with fine jewels and precious stones. The homes of the leading merchants are still being searched, torn down, actually. It's faster than trying to torture the information out of them."

Last night, under the threat of torture, Naran had revealed two hiding places where he kept his hoard of gold and other valuables. But despite his protestations, the king of Larsa had given them up too easily, and Eskkar had suspected there would be a third. He stood, tossing the remains of the bread on the floor. "Are the commanders here?"

"Waiting in the courtyard."

"Then it's time to begin."

Before leaving the upper chambers, Eskkar stopped to see Naran and his three wives, four daughters, two young sons, and three concubines. All of them spent the night huddled together in the adjacent chamber. Eskkar hadn't heard any sounds of weeping or wailing. The guards must have threatened to cut the tongue out of anyone who disturbed the king of Akkad's rest.

Now the royal prisoners stared up in fear when they saw Eskkar standing in the doorway. The chamber was just large enough to hold all of them. Two Hawk Clan soldiers, both looking tired but still alert, guarded the former king of Larsa and his women. Both guards held bread in their hands. Eskkar nodded a greeting and let them return to their own breakfasts.

Naran's house had a private well, of course, and Eskkar drank his fill of fresh water, then stripped and rinsed out his tunic, while he washed his face and hands. By the time he had finished, his commanders had gathered at a small table, awaiting the day's orders.

One empty seat awaited him. Before he took his place, he looked at each of his men. Tired but grinning faces greeted him. Probably none of them had snatched more than a few moments of sleep since the night before.

"My thanks to all of you. Your bravery has let us take Larsa, and now its food and supplies will sustain us – not Shulgi." He turned to Gatus, yawning at the opposite end of the table. "How long before Shulgi arrives?"

"At least a day and a half, probably two and half. Whenever he gets here, I doubt if his army will be in any condition to fight that day. So we've probably got three days before we have to worry."

"Good. That gives us more than enough time. The first thing we need to do is move all the supplies across the river."

"A few boats got away last night," Yavtar said. "But we captured nine that had been pulled from the river and taken inside the walls. I'll put them all to good use. When our own boats return today or tomorrow, we should be able to ferry everyone across the river in a single day. Meanwhile, I'll send three or four ships north with the wounded and the spoils."

"Move the supplies first," Eskkar said, then regretted his words. He hated giving useless orders about trivial details. His leaders knew what needed to be done. Eskkar decided his head must still be stuffed with sleep. "Anything we can use goes across," he corrected himself. "Everything else is to be burned or tossed in the river."

"What about the people?" Alexar looked as weary as Gatus. "Are we going to let them go? Many of them slipped out through the gates before we could close them off. Others went over the walls."

"Turn all the women and children out of the city first. That may get our men to stop chasing them. Any men too old or infirm for work can leave, too. Make sure they take nothing of value with them, including their clothes. Have our men collect all the loot and turn it over to Yavtar."

"What about the men?"

"The able-bodied men and boys will help us move the supplies. Then use them to help burn down the rest of the city. What won't burn is to be torn down. After that, we'll let the prisoners go free. That will be more mouths to feed when Shulgi arrives. Since he's got thousands of soldiers from Larsa in his army, he won't be able to just ignore them. He'll have to share some of his supplies with them. But when Shulgi gets here, I don't want him finding anything he can use, or seeing one stone standing atop another. Larsa will teach the Sumerians a lesson they will remember for a long time."

Terror, as Trella reminded him, can be a useful weapon. Eskkar intended to use it to the fullest on Larsa.

He studied his commanders' faces. None of them showed the slightest sympathy for Larsa or its inhabitants. Too many raids over too many years – most launched from and supported by Larsa – had long ago hardened the Akkadians against the city and its rapacious rulers. Larsa's raiders had terrorized Akkadian lands. Now they would be repaid in full.

"Meanwhile, we've accomplished two of our goals. Our army marched unscathed to Larsa, and we captured the city. Now we've plenty of time to destroy it. By sunset tomorrow our men can rest in safety, across the river. Then we'll resume the march."

Heads nodded approval. His commanders knew what to do, and how best to accomplish their tasks.

"I wonder how Hathor is doing?" Gatus voiced the question, though he knew that no one knew anything about the Akkadian cavalry.

Eskkar had almost forgotten about the Egyptian and his mission.

"Let's hope he's as lucky as we've been."

Surrounded by a dozen Hawk Clan guards, Eskkar spent the rest of the morning walking the city, making sure the detachments of soldiers knew and understood what he wanted done. His men started gathering the women and children and herding them toward the west gate. That at least put a stop to the raping. The Akkadians had been in no mood for mercy. The city had resisted them, and its women were fair game. Eskkar couldn't have stopped the men even if he'd wanted to. And as a commander, he knew better than to give foolish orders that couldn't be enforced.

By mid-morning, the last of the sobbing women and crying children were streaming across the countryside. Everyone had passed through the river gate. Soldiers searched them for jewels, even making them open their mouths and examining their hair. Their clothing – ripped from their bodies by force – if necessary, had to be checked as well, as there had been enough time for jewels or coins to be sewn into the garments.

Only then, and as naked as the day they were born, were the women, children and elderly allowed to pass through the gate. Many still feared for their lives, though Eskkar's commanders had told them again and again they would not be harmed once they left. Many wailed at their fate. Most of them had been raped, some many times. Now they had to leave their husbands and family behind. Almost all of them headed south, as Eskkar's soldiers had ordered them, but a few ran to the north or east.

Meanwhile, Alexar took charge of the city's destruction. About nine hundred of the city's inhabitants remained. None of them resisted, as the Akkadians greatly outnumbered them. Those who had tried to fight for their women or possessions had died during the night. The survivors had no strength or will to continue a hopeless battle. Their wives and children were either safe in the countryside as promised, or dead. Now they only worried about their own existence.

Dividing the men into two groups, Alexar set five hundred of them to tearing down the houses, starting with those of the wealthy merchants and tradesmen. Everything that could burn, clothing, furniture, leather, even baskets, was collected and tossed onto the embers of last night's fires. Every clay pot was smashed. Fresh smoke broiled up into the sky. Anything of military value, weapons or food, went to the docks. Everything else went into the flames.

The houses, made of the usual mud brick, wouldn't burn, but men wielding hammers, chisels and any other tool that could be used to dislodge the bricks, knocked them down. Thick logs were also used to smash down walls. The soldiers worked their prisoners hard. Eskkar's men learned that the people of Larsa had celebrated with a feast when Kanesh fell, and every Akkadian soon knew the story.

The remaining four hundred prisoners began emptying the city of anything edible. All food, grain, wine, ale, livestock, captured horses, anything that could be eaten or useful to the Akkadians were carried down to the river and ferried across, boat load by boat load. Soon a mound of supplies began to arise on the western bank of the Tigris.

When Gatus and Yavtar complained that they had more food than the Akkadians could possibly eat, Alexar ordered the prisoners to start dumping the remaining food stocks into the river. Shulgi, when he arrived, would have to do something to prevent the starvation of the city's inhabitants, but Eskkar had no sympathy either for them or Shulgi. The destruction went on all day, and by dusk only the city's gates remained intact, and Naran's house was the only one still standing. Rubble from the houses around it stretched all the way to the courtyard walls, and thick clouds of dust hung in the air, drawn toward the flames or blown about by the evening breeze off the river.

When Eskkar returned to Naran's house, Drakis and two men waited for him in the courtyard. Eskkar headed toward the well. A thick coat of dust and dirt had accumulated on his tunic, and it stank with the odors of burning wood and animal flesh. Taking his time, he washed his body. Grond had found a clean garment somewhere suitable for Eskkar's stature, so he kicked the old one aside, and slipped the clean one over his frame.

Inside the house, the common-room table was covered with platters of food and pitchers of wine and ale, more than enough for Eskkar and his commanders. The food tempted him, but Eskkar wanted to get one last task over with.

With Grond at his side, he climbed the stairs, followed by Drakis and his companions, and entered the room where Naran and his women still awaited their fate. Now the once spotless chamber stank of urine and worse. No one bothered to empty the chamber pots. Any wealth the room might have contained had disappeared as well. Curtains, bedding, garments and sandals had been tossed through the window and burned, along with all the other goods from the house. Naran's hoard of gold and precious stones had departed at midday, by now well on its way to Trella's vaults. Naran, his swollen hands still bound, lifted his eyes when Eskkar entered.

He stopped two paces away and stared down at Larsa's king for a moment. "I wanted you to know your city is in ruins, Naran. It will be many, many years before anyone tries to build on this site again. Larsa will suffer the same fate that you plotted for Akkad."

"What are you going to do with me?" The former ruler of Larsa looked haggard, his hair hanging limp on his shoulders. He'd soiled himself, probably more than once. His hands shook, and his lips quivered from fear. The fate of his city meant nothing to him now, only his own life.

"Do with you? Nothing. But your wives and children are going to Akkad. They'll be slaves there for the rest of their lives, unless anyone bothers to ransom them. At least they'll be alive."

A gasp came from the women as they heard their fate, but no one cried out. They had emptied themselves of tears during the night.

"What about me?" Naran had to pause to get the words out. "You've taken all my gold. There's nothing left here to pay a ransom, but my sons might be able to raise enough."

Eskkar ignored the words. Naran had two grown sons, no doubt leading Larsa's contingent under Shulgi. Instead, Eskkar glanced behind him to where Drakis, who had stopped just outside the chamber, waited. "Come in, Drakis, and bring our friends. I want them to meet Naran, king of Larsa." He turned to Naran. "Do you know these two men?"

Naran squinted at the two poorly dressed men who shuffled slowly into the room. "No, I've never seen them."

"This is Dragan and his brother Ibi-sin. Come closer. Naran can't hurt you now."

The two stepped forward, one limping, his hand on the other's arm for support.

"These men are the ones who risked their lives to lower ropes to my men. Without their help, I might not have gotten inside Larsa so easily. I told them to help themselves to whatever they wanted from your gold, but they said they wanted only one thing. Best you tell him, Dragan."

Still leaning on his brother's arm, Dragan moved closer. "Your men killed my family, King Naran. One of your sons led the raid. Ten days ago, I watched him leave the city. He rode proudly to fight with King Shulgi's army, but I will pray to the gods that King Eskkar kills him in battle. Your men raped and killed my sisters, murdered our parents, blinded Ibi-sin in one eye, and wounded me in the leg so badly that to this day I cannot walk without pain. They did all this to us for no reason. We were farmers, without any weapons. We had done no harm to anyone. When King

Eskkar asked me what I wanted, I told him I wanted you, so that I could take my revenge for my family."

Naran's eyes had widened in horror at Dragan's words.

"And I told Dragan he could have you, Naran," Eskkar added. "Since I first came to Akkad years ago, I've heard many such tales, how you sent your riders north across the Sippar time after time, to kill and loot those who placed themselves under my protection. You should have surrendered your city yesterday when I gave you the chance. I would have kept my word, would have let you go. But this is better. Your death will be a warning to the other kings of Sumeria. They will hear of Larsa's fall and your death at the hands of those you murdered. They will learn to stay south of the river."

"No, please . . . King Eskkar, please spare my life. I have relatives in Sumer . . . they can pay . . ."

"Too late for that, Naran." Eskkar called to the guards outside. "Take the women to the docks. Give them to Yavtar. A boat will be leaving as soon as it's dark."

The room erupted in screaming and wailing. Naran fell to the floor, his hands outstretched, his eyes wide with fright. The waiting guards had already prepared ropes, and they quickly bound the crying women, and led them away. When they were gone, Naran looked around at the empty room, his eyes wide, as if searching for his followers, his possessions, anything that might save him. He lifted his head, tears streaming down his face, and held up his bound hands piteously. "Mercy, King Eskkar! I plead for my life. I can raise more gold. I will pay whatever ransom you wish."

Eskkar didn't bother to reply. He turned to the brothers. "He's yours, Dragan, Ibi-sin. But you must not take too long. Yavtar's boat will be leaving soon, and you must be at the docks so you can return to Akkad."

Dragan shrugged off his brother's arm. "It will not take long." He drew his knife from his belt. "Come, Ibi-sin. You may strike first." Holding onto his brother's arm, they stepped forward together.

As Eskkar left the chamber, the first scream erupted behind him. He touched Drakis's arm. "Stay with them. When they're finished, make sure Naran is dead, and bring me his head. Then give Dragan and his brother two sacks of gold, and get them to the boat."

Outside, the sun was touching the western horizon. A hundred prisoners sat on the ground in the fading light, awaiting the command to destroy Naran's house. Exhaustion and despair covered every face, and they barely raised their eyes at the sight of the Akkadian king. An equal number of soldiers guarded them.

"There are three men still inside. As soon as they come out, destroy the Compound. Leave nothing standing, and burn everything. He saw the two large pots of oil that the prisoners had prepared.

Eskkar gazed about him in satisfaction. Naran and his fine house would soon be turned into rubble, like the rest of Larsa. Now it was time to go. He strode through the Compound's gate. After a short walk through the debris that filled the lane, he reached the main gate. Fifty of Alexar's men waited there, guarding about a hundred slaves.

"Tear down the gates. Feed them to the fire."

With his guards, Eskkar walked one last time through the ruined city, trying to ignore the stench of death and dust that lingered everywhere. The docks were a frenzied scene of chaos and confusion. Slaves were busy tearing them apart, piling the wood up for yet one more gigantic bonfire. The last pots of oil in Larsa would feed those flames.

Eskkar watched the final preparations. Most of his men had already crossed the river, and by now were busy setting up camp. With a loud snapping sound, the river gates came crashing down, and men with axes broke the logs apart, hewing through the ropes and staves that held the logs together. Soon those logs were added to the growing piles of what remained of the dock, and flames again leaped and twisted high into the sky.

One of Drakis's men arrived, escorting Dragan and Ibi-sin. Their hands were clean – no doubt washed in Naran's well – but blood still clung to their clothing. They would travel north on the same boat that held Naran's women. With all the gold Eskkar had given them, they'd never have to work again.

"When you reach Akkad," Eskkar said, "tell Trella everything that happened. She will make sure you are taken care of."

He wasn't sure that Dragan even heard him. But the brothers climbed into the boat, each clutching a sack to their body. They'd help row the craft upriver, and that would take their minds off the horror they had left behind.

From within the city, fresh flames climbed into the darkening sky, and Eskkar knew the two other gates had been set afire. Two hundred slaves who had helped destroy the last of Larsa were marched up, and the final embarkation began. Eskkar planned to bring them across the river. Boats were waiting for them, and soon prisoners and their guards were ferrying across the darkening water. The rest of the prisoners were abandoned, left to fend for themselves as best they could among the wreckage of the city.

With Grond, Eskkar boarded the last boat. They put off from the dock, but a rope held them a few paces from the riverbank. He watched his men tear up the remaining dock, then saturate everything with the oil. They scrambled through the water, and the last man tossed a torch onto the dock. It erupted in flame, a wave of fire sweeping back to the inferno that had marked the remains of the gate.

The man swam to the ship and waiting hands pulled him aboard. The captain gave the order, the rope was slipped from its fastening and hauled aboard. The boat swung with the current for a moment, then the men worked the oars, and the vessel began its journey across the Tigris.

Eskkar remained in the stern, facing the gathering dusk and watching Larsa burn. This was war, war the way barbarians waged it. Devastation, destruction and terror. Larsa would likely never be rebuilt, and when men sailed the river or led caravans past the ruins, they would tell the tale of the city's destruction, as a penalty for bringing war to Akkad's lands. He hoped the lesson would linger for a hundred years, but Eskkar knew how quickly men can forget.

Nevertheless, when Shulgi arrived, he would find nothing useful, not even a roof to cover his head. Meanwhile, thousands of people roamed the land begging for something to eat. All the crops in the nearby fields had been burned. No food, weapons, supplies of any kind remained in the ruins. The dead – hundreds of bodies – had been dumped in the city's wells. They would poison the water for months, maybe longer. The city's gold and valuables would travel to Akkad. Trella would sell them, to help pay for the war.

Larsa had ceased to exist. No one would organize raids to the north from this place again. Eskkar nodded in satisfaction and turned to the west. Tomorrow would be the sixth day, and then there would be only six more days remaining to defeat Shulgi's army. Until today, he hadn't spared much thought for Hathor. He wondered how his horse commander was faring. Everything would now depend on him.

50

S hulgi, Razrek, Vanar and the rest of Sumer's commanders rode up to what was left of Larsa's wall, two hundred horsemen following behind and another hundred leading the way, all of them alert for any possibility of an ambush. The sun drifted down toward the horizon in the west, but Shulgi wanted to see the damage for himself before it grew dark. The rest of his army remained half a day's march behind, and wouldn't arrive at Larsa until midday tomorrow.

A rage burned in Shulgi's chest at the sight of Larsa's devastation. The stench of death mixed with the acrid smell of burnt wood. Uncountable flies buzzed about, feasting on the rotting flesh of men and animals. Shulgi wanted to rail at Razrek once again, but he had already done that, bitterly accusing the cavalry commander of cowardice and of failing to defend Larsa. The two had nearly come to blows, and Shulgi knew he couldn't afford that luxury yet. He still needed Razrek and his horsemen.

"They're still across the river," Razrek remarked, breaking the silence that lasted far too long.

Shulgi didn't answer, but he lifted his eyes from the smoking ruins. On the other side of the Tigris, part of the Akkadian camp showed atop the bluff. No death odors up there, only clean breezes blowing off the river. At the base, more than a dozen boats lined the west bank. The camp looked peaceful. No ranks of warriors, no line of sentries stared at the riders approaching Larsa. The Akkadians didn't care about Shulgi's army, at least not today. All the Sumerians understood the humiliating situation. King Shulgi's men had no way to cross the river.

Larsa had always boasted the easiest crossing for miles in either direction. That's why the city had sprung up here, to take advantage of the easy crossing. But while its current might flow slowly, the Tigris remained too wide and deep for horses or men to swim across. Boats and rafts would be needed to get the soldiers and supplies across, and any crossing would be vulnerable to attack until enough soldiers were established on the far side.

"I can ride north." Razrek's voice seemed loud in the stillness that hung over Shulgi's commanders. "There's a village ten or twelve miles from here where we can get some horsemen over."

"No. We'll cross here." Shulgi had already made his decision. "Have the men scour the countryside. We'll build the rafts just above Larsa."

"Why cross the river at all? We can reach Sumer just as quickly from this side of the river."

"If we want to close with Eskkar, we need to cross here."

"The Akkadians will stop us. From those bluffs, they could pour arrows down on us."

"They won't be here to stop us," Shulgi said. "They haven't bothered to establish outposts or watchtowers. I think they'll soon be on the march once again, tomorrow or the next day."

"Heading to Sumer."

Shulgi's advance force had encountered dozens of naked survivors, most of them women and children, and all of them exhausted, hungry, and full of despair. The Akkadians had driven them out of the city with nothing, and the dazed inhabitants had begged Shulgi's men for food and water. Eskkar's men had poisoned every well with dead bodies, man and beast, that now rotted in the warm water.

Shulgi understood the trap Eskkar had set for him. If he ignored the wretched survivors, left them to starve, his troops would begin muttering against him. If he ordered his men to share their own meager food with them, his soldiers would be forced to do with less, and his entire army would be slowed down in the process. Gritting his teeth, Shulgi acceded to the need to share his supplies.

Almost all who had survived the city's fall repeated that the Akkadians planned to march on Sumer. Shulgi wasn't so sure. The further south Eskkar went, the greater the danger to the Akkadians increased. Even if he reached Sumer, the city wasn't likely to fall overnight, like Larsa. Shulgi had already dispatched a company of horsemen to warn Kushanna that the Akkadian army might be on the march toward them and to take extra precautions. And with every step farther southward, the Akkadian supply line would be stretched thinner and thinner. Shulgi already had men working to stop the infernal boats that carried men and supplies to Eskkar's forces.

None of these thoughts gave Shulgi any satisfaction. He had to cross the river somewhere, and the easiest route to Eskkar's army lay across the river. If Shulgi moved to some other crossing, he would waste another day marching, and still have to find or build boats. Better to do it here, where the abandoned men of Larsa could at least provide a labor force.

"Razrek, set up the camp over there, away from the stink of Larsa." The horses sensed the odor of death, too, and pawed the ground nervously, unwilling to move closer to its source. The gagging smell would last for days, perhaps longer.

"As soon as the camp is started, send riders up and down the river, looking for boats, wood, ropes, anything we can use to build rafts."

He turned his horse away and trotted back to where he ordered his command tent erected. For once the servants and soldiers doing his bidding had nothing to say. Everyone avoided his gaze. Shulgi handed off his horse and sat cross-legged just outside the tent flap. He spread a map out before him and stared at its symbols. He hadn't moved when Razrek returned.

"I've sent fifty horsemen up and down the river, searching for boats." Razrek squatted down across the map from Shulgi. "We should be able to start crossing as soon as the army arrives. That is, if Eskkar's men are gone. Though I still think it's a waste of time to cross if we're going back to Sumer."

Shulgi lifted his gaze from the map. "Eskkar has no intention of marching to Sumer. He's going to Isin. He wants us to dash off toward Sumer, to give him more time to take the city."

Razrek glanced at the map. "Why Isin? Why not Sumer? It's not that much further."

"Have you wondered where Eskkar's cavalry is?"

"Not lately." Razrek shrugged. "No one has seen any sign of them. As long as they're not a threat, who cares where they've gone?"

Shulgi bit off the cutting reply. Razrek had his uses, but strategy wasn't one of them. "Eskkar cares. I think he's sent them out into the desert. They've ridden north, circled around Lagash, and are probably attacking Nippur right now. Unless they're headed to Uruk."

"Uruk! They'd have to ride halfway across the desert, and the Tanukhs still have plenty of men there to stop them. And they wouldn't have any supplies."

"Unless there were more of those cursed boats coming down the Euphrates to resupply them."

"There's no way, not by boat. Lagash sits on the Euphrates. If that many boats tried to run past them, we'd have heard about it."

"These maps don't show every stream and creek in Sumeria, and the Euphrates has more than one branch going south. I spoke with several men from Lagash. They say there's a good-sized stream that bypasses Lagash before running down to Uruk."

"Even if Eskkar's horsemen did reach Uruk, they would never be able to take the city. They have no archers. There's not enough of them to force an attack."

"True. Unless they rode in from the west unexpectedly and stormed the city at night. Or if Eskkar has more agents in Uruk to open the gates for him. Larsa fell almost as soon as he arrived, remember that."

That city's survivors had related the story of men climbing unhindered over the wall.

Razrek licked his lips. The less he heard about Larsa the better. "We should send a warning to Uruk and Nippur, and Lagash, too. Let them know –"

"It's too late for that." Shulgi shook his head. "I should have thought of this earlier. The Akkadian cavalry rode off six days ago. It would take us three days to get a rider to Lagash, and at least two to reach Uruk from here, probably two and a half days. There are two wide rivers to cross, remember. If Eskkar's cavalry is going to Lagash, they're already there. If they're going to Uruk, they'll be there the day after tomorrow."

"They'll be spotted. Lagash will send word down the river to warn the other cities."

"Unless Eskkar's horsemen ride deeper into the desert. This Hathor that commands them, they say he came to Akkad across that very desert. That he knows much about desert fighting. And the Tanukhs would be caught off-guard. With the Salibs destroyed, they have no enemies to raid them. "

Razrek grimaced. "Hathor is a renegade Egyptian who begged for his life, and was saved from the torture by Eskkar's witch-wife. No one knows why. But even if Hathor knows the desert, it still makes for hard traveling. He would need supplies, hay for the horses, food for his men."

"All of which could have been prepared and stored months ago. Or there's an even easier way. The villages of the Tanukhs have plenty of food and fodder in them, especially now."

Even Razrek knew enough to glance around, to make sure no Tanukhs could hear the conversation. The Tanukh horsemen made up almost a third of Razrek's cavalry. They retained their own leaders, and fought only for gold and the chance to loot their enemies. Razrek had unleashed them on the Akkadian farmlands, but they somehow managed to devastate and pillage almost as many Sumerian farmers in the process. Brutal and cunning, they were like jackals. They struck only when their enemy appeared weak, and stole anything and everything they could get their hands on. Against a strong enemy, they were as likely to turn and run.

"If the Tanukhs think that Akkad has horsemen raiding their lands," Razrek said, "they'll race home as fast as they can ride."

"It might almost be worth it, for all the trouble they've caused."

The Tanukhs had created more problems for Razrek and the rest of the Sumerian army than any other group. Everyone hated them. They had only joined the Sumerian cause because of Shulgi's gold, and the promise of more loot from Akkad when the city fell.

"If they left, they would keep Eskkar's cavalry off our backs."

Shulgi shook his head. "Even if they stayed together, the Tanukhs wouldn't number much more than the Akkadians. They'd never face Eskkar's horsemen in battle. Hathor would ride right through them, if they tried to stop him. No, better to keep them here, where they can be useful."

"Well, what are we going to do?"

"We're not going to tell anyone about our suspicions of where Eskkar's cavalry might be. We're going to need every horseman we have, even the Tanukhs, when we come to grips with the Akkadians."

"You think Eskkar will stand and fight?"

"When he's ready, he'll attack us. He intends to wear us down, weaken us by marching up and down Sumeria, wait until our supplies are low. Then he'll attack."

Razrek wasn't convinced. "You think Eskkar has planned all this out in advance? It would have taken days, months . . ."

"Yes, I think he has. The barbarian – or perhaps his witch-wife Trella – has prepared for this war for at least a year, maybe longer. We thought we had given him only two choices, to march south and fight us at Kanesh, or wait for us to come to Akkad. Instead, he's devised another way, and unless we start out-thinking him, Eskkar may end up nailing our hides to Akkad's gate."

"But he doesn't have enough men," Razrek protested. "He'll never face us in battle."

"I underestimated Eskkar once," Shulgi said. "And now Larsa is gone, along with most of our supplies. I'm not doing it again. We're going to make him fight us when we're ready."

"How will we do that? He's already proven he can out-march our men, and we don't have enough horsemen to stop his army."

"First we have to make sure Isin holds. If he captures that city, he can march in any direction, south toward Sumer or north to Lagash and Nippur. Whichever way we march, he'll move in the opposite direction."

"Isin's been warned. Eskkar won't be able to take it, not before we can reach him. Naxos is not some merchant who can be brushed aside, like Naran."

"I'm telling you, Eskkar already has a plan to take the city. Just like he did at Larsa. The best way to stop him is to send all the soldiers and horsemen from Isin back to their city. We've got three thousand men from Isin in our ranks, and a third of them are cavalry. Send as many as you can get on horseback at once. They should be able to reach the city before Eskkar's foot soldiers get there."

"And if they can't, if they arrive too late?"

"Tell them to ride the horses to death, whatever it takes to save their city. Send any horsemen from Larsa, too. They'll understand what losing Isin means. Meanwhile, I'm going to stop these boats that have been resupplying Eskkar's forces. Without them, he can't move as fast or as far. If Isin can hold out for a few days, we'll catch up with him and crush him there."

"What about our own supplies?"

The mountain of supplies that had been laboriously transported to Kanesh now languished there. Shulgi knew it would take more than a few days to get even a portion of those goods moving south again.

"I've already sent word to Sumer. They'll load every boat they can find and send it upriver to Isin. Your horsemen will have to make sure that we get those supplies, not the Akkadians. And you can do that while you find and finish the Akkadian cavalry. When they're finished with Lagash, or more likely, Uruk, they'll head east to rejoin Eskkar. Once they're reunited, that's when they'll be ready for the final battle."

"And if you're wrong, if Eskkar marches toward Sumer?"

"Then Sumer will have to hold out. But even if it falls, the barbarian will have no way to escape."

"You don't care about your own city, Shulgi?"

"The city can always be rebuilt, Razrek. If Eskkar is dead and his army smashed, we can take Akkad at our leisure, and win the war. A few cities lost along the way are a small price to build an empire. Now get moving, and get those men on their way to Isin. By tomorrow I want them well on their way."

51

Day 7

Well after dawn, Eskkar and Grond rode to the top of the bluff overlooking the Tigris. Across the river lay the ruins of what had been Larsa, where a few fires still smoldered and sent wisps of smoke into the air. The advance elements of Shulgi's army had arrived yesterday afternoon and established a camp just beyond the ruined walls. Before long, scouting parties rode north and south, no doubt looking for anything they could use to get men across the river. Today would see the rest of the Sumerians march into view.

Shulgi must have decided to cross here, which meant he wouldn't waste any time going north toward Akkad or south to defend Sumer. Eskkar hadn't expected that, and frowned at the implications. "He's going to stick to our heels."

"Well, you couldn't expect Shulgi to keep making mistakes. Sooner or later, he had to do something right."

The Sumerian king had lost the tactical advantage twice, once when he let the Akkadians slip past him at Kanesh, and again when he let Hathor's cavalry ride off uncontested. Perhaps even a third time, when he wasted Razrek's horsemen trying to save Larsa.

"I almost wish we had the means to send a raiding party back across the water. With some luck, they might catch Shulgi off guard. His death would go a long way to ending the war."

"No doubt Shulgi has the same ideas about you."

488

Neither force could cross the river for now. Shortly after the Sumerians were sighted, the boats that had ferried the Akkadians across the river were dragged onto the riverbank, broken up and burned. Without boats, neither side could harm the other. Instead, the tired Sumerian cavalry would now have to search up and down the river, looking for boats or anything else that would float to help them ferry their soldiers across.

Meanwhile, Eskkar's soldiers rested in their camp, while he and Grond stared across the Tigris, watching the weary enemy straggle into camp. The Sumerians arrived in ragged groups, the result of their rush to Larsa, which had spread their force as the better-trained and conditioned elements moved faster than those slower of foot. Nevertheless, the entire Sumerian army would be at Larsa by midday, joining with those who had ridden in yesterday.

Eskkar watched as the enemy soldiers – no doubt as soon as their commanders dismissed them – moved toward the river, to get a better view of the ruins of the city. He remembered a saying of his clan: a sword can cut two ways. According to Trella's spies, the Sumerians had begun this war with high spirits, eager for conquest and glory. Now those same soldiers had learned a grim lesson. War had come to their land, and struck down their own kind as mercilessly as they had killed the farmers and villagers living along the Akkadian border.

Even more important, Shulgi and his commanders had learned that same lesson. The Sumerians had captured a few outposts and destroyed crops. Outposts could be rebuilt and new seeds planted. Meanwhile, Eskkar had overwhelmed and destroyed one of their cities. That loss would not be replaced easily, as new supply lines and depots would have to be established, a lengthy and laborious process.

Eskkar had ridden to the bluff so that the enemy could see him, just out of reach of Shulgi's vast army. Some of the Sumerians would be angry and eager to strike a blow in revenge. But others would be worrying about losing their own lives, or their own city. When men ride to war, the sword indeed can cut two ways.

"They don't look very happy," Grond remarked.

The Sumerians had noticed the little party of Akkadians watching them from the bluffs. A distant muttering of angry voices floated across the river, and Eskkar saw men jumping up and down in anger, unable to control their rage at the Akkadians who had burned their city. Voices couldn't carry over such a distance, but a few began to bang their swords against their shields, unable to do anything more.

"Many of those soldiers are from Larsa," Eskkar said. "They're wondering what happened to their families, their wives, whether they are alive or dead."

"Some will go off looking for their kin, I expect."

"Shulgi won't allow that. None of them dare come closer to the ruins. If he lets even one of Larsa's soldiers depart, they'll all desert."

"And we just stay here all day?"

"Our men need to rest, and we might as well do it here as anywhere. Besides, this way we can use up most of the food we took from Larsa. It will be that much less to carry. Shulgi's soldiers will be tightening their belts tonight. They'll find little to eat but what they carried with them."

"And you think Shulgi will cross here and follow us to Isin?"

"If not here, then somewhere nearby. He must know where we intend to go by now. I just hope he hasn't figured out where Hathor has gone."

"Even if Shulgi does, Hathor will be fine. He knows ..." Grond moved his eyes to the north. "There's a boat coming down the river."

Eskkar gazed up the expanse of the Tigris, lined on both sides with small trees and rushes. The height of the bluff, about a hundred paces, provided a good vantage point. A faint blur of white showed a ship under sail, taking advantage of a favorable breeze to race down the waterway. "We're not expecting any more of Yavtar's ships. It could be Sumerian."

The last of the river craft had set out yesterday for Akkad. No more boats would be linking up with Eskkar's army until he reached his next destination.

"I don't think that's ... it's moving too fast to be Sumerian," Grond said. "It must be one of Yavtar's messenger boats."

Built for speed, the small but trim craft carried a taller sail and more than enough rowers to race a boat up or downriver.

By now Eskkar's eyes picked up more detail. Definitely a messenger boat piloted by a fearless master, to sail his craft right toward the heart of the Sumerian army. "Let's get down to the water before Shulgi finds some way to sink the boat."

They wheeled their horses around and cantered away from the edge of the bluff. It took a few moments to reach the bottom. They rode along the back of the hill until they reached the opening that led to what had been the western side docks for the city of Larsa.

When they reached the water's edge, they found themselves joining a growing crowd of Akkadian soldiers. Other eyes had spotted the boat and come to the same conclusion. Every man in the army wanted to know what news it carried.

Eskkar didn't have to wait long. The boat moved towards them, six rowers on each side propelling the craft through the calm waters. When the ship drew closer, the sail came down. Eskkar saw the oarsmen slow their strokes and lean back, letting the steersman guide the vessel through the currents. A man stood in the prow of the boat.

"It's Draelin!" Someone with keen eyes recognized one of Daro's subcommanders.

A moment later, the craft hissed onto the sandy riverbank. Before it stopped moving, Draelin leapt off the bow and splashed his way through the mud, ignoring those soldiers helping pull the boat up on the shore. Instead, he headed straight for the king.

Eskkar swung down from his horse just as Draelin arrived. Whatever news the soldier carried, it couldn't be bad, not with a grin that broad on his face.

"Lord Eskkar," Draelin began, but words failed him. He threw his arms around Eskkar and hugged him tight. Some of the soldiers standing around laughed at the sight. Before Eskkar could react, Draelin pushed away. "Lord Eskkar, I bring you –"

A powerful voice from one of the boat crew spoiled whatever speech Draelin had prepared. "We won! We defeated the barbarians and drove them from the walls!"

The words echoed off the cliff and out over the river. In a heartbeat the soldiers broke out in a cheer. By now more Akkadians had wandered down to the river. They took up the cry, everyone shouting and pounding their companions on the back.

"We won! Akkad is safe! The city is safe!"

Like a raging hillside fire, the word swept through the camp. Soldiers ceased whatever task occupied them and rushed to the river's edge. In moments every Akkadian fighter joined in the celebration. The cheers and cries of five thousand voices swelled and soared over the river, a jubilation of pure joy mixed with relief. Since leaving Kanesh six days ago, the men of Akkad had worried about the dangers facing their city. By unspoken agreement, no one had said anything about the threat to their family and friends left behind, but every man had struggled to keep the dark thoughts from his lips.

Across the river, the Sumerians clenched their fists in rage. They'd seen the ship come sailing down the Tigris, unafraid of their vast army. The enemy knew of the other ships that plied the river with the same impunity, carrying food and supplies to Eskkar's army. And the Sumerians knew that only some great victory would have occasioned such an outburst, and that whatever good fortune cheered the Akkadians would bring only anger and gloom to their own cause and hearts.

By now Eskkar had regained his composure. Men from the boat had jumped ashore, each one shouting news about the attack. Draelin couldn't be heard above the din, so Eskkar swung back up on his horse, then leaned down and grabbed Draelin by the arm. With one powerful swing Eskkar pulled the messenger up behind him. A touch of Eskkar's heels sent the horse in motion, clearing a way through the still growing crowd of happy soldiers.

With Grond following, Eskkar finally broke free of the soldiers. He guided the horse back up the bluff, leaving the thousands of milling soldiers still celebrating beneath them. When he eased the horse to a stop, the cheering had started to die down.

"At least we can talk up here," Eskkar said, as Draelin slid down from the horse. Eskkar followed, and with Grond accompanying them, they moved to the edge of the bluff, where they could see the camps of the Sumerians. "Now, tell me what happened!"

Draelin's smile had returned. He told the story of Trella's victory, how she had unearthed the plot and lured the Alur Meriki into the city, where the archers had riddled them with arrows.

"In the morning, we counted over seventy dead and wounded. That included another dozen cut down in the ditch as they fled. Horsemen from Bisitun arrived and even though they were outnumbered, they chased after the fleeing barbarians and killed a few more. The Alur Meriki didn't even stop to attack or loot the outlying farms. By then they had no stomach for facing our fighters."

As Draelin's story unfolded, Eskkar felt a vast weight ease from his shoulders. Like his men, he had refused to think about Akkad and the danger to Trella. Now that burden could be set aside. With Shulgi's army here, instead of ravaging Akkad's lands and storming its walls, Trella and little Sargon would be safe. The countryside and the all-important crops would be protected. And no matter what happened to Eskkar, it would be many months before Sumer could mount another assault on the northern lands.

Another emotion grew in his breast. The Sumerians had made a pact with their hated enemy, the common enemy of all city- and village-dwellers. Shulgi sought to unleash the fury of the Alur Meriki. Eskkar determined to turn that same fury against the Sumerians.

He made Draelin tell the story again and again, each time dragging a bit more information from the messenger. At last he could think of no more details to add.

"Lady Trella asked me to give you this message. She said to tell you that the city is safe, and well-stocked with provisions. Another cargo of silver just arrived from Nuzi, and all the soldiers received their pay. She wished you good fortune in your attack on Larsa."

By now the boats that had departed after the capture of Larsa would have carried word of the city's destruction to the north.

"You'll stay the night with us, Draelin," Eskkar said. "There's enough wine to celebrate Trella's victory."

Draelin stared at the ruins across the river. "I stopped in Larsa only a few months ago. People spat at me in the lanes when they heard I was from Akkad." He shook his head. "It's hard to believe it's all gone now."

"They brought it on themselves," Grond said. "Now I think we should take advantage of the wine, before the men drink it all."

"I'll drink a cup to your victory, Lord Eskkar. But as soon as darkness falls, we'll push off for Akkad. Shulgi is positioning men all along the river, to stop our boats. It's best to get as far north under cover of darkness as possible."

With so many crewmen, the little craft could row all night, even against the current.

"Then a good journey to you, Draelin," Eskkar said. "And tell Trella that we'll be home soon."

"Yes, only a few more battles to go," Grond added. He took one last look at the vast Sumerian army camped across the river and shook his head.

52

The great western desert . . .

Hathor hated the desert, had always hated it, even when he lived in Egypt, where the desert sands lapped ever closer as one moved away from the Nile. Growing up along the mighty river's banks, Hathor never experienced the cruel heat and burning sands of the desert until his fifteenth season, when his parents were killed. To fill his belly and seek revenge against their murderers, he joined Korthac's marauders and fought against Korthac's enemies for the next nineteen years. In time, he became a feared and powerful subcommander.

Most of those years he lived on the border of what the Egyptians called the eastern desert, cursing the fate that brought him there. The Akkadians called it the great western desert, but it remained the same sand, dust and searing rocks that spread from the land between the rivers almost to Egypt's border.

But Korthac, despite his cunning, had lost his great battle to seize control of all Egypt. His army almost completely destroyed and his enemies – burning with a desire for revenge – closing in on him, Korthac and a few surviving followers fled into the great desert. For months Korthac led the remnants of his men through this dry and useless land, watching them die one by one, the living feeding on the bodies of those too weak to defend themselves. The survivors had crawled out of the desert just in time to avoid dying of thirst. Hathor still remembered lying on his stomach, his face buried in a muddy irrigation ditch, drinking the sweetest water he'd ever tasted in his life.

Now once again Hathor found himself challenging the hot sands. He might well end up dead on this journey, but at least this time it wouldn't be the desert that killed him. Death would more likely come from a Tanukh arrow or Sumerian spear. But despite his distaste for these barren and arid lands, no man in Akkad knew more about fighting in this environment than he did. So Hathor had volunteered to lead the cavalry.

With Klexor and seven hundred and fifty horsemen, Hathor had ridden north after separating from Eskkar and bypassing Kanesh, taking a little-used trail that bypassed most villages. That day they covered almost forty miles and reached the first of their supply points. Yavtar's bobbing boats waited for Hathor's arrival, riding low in the water with extra food for the men and grain for the horses. Another thirty horses waited there as well, guarded by a dozen Akkadians who had herded them across the river and down to meet the cavalry. The spare mounts, all of them battle trained, would carry food and weapons, but their main function would be as reserves for any animals lost on the long journey before them.

Akkad's defenders would sorely miss the mounts. The decision to send them to Hathor would weaken the city, and only Trella's resolve and support had overridden Bantor's objections.

"A few more mounted riders won't save the city," Trella said, "but they may make the difference between Hathor's success or failure."

He wished the men who delivered the mounts could accompany him, but they needed to return to Akkad as quickly as possible. The city would be in danger, and craved every man who could swing a sword in its defense. Eskkar's war plan had much that could go wrong, and not least was the possibility that Akkad might fall while her army struggled in the south. Hathor had observed Korthac take many a desperate gamble, but never one such as this, that required so much from so many. The blessings of the gods – or Eskkar's famous luck – would be stretched to the limit.

With Hathor's horses and men resupplied, his cavalry started their journey at dawn the next morning. This time he led the way north-west. They had to get far enough away from anyone who might report a large body of horsemen moving toward the desert or the vicinity of Lagash. If King Shulgi learned of their position or even their general direction, it wouldn't be difficult to guess their destination. Once that happened, the warning would flash down the rivers, and Akkad's enemies would be alerted to a new danger.

All those worries mattered little now. Hathor and his force were as committed as Eskkar's own. If the Akkadian cavalry reached their destination and found a well-armed and well-prepared foe waiting for them, they would just have to deal with the situation as best they could. Attack if possible, or extricate themselves from whatever trap the enemy might have set.

That day passed without incident. The following day, just before sunset, the Akkadian cavalry splashed across the Euphrates river two hundred miles north of Lagash. Their course, however, continued westward, as they needed to swing wide of the city, so as to avoid detection.

Every horse and pack animal now labored under the need to carry extra water. Wells and streams would grow fewer and smaller as they rode west, and those sources of water would likely be in camps or villages settled by Tanukh or the few Salib survivors that had escaped King Shulgi's wrath.

As the sun rose and set, Hathor grunted with satisfaction at his men's progress. The rare travelers they did encounter fled at first sight, and never came close enough to identify Hathor's men as Akkadians. In this part of the countryside, any larger band of horsemen would more likely be either barbarians from the north, or desert-dwellers. At least, Eskkar had assured him, that was the likely assumption. Now it became Hathor's fervent hope, and he muttered a prayer for protection to the Egyptian gods he no longer believed in, and who, if they even existed, likely had no power this far from the Nile.

Each morning they rose before dawn, gulped down a mouthful or two of stale bread, watered the horses, and continued their journey. They rode hard, but always with an eye to caring for their mounts. Hathor couldn't afford to exhaust his valuable and well-trained animals. Whenever and wherever this journey ended, the horses would need all their strength for whatever fighting awaited them.

Another day passed without incident, and he decided that his cavalry had slipped past Lagash without encountering any of its patrols, a good omen. Late in the afternoon on the third day, Hathor lay on his belly and looked down into a vast desert basin, where he saw the first Tanukh village, a dreary-looking place named Margan. At this distance, he couldn't make out individual tents, but saw many had fires already lit in preparation for the evening meal.

Hathor took his time counting and guessed that a hundred or so tents comprised Margan, more than he'd expected this far north. Three rope corrals held about the same number of horses. He saw few warriors, though an encampment that size should have at least three hundred men of fighting age, maybe more. No doubt many of these Tanukhs had flocked to Shulgi's army, drawn by the promise of gold and the chance to loot the lands of Akkad.

Klexor and Fashod lay on Hathor's left, and Muta, once a farmer whose family lived just west of the Euphrates, crouched on his right. "How many warriors able to fight remain?"

"Not much more than a hundred," Muta said, "probably less than a hundred and fifty. And many will be boys and old men."

Hathor took one last look at the camp. "I've seen enough." He glanced up at the sun. "We've just enough time before sunset. Let's go."

He pushed himself backwards from the crest of the hill, then led the way down to where the rest of the men waited, tending to their horses and weapons.

Squatting down, Hathor used his knife to draw a crude map in the dirt, while his subcommanders crowded around to learn what they would face. It didn't take long to give the few orders needed. They had trained for such an attack before, and Muta's knowledge of the land had prepared them for this moment even before they started out from Akkad.

"Remember, we must make sure none escape." Hathor looked at each of his subcommanders in turn. "If any do get away, it must be to the west, into the desert. This village is only two days' ride from Lagash, and word of our presence must not reach them until we are well to the south."

Klexor, commanding a third of the cavalry, led his men out first. They would swing to the south, and make sure no one fled eastward, toward Lagash. Muta took another third, and led them to the west, deeper into the desert. When both his subcommanders were in position, Hathor would start the attack from the north, and the Akkadians would strike from three directions. With any luck, they would trap all the Tanukhs between them.

As soon as his commanders departed, Hathor returned to the crest of the hill to study the camp. Nothing had changed, and if the Tanukhs had patrols guarding the village, they had all returned for the night. From so far away, he couldn't detect any sentries, but the village would surely have a few in place.

When he saw that Klexor and Muta had nearly reached their positions, Hathor descended the hilltop and gave the order to advance. In moments, he and his men rode up and over the top of the low hill that had concealed them. They moved at a steady trot, the usual pace for desert horsemen trying to conserve their mounts, and one that kept their dust trail low to the earth.

They rode in no particular order, just a straggling column of riders. That took some doing, as both the men and horses tended to want to form the usual column that they had trained for over the last year or two. So the leaders of ten and twenty kept up a constant stream of orders, mixed with a good amount of curses at men who either couldn't or forgot to control their mounts.

Hathor hoped anyone noticing them would think – for a few precious moments – that they were a band of returning Tanukh horsemen. The twenty two Ur Nammu warriors under Fashod rode in the rear, where their different clothing and weapons might alert the villagers. The Ur Nammu all rode powerful mounts, the best in Hathor's force, and could run down almost any horse and rider.

The Akkadians covered nearly half the distance before they were detected, and managed another few hundred paces before those in the camp heard and understood the alarm. Hathor didn't bother giving an order. As soon as he saw men scrambling about, he touched his horse's flanks with his heels, and the big stallion jumped into a gallop. In moments, nearly three hundred men thundered in a wild charge at the Tanukh camp, a large cloud of dust erupting up into the air behind them.

The Ur Nammu warriors, at last free of the restriction that kept them in the rear, pounded past Hathor, angling their horses to the right. Their frightening war cries rose above the pounding of the horses' hooves. They would ride around or through the edge of the village, to prevent any from escaping to the west and south.

By now Hathor could see the confusion and panic in the camp. Women fled in all directions. Some men struggled to string bows, others readied their weapons, while most rushed to get to their horses. But the Tanukhs had no time to prepare a defense. As soon as they saw the great number of the approaching horsemen, most abandoned any hope of resistance, and tried to flee. By then it was much too late.

The Akkadians greatly outnumbered the Tanukhs. Hathor's men launched their first flight of arrow as soon as they were in range, about two hundred paces. Two more flights followed, before the Akkadian cavalry tore past the first tent.

Any resistance had vanished. Men fled, abandoning their wives and children, desperate to reach their horses and escape. But Muta and Klexor's forces arrived right after Hathor's, slamming into the village from either side, and sealing the village's fate.

Pulling hard on the halter, Hathor slowed his horse near the center of the village, his eyes searching for any resistance. The trap had been well sprung, and all he saw was death and slaughter. His men – most of whom had felt the wrath of the Tanukhs or knew of those who had – now offered no mercy to the desert-dwellers. They had raided and pillaged Akkadian lands for too many years, and now they would be repaid for that blood debt.

Every one of the Tanukhs died in the assault. Men, women, children, the young, the old, all were killed. The Akkadians had thoughts only of vengeance for the savage attacks on Kanesh and the border outposts. Even before the fighting ended, the women were shoved to the ground and raped, most more than once. Then they, too, were slain.

Hathor watched it all without showing any emotion. They all had to die, so that none remained who could give warning of the Akkadian presence. Better a thousand Tanukh deaths than the loss of a single one of his own force. The same brutal tactics used by the Tanukhs would be turned on them, only with even more ruthless efficiency. Terror indeed was a two-edged sword.

When the screams ended and the blood stopped flowing, the task of rounding up the Tanukh horses started. Other men emptied the tents of grain, food, or anything of value, and the herd animals were butchered to provide fresh meat for the Akkadians. They rinsed and refilled their water skins from the well. Then the destruction began. His men torn down every tent and piled them together, along with everything else that would burn. As the flames took hold throughout the camp, Hathor gave orders to dump all the dead bodies – both men and animals – into the well, a horrifying symbol for any desert-dweller. He intended to make sure the water source would be poisoned for many months, so that the Tanukhs could not return and re-establish the village. Akkad wanted no more raids originating from this part of the desert.

Survivors – if any remained hiding in the sand – must be left to die from thirst and hunger. The Akkadians would have no need to return this way. They would live or die along another route out of the desert.

Hathor had delivered Eskkar and Trella's first message of terror to the Tanukhs: those who ride to war against Akkad and its people will be destroyed.

Hathor established his night camp five hundred paces from the still smoldering village. His men, grinning and laughing at their easy victory today, ate well, and the horses had plenty of grain. Margan's fires burned and smoked with the stench of death long into the night, as Hathor knew they would. He'd waged this kind of war before, and that knowledge ensured that the devastation would be complete. Soon word of Margan's destruction would spread, and fear and apprehension would travel across the desert.

In Akkad, Lady Trella's comprehension of the use of terror had surprised Hathor. She understood – in some ways even better than her husband – how such a massive raid would keep the Tanukhs in check for many years. Always eager for knowledge, Trella had spoken to Hathor many times about his days with Korthac and his brutal ways.

Terror – she explained once to answer his question – was merely another way to defend Akkad and keep its enemies off-balance. Both our friends and enemies must know that it will not be used first, she declared, but if provoked, then terror would be employed to punish Akkad's attackers. Tanukh raids into Akkadian lands must stop, once and for all.

In Hathor's eyes, Lady Trella was more than just a keen mind. As he soon discovered, she also understood the many ways to use power.

The first six months had been difficult for Hathor. First his wounds had taken longer to heal than expected. When he grew strong enough to hobble about, he encountered many Akkadians who had suffered from Korthac's short rule, and now only Hathor remained alive to remind them of those unhappy days. But gradually the rancor had faded. As Eskkar trusted Hathor with more and more responsibilities, the populace started to change their minds about the dour Egyptian.

About that time, Trella had summoned him to meet her. When Hathor arrived, he found her speaking with another woman, Cnari, who not long before had lost her husband of eight years. Now in her early twenties, Cnari stood tall and slim as a willow, with fine features, long brown hair, and the slightly darker skin that, like Lady Trella, marked her as being born in the lands of Sumeria.

Trella introduced them, then found a reason to leave the chamber. Cnari appeared nervous, and Hathor realized this was no chance encounter, that Trella must have prepared Cnari for his arrival. For his part, he spoke haltingly, afraid to say much, and certain that his appearance and grim visage would frighten any Akkadian woman. Later he learned that Trella had softened that initial impression by relating to Cnari the story of how Trella first met Eskkar, and the fear and doubts she had experienced that night.

Trella didn't return to her chamber for some time, and Hathor and Cnari spoke awkwardly about meaningless things. When Trella rejoined them, Cnari took her leave. But before she departed, she favored Hathor with a brief smile that enhanced her fine features. He stared at the doorway, aware for the first time of the scent Cnari used, still lingering in the air.

"What do you think of Cnari?" Trella's words brought Hathor out of his reverie. "She is a good woman, but she needs a strong man to protect her. And it's not fit that one of Eskkar's commanders does not have a woman of his own. I can think of no better man in Akkad for her than you."

Hathor had not had a woman of his own for almost two years, since he left his family in Egypt to fight with Korthac. He hadn't thought of them in months, and felt no particular sense of loss at their absence. Here in Akkad, the women turned their eyes from him, remembering the horror Korthac had brought to the city.

"Cnari is . . . too beautiful, Lady Trella, for a man like me. All the men of Akkad will want her."

"And that has frightened her. She has no family of her own, no children, no one to guide her, so she came to me for protection and help in finding a new husband."

Trella had arranged dozens of marriages in the last few years. Her skill at matching men and women had proved as good as everything else she undertook, and men as well as women often sought her guidance.

"You honor me, Lady Trella. But I am not sure . . . she needs a man with more skills than a mere soldier."

"Perhaps you should ask Eskkar about that," Trella said with a smile. "For now, Cnari is living downstairs. If you wish, call on her, speak to her, listen to her. If you find she is not to your choosing, I will try to find you another. There are many women in Akkad who would now look with favor on you. "

Hathor doubted the truth of that statement. Trella said nothing more about the matter, and when Hathor departed, he decided to avoid Cnari. But at Eskkar's table that evening, chance seated Cnari beside him. They began to talk, and soon were ignoring the rest of the guests. The next evening, after he completed his duties, Hathor took a long swim in the river. Then he called on her, and they sat in Trella's garden at the back of the house, talking long into the night.

Just as much as the day Trella spared his life, that evening changed his fortune once again. When Hathor returned to his quarters, all he could think about was Cnari, her hair, her eyes, the hand she placed on his arm for a fleeting moment while they spoke. A few days later, they went to Lady Trella and asked to be wed in the temple of Ishtar.

That had been over a year ago, and now she had become part of his life. She had clung to him the morning the army marched to war, tears streaming down her cheeks, and he could scarcely free himself from her grasp.

No woman had ever cried over him before, and to his surprise, Hathor had had to bite back his own tears. Cnari was heavy with her first child, would probably give birth while he was fighting in Sumeria. But for the gift of Cnari's love that Trella had given him, to both of them, Hathor would fight a dozen battles for her and Lord Eskkar.

Tonight he put aside his thoughts of Cnari and the child that was to come. No matter what happened, he would have a son to carry on his line, or at least a daughter to hold his memory. Now was the time to make war, to destroy Akkad's enemies, and to ensure that no danger ever threatened either Trella or Cnari and her child again.

In the morning, Hathor mounted and led the men south. They left the smoking remains of Margan behind them, fit only for the flies and scavengers already boldly foraging for food among its dead.

53

Two days later, Hathor and his men swept down on the next Tanukh village in their path. They had ridden hard, pushing the horses as much as they dared, and hoping to outrun any news of their approach. Tibra, the next Tanukh encampment, was much larger than Margan. Situated beside a fair-sized oasis bordered with willow and palm trees, over two hundred tents ringed the glistening, green-encircled waterhole. Tibra also boasted several fields irrigated by channels dug out of the sand. Slaves had done the digging, Hathor knew, from hearing Muta's tales. Such labor was beneath a Tanukh's dignity.

The camp lay in the center of a wide basin, with no way to draw near without being seen.

"This is the village where I was enslaved." Muta's harsh words sounded different from his usual tone. "My brother died here."

"Then today you will take your revenge for your brother." Hathor gave the order to advance. The Akkadians formed a wide line of riders, and cantered toward the Tanukh village, his men readying their weapons. "Just don't get yourself killed taking your revenge," Hathor shouted over the drumming hooves to Muta. "We need you alive."

Muta's parents had been killed, and he and his brother taken as slaves, brutalized and beaten almost every day. For five years he and the other slaves had carried supplies from one Tanukh village to another, mere beasts of burden treated worse than the weakest pack animal by the ever-grasping Tanukh traders. His brother had died under the overseer's lash, after falling sick from hunger and exhaustion. The desert had as little pity on the slaves as did their Tanukh masters. One day Muta was sold to a Sumerian trader who needed extra slaves to carry his goods.

A year later, Muta was left for dead after he collapsed from exhaustion under his burden. Certain of his property's demise, Muta's latest master hadn't even bothered to cut Muta's throat or give him the hammer stroke to the temple. But Muta recovered, and somehow made his way to Orak, arriving a few months before the great siege. Eskkar and Gatus, desperate for men to defend the village, cared nothing about Muta's past life as a slave. They needed strong and willing men to fight the barbarians, and so, for the first time in his life, Muta learned the trade of war. Trained as an archer, he fought on the wall against all the Alur Meriki attacks.

Two years later, after King Eskkar defeated King Eridu in the first Sumerian war, Gatus had sent Muta to meet with Hathor. That foresight now benefited Hathor. Muta had not only lived in those lands, but had labored on caravans moving from village to village. He had walked most of the desert trails and knew the location of watering holes.

Hathor's horsemen shifted to a gallop and widened their front. The orderly formations used for traveling and training vanished, replaced by the need to get as many horsemen into the Tanukh camp as fast as possible. No need for silence or stealth. No force of this size could be anything but the enemy of the Tanukhs.

Nevertheless, Hathor had hoped to overwhelm Tibra before any could escape. But before his men had closed to within five hundred paces, he saw horsemen streaming out of the village, lashing their mounts and scattering in all directions. This camp might not have had any advance warning, but they had reacted swiftly the moment they caught sight of Hathor's cavalry bearing down on them.

More Tanukhs reached the corrals, wrenching open the gates and catching the first horse they could. The Tanukh menfolk felt no compunction about sacrificing their women and children, as long as they could save themselves and their horses.

In a way Hathor was glad to see them run. Two or three hundred Tanukh warriors wouldn't have presented much difficulty, but there still would have been many Akkadian casualties with no guarantee that word of Hathor's cavalry would not be spread far and wide.

His eight hundred men swept through the camp, ignoring the few arrows fired at them by the defenders. The inhabitants of Tibra were hunted down and slain as mercilessly as those of Margan. Those who could reach a horse galloped away, safe for the moment from Hathor's tired horses. Those who couldn't escape on horseback, mostly women and children, fled into the desert, running for their lives, each desperately hoping someone else would be hunted down and killed.

In moments, the Akkadians had swept through the camp. Hathor heard Klexor shouting to his men to collect the remaining horses. The more mounts the Akkadians could capture, the weaker their enemy would be.

At the same time, the burning started. One running man with a torch could set a great deal of fires, and soon flames from every tent sent a wall of heat up into the sky. This time Hathor gave his men little time to enjoy their victims. Food and grain were loaded onto captured horses, the oasis water fouled with the bodies of the dead, and anything that would burn was heaped in piles and set afire.

Only one life was spared. Hathor found the old man standing before his burning tent, a sword in his hand that he barely had the strength to raise. Hathor rode up just as one of his men was about to kill the Tanukh.

"Wait! Let this one live." Hathor glanced around him. This trembling old man might be the only Tanukh still alive within the camp. "Find Muta. Tell him to come here."

Hathor swung down from his horse and stared at the old one. The man made no move to attack, just stood there, his mouth flecked with saliva, his chest rising and falling with his fear.

Muta, his sword and right arm splattered with blood, walked over, a wide grin on his face. "Is this one the only one left?"

"Tell him who we are and why we came."

Muta took two steps toward the Tanukh. With a sudden movement, he struck the sword from the old man's trembling hand. Both sword and man went to the ground.

Muta put his sword to the man's throat. "When your cowardly men return, tell them the soldiers of Akkad have destroyed your village as a warning. Tell them that if they ever raid the lands claimed by Akkad again, we will return, and kill every one of you, no matter where you hide. Remember what I say, and tell your leaders. Do you understand?"

The old man nodded, unable to speak.

Muta spat in his face. "Don't forget!"

Hathor grunted with approval. "Now let's get our men on the move. We've still a long way to go today."

Before the sun had moved much more than a hand's breath across the sky, Hathor and his men departed Tibra. Behind them, fires burned and smoke slid high into the cloudless sky before disappearing. Hathor felt as much satisfaction as any of his men. Two Tanukh camps had been destroyed, but now the Akkadians' presence in these lands was known. He had to continue to move and to strike, and strike again as quickly as possible, before the Tanukhs had time to combine their scattered forces against him.

At least the Akkadians had plenty of food and water as they rode south. By mid-morning of the next day, Hathor's scouts spotted a band of Tanukh horsemen following them. They stayed far out of bowshot, but hung on Hathor's trail most of the day.

When the Akkadians camped for the night, a stronger than usual guard had to be posted. Hathor expected that the Tanukhs would try to steal back their horses, or perhaps attack the sleeping soldiers. Throughout the night, two hundred soldiers guarded the camp, every man taking his turn, until the morning sun lifted above the horizon and showed an empty landscape.

After eating and drinking their fill, the Akkadians started moving again. Hathor pressed for all possible speed. The quicker they could move through this land, the less likely the Tanukhs would be able to muster enough horsemen to dispute their passage. Hathor's cavalry rode south, continuing straight into the desert. By now frantic Tanukh messengers, leading extra mounts, would be racing around his force, desperate to warn the villages and camps that lay before these new invaders.

That night, the Tanukhs crept up as close as they dared, and launched arrows from out of the darkness. The shafts were intended not only to kill Akkadians, but to stampede the horses. All night long the attacks continued, sometimes only an arrow or two, other times a dozen at a time. It took all the Akkadians' skill to restrain the horses and prevent them from bursting through the rope corrals. None of the Akkadians got much sleep. Nevertheless, Hathor's men took it as a point of honor to deny the Tanukhs any chance to get at the horses, and each man hung on to two or three mounts most of the night.

When the sun rose, Hathor had lost two men killed, and nine wounded. But none of the horses had broken free or been stolen, and they found the bodies of seven dead Tanukhs scattered around the camp, killed by Fashod's men who hunted the Tanukhs in the darkness and took extra pleasure in the killing.

"Get the men moving, Klexor," Hathor shouted.

The men were just as eager to leave this place. The Tanukhs, their number increasing, resumed their shadowing of the Akkadians, but only once did they venture close. Muta wheeled suddenly with a hundred riders and charged toward the Tanukhs. They turned and fled, but not before Muta and Fashod's warriors drew close enough to launch three flights of arrows, shooting them at a dead run, just as they had been trained by the Ur Nammu. Four Tanukhs died, and as many horses, while the rest fled for their lives. After that, the desert dwellers kept their distance.

Hathor pressed on. Only one more village remained between him and his destination. When they camped for the night, they were able to find suitable ground between two low hills. It gave them a place to hold the horses, and surround them with guards. Once again, Hathor let the Fashod and his Ur Nammu warriors patrol the darkness. Whether due to the defendable location or Fashod's men, no arrows reached the Akkadians that night. Hathor and his commanders sat in the shadows and made their plans for the coming day, grateful for the chance to get some rest.

In the pre-dawn of the eighth day since leaving Esskar, Hathor moved through the camp making one last check of his men. Everyone had to know their mission and be prepared to move as fast as possible. He led the way out at first light, still heading south. He pushed the pace. Today they had to cover a great distance, and the horses would get little rest until tomorrow.

Another Tanukh village lay to the south-west, about a day's ride, and Hathor wanted to give the enemy shadowing his movements the impression that it remained his destination. A little after dawn Hathor spotted a dozen Tanukh horsemen riding at full speed and leading spare mounts, intending to warn the village of his approach. No doubt the main force of Tanukhs assembling to attack him had headed in the same direction.

At mid-morning Muta, who'd been leading the men, slipped back to Hathor's side. "We're here."

They had just ridden to the crest of a hill, and its height gave Hathor a good view of the desert before him. He gave the order to halt and let his eyes scan the empty landscape before him, taking his time and searching the land from horizon and back. No landmarks, not even a trail showed on the shifting sands and rocks. As he finished, Klexor rode up to join them.

"This is the place?"

Muta nodded. "From here, we turn east. The trail is unmarked, and it's a long dry march for men on foot, at least two days, but it leads to Uruk. On horseback, we should be able to make it in a single day. Once we reach the river, we'll need some luck crossing over. But the river shouldn't be too high at this time of year."

Hathor knew they had to ride almost fifty miles, then cross a branch of the Euphrates. If they could manage that, they would reach Uruk just before the sun went down. With luck, no word would have reached the city of the presence of a large force of Akkadian cavalry driving toward them. If Hathor hoped to take the city by surprise, his men would have to cover nearly eighty miles from dawn to dusk. There was only one way to find out if the horses could maintain that pace.

Such an opportunity, to appear out of the desert without warning, would give him a real chance to strike Uruk hard. Even if he couldn't gain entry to the city, Hathor could ravage the countryside, destroy crops and herds, and break Uruk's ability to support the war for some time.

He glanced up at the sun, which appeared to have jumped higher in the sky in the last few moments. Hathor raised his voice and let his bellow cover the entire column. "Mount up! We turn east here! Today we show the Sumerians the danger of attacking Akkad. We ride for Uruk!"

The men gave a cheer. They had had enough of the desert and its heat, and each step eastward would bring them closer to the fertile lands of Sumeria.

Hathor tugged on the halter and turned the animal's head toward the east. He and his commanders had trained these men for years, and now the long months of training would be put to the test. Like a long sword pointed at an unsuspecting foe, the column cantered toward the lands of Sumeria. The horses responded well, moving easily, as strong and well conditioned as their riders. Even the pack animals and spare mounts had no trouble keeping pace. With luck, the Akkadians would attack from a direction the unsuspecting enemy least expected.

The long ride began. With such a great distance to cover, they rested only briefly. To ease the strain on their mounts, Hathor periodically swung down from his horse's back and ran beside the animal. His men followed, of course. No horse fighter would ever admit that the old man commanding them could perform any feat of horsemanship or physical effort that they couldn't match. And they knew that today of all days, the Akkadian cavalry had to outrace the sun.

"Run, damn you lazy bastards!" Hathor shouted, again and again. "You can rest tomorrow, in Uruk!"

Scouts moved out ahead and to the flank. The Tanukhs would not be expecting a turn eastward. After two attacks on their own camps, they had no reason to think the Akkadians would suddenly turn their attention toward Uruk, nor would they likely be too concerned about such a move even if they knew. If the Akkadians moved out of their lands, so much the better. Let the Sumerian city with its thick walls deal with this new enemy. At least, that remained Hathor's earnest hope.

They rode and ran beside their mounts, every man giving his utmost, running and riding, the miles passing swiftly beneath them. Before long, each step became easier, as they gradually left the sandy wastelands behind and moved onto firmer ground. They crossed a riverbed, nearly dry now at the height of the summer, pausing only long enough for horse and rider to drink the brackish liquid and refill the water skins.

They resumed the punishing ride, racing the sun now at their backs. Mile after mile passed, and Hathor's feet burned and stung with every step. He ran until he could no longer draw a breath, then pulled himself onto his horse's back. Every time he glanced up, the sun moved lower across the sky, moving ever faster toward the horizon.

Suddenly, one of the scouts riding point halted, waving his arms and shouting that the Euphrates lay ahead. A few moments later, Hathor crested a low rise and saw the wide ribbon of brown water in the distance. By now every rider's dry throat burned with thirst, and the horses' necks and chest were covered with dried froth. Every water skin had gone dry long ago. Hathor had pushed every man and beast to the limit, but now that the horses caught the scent of water ahead, they renewed their own strength, pressing on until the Akkadians cantered right into the river before halting.

Men slipped from their mounts and fell into the water, shouting in delight and relief. Horse and rider drank together. The cool water refreshed them all, and man and beast drank and drank until every belly was stretched to its limit. The water soothed Hathor's feet, washing some of the pain away. After a brief rest, the men walked their reluctant horses across the river. The horses would be more likely to stumble and injure themselves carrying a man's weight through the water. The Euphrates was wide here, but moved slowly. Only near the center did they need to cling to their mounts and swim for a few dozen paces. When they emerged, they rested again on the east bank. According to Muta, Uruk lay about ten miles due south.

Hathor took one last look at the horizons. Nothing moved, not even a farmer tending his fields. The scouts had seen no one, which meant their presence might yet be unknown.

"Klexor, you take command of the main force. Muta and I will ride ahead with the picked men."

Hathor, accompanied by Muta and thirty men, prepared themselves. Hathor inspected every mount, to make sure it was fit to ride. Then he and his troop gathered the weapons and tools they needed, and cantered off. The rest of the Akkadians fanned out, to follow their commander at a somewhat slower pace, and to block the route of anyone who might see them.

All the horses were weary now, after a long day, and Hathor could feel his mount starting to tire. Nevertheless, Uruk drew closer with each stride. The sun sank nearer to the horizon, but now that worked in the Akkadians' favor.

On the main trail to the city, they encountered few travelers this late in the day, and those they did meet were all on foot. Farmers and traders shrank away at their approach, and none would be able to outrun them to Uruk. The city's gates would be closing at sundown. Hathor wanted to reach the city just before then.

Finally, the city's walls rose up. At this distance, Hathor had to rely on one of his men's eyesight. He couldn't tell if the gate were open or closed. If word of their approach had reached Uruk, the gate would be closed and the wall bristling with armed men. If it remained open, it would mean that Uruk had not yet learned of the presence of the Akkadian force within their heartland.

He knew a little about the history of Uruk. Supposedly the oldest city in the land between the rivers, farming and trade had flourished here long before anyone began working the land around Akkad. For a while, or so its inhabitants claimed, Uruk had stood above the other villages, but in the last few generations, Sumer and the other cities, with their emphasis on trade, had surpassed it. Uruk's walls reflected its status. Raised in the last few years, they were just high enough to keep out the occasional desert raiders.

Hathor halted his men for one last brief rest, and to allow them a few moments to ready themselves. The riders swung down from their horses. Twenty men, already dressed to look like slaves, wrapped ropes around their wrists as if bound. They would complete the journey on foot. Weapons were placed in sacks and tied on the backs of the horses. The change over took little time, because the men had prepared for it last night. Leading the way, Hathor rode slowly toward Uruk's northern gate, with Muta at his side.

Behind them came the twenty "slaves", trailed by ten mounted men leading the rest of the horses. The riders wore rope whips fastened to their wrists, the usual means to keep slaves in order. A single rider brought up the rear, leading two pack animals. Hathor's pace kept the supposed slaves staggering to keep up. He heard them cursing at the effort, but slaves often were pushed to the limits of their endurance and beyond. No one cared about a few slaves staggering along or falling down from exhaustion. More important, Hathor didn't want to find the gate slammed in his face just as they drew near. This close to the city, he couldn't see any extra guards appeared on the walls, and step by step, the little caravan moved closer.

"We've done it, Muta. They haven't heard about us."

If the Uruks had been warned and the city on alert, Hathor's orders were to raid the countryside and cause as much damage and confusion as possible. But if they could get into the city …

"They will soon enough." Muta couldn't conceal the excitement in his voice. "Just a few moments longer."

Hathor wanted to see if Klexor and the rest of the Akkadians had closed up the gap behind them, but didn't dare to turn around and draw the guards' attention to their rear. At last, only a hundred paces lay between Hathor and the gate. Then they were within hailing distance.

"Who are you?" The words came from the guard tower on the right.

"Answer him, Muta." Hathor tried to look unconcerned.

"Muta of Margan, bringing slaves and horses for Uruk's market."

"Hurry, then," the guard called down. "We're about to the close the gate for the night."

Another forty paces and Hathor's horse stepped its way through the open gate. A half dozen slaves stood there, ready to close the heavy panels that would secure the city for the night. He slid off his horse and moved aside.

"Where are you from? I don't recognize you."

Hathor turned to find the same guard who had hailed him approaching. He wore some emblem of rank on his tunic and appeared in charge of the soldiers at Uruk's main entrance. By now the first of the "slaves" had trudged through the opening, shoved along by their overseers.

"My master doesn't speak your language," Muta said, moving beside Hathor. "We come from the desert to the west of Margan."

A cry went up from one of the guards on the tower. "Commander! I see horsemen! Hundreds of them approaching!"

"Close the gate," the commander shouted, then turned to Hathor. "Get your men inside!"

The man's slow wits hadn't connected Hathor's party with those approaching at a canter. Hathor's sword flashed from its sheath and he drove the point into the man's stomach. The gatekeeper's eyes showed surprise and understanding in the brief moment before life fled his body.

Shouts echoed across the towers and along the walls. Hathor's men were already casting off their ropes and seizing their weapons. Bows and quivers were scooped up from the packs. Men raced into the towers, to climb the steps and kill the guards. The slaves about to close the gate fled down the nearest lane.

Two Akkadians had a different role. Each carried a hammer and a thick stake, and each was already hammering the stakes into the ground. A few mighty swings, and the sharpened stakes penetrated deep into the earth, preventing the gates from closing.

An arrow struck the wall just behind Hathor. He ducked into the doorway of the nearest tower. Soldiers from inside the city were rushing to the walls, but they had to fight their way through those inhabitants trying to get as far away from the gate as possible.

Hathor's men took their station inside the towers, shooting arrows at anyone attempting to drive them out. Arrows from the defenders rained down on the gate from the walls, but the gates remained open. Until the stakes were removed, a task that would take several men some time, the gates could not be closed.

Leaving his men at the base of the tower, Hathor rushed up the steps. Bodies were strewn about the top of the tower, including a few of his own men.

"Keep down!" a voice shouted.

Defenders from along the wall on either side were targeting the Akkadians. Nevertheless, Hathor risked a quick glimpse over the wall. Klexor and his men were only a few hundred paces away, screaming their war cries and kicking their exhausted horses at a dead run. Nothing could stop them now.

Hathor dashed back down the steps. By the time he reached the bottom, over seven hundred heavily armed men were riding through, all shouting war cries at the tops of their lungs. They split into three groups, one heading for the barracks, one for the marketplace, and one for the main stables.

Uruk had close to four thousand people living within its walls, but many of its fighting men had joined Shulgi's army. The city probably only had three or four hundred armed men capable of mounting a resistance, and these were scattered throughout the city, their day's work ended. Leaderless, they tried to resist, to gather themselves into units, but soon hundreds of people were streaming toward the south and east gates, escape the only thought in the minds. A few of the defending soldiers had the same thought, and the city's defense collapsed before it could even get organized.

Flames sprang up, as Akkadians found torches and oil, and set fires, as much to panic the inhabitants as to light the city against the gathering darkness. Women wailed and men shouted, all of them rushing about trying to save themselves. Hathor had never seen anything like this before, the entire population of a large city thrust into a complete panic within moments. Most had no idea who had attacked them. He heard the word "Tanukhs" again and again, despite the Akkadians using their city's name as their war cry. It seemed like everyone within the walls was screaming in terror.

By the time Hathor reached the south gate, the sun had started its descent below the horizon. As far as he could see, and in every direction, people streamed away from the already burning city, carrying their children or whatever possessions they had managed to snatch up. They would run and run until they collapsed in exhaustion.

Klexor rode up. "We captured the stables and many horses before they could escape. I've told our men not to pursue those running away. Otherwise, any who resist are to be killed.

"Keep the fires burning." Hathor had to shout to be heard over the din. "Burn everything. And make sure the horses we don't need are slaughtered, too."

There must not be any pursuit after the Akkadians had left. His men knew what needed to be done. One by one, as they found no foe to face them, they put down their bloody weapons and began heaping the fires. Doors, corrals, clothing, anything that would catch fire was put to the torch.

The sun slipped below the horizon, but the light from the fires that had sprung up everywhere made the city as bright as day. Uruk would burn through the night. This city, like the camps in the desert, would pay the price for helping recruit and arm the Tanukhs, so they could wage war on Akkad.

Day 9

In the morning, the stench of burning wood and flesh – both human and animal – hung in the air. Hathor's commanders counted at least two hundred bodies, mostly men who had died either fighting or trying to escape. The rest had abandoned their homes and fled. The countryside would be full of people running or trying to hide.

Hathor give his tired men no rest during the night. Guarding the captured horses, loading supplies and water skins, and even collecting loot, all had to wait until his men gathered everything that would burn and set it afire. Twice he rode through the wreckage of Uruk, pointing out huts or corrals still standing that his men had overlooked.

His soldiers cursed and swore at him as they labored, covered with sweat, dust and soot from the fires. Nevertheless, every man took satisfaction in the destruction. Uruk had provided men and supplies to both Sumer and the Tanukhs, and now terror had come upon them.

Just before mid-morning, Hathor swung himself onto his horse, and led his men out of the north gate. The Akkadian cavalry now resembled a vast caravan, with over a hundred captured horses loaded down with loot, the spoils of an entire city. Behind them, they left an empty shell, inhabited only by the dead, and possibly a handful who might have saved themselves by concealing themselves in their hiding holes. Hathor had even ordered the captured women, some still crying after being raped, driven out of the city. Some would return, but they would find little to sustain them.

The supply animals forced the Akkadians to travel slowly. The horses had a night's rest, but they were still weary from the great distance they had traveled yesterday. Still, Hathor knew he had to balance his men's need for rest with the need to keep moving. By now word of his raid would be spreading throughout the land, and every city and village would be scrambling to assemble a force large enough to hunt him down. This deep into enemy territory, anything could happen. Given enough time, the Sumerians could raise enough men to trap him.

Hathor led his men back up the Euphrates, to the place where he had crossed only yesterday. They pitched camp there and set up picket lines. Not only was the crossing a good place to camp, with plenty of fresh water, but they could see a good way in every direction, which meant no enemy could surprise them. Everyone not on guard duty slumped to the ground to fall asleep within moments. Hathor wanted to do the same, but he forced himself to remain awake, letting Klexor and Muta get some rest first. That would ensure that at least one of the senior commanders stayed awake and alert.

When they woke Hathor, the sun was falling toward the horizon.

"Commander, boats are approaching. It must be Yavtar."

Hathor accepted the soldier's hand and pulled himself to his feet. By the time he reached the river, six boats were heading for the shore, three of which were Yavtar's fighting ships. Hathor recognized Maralla, the commander of this little fleet. He stood in the prow of the lead boat, then jumped into the river and splashed his way to where Hathor stood.

"Welcome, Maralla." Hathor clasped the man's shoulder.

"Welcome, Hathor. We saw the smoke, and knew Uruk was burning."

"We were fortunate. They had no idea any Akkadians were within two hundred miles of Uruk."

"Did you lose many men?"

"About twenty dead, and thirty-six wounded. Can you take all of them?"

"Yes, and whatever loot you want us to carry, as soon as we unload the grain, food and arrows."

"You may need more boats. My men brought plenty of valuables with them. And the horses need the grain. We didn't have time to take much food from Uruk. We'll stay here and rest for a day or two, before moving east."

"As soon as we've exchanged cargoes, I want to be out of here." Maralla glanced up and down the river, as if expecting a fleet of enemy ships at any moment. "It's a long haul upriver, and we'll need to stay off the main branch of the Euphrates until we're past Lagash. If we row through the night, we may slip past anyone watching for us."

Maralla had come down from the north, bypassing Lagash, but word of his passage would have been dispatched, and no doubt foes would soon be waiting for him on his return. The sooner he got out of Sumeria, the better.

"We'll be moving out tomorrow as well. One day of rest is all we can risk this far south."

Hathor gave the orders, and soon the wounded were carried to the shore and handed down into the boats, the men returning with whatever cargo they were handed. It didn't take long to empty the boats, but it was well past dusk when Maralla and the last of the ships pushed off and headed north, their small sails catching a breeze that helped the rowers.

"I hope they make it," Klexor said. "It's a long way home."

The mention of home brought Cnari back to Hathor's thoughts. For the first time in his life, Hathor wished he, too, were home. He took a breath and put his wife out of his mind. "Even if they don't, they've fulfilled their task. Our horses will be well fed, the men rested, and we've plenty of arrows."

"Let's hope we don't need to use them until we rejoin Eskkar's forces."

Day 10

After a day and a night of rest, Hathor's forces moved out with the dawn. If he were to keep his rendezvous with Eskkar, he had two days to reach Isin, a journey of over one hundred miles. Hathor would have preferred to depart yesterday, but the horses needed rest and a chance to stuff their bellies with grain. It would be of little benefit if either his men or their mounts were unable to fight when they joined Eskkar's forces.

They traveled light, carrying only enough food for the two-day journey. The water skins stayed empty, as there would be at least a dozen streams to cross between Uruk and Isin. The horses had already devoured all the grain carried on Maralla's ships, and for the next few days would have to forage as they traveled. To make that easier, Hathor spread his men out over a wide front. He stayed in the center of the line, with Klexor on the right, and Muta commanding on the left. The temptation to burn and kill everything in his path was strong, but he knew he had no time to waste, and so the countryside was spared the worst.

They stopped at midday, after crossing over a small stream.

"I wish we knew how Eskkar is doing." Klexor had ridden in from the flank.

"We'll know when we get to Isin." Hathor had asked himself the same question, but refused to let his men see that he shared their concerns, not even his commanders. If they reached Isin and didn't find Eskkar waiting, they would probably all end up dead.

"If he's not there, we'll have a hard time getting back north."

"If Eskkar isn't there, word will still come down the river." Hathor didn't really believe it. If Eskkar wasn't there, it meant he'd been defeated in battle.

"And if we meet Razrek's cavalry . . . ?"

"Then we'll have a good fight before we get home." He clasped his hand on Klexor's shoulder. The two men had become good friends during the last year, training side by side. "Now we just need to get to Isin. Tell the men to start moving. We've still got a long ride ahead of us."

54

Eskkar and his commanders crested a low hill at mid-morning and caught their first glimpse of Isin, less than two miles away. The Akkadian army had approached the city from the north, and as soon as they reached the Euphrates, Yavtar's boats had joined them.

Like Akkad, Isin nestled in a gentle curve of the river. And, like Akkad, it had three gates. Eskkar had visited this city several years ago, but it was good to match what he remembered against the actual sight. Isin boasted a good anchorage, and he could see a dozen river boats crowded against each other. High walls ringed the city, and a fresh scar in the earth showed that the surrounding ditch had only recently been dug out, expanded and deepened.

"Won't be easy to get in there," Gatus said, his eyes scanning the possible field of battle. "Not with the reinforcements they got yesterday."

Over a thousand horsemen had ridden past Eskkar's infantry yesterday just after midday. The Sumerians hadn't bothered to avoid Akkadian scrutiny, and Eskkar frowned when he saw that these men were not the rabble Tanukhs or regular Sumerian cavalry. Shulgi had no doubt sent men to Isin who could be expected to stand and fight.

"It's not likely Trella's spies will be able to help us this time." Eskkar's eyes told him there would be no easy way into Isin. "They'll keep a better watch over the walls after what happened at Larsa."

"Too bad there was no time to dig the tunnel."

One of the many plans discussed at the war table was the digging of a tunnel under the city's walls. But such a task proved too daunting for the few men inside Isin working for Trella.

The last report Eskkar had received from Akkad's spies within Isin was that King Naxos had retained four to five hundred fighting men within the city. With the reinforcements sent by Shulgi, at least fifteen hundred fighting men would be preparing to defend the city.

"I never believed they could dig a tunnel without getting caught," Eskkar said. "If Shulgi hadn't sent those horsemen, we could have taken the city, despite the losses. But now, we'd lose too many men, and even then might not break through the defense."

"Let's hope that Corio's plan works."

The master builder who had erected Akkad's walls had dispatched his son, Alcinor, to each of the six Sumerian cities last year, ostensibly on trading missions. His "bodyguards" for that journey were veteran soldiers who focused their attention on the forces defending the cities and to the quality and quantity of men and weapons. Alcinor, who already equaled or possibly surpassed his father's skill as a master builder, had returned with much good information on the Sumerian cities, their strengths and weaknesses, and how and where they could best be attacked. Isin, however, had one feature that made it unique. Taking advantage of that, Alcinor and his father had come up with a dubious plan for taking the city.

In many ways, Isin appeared the strongest of the six cities. Its walls, while not as high or as thick as Akkad's, stood tall enough to require the construction of ramps for scaling. No easy approaches would provide any cover. Even if it could be taken by direct assault, Eskkar didn't dare risk losing half his army. King Shulgi would finish them off with ease after that.

"We'll have to give Corio's scheme a try. If it fails, we'll look like bigger fools." Eskkar took a deep breath and let it out. "Best to get started on the preparations."

"I don't think King Naxos will scare too easily."

The name of the king of Isin always awoke memories in Eskkar. His long travails toward the kingship of Akkad had begun when he had slain a man named Naxos, who had received orders to kill Eskkar from one of the ruling nobles. Trella's insight had provided Eskkar with enough warning, and Naxos had died with Eskkar's sword in his belly, a slow and painful death. The death of Naxos precipitated Eskkar's decision to stay and fight against the barbarians.

Now another man named Naxos ruled in Isin. Unlike merchants such as Eridu or Naran who bought their way into power, Naxos was a true warrior and he had won his kingship by fighting for it. The lands around Isin were some of the most fertile in Sumeria, and never failed to produce good harvests. Palm trees provided shade and numerous streams bordered with willows made irrigating the crops even easier than at Akkad. The people of Isin had grown prosperous in the warmth of the Sumerian sun.

The bountiful land with its warm climate had not made them soft or lazy. Eskkar knew that it was not only the hard lands that bred strong and ferocious fighters. All Isin's neighbors coveted the land that Isin claimed, and Naxos had built a strong fighting force to keep the other cities at bay. The city's inhabitants knew that their land and families remained safe only because of the weight of their soldiers' swords. Some of the strongest and best-trained forces that Shulgi would array against the Akkadians would have come from the levies that Isin provided.

Though Eskkar had never mentioned it to anyone except Trella, ten years ago he had briefly fought with the forces of Isin against an invasion from Nippur. His respect for the fighting skills that Naxos possessed was based on that experience. But Eskkar had never crossed paths with Naxos, who had also risen from nothing to assume control of the city. What he had fought so hard to take, Naxos would not relinquish without a hard struggle.

The city's sentries had spotted Eskkar and his company. The north rampart now thronged with soldiers, and even at this distance Eskkar could see them waving bows and spears in defiance.

Eskkar ignored them. "Let's get busy, Gatus. We only have two days, possibly three before Shulgi arrives with his army." He turned his horse aside, and rode back to the camp, Gatus and the others following.

By the time Eskkar reached the river, the last of the seven boats was being unloaded. Grain for the horses, bread and fruit for the men made up the bulk of the cargo, in addition to another three thousand fire-arrows, a hundred torches and twenty jugs of the oil that burns. But Alcinor's plan required something else, and two of the boats had carried nothing but shovels, six hundred in all.

The men unloading that odd cargo stared at the digging tools with quizzical looks, already spreading rumors about tunneling their way into Isin. Eskkar smiled at the sight. His men would soon have plenty of experience handling a shovel.

"Good morning, Lord Esskar."

He turned to find Alcinor standing there. "You came? I thought that your father was sending another to join me."

Tall and earnest-looking, the young man shook his head. "He wanted to, but I insisted on coming. This is too important to delegate to someone else. It was my idea, and I wanted to be sure it was carried out properly."

Corio would not have relished the idea of risking the life of his eldest and ablest son by sending him into a battle. In Esskar's eyes, Alcinor had already proved his valor by challenging his father's decision and risking his life by coming downriver to join the Akkadian forces.

"Then you can take charge of the men. Just tell Grond what you need, and he will inform the commanders. But we must make haste, Alcinor. Your plan seems to be more of a dream now that we're here than it did in Akkad."

"It's no dream, Lord Esskar. It will work."

Esskar still had his doubts, but he gave Alcinor an encouraging smile. "Then your name will surpass your father's. But I think you'd better start now, and work through the night. We may not have much time."

Gatus established a camp strong enough to stop any of Razrek's horsemen from attacking, even if reinforced by soldiers from within Isin. Protected by the river at their backs, the men took their positions facing outward, while the horsemen and archers patrolled the outskirts of the encampment, to make sure no spies from Isin drew close. Esskar wanted no word of what his men were doing to find its way into Isin. The low hills blocked sight of the camp and its activity from Isin's walls.

Under Alcinor's direction, Grond soon had a thousand men stretched out along the river, the shovels distributed among them. Some would dig, others would shift the loosened sand and dirt. Anything that could be used to dig or carry was pressed into service. The sacks used for ballast in the riverboats were utilized. Filled with dirt, they were hauled away, to be emptied and returned to carry another load. Eventually most of them fell apart from the heavy loads, which forced the soldiers to work even harder. Esskar knew there would be little sleep for any of his men tonight, and plenty of hard labor.

The soldiers complained, of course, loudly and often. They'd marched all day, and had hoped for at least a night of rest. Gatus ignored their comments. "What would you rather do," he shouted again and again, "dig or fight?"

Before long, they were shouting back at him. "Fight! We'd rather fight than dig!"

But Gatus had an answer for that, too. "You'll all be fighting soon enough. Keep digging!"

Day 11

Eskkar watched the work progress until almost midnight. Finally, after Grond's repeated suggestions, Eskkar took the hint and decided to get some rest. When he woke, the sun was well above the horizon, but he felt as rested as if he'd slept all night.

With a handful of bread, he mounted and rode toward the river. The progress in the ditch surprised him. Working in shifts, the soldiers-turned-diggers had moved an enormous quantity of earth. Grond, who had slept only briefly through the night, professed both Alcinor and himself well satisfied with the men's labors. Nevertheless, the work continued. There was still much more dirt to be moved. Now as impressed as any of his men, Eskkar decided that this whole scheme might just possibly work.

At midday, Eskkar studied the three men standing before him. Simple farmers, they'd been unlucky enough to be taken prisoner during the march to Isin. All of them showed fear, either on their faces or by their trembling limbs. Eskkar selected the one who trembled the least, and whose eyes showed a hint of steady wits. He moved to stand directly before the man.

"What's your name?"

"Harno, noble one."

"Look at me when you speak, Harno. Unlike your Sumerian rulers, I like to see a man's face when he talks to me, not the top of his head." Eskkar towered over the man, who appeared to have about thirty seasons. "Do as I say, and you won't be harmed. I want you to take a message to King Naxos. Tell him I wish to meet him. Tell him to bring his master builder with him, but no others. I will meet him alone, save for my clerk. We'll meet in the open, halfway between the hills and the walls. Tell him to come at once, if he wishes to save his city. Can you remember all that, Harno?"

"Yes, lord. But if he does not come . . ."

"You will be safe inside Isin's walls – at least for a little while."

"My brother." Harno gestured toward one of the other captives. "What will happen to him?"

"Ah, your brother. Well, his life will depend on how well you convince Naxos to meet me. Make sure your king knows that there is only this one chance to save his city. Remind him that I gave the same offer to King Naran of Larsa before I destroyed that city. If Naxos fails to meet me, you'll find your brother floating in the river, without his head. And make sure Naxos brings his master builder with him. That's as important as the king coming himself."

"Yes, noble one. I'll give him the message."

Eskkar made Harno repeat the message three more times, until he felt certain the man could remember everything Eskkar had said, at least until he reached Isin's walls. Then he and Grond escorted the man to the edge of the camp.

"Harno, there is something else. I want you to give this to King Naxos as a gift." Eskkar turned to Grond, who unwrapped a bundle he carried. A lustrous sword, with a carved hilt embedded with jewels, glinted in the sun. "This was the sword of the King of Larsa. He doesn't need it any more, so I'm giving it to Naxos as a gift. Give it to none but the king. He'll know what it means."

Grond rewrapped the sword and handed the weapon to the messenger, whose unsteady hands nearly dropped it. "The sword should convince the guards to take you to the king. Make sure no one takes it away from you. No matter who demands you speak to them, tell your message only to King Naxos. Remember that. Others will try to learn what words you carry. Do not heed them. And call out as you approach the walls, that you bear a message from Eskkar of Akkad for King Naxos. Go!"

Harno, holding the bundle awkwardly with both hands, had to be pushed on his way.

Eskkar and Grond watched the man stumble his way down the hill and break into an unsteady trot toward the city walls.

"Do you think Naxos will come?"

Eskkar shrugged. "Perhaps. He's a warrior, so he'll understand what the sword means. I don't think he'll be afraid. But he might suspect a trap. If he doesn't come, he should at least send someone else out to talk to us. Let's hope some eager subcommander doesn't force the message from Harno's lips and twist its meaning. We'll see soon enough, either way."

They remained on the crest of the hill until Harno reached the city's gate. For a long moment, nothing happened, then one portal of the gate opened a trifle, and Harno disappeared inside the city.

"Well, at least they let him in. I was half expecting they'd riddle him with arrows."

"Bring my horse, Grond. And tell Alcinor it's time."

Eskkar and Alcinor rode down the hill and moved out of bowshot from the crest. They stopped a little less than half a mile from the city's walls, just out of range of any bows. Eskkar dismounted, tied his horse to a scraggly bush, and sat on a small boulder to wait. The land – part of a grain field – lay empty after the recent harvest. Only a flat expanse of short grass remained. That should make it clear to Naxos that there would be no attempt to capture him.

The sun crawled across the sky, and started its descent. When the rock grew too hard to sit, Eskkar slid to the earth and stretched out his long legs on the ground, with his back to the boulder, and closed his eyes. Alcinor, too nervous to remain in one place, paced back and forth, his eyes wide as he stared at the city, unable to control his excitement.

"Your messenger has been gone a long time, Lord Eskkar. More than enough time for them to hear your message and act on it."

"He's a king, Alcinor. He can't appear to run when someone calls. Besides, the longer he takes, the closer your men get."

Nevertheless, sun had traveled a good distance across the sky. At last Eskkar decided that Naxos wasn't coming. He stood and stretched. Just then the gate opened, and twelve men rode out. They rode leisurely toward Eskkar's position.

He loosened the sword in its scabbard and moved toward his horse. If the men kept coming, he and Alcinor would ride back up the hill. Mitrac and fifty archers waited there, in case they were needed.

But ten of the men halted halfway, while two continued to ride. Eskkar checked the fastening that tethered his mount, then studied the men approaching. One was old and thick-waisted. Even at this distance, Eskkar could see the man's wispy gray hair floating around a mostly bald pate. Isin's master builder rode awkwardly on an old brown horse that looked more suited to pulling a plow than to carrying a man.

Naxos rode a rangy red stallion bigger than Eskkar's. Tall and broad, Naxos wore a bronze helmet and breastplate. Thick legs kept the horse under firm control, and a sword hung from his left hip. He stopped about fifty paces from Eskkar and looked around, taking his time and checking for any possible ambush. Naxos's nose, like Esskar's, had encountered something solid in his youth. Then Naxos turned his gaze to Alcinor for a few moments, before giving his attention to Esskar.

Esskar said nothing. Anything he could say now, any words or assurances, would mean little to Naxos. The sword had brought Isin's king out from behind his walls, but the man still needed to make up his own mind, and Esskar knew there was no need to rush him.

Naxos made his decision. He said something to his companion, tapped his horse's flank, and stepped his horse closer, his master builder following with obvious reluctance. When Naxos halted again, he was only ten paces away.

"You're Esskar."

It wasn't a question, just a statement.

"I am. You're as men have described you, Naxos of Isin."

"What do you have to say?"

"In a moment. Is this your master builder?"

Naxos snorted in disgust. "One of them. The other was too frightened to come. He fell to his knees and couldn't stop shaking. He thought you would cut out his heart and eat it before his eyes."

Esskar grunted. He'd seen such stupidity before. He turned to Alcinor. "Take Isin's master builder . . . what is your name?"

The man had to lick his lips and clear his throat before he could get the words out. "Sardos, King Esskar." He gave a fearful glance not to Esskar, but to his king, to see if Naxos approved of the use of Esskar's title.

"Well, Sardos of Isin, I want you to go with Alcinor here to the top of the hill. There's something you need to see. Nothing will happen to you. And when you get there, make sure there are no soldiers lurking about. King Naxos will want to know that."

Sardos turned to Naxos, licking his lips in fear. "Lord, do I have to go . . . ?"

"Get going, you fool, or I *will* cut your heart out myself. Do you think he's lured me out of Isin just to take your fool head?"

Alcinor, who appeared almost as nervous as Sardos, gingerly mounted his horse and started trotting up the hill. Naxos slapped the rump of Sardos's horse, to send him along.

Naxos watched as the two rode slowly up the hill, then turned his gaze to Esskar. "You know, I'm tempted to kill you right here." He let his left hand drop to the scabbard of his sword. The weapon would slide easily when held that way. "Shulgi thinks that killing you would end the war in one stroke."

Eskkar met Naxos's gaze. "Don't you want to hear what I have to say?"

"Your death scream would tell me all I need to know."

"Bigger and better men than you have tried to take my head." Eskkar kept his voice calm, with no trace of emotion, as all barbarians did when they faced their foe before battle. "But if you think you're good enough . . . think how happy Shulgi would be. I'm sure he would give you a suitable reward. Or perhaps he would be even more satisfied if I killed you. I'm sure I can deal with your successor just as well."

Naxos tightened his lips at the taunt. Eskkar could see the man considering his chances. He was on horseback, facing a man on foot. It should be easy enough to ride him down, one quick slash of his blade, but . . . Naxos took his hand off the hilt of his sword.

"Damn you, Eskkar, and damn Shulgi even more! I'll not do his dirty work for him, at least not yet. What is that old fool doing up there?"

That last was directed toward the top of the hill. Eskkar turned to stare upwards. Alcinor and Sardos had reached the crest, and now the two were exchanging words. Alcinor pointed to the north, moving his hands for emphasis. In a moment Sardos's high-pitched voice floated down the hill, but not his words. Both men continued talking, and the discussion went on and on. Every few moments, Sardos gestured impatiently. Even Eskkar grew tired of watching them.

"Alcinor is showing your man . . . Sardos? . . . how we're going to destroy Isin. I thought it best to have it explained to a builder who can understand such things. The idea is hard to grasp. I didn't believe it possible myself, but Alcinor and my other builders kept assuring me it would work."

Naxos stared up the hill, unimpressed by Eskkar's comment. The conversation between the two builders ceased, but Sardos continued to keep his gaze fixed to the north. Finally, he dragged his horse's head around, and started coming cautiously back down the hill, Alcinor following.

"Well, here they come." Eskkar's eyes followed the two as they approached. One good look at Sardos's face and wide eyes told Eskkar what he needed to know. "After you've heard what they say, you might want to see for yourself."

Sardos managed to pull his horse to a stop facing his king, his back to Eskkar. Apparently, the man no longer feared that the Akkadian would murder him. "Lord Naxos, the Akkadians have dug a channel from the river to just beyond this hill. It's almost completed. They're preparing to flood the city."

"Flood the city? What kind of fool are you? The city's a half a mile away, more even."

Sardos shook his head. "The ditch is nearly complete. Once they break through the last few paces of earth to breach the riverbank, the force of the water will widen the opening and deepen the channel. Since the river runs higher here than at Isin, the breach will continue to widen. The whole river . . . the course of the river will change. It will flood the basin. Isin will be surrounded by the river."

Naxos's brow furrowed in anger, and his words came more rapidly than before. "So? So let the water come. It won't reach the top of the walls."

Eskkar laughed, and both men turned toward him. "Ah, I'm not laughing at you, Naxos. That's what I said, when I first heard it explained." He moved toward his horse. "But as Akkad's builders explained to me, the water will quickly wash away the loose soil surrounding the city's walls. Then the base of the walls will begin to weaken. The bricks are mostly mud, after all, and as soon as they get too wet, they'll simply start to crumble under the weight from above. Once the foundation is loosened, the walls will come down, and the city will be under water. How high will it get, Alcinor?"

"About the height of a man, Lord Eskkar. Maybe a little higher."

"And how long will this take?"

"Once we open the breach, it will take less than half a day to surround Isin with water, perhaps sooner. Another half day should see the walls crumble and start to collapse. No longer than that, I think."

Naxos glanced at Eskkar, then fixed his gaze on Sardos. "Is this true? So help me, if they're trying to trick you, I'll cut your balls off and make you eat them myself!"

"Lord . . ." Sardos had to lick his lips again. "I think it will happen as Alcinor and King Eskkar say. Go see for yourself what they have done."

"Come, Naxos." Eskkar unfastened his horse. "Use your own eyes. Then we'll talk about how you can save your city."

"Damn you all!" Naxos didn't bother to wait for Eskkar. He kicked his horse and galloped up the hill alone.

Taking his time, Eskkar followed him. When he reached the crest, Naxos was still staring in amazement.

Since they had made camp yesterday, Gatus, Grond and Alexar had over three thousand men working in shifts, digging out a channel that already stretched more than a quarter mile. The soldiers still labored, moving dirt, widening the channel. The site impressed Eskkar almost as much as it did Naxos. Neither had ever seen so many men working together on such a task. After one look, even someone untrained in the force of the river could imagine what would happen when the riverbank collapsed, and likely Naxos knew more about the flow of water than most of those living in his city. Isin, like Akkad, depended on the river to survive, and Naxos would understand the river's strength.

When the riverbank was breached, the water would flow through the channel, widening it on the downriver side, as more and more of the bank was washed away. The unchecked water, pushed by hundreds of miles of river behind it, would flow out over the plain and engulf Isin, not in a fury of rushing water, but in a slow but powerful force that would make what remained of the city an island.

Alcinor and Sardos had rejoined them. Alcinor pointed out how the water would move, while Sardos explained the effects. Eskkar soon saw that both were wasting their words. A merchant might buy his way into a kingship with gold, but a fighting man needed to know how to think on his feet to accomplish the same goal.

"Come, Naxos. I think you've seen enough. Let's ride back down the hill, before your men waiting out there decide to do something foolish. Then we'll talk."

Without waiting for a reply, Eskkar turned his horse around and started down. "You can return to camp, Alcinor. Make sure everything is ready."

Eskkar stopped at the same boulder, dismounted and fastened his horse. "Send Sardos back to your men. I don't think we need our master builders anymore."

Naxos jerked his head. "Get back to the city. Start making preparations to hold back the water. Put every man and woman in Isin to work on it." He swung down from his horse and tied it to the same bush as Eskkar's.

"All right, damn you, now let's talk. Then I'll decide whether or not to kill you."

"Why did you join forces with Shulgi?"

The question caught Naxos by surprise. "Why not? He had plenty of gold, and too many of my men were eager to fight. It's always the fools who know nothing about battle that want to rush out and fight the most."

"Why didn't you go with him?"

"He didn't ask me. Like his father, I suppose he didn't want to share the glory of destroying Akkad. Besides, he trusts his own commanders, and he has a few good ones."

"His war has already cost Sumeria two of its cities. First Larsa, and now Uruk."

"Uruk! How did you . . . ?"

"My cavalry slipped away from Shulgi, crossed over the desert, and took Uruk by surprise from the west. I just received word before I sent the messenger to you. My horsemen will be here by sundown. Then I'll be ready to face Shulgi."

"He'll smash your forces, horsemen or not. He outnumbers you five, maybe six to one."

"Perhaps. But if I win, I'll move south to take Sumer, then return here to finish you. Isin will be isolated. I'll cut your supply lines and starve you out, if I have to. Or I'll just drown you and your city. There are other places where the river can be breached, and you won't be able to guard them all. You'll have to come out and fight, to stop me from unleashing the river, and this time you'll be outnumbered four or five to one."

Esskar paused for a moment to let that sink in. "Unless you're willing to consider another way."

Naxos frowned again. "What other way?"

"Stay out of the battle. Don't try to join forces with Shulgi, or attack my rear. If you do that, you can save your city."

"And if Shulgi defeats you?"

"Then you can say you were trapped by my threats against Isin, forced to remain behind your walls. I don't think Shulgi knows about Uruk, not yet. If Shulgi wins, then your troubles are over. If Akkad wins, then you and Isin will be the most important city in Sumeria."

"Sumer always profits more from the river trade than we do."

"Not after I tear it down. Or better yet, if I directed that all goods coming downriver from Akkad and the north go not to Sumer, but cross over to Isin. That would make your city the center of river trading in Sumeria. With all the merchants and goods passing through your gates, King Naxos of Isin would soon make the decisions for Sumeria, not Shulgi."

Naxos considered that for a moment. "As long as Shulgi lives, Sumeria will do his bidding. The boy's young, but he's no fool. Even now, his sister rules in Sumer in his name, of course. She is promised to me as a prize after the victory over Akkad."

"She's a cunning bitch who will probably poison you in your sleep on your wedding night. Since she and Shulgi took power, I've learned much about her. Kushanna belongs to Shulgi, apparently by choice, for many years. He might give her up for a few months, to lull you into relaxing your guard, but not longer. By telling you this, I've probably saved your life. Besides, your marriage wedding bed will likely be empty. With any luck, she's already dead by now. I have spies in Sumer prepared to strike her down."

Eskkar doubted that was true, but Naxos had no way of knowing if she were alive or dead.

"How . . . never mind her. And all I have to do to save my city and reap these new trade routes is stay inside Isin?"

"I know many of Razrek's men are with you. Is he inside with you, too?"

"No. He sent Mattaki, one of his commanders. Most of the men he brought are from Isin."

"Good. Without Razrek, his men will be easier to deal with. Still, they'll want to leave Isin, to attack my rear. Since I can't trust them, I want all their horses and yours, too, driven out of the city. My men will scatter them, so that it will take days before they can be recaptured. I want all your spears and shields carried outside the gate and burned. And I want five thousand bowstrings handed over. If you meet those terms, you can keep your city dry."

"Why the bowstrings? I don't have five thousand anyway."

"Every archer has at least two or three, and I'm sure you have another thousand or two stored somewhere within Isin. Without them, and without spears and shields, and with no horses, I won't have to worry about your men attacking my rear anytime soon."

"I need those weapons to defend Isin."

"Shields and spears won't help you on the walls, Naxos, nor will the horses. Not once the water begins to rise."

Naxos considered that for a moment. "Shulgi won't be happy if I do as you say."

"You did what was needed to save your city. Besides, if he wins, he'll be willing to overlook your actions. With Larsa and Uruk gone, he'll need Isin even more."

"Is Larsa really destroyed?"

"Everything except the walls was torn down and burned. The inhabitants, those that survived, were stripped naked and driven from the city. I turned Naran over to those he tortured over the years. Everything of value went north to Akkad, by riverboat. There will be no more raids north from Larsa. It will be five, maybe ten years before anyone even thinks about rebuilding anywhere near the place. By then, it will be an insignificant village, unimportant to the river trade. Isin will be the first to benefit from Larsa's destruction."

"Some of Razrek's men will resist giving up their horses."

Those words told Eskkar that Naxos had made his decision. Eskkar shrugged. "Make them. Most of the fighting men in Isin are loyal to you. How you convince the others is your problem. Put a sword to Mattaki's throat if need be. From what I've heard of him, he's not likely to sacrifice himself for Razrek or even Shulgi, for that matter."

"How do I know you'll keep your word? That after I make my city defenseless, you won't still breach the river?"

"Because I give you my word, on my honor as a warrior. That might not be enough for Shulgi or Razrek, but it should be enough for you. A steppe warrior has honor, or he has nothing. Even a Sumerian bandit like you should know that."

Eskkar knew that Naxos had started his rise to power by raiding villages up and down the Euphrates. When he took power in Isin, the first thing he did to restore order was drive off all the other bandits, including many of his former companions.

Naxos stared at him. By now they stood only a few paces apart. He swallowed both his anger and his pride. "All right, I'll do it. But if the river is breached, I'll hunt you down and kill you if it's the last thing I do."

"I'll send men for the horses and bowstrings. Make sure no one shoots any arrows at them from the wall. And if I see one rider on a horse leave Isin, one boat go upriver or down, I'll loose the last bit of riverbank myself. Even one rider, Naxos. Remember that."

"You're a fool, Eskkar, to let yourself be trapped like this, between Shulgi's army and Isin. The man's no fool, and he knows how to move his men."

"Perhaps. But better to fight him here than outside Akkad. Even if I lose, my city will hold out. Another army will be raised against him. This is a war Shulgi can't win. He was foolish to even start it, even more foolish than his father."

"But you can still end up dead, Eskkar."

"Perhaps. If not, you can come visit me in Akkad one day. I think Trella would enjoy your company. If I'm victorious, I'll send word to you in a few months. I think you'll find Akkad a better friend to Isin than Sumer ever was or will be. Think about that for the next few days."

Eskkar jerked the halter loose from the bush. "Meanwhile, stay in Isin until the battle is over. After that, you'd better send men out to fill in the ditch. The river might be stronger than Alcinor thinks."

He swung up onto the horse, and cantered away, without looking back, satisfied that he had rendered helpless one of his enemies and struck terror to an entire city. Sardos would have blurted the threat at the top of his lungs to everyone he met. All this accomplished, and all without losing a man. Trella would be pleased.

Day 11

The next day, Hathor crossed the Euphrates ten miles south of Isin just after midday. He and his men rode north at an easy pace. Both men and animals were tired after two days of hard riding since leaving Uruk, and he wanted to conserve their strength. No patrols or force from Isin appeared to challenge his presence, but he kept a wary eye on his flanks until his men had moved north of the city and he saw Eskkar's camp. Cheers broke out from the soldiers when they saw Hathor's riders approaching.

He sent a messenger on ahead, and found Eskkar and Gatus waiting for him when he rode up.

"Welcome, Hathor." Eskkar smiled for the first time all day. "Your wild ride through Sumeria will be talked about for many years."

"We had plenty of luck in the desert and at Uruk. We might have been here sooner, but we had to rest the horses after taking the city. And they're weary again."

"We've boatloads of grain waiting for them," Gatus said. "But you'd better hurry. We're moving north soon."

Hathor gave the orders to Klexor and Muta, then swung down from his horse. "Where's Shulgi?"

"Not far, now. Half a day's march, maybe less. His scouts are already nearby, keeping an eye on us. They've been watching us all day."

"And Isin?"

"Their horses are scattered, and the gates remain closed. Naxos wouldn't even open them for Shulgi's messengers. They had to shout their messages to those on the wall. I'm sure Shulgi won't be pleased when he learns about it."

Hathor laughed at the idea. "Any problems?"

"Just Yavtar. He and his ships should have been here this morning. Shulgi may have found a way to block the river."

"What was he carrying?"

"Food, mostly. And the bronze stones for the slingers. We already have most of the weapons."

"And you've picked the battleground?"

"Yes. It's not ideal, but it will have to do. There's not enough food for another day's march. Shulgi's probably as short of supplies as we are. He hasn't been able to move much of what he stored at Kanesh. Yavtar's boats have been raiding his ships. So our battle will be tomorrow, and only the victor will get a decent meal."

"Then I can get a good night's rest." Hathor stretched. "My ass is sore from twelve days of hard riding."

Eskkar smiled in sympathy. "I've ridden hard many a time in my life, but never for so long."

"Well, next time you can lead the cavalry, and I'll stroll along with the infantry."

"Agreed. But now listen to Gatus. We need to get moving once again."

The Akkadian army, foot soldiers and horsemen broke camp before the sun touched the horizon. They didn't have far to go, a mere three miles, but Eskkar wanted to secure the battle site before Shulgi's forces reached it. The Sumerians had shifted a bit north as they drew near Isin, to make sure they stood between Eskkar and any escape route back to the north and Akkad. They needn't have bothered. Eskkar had no intention of trying to escape, even if he could somehow manage it. Without food and surrounded by enemies, he had to fight.

Gatus left fifty men behind, including three on horseback to keep watch on Isin, and the rest ready with shovels to open the riverbank at the first sign of treachery from Naxos.

The army moved north, traveling at a steady pace even as dusk settled over the land. They reached the location Eskkar had scouted yesterday just as the last of the day's light faded from the sky. As the Akkadians settled in to make camp for the night, they saw the first of Shulgi's fires glowing in the north. The Sumerians had finally caught up with Eskkar's forces, and now they camped less than three miles away. The time for battle had nearly arrived. One way or the other, tomorrow would decide which city ruled in the land between the rivers.

55

Shulgi and Razrek sat side by side on the ground, hunched over the map spread before them. Vanar and the other commanders craned over their shoulders to get a better view. A fire crackled and hissed nearby, shedding its flickering light over the Sumerian leaders.

"He'll attack tonight, probably just before dawn." Shulgi tapped the map with his dagger. "That's why he's marched north, to get closer to our camp. Otherwise he would have stayed where he was, and tried to fortify his position."

"Why would he attack at night? He can't use his cavalry very well, and his archers will be shooting blindly."

"The barbarian always seems to do what we least expect," Shulgi said. "Move the men into battle order and have them sleep in shifts in their positions."

"Our men and horses are tired and hungry. They'll be even more weary if they're up half the night."

"And if Eskkar attacks while we're sleeping, how weary will they be then? The men can sleep tomorrow, after we've driven the last of the Akkadians into the river and watched them drown."

Razrek hesitated, then shrugged in resignation. Shulgi had been right about Eskkar's movements, and even about Uruk, and Razrek didn't have any good reason to challenge the king's orders. Especially since word of Uruk's fall had arrived, delivered by a single exhausted rider who had trailed the Akkadian force halfway across Sumeria. They had only heard about the sacking of that city as they ceased the day's march. To Razrek's surprise, Shulgi didn't seemed too concerned about Uruk.

"If he doesn't come at night, he'll dig in in the morning. We'll have to attack him."

"The ground here is as favorable to us as to him," Shulgi said. "The river will protect our right flank, and he doesn't have enough men to flank us. That is, assuming your precious cavalry can finally start earning their pay."

Razrek ignored the insult. They'd been over that argument at least once a day for the last ten days. "We'll brush aside his horsemen, assuming you can keep his archers occupied."

"As soon as you do, send a few hundred to Isin. If the Akkadians don't flood the city, your men can do it. I'll teach Naxos to keep a thousand good men out of the battle."

Despite both Naxos and Eskkar's efforts, word of Isin's plight had reached the Sumerians. Shulgi had flown into a rage when he heard of Naxos's refusal to join the fight, and for once Razrek couldn't blame him. Somehow the barbarian had managed to pin Naxos, of all people, inside his own walls without shooting a single arrow.

"Eskkar will have some tricks for us tomorrow."

"Yes, I'm sure he will," Shulgi agreed. "We're not going to fall for any of them. When the battle starts, we'll march straight at his center. All you have to do is keep his horsemen off our flank, and I'll finish Eskkar's spearmen. Once they're gone, the rest of his men will turn and run."

Shulgi turned to the rest of his commanders. "You know your positions. Tomorrow there will only be one command: to close with the enemy as soon as I give the order. We've cut off Eskkar's supply ships, and now he's as short of food as we are. Once we're finished with him, Isin will provide all the food we need, or I'll have Naxos's head on a spear right next to Eskkar's. Otherwise, I'll flood the city myself. A few hours fighting tomorrow and the spoils of Akkad will be ours. Just keep the men alert tonight."

Shulgi glanced at his commanders. Heads nodded in agreement. Even Razrek's. The Akkadian was trapped against the river with no way to cross, outnumbered, and short of food and supplies. Tomorrow would see the end of Akkad's barbarian leader.

As the darkness fell, some soldiers built a fire near Eskkar's command post, despite the mild summer evening. No one had ordered them to do it, but they did it anyway, to help their leader meet with his men. One by one, his commanders joined him, to report on their men, review their orders for tomorrow, and take into account any new instructions. They formed a tight circle around him, some kneeling so that as many could see the map as possible.

While Eskkar waited for the last of his subordinates to arrive, he studied the map on the ground before him, though its frayed edges and grimy appearance showed how often Eskkar and his commanders had consulted it during the last eleven days. This map depicted the land around Isin, and had first been detailed by Trella's map makers back in Akkad almost a year ago. It had proved its use already by determining where to dig the canal to threaten Isin.

But Trella's map makers had done more than just identify the landscape. They had walked this land, studying possible battle sites, just as they had done in and around Larsa, and even Sumer itself. Finding likely places for two armies to clash wasn't as difficult as it first appeared. Troops from both sides needed water and supplies, which kept everyone close to the rivers and streams. Commanders needed to communicate with their respective cities as well as their own garrisons, which suggested other likely trails for troops to move and establish camp. All in all, nearly a dozen such sites had been studied around the city of Isin, and Eskkar's clerks carried maps of all of them.

Sitting cross-legged on the ground, he studied the map in silence, though by now he knew every line and symbol. Gatus arrived and took his place beside his captain, along with Drakis; they would lead the spearmen in tomorrow's attack, and face the brunt of Shulgi's forces. Hathor sat on Eskkar's right, with Klexor and Muta; they commanded the cavalry. Alexar and Mitrac would lead the bowmen in support of Gatus, and Shappa and Nivar commanded the slingers, who would follow Hathor. Yavtar and Daro would command the riverboats and their archers. The smallest force was that of the Ur Nammu warriors, led by Fashod and Chinua. Grond completed the circle, facing his friend and commander across the fire. Of all those present, only he had no need to see the map. Grond's place would be wherever Eskkar was.

When they had all taken their places, Eskkar turned the map over. One of his clerks could sketch and draw. Eskkar and Gatus had spoken to the artist the day before yesterday, when they traversed what appeared to be the most likely battleground. The man had created a new drawing that showed in detail where Eskkar wanted to place his men, and where he expected the Sumerians to place theirs. Nothing fancy, just blocks with a single symbol within, to identify the particular force and its position.

Every head craned forward to get a closer look, each commander intent on studying the battleground. While they examined the map, Eskkar lifted his eyes and studied the men surrounding the camp fire. Hundreds of soldiers had jammed themselves in as close as they dared, to hear the words of their leaders. They made no sound, didn't even talk among themselves, and Eskkar wondered if some of them weren't holding their breath. No doubt they expected to be ordered away, but Eskkar didn't mind. The more his men knew about what they would face, the easier it would be in the morning. With that in mind, he raised his voice, so that as many as could would hear his words.

"The last report from Trella's agents estimates that Shulgi had about twenty-two thousand men with him when he left Larsa. Almost a thousand of those are now behind us, in Isin. I expect King Naxos will keep them there, but our men are still watching Isin and guarding the ditch in case those in the city try anything tonight."

He looked around the circle of commanders. "So in the morning we'll face at least twenty one thousand men, perhaps more. We'll be outnumbered more than four to one." He paused to let the numbers sink in. Better they heard about the enemy's strength tonight than when they first saw the enemy host in the daylight.

"But many of the men Shulgi commands are unproven. They've been drawn from all over Sumeria, and they fight only for the prospect of loot, or because they've been ordered to war by their leaders. Almost ten thousand are nothing more than men carrying swords. Most have never fought a battle. Just as important, most of them have little loyalty to Shulgi. Their cavalry is well trained, and they've had plenty of experience fighting the desert tribes. Altogether, Shulgi still has at least three thousand horsemen, but almost half that number is drawn from the rabble of Tanukh desert-dwellers. That scum of the desert fight like jackals, attacking only when they have the advantage. Fashod has fought them in the past, even hunted them for sport. Hathor and his men have swept through two of their villages. He saw Tanukh men abandon their wives and children to flee with their horses. Tell them what you saw."

Eyes turned toward Hathor. "It's true. They left their women, old men, and boys behind, to die defending their honor and tents. Very few stood and fought, and most of those only because we caught them before they could escape. Only a coward would leave his family to face death."

"The rest of Shulgi's army is little better," Eskkar went on. Our men have trained for this fight, some for as long as two years. We've out-marched the Sumerians in the last eleven days. We've destroyed Larsa, burned Uruk, and forced Isin to abandon its support for Shulgi's cause. Even this place of battle is known to us, and the ground will favor our fighters. Shulgi will have only one tactic, to close with us as quickly as possible, and try to overwhelm us with their numbers. We have prepared even for that."

Again Eskkar looked out at the men standing behind the commanders' circle. He saw no fear, no doubts. "Tomorrow we will do what the Sumerians least expect. They expect us to dig in and wait for their assault. Instead we will attack them. Our cavalry will strike their rear like a hammer, while our infantry will attack their front lines, an anvil of unbreakable strength. The Sumerians will be caught between the anvil and the hammer, and they will be crushed."

He paused to look around the circle once again.

"Now it is time for the commanders to speak. If any of you have questions or doubts, speak now." Eskkar had learned long ago to let the most junior commander speak first, so as not to be intimidated by the more experienced leaders, but this time he turned to Gatus, as the senior commander.

"We could still attack at night," Gatus said, "catch them off guard. My spearmen have practiced for a night battle."

Earlier, Eskkar had asked Gatus to speak of a night attack. Eskkar wanted the men to hear and understand all the reasons for the decision not to try and fight at night.

"No." Eskkar put all the firmness into the single word that he could. "The Sumerians wait even now for us to attack. They are prepared for it, and if we attack now they will fight, because there is no place to run in the darkness. As the night passes, they will grow even more certain that we will come, if not during the night than at first light. Their soldiers will get little sleep tonight, and tomorrow their legs will be weak. In the morning, the Sumerians will be weary. They will see us advancing on their position. Doubt and fear will fill their throats, weaken their knees. What courage they have will fade away. They will look for any excuse to turn and run."

"And that excuse, what will it be?"

Gatus's rehearsed words sounded a bit awkward, but Eskkar doubted any of the soldiers listening nearby with open mouths would notice.

"We are going to strike at the head of the Sumerians. Shulgi is all that holds them together, when they see him fall, or turn to flee, the battle will be over. He has only fought against the desert horsemen, never fought a real battle. So I will take the fight to him. Let us see if he is willing to face me."

One by one, he spoke to each commander, listened to what they had to say, answered any questions. None, he saw with satisfaction, needed any reassurance. All of them wanted to close with the enemy as much as he did.

When everyone had had their say, Eskkar stood. "Make no mistake. Shulgi is a strong leader and his men will fight hard. But he lacks experience, and we will take advantage of that. We've trained for this battle for months. Tomorrow is the day we will win it. Commanders, repeat my words to those who could not be close enough to hear our voices. I want every man to know what he'll face, and what to do. Then tell them to get as much rest as they can."

He picked up the map and tossed it to his clerk, who had stood nearby, open-mouthed, during Eskkar's speech. The map wouldn't be needed any more. "All of you will lead your men bravely, I know. Our soldiers have already proven themselves. They, like you, will know what to do. And tell them that I am proud to lead them into battle. And after we win, the spoils of Sumer will be ours. Good hunting to all of us tomorrow."

The fire had nearly burned out, and this time no one thought to replenish it. Eskkar strode into the darkness, but not to try and rest. Instead, he walked through the camp, talking to the men, repeating parts of what he'd said earlier. Again and again he spoke, each time with a hundred or more men clustered about him, more than a few reaching out to touch his arm. Many were in awe of him, of his reputation. He used that trust now. He had to rely on them tomorrow, and they needed to know that.

As Trella had told him time after time, win the loyalty of your men and they will follow you wherever you lead. Long ago she had foretold him that that someday a thousand men or more would follow him into battle, no matter what the odds. At the time, he thought she spoke without thinking, or more likely, without understanding how hard it would be to command so many men. But as he'd often found with Trella, she always chose her words with care, and meant what she said. Tomorrow her prophecy would come true. Esskar intended to lead Akkad's soldiers against a mighty host, and he knew how much risk they all faced.

At last Grond, who had stayed at Esskar's side as he moved throughout the camp, put his arm around his friend's shoulder. "It's past midnight, Captain. You've spoken to enough of our men. They'll spread your words. Time to get some rest, or you'll be too tired to stand in the morning, let alone fight."

They returned to the camp fire, one of the few that still burned this late into the night. Esskar threw himself down on his blanket. The stars shone overhead, and he remembered another night watching the stars cross the heavens, and knowing a fight to the death waited in the morning. Balthazar, an old shepherd, had taught him about the mysteries of the starry heavens that night. Esskar wondered if the old man had found the peaceful life that he sought, surrounded by his kin. Balthazar might even still be alive. When this battle was over, if Esskar survived, he decided he would send word to the shepherd, perhaps invite him to come visit Akkad. He was, after all, a companion in arms, one of the few who had fought at Esskar's side in the old days.

Tired as Esskar felt, sleep would not come. He knew that many of his men would be lying there, staring at the same heavens and wondering if they would live to see the sun set once again. Or wondering if they could face the enemy with courage. Tonight they would think about death and dying, about pain and blackness. Tomorrow they would stare into the eyes of their enemies. Each man would fight, not for Akkad, not for Esskar, but to hold the respect of the men who stood beside him, his friends and companions. These men had trained together for months or even longer, and now the bonds of brotherhood would hold them fast, side by side, in the face of the enemy.

He knew one thing for certain. Tomorrow a lot of men were going to die. His soldiers would follow him because he would lead, and they would show no fear. But deep down, inside their bowels, they would be afraid nonetheless.

Eskkar had experienced fear before, but never felt the battle dread, nor the fear that sometimes gripped men the night before a battle, banishing sleep. But he worried nevertheless. The fate of Akkad might be decided tomorrow, even Trella's life and that of his son, determined by the deaths of thousands of men he would lead into battle.

He looked again at the sky. The stars seemed so peaceful as they moved across the night, but the priests claimed that the tiny sparks of light could foretell a man's future. Eskkar wished he knew more about them, enough to read the ending to tomorrow's battle. That meant more than his own fate. As long as Akkad defeated the Sumerians, he would be satisfied.

Finally, he decided there was no use lying there, that he might as well be up and about. Instead, he closed his eyes for one last moment of rest, and fell into a troubled sleep.

Grond, stretched out beside his friend, saw his captain's body relax, and heard the soft snoring. Thank the gods, he thought. His friend would need all his strength in the morning. Grond let his own eyes close, though he slept lightly through the darkness, waking often and making sure each time that all was well, and that Eskkar's restless sleep continued without interruption.

56

Day 12

It seemed to Eskkar that he had just closed his eyes when Grond awoke him. Eskkar jerked himself upright. Sounds of men moving about were all around him, not the loud morning sounds of men yawning and complaining themselves awake, but the softer sound of men rising and preparing for battle, and trying to do it with as little noise as possible. When he got to his feet, Eskkar realized that everyone else was already fully awake. A quick glance at the fading moon told him dawn approached.

"Nothing to see yet, Captain." Grond held a heavy sack in his hand. "Gatus is moving the men in shifts down to the river and back, telling them to drink all they can hold. Every water skin will be filled."

Grond dropped the sack, and Eskkar heard a clanking noise from within. "A gift from Trella," Grond said, as he untied the cord that held the sack closed. He lifted a bronze breastplate. "She says you're to wear this when you ride to battle. Yavtar's been lugging this up and down the Tigris and Euphrates for days. Says he's glad to finally be rid of it. I think he was afraid someone would steal it."

Eskkar started to protest but Grond cut him off. "Don't argue, Captain. You'll need this today. Every archer will be aiming at your heart, and we can't afford to lose you. At least until the battle's won. Trella told me not to give it to you until just before the battle, so that you wouldn't have a chance to lose it."

"Naxos had one like that." Eskkar had never worn a breastplate. They were difficult to make and cost a great deal of gold. "Will it even fit me?"

"We'll see. Hold this." Grond handed Eskkar the breastplate, picked up the back protector and began lacing the two parts together across Eskkar's shoulders. A few quick tugs, and it slid into place. The two pieces fit perfectly, and Eskkar suddenly remembered Trella a few months ago spending what seemed like half a morning measuring him for a new tunic.

Grond fastened the sides together just above Eskkar's waist, and the breastplate settled onto his chest.

Eskkar took a deep breath, half expecting to find some excuse to avoid wearing the armor. He felt the weight of the bronze, but it moved smoothly and didn't seem to affect his breathing. Nor did it seem that heavy, with its weight distributed over his shoulders. At least for now.

Gatus strode over. "About time you were up. Thought you were going to sleep right through the fight. Did he give you any trouble about the bronze?" Gatus wore armor himself, but made of thick leather.

"No, Gatus. I think I caught him before he fully woke. He hardly protested."

"Well, then that's taken care of. I had half a dozen men waiting to force him into it."

Gatus laughed at the thought, and Eskkar wasn't sure if he meant it or not. With Gatus, you never knew for certain.

"The last of the food has been handed out, and the men are swelling their bellies with water. Everyone's pissing like mad, either from too much to drink or because they're scared to death. Watch where you step, there's shit everywhere. I swear there's not a tight bowel in any of them. Even I dropped a good load, always a good sign."

With the reminder, the strong odors of urine and shit caught Eskkar's attention. The urge to relieve himself became urgent, and he, too, decided to walk down to the river. It was going to be a long and hot day. He splashed into the cool water and washed his face and hands, then drank until he could hold no more, forcing himself to swallow long after his thirst was satisfied, until his belly protested it could hold no more.

His commanders were moving everyone into position when he returned. Grond waited there, holding Eskkar's horse. The first rays of the sun were starting to lighten the eastern sky, and soon the sun would lift itself above the land of Sumeria. If the Sumerians planned to attack at dawn, they would find the Akkadians ready and waiting.

Grond handed Eskkar a loaf of bread. Eskkar saw there was only one loaf, and broke it in two, giving half back to his bodyguard. "Don't argue. You'll need your strength today, too."

He swung up onto the horse. Boy snorted and pawed the earth, sensing the excitement in the air. To Eskkar's surprise, he felt relief. For two years he dreaded the coming of this day, even hoped it would never come. Now there was nothing left to think about. He recalled his father's words: Just kill the man in front of you, and don't worry about anything else. Well, father, today we'll see how well you've taught me.

The edge of the sun cleared the horizon, and flooded the land with the day's first light. Everyone searched the landscape, but no enemy moved toward them, though in the distance Eskkar could see plenty of movement from the enemy camp. Sumerian commanders would be moving their men into position as well, though he doubted the task would be done as smoothly as the Akkadians.

"Move the men out, Gatus. And good hunting to you today."

The old soldier had replaced his usual wide-brimmed hat with a bronze helmet that covered his forehead and protected the back of his neck almost to his shoulders. But he kept the hat with him, hanging by a loop from his belt. Eskkar understood. The battle might not start for some time, and the bronze helmet would heat quickly in the sun.

With the first rays of the sun, the men's spirits rose. Throughout the camp, men shouted orders, heard them repeated and expanded. Leaders of ten cursed their slow-moving men, pushing the laggards still brushing the sleep from their eyes into position. The spearmen moved out first, leading the way. They marched in a three-deep formation. The archers wearing their leather caps and vests fell into place behind them. Eskkar and Grond guided their horses out of their way, and joined Hathor and Fashod. Shappa and Nivar followed the horsemen, striding along behind them.

"Well, we've given them the first surprise." Hathor jerked his head toward the Sumerian camp. "I don't think they expected us to be marching toward them."

"Let's hope that's not all they don't expect. Fashod, your men are ready?"

"Ready? I can scarcely keep them in check. The thought of killing so many dirt-eaters at one time is more than they can stand."

Eskkar smiled at the Ur Nammu warrior's words. He hadn't used the term "dirt-eater" for months now, out of politeness to his allies. "Just keep them under control until I give the signal. Hathor, you'd better take your place as well. Good hunting to you."

"And to you, my king." No mere title of courtesy sufficed this day.

The Akkadians kept moving, taking their time. The spearmen marched with their left flank against the Euphrates. They carried their spears loosely, dangling them at arm's length in their right hands. Each spear now showed a thick wrapping just behind the center of the shaft, to provide a better grip. Bronze helmets glinted in the rising sun. As they stepped forward, Eskkar heard the subcommanders keeping order, making sure the line moved as one. Even today – or maybe today of all days – discipline had to be maintained, and a united front presented to their enemies. Leaders of ten and twenty gave their own commands, to keep each group in its proper place and position.

Just as they were trained, Eskkar thought, watching the familiar spectacle of men moving in formation. He'd seen Gatus march his men out a hundred – maybe two hundred – times before. Well, the routine orders would keep everyone's mind off the enemy waiting for them. Eskkar knew that the Sumerians would be sweating already. Despite their greater numbers, they knew they would face a determined force.

Eskkar reached his position, at the spearmen's right flank. He kept the horse at a slow walk, to stay even with the infantry. From his right, nearly eight hundred Akkadian cavalry extended out in a line, also falling into three ranks. Grond moved his horse to Eskkar's left, while Fashod and Chinua rode on Eskkar's right. Behind them rode the forty Ur Nammu warriors. They had argued and fought for the honor of riding with Eskkar into battle, and he had finally agreed, as long as they promised to follow orders.

For them, allowing dirt-eaters to lead the way into battle was almost unthinkable to their sense of honor, especially against other dirt-eaters, but they had promised to wait until Eskkar gave the signal to attack. They sat their horses with ease, showing none of the tension or stress that betrayed itself with the slight and nervous movements that the other cavalrymen displayed. While most men dreaded battle, these warriors lived for it.

The small signs of nervousness didn't concern Eskkar. He knew the cavalry would follow where he and Hathor led them. These men had just raided across Sumerian lands, and already proved their valor.

Eskkar saw Hathor take his station, a third of the way down the line of horsemen. Some of the horses showed as much excitement as their riders. The animals – tossing heads and pawing the ground – sensed the oncoming danger, and relied on their riders to reassure them. For some of the more nervous riders, controlling their mounts now occupied all their attention, to the soft swearing of the companions on either side.

The first third of the cavalry would follow Eskkar. Hathor would lead the next third, to deliver the first blow from the hammer. Klexor and Muta had the next position, with the last third, ready to deliver the second hopefully fatal hammer blow. Drakis commanded the spearmen on Eskkar's left, expected to be the most dangerous position today. He not only had to lead his men, but ensure that the Sumerian horse fighters didn't flank him, to attack from behind.

By now every infantry man, every horse and rider settled into their proper place. The Akkadians, despite moving at a slow pace, had traversed almost half the distance to the Sumerians.

"Demons below, look at them!" Grond spoke just loud enough to be heard at Eskkar's side. "How many men did you say Shulgi had?"

Eskkar, too, had his eyes fixed on the enemy. He needed to grasp their positions and notice their leaders. "More than enough. But Shulgi's the key to this battle. It's him that we have to kill. No matter what happens, you make sure he ends up dead."

"Let's just hope he isn't thinking the same thing about us."

Shulgi and Razrek had finally readied their weary men. Once again, the cursed Akkadians had failed to attack during the night. The stake-filled ditch the Sumerians had dug to entrap the attackers remained empty, another wasted effort. When dawn showed an empty expanse between the two forces, Shulgi had been ready to give the order to advance until he saw Eskkar's forces on the move, coming straight toward him, spread out in a line, the infantry along the river on Shulgi's right, the cavalry on his left.

"They're going to attack us." Razrek couldn't believe his eyes. "They're bigger fools than I thought. They don't have enough men. We'll flank them and take them from the rear."

Shulgi saw the same thing. His line of spearmen and infantry – four and five deep – stretched from the riverbank, across the Akkadian spearmen, and reached past almost half of Eskkar's cavalry. Razrek's horsemen,

Shulgi's left flank, extended far to the east, well beyond Eskkar's line of horsemen.

"Get to your men," Shulgi said. "When I give the signal, charge straight at him, and let your left flank swing around and attack his rear."

"Are you going to attack first?"

"No. If they want to come to us, we'll wait here for them, behind the stakes."

Shulgi examined his forces, looking up and down the line. His men were regaining their courage, now that they saw how few were the numbers of their enemy. No matter how strong the Akkadians might be, it would only be a matter of time before Razrek's forces turned their flank and delivered the death blow to their rear. No line of spearmen could fight both front and rear.

"I don't see any reserves." Razrek stretched upright on his horse. "Nothing to protect their rear."

"Good. Then all we need to do is flank them, or punch one hole in their line, and they're finished. Now get moving. And I don't care how many men you lose, just get behind them."

Gatus halted the men halfway across the empty grassland that separated the two forces. The Akkadian line rippled and shifted as the men stopped advancing. Sunlight glinted from the bronze helmets and spear tips. The men gulped from their water skins. More than a few had to piss again, but now they had to remain in place, and try not to spray the legs of the man in front of them. When they had finished taking care of their needs, they rested the butts of their spears on the earth and waited for the next order.

The two armies were less than a mile apart. Eskkar glanced to his left, just as Gatus gave the order to resume the slow advance. The initial stage of the attack depended on Gatus getting his men into the proper position, so the old soldier had command of the first portion of the advance.

The Akkadian spearmen resumed moving forward, matched by the cavalry, and gradually closed the gap between the two forces. This march didn't need to cover much distance, and Gatus stopped the spearmen for the second time just out of bowshot from the Sumerian archers. About a quarter of a mile separated the two forces, but Eskkar guessed that Mitrac's men might have the range to put a few shafts into the enemy ranks. Eskkar twisted on his horse, and saw that Mitrac had his hand to his mouth, calling out something to Gatus.

Meanwhile, the Sumerians started shouting at their enemies, daring them to come closer. They waved their weapons in the air, and called curses down on the Akkadians. Eskkar couldn't quite make out the words, but he had no doubt what was being said. Gatus's men remained silent. Only women and boys talk before a fight, Gatus had reminded them often enough.

One of the Ur Nammu warriors, a young man named Teadosso, disobeyed orders and moved his horse a dozen paces out in front of the first rank. Before Eskkar or anyone could order him back, Teadosso stood up and balanced himself on his horse's back, both feet pointed the same direction, as he guided the animal down the line of Akkadian horsemen at an easy canter. At the same time, he lifted his tunic and waved his bare backside toward the Sumerian cavalry.

Eskkar, caught by surprise as much as any of his men, couldn't help laughing at the sight. Teadosso galloped his horse to the end of Hathor's riders, then, still standing astride the animal, skillfully turned it around and headed back toward Eskkar's position at the other end of the line. As the horse reversed itself, Teadosso changed his position, so as to keep his rear facing the enemy. More curses from the Sumerians filled the air, but even the enemy probably had to admire a good bit of horsemanship.

Everyone was laughing now. Teadosso returned to Eskkar's end of the line.

"Get back to your place, you fool!" Fashod ordered, but his tone softened the rebuke. Teadosso dropped down onto the horse's back and guided his mount back to its original position, and two or three of his grinning companions clapped him on the shoulder in approval.

Eskkar turned toward Gatus, a few hundred paces away. The old soldier rode just behind his men. He waved his sword toward Eskkar.

"It's time." Eskkar took a deep breath, drew his own sword, and held it high, then pointed it, not toward the enemy, but toward Hathor. "Move your men out. Nice and slow." His heart beat strongly in his chest as he gave the order, and he felt that familiar mix of fear and exhilaration that preceded a battle. But it didn't matter now. Eskkar had committed his men to this battle plan and there was no way to turn back. They could only go forward, to victory or death.

Hathor repeated the signal, and at the last part of the line, Klexor saw the waving sword. He repeated the signal to Muta, who sat on his horse alone at the far end of the line. When he saw the signal, Muta turned his horse to the flank and started walking eastward, as slow as he could make his mount move. Horse by horse, and always remaining in the three-abreast formation, the whole line of Akkadian cavalry faced to the east and plodded after Muta. Screened by the slow-moving cavalry, the slingers walked east as well, always keeping the horsemen between themselves and the enemy.

Eskkar and his Ur Nammu guards were the last to move. Now he was at the rear of the cavalry, which was now being led by Muta at the other end. Behind them, they left the right flank of the spearmen exposed, but two hundred archers moved up to form a double column, not a line, along the infantry's right flank. When Razrek's cavalry arrived to turn Gatus's flank, these archers would have to hold them off.

From behind his infantry, Shulgi stared in surprise as he watched the Akkadian cavalry. They were moving east, the horses plodding along slowly, almost as if they were leaving the scene of the battle. As the line extended, a gap appeared between the Akkadian infantry and the cavalry. As Shulgi watched, that gap began to widen.

Razrek galloped up beside him. "Is he trying to flank us? The fools don't have enough men."

Shulgi ignored Razrek's excited utterance and studied the battle-ground. The Akkadian infantry wasn't moving. Every spear still pointed toward the sky. Either Eskkar was abandoning his spearmen and leaving the field of battle, or he intended to try and position himself to ride around the end of Razrek's horsemen and launch an attack at their rear.

"I can see men behind his cavalry," Shulgi said. "I don't see them carrying bows. Are they the boy slingers he's brought with him?"

"He's going to turn our flank, and attack from there," Razrek said, ignoring the comments about the slingers. "Your bowmen and infantry won't be of any help if he attacks from that direction. They'll be too far away. Let me attack now."

Shulgi had already considered that option. If he let Razrek attack without support, the Akkadian cavalry might be able to deliver a powerful blow to his own horsemen, while keeping their infantry intact. And if he moved to the attack with his infantry, Shulgi's forces would be giving up their strengthened position behind the row of stakes. But if Eskkar's spearmen retreated, Shulgi's forces would have to chase after them.

As long as he kept his forces together, Eskkar's men couldn't attack him effectively. He decided on a third course of action.

"Stop your whining, Razrek. Get back to your men. Keep your horsemen in front of Eskkar's. Don't let him flank you, no matter what. Match his movement, but stay in line with our infantry."

Whatever trick Eskkar might be planning, Shulgi intended to counter it with overwhelming force.

Razrek whirled his horse around and galloped back to the center of his men. "Form a column and move to the east. Keep the Akkadians in front of you."

The jeers and curses had all disappeared now, replaced by grim expressions. Word spread through the ranks of the Sumerians that King Eskkar was trying one of his usual cunning tricks. Razrek's horsemen began to move to their left, trying to stay even with Eskkar's slow-moving cavalry force. It took longer for the larger mass of Razrek's horsemen to wheel to their left, but once it did, the entire Sumerian cavalry began to shift along with the Akkadians.

Gatus, seated astride his faithful mare behind his lines of spearmen, watched the Sumerian ranks in front of him as they stared at Eskkar's movement to the east. It was obvious that Shulgi intended to remain behind his stakes. Nevertheless, Gatus could see the heads of the Sumerian spearmen following the movement of their cavalry. Without raising a sword, Eskkar had sown some confusion in the enemy's ranks.

Mitrac came over to stand beside him, his longbow held easily in one hand. The archer carried two quivers slung over his shoulder. "What's happening?"

Gatus had the advantage of the horse's height to give him a better view. The rest of the archers standing behind the front ranks couldn't see much.

"Lots of movement in the lines, but they're holding firm. They're sure Eskkar is up to something, but they don't know what. But don't worry about him. We'll be busy soon enough."

Eskkar had given him the most dangerous and difficult assignment.

Gatus had to not only hold off the Sumerian infantry, he also had to distract them to give Esskkar enough time to make his plan work. And the time to begin that distraction had arrived.

"Alexar! Drakis! Move the men forward. And keep it slow!" He turned to Mitrac. "Now it's up to you."

Orders were barked, and the line of spearmen rippled and shifted, spears lowered once again to the marching position. Then the three ranks began to move, taking their time, as the formation moved ever closer to Shulgi's forces waiting behind their line of stakes.

The Akkadians moved slowly across the gap. Mitrac trotted a dozen paces away from Gatus, to keep a better view of his own men. Now Mitrac had to worry more about the disposition of his bowmen than anything else. He was the one who would decide when to halt the formation.

"Far enough, Gatus!" Mitrac had both hands to the sides of his mouth as he shouted the words. "We've a bit of a breeze behind us."

"Halt!" Gatus bellowed the command, repeated by his commanders and subcommanders. The advancing spearmen stopped moving, the line almost as straight and smooth as if they were practicing back in Akkad's barracks. According to Gatus's count, they had advanced a little more than a hundred and twenty paces.

Mitrac shouted another command, and his seven hundred bowmen halted, braced their feet wide apart, and put shafts to the bowstrings. The master archer paused to glance up and down the line of archers. Everyone appeared ready. His was the command that would start the actual fighting. "Draw your shafts! Loose! Shoot at will!"

Gatus watched the first flight of arrows whistle high into the sky, level off, and begin its descent. Before they reached the highest part of their flight, another seven hundred shafts were launched. A third wave of arrows flew upwards even as the first wave descended on the enemy. At first Gatus thought Mitrac's bowmen had stopped too soon, but then Gatus saw the arrows strike the enemy shield wall. Many shafts fell short, but most rained down on the upraised shields. The arrows sounded a soft drumming note when they struck, but Gatus also heard men screaming, as a few shafts found crevices and gaps between shields.

"Keep shooting!" Mitrac bellowed the commands, even as he worked his own bow. "Pull every shaft to the ear! Get them up in the air!"

The Sumerian archers fired their own weapons, but almost all the arrows landed twenty or thirty paces short of the Akkadians. A small enough distance, Gatus realized. A shift of the wind to the opposite direction could bring the enemy bowmen within range.

But for now, at least, most of the Sumerian weapons did not have the same reach. The Akkadian archers needed months of practice to build up their strength, so as to draw the heavy bows to the maximum. Some of these men had trained with their weapons for as many as four years, had fought from the wall against the Alur Meriki horsemen.

Gatus whirled the mare around and glanced at his rear. A steady stream of men trotted from the water's edge, each carrying four quivers of arrows in their arms. Six of Yavtar's supply boats had managed to reach Eskkar's forces just after midnight, along with three fighting ships. Yavtar's force had encountered King Shulgi's boats and archers almost twenty miles upriver, and it had taken a hard battle before the Akkadian ships broke through, at the cost of losing five boats. Now the surviving vessels crept along the river behind the marching soldiers, carrying thousands of extra shafts, and stones for the slingers as well, although those weren't needed yet.

Gatus raised his eyes to the horizon, and saw nothing. Eskkar had assured him that Naxos wouldn't come out of his city, but Gatus hadn't been so sure. But the land behind them lay empty. Not even any of Razrek's men had attempted to swing around behind them yet.

Turning the horse back toward the Sumerians, Gatus glanced to his right. Eskkar and the cavalry had ever so slowly opened a gap of about two hundred paces between the two halves of the Akkadian army. That gap would tempt the Sumerians soon enough.

The bowmen kept launching shafts into the sky, grunting now with the effort to pull each arrow back to the ear before releasing. Empty quivers littered the ground beneath them. Each archer had already emptied one quiver, and their second would be exhausted soon. Those arrows, already more than twenty thousand, would be taking their toll on the enemy, despite the Sumerian shields.

No more carefully timed volleys now. Better to have the arrows arrive continually, Gatus knew, so that every enemy would be afraid to show his face.

Many arrows fell short, but most reached the enemy position. The Sumerian infantry had their shields raised up to cover their heads, but a few shafts here and there would slip over or under the protection, wounding or killing when they did. A shield couldn't cover every part of the soldier's body, not unless the man hunched himself down like a dog behind it.

The Sumerian archers returned the volleys. Supposedly, Sumer had two thousand archers, more than twice the number of Akkadian bowmen, but, as Gatus knew, giving a man a bow didn't make him a bowman. He turned to his right, to see Eskkar still moving slowly away from the Akkadian spearmen. At least Eskkar and his horsemen wouldn't be under attack by Shulgi's archers.

Gatus knew they had reached the most dangerous time of the battle. The arrows raining down on the Sumerians would make it difficult to get their infantry moving. But if Shulgi sent his men charging toward the Akkadians spearmen, they would likely be overwhelmed by sheer force of numbers. Nevertheless, the Sumerians remained behind their line of stakes. They wouldn't want to give up that position readily. And the odd movement of the Akkadian cavalry would be proving a distraction. Eskkar and Gatus had to give young Shulgi the chance to make a mistake. And making him worry about bowmen on the one side, and Eskkar's odd maneuvering on the other, just might do the trick.

Gatus turned his mare to the side and trotted over to where Mitrac stood, just behind his double line of bowmen. The young master archer was using his own bow, but Gatus saw that he kept his eyes on his men as well.

"It's up to you, Mitrac!" Gatus shouted. "You'll have to loosen that position."

Mitrac nodded. "We will. Their archers can't reach our men. We can keep shooting all day if we have to. They can't stand up to this for long."

Even as Mitrac said the words, another handful of panting men arrived, carrying fresh bundles of arrows that they distributed to replace those already launched. Thanks to Yavtar's boats, the Akkadians had plenty of shafts. The old sailor had delivered thousands of arrows with the last of his boats.

Gatus wondered how many arrows Shulgi's archers had with them. They'd likely lugged those arrows from Sumer to Kanesh to Larsa and now to Isin. The Sumerians would get their first surprise soon enough. They'd be expecting the number of Akkadian arrows to diminish, as the archers shot most of their shafts, but with Yavtar's last cargo, that wasn't going to happen, not for some time.

The Akkadian bowmen continued their assault on the Sumerian lines.

Gatus could see men going down, despite the shields. And many of the shafts were falling behind the line of spears, no doubt striking at the Sumerian archers, who had to be as close as possible to their front line to have even a hope of reaching the Akkadians. The enemy would be growing nervous, fearful, aware that death could strike at any moment from the sky. Thousands of arrows had already been loosed, with only a few Sumerian shafts able to reach Gatus's men.

Again Gatus stretched himself upright on his horse. He'd seen movement in the Sumerian ranks. The center, where the enemy cavalry butted against the infantry, had started to thin. Gatus snorted. Perhaps Esskar's luck might hold up one more time. He knew Esskar and the cavalry would begin their charge any moment. Now was the moment to give Shulgi something else to think about. He filled his lungs with air.

"Spearmen! Ready your weapons. Prepare to advance!" Gatus looked up and down the line, to make sure every commander stood ready. "Advance!"

The battle cry "Akkad!" roared from more than three thousand warriors, the first sound they'd uttered today. The spearmen began marching toward the Sumerians, the front rank holding their shields to the front, the second and third ranks holding their shields high, to protect against descending arrows that would soon be arriving in greater numbers, as they closed within range of their enemy.

Behind the spearmen, Mitrac issued his own orders. Seven hundred bowmen continued their shooting, arcing their shafts up into the air, to fall on the crowded Sumerian ranks of infantry and archers. The Akkadian archers moved forward as they shot their shafts, spread out in a ragged line and staying just far enough behind the spearmen so that they could launch their arrows. Without shields, the only protection the bowmen had came from the spearmen, and the fact that the Sumerian archers were now directing their arrows at the advancing infantry, to stop the Akkadian advance.

"Spearmen! Halt!"

Gatus gave the order before the men had moved another hundred paces. His soldiers expected the command, so they maintained their ranks. He waited until all the forward movement had ceased. "Spearmen! Retreat!"

The subcommanders and leaders of ten repeated the command, and the spearmen began backing up, moving with care since they had to keep their shields up and maintain their ranks. Mitrac's bowmen retreated also, but they kept loosing shafts as they moved, maintaining their position just behind the spearmen. For the Sumerians, this must seem a strange sight, to see their enemy first advancing, then retreating in good order and all the while maintaining their shield wall. Gatus's men had trained for months to execute such a maneuver. It was an infantry movement he doubted the Sumerians could duplicate.

When the men had returned almost to their starting point, Gatus called a halt. A few bodies lay scattered on the ground in front of his men, so the Sumerians had caused some damage. He saw that Mitrac, too, had lost a few bowmen dead or wounded. They had little protection, just their leather helmets and vests that might stop a shaft at this range, but not if the distance diminished.

But the archers kept firing, and arrows kept leaping off their bows, to rise into the sky and descend on the enemy. Already the front wall of Sumerian shields appeared to be covered with arrows. Something had to break soon, he knew. Shulgi should be getting rattled by now. At least, that's what Gatus hoped.

57

On the river, Yavtar watched the soldiers form up and move northward. As soon as they moved out, he issued orders and his own three fighting boats pushed away from the riverbank just after dawn. Three of the cargo ships had departed in the middle of the night, carrying wounded men and sacks of loot intended for Akkad. Yavtar had wished the boat captains good luck, and guessed they would need it. For them, the first stage of the slow passage upriver might be more dangerous today than fighting Shulgi's army.

Yavtar had hoped to have five or six of the big war boats here today, but Shulgi's blockade had left him with only three. At least he had some of the rowers and archers from the lost boats, so each craft had more than its usual compliment of bowmen. His three vessels would deliver a deadly sting to the Sumerian army, but whether any of them would survive the encounter remained an unanswered question. No one – at least as far as he knew – had ever used boats as floating platforms for archers, or contemplated using them against a massive land army.

With his three craft well away from shore, they rowed up river, already struggling to keep station with Gatus's spearmen, whose easy strides covered the ground faster than his boat crews could row. Each ship had raised its sail, but the linen squares hung limp in the still air. Later in the morning Yavtar expected a slight breeze from the south that might help, but this early in the day, such winds seldom appeared.

The boat crews had to row hard just to keep from being shoved downriver by the current. Since the boats carried extra men, the heavily laden vessels handled even worse than usual, each craft carrying more than twenty archers and a dozen rowers. His men struggled with the oars, thrusting them deep into the brown waters of the Euphrates and pushing with all their strength, forcing the craft forward against the current.

The archers provided some assistance. They used the few extra paddles to help drive the boats. Yavtar had intended to take the lead, but another craft slid easier through the water, despite Yavtar's steady cursing at his own rowers, and until finally he waved the other boatmaster ahead, settling into the second position.

Daro, in command of all the archers, also directed the bowmen on Yavtar's craft. Daro kept moving up and down the line, making sure the broad shields sat firmly in their place, and that every man had plenty of arrows and extra bowstrings at hand.

"Pull, you dogs!" Yavtar's bellow carried across the water to all three craft. "Gatus is moving ahead. Damn you, pull!"

A few men had enough breath to laugh at their commander's eagerness to get into battle.

Stroke by stroke, the ships clawed their way upriver, until they rode alongside Gatus and his spearmen, only a hundred paces away. "Keep rowing. We need to be ahead of them."

When the spearmen launched their real attack, they'd be running as fast as they could cover the ground. The sooner the infantry could close the distance, the less time the enemy archers would have to launch shafts at them. That meant Yavtar needed to be well ahead of Gatus's infantry. Fortunately, the river widened a bit, and the boats began to move faster through the water, slowly drawing ahead of Gatus and his spearmen.

As soon as Yavtar saw that he'd be in position, he took a moment to study the enemy. His eyes widened at the sight of so many men. No one had ever assembled such a host before. He could scarcely believe what he saw. Yavtar had heard the estimates, seen the numbers, but to actually face so many, their upright spears glinting in the sun . . . he wondered how Eskkar could maintain his steadfastness of purpose, let alone his belief in victory. Even more, Yavtar wondered how the soldiers marching forward maintained their trust in their commander. Eskkar's reputation had much to do with that, of course, but most of all Eskkar believed in himself, and the men sensed and shared in that belief.

The king had once remarked that every battle he'd ever fought, he'd been outnumbered.

"Did you ever think of run . . . not fighting?" Yavtar had corrected himself just in time.

"Every time," Eskkar replied, smiling at his friend.

Seeing the enemy host, Yavtar wondered what thoughts might be tempting the king today.

"What a sight." Daro finished checking his bowmen, and joined Yavtar at the rear of the boat, just ahead of the steering oar. He stared in amazement at the enemy army.

Two crewmen crouched right behind Yavtar, one holding the steering oar and the other ready to take his place should an arrow take him. A larger than usual shield gave them good protection, but under no conditions did Yavtar want to end up with his boat beached on the riverbank due to the loss of the steersman.

"I think I'm glad to be on the water," Yavtar said, following Daro's gaze to the shore.

If disaster struck the Akkadians, the boats would have a chance to escape, though they would still have to maneuver past the narrow bend in the river a few miles from here. Yesterday Shulgi had spread his boats and men across the water and caused the sinking of half a dozen boats before Yavtar could break free. But the Sumerians might have abandoned that place once the battle started.

"It's a long way back to Akkad." Daro strung his own bow, then tested the pull. Thumb-ring and wrist gauntlet were already in place. "Let's hope we don't have to row all the way there."

"Look! There goes the cavalry!" Yavtar couldn't keep the excitement from his voice.

Eskkar's horsemen were on the move, walking slowly away from the spearmen. Gatus had already halted his men. The boat crews caught their breath. Now they just had to hold their position until the next advance.

"My bowmen are ready to fight," Daro said. "They'd rather shoot arrows than row any time."

"Good luck and good hunting to you, Daro."

"And to you, Yavtar. Remember to keep low and stay behind the shields. I think we're going to have thousands of arrows launched at us."

The idea of a thousand arrows striking the boat made Yavtar's mouth go dry. The archers would be behind shields, but they would still have to expose part of their bodies to launch their shafts. And his crew would still have to work the boat, despite the enemy's missiles. Many on board were going to die.

Yavtar reached down and scooped up a water skin half hidden beneath the steering bench. "Better take one last drink before we start." He took a few swallows then handed the skin to Daro. While the archer drank, Yavtar retrieved another skin from a deeper recess. "And a few swallows of wine can't hurt, either."

Deciding there would always be plenty of water from over the side to drink, Yavtar took a deep pull from the wine skin, then handed it to Daro.

Daro accepted that skin as well. "To victory." He lifted the skin as if it were a cup, and drank deep.

Yavtar took another look at Shulgi's army. "I'll drink to that. I'll even drink to having a drink tomorrow night, if we're still alive." He took back the wine skin and swallowed as much of the strong liquid as he could force down his throat. "It's going to be a long day," he explained, "and I don't want to get thirsty later."

From the shore, Gatus's spearmen gave their battle cry, and began moving forward, the men maintaining their position. It appeared as though a solid block of shields and spear points were on the move.

"It's time." Daro moved forward, to his place in the center of the boat.

"Pull for all your worth," Yavtar shouted. He tossed the wine skin to the two men behind him. "Might as well finish that. We're going to need it."

Once again, the three ships slowly gathered way against the current. For the first time in anyone's memory, boats were going to be in the thick of a land battle. Yavtar checked his sword for the tenth time, and moved toward the bow of the vessel. Soon they'd be far enough upriver to see what lay behind the enemy lines.

Gatus's infantry halted for the second time, but Yavtar continued moving forward, and soon his three little boats had drawn almost even with the enemy ranks. So far no one had loosed an arrow at them, but Yavtar knew that would soon change, once they saw how powerful a sting rode the river.

Daro's voice rose up, echoing out over the calm water. "Bowmen! Loose at will!"

After the training volleys that Yavtar had seen in Akkad's training ground or the northern camps, the few shafts from Daro's archers seemed puny indeed. But soon more than sixty bowmen spread out over three ships were launching shafts at Shulgi's right flank. Many fell short, but Yavtar knew that would change in a few moments as the range shortened, as the ships continued making headway against the river.

The archers were on their fifth or sixth shaft before the Sumerians returned the first volley. Daro shouted a warning, and Yavtar looked up to see a cloud of shafts arch up into the sky, then begin to fall toward his ship. For a moment it seemed as if every single arrow were aimed right at him. He ducked down behind the shield, practically shoving his face into the bilge water, just as the shafts struck home.

In a moment, the ship was riddled with shafts protruding from every surface. As the arrows struck the wooden hull or shields, a loud drumming came from the wood, as if each shaft were a hammer blow. To Yavtar's surprise, not a bowmen went down under the first volley. He picked up his own round shield, and held it between his head and shore, so he could see what was happening. The lead ship was shooting arrows as well, already in range to reach targets well back from the river. To his rear, Yavtar saw that the third boat had turned away from the shore for a moment, then righted its course once again. A body fell into the water, but its archers continued to launch their arrows.

A quick glance toward shore saw that Gatus's spearmen continued moving slowly toward the Sumerian line. But as they drew within a quarter mile or so, they halted. The front rank had its shields held up, while the second and third ranks raised them over their heads. Behind them, he saw Mitrac's archers begin shooting.

"Yavtar! Can you get us a little closer to the shore?" Daro's bellow shook Yavtar out of his fascination with the battle on shore.

Yavtar took a quick glance at the water flowing beside the hull, then at the riverbank. The water would be deep enough and the current about the same. It seemed madness to draw closer to the enemy bowmen, but today no one worried about that. He scrambled back to the rear of the craft, hunched over the whole way. He found himself muttering prayers to the god of the rivers, and hoping an arrow wouldn't find his backside as he wriggled past the grunting archers and sweating rowers.

"Move us in closer, about twenty paces." The steersman's face went a shade whiter at the order. "Hurry, Daro wants a closer shot!"

The man nodded his understanding, and he pushed on the oar with hands that shook more from fear than the force of the river. The craft responded well, turning slightly and edging closer to the shore.

Yavtar glanced at the other boats. Hopefully they would remember their orders to take station wherever Yavtar's vessel went.

Daro shouted orders to his men. Soon arrows from sixty archers again began striking the partially exposed right flank of the Sumerian spearmen. The enemy had their shields raised up for protection against Mitrac's shafts, and Daro's arrows weren't a numbing volley, but even Yavtar's hurried glimpses over the side of the boat showed the attack's effect. The Sumerian spearmen anchoring Shulgi's right flank had to shift some shields to protect their exposed right sides. Meanwhile, arrows from the Akkadian archers behind the ranks of Gatus's spearmen continued to fall on them. Daro's men had an unheard of opportunity to loose their shafts down the solid mass of the enemy's main battle line. Even shafts that glanced off an upraised shield might strike another target before they came to rest.

No infantry expected to be under continual fire like that, from two directions, especially not at such close range. If the Sumerians could have mounted even a brief charge, the Akkadian bowmen would be slaughtered. But at least seventy-five paces of water remained between the boats and the river bank, and Daro's archers were as much out of reach as if they were on the other side of the river. Unless Shulgi wanted to order swimmers into the river to try and board the boats, he could do nothing except have his archers shoot back at them.

By now the sides of the boat and the shields were riddled with arrows. At least two of Daro's men were down, one wounded in the leg and out of the fight, another dead with an arrow in his throat.

But the Akkadian shafts continued to fly at the Sumerian ranks. Each boat had pushed away from shore that morning with two hundred and fifty shafts for every archer, an enormous reserve of arrows and more than enough to allow a steady fire. And Yavtar knew these bowmen could do it, shooting shaft after shaft, drawing each feather to the cheek before releasing the arrow.

The bowmen ignored the bellowed threats and curses from the shore, Yavtar's shouting of orders that passed up and down the length of the boat, and even the harsh breaths and grunts each man made as he released his missile. The snapping of bowstrings mixed with the steady drumming of Sumerian arrows striking every wooden surface on the boat added to the din. Yavtar had fought before, but nothing compared to this frenzy of conflicting noise.

On the shore, Shulgi's commanders soon recognized the danger in the boats attacking them. An entire company of Sumerian bowmen shifted their position and started launching arrows at the three vessels that lay just out of reach.

"Bowmen!" Daro's voice boomed out over the battle din. "Maximum range. Aim for their leaders. Aim for the red banner!"

Yavtar risked another glance, but couldn't see any banner. Daro must have caught sight of a worthy target, perhaps Shulgi himself or one of his commanders. Yavtar saw the bowmen elevate their weapons even higher, sending the shafts high into the sky, to rain down well away from the riverbank, and close to the position occupied by the Sumerian leaders.

It seemed odd to be shooting at something that wasn't shooting back at you, but the archers didn't seem concerned about that. They just kept launching their shafts at whatever target their leaders selected, grunting with every effort to draw the string back to the full force position before letting fly.

Yavtar wondered if these latest shafts, aimed high into the sky, were having any effect. He watched Gatus's men first advance and then fall back, an orderly movement that kept their lines and shield wall intact. Still, the Sumerians hadn't budged from their position, which wasn't a good sign. By now Yavtar expected that the enemy would have abandoned their defensive positions to come to grips with their attackers.

He decided to move the boats a little more upriver, to catch a glimpse what lay behind Shulgi's main battle line. It might confuse the Sumerians who would be expecting the ships to stay just ahead of Gatus's spearmen.

"Move the boats upriver!" With both hands cupped to his mouth, Yavtar's bellow carried to the other two ships, and he repeated the message twice in each direction. "At least three hundred paces. Pull, you lazy bastards, pull!"

He turned to find Daro staring at him, but the questioning look on the master bowman's face gave way to approval.

"Good idea!" Daro, too, had to shout to be heard. "We'll be able to see behind them." He raised his voice. "Keep shooting! As fast as you can!"

The three ships moved ponderously forward, pulling well ahead of Gatus's line. If Yavtar could maneuver the boats even a small distance behind the Sumerian front, Daro's archers should be able to create havoc.

The ships crept steadily upriver. The enemy either didn't notice, or didn't care. Yavtar's vessel, still in the center of the little fleet, had drawn almost even with the Sumerian line when the arrows stopped arriving. The cessation of enemy arrows drumming against the hull tempted Yavtar to take a good look at the Sumerians.

On the shore, at least a thousand bowmen had shifted their positions, readying themselves to fire directly at the boats. The men moved quickly, formed ranks facing the river, and drew their bows. Yavtar turned to Daro, but the archer had already grasped the significance and shouted new orders to his men.

A few moments later the first volley hurtled toward the ships. Yavtar hunched down below the boat's hull, and shouted a warning to his steersmen and rowers to do the same. Daro and his men ducked behind their shields. The thudding impact of the first volley was strong enough to make the boat lurch in the water. Before Yavtar had time to congratulate himself on being alive, more arrows struck, creating a hammering sound that went on and on. The limp sail even captured a dozen shafts entangled in the thick linen, while plenty of others just passed through.

Looking forward, he saw more arrows protruding from the vessels' sides like blades of grass in a field. If it weren't for the outriggers, slipped into place right after the morning launch, the boats might have capsized from the extra weight of all those arrows alone. Every one of the archers had dropped to his knees and huddled close to the shields, while the rain of death poured down on them.

But the moment the volleys ended, Daro ordered his men to return to their shooting positions. Yavtar counted four more bowmen down, victims of the savage volleys, either dead or out of the fight. Probably the losses would be about the same on the other boats. But Daro still had a battle grimace on his face, and every man that could fight still launched his shaft with a full pull of his bow.

Something burned along his cheek, and Yavtar realized a shaft had just missed his eye. He felt the warm blood dripping down his face, and he hunched a little closer to the wooden shield, not much thicker than the width of his thumb, all that stood between himself and almost certain death.

58

From the slight incline that provided some height, Shulgi still had to strain upwards on his horse to take in the entire battlefield. What he did see caused his brief moment of exultation to turn to anger again. The Akkadians had finally advanced within bowshot, but then they retreated almost as quickly. Meanwhile, their cursed archers were wreaking havoc on his bowmen and infantry. The spearmen at least had their shields, but the rear ranks of archers and foot soldiers were taking losses at an alarming rate.

Now those damned riverboats had crept further up the river, almost level with his own position, and launched arrows at his spearmen's right flank, and even toward his command post. Once again the main force of Akkadian archers remained just out of reach of his smaller bows, and though he had three times as many archers, they might as well have stayed in Sumer for all the good they were doing. They couldn't even stop the handful of enemy archers on the ships, who kept shooting despite the massive volleys that he'd ordered directed at them.

"Shulgi! We have to advance! Now! Their archers are cutting our men to pieces!"

He turned to find Vanar beside him, a shield held up high to protect his head. His commander's wide eyes reflected his concern. Shulgi took another look toward Eskkar's horsemen, still moving slowly to the east.

"Not yet. I want to see what Eskkar's cavalry are doing."

"Damn Eskkar! Whatever he's up to, we've got to close with those bowmen. The men are already looking behind them. They'll be running soon."

"The Akkadians should have been out of arrows by now."

"The riverboats must have resupplied them. We have to attack. Now."

Shulgi gritted his teeth. He wanted to wait at little longer, but if even a few men started to run . . . he knew what that would lead to. "All right, give the order to advance. Move them all forward. Make sure they all move together. We need to strike the enemy with a solid line."

"They will, and the sooner the better."

Vanar shouted the orders as he turned away, and the subcommanders repeated it. The Sumerian spearmen raised a cheer as the preliminary commands worked their way up and down the ranks. They welcomed the order. Better to move forward on the attack than just stand there taking enemy fire, and plenty of men in the Sumerian ranks wanted revenge for Larsa.

As Shulgi watched, the first rank, after some pushing and shoving, moved forward, slipping between or knocking aside the stakes driven into the ground yesterday in preparation for the Akkadian night attack that had never come.

Shulgi urged them on. His Sumerians looked as eager to close with the Akkadians as he was. They'd chased Eskkar's army for days, and now wanted nothing better than to cut them apart. Shields held high, they moved forward.

He turned to see Razrek's cavalry on the move, continuing to shift so as to contain Eskkar's moving horse fighters. Then Shulgi saw the gap between his infantry and horsemen begin to grow. Razrek was supposed to keep the left flank of the spearmen protected. Instead he'd left it exposed as he moved his men eastward.

Shulgi turned to one of his messengers. "Move up the Tanukhs! Have them close that gap! And send a rider to Razrek and tell him to protect our flank!"

Shulgi had kept a quarter of the Tanukhs in reserve, almost three hundred fighters, intending to send them in where they might be needed. They might not be as steady as Razrek's men, but they would do until Razrek got his horsemen under control. For now, Shulgi wanted to maintain a solid line, as much to overawe his enemy as protect his center.

Out of the corner of his eye, Eskkar watched the movement in the Sumerian lines. He saw the small gap developing, but forced himself to continue plodding east. He needed to get all of the Sumerian horse in motion. And once they started, he knew they would find it hard to stop. The horses would want to keep moving, if nothing else.

Across the gap between the two cavalry forces, Razrek's men – not as well trained or used to following orders – began to move faster and faster to the east, determined to stay ahead of Eskkar's horsemen, so that when the attack command came, they could easily sweep around Eskkar's flank.

"Eskkar, I think it's time . . ." Grond's voice betrayed his excitement.

More than five hundred paces now separated Eskkar from Gatus and the spearmen, and the rest of the line stretched far ahead.

"Keep steady! Not yet." Eskkar kept his eyes on Klexor and Muta, at the far end of the line, still pacing their horses steadily to the east. Eskkar had ordered his commanders not to turn their heads around, but to keep their eyes and those of their men straight ahead until they heard Eskkar's signal.

He gritted his teeth and let the horse take another dozen steps before he allowed himself to turn his head toward the Sumerians. The small gap shifted and opened a bit more as the horses kicked some dust into the air. He glimpsed men milling around in the rear of the infantry, behind Shulgi's command post. A force of horsemen remained in the rear, no doubt a reserve. Suddenly, he saw a cluster of men that must be Shulgi's guard, surrounding a trio of tall red banners. That would be where he would find Shulgi. If Eskkar could see Shulgi, that meant the moment had come. He took a deep breath.

"Fashod! Now! Akkadians, attack!"

The bellowed order carried down the line, and even as he uttered it, Eskkar wheeled his horse around and kicked it into a gallop. Fashod barked his own command in the harsh gutturals of the Ur Nammu, and Eskkar heard it repeated up the warriors, though by now it didn't matter. The pounding of the horses' hooves relayed the moment of attack as well as any words. As soon as he had the horse moving at a dead run, he brought up the two javelins that he'd carried in his right hand, held along the side of the horse. Eskkar might not be able to shoot a bow from horseback like his kinsmen or some of his own cavalry, but his powerful arm could still hurl the javelin as hard and as accurately as any of his followers.

Like the tip of a spear, he headed straight for the small break in the

Sumerian lines that had opened between the Sumerian foot soldiers and their cavalry. Behind Esskar, his gleaming helmet and breastplate catching the sun, charged the Ur Nammu warriors, already fitting shafts to their bows. Their war cries burst across the gap and managed to rise above the din of the Akkadian archers, the frightening sounds of the steppe barbarians riding to war. In a few dozen strides – and determined to lead the charge – they drew abreast of Esskar's stallion and he had to urge his horse again just to keep up with them.

As soon as Esskar began the charge, Hathor and Klexor also tugged their horses around and followed, the entire Akkadian cavalry aimed directly – like the shaft of a spear – at Shulgi's command post, driving at a full gallop, every rider shouting his war cry, as they cut diagonally across the open space.

Months and years of training to teach horse and rider to respond to every command, no matter how odd, now proved its worth. The Akkadian charge, led by Esskar and Fashod, was only thirty horses wide, but the entire mass of Hathor's cavalry followed in their steps. They rode as wildly as any barbarian horde, with the fastest moving to the front and the slower following behind, all intent on closing with the enemy as fast as possible.

Arrows flew toward Esskar and those leading the charge, a few striking the horsemen, but the Sumerian archers were far to the left of the line, many having been shifted to the river to deal with the Akkadian boats, and not all that remained had a clear shot. And at a full gallop, the moments Esskar and his men were under fire from the enemy archers would be brief indeed.

Esskar shifted one lance to his left hand and raised the other in his right hand. The horses thundered across the shaking ground, and already he could see his foes shouting at each other in confusion. No one had expected the Akkadians to attack the Sumerian infantry at their flank, especially not with so many of Razrek's horsemen ready to oppose such an attempt. Esskar saw one or two already taking a few steps backward, unsure of what to do.

At about one hundred and fifty paces from the enemy, Esskar heard Fashod signal the Ur Nammu warriors to loose their arrows. Some had already launched their shafts, counting on the speed of their horses to propel the arrow the extra distance. All the missiles flew straight at the Sumerians directly in their path, those still trying to fill the gap. That first flight didn't have much effect, but in moments, every one of Esskar's mounted bowmen were loosing shafts as fast as they could, guiding their horses with their knees and still managing to give their war cries. With so many men before them, they had no need to aim, just launch as quickly as possible.

Eskkar glimpsed horsemen urging their horses forward to fill in the gap, but now arrows were striking at them. Horses were hit, disrupting the movement. Wounded animals tried to flee, frightened at the mass of horses approaching them. Others reared up in simple fright. Eskkar took all this in as he galloped. From behind, more arrows from his own riders flew just over his head, striking at the Sumerian horsemen moving to fill the gap. Caught in the battle rage, Eskkar gave voice to the battle cry of his fathers, as he hurled himself toward Shulgi's forces.

Nevertheless, the enemy horsemen kept moving forward from the rear, and the empty gap began to disappear. However, the number of defenders moving into position remained small for the moment, and by now nothing could stop the Akkadians hurtling down on them.

The distance between the forces vanished. Eskkar saw a Sumerian horse fighter, struggling to control his horse, and aiming an arrow at him. Eskkar flung the lance with all his strength, arching it up slightly, its flight intensified by the speed of his horse. The shaft struck the man in the chest, the force of the blow knocking him backward off the horse.

Eskkar had just enough time to snatch the second lance from his left hand, and hurl it toward the mass of riders moving toward him. Then he jerked the sword from his scabbard as his horse burst in the midst of the Tanukh riders, the Ur Nammu warriors screaming like demons beside and behind him.

A touch of the halter guided the stallion between two Sumerians. One man went down from Eskkar's sword, swinging down with all his strength, while the second was knocked from his horse by the stallion's shoulder. More arrows, fired at a dead run by both the Ur Nammu and the Akkadians still charging behind their leaders, hissed through the air, striking down men and horses alike, everything in their path. Javelins, too, flung by most of the cavalry, struck with devastating effect. Behind Eskkar, Hathor and his men were screaming their war cries, the sound drowning out any Sumerian battle cries.

Eskkar and Grond, at the head of the Ur Nammu, broke through the thin first rank and smashed their way deep into the Tanukhs moving to fill the gap. The desert horsemen, still shifting into position, recognized the barbarian war cries, though they had no idea of how few such men Eskkar had with him. A handful took one look at Eskkar's forces and decided they wanted no part in fighting steppe warriors. They turned their horses away, unwilling to face their hereditary foes.

Nevertheless, the sheer mass of Tanukhs slowed Eskkar's charge, and soon his stallion labored to push its way forward, urged on by the pressure of Eskkar's knees. The great sword rose and fell, striking at anything that came within reach, man or beast.

Just as the charge's momentum seemed about to stall, Ur Nammu shafts, fired with rapidity, cleared the path ahead. With one last blow of his sword, Eskkar burst through the last of the Tanukhs, Grond at his side. A savage kick to his horse's ribs drove the animal forward.

A hundred paces away Shulgi's guard had formed up around their leader. Some had bows and they launched arrows at the charging Akkadians toward Shulgi's guard. A shaft rattled against Eskkar's bronze breastplate before glancing off, and he felt the force of the blow. Another shaft hissed by his face, and he felt something else glance against the bronze helmet.

Then arrows didn't matter, as the two forces collided. Eskkar's sword came down with all his strength, knocking aside an enemy blade raised in defense. With Grond and the Ur Nammu and two hundred other horse fighters, Eskkar had thrust himself deep into the rear ranks of the Sumerians.

Shulgi's fighters, driven back at first, finally managed to slow the attack by sheer numbers. Now swords rose and fell, as Eskkar kept pushing his horse forward, determined to close with Shulgi. The Sumerian king's men – no less determined – tried to halt the deadly advance toward their leader. The jam of horseflesh and men blocked the way, and Eskkar found himself fifty paces from Shulgi's red standards, still waving gaily in the gentle breeze.

Surrounded on all sides by desperate men fighting to the death, all Eskkar could do was strike as hard and fast as he could. He struck a horse in the forehead, and it reared up, screaming in pain. A following thrust caught its rider in the belly. Another rider pushed forward to take his place, and Eskkar's stallion butted shoulders with the new attacker.

On all sides, horses neighed and screamed, either from fright or wounds, as they pushed against each other at the brutal urging of their riders. Men, too, screamed in pain or in rage, as swords – swung with all the force each man could muster – clashed against the bronze blades raised against them. Grond's horse went down, it's legs in a tangle, and Eskkar saw his bodyguard crash to the ground.

In spite of his fury, Eskkar's advance slowed and stopped. He found himself beset on all sides with thrusting blades and spears. His horse reared up, screaming in pain and sending Eskkar sliding down the animal's rump, unable to maintain his seat. He landed on a still-moving body, as the horse turned into a kicking and biting beast, striking at anyone within reach.

A twitching Tanukh body beneath him had taken a lance in the throat. Eskkar seized it with his left hand and jerked it free. He'd managed to hang onto his sword. The battle rage still swept over him. A war cry burst from his lungs, and he charged forward into the mass of men and horses before him.

Two strikes of the sword cleared his advance and he thrust the lance into a horse's open mouth before the rider could get close enough to bring his blade to bear. Ducking under another wild swing, he extended his body and drove the point of the sword through a man's stomach. Using lance and blade, he cut his way forward.

Ignoring Eskkar's battle, Hathor and three hundred men closed the gap, shifted slightly to their left, and smashed into the flank of the Sumerian spearmen. Disrupting the enemy infantry remained his primary task. Arrows and javelins flew through the air, striking into the midst of the spearmen, still trying to advance against the Akkadians.

Sumerian commanders screamed orders, and tried to turn the line to face Hathor's horsemen. A few managed to do so, and raised their shields and spears against this new foe. But the Sumerians had only a small number of men opposing Hathor's three hundred, and he had the advantage of numbers at the point of contact.

Akkadian javelins hurtled through the air. At such close range, many found their target. Even those that missed striking flesh penetrated the Sumerian shields, entangled themselves, and hindered the spearmen's efforts to form a line.

Hathor grunted in satisfaction at what he saw. Spearmen – to withstand infantry – need to be in a formed line and moving forward. Now horses and men clashed over the ragged remnants of the Sumerian left flank, stepping over the dead and dying. The enemy continued to try and shift their position to face this sudden threat, urged on by the desperate shouts of their commanders. Despite those efforts, the left flank of Sumer's spearmen crumbled under Hathor's ferocious onslaught, then started to collapse as the men were driven backward, pushing and shoving against others still in ranks, disrupting them further and preventing them from facing the Akkadians.

Nevertheless, the dense mass of infantry slowed Hathor's advance. Horses went down, stabbed by enemy spears. Wounded animals, mad with pain, lashed out at friend and foe alike. Horsemen, flung to the ground, found themselves scrambling away from spears thrust at them. The Akkadians drew their swords and kept fighting. They had no other choice. The Sumerians had to be broken, or all was lost. Any retreat would give the Sumerians time to reform ranks, and drive the Akkadians before them. But Hathor's men knew they only needed to roll up the end of the Sumerian flank. And help was on the way. He glimpsed Klexor leading a wild charge into the rear of the enemy.

Still at the tip of his men, Hathor screamed his war cry. The Sumerians had never managed to shift their line. By now the Akkadians had hurled all their lances. Swords rasped from scabbards as Hathor's horse-fighters flung themselves into what remained of the left flank of the Sumerian spearmen. In his excitement, he fell back into his native language, but the harsh Egyptian challenge needed no translation.

Hathor's horse ploughed deep into the confused mass of Sumerians, knocking one man backwards into the ranks. Hathor's sword swung down, crunching loudly through another man's shoulder. His horse lashed out with his hooves, knocking another spearman to the earth. Hathor urged the horse forward, leaning aside to let a thrust spear slip past, then striking hard the man's arm. The shriek of pain added to the din of men shouting, horses neighing, and bronze blades clashing against shields and spears. By now the enemy left flank had crumbled into a disorderly mass of men struggling to get away from the Akkadian horsemen.

Nevertheless, some Sumerians fought bravely. With a scream of panic, Hathor's horse stumbled and went down, a spear thrust between its forelegs. Hathor felt the first trembling through his legs, and leapt aside as his horse crashed into the earth, kicking and biting at anything that moved.

Another horse brushed past him as he struggled to regain his footing, the snorting beast hurtling over Hathor's downed mount. An enemy spearman lunged at Hathor, but he struck the spear aside, stepped inside the length of the weapon, and drove his sword into the face of the Sumerian. Blood spurted over the length of his arm, as the dying man shrieked in agony.

At close quarters and without the support of orderly ranks knitted together, the Sumerian spears turned into clumsy weapons. Hathor dodged and weaved his way between them, striking at everything – shield, spear or man – that he could reach.

Two Sumerians, shields locked, moved toward him. But before they could get close enough, an arrow split the skull of one of the men, transfixing its length just below his mouth. Hathor struck aside the other spear, and flung his weight against the man's shield. The foe lacked Hathor's size, and he stumbled back, exposing his right side.

Hathor swung his sword with both hands, the sharp blade cutting through the man's upper arm, and eliciting a scream of agony. Hathor had no idea of how the battle was progressing. All he could do was try to stay alive, and strike at anyone within reach. All around him, men were fighting, struggling, some even without weapons in their hands.

Suddenly, a riderless horse reared up before him, kicking out with both its front hooves. Hathor ducked under an enemy sword and shoved the man to the earth. Two quick steps allowed him to catch the panicky animal's halter, and he leapt up onto the beast's back. The horse responded to the pressure of his knees. A quick glance showed the mass of Sumerian spearmen ahead, most trying to reform their lines to face the savage attack from the Akkadian cavalry.

At least from the back of the horse, Hathor could see the battle developing. Horses were still moving forward. He saw Klexor's men join in the attack, shouting their war cries and hurling lances and arrows into the rear of the enemy infantry. The first two blows of the hammer had struck, and now parts of the Sumerian line began to collapse, faced with ferocious spearmen on one side, and frenzied horsemen at their flank and rear. Hathor could see nothing of Eskkar or his men, and could only hope his leader had survived the wild charge.

"Akkad! Akkad! Kill the Sumerians!" This time Hathor remembered to avoid Egyptian, as he pointed with his sword. His distinctive voice rallied his men, and a handful of horsemen, as well as an equal number on foot, rallied to his side, their war cries echoing his own. He swept back into the battle, waving his bloody sword high over his head.

"Kill! Kill the Sumerians!"

Kill them all, he thought, before they kill us.

59

The moment Eskkar turned to the attack, as the cavalry thundered by them, Shappa and his four hundred slingers were exposed. Scattered behind the galloping horsemen, the slingers carried only their knives, slings and as many missiles as they could fit into the two pouches attached to every man's waist. In addition, they all carried at least one extra bag of stones in their left hand, and some of the stronger men carried two. Shappa didn't want to take any chance of running out of missiles or, even worse, having his men waste time trying to find something on the battlefield they could use.

"Good hunting, Nivar!" Shappa and his friend had grown closer during the last two years and now they were fighting side by side, attempting to do something few Akkadian soldiers believed possible – stop a massed charge of horsemen with nothing but slingshot. The small force of slingers had the most exposed and difficult task of all this day, to slow down the huge force of Sumerian cavalry and prevent them from falling on Eskkar's rear.

As soon as Eskkar gave the order to charge, Shappa burst into a run, keeping a tight grip on his two bags of stones. He didn't bother shouting any commands. His men knew what needed to be done. Running as fast as he could, he led them toward what had been the center of the open ground between the two forces. Unlike Eskkar's diagonal charge, Shappa moved directly toward the enemy line.

He had time for one glance behind him, and saw the entire force of slingers following his steps. They didn't look graceful or organized, each lumbering along and carrying the extra projectiles, but they were young and fleet of foot. For the short distance they had to travel to block the gap, they covered the ground almost as fast as a man on horseback.

They clutched their slings as they raced forward, and every man had their roundest and heaviest bronze ball already held fast within the leather. Breathing hard, Shappa reached the midpoint just as the Sumerian cavalry – caught off-guard by Eskkar's unexpected attack – realized what had happened. Some turned their horses around, intending to pounce on Eskkar's exposed rear.

Shappa dropped the extra bag of stones he carried, then scooped out three missiles with his left hand. His sling, carried in his right hand, already contained a stone.

The Sumerian cavalry had finally halted all movement to the east. Despite their confusion, they wheeled their horses around, delighted at the chance to fall upon Eskkar's rear, and Shappa could see the commanders urging their men to attack. He spun the sling and loosed the first stone, flinging it into the mass of horsemen less than a hundred and fifty paces away. Beside him, Shappa heard the pants and grunts of the rest of his men arriving, followed a moment later by the sound of whirling slings.

The Sumerian horsemen needed only moments to turn around and countercharge. Shappa didn't intend to give them that moment. "Throw! Throw! Slow them down!"

A few of the slingers let loose their missiles while they pressed ahead, but most slowed down enough to put all their force into the throw. Hundreds of stones rose up into the air, to descend on the Sumerian cavalry. In moments, the air hummed with the steady sounds of slings snapping as they hurled their small but deadly projectiles at the enemy horsemen.

By now all four hundred slingers were in range, and missiles filled the air, striking horse and rider in what seemed like an unceasing rain of bronze. It was almost impossible not to hit something, with so many horses jammed together. The animals began bucking and rearing, whinnying in pain as the heavy round pellets stuck their necks and chests, or glanced off their flanks. Some of the riders turned aside, moving either toward their own rear or trying to get to the slingers' flank or rear.

Shappa had to prevent that. If he could move his men directly between Eskkar's cavalry and the enemy horsemen, at least he wouldn't have to worry about anyone in his rear. The thought that he might get run down never entered his head.

"Keep moving forward! Move closer!" Shappa gave the order and set the example, moving forward, determined to put his slingers directly between Eskkar's force and the Sumerian horsemen. Off to his right, he caught a glimpse of Nivar urging his men in the same direction, even as his friend loosed his own weapon.

Enemy riders went down, struck by stones or pitched from their mounts. The countercharge against Eskkar's riders hesitated, then stopped, as men fought to control their animals. None of the Sumerians or Tanukhs had ever faced slingers before, and this new tactic by this strange foe had them confused. Their horses, too, reacted with fear to these men whirling things through the air.

Shappa knew his men looked helpless and vulnerable, without any real weapons. The obvious Sumerian tactic would be to ride them down. To accomplish that, the great numbers of Sumerian cavalry needed only to move as a concerted force, ignoring their losses until they could ride into the slingers' midst. But the stones kept coming, smashing into the enemy horsemen with even greater force as the slingers drew closer.

A few riders charged the slingers. Some even managed to evade the dozens of stones flung at them. But when those hardy Sumerians tried to strike down the apparently helpless slingers, they saw their opponents throw themselves to the ground beneath the Sumerian swords, only to rise up an instant later and strike with their long knives at the rear legs of the horses. Wounded animals reared out of control, unhorsing their riders, who then became easy targets for the slingers' stones or long knives.

Shappa had trained his men well, and they knew to seek out enemy commanders as targets for their missiles, those men who would be trying to restore order and rally their ranks. Without commanders urging them forward – ordering them to run down the slingers and kill them at any cost – the Sumerians continued to hesitate, then some began turning away from the rain of missiles. They saw the fate of those who had rushed into the slingers' midst, and decided a more prudent course of action was to ride around them. A few galloped off, as much to get out of range of the slingers as to reach the Akkadian rear.

Shappa ignored them. He kept directing his slingers against the mass of horsemen still milling about. The stones sought them out, arcing higher in the sky before falling. When they struck the horses, the animals bolted or started bucking, often tossing their riders to the earth at the same moment. Shappa had to keep up the pressure. The Sumerians had thousands of riders, and if it occurred to all of them to simply ride around the flanks of the slingers, both Eskkar and the spearmen would be in trouble.

But the havoc and commotion of Eskkar's charge had driven reason from their heads. They had thought only of attacking Eskkar's smaller force, hitting them from the rear and wiping them out. They wanted to reach the Akkadian king, not waste time on insignificant slingers, and risking their own lives in the process.

Shappa had no time to worry about that. He kept dropping stones into his pouch, and flinging them toward the enemy. Suddenly his hand came up empty from the first pouch. He had already thrown over thirty stones. He ripped open the second sack, and hoped that the Sumerians turned back, or help arrived, before he emptied that one as well. Off to one side, he saw a large force of enemy horsemen moving across the battle line, intending to attack Gatus's rear.

That didn't concern him. His task this day was to halt or slow down the Sumerian cavalry, and by all the gods, he intended to do just that.

Razrek picked himself up from the ground. He didn't remember falling, but a stone must have struck his bronze helmet and knocked him from his horse. He needed both hands to push himself to his feet. His sword had vanished, lost in the debris that now littered the battlefield. Bodies of men and horses lay scattered on the ground all around him. Those cursed slingers continued to hurl their missiles into his horsemen, many of them milling around like a bunch of frightened women.

With an oath he stumbled toward the rear. A horse kicked its heels, its halter tangled around its dead rider. The man's body kept the frightened animal from bolting. A vicious cut with his knife freed the rope, and Razrek jerked the halter so hard that the stunned animal ceased its frantic efforts to get away. Still, it took all his strength to pull himself onto the animal.

"Razrek! Razrek! We can't get through!" Mattaki pulled up beside him. "Those slingers are blocking the way . . ."

"I can see, you fool! Forget Shulgi, and forget these slingers. Get our men to the rear of the Akkadian infantry. We can ride them down. They've no one behind them."

"I'll rally the men . . ."

Two stones arrived at the same time. One hit Mattaki's horse in the chest, and the other glanced off Razrek's forehead.

For a few moments, Mattaki fought to regain control of his bucking mount. When he finally got the animal under control, he turned toward Razrek, and saw his leader motionless, flat on his back with his forehead a mass of blood, either dead or dying. More stones hissed through the air. The accursed Akkadian slingers still had a plentiful supply of missiles.

Mattaki thought of all the gold he'd buried deep in the earth near the edge of the desert, and decided he had had enough fighting for the day. Razrek was dead and, win or lose today, Shulgi wasn't going to be too happy with the commanders of his cavalry. Mattaki wheeled his horse around and galloped at full speed away from the battle. A few other horsemen had already reached the same conclusion. By twos and threes, then by twenty and thirty, many of the Sumerian cavalry followed, riding away from the battlefield.

Gatus heard the wild roar that signaled Eskkar's charge. The enemy spearmen had pushed forty or fifty paces past their line of stakes, their bowmen moving up behind them. The first Sumerian arrows began to strike the Akkadian shield wall, and he knew that soon every Sumerian bowman would have the entire Akkadian force within range. But that didn't matter any longer. The line of deadly stakes had vanished, overrun by the advancing enemy. The time had come. The anvil had to move forward.

"Spearmen. Ready to advance!" One brief moment to make sure the command reached up and down the line. "Advance! Fast march! Advance! Attack!"

Up and down the line, leaders of ten and twenty repeated the commands. The line moved forward. No slow step this time. The Akkadian infantry took full strides, moving as quickly as the ground permitted, determined to close with their enemy and get past the arrows beginning to rain down on them. Ignoring the noise and cries of battle all around them, they quick marched in silence, shields raised, spears still carried low in the right hand.

The two soldiers responsible for guarding Gatus pulled him from his horse. One handed him a sturdy shield. As the only mounted man, he would have drawn every Sumerian arrow, and Eskkar himself had warned them about that possibility. One guard smacked the mare on the rump, sending it away from the coming battle.

Gatus had no time to do more than swear at his guards. He rushed forward, slipping his arm through the shield's leather grip and hitching it into position. His two guards stayed in front, using their shields to protect his sides from any stray arrow. Behind him, he heard Mitrac ordering the bowmen forward as well. If the archers were going to face a Sumerian arrow storm, they'd be safer as close behind the spearmen as they could get.

Arrows now flew in both directions, and the Sumerian arrows started to take their toll. Men dropped out of the advancing line, killed or wounded, but the line kept its cohesion and those in the rear ranks moved forward to fill the spaces of those who'd fallen.

Gatus stretched his body upward, jumping every few steps so that he could see the men's progress and gauge the remaining distance to the enemy spearmen. A dozen more paces. The approaching enemy had closed to within a hundred and fifty paces. Close enough, he decided.

"Spearmen! Ready to charge!"

Those words rippled up and down the line, the men growling impatiently. Voices called out from the ranks, to add their own encouragement to their leaders orders, as they waited for the final command that would release them to the attack. But they never stopped moving forward.

Gatus's bellow rolled out over the battlefield. "Spearmen! Charge! Charge! Charge!" The two Akkadian drummers, silent up to this moment, now pounded the attack drumbeat.

With a roar that drew every head on the battlefield, the Akkadian spearmen broke into a run. The spears were lifted to the attack position, raised just over the shield, which they held at eye level. With their bronze helmets, only Akkadian eyes and spear points were visible to the enemy.

Everyone shouted as loud as they could. The line surged forward. They'd been silent throughout the battle so far, and now they intended to make up for it. War cries filled the air as the line rushed forward. Some parts moved a bit quicker than others, but the three-man-deep attack line remained in good order, holding its cohesion. For long months the men had trained to charge together, spears raised, shouting as loud as they could. Now all that training would be put to the real test.

The Sumerian line, which had moved at a regular marching pace, heard the savage drumbeats and saw the enemy approaching at a run, screaming war cries as their spears moved up and down with each stride. The Sumerian line slowed slightly. They had expected the two lines to close together at the fast marching pace. No one expected a wild charge by the smaller force, still only three ranks deep.

Most of the others didn't notice the slight slowing, the doubt creeping into the Sumerian forward line. Gatus, however, had been searching for it. By now he could see wide-eyed Sumerian faces showing the first hint of fear. The Sumerian army might win the battle, but those spearmen in the front line knew who was going to take the full brunt of the collision.

"Attack! Charge! Kill them all! Akkad! Akkad! Attack!"

Gatus's words, bellowed with every breath within him, swept over the ranks. The frenzied spearmen repeated the war cries. They all screamed like demons possessed. Then the gap between the forces disappeared.

The Akkadian spearmen crashed into the still advancing Sumerian line. At the moment of contact, spears were driven forward with every bit of strength the men could summon. Sounds of splintering wood crackled over the deeper crash as shield wall met shield wall, both overshadowing the sudden cries of the wounded and dying. The noise drowned out every other part of the battle, as the shields smashed together up and down the line.

In the front rank, bronze spear points tore right through Sumerian shields, to impale the shrieking body behind it. The Akkadian second rank pushed their shields into the backs of the men in front of them, leaned forward, and drove their spears into the faces of the enemy, jabbing again and again at any thing that moved, any flesh that showed itself.

The Sumerian front line went down by the dozens. Despite having twice as many men in the ranks, and overlapping the Akkadians to some extent, the Sumerian countercharge slowed, and stopped.

As the Akkadian second and third ranks closed up, the six-deep Sumerian line found themselves, to their own surprise, being pushed back by the smaller force. To the Sumerians, these Akkadians were indeed demons, unafraid to attack a superior force. The Sumerian spearmen – forced to take a step or two backward to regain their momentum – found themselves incapable of moving forward again. Instead they found themselves slipping or stumbling, unable to use their weapons. Some tried to duck behind the shield of another, to gain a moment's protection from the spears and swords now being thrust at their faces.

The Akkadians kept pushing, pushing, driving the heavier line backwards, their powerful leg muscles thrusting furiously against the earth, as they tried to shove the Sumerian line into the ground. Men tripped and stumbled over dead bodies, and live ones, too, whose howls rose up from the ground as they were trampled on.

The smell of dying men was in the air and blood now soaked the ground. Shields, helmets, faces, all were splashed in hot liquid that spurted from open veins and splattered like rain against men's faces and shields. Soldiers shouted their battle cries into the faces of their enemy, sometimes only a hand's width away from their own. Other men screeched in agony as sharp spear points thrust into their bodies.

Many in the Akkadian front rank had lost their spears, either splintering from the collision or hopelessly entangled with the enemy. But despite the press of bodies at their front and rear, each could still manage to draw his short sword. Some men – squeezed in front and back by the pressure of opposing shields – had no room to use a blade. Instead they smashed the pommel of the weapon into their opponents' faces. Others jabbed the sword's point into the heads and necks of those pressed against them, or those in the rank behind. They struck again and again, until the man in front of them went down. When that happened, the now ragged line would surge another half-step forward, bringing a new opponent into reach.

Some of the dead had no room to fall, kept upright for a few moments by the sheer press of numbers. Others, their bodies slippery with blood, slid to the ground, many still alive and gasping at the thought of what awaited them. To fall meant never to rise again. Scrambling feet from both sides trampled those underfoot, adding new pain to existing wounds or simply crushing the life from their bodies.

The battle had degenerated into individual combat, with each man pressed against the opposing man's shield. But the Akkadians had trained hard for just such an encounter. They welcomed the pressure of their companion's shield in their back, and as Gatus had taught them, they never stopped struggling to move forward. They knew their legs would win the battle for them, as long as they pressed ahead. The days of long and hard training under Gatus's tutelage kept the shield wall not only intact, but moving forward, a half-step every few moments. The smaller force had not only stopped the advancing Sumerians, but now began to drive them backwards, step by step.

For the Sumerians, to reach the front rank meant death, but still they held their ground, clinging stubbornly to their position. The Sumerian commanders urged their men forward, and determined men hurled themselves against the backs of their ranks. The Akkadian advance slowed, then stopped. The greater weight of numbers on the Sumerian side began to weigh against the tiring Akkadian infantry. The battle line surged and rippled, but the Sumerians, now in a battle frenzy of their own, halted the onrush and began to push their enemy backwards.

Klexor led his men at the charge, at first following the path of Eskkar and Hathor. Klexor's orders were to take his men between the other Akkadian commanders. The battle plan required that the king break through the line with his men and seek out Shulgi. Hathor would attack the Sumerian left flank. Klexor's objective was to guide his three hundred men between Eskkar and Hathor's forces, and crumple the Sumerian spearmen's rear, to disrupt the Sumerian infantry from behind. Only by attacking from the front and rear could the Akkadians hope to prevail over the superior numbers of their enemy. Nevertheless, this meant Klexor's men had the greatest distance to cover before they came to grips with the enemy. To make sure his horsemen followed his lead, Klexor had the steadiest men under his command. All of them knew where to go, and what to do.

Eskkar's men had vanished into a mob of swirling horses and screaming men. Still, Klexor found the tiniest of gaps, only a few paces wide, between Hathor and Eskkar's fighters. Klexor raised his sword and guided his horse toward the opening. "Attack! Follow me! Attack!"

He swept past Hathor's still struggling horsemen. In front of Klexor the enemy spears loomed up. The enemy left flank still extended beyond the line of Gatus's spearmen, and hadn't yet engaged in battle. Now they saw Klexor's thundering horsemen approaching, and tried to turn to their rear to meet this new threat. But that maneuver required some doing. Men had to shift and reform ranks, a task that would take precious moments. If they could raise a wall of spear points between them and Klexor's men, they would be able to stop the advance.

But before the Sumerians could form up, Klexor's cavalry began hurling their javelins at the mass of men struggling to regroup. Flung with all a man's strength, and aided by the speed of the galloping horse, the deadly missiles rained down on the reforming ranks. Arrows, too, flew into the Sumerians, disrupting their effort to form a solid line. Some men panicked, trying to shift out of the path of the onrushing horsemen that had suddenly appeared in their rear.

Klexor saw the fear in their faces as he swung his sword down with all his might, striking right and left at anything that moved, pushing the horse ahead with all his strength.

"Attack!" he shouted. "Kill them all! Kill them all!"

His horse killed beneath him, Fashod broke through his own ring of attackers, and saw Esskar a dozen paces ahead, swinging his sword and surrounded by enemies. Fashod's bow was gone, wrenched from his hands, and he'd seen Grond go down, crushed by a mass of surging Tanukhs. Fashod saw Chinua jump his horse over the mounting bodies of the dead, to move to Fashod's side.

"Esskar!" Fashod used his sword to point at the Akkadian.

Chinua still had his bow. Gripping his horse hard with his knees, he fit a shaft to the string and shot it, striking a Tanukh horseman trying to ride down the king. Three more shafts followed, launched faster than any Fashod had ever seen, and the rush that threatened to overwhelm Esskar slowed. His quiver empty, Chinua dropped his bow and snatched out his sword.

Behind them, the Ur Nammu war cry sounded, and a half dozen warriors broke through their enemies and swept past Fashod and Chinua. Kicking their horses to the gallop, they charged the Tanukhs, brushing past Esskar as they hurled themselves into the mass of enemy horsemen. Behind them rode another shouting handful of Akkadians desperate to reach the king's side. If Esskar went down, the battle could still be lost.

60

Shulgi's voice rasped with every order he shouted. The Akkadian bowmen had raked his men with their shafts, the puny boats on the river had taken their toll on his right flank, and now Eskkar's horsemen had charged deep into the gap created by Razrek's carelessness.

"Hold them off!" Shulgi shouted, turning to the Tanukh beside him.

Kapturu, the leader of the Tanukhs, heard the war cries of the approaching men and hesitated.

"Order your men forward or I'll kill you now!" Shulgi said, his sword suddenly in his hand. The king's guards moved in closer, both to protect their leader and prevent Kapturu's leaving.

The Tanukh weighed his chances, then gave the order. Raising his arm, he pointed toward Eskkar's charging horsemen. "Tanukhs! Forward! Attack! Attack!"

The mass of Tanukh horsemen surged forward, whatever their misgivings. In a few strides, the Sumerian reserve moved toward the gap, gaining speed as they moved. Then the wave of Akkadians tore through the tiny opening and crashed into the Tanukhs. In moments the fighting had surged past his once orderly ranks and into his rear. The battle Shulgi had sought for two years now threatened to overwhelm him.

Shulgi stared at the carnage surrounding him. His cavalry had vanished, and only the Tanukhs were keeping the Akkadians from breaking through the line. But his infantry's flank was in ruins, and some of Eskkar's cavalry had slipped past and smashed into the rear of the line.

Still, if the Tanukhs could hold a little longer, until Razrek's men counter-attacked, the Akkadians would be caught between two forces and broken.

The mass of Sumerian and Tanukh fighters to his left thinned out, and Shulgi saw Esskar's tall figure, now dismounted, but still leading the attack and trying to break through to the rear.

"Bowmen!" Shulgi's bellow turned every one of his men's heads toward him. He pointed toward Esskar. "Get bowmen on the king! Kill Esskar!"

Two archers ran up, pushing their way through Shulgi's protective ring of horsemen, trying to scramble onto the tiny hillock and get high enough above the mass of men to take a shot at Akkad's king. Shulgi reached down and grabbed the nearest by the shoulder and pointed towards Esskar. "Hurry! Don't let him get away!"

The first archer drew back his shaft and let fly. A good shot, and Shulgi saw the arrow strike Esskar in the chest, but the king was turning when the missile struck, and it merely glanced off the Akkadian's breastplate. The other archer, still struggling to find his footing amidst Shulgi's personal guards, drew back his shaft for a carefully aimed shot . . .

On the river, Yavtar saw the Sumerians start their advance, and a quick glance showed the Akkadian spearmen also moving forward. They looked helpless against such a large force. Their flanks would be turned, or they'd be overrun and pinned against the river and slaughtered.

"Boats!" Yavtar had to shout the word with all his lungs. Fortunately, the emptiness of the river carried his voice to the other two boats. "Move in closer to shore! We have to hold the spearmen's flank!"

He turned to his steersman, still crouched as low as he could and just as frightened as when the battle began. "Move us closer to the shore! Get us within fifty paces, and keep us there!"

Daro dropped down beside him, an arrow still strung on the bow. "Good move. We'll cut them apart at that distance."

Unless a few hundred suddenly jumped in the river and swam toward them, Yavtar thought. Then we're all going to be dead.

But the boat crept toward the riverbank, the men still straining at their oars. It took more effort to hold the boat in position as the land drew near, and these men had been pulling at the oars for some time. A look ahead and behind showed that the other two vessels had heard and understood the order. Either that, or they were just keeping their station on Yavtar's boat, as they'd been ordered.

"Daro! We need to lighten the boat. Throw the dead overboard."

At least five bowmen were dead, and two or three were cursing in pain from their wounds. Still, getting rid of the dead would help the oarsmen.

Daro nodded, and soon bodies were shoved over the side, to splash loudly in the water before drifting away on the current.

By the time his men dumped the dead overboard, Yavtar's boat had pulled within twenty paces of the fighting. The three craft, which had drifted a few dozen paces apart since the start of the fighting, now drew closer together. Yavtar could have jumped from his boat into either of the other two. He could see the drawn faces of the Sumerians and hear the shouts and curses as they advanced.

On shore, all the Sumerians were on the move forward, their attention for a moment fixed on the advancing Akkadian infantry as the two forces converged. The archers on board the riverboats noticed the slackening of arrows directed toward them. Emboldened, they aimed their shafts and launched at the Sumerian flank, now unprotected by either shield wall or the Sumerian archers.

As the enemy advanced, the boats compensated to keep themselves level with the Sumerians. Yavtar's boat, and the one following behind him, slowed their rowing to keep themselves in the same position. But a gap opened up between those two craft and the remaining boat, the one that had been farthest north. It was now well behind the advancing enemy lines, and drifted even nearer to the shore.

For a moment, Yavtar thought the wayward craft might be sinking. Then he saw the arrows that flew from that craft were aimed not at the moving infantry, but deep toward the center of the Sumerian line. What targets drew their shafts Yavtar couldn't see, but the boat captain knew his business, and the leader of his boat's archers had been picked by Daro for that command. Still, their orders were to stay close to Yavtar's boat, and to follow his lead.

"Daro!" He pointed with his hand at the other boast, now a hundred paces ahead of the other two boats.

After launching the shaft on his bowstring, Daro ducked back behind the shield. Yavtar again jabbed his hand toward the lead boat.

Breathing hard, Daro had no time for more than a glance at the wayward craft.

"Forget them, Yavtar. Keep us abreast of the enemy line."

On the first ship, a young archer named Viran commanded the force of bowmen. He saw Yavtar's and the other boat slipping southward to maintain close contact with the Sumerian line. But as the enemy spearmen, infantry, and their supporting archers moved forward, Viran glimpsed a cluster of horsemen near the center of the Sumerian line. Three red banners floated in the air just around them. Viran couldn't see much, but he knew what the banners floating softly in the morning breeze likely meant. Some Sumerian commanders had marked their position, and the banners dipped and rose to signal movements to their men.

Alexar, Drakis, even Esskar, had all ordered their bowmen, time after time, to aim for the leaders of the enemy. Viran saw that the banners neither advanced nor retreated. That might not mean much. He took but a moment to decide.

"Boatmaster! Forget Yavtar's order. Keep us where we are!" Viran turned his attention to his own men. "Archers! See those three red banners? Let's give them a few volleys!"

By this stage of the battle, Viran only had nine archers still fit to draw a bow. But if even one or two arrows struck the enemy commanders, it would be worth the effort. The arrows' flight would be a long one, and his bowmen would have to put plenty of arc on the shot, but they should be just within range.

"Halt! At my command! Draw your bows! Shoot! Again! Hit those red banners, damn you! Draw! Shoot! Keep shooting!"

Viran barked the same commands used on the training ground, but now his voice added urgency to his men, and they dug deep into their waning reserves of strength to obey. Fortunately, no enemy archers were targeting Viran's boat, though out of the corner of his eye he saw plenty of shafts still striking Yavtar's vessel.

The first volley from Viran's ship rose up into the air almost like a flight of birds, one shaft leading the others. At this distance, and without a high place to observe the targets, Viran knew he wouldn't be able to see the effects of his men's arrows. But like all of Akkad's finer marksmen, he had faith in both his weapon and his men's ability. He glanced at his bowmen on either side.

"Pull those shafts, you lazy dogs! Make sure every arrow reaches those banners!"

As he gave the command, Viran set the example. Aiming his arrow high toward the still climbing sun, he dragged the feathered end to his ear, fighting against the tension and the tiredness in his arms, and released. The thick bowstring twanged and slapped hard against his wrist guard as the shaft tore its way up into the air. A puff of air pushed it forward, before it began its descent.

As he nocked another shaft, he wondered if he would ever know what effect his men's arrows would have this day.

The small flight of arrows rained down on Shulgi's bodyguards. Only a half dozen reached the place where the Sumerian king stood. A bodyguard took a shaft in the thigh, but despite the knot of men surrounding the king, the rest failed to strike any other targets. Except one. One arrow dove deep into the rump of a horse, ridden by a bodyguard positioned just behind Shulgi. The wounded beast bolted forward, crashing into Shulgi's mount, and driving the Sumerian king and his horse into the two archers. The arrow aimed at Eskkar's head flew wide, and both archers were knocked to the ground. The terrified animal, wild with pain from the thick shaft and unable to move forward, then reared up and began striking out with its hooves.

With a curse, Shulgi found himself fighting to keep his seat. His horse was struck in the neck by a flying hoof from the enraged animal beside him. Both horses reared up, biting and kicking at each other, but Shulgi's mount lost its footing and crashed to the earth, taking the king with him.

His shoulder took the brunt of the fall, knocking the breath from his lungs. For a moment he lay pinned beneath his kicking horse. Then the frantic animal found its footing, struggled to its feet, and bolted off to the rear, away from the noise and confusion. The other horse, maddened by the pain in its rump, continued bucking and rearing, until one of the guardsmen struck it across the head with his sword, sending the animal stumbling dead to the ground. Two of Shulgi's red banners went down with it, entangled with the beast.

Another half dozen or so arrows rained down on the Sumerian king's position. One man took a shaft in the side, but no other missiles found a target. Shaking his head, Shulgi climbed to his feet. The first thing he saw was Kapturu, the leader of the Tanukhs, wheeling his horse around and kicking it hard, away from the edge of the battle front that had come too near for Kapturu's liking. Other Tanukhs followed their clan leader's example.

"King Shulgi is dead! The king is dead!"

Some fool had seen Shulgi fall, and given voice to the lie. Others took up the cry at the sight of the king's riderless horse. He knew he had to stop the panic from spreading.

"Sumerians! To me! To me!"

Except for those surrounding him, Shulgi's shout went unheard, almost lost in the clamor of the conflict. Men shouted at each other, horses neighed and screamed, and the clash of bronze sword rang on both wooden shields and naked blades.

He tried to drag his sword from its scabbard, but the blade resisted, the scabbard bent by the fall. Shulgi finally ripped it free and raised it up over his head. "To me! Rally to your king!" He trod over two bodies to reach the lone red standard and stood beside it. "Rally to your king!"

A few heads turned his way. Others picked up his words, and passed them on. Shulgi knew he needed to hold his position long enough to give his spearmen time to break the Akkadian ranks. Victory remained within his grasp.

His shield held close to his eyes, Gatus stood behind his ranks of spearmen, watching the battle line ripple and waver as the bloody fighting continued. His left flank, anchored against the river, was holding fast, no doubt helped by the two of Yavtar's fighting boats that Gatus could see. What should have been the weakest part of the line, the right flank, also stood firm, no doubt helped by the confusion that Hathor and Klexor's men had brought to bear. Only at the center, facing the greatest concentration of Sumerian might, had the advance ground to a halt, and even as he stared, it started giving way.

Gatus turned his head. By now he'd expected the Sumerian cavalry to be on his back, but the grassy field, trampled down by his men, remained empty as far as he could see. The slingers must still be engaging the enemy horsemen.

Shouts from his infantry snapped his head around. His precious spearmen were being driven back, killed as they tried to hold the line. They had started out in ranks three or even four deep, but now he saw many gaps where only one or two ranks remained, struggling to resist the enormous mass of Sumerian infantry, many shouting the war cries of Larsa, only a dozen paces away. Gatus knew they couldn't withstand so many for much longer.

"Mitrac! Alexar! Help hold the line!"

Without waiting for a reply, Gatus charged ahead, his two cursing bodyguards caught by surprise at the old man's sudden burst of speed. Drawing his sword, Gatus ran straight toward the largest bulge in the line. He arrived just as three men went down, losing their footing against the pressure of the Sumerians. Sumerian shouts rose, as the enemy saw only a handful of archers before them.

With an oath, Gatus thrust himself into the breech. Despite his age, his muscles were fresh, unlike those of all the men fighting. "Akkad! Spearmen, hold! Hold the line!"

His shield knocked one man back, and he thrust his sword into the face of another. The ground had good footing here, and his guards crashed against the line on either side of their leader, all three using their swords and shouting their war cries.

Hacking and stabbing, the three men halted the advance, and Gatus managed to take a step forward before the Sumerians regained their footing.

The Sumerians, nipped and harried by the Akkadians all morning, with many of their own men killed in the initial charge, now saw empty space only a few paces ahead. The sight rallied their strength and they pushed forward. One of Gatus's guards went down, struck in the head with a sword. Gatus redoubled his efforts, thrusting and hacking with his sword, and keeping his shoulder pressed against his shield.

Something burned his side, and he staggered back, shoved by the force of the spear that entered his body. His surviving bodyguard struck at the enemy spearman's face, knocking the man down and ripping the spear's point from Gatus's side. Ignoring the pain, Gatus moved forward again, swinging his sword down on another enemy head. Then a crazed Sumerian shoved a shield against Gatus's, and once again drove the Akkadian back. He slipped and fell, as the way opened up for the Sumerian spearmen to burst through the Akkadian line.

Mitrac had arrived with one hundred archers. The enemy horsemen hadn't appeared on the infantry's flank yet, and he'd seen Gatus's line bend and begin to break. Mitrac's men gathered into two ranks, a dozen paces behind the center of the line. "First rank aim high, second rank low. Shoot!"

Without seeming to aim, he put a shaft right through the eye of the first battle-crazed Sumerian to step over Gatus's still struggling body. Shaft after shaft, propelled from the powerful bow, tore into the enemy, many of them too weary to lift their shields high enough to protect their faces.

The second rank of archers targeted the enemy's legs, shooting downward into the mass of churning limbs that were packed so close together that almost every shaft had to strike something before it buried itself in the earth. Mitrac realized those facing him were not spearmen. Most of those had fallen victim to the Akkadian spears. These men lacked the large shields that the Sumerian infantry carried. Most were armed only with swords and small shields.

The deadly flight of arrows halted the surging Sumerians. Even those with shields found their protection of little use. At such close range, many bronze-tipped shafts bored through the hide-covered wood with enough strength to kill or wound the flesh pressed against it. Mitrac's bowmen had plenty of arrows, and in moments they'd launched a thousand arrows at the concentrated enemy line.

The Sumerians halted, unable to advance in the face of the withering arrow volleys. A few glanced up, to see even more archers racing toward them. Cries went up from behind them, as Klexor's horsemen continued to pound their rear, the sound of Akkadian war cries at their back adding to their confusion. In a few heartbeats, panic raced through the Sumerians.

Mitrac saw the effect of his arrow storm. "Advance! Keep shooting!" Even as he bellowed the words, he stepped forward, still loosing shafts as fast as he could. "Kill the Sumerians! Death to Sumeria!"

"Akkad!" The shout burst from his men's lungs, as they took a dozen steps forward. More arrows tore into the Sumerian center. More archers arrived, to add their shafts to the carnage.

It was more than the Sumerians could bear. Some took a step backward, others turned and tried to shove their way out of the line. They'd fought bravely enough, but there seemed to be no end to these blood-crazed Akkadians.

Even those men from Larsa, still driven by their thirst for revenge, began to fall back. Some turned to run. Arrows ripped through the mass of men. Without shields to protect their backs, every arrow brought a man down. The retreat turned into a rout. Then it became a slaughter as the Akkadian spearmen – freed from the pressure of the enemy – summoned up one last effort, regained their footing, and returned to the attack.

Mitrac expended his last shaft. Clutching his bow in his left hand, he drew his sword and charged. "Kill them all! Kill them all!"

Breathing hard, Eskkar ran after the Ur Nammu horsemen. The Tanukhs were falling back, despite the smaller number of Akkadians facing them. Blood covered the slippery ground, and bodies of the dead and wounded lay everywhere. One red standard still stood, and he raced toward it, still gripping the lance in his left hand.

The battle now raged at close quarters. Victory or defeat depended on dozens of individual combats raging all over the battleground. All Eskkar could do was try and kill as many of his enemies as possible.

"Akkad!" His powerful voice bellowed above the din of battle. "Follow me! Akkad!" No matter what happened, he swore to cut his way through and reach the Sumerian king.

Men fought all around him, but almost all were mounted. A Tanukh fought against one of the Ur Nammu warriors. Ducking between the two, Eskkar thrust up with the lance at the Tanukh, the bronze tip digging into the man's left side. The wounded man broke away with a cry, wheeling his horse and bolting for the rear. Eskkar kept moving, ducking and shifting his way through the mass of milling men and animals. He burst past the last of the Tanukh line, astonished to see the entire force falling back, some already galloping off to the rear.

The lone red standard stood atop a slight rise in the ground, and he advanced toward it. Bodies lay all about, many with arrows protruding from them. A handful of Sumerians, most struggling to control their mounts, saw him coming. One man on foot wore a burnished breastplate, and held a sword upright in his hand. Shulgi.

Eskkar moved forward. "Akkad!" His cry pierced the clash of weapons and the shouts of men fighting. To the right of Shulgi's standard, Eskkar saw the Sumerian infantry giving way. Their archers led the retreat, some tossing their weapons away to run all the faster. What remained of the

Sumerian spearmen followed, some still trying to retain their ranks as they moved backwards. A few started to run, and once that started, Eskkar knew it wouldn't stop. The Sumerians had broken, and not even a counter-attack from Razrek's cavalry could save them now.

Three of Shulgi's guards kicked their horses forward. Esskar never slowed. When only a few paces from the oncoming riders, he flung his arms up, lance and sword jutting toward the face of the center horse, trying to panic it. "Akkad!!"

Either Esskar's bellowing charge or the lance flashing before its face made the lead animal dig in its heels, its rear haunches sliding to the ground. Esskar shifted to his left and drove the lance into the horse's shoulder, while his sword, thrust forward with all his strength, slipped under the center horseman, still trying to regain control of his mount. Esskar's blade passed completely through the man's stomach.

The remaining rider, after taking a wild cut at Esskar's head, pulled his mount around, his sword swinging down. Ripping lance and sword free, Esskar flung himself to the ground, and the sword stroke passed a hand's length over his head. Then he pushed himself to his feet. The lance bit again, this time into the horse's hindquarters.

The horse reared, and Esskar felt something strike his chest. He stumbled backwards, then tripped over a body. Another Sumerian fighter – this one on foot – appeared, his sword thrust down to pin Esskar to the earth. Esskar rolled toward him, flinging his body into the man's legs.

A sword hissed through the air, as Chinua thundered by, his long sword taking the surprised man's head from its shoulders and sending a spray of blood into the air. Shulgi thrust at Chinua as he galloped past, but missed the Ur Nammu warrior. Other Akkadian horsemen arrived, killing a few of the Sumerian king's guards and driving off the rest. In a few moments they'd cut Shulgi off from the rest of his men. Soon a ring of Akkadian and Ur Nammu warriors surrounded the king of Sumer.

Esskar used the haft of the lance to help himself to his feet, drinking air into his lungs. He realized the battle was over. Everywhere he looked men were fleeing the battlefield, avoiding the circle that held their king. Sumer's army was finished. All Esskar had to do was give the word, and his men would cut Shulgi down or take him prisoner. Esskar saw Chinua ride back to the edge of the ring and halt. He knew what the Ur Nammu expected.

His army defeated, his guards driven off, Shulgi saw death circled all around him. But the Akkadians and their barbarian allies held back. They wanted to see the two leaders battle. Shulgi hefted his shield into position and waited.

Eskkar gulped more air into his chest. The fierce fighting had tired him, while Shulgi still possessed all his strength. But Eskkar's honor demanded that he fight. His men had followed him into battle, and they had done what he asked of them. It had taken many of their lives to bring him to the heart of the enemy. Now it was up to Eskkar to finish the conflict.

Shulgi looked around him and understood. Unafraid, he moved forward, now only a dozen paces from Akkad's king. "At least I'll have the satisfaction of killing you before I die."

Eskkar shifted the lance in his hand and tightened his grip. Days of practicing with the cavalry had taught him how to use the weapon that way. Shulgi either didn't understand its use, or didn't care. The Sumerian edged forward, making sure of his footing as he advanced.

"Throw down your sword, Shulgi. I'll let you live. You can surrender your –"

"Better to die after I kill you, you filthy –!"

Eskkar knew better than to heed an enemy's words. He struck first, jabbing the lance toward Shulgi's face. The shield rose to deflect it, and Eskkar struck at Shulgi's left leg with a vicious overhand stroke from his sword. But the Sumerian recovered and shifted away before the blow could strike, though the blade knocked a clod of dirt and sand from the earth.

Shulgi laughed and circled to his right. "You're slow, old man, with your clumsy weapon. I've killed a dozen horse-fighters with their long swords."

Behind Eskkar, the sounds of battle began to fade. More and more men joined the circle, to watch the two leaders fight. Even a few Sumerians, having thrown down their weapons in surrender, now stood on the ring that encircled the two fighters. Eskkar gritted his teeth. No matter what the cost, he could not allow Shulgi's taunts to continue.

At least Eskkar had recovered most of his breath. He attacked again, sword and lance, thrusting and cutting, shifting his feet, even leaping over a body. But Shulgi danced away each time, using his shield and short sword effectively, counter-striking at every opportunity.

Eskkar kept up the attack, trying to overwhelm the younger man with sheer strength. Blade clashed against blade, and this time Shulgi stood toe to toe. Twice he used his shield to force Eskkar back. The bloody grass littered with weapons and debris hindered both fighters. Eskkar knew what would happen to the first man to slip and fall.

"Better summon your archers to finish me, barbarian, before it's too late."

Shulgi attacked for the first time, his short sword flashing in the sun as it sought to weave a deadly web of bronze around his enemy.

After three hard strokes, Eskkar broke off the contact, leaping back and to his right, away from Shulgi's sword arm. The Sumerian's strokes were too quick, too powerful for Eskkar's long sword to counter for long. By now his chest again heaved with the exertion.

"Too proud to call on your men, old man?" Shulgi taunted. "They see what's happening."

Eskkar used his anger to attack, but Shulgi met his advance, his shield absorbing the vicious overhand strike of Eskkar's blade. Only the slim lance in Eskkar's left hand kept Shulgi's sword at bay. Another four or five hard strokes forced Eskkar to give up the attack, once again moving back and to his right. His right arm was weakening, and he knew Shulgi could feel it, too.

And then he remembered. Many years ago Eskkar had fought a skilled and powerful swordsman, a warrior so strong that even Eskkar's strength and youth could not defeat the man. A trick had saved Eskkar's life then, a gamble that would leave him open to a deadly stroke if it failed. Still, he felt the sword growing heavier in his hand, the blade sagging a little lower after each attack. Eskkar realized he would not last much longer against his younger opponent. He took one deep breath.

"Time to die, boy king!"

As the last word left his lips, Eskkar attacked with a ferocity that took every bit of his remaining strength. The blades clashed again and again, mixed with the dull thud of sword against shield. Stroke followed stroke, until Eskkar felt himself weakening. He threw himself back and to the side, as he'd done twice before.

Shulgi had waited for the same moment. As soon as Eskkar shifted, Shulgi, moving with a blur of speed, turned to his left, lunged forward, and struck at where Eskkar's unprotected sword arm would be.

But Eskkar had not fully shifted his body, and instead of dodging to the right, he flung himself forward and to his left, diving under Shulgi's overhand swing that would have cut Eskkar's arm in two if he'd moved as Shulgi expected. Instead, Eskkar slid onto his left knee, and thrust the point of his sword into Shulgi's exposed armpit, the weapon's tip piercing the laces that bound Shulgi's breastplate and stopping only when the blade bit against the shoulder bone.

Shulgi whirled around and struck downwards, but Eskkar had already rolled away, wrenching his sword loose and regaining his footing. Blood poured down Shulgi's side as he advanced again. He lunged at Eskkar's head with his sword, and Eskkar nearly failed to raise his blade in time to parry the stroke.

The Sumerian king tried to raise his sword for another attack, but his arm muscles refused to obey, and Eskkar struck the weapon aside with his own. Shulgi flung himself forward, raising his shield and trying to smash into Eskkar and bring him to the ground.

Eskkar closed in, lowering his left shoulder and smashing his body against the shield. Shulgi, moving slower, couldn't shift to the side as he done before. Eskkar's weight now flung Shulgi backwards. The Sumerian's heel caught on the outflung leg of a body and he crashed onto the trampled earth. The sword fell from his hand. Shulgi looked up, unable to lift his right arm, already growing weak from the blood loss that streamed down his right arm and side.

Shulgi tried to recover his sword, but Eskkar placed his left sandal on the blade, pinning it to the ground. He had to take two breaths before he could get control of his words. "I told your father ... he should have stayed in Sumer. You should have learned from what happened to him."

Blood now soaked the ground beneath Shulgi's arm. The Sumerian glanced at his right arm, already covered in blood, and then laughed. "A trick ... to keep yourself alive. The mighty Eskkar." He coughed, tried to laugh, then coughed again, this time spewing blood from his mouth onto his chest.

"Enough talk, Sumerian." Eskkar thrust down, not with his sword, but with the lance in his left hand. The slim bronze tip tore into Shulgi's throat and buried itself in the earth. His eyes bulged with pain, then rolled up into his head. The body twitched for a moment, then lay still. The boy king of Sumer had at least died bravely, fighting to the last. A warrior's end, and better than his father's.

Eskkar didn't care. He straightened up, letting go of the lance, and looked around the circle of men. It had grown in depth, and it seemed as though half the Akkadian army had stopped and watched the brutal demise of Shulgi's ambitions.

A cheer started, at first just a few men, then more, until everyone joined in. The realization that they had not only won the battle, but destroyed the enemy and killed its king sank in. They had survived and would live. The jubilation rose in intensity, until every voice shouted the same refrain. "Akkad! Akkad! Akkad!"

He let the chant go on, until their voices ran out of breath. Eskkar raised his sword, forcing himself to keep the blade steady. "You've won a mighty victory!" Another cheer answered him. "Now on to Sumer!"

This time the roar shook the battlefield. A new cry went up. "Death to Sumer! Death to Sumer!" It went on and on, this time accompanied by the clamor of men crashing swords against shields, until the sound came from every voice and floated from horizon to horizon on the warm air.

Two miles away King Naxos of Isin sat on his horse, his advisor Kuara at his side. The two men had slipped out of the city, and ridden south before swinging around to the east, taking care not to be seen by the handful of Eskkar's men still guarding the ditch. All over the horizon, they saw hundreds and hundreds of men running or riding away, all of them heading south. Many would flee to Isin, but Naxos had already given orders to admit only those who could prove they lived there.

Suddenly, a roar ascended into the heavens, a mighty cheer that echoed over the ground.

"That will be Shulgi's death knell," Kuara said, shaking his head in disgust. "His army is destroyed. Now Eskkar will march to Sumer and tear it down."

Naxos shook his head. "I doubt it. The Sumerians would be fools to resist, and Kushanna is anything but a fool. She'll slip away, or come up with some idea to turn aside the Akkadian's sword."

"Well, if anyone can talk their way out of trouble, she's the one. Do you think Eskkar will turn his fury on Isin?"

"He may be a barbarian," Naxos said, "but he's no fool, either. He knows he'll need as many allies in Sumeria as he can get. With Larsa gone and Sumer's wealth exhausted, Akkad needs our trade to recover, just as we need theirs. No, he'll keep his word and spare our city."

"Then we'll have to ally ourselves with him." Kuara sighed. "Still, it may not be so bad, if Akkad directs its trade to Isin. In a few years, we'll be strong again."

Naxos had reported his encounter with Eskkar to his advisor, but hadn't mentioned that Eskkar had invited him to visit Akkad. "Perhaps I will visit the barbarian's city for myself."

Kuara glanced at him. "You'd put yourself within reach of Trella's power? Why would you risk your life to go there?"

"Ah, to meet Lady Trella, of course." Naxos laughed. "Sooner or later, Eskkar is going to get himself killed. Some day she may need another strong leader to protect her."

Kuara shook his head. "If what Eskkar told you is true, you just escaped Kushanna's poison, my king. I don't think you should be taking yourself from the path of one viper and placing your neck in front of another."

"Well, we'll see about that. After all, only the gods know what the future holds."

"I doubt if that particular future is in the stars."

Naxos laughed. "Well, the years will tell us. Now let's get back to Isin. We've got to fill in that ditch as soon as possible."

The first thing Razrek felt was a fly buzzing around his face. He lay flat on his back, something hard pressing against his spine. His eyes refused to open, and all he could make out was a reddish haze. Blood, he decided. It took all his strength to raise his hand and rub it across his eyes. First one eyelid, then the other broke loose from the dried blood, and the fierce mid-morning sun nearly blinded him. Razrek closed his eyes and tried to ignore the pain. Something had struck his head, but he couldn't remember . . .

The silence washed over him. He heard no sounds of fighting, no horses crying out, nothing. Razrek used the pain to force himself fully awake. The battle had ended. No matter which side had won, he had to get to a horse.

"Here's another one still alive."

Razrek squinted into the sun, but couldn't see the speaker. He tried to sit up, but a foot planted itself firmly on his chest.

"This one's a commander, at least," another voice remarked. "Look at that fancy knife!"

Razrek twisted his head and gazed upward. A boy had moved into view over him, a bulging sack slung over his shoulder and a long knife in his hand.

"Should be good for a few coins."

Another boy joined the first, his shadow blocking out the sun. Razrek saw a sling hanging from the second boy's neck. He, too, carried a long knife in his hand. Both blades, Razrek realized, were stained with fresh blood.

"Should we take him to Shappa? He may be someone important."

"And give up what he's carrying? Your wits are slow today, little brother."

Before Razrek could reach for his knife, the second youth dropped down and thrust his blade into Razrek's neck. The powerful stroke sent the sharp point straight through the flesh and into the earth.

Pain lanced through Razrek's throat and head. He flailed his arms, trying to grasp the knife, but already he felt blood gurgling up. Choking, he thrashed about, but the pressure on his chest increased. His muscles failed him, and the pain slipped away. His eyes remained open, and words still reached his ears.

"Look at this purse! We'll never have to work again!"

"Hurry, before anyone sees! Strip the body. He may have more concealed in his tunic."

For Razrek, the bright morning sun faded to darkness as the two slingers finished looting his dead body.

By sundown the Akkadians had established a camp about a mile north of the battlefield, every man and beast stumbling wearily northward until they reached the chosen site. The burst of energy after the defeat of the Sumerians had faded. Exhaustion set in, as well as sadness. Many in Eskkar's army had died, though not as many as he'd expected. The wounded – and there were many – needed to be cared for. With the river now clear of Shulgi's men, more riverboats arrived to deliver food and take those who could not walk back to Akkad.

Eskkar sat before the fire, staring into the flames. Every muscle in his body ached. His right arm still felt numb, and he'd had trouble controlling his horse on the brief ride upriver.

A wine skin lay close at hand, and he'd already finished at least two cups of the strong drink. One more and he'd sleep well tonight, though he'd pay for it in the morning. Right now, it didn't seem to matter.

Alexar limped up, as weary as any man in the army. He had taken a spear in his leg. Despite that, Alexar had been the first to recognize the black mood that descended over Eskkar after Shulgi's death. Alexar regrouped the men and organized the brief march north. He slumped to the ground beside Eskkar.

"I've got a rough count of our dead, Captain."

"How bad?" Another grim aftermath of every battle – the dead friends and companions, the wounded who would die later. Eskkar knew there was no escape from Alexar's tidings.

"About two hundred cavalry dead. Less than fifty archers, and almost half of those died on the boats. The slingers did better than anyone expected. Only forty dead."

"The infantry?"

"Two hundred and forty dead. Many of the survivors took wounds."

Including Gatus, who had died with Eskkar's arms around his shoulders. Eskkar had wept for the old soldier, who had flung his life into the battle to save his line from breaking. At least he died as he would have wanted, standing alongside his men and fighting to the end.

Grond had died as well, overwhelmed by a dozen men after he raised a mound of dead around himself. And probably still struggling to reach Eskkar's side. Klexor had died, too, riddled by enemy spears when his horse went down almost as the fighting ended. Muta had taken his command when his leader fell. A dozen paces away from where Eskkar sat, Drakis lay wrapped in bandages. Four years ago the man had nearly died fighting in Akkad, and now he was gravely wounded again. He would be on the first boat returning to Akkad in the morning.

The list of dead could have been far worse, Eskkar knew. The gods had favored him once again. Either that, or Gatus's training had kept most of the men alive, including himself. The slim Akkadian lance had kept Shulgi's sword at bay just long enough.

Eskkar's own victory over Shulgi counted for little. Every man watching had seen the younger man wear down his older opponent. In truth, Eskkar had won only by a trick, a desperate gamble that should have failed the first time he tried it, let alone the second. It bothered him that he hadn't been able to kill Shulgi outright, but staying alive was what counted, not how you did it. Eskkar knew what Trella would say when he told her. "In time they will only remember that you faced the king of Sumer in battle and slew him."

He would send her word of the victory tomorrow. She'd had her own victory over the Alur Meriki to celebrate. That didn't matter, either. Only that the city would remain safe and free, and that Sargon would grow stronger every day. The threat from Sumer had been eliminated. Once Eskkar stamped out Kushanna and her nest of snakes, peace would return to the land, at least for a time.

In the morning, Hathor would take the brunt of the cavalry and ride south. Despite today's victory, Eskkar intended to give Sumer no time to recover, raise more troops, or prepare a defense. Hathor had somehow come through the fighting almost unscathed. His dark Egyptian gods must still be protecting him. He would ravage the lands around Sumer, and seal it off from any river traffic. By the time Eskkar's army arrived, the city might have already surrendered.

"Drink some more wine, Captain, and get some sleep," Alexar said. "You need the rest."

Eskkar glanced up. Alexar's voice showed his concern. It always surprised Eskkar when others showed honest affection for him. And Alexar had his own wound to prove his courage. At least his commander knew how great the danger had been, and how lucky they were to survive it.

Without stopping, Eskkar emptied the wine cup, tossed it aside, then fell back against the hard ground. More than two years had passed since this war began, but it had finally ended. Once again Trella would be kept busy helping the city recover. Better than anyone, she knew how to heal the wounds in the countryside and in the city. But peace would soothe the pain, and in time, Akkad would grow strong again, with its walls raised ever higher until, like mighty arms, they spread their protection around Trella, their son, and their children yet to come.

Eskkar looked up at the stars blazing overhead. Now he knew what they foretold. Long life for himself and Trella. A son to carry on their line, other descendants who would live through them and through the ages. Most of all, Akkad would grow strong and prosperous again. The empire encompassing all the land between the two rivers would be ruled from Akkad, not Sumer. And that, Eskkar decided before he fell into an exhausted and troubled sleep, made all the fighting worthwhile.

61

In Sumer, the days rushed by, each filled with excitement. The war talk dominated every conversation. Rumors abounded about King Shulgi's army, its mighty size and power, its rapid march to the north. Everyone spoke proudly of how the other Sumerian cities already acknowledged Sumer's leadership. Others boasted about the coming destruction of Akkad and the creation of a mighty Sumerian Empire that stretched between the two rivers all the way to the far north.

When word of the fall of Kanesh arrived, the city's inhabitants celebrated. The fertile fields of the north would soon supply Sumer's every need, and slaves from the Akkadian lands would abound in the slave market.

Nevertheless, many suffered hardship. With the resumption of hostilities, trading ceased almost at once. Every boat that arrived at the docks was taken into King Shulgi's service, as the soldiers commandeered every craft. Wine and ale, grain and bread, chickens and herd animals, all were rushed aboard boats and sent north. Since the only vessels moving on the river carried cargoes to support King Shulgi's army, food supplies within Sumer grew scarce. Queen Kushanna's men had already emptied the city's storage places to feed the ravenous army. And still supply caravans departed each day, taking what little remained and collecting supplies along the way.

The shortages caused every merchant to raise prices, though few buyers had enough coins remaining to purchase anything but necessities. Even En-hedu's massages slowed, as the tight-fisted upper classes, staggering under Kushanna's ever-rising taxes, ordered their pampered women to cut back. Without a steady supply of ale, business at the Kestrel dropped off as well, and En-hedu and Tammuz suddenly found they had plenty of time on their hands.

Still, the mood in Sumer remained jubilant until the ninth day after the start of hostilities. Late in the afternoon, boatmen returning from Kanesh reported the disquieting news that Eskkar's army had slipped by King Shulgi's forces at Kanesh. The Akkadians were reputed to be marching toward Larsa or possibly even Sumer. Before the sun set, word had reached every hut in every lane. Many refused to believe it. For the first time, worried looks appeared on many faces. The city's soldiers doubled their efforts to strengthen the walls.

A king's messenger arrived the next day demanding more troops. Half the city's remaining garrison departed, ordered north to protect the caravans moving supplies. For En-hedu and Tammuz, that resulted in one piece of good tidings – Jarud was promoted to Captain of the Guard. He celebrated with his friends and companions at the Kestrel the next evening.

Three days later, a boat carrying no cargo docked with word of the fall of Larsa. The grim news swept through Sumer. Over the next few days, more reports arrived, many of them conflicting, all of them adding shocking details about the destruction of Larsa. King Shulgi remained in pursuit of Eskkar's forces, but now that meant little to the city's inhabitants. Rumors insisted that the Akkadians were on the march to Sumer, intending to tear down the walls and kill everyone within.

The inhabitants started hoarding what little they had. Many shops and stalls in the lanes closed. Dozens left the city, before Queen Kushanna ordered the gates closed. No one was allowed to depart the city without her permission. The mood in Sumer turned sullen, as hard-eyed messengers from King Shulgi returned and departed, forbidden by Kushanna to speak to any. Desperate people, trapped in the city without any means of livelihood, formed gangs that roamed the lanes at night, searching for anything of value or even food to eat.

The gloom worsened when Sumer learned of the raid on Uruk, the city burned and its inhabitants driven into the countryside by Eskkar's horsemen, who had magically appeared out of the desert, wreaked their havoc, and disappeared. Everyone agreed that the king of Akkad was a demon from the underworld. How else could his armies be in so many places, and move about unopposed?

Twenty days after the start of the war, horsemen arriving at midday brought word of a mighty battle outside Isin, and the destruction of the Akkadian army. Eskkar's soldiers had been crushed and the survivors driven into the Euphrates to drown. The welcome news swept through the city like the fresh breeze from the Southern Sea. Smiling and relieved people gathered in the marketplace and outside the queen's quarters to give thanks, happy to learn that their sons and husbands would soon be returning home victorious over their enemy. En-hedu and Tammuz cheered as loudly as any.

"This is bad," Tammuz said when they were alone.

En-hedu shook her head. "No, it's just another rumor. Even if Eskkar were defeated, he would not have let his army be completely destroyed. He's far too good a fighter to let that happen. Eskkar may have lost a battle, but we mustn't give up hope yet."

That evening a good number of customers returned to the Kestrel, eager to drink to the success of Shulgi's soldiers.

Later that night, as the raucous patrons began to depart, Jarud strode into the Kestrel accompanied by three of his men. En-hedu took in their scowling faces and felt her heart jump, afraid that she and Tammuz had been discovered. But the newly appointed Captain of the Guard called out for ale, and plenty of it, as he slumped onto a bench.

En-hedu carried a pitcher with the last of the night's brew to the table, and filled everyone's cups. "You look too serious to be celebrating, Captain. Is anything wrong?"

Jarud downed his ale before replying. "Nothing to celebrate." He ignored her questioning look for a moment. "Damn all the demons! I just found out . . . you'll hear the news soon enough." He lowered his voice. "A handful of soldiers from the north arrived this evening." He filled his cup. "Not soldiers any more! Rabble. King Shulgi's army was defeated at Isin. King Naxos and the rest of his traitors refused to fight, and the Akkadian scum caught Shulgi unprepared. Our soldiers broke and ran. Hundreds, maybe thousands are dead, including the king."

Eyes wide, En-hedu sank down on the bench beside Jarud. "Are you sure? I mean . . ."

"I'm sure. I spoke to some of the scum myself. The army was . . ." Jarud couldn't find words to describe what he felt.

Tammuz joined them, and she whispered the news to him. It didn't matter. The remaining patrons needed only a look at Jarud and his companions to guess the worst. Then faint shouts from the lane could be heard. The news had already begun to spread.

En-hedu clasped her hands to her bosom. "The gods preserve us! What will happen now?"

"Who knows?" Jarud shrugged. "Whenever he's ready, Eskkar will march on Sumer. The last messenger brought news that Isin has changed sides and is now supporting the Akkadians. King Naxos will allow free passage across his lands, the filthy coward."

"Sumer will not fall," En-hedu declared. "It's walls are high . . ."

"Larsa fell, and Uruk, too. The other cities will not come to our aid now. Like Isin, they'll rush to make their peace with Akkad. On Kushanna's orders, I sealed the city, to keep everyone within, but that's not going to work for long. With Eskkar on the march, everyone will want to flee."

No longer "Queen" Kushanna, En-hedu noted. Just the woman's name, spoken unflatteringly. "Perhaps things are not as bad as we think. Tomorrow may bring better news." But in her heart, and for the first time, En-hedu started to believe that Eskkar had succeeded.

She rose and fetched two more cups, and she and Tammuz joined in with Jarud, consuming the last of the ale, and all of them wondering what word would arrive tomorrow.

Just before dawn, Kushanna raged at the wretched soldier cringing before her, his right arm bound in a clumsy sling. A leader of twenty, he'd ridden through the night to bring his news. "My husband is dead? You saw him fall?"

"Yes, my queen. He fought with Eskkar and was slain. King Shulgi fought well, but the barbarian was too strong. Afterwards, the Akkadian king spared my life. He set many of us free, gave us horses, and told us all to deliver word of Shulgi's defeat and death to you. And to tell you that he is coming to destroy Sumer."

Of all those given the message, only this man had bothered to return. Probably the others had already disappeared into the countryside.

"And our army? How many men remain to fight? When will they return?"

The subcommander shook his head. "Not many escaped. Sumer's soldiers fought to the last, even when the other contingents lay down their weapons. However many survived, it will not be enough to stop the Akkadians. They fought like demons, my queen, attacking our men despite their few numbers."

She cared nothing about how either side had fought. "How long before Eskkar arrives?"

"A few days, four or five at most. I expect his horsemen will be here tomorrow. They were already preparing to ride south when I and the others left. The main force won't be far behind."

Kushanna tried to control the sinking sensation in her stomach. How had this happened? How could everything have gone so horribly wrong? Twenty thousand men defeated by a handful? "Get out. All of you, get out!"

She turned away, ignoring them, and stepped onto the balcony. The courtyard appeared different, and she realized that many of the soldiers who should have been standing guard had gone, slipping away in the night as soon as they heard the news. The morning would find more deserters abandoning their posts.

"Damn you, Shulgi, you fool!"

Kushanna took a deep breath, and tried to control her rage. She needed to think. Something must be done. She could leave the city, but where could she go that Trella's agents wouldn't find her? Nippur and Lagash wouldn't take her in, and there would soon be a bounty on her head. Trella knew of Kushanna's involvement in the war, and wouldn't rest until she'd been captured or killed. Besides, who could she trust to protect her if she ran? Whoever Kushanna turned to would want her gold and jewels more than they wanted her body, and she would be helpless to protect either of them.

Sumer might be held, at least for a time, perhaps long enough to wring some concession from Eskkar. But another look at the quiet courtyard convinced her that wouldn't happen. Without enough fighting men to man the walls, the soldiers wouldn't continue the battle for her. They'd throw down their weapons at first sight of Eskkar's riders.

In fact, the longer she thought, the more she realized only one man could save her: Eskkar. The king of Akkad. Kushanna would have to turn him to her side. She had dominated every man she'd ever met, and had no doubt that she would succeed with the barbarian king. It would take some doing, but perhaps it could be managed.

She thanked the gods that she hadn't killed Trella's brother. Now the half-witted slave might prove useful. She would send word to the farm and have him delivered to her.

By the time Kushanna worked out what to do, the first rays of the sun broke into the morning sky. She left her chambers and descended to the courtyard, grateful to see at least a few loyal soldiers still awaiting her commands. Her eyes rested on Jarud, the new Captain of the Guard.

"Jarud! Round up every one of the nobles, every merchant, every trader." She rattled off the names of Sumer's wealthiest. "Bring them here at once. Make sure you find every one." They would protest, but that didn't matter. "And spread the word throughout the city. I will speak to the people at mid-morning in the marketplace. Go! And do not fail. Sumer's fate may rest on how well you obey my commands."

And more important, her own.

En-hedu and Tammuz arrived at the marketplace well before mid-morning, determined to get a good place to stand and hear Queen Kushanna's words. Rimaud joined them, as much to keep them safe as to hear the queen speak. With the city in an ugly mood, Rimaud wore his sword, and Tammuz carried his knife on his belt.

Others arrived early as well, and soon at least eight or nine hundred people of all ages packed their way into the marketplace, with more arriving every moment. Everyone had questions, and shouts echoed back and forth as people sought to learn what had happened. Many had news, probably most of it wrong, to share with whomever would listen. En-hedu shook her head at their foolishness.

Mid-morning came and went before Jarud and ten soldiers arrived, escorting thirteen of Sumer's richest men. Some showed bruises and marks on their face and arms, so En-hedu knew they hadn't come willingly. Every one of them had sullen looks on their faces. She saw Merchant Gemama there, along with Puzur-Amurri, and Jamshid, Bikku's husband. En-hedu had given massages to most of their women.

She leaned closer to Tammuz. "Too bad I never got invited to service Kushanna." She fingered the knife under her dress.

The crowd – now numbering close to two thousand – surged forward, shouting questions at the merchants, demanding to know what had happened. The former leaders of Sumer stared at the angry people confronting them, but said nothing.

"They've been ordered not to speak," Tammuz said.

"Queen Kushanna had better arrive soon," En-hedu whispered. "The people are getting angry. There aren't enough soldiers here to control this many."

They both sensed the rising tension. No one enjoyed standing around in the hot sun, which added to the crowd's anger. The smell from so many bodies filled the still air. The incensed mutterings grew louder and angrier. The soldiers glanced at each other and fingered their weapons.

"Where is our army?" An old man shouted the question with a quavering voice. "What happened to my sons?"

Everyone joined in, and soon the crowd began to shift and move under the pressure of so many struggling to make themselves heard.

"This could get out of hand," Tammuz said. "Stay close to me."

A column of eight soldiers strode down the lane, shoving anyone in their path out of the way. Queen Kushanna walked in their midst, wearing one of her finest gowns, her hair combed and arrayed. She wore a necklace of pearls, gold rings on her fingers and bracelets on her arms. Her escort started for the top of the market, but she halted them. Too many people blocked the way. "Stop here. I'll speak to them from here."

Kushanna ignored both the people and their cries for answers. A soldier carried over a stool, and helped her step onto it, so Kushanna could be seen and heard. She stared at the crowd, and waited until the din had died down.

"People of Sumer. People of Sumer. Hear me." Her melodious voice quieted the crowd. "I bring you evil tidings. Our army has been defeated by the Akkadians."

En-hedu noted the use of just the name, no longer demons or barbarians.

"Our king, my husband, is dead. Now the Akkadian army marches toward Sumer."

A groan went up from the crowd, along with a few curses.

"To save our city, and protect your lives, I will offer a ransom of gold to King Eskkar when he arrives. These men," Kushanna lifted her shapely arm to point at the nobles under Jarud's guard, "will be required to give up their wealth to save the city. With all their gold and possessions, and what little is left of King Shulgi's goods, we should be able to raise at least a thousand gold coins."

A cheer burst forth at the nobles' discomfort. "Let the bastards pay!"

Others grew angry, as they grasped the size of the merchants' wealth, flaunted at them while they went hungry.

Kushanna raised her arm again to quiet the now angry mob. "To ensure that Sumer and your safety is protected, I will also offer myself to King Eskkar, begging him to spare our city. I will kneel before him and throw myself at his mercy. King Eskkar has shown forgiveness in the past. Now I will sacrifice myself to save your lives, and to save our city. And I will present him with the gift of the brother of Lady Trella, who we rescued from the mines."

Cheers greeted the news, the first bit of hope they'd been offered.

En-hedu exchanged a brief glance with Tammuz. Neither of them had ever heard that Trella had a brother.

Listening to the crowd, En-hedu decided that Kushanna might just manage to do it. She would win over the mob with the sacrifice of the nobles. With more than a little apprehension, En-hedu wondered if Eskkar would fall under Kushanna's spell. The woman was indeed a witch.

A shrill voice broke through the clamor. "You murdered my sons! I had three sons, and now they're all dead!"

An old woman with long gray hair hanging limp around her face had pushed her way through the crowd, shoving grown men aside. She flung a stone at Kushanna, only a few paces away, narrowly missing the queen, whose eyes went wide in surprise. No one had ever dared raise a hand toward her.

The woman refused to be silent. "You sent them all to their deaths!" She reached down and scooped up a handful of dirt and threw that as well.

A soldier stepped forward and struck the woman in the face with the haft of his spear, knocking her back into the arms of those behind. Whatever sympathy the crowd had started to give Kushanna vanished in a moment.

"Murderers! She sent our husbands to their deaths!"

The soldiers lowered their spears and pushed the now angry crowd back, while a frowning Queen Kushanna looked on, her lips clenched in anger at the insolence. The throng of people pushed and shoved, moving in all directions, everyone cursing and shouting.

En-hedu realized what could happen. This crowd could be turned. Her elbow jabbed Tammuz in the ribs. "Death to the queen!" She yelled the words with all her strength. "Death to those murderers who led us to war! Death to the queen!"

Tammuz, shocked at his wife's outburst, took a moment to grasp the situation. Then he, too, joined in. "Death to the queen! Death to those who betrayed us!" In a moment, every voice in the marketplace repeated the same words.

The soldiers, greatly outnumbered, hesitated at the sudden ferocity from the mass of men and women facing them. Most of Sumer's remaining soldiers guarded the gates and the wall. And Queen Kushanna's guards were not hardened veterans. Most were either too young or too old to go off to war, and none had ever seen naked anger and hatred such as this.

The crowd saw the doubt and fear on their faces. A wave of people surged forward, as ten, fifty, a hundred voices joined in, all shouting death to Queen Kushanna.

Tammuz pushed his way to the front. "Death to Kushanna!" A soldier tried to hold him back, but Tammuz's knife lashed out, and the guard staggered back, his nose broken by the weapon's hilt. A few people in front died, impaled on the spears, but the screaming mob now could not be stopped. "Death to Kushanna!" The words came from every voice, and this time the cry didn't stop.

Chaos erupted. The people of Sumer had been demeaned and crushed down for many years, and now they saw a chance for their revenge. The soldiers grasped the situation, too. Many shrank aside, others dropped their spears. Some turned toward the queen, as eager to strike as any of the mob. The nobles, released by the captors, added their voices to the din.

Jarud saw the danger. He abandoned the nobles and closed up his men around the queen, shouting at his soldiers to keep together. Enough heeded his words. In moments, they formed a protective ring around Kushanna. They struggled and shoved their way through the clawing mob, moving toward the lane that had brought Kushanna into the marketplace. A few more steps and . . .

En-hedu saw Kushanna slipping away. She ducked low, practically slithering between the legs of the crowd shrieking hatred and venom above her. Then she saw the legs of the soldiers forcing their way forward, then the hem of Kushanna's gown. Rising up, En-hedu's long arm stretched out. She meant to strike at Kushanna's heart, but an unheeding arm knocked the blade down, and instead the weapon sank to the hilt just above the queen's hip, before it was wrenched from En-hedu's hand by the forward momentum of the guards. Kushanna's scream could scarcely be heard in all the confusion. Because the stroke landed so low, none of the soldiers realized what had happened.

Only one man saw En-hedu strike – Jarud.

Her knife gone, En-hedu moved back, trying to return to Tammuz's side. A dozen paces away, her husband pushed and shoved against the nearly unmovable mass of people to reach her. She looked back, and saw Jarud knocking people aside, determined to get his hands on her. En-hedu struggled as hard as she could, trying to move away from Jarud. But the Captain of the Guard was bigger and stronger, and the crowd gave way before him as he forced his way closer.

Looking up, she saw the nobles fighting the angry crowd for their own lives. Stones and clods of dirt flew through the air. Gemama had both arms raised, trying to protect his head from the people's wrath. The sight gave En-hedu another idea.

"Gemama for king! Gemama for king!" She snapped her gaze at Tammuz. The soldiers escorting Kushanna had pushed their way clear, dragging the faltering queen with them. Jarud had moved almost within arm's length.

"Gemama for king!" Unable to reach his wife through the surging mob, Tammuz bellowed the words. "Gemama for king!" Rimaud took up the cry, and others joined in, a few at first, then dozens and more.

At the head of the market, Gemama lowered his hands, looking at the shouting mob, as surprised as anyone. At least the stones pelting him and the other nobles ceased. His eyes sought the place where the call started, and he picked out En-hedu and Tammuz.

"Gemama will save us!" En-hedu shouted the words as loud as she could.

Those standing beside Gemama stopped their attacks. One man, his anger vanished in a heartbeat, grabbed the merchant's arm and lifted it high. "Gemama will be our king!"

The sight of the stout merchant's arm raised high turned the mood of the mob. "King Gemama! King Gemama!" The chant filled the marketplace, repeated again and again.

Jarud pushed aside the last of those blocking his way, and his hand closed on En-hedu's shoulder with a grip of bronze. Tammuz and Rimaud struggled a few paces away, helpless to reach her side. The words "King Gemama" came from every voice now, along with appeals for him to save their city.

En-hedu saw Jarud's sword jerked from its scabbard.

"Wait! Listen to me!" She leaned toward him, shouting the words into his face to make herself heard over the noise. "You will be commander of all of Sumer's forces!" The sword's tip reached her breast. "Gemama will need you! You will lead his soldiers! We can help you!" She tried to push herself away from the blade, but the crowd held her fast, swirling around the two of them. No one paid any attention to them. Every eye now remained fixed on Gemama, standing dazed before the chants of the crowd.

Two soldiers moved forward to protect the merchant, who now held both arms high.

Jarud's eyes burned into hers, but he stayed his sword. He glanced at Gemama, then at her. Understanding came, as he worked out what had happened.

"Help him, Jarud!" she said. "To save Sumer, help him!"

Tammuz and Rimaud pushed their way to her side, both with weapons in their hands. Whether it was their presence or his own choice, Jarud lowered his weapon.

"Make way for the king's men!" he shouted. "Soldiers, defend King Gemama! Protect Sumer's king!"

Then he was gone, knocking people left and right until he reached the forefront, to clear the way for Gemama.

En-hedu breathed a sigh of relief and fell against her husband. Her heart still raced in her breast.

"Let's get out of here," Tammuz said. "Rimaud, lead the way home."

They headed toward the same lane that Queen Kushanna had used. They pushed through the last of the crowd. A dozen paces farther, Kushanna lay in the dirt, a large pool of blood staining her dress and the ground beneath it. The pearl necklace and gold rings had vanished. Her guards had abandoned her.

En-hedu stared down in astonishment. Her knife stroke had managed to cut the big blood carrier. Queen Kushanna was dead.

The next day, at mid-afternoon, Hathor and four hundred horsemen appeared outside Sumer's walls. They had made a fast passage, encountering no resistance and finding a steady source of supplies originally intended for King Shulgi. Now to Hathor's surprise, he stared at

Sumer's walls and found them undefended, the gates standing open, and a delegation of the city's inhabitants stepping outside the city and walking toward the Akkadians. Hathor halted his men just out of bowshot of the walls and waited.

A portly man led the way, a single armed soldier accompanying him, but Hathor's gaze went to the dozen or so frightened men and women walking respectfully behind. Only two strode upright and met his eyes unafraid. Hathor saw the hint of a smile on Tammuz's lips, while the slight incline of En-hedu's head told Hathor everything he needed to know.

The man leading the little troop stopped a few steps from the Akkadians. He announced himself as King Gemama. He offered to surrender the city and pay a ransom if they would spare Sumer and its inhabitants. He pleaded for mercy, and blamed the war on Shulgi and his evil wife, both dead.

Gemama's voice droned on, but Hathor scarcely heard him. The man's words didn't matter. Later on, Hathor would find an excuse to speak to En-hedu in private, and she would tell him what had happened and how to resolve Sumer's future.

Whatever happened, King Eskkar would get quite a shock. Sumer taken without a battle, Queen Kushanna dead, a ransom offered, and all with En-hedu and Tammuz standing directly behind the city's new king and the leader of his guards. Incredible.

Perhaps, Hathor decided, the gods of Egypt did have power even this far east of the Nile. They had stayed his hand and spared Tammuz's life. That mercy had saved Hathor's own life, and in time delivered Cnari into his arms. No man, it seems, could fathom the ways of those who ruled the heavens above and earth below. The conflict between Sumer and Akkad had ended, and neither Hathor nor any of his men needed to risk their lives in battle any more.

Hathor offered a silent prayer to the mighty Egyptian god Ra for this new gift of life. Then, just to be certain, Hathor muttered the same prayer to every single one of the gods that held sway over the land of the Nile.

Epilogue

E
skkar guided Trella up the last and steepest flight of stairs until they reached the open space at the top. The two watchtowers that overhung the city's main gate were the highest structures in the land, climbing more than twenty-five paces above the ground. No other city, including those in Sumeria, had dared to raise any structure that high. Sunk into the battlement, a tall staff rose even higher into the sky. From its tip, the lion pennant fluttered over their heads, the symbol of the city's power. Opposite, on the right tower, flew the pennant of the Hawk Clan, its bronze cap catching the rays of the setting sun.

Trella rested her elbows on the waist-high wall and gazed out over the countryside. Esskar stood behind her, his arms wrapped around her. He touched her stomach, and felt the swell of the child within. Soon there would be another son or daughter to carry on their line. Esskar hoped for a boy, but Trella shook her head. "This one feels different, husband. I think you will soon have a daughter."

Behind them, the city of Akkad celebrated once again, its people happy in their deliverance. The Sumerians had pillaged the southern lands, but Akkad itself had avoided the devastating horror of war. The inhabitants had suffered through hardships, but already that memory was fading, as trade resumed and new crops burst from the rich soil. Akkad's victory turned the city into the hub for every merchant, trader and shipmaster throughout the land. Once again, hundreds, perhaps thousands of people would converge on the city, eager to pass through its gates. Commerce would flourish, and the people would be happy and secure.

Eskkar had returned to Akkad last night, little more than a month after he marched the army south to meet the Sumerians. In that time, the world had changed. Larsa destroyed, Uruk humbled, Isin turned into an ally and trading partner, and Sumer now ruled by Trella's agents. Shulgi and Kushanna dead and already forgotten.

Even Trella's brother had survived, rescued by Tammuz and Enhedu from the chaos of Sumer. As soon as Almaric recovered his strength, he would journey north to be reunited with his sister. Whether he would ever fully regain his wits, only time and the gods would decide.

With all its enemies vanquished, Akkad reigned supreme over the land between the rivers. There was no place her soldiers could not march, no land so distant her horsemen could not penetrate, no enemy so bold as to offer challenge. Soon her influence, if not her soldiers, would spread even beyond those boundaries.

Trella raised her arm and pointed toward the north, where the wide ribbon of the Tigris glistened in the setting sun. "That's where the future of Akkad will lie. Those empty lands will fill with farms and villages. In five or ten years, they will be the source of our strength."

"Sargon will rule over those lands," Eskkar said. "He will grow up to be their king as much as Akkad's. No one will challenge his right to rule now."

In another few months, the boy would be five seasons old, and already he'd begun to outgrow his childish toys.

"He will be safe for a time," Trella said, "perhaps for many years. But there will be new enemies, if not from outside these walls then from within. There will always be those who will seek to take what belongs to him."

"When he is old enough, I will send him north to the lands of the Ur Nammu. They will teach him how to be a warrior. When he returns, you will teach him how to be a king."

"We'll talk about that when the time comes."

Eskkar knew she wasn't convinced of the wisdom of sending the boy away. But that day of reckoning lay seven or eight years in the future.

"En-hedu is also carrying a child," Trella said. "Though he may grow up to be more Sumerian than Akkadian."

"And Cnari has given Hathor a son. Our children and those of our friends will all grow up together."

"And you and I, Eskkar, will make sure they do. We must never forget that our strength lies in the hearts of our people. As long as we care for them as much as we care for Sargon, they will give us their allegiance. Sumer and Larsa showed what happens when rulers place their own desires above those of their subjects."

"You will make sure of that," Eskkar said, "while I will make certain our army remains strong. Gatus would have made sure of that. And who knows from what direction the next danger will come?"

She turned away from the expanse, and put her arms around his neck. "Our blood is still in these walls, husband. And soon our children will draw their strength from these same walls."

He kissed the top of her head. "I think you will give them more strength than any wall, no matter how high or strong."

Eskkar glanced up at the heavens. One by one, the stars were breaking through the darkness. Perhaps because of them, he'd survived another battle, another conflict. Whatever role they planned for his future was yet to be played out. But for now, they had given him what he wanted, and he didn't intend to waste the moment.

"Come, Trella. Let's go home. I want to play with my son."

Acknowledgements

W riting about historical events has turned out to be a tricky business. There are so many experts in the various fields, and sometimes it seems they are all arrayed against the lonely writer, who has to get it right while attempting to write an engaging story. Fortunately, for me at least, one author has unwittingly come to my assistance. I want to give special mention to Philip Sidnell, author of *Warhorse: Cavalry in Ancient Warfare*. His research into the use of horses in warfare confirms what I always believed but could not convincingly prove – that warhorses were used as far back as 3500 BC. Many thanks to Mr Sidnell, who crafted an engaging and well-written history of early cavalry.

Other readers will no doubt find fault with Eskkar's final battle plan – too ambitious, too risky, too bold, and doomed to failure from the start, especially against such overwhelming odds. Before these helpful readers dash off their communications advising me such a plan could never have succeeded, I would suggest they read up on Alexander the Great, and the defining Battle of Gaugamela. Alexander used the same battle plan against the same relative odds (with even more complex troop movements) to defeat Darius and bring down the Persian Empire.

So the real question is, whose plan was it? Did the author take it from Alexander? Or did Alexander somehow learn of Eskkar's tactics and victory at the earlier Battle of Isin? Only Eskkar and Trella know for certain.

Finally, let me offer my gratitude to those who helped make this book a reality. My literary agent Dominick Abel as ever offered many useful and positive suggestions. My editors at Century, Oliver Johnson and Katie

Duce, provided in-depth comments and recommendations at every stage of the story, and pointed out many of the countless flaws that creep into every manuscript. Oliver truly helped improve the story.

Special thanks go to my critique group, Thelma Rea and Martin Cox, who provided their usual and invaluable assistance, almost always at short notice. Linda Roberts also contributed to the final draft, even as she helped the author in ways too numerous to mention.

Sam Barone
Scottsdale, AZ